cloud atlas

David Mitchell

SCEPTRE

Copyright © 2004 David Mitchell

First published in Great Britain in 2004 by Hodder and Stoughton
A division of Hodder Headline

The right of David Mitchell to be identified as the Author of
the Work has been asserted by him in accordance with the
Copyright, Designs and Patents Act 1988.

A Sceptre Book

10 9 8 7 6 5 4 3 2 1

A CIP catalogue record for this title is available
from the British Library

Hardback ISBN 0 340 82277 5
Trade Paperback ISBN 0 340 83237 1

Typeset in Sabon by
Rowland Phototypesetting Ltd, Bury St Edmunds, Suffolk
Printed and bound in Great Britain by
Clays Ltd, St Ives plc

Hodder and Stoughton
A division of Hodder Headline
338 Euston Road
London NW1 3BH

For Hana and her Grandparents

The Pacific Journal of
Adam Ewing

Thursday, 7th November —

Beyond the Indian hamlet, upon a forlorn strand, I happened on a trail of recent footprints. Through rotting kelp, sea cocoa-nuts & bamboo, the tracks led me to their maker, a white man, his trowzers & Pea-jacket rolled up, sporting a kempt beard & an outsized Beaver, shovelling & sifting the cindery sand with a tea-spoon so intently that he noticed me only after I had hailed him from ten yards away. Thus it was, I made the acquaintance of Dr Henry Goose, surgeon to the London nobility. His nationality was no surprise. If there be any eyrie so desolate, or isle so remote that one may there resort un-challenged by an Englishman, 'tis not down on any map I ever saw.

Had the doctor misplaced anything on that dismal shore? Could I render assistance? Dr Goose shook his head, knotted loose his 'kerchief & displayed its contents with clear pride. 'Teeth, sir, are the enamelled grails of the quest in hand. In days gone by this Arcadian strand was a cannibals' banqueting hall, yes, where the strong engorged themselves on the weak. The teeth, they spat out, as you or I would expel cherry stones. But these base molars, sir, shall be transmuted to gold & how? An artisan of Piccadilly who fashions denture-sets for the nobility pays handsomely for human gnashers. Do you know the price a quarter pound will earn, sir?'

I confessed I did not.

'Nor shall I enlighten you, sir, for 'tis a professional secret!' He tapped his nose. 'Mr Ewing, are you acquainted with Mar-chioness Grace of Mayfair? No? The better for you, for she is a corpse in petticoats. Five years have passed since this harridan besmirched my name, yes, with imputations that resulted in my

3

being blackballed from Society.' Dr Goose looked out to sea. 'My peregrinations began in that dark hour.'

I expressed sympathy with the doctor's plight.

'I thank you, sir, I thank you, but these ivories,' he shook his 'kerchief, 'are my angels of redemption. Permit me to elucidate. The Marchioness wears dental-fixtures fashioned by the afore-mentioned doctor. Next yuletide, just as that scented She-Donkey is addressing her Ambassadors' Ball, I, Henry Goose, yes, *I* shall arise & declare to one & all that our hostess masticates with cannibals' gnashers! Sir Hubert will challenge me, predictably, "Furnish your evidence," that boor shall roar, "or grant me satisfaction!" I shall declare, "Evidence, Sir Hubert? Why, I gathered your mother's teeth *myself* from the spittoon of the South Pacific! Here, sir, *here* are some of their fellows!" & fling these very teeth into her tortoise-shell soup tureen & that, sir, that will grant me *my* satisfaction! The twittering wits will scald the icy Marchioness in their news-sheets & by next season she shall be fortunate to receive an invitation to a Poorhouse Ball!'

In haste, I bade Henry Goose a good day. I fancy he is a Bedlamite.

Friday, 8th November —

In the rude shipyard beneath my window, work progresses on the jibboom, under Mr Sykes's directorship. Mr Walker, Ocean Bay's sole taverner, is also its principal timber-merchant & he brags of his years as a master shipbuilder in Liverpool. (I am now versed enough in Antipodese etiquette to let such unlikely truths lie.) Mr Sykes told me an entire week is needed to render *Prophetess* 'Bristol fashion'. Seven days holed up in the *Musket* seems a grim sentence, yet I recall the fangs of the banshee tempest & the mariners lost o'erboard & my present misfortune feels less acute.

I met Dr Goose on the stairs this morning & we took breakfast together. He has lodged at the *Musket* since middle October after voyaging hither on a Brazilian merchantman, *Namorados*, from Feejee, where he practised his arts in a mission. Now the doctor awaits a long-overdue Australian sealer, the *Nellie*, to convey him to Sydney. From the colony he will seek a position aboard a passenger ship for his native London.

My judgement of Dr Goose was unjust & premature. One must be cynical as Diomedes to prosper in my profession, but cynicism can blind one to subtler virtues. The doctor has his eccentricities & recounts them gladly for a dram of Portuguese *pisco* (never to excess) but I vouchsafe he is the only other gentleman on this latitude east of Sydney & west of Valparaiso. I may even compose for him a letter of introduction for the Partridges in Sydney, for Dr Goose & dear Fred are of the same cloth.

Poor weather precluding my morning outing, we yarned by the peat fire & the hours sped by like minutes. I spoke at length of Tilda & Jackson & also my fears of 'gold-fever' in San Francisco. Our conversation then voyaged from my home-town to my recent notarial duties in New South Wales, thence to Gibbons, Malthus & Godwin via Leeches & Locomotives. Attentive conversation is an emollient I lack sorely aboard *Prophetess* & the doctor is a veritable polymath. Moreover, he possesses a handsome army of scrimshandered chessmen whom we shall keep busy until either the *Prophetess*'s departure or the *Nellie*'s arrival.

Saturday, 9th November —

Sunrise bright as a silver dollar. Our schooner still looks a woeful picture out in the bay. An Indian war-canoe is being careened on the shore. Henry & I struck out for 'Banqueter's Beach' in holy-day mood, blithely saluting the maid who labours for Mr Walker. The sullen miss was hanging laundry on a shrub & ignored us. She has a tinge of black blood & I fancy her mother is not far removed from the jungle breed.

Passing below the Indian hamlet, a 'humming' aroused our curiosity & we resolved to locate its source. The settlement is circumvallated by a stake-fence, so decayed that one may gain ingress at a dozen places. A hairless bitch raised her head, but she was toothless & dying & did not bark. An outer ring of *ponga* huts (fashioned from branches, earthen walls & matted ceilings) grovelled in the lees of 'grandee' dwellings, wooden structures with carved lintel-pieces & rudimentary porches. In the hub of this village, a public flogging was under way. Henry & I were the only two Whites present, but three castes of spectating Indians were demarked. The chieftain occupied his throne, in a feathered cloak, while the tattooed gentry & their womenfolk & children stood in attendance, numbering some thirty in total. The slaves, duskier & sootier than their nut-brown masters & less than half their number, squatted in the mud. Such inbred, bovine torpor! Pockmarked & pustular with *haki-haki*, these wretches watched the punishment, making no response but that bizarre, bee-like 'hum'. Empathy or condemnation, we knew not what the noise signified. The whip-master was a Goliath whose physique would daunt any frontier prize-fighter. Lizards mighty & small were tattooed over every inch of the savage's musculature: – his pelt would fetch a fine price, though I should not be the man assigned to relieve him of it for all the pearls of O-hawaii! The piteous prisoner, hoarfrosted with many harsh years, was bound naked to an A-frame. His body shuddered with each excoriating lash, his back was a vellum of bloody runes but his insensible face bespoke the serenity of a martyr already in the care of the Lord.

I confess, I swooned under each fall of the lash. Then a peculiar thing occurred. The beaten savage raised his slumped head, found *my* eye & shone me a look of uncanny, amicable knowing! As if a theatrical performer saw a long-lost friend in the Royal Box and, undetected by the audience, communicated his recognition. A tattooed 'blackfella' approached us & flicked his nephrite dagger to indicate that we were unwelcome. I enquired after the nature of the prisoner's crime. Henry put his arm around me. 'Come, Adam, a wise man does not step betwixt the beast & his meat.'

Sunday, 10th November —

Mr Boerhaave sat amidst his cabal of trusted ruffians like Lord Anaconda & his garter-snakes. Their Sabbath 'celebrations' downstairs had begun ere I had risen. I went in search of shaving water & found the tavern swilling with Tars awaiting their turn with those poor Indian girls whom Walker has ensnared in an impromptu *bordello*. (Rafael was not in the debauchers' number.)

I do not break my Sabbath fast in a whorehouse. Henry's sense of repulsion equalled to my own, so we forfeited breakfast (the maid was doubtless being pressed into alternative service) & set out for the chapel to worship with our fasts unbroken.

We had not gone two hundred yards when, to my consternation, I remembered this journal, lying on the table in my room at the *Musket*, visible to any drunken sailor who might break in. Fearful for its safety (& my own, were Mr Boerhaave to get his hands on it), I retraced my steps to conceal it more artfully. Broad smirks greeted my return & I assumed I was 'the devil being spoken of', but I learned the true reason when I opened my door: – to wit, Mr Boerhaave's ursine buttocks astraddle his Blackamoor Goldilocks in *my* bed *in flagrante delicto*! Did that devil Dutchman apologise? Far from it! He judged *himself* the injured party & roared, 'Get ye hence, Mr Quillcock! or by God's B—d, I shall snap your tricksy Yankee nib in two!'

I snatched my diary & clattered downstairs to a *riotocracy* of merriment & ridicule from the white savages there gathered. I remonstrated to Walker that I was paying for a private room & I expected it to remain private even during my absence, but that scoundrel merely offered a one-third discount on 'A quarter-hour's gallop on the comeliest filly in my stable!' Disgusted, I retorted that I was a husband & a father! & that I should rather die than abase my dignity & decency with any of his poxed whores! Walker swore to 'decorate my eyes' if I called his own dear daughters 'whores' again. One toothless garter-snake jeered that if possessing a wife & a child was a single virtue, 'Why, Mr Ewing, I be ten times more virtuous than you be!' & an unseen hand emptied a tankard of sheog over my person. I withdrew ere the liquid was swapped for a more obdurate missile.

The chapel bell was summoning the godfearing of Ocean Bay & I hurried thitherwards where Henry waited, trying to forget the recent foulnesses witnessed at my lodgings. The chapel creaked like an old tub & its congregation numbered little more than the digits of two hands, but no traveller ever quenched his thirst at a desert oasis more thankfully than Henry & I gave worship this morning. The Lutheran founder has lain at rest in his chapel's cemetery these ten winters past & no ordained successor has yet ventured to claim captaincy of the altar. Its denomination, therefore, is a 'rattle-bag' of Christian creeds. Biblical passages were read by that half of the congregation who know their letters & we joined in a hymn or two nominated by rota. The 'steward' of this demotic flock, one Mr D'Arnoq, stood beneath the modest cruciform & besought Henry & I to participate in likewise manner. Mindful of my own salvation from last week's tempest, I nominated Luke ch. 8, *And they came to him, & awoke him, saying, Master, master, we perish. Then he arose, & rebuked the wind & the raging of the water: & they ceased, & there was a calm.*

Henry recited Psalm the Eighth, in a voice as sonorous as any schooled dramatist, *Thou madest him to have dominion over the works of thy hands; thou has put all things under his feet: all sheep & oxen, yea, & the beasts of the field; The fowl of the air, & the fish of the sea, & whatsoever passeth through the paths of the seas.*

No organist played a *Magnificat* but the wind in the flue-chimney, no choir sang a *Nunc Dimittis* but the wuthering gulls, yet I fancy the Creator was not displeazed. We resembled more the Early Christians of Rome than any later Church encrusted with arcana & gemstones. Communal prayer followed. Parishioners prayed *ad lib* for the eradication of potato blight, mercy on a dead infant's soul, blessing upon a new fishing boat, &c. Henry gave thanks for the hospitality shown us visitors by the Christians of Chatham Isle. I echoed these sentiments & sent a prayer for Tilda, Jackson & my father-in-law during my extended absence.

After the service, the doctor & I were approached most cordially by an elder 'mainmast' of that chapel, one Mr Evans, who introduced Henry & I to his good wife (both circumvented the handicap of deafness by answering only those questions they *believed* had been asked & accepting only those answers they *believed* had been uttered – a stratagem embraced by many an American advocate) & their twin sons, Keegan & Dyfedd. Mr Evans made it known that every week he had the custom of inviting Mr D'Arnoq, our Preacher, to dine at their nearby home, for the latter dwells in Port Hutt, a promontory some miles distant. Would we, too, join their Sabbath Meal? Having already informed Henry of that Gomorrah back at the *Musket* & hearing cries of 'Mutiny!' from our stomachs, we accepted the Evanses' kindness with gratitude.

Our hosts' farm-stead, seated half a mile from Ocean Bay up a winding, blustery valley, proved to be a frugal building, but proof against those hell-bent storms that break the bones of so many hapless vessels upon nearby reefs. The parlour was inhabited by a monstrous hog's head (afflicted with droop-jaw & lazy-eye), killed by the twins on their sixteenth birthday, & a somnambulant Grand-father clock (at odds with my own pocket-watch by a margin of hours. Indeed, one valued import from New Zealand is the accurate time). An Indian farmhand peered through the window-pane at his master's visitors. No more tatterdemalion a *renegado* I ever beheld, but Mr Evans swore the quadroon, 'Barnabas', was 'the fleetest sheep-dog who ever ran upon two legs'. Keegan & Dyfedd are honest woolly fellows, versed principally in the ways of sheep (the family own two hundred head), for neither has gone to 'Town' (the islanders thus appellate New Zealand) nor undergone any schooling save Scripture lessons from their father, by dint of which they have learnt to read & write tolerably well.

Mrs Evans said grace & I enjoyed my most pleasant repast (untainted by salt, maggots & oaths) since my farewell dinner with Consul Bax & the Partridges at the Beaumont. Mr D'Arnoq told us tales of ships he has supplied during his ten-year on Chatham Isle, while Henry amused us with stories of patients, both illustrious & humble, he has benefacted in London & Polynesia. For my part I described the many hardships overcome by this American notary in order to locate the Australian beneficiary of a will executed in California. We washed down our mutton-stew & apple-dumpling with small ale brewed by Mr Evans for trading with whalers. Keegan & Dyfedd left to attend to their livestock & Mrs Evans retired to her kitchen duties. Henry asked if missionaries were now active on the Chathams at which Mr Evans & Mr D'Arnoq exchanged looks, & the former informed us, 'Nay, the Maori don't take kindly to us *Pakeha* spoiling their Moriori with too much civilization.'

I questioned if such an ill as 'too *much* civilization' existed or no? Mr D'Arnoq told me, 'If there is no God west of the Horn, why there's none of your constitution's *All men created equal*, neither, Mr Ewing.' The nomenclatures 'Maori' & 'Pakeha' I knew from the *Prophetess*'s sojourn at the Bay of Islands, but I begged to know who or what 'Moriori' might signify. My query unlocked a Pandora's Box of history, detailing the decline & fall of the aboriginals of Chatham. We lit our pipes. Mr D'Arnoq's narrative was unbroken three hours later when he had to depart for Port Hutt ere nightfall obscured the dykey way. His spoken history, for my money, holds company with the pen of a Defoe or Melville & I shall record it in these pages, after, Morpheus willing, a sound sleep.

Monday, 11th November —

Dawn sticky & sunless. The bay has a slimy appearance, but the weather is mild enough to allow repairs to continue on *Prophetess*, I thank Neptune. A new mizzen-top is being hoisted into position as I write.

A short time past, while Henry & I breakfasted, Mr Evans arrived hugger-mugger, importuning my doctor friend to attend to a reclusive neighbour, one Widow Bryden, who was thrown from her horse on a stony bog. Mrs Evans was in attendance and fears that the widow lies in peril of her life. Henry fetched his doctor's case & left without delay. (I offered to come, but Mr Evans begged my forbearance, as the patient had extracted a promise that none but a doctor should see her incapacitated.) Walker, overhearing these transactions, told me no member of the male sex had crossed the widow's threshold these twenty years & decided that 'The frigid old sow must be on her last trotters if she's letting Dr Quack frisk her.'

The origins of the Moriori of 'Rēkohu' (the native moniker for the Chathams) remain a mystery to this day. Mr Evans evinces the belief they are descended from Jews expelled from Spain, citing their hooked noses & sneering lips. Mr D'Arnoq's preferred theorum, that the Moriori were once Maori whose canoes were wrecked upon these remotest of isles, is founded on similarities of tongue & mythology, & thereby possesses a higher *carat* of logic. What is certain is that, after centuries or millennia of living in isolation, the Moriori lived as primitive a life as their woebegone cousins of Van Diemen's Land. Arts of boat-building (beyond crude woven rafts used to cross the channels betwixt islands) & navigation fell into disuse. That the terraqueous globe held other lands, trod by other feet, the Moriori dreamt not. Indeed, their language lacks a word for 'Race' & 'Moriori' means, simply, 'People'. Husbandry was not practised, for no mammals walked these isles until passing whalers wilfully marooned pigs here to propagate a parlour. In their virgin state, the Moriori were foragers, picking up *paua* shellfish, diving for crayfish, plundering bird-eggs, spearing seals, gathering kelp & digging for grubs & roots.

Thus far, the Moriori were but a local variant of most flaxen-skirted, feather-cloaked heathens of those dwindling 'blind-spots' of the ocean still unschooled by the White Man. Old Rēkohu's claim to singularity, however, lay in its unique pacific creed. Since time immemorial, the Moriori's priestly caste dictated that whosoever spilt a man's blood killed his own *mana* – his honour, his worth, his standing & his soul. No Moriori would shelter, feed, converse or even *see* the *persona non grata*. If the ostracised murderer survived his first winter, the desperation of solitude usually drove him to a blow-hole on Cape Young where he took his life.

Consider this, Mr D'Arnoq urged us. Two thousand savages (Mr Evans's best guess) enshrine *Thou Shalt Not Kill* in word *& in deed* & frame an oral 'Magna Carta' to create a harmony unknown elsewhere for the sixty centuries since Adam tasted the fruit of the Tree of Knowledge. War was as alien a concept to the Moriori as the telescope is to the Pygmy. *Peace*, not a hiatus betwixt wars but millennia of imperishable peace, rules these far-flung islands. Who can deny Old Rēkohu lay closer to More's Utopia than our States of Progress governed by war-hungry princelings in Versailles & Vienna, Washington & Westminster? 'Here,' declaimed Mr D'Arnoq, 'and here only, were those elusive phantasms, the noble savages, framed in flesh & blood!' (Henry, as we later made our way back to the *Musket* confessed, 'I could never describe a race of savages too backward to throw a spear straight as "noble".')

Glass & peace alike betray proof of fragility under repeated blows. The first blow to the Moriori was the Union Jack, planted in Skirmish Bay's sod in the name of King George by Lieutenant Broughton of HMS *Chatham* just fifty years ago. Three years later, Broughton's discovery was in Sydney & London chart agents & a scattering of free settlers (whose number included

Mr Evans's father), wrecked mariners & 'convicts at odds with the New South Wales Colonial Office over the terms of their incarceration' were cultivating pumpkins, onions, maize & carrots. These they sold to needy sealers, the second blow to the Moriori's independence, who disappointed the Natives' hopes of prosperity by turning the surf pink with seals' blood. (Mr D'Arnoq illustrated the profits by this arithmetic – a single pelt fetched 15 shillings in Canton & those pioneer sealers gathered over two thousand pelts *per boat*!) Within a few years the seals were found only on the outer rocks & the 'sealers' too turned to farming potatoes, sheep & pig-rearing on such a scale that the Chathams are now dubbed 'The Garden of the Pacific'. These *parvenu* farmers clear the land by bush-fires that smoulder beneath the peat for many seasons, surfacing in dry spells to sow renewed calamity.

The third blow to the Moriori was the whalers, now calling at Ocean Bay, Waitangi, Owenga & Te Whakaru in sizeable numbers for careening, refitting & refreshing. Whalers' cats & rats bred like the Plagues of Egypt & ate the burrow-nesting birds whose eggs the Moriori so valued for sustenance. Fourth, those motley maladies which cull the darker races whene'er White civilization draws near, sapped the aboriginal census still further.

All these misfortunes the Moriori might have endured, however, were it not for reports arriving in New Zealand depicting the Chathams as a veritable Canaan of eel-stuffed lagoons, shellfish-carpeted coves & inhabitants who understand neither combat nor weapons. To the ears of the Ngati Tama & Ngati Mutunga, two clans of the Taranaki Te Ati Awa Maori (Maori geneaology is, Mr D'Arnoq assures us, every twig as intricate as those genealogical trees so revered by the European gentry, indeed, any boy of that unlettered race can recall his grandfather's grandfather's name & 'rank' in a trice), these rumours promised compensation for the tracts of their ancestral estates lost during the recent 'Musket Wars'. Spies were sent to test the Moriori's mettle by violating *tapu* & despoiling holy sites. These provocations the Moriori faced as Our Lord importuned, by 'turning the other cheek', & the transgressors returned to New Zealand confirming the Moriori's apparent pusillanimity. The tattooed Maori *conquistadores* found their single-barked armada in Captain Harewood of the brig *Rodney* who, in the dying months of 1835, agreed to transport nine hundred Maori & seven war-canoes in two voyages, in guerno for seed potatoes, firearms, pigs, a great supply of scraped flax & a cannon. (Mr D'Arnoq encountered Harewood five years ago, penurious in a Bay of Islands tavern. He at first denied being the *Rodney*'s Harewood, then swore he had been coerced into conveying the blacks, but was unclear how this coercion had been worked upon him.)

The *Rodney* embarked from Port Nicholas in November, but its heathen cargo of five hundred men, women & children, packed tight in the hold for the six-day voyage, bilged in ordure & seasickness & lacking the barest sufficiency of water, anchored at Whangatete Inlet in such an enfeebled state that, *had they but the will*, even the Moriori might have slain their Martial brethren. The Goodly Samaritans chose instead to share the diminished abundance of Rēkohu in preference to destroying their *mana* by blood-letting, & nursed the sick & dying Maori back to health. 'Maori had come to Rēkohu before,' Mr D'Arnoq explained, 'yet gone away again, so the Moriori assumed the colonists would likewise leave them in peace.'

The Moriori's generosity was rewarded when Cpt. Harewood returned from New Zealand with another four hundred Maori. Now the strangers proceeded to lay claim to Chatham by *takahi*, a Maori ritual transliterated as 'Walking the Land to Possess the Land'. Old Rēkohu was thus partitioned & the Moriori informed they were now Maori vassals. In early December, when some dozen Aboriginals protested, they were casually slain with tomahawks. The Maori proved themselves apt pupils of the English in 'the dark arts of colonization'.

Chatham Isle encloses a vast eastern saltmarsh lagoon, Te Whanga, very nearly an inland sea but fecundated by the ocean at high tide through the lagoon's 'lips' at Te Awapatiki. Fourteen years ago, the Moriori men held on that sacred ground a parliament. Three days it lasted, its object to settle this question: Would the spillage of Maori blood also destroy one's *mana*? Younger men argued the creed of Peace did not encompass foreign cannibals of whom their ancestors knew nothing. The Moriori must kill or be killed. Elders urged appeasement, for as long as the Moriori preserved their *mana* with their land, their gods & ancestors would deliver the race from harm. 'Embrace your enemy,' the elders urged, 'to prevent him striking you.' ('Embrace your enemy,' Henry quipped, 'to feel his dagger tickle your kidneys.')

The elders won the day, but it mattered little. 'When lacking numerical superiority,' Mr D'Arnoq told us, 'the Maori seize an advantage by striking first & hardest, as many hapless British & French can testify from their graves.' The Ngati Tama & Ngati Mutunga had held councils of their own. The Moriori menfolk returned from their parliament to ambushes & a night of infamy beyond nightmare, of butchery, of villages torched, of rapine, of men & women, impaled in rows on beaches, of children hiding in holes, scented & dismembered by hunting dogs. Some chiefs kept an eye to the morrow & slew only enough to instil terrified obedience in the remainder. Other chiefs were not so restrained. On Waitangi Beach fifty Moriori were beheaded, filleted, wrapped in flax-leaves, then baked in a giant earth oven with yams & sweet-potatoes. Not half those Moriori who had seen Old Rēkohu's last sunset were alive to see the Maori sun rise. ('Less than an hundred pure-blooded Moriori now remain,' mourned Mr D'Arnoq. 'On *paper* the British Crown freed these from the yoke of slavery years ago, but the Maori do not care for paper. We are one week's sail from the Governor's House & Her Majesty maintains no garrison on Chatham.')

I asked, why had not the Whites stayed the hands of the Maori during the massacre?

Mr Evans was no longer sleeping & not half so deaf as I had fancied. 'Have you ever seen Maori warriors in a blood-frenzy, Mr Ewing?'

I said I had not.

'But you have seen sharks in a blood-frenzy, have you not?'

I replied that I had.

'Near enough. Imagine a bleeding calf is thrashing in shark-infested shallows. What to do – stay out of the water or try to stay the jaws of the sharks? Such was our choice. Oh, we helped the few that came to our door – our shepherd Barnabas was one – but if we stepped out in that night we'd not be seen again. Remember, we Whites numbered below fifty in Chatham at that time. Nine hundred Maoris, altogether. Maoris bide by Pakeha, Mr Ewing, but they despise us. Never forget it.'

What moral to draw? Peace, though beloved of our Lord, is a cardinal virtue only if your neighbours share your conscience.

Night –

The name of Mr D'Arnoq is not well-loved in the *Musket*. 'A White Black, a mixed-blood mongrel of a man,' Walker told me. 'Nobody knows *what* he is.' Suggs, a one-armed shepherd who lives under the bar, swore our acquaintance is a Bonapartist general hiding here under assumed colours. Another swore he was a Polack.

Nor is the word 'Moriori' much loved. A drunken Maori mulatto told me that the entire history of the aboriginals had been dreamt up by the 'mad old Lutheran', & Mr D'Arnoq preaches his Moriori gospel only to legitimise his own swindling land-claims against the Maori, the true owners of Chatham, who have been coming to & fro in their canoes since time immemorial! James Coffee, a hog-farmer, said the Maori had performed the White Man a service by exterminating another race of brutes to make space for us, adding that Russians train Kossacks to 'soften Siberian hides' in a similar way.

I protested, to *civilize* the black races by conversion should be our mission, not their extirpation, for God's hand had crafted them, too. All hands in the tavern fired broadsides at me for my 'sentimental Yankee clap-trap'! 'The best of 'em is not too good to die like a pig!' one shouted. 'The only gospel the Blacks *savvy* is the gospel of the d—d whip!' Still another: 'We Britishers abolished slavery in our empire – no American can say as much!'

Henry's stance was ambivalent, to say the least. 'After years of working with missionaries, I am tempted to conclude that their endeavours merely prolong a dying race's agonies for ten or twenty years. The merciful ploughman shoots a trusty horse grown too old for service. As philanthropists, might it not be our duty to likewise ameliorate the savages' sufferings by *hastening* their extinction? Think on your Red Indians, Adam, think on the treaties you Americans abrogate & renege on, time & time & time again. More humane, surely, & more honest, just to knock the savages on the head & get it over with?'

As many truths as men. Occasionally, I glimpse a truer Truth, hiding in imperfect simulacrums of itself, but as I approach, it bestirs itself & moves deeper into the thorny swamp of dissent.

Tuesday, 12th November —

Our noble Cpt. Molyneux today graced the *Musket* to haggle over the price of five barrels of salt-horse with my landlord (the matter was settled by a rowdy game of *trentuno* won by the captain). Much to my surprise, ere he returned to inspect the progress in the ship-yard, Cpt. Molyneux requested some confidential words with Henry in my companion's room. The consultation continues as I write. My friend has been warned of the captain's despotism, but still, I do not like it.

Later —

Cpt. Molyneux, it transpires, suffers from a medical complaint which, if untreated, may impair those divers skills demanded of his station. The captain has therefore proposed to Henry that my friend voyage with us to Honolulu (victualling & private berth *gratis*), assuming the responsibilities both of Ship's Doctor & personal physician to Cpt. Molyneux until our arrival. My friend explained he had intended to return to London, but Cpt. Molyneux was most insistent. Henry promised to think the matter over & come to a decision by Friday morning, the day now set for *Prophetess*'s departure.

Henry did not name the captain's illness, nor did I ask, though one needs not be an Aesculapian to glean Cpt. Molyneux is a slave to gout. My friend's discretion does him much credit. Whatever eccentricities Henry Goose may exhibit as a collector of curios, I believe Dr Goose is an exemplary healer & it is my zealous, if self-serving, hope that Henry returns a favourable answer to the captain's proposal.

Wednesday, 13th November —

I come to my journal as a Catholick to a confessor. My bruises insist these extraordinary past five hours were not a sickbed vision conjured by my Ailment, but real events. I shall describe what befell me this day, steering as close to the facts as is possible.

This morning, Henry paid Widow Bryden's hut another call to adjust her splint & re-apply poultice. Rather than submit to idleness, I resolved to scale a high hill to the north of Ocean Bay, known as Conical Tor, whose lofty elevation promises the best aspect of Chatham Isle's 'back-country'. (Henry, a man of maturer years, has too much sense to tramp unsurveyed islands peopled by cannibals.) The tired creek who waters Ocean Bay guided me upstream through marshy pastures, stump-pocked slopes, into virgin forest so rotted, knotted & tangled, I was obliged to clamber aloft like an orang-utan! A volley of hailstones began abruptly, filled the woods with a frenzied percussion & ended on the sudden. I spied a 'Robin Black-Breast' whose plumage was tarry as night & whose tameness bordered on contempt. An unseen *tui* took to song, but my inflamed fancy awarded it powers of human speech: – 'Eye for an eye!' it called ahead, flitting through its labyrinth of buds, twigs & thorns. 'Eye for an eye!' After a gruelling climb, I conquered the summit grievously torn & scratched at I know not What o'Clock, for I neglected to wind my pocket-watch last night. The opaque mists that haunt these isles (the aboriginal name 'Rēkohu', Mr D'Arnoq informs us, signifies 'Sun of Mists') had descended as I ascended, so my cherished panorama was naught but tree-tops disappearing into drizzle. A miserly reward for my exertions, indeed.

The 'summit' of Conical Tor was a crater, a stone's throw in diameter, encircling a crag-walled depression whose floor lay unseen far beneath the funereal foliage of a gross or more *kopi* trees. I should not have cared to investigate its depths without the aid of ropes & a pick-axe. I was circumambulating the crater's lip, seeking a clearer trail back to Ocean Bay, when a startling *hoo-roosh!* sent me diving to the ground: – the mind abhors a vacancy & is wont to people it with phantoms, thus I glimpsed first a tusked hog charging, then a Maori warrior, spear held aloft, his face inscribed with the ancestral hatred of his race.

'Twas but a mollyhawk, wings 'flupping' the air like a windjammer. I watched her disappear back into the diaphanous fog. I was a full yard shy of the crater's lip but, to my horror, the turf beneath me disintegrated like suet-crust – I stood not on solid ground but an overhang! I plunged to my midriff, grasping some grasses in desperation, but these broke in my fingers & down I plummeted, a mannikin tossed into a well! I recall spinning in space, yelling & twigs clawing my eyes, cartwheeling & my jacket snagging, tearing loose; loose earth; the anticipation of pain; an urgent, formless prayer for help; a bush slowing, but not halting my descent & a hopeless attempt to regain balance – sliding – lastly *terra firma* careering upwards to meet me. The impact knocked my senses out of me.

Amid nebulous quilts & summery pillows I lay, in a bedroom in San Francisco similar to my own. A dwarfish servant said,

'You're a *very* silly boy, Adam.' Tilda & Jackson entered, but when I voiced my jubilation not English but the guttural barkings of an Indian race burst from my mouth! My wife & son were shamed by me & mounted a carriage. I gave chase, striving to rectify this misunderstanding, but the carriage dwindled into the fleeing distance until I awoke in bosky twilight & a silence, booming & eternal. My bruises, cuts, muscles & extremities groaned like a court-room of malcontent litigants.

A mattress of moss & mulch, lain down in that murky hollow since the second day of Creation, had preserved my life. Angels preserved my limbs, for if even a single arm or leg had been broken I should be lying there still, unable to extricate myself, awaiting death from the elements or the claws of beasts. Upon regaining my feet & seeing how far I had slid & fallen (the height of a foremast) with no worse damage to my person, I thanked our Lord for my deliverance, for indeed, *Thou calledst in trouble, & I delivered thee; I answered thee in the secret place of thunder.*

My eyes adjusted to the gloom & revealed a sight at once indelible, fearsome & sublime. First one, then ten, then hundreds of faces emerged from the perpetual dim, adzed by idolaters into bark, as if Sylvan-spirits were frozen immobile by a cruel enchanter. No adjectives may properly delineate that basilisk tribe! Only the inanimate may be so alive. I traced my thumbs along their awful visages. I do not doubt, I was the first White in that mausoleum since its pre-historic inception. The youngest dendroglyph is, I suppose, ten years old, but the elders, grown distended as the trees matured, were incised by heathens whose very ghosts are long defunct. Such antiquity surely bespoke the hand of Mr D'Arnoq's Moriori.

Time passed in that bewitched place & I sought to effect my escape, encouraged by the knowledge that the artists of the 'tree-sculptures' must earn regular egress from that same pit. One wall looked less sheer than the others & fibrous creepers offered a 'rigging' of sorts. I was readying myself for the climb when a puzzling 'hum' came to my attention. 'Who goes there?'

I called (a rash act for an unarmed White trespasser in a heathen shrine). 'Shew yourself!' The silence swallowed my words & their echo & mocked me. My Ailment stirred in my spleen. The 'hum' I traced to a mass of flies orbiting a protuberance impaled on a broken-off branch. I poked the lump with a pine stick & nearly retched, for 'twas a piece of stinking offal. I turned to flee but duty obliged me to dispel a black suspicion that a human heart hung on that tree. I concealed my nose & mouth in my 'kerchief &, with my stick, touched a severed ventricle. The organ pulsed as if alive! & my scalding Ailment shot up my spine! As in a dream (but it was not!) a pellucid salamander emerged from its carrion dwelling & darted along the stick to my hand! I flung the stick away & saw not where that salamander disappeared. My blood was enriched by fright & I hastened to effect my escape. Easier written than done, for had I slipped & plunged anew from those vertiginous walls my luck may not have softened my fall a second time, but foot-holes had been hewn into the rock & by God's grace I gained the crater's lip with no mishap.

Back in the dismal cloud, I craved the presence of men of my own hue, yes, even the rude sailors in the *Musket*, & began my descent on the nonce in what I hoped was a southerly direction. My initial resolve to report all I had seen (surely, Mr Walker, the *de facto* if not *de juro* Consul should be informed of the robbery of a human heart?) weakened as I approached Ocean Bay. I am still undecided what to report & to whom. The heart was most likely a hog's, or sheep's, surely. The prospect of Walker & his ilk felling the trees & selling the dendroglyphs to collectors offends my conscience. A sentimentalist I may be, but I do not wish to be the agent of the Moriori's final violation.*

---

* My father never spoke to me of the dendroglyphs & I learnt of them only in the manner described in the Introduction. Now that the Moriori of Chatham Island are a race over extinction's brink, I hold them to be beyond betrayal. – J.E.

Evening –

The Southern Cross was bright in the sky ere Henry returned to the *Musket*, having been detained by more islanders seeking to consult 'Widow Bryden's Healer Man' on their rheums, yaws & dropsy. 'If potatoes were dollars,' rued my friend, 'I should be richer than Nebuchadnezzar!' He was concerned by my (much edited) misadventure on Conical Tor & insisted on examining my injuries. Earlier I had prevailed upon the Indian maid to fill my bath & emerged much recruited. Henry donated a pot of balm for my inflammations & refused to take a cent for it. Fearing this may be my last chance to consult with a gifted physician (Henry intends to refuse Cpt. Molyneux's proposal), I unburdened my fears *vis-à-vis* my Ailment. He listened soberly & asked about the frequency & duration of my spells. Henry regretted he lacked the time & apparatus for a compleat diagnosis, but recommended, upon my return to San Francisco, I find a specialist in tropical parasites as a matter of urgency. (I could not bring myself to tell him there are none.)

I slumber not.

Thursday, 14th November –

We make sail with the morning tide. I am once more aboard the *Prophetess*, but I cannot pretend it is good to be back. My coffin now stores three great coils of hawser which I must scale to attain my bunk, for not one inch of floor is visible. Mr D'Arnoq sold half a dozen barrels of sundry provisions to the quartermaster & a bolt of sailcloth (much to Walker's disgust). He came aboard to supervise their delivery & collect payment himself & bid me God-speed. In my coffin we were squeezed like two men in a pot-hole so we repaired to the deck for it is a pleasant evening. After discussing divers matters we shook hands & he climbed down to his waiting ketch, ably crewed by two young manservants of mongrel race.

Mr Roderick has little sympathy with my petition to have the offending hawser removed elsewhere, for he is obliged to quit his private cabin (for the reason stated below) & move to the fo'c'sle with the common sailors, whose number has swollen with five Castilians 'poached' from the Spaniard at anchor in the Bay. Their captain was the portrait of a Fury, yet short of declaring war on the *Prophetess* – a battle sure to bloody his nose, for he pilots the leakiest tub – he can do little but thank his stars Cpt. Molyneux required no more deserters. The very words 'California Bound' are dusted in gold & beckon all men thitherwards like moths to a lantern. These five replace the two deserters at the Bay of Islands & the hands lost in the tempest, but we are still several men short of a full crew. Finbar tells me the men grumble over the new arrangements for, with Mr Roderick lodged in their fo'c'sle, they cannot yarn freely over a bottle.

Fate has dealt me a fine compensation. After paying Walker's usurous bill (nor did I tip that scoundrel a cent), I was packing my jackwood trunk when Henry entered greeting me thus: – 'Good morning, Ship-mate!' God has answered my prayers! Henry has accepted the post of Ship's Doctor & I am no longer friendless in this floating farmyard. So ornery a mule is the common sailor that, instead of gratitude that a doctor shall be on hand to splint their breakages & treat their infections, one o'erhears them moaning, 'What are we, to carry a Ship's Doctor who can't walk a bowsprit? A Royal Barge?'

I must confess to a touch of pique that Cpt. Molyneux afforded a fare-paying gentleman such as myself only my lamentable berth, when a more commodious cabin lay at his disposal all along. Of far greater consequence, however, is Henry's promise to turn his formidable talents to a diagnosis of my Ailment as soon as we are at sea. My relief is indescribable.

Friday, 15th November —

We got under weigh at daybreak, notwithstanding Friday is a Jonah amongst sailors. (Cpt. Molyneux growls, 'Superstitions, Saints' Days & other blasted fripperies are fine sport for Popish fish-wives but *I* am in the business of turning a profit!') Henry & I did not venture on deck, for all hands were busy with rigging & a southerly blows very fresh with a heavy sea; the ship was troublesome last night & is not less so today. We passed half the day arranging Henry's apothecary. Besides the appurtenances of the modern physician, my friend owns several learned volumes, in English, Latin & German. A case holds 'spectra' of powders in stoppered bottles labelled in Greek. These he compounds to make various pills & unguents. We peered through the steerage-hatch towards noon & the Chathams were ink-stains on the leaden horizon, but the rolling & pitching are unsafe for those whose sea-legs have vacationed the week ashore.

Afternoon —

Torgny the Swede knocked on my coffin door. Surprized & intrigued by his furtive manner, I bade him enter. He seated himself upon a 'pyramid' of hawser & whispered that he bore a proposal from a ring of ship-mates. 'Tell us where the best veins are, the secret ones you locals are keeping for yourselves. Me 'n' my fellows'll do the pack-work. You'll just sit pretty & we'll cut you in a tenth share.'

I required a moment to understand that Torgny was referring to the Californian mining-fields. So, a widespread desertion is in the offing once the *Prophetess* reaches her destination &, I own, my sympathies are with the seamen! Saying so, I swore to Torgny that I possessed no knowledge of the gold deposits, for I have been absent this twelvemonth, but I would *gratis* compose a map illustrating the rumoured 'Eldorados' & gladly. Torgny was agreeable. Tearing a leaf from this journal, I was sketching a *schema* of Sausalito, Benecia, Stanislaus, Sacramento, &c., when a malevolent voice spoke out. 'Quite the oracle, no, Mr Quillcock?'

We had not heard Boerhaave descend the companionway & nudge open my door! Torgny cried in dismay, declaring his guilt in a trice. 'What, pray,' continued the first mate, 'what business have you with our passenger, Pustule of Stockholm?' Torgny was struck dumb, but I would not be cowed & told the bully I was describing the 'sights' of my town, the better for Torgny to enjoy his shore-leave.

Boerhaave raised his eyebrows. 'You allot shore-leave now, do you? New news to my old ears. That paper, Mr Ewing, if you please.' I did not please. My gift to the seaman was not the Dutchman's to commandeer. 'Oh, begging your pardon, Mr Ewing. Torgny, take receipt of your *gift*.' I had no choice but to hand it to the prostrate Swede. Mr Boerhaave uttered, 'Torgny, give me *your* gift instanter or, by the hinges of hell, you shall regret the day you crawled from your mother's [my quill curls at recording his profanity].' The mortified Swede complied.

'Most educational,' remarked Boerhaave, eyeing my cartography. 'The captain will be delighted to learn of the pains you are taking to better our scabby Jacks, Mr Ewing. Torgny, you're on mast-head watch for twenty-four hours. Forty-eight if you're seen taking refreshment. Drink you own p— if you get a thirst.'

Torgny fled but the first mate was not finished with me. 'Sharks ply these waters, Mr Quillcock. Trail ships for tasty jetsam, they do. Once I saw one eat a passenger. He, like you, was neglectful of his safety, & fell o'erboard. We heard his screams. Great Whites *toy* with their dinner, gnawing 'em slow, a leg here, a nibble there & that miserable b— was alive longer than you'd credit. Think on it.' He shut my coffin door. Boerhaave, like all bullies & tyrants, takes pride in that very hatefulness which makes him notorious.

Saturday, 16th November —

My Fates have inflicted upon me the greatest unpleasance of my voyage to date! A shade of Old Rēkohu has thrust *me*, whose only desiderata are quietude & discretion, into a pillory of suspicion & gossip! Yet I am guilty on *no counts* save Christian trustingness & relentless ill fortune! One month to the day has passed since we put out from New South Wales when I wrote this sunny sentence, 'I anticipate an uneventful & tedious voyage.' How that entry mocks me! I shall never forget the last eighteen hours, but since I cannot sleep nor think (& Henry is now abed) my only escape from insomnia now is to curse my Luck on these sympathetic pages.

Last night I retired to my coffin 'dog-tired'. After my prayers I blew out my lantern & lulled by the ship's myriad voices I sank into the shallows of sleep when a husky voice, *inside my coffin!*, awakened me wide-eyed & affright! 'Mr Ewing,' beseeched this urgent whisper, 'Do not fear – Mr Ewing – no harm, no shout, please, sir.'

I jumped involuntarily & knocked my head against the bulkhead. By the twin glimmers of amber-light through my ill-fitted door & star-light through my port-hole, I saw a serpentine length of hawser uncoil itself & a black form heave itself free like the dead at the Last Trump! A powerful hand seemed to sail through the blackness & sealed my lips ere I could cry out! My assailant hissed, 'Missa Ewing, no harm, you safe, I friend of Mr D'Arnoq – you know he Christian – please, quiet!'

Reason, at last, rallied against my fear. A man, not a spirit, was hiding in my room. If he wished to slit my throat for my hat, shoes & legal-box, I would already be dead. If my gaoler was a stowaway, why, he, not I, was in peril for his life. From his uncut language, his faint silhouette & his smell, I intuited the stowaway was an Indian, alone on a boat of fifty White Men. Very well. I nodded, slowly, to indicate I would not cry out.

The cautious hand released my lips. 'My name is Autua,' he

said. 'You know I, you seen I, aye – you pity I.' I asked what
he was talking about. 'Maori whip I – you seen.' My memory
overcame the bizarreness of my situation & I recalled the
Moriori being flogged by the 'Lizard King'. This heartened him.
'You good man – Mr D'Arnoq tell you good man – he hid I in
your cabin yesterday night – I escape – you help, Mr Ewing.'
Now a groan escaped my lips! & his hand clasped my mouth
anew. 'If you no help – I in trouble dead.'

All too true, I thought, *& moreover you'll drag me down
with you, unless I convince Cpt. Molyneux of my innocence!* (I
burned with resentment at D'Arnoq's act, & burn still. Let *him*
save his 'good causes' & leave innocent bystanders be!) I told
the stowaway he was already 'in trouble dead'. The *Prophetess*
was a mercantile vessel, not an 'underground rail-road' for
rescued slaves.

'I able seaman!' insisted the black. 'I earn passage!' Well &
good, I told him (dubious of his claim to be a sailor of pedigree),
& urged him to surrender himself to the captain's mercies forth-
with. 'No! They no listen I! *Swim Away Home, Nigger*, they
say, & throw I in drink! You law-man aye? You go, you talk,
I stay, I hide! Please. Cap'n hear you, Missa Ewing. Please.'

In vain I sought to convince him, no intercessor at Cpt. Molyneux's court was less favoured than the Yankee Adam Ewing.
The Moriori's adventure was his own & I desired no part in it.
His hand found mine & to my consternation closed my fingers
around the hilt of a dagger. Resolute & bleak was his demand.
'Then kill I.' With a terrible calmness & certitude he pressed its
tip against his throat. I told the Indian he was mad. 'I not mad,
you no help I, you kill I, just same. It's true, you know it.' (I
implored him to restrain himself & speak soft.) 'So kill I. Say
to others I attack you, so you kill I. I ain't be fish-food, Mr
Ewing. Die here is better.'

Cursing my conscience singly, my fortune doubly & Mr
D'Arnoq trebly, I bade him sheath his knife & for Heaven's sake
conceal himself lest one of the crew hear and come knocking. I
promised to approach the captain at breakfast, for to interrupt

his slumbers would only ensure the doom of the enterprise. This satisfied the stowaway & he thanked me. He slid back inside the coils of rope leaving me to the near-impossible task of constructing a case for an Aboriginal stowaway, aboard an English schooner, without attainting his discoverer & cabin-mate with a charge of conspiracy. The savage's breathing told me he was sleeping. I was tempted to make a dash for the door & howl for help, but in the eyes of God my word was my bond, even to an Indian.

The cacophony of timbers creaking, of masts swaying, of ropes flexing, of canvas clapping, of feet on decks, of goats bleating, of rats scuttling, of the pumps beating, of the bell dividing the watches, of mêlées & laughter from the fo'c'sle, of orders, of windlass shanties & of Tethys' eternal realm; all lulled me as I calculated how best I could convince Cpt. Molyneux of my innocence in Mr D'Arnoq's plot (now I must be more vigilant than ever that this diary should not be read by unfriendly eyes) when a falsetto yell, beginning far-off but speeding nearer at a crossbolt's velocity, was silenced by the deck, mere inches above where I lay.

Such a terrible finality! Prone I lay, shocked & rigid, forgetting to breathe. Shouts far & near rose, feet gathered & an alarum of 'Raise Doctor Goose!' cried forth.

'Sorry b— fall from rigging, dead now.' The Indian whispered as I made haste to investigate the disturbance. 'You can nothing, Missa Ewing.' I ordered him to stay hidden & hurried out. I fancy the stowaway sensed how tempted I was to use the accident to betray him.

The crew stood around a man lying prone at the base of the mid-mast. By the lurching lantern-light I recognized one of the Castilians. (I own that my first emotion was relief, that not Rafael but another had fallen to his death.) I overheard the Icelander say the dead man had won his compatriots' arrack ration at cards & drunk it all before his watch. Henry arrived in his night-shirt with his doctor's bag. He knelt by the mangled form & felt for a pulse, but shook his head. 'This fellow has no need of a doctor.' Mr Roderick retrieved the Castilian's boots & clothes for auction & Mankin fetched some third-rate sack-cloth for the cadaver. (Mr Boerhaave will deduct the sackcloth from the auction's profits.) The Jacks returned to their fo'c'sle or their stations in silence, every man made sombre by this reminder of the fragility of life. Henry, Mr Roderick & I stayed to watch the Castilians perform their Catholic death-rites over their countryman before knotting up the sack & committing his body to the deep with tears & dolorous *adios*! 'Passionate Latinos,' observed Henry, bidding me a second good-night. I yearned to share the secret of the Indian with my friend, but held my tongue lest my complicity infect him.

Returning from the melancholy scene, I saw a lantern gleam in the galley. Finbar sleeps there 'to ward off pilferers', but he too was roused by the night's excitement. I recalled that the stowaway may not have eaten for a day & a half, fearfully, for what bestial depravity might a savage not be driven to by an empty stomach? My act might have stood against me on the morrow, but I told the cook a mighty hunger was robbing me of sleep & (at double the usual expence 'on account o' the unseason'ble hour') I procured a platter of sauerkraut, sausage & buns hard as cannonballs.

Back in the confines of my cabin the savage thanked me for the kindness & ate that humble fare as if it were a Presidential Banquet. I did not confess my true motives, *viz.*, the fuller his stomach, the less like he was to consume me, but instead asked him why, during his flogging, he had smiled at me. 'Pain is strong, aye – but friends' eyes, more strong.' I told him that he knows next to nothing about me & I know nothing about him. He jabbed at his eyes & jabbed at mine, as if that single gesture were ample explanation.

The wind rose higher as the middle watch wore on, making the timbers moan & whipping up the seas & sluicing over the decks. Sea-water was soon dripping into my coffin, trickling down the walls & blotting my blanket. 'You might have chosen a drier hidey-hole than mine,' I whispered, to test the stowaway's wakefulness. 'Safe better 'n dry, Missa Ewing,' he murmured, alert as I. Why, I asked, was he beaten so savagely in the Indian hamlet? A silence stretched itself out. 'I seen too much o' the world, I ain't good slave.' To ward off seasickness during those dreary hours, I teazed out the stowaway's history. (I cannot, moreover, deny my curiosity.) His pidgin delivered his tale brokenly so its substance only shall I endeavour to set down here.

White men's ships bore vicissitudes to Old Rēkohu, as Mr D'Arnoq narrated, but also marvels. During my stowaway's boyhood, Autua yearned to learn more of these pale peoples from places whose existence, in his grandfather's time, was the realm of myths. Autua claims his father had been amongst the natives Cpt. Broughton's landing party encountered in Skirmish Bay, & spent his infancy hearing the yarn told & retold: – of the 'Great Albatross', paddling through the morning mists; its vividly-plumaged, strangely-jointed servants who canoed ashore, facing backwards; of the Albatross-servants' gibberish (a bird language?); of their smoke-breathing; of their heinous violation of that *tapu* forbidding strangers to touch canoes (doing so curses the vessel & renders it as unseaworthy as if an axe had been taken to it); of the pursuant altercation; of those 'shouting-staffs' whose magical wrath could kill a man across the beach; & of the bright skirt of ocean-blue, cloud-white & blood-red that the servants hoisted aloft a pole before rowing back to the Great Albatross. (This flag was removed & presented to a chieftain who wore it proudly until the scrofula took him.)

Autua had an uncle, Koche, who shipped aboard a Boston sealer, *circa* 1825. (The stowaway is unsure of his exact age.) Moriori were prized crew amongst such vessels, for in lieu of martial prowess, Rēkohu's manhood 'won their spurs' by seal-hunting & swimming feats. (To claim his bride, as a further example, a young man had to dive to the sea-bed & surface with a cray-fish in each hand & a third in his mouth.) Newly-discovered Polynesians, it should be added, make easy prey for unscrupulous captains. Autua's uncle Koche returned after five years, garbed in *pakeha* clothes with rings in his ears, a modest pouch of dollars & *réals*, possessed of strange customs ('smoke-breathing' amongst them), dischordant oaths & tales of cities & sights too outlandish for the Moriori tongue to delineate.

Autua swore to ship on the next vessel leaving Ocean Bay & see these exotic places for himself. His uncle persuaded a second mate on a French whaler to ship the ten-year-old (?) Autua as an apprentice. In the Moriori's subsequent career at sea he saw the ice-ranges of Antarctica, whales turned to islets of gore, then barrels of sperm-oil; in the becalmed ashy Encantadas he hunted giant tortoises; in Sydney, he saw grand buildings, parks, horse-drawn carriages & ladies in bonnets & the miracles of civilization; he shipped opium from Calcutta to Canton; survived dysentery in Batavia; lost half of an ear in a skirmish with Mexicans afore the altar at Santa Cruz; survived shipwreck at the Horn & saw Rio de Janeiro, though did not step ashore; & everywhere he observed that casual brutality lighter races show the darker.

Autua returned in the summer of 1835, a worldly-wise young man of about twenty. He planned to take a local bride & build a house & cultivate some acres but, as Mr D'Arnoq relates, by the winter solstice of that year every Moriori who had not perished was a slave of the Maori. The returnee's years amongst crews of all nations did not elevate Autua in the invaders' estimation. (I observed how ill-timed was the prodigal's homecoming. 'No, Missa Ewing, Rēkohu *called* me home, so I *see* her death so I *know*,' he tapped his head, 'the truth.')

Autua's master was the lizard-tattooed Maori, Kupaka, who told his horrified, broken slaves that he had come to cleanse them of their false idols ('Have your gods saved you?' taunted Kupaka); their polluted language ('My whip will teach you pure Maori!'); their tainted blood ('Inbreeding has diluted your original *mana*!'). Henceforth Moriori unions were proscribed & all issue fathered by Maori men on Moriori women were declared Maori. The earliest transgressors were executed in gruesome ways & the survivors lived in that state of lethargy engendered by relentless subjugation. Autua cleared land, planted wheat & tended hogs for Kupaka until he won enough trust to effect his escape. ('Secret places on Rēkohu, Missa Ewing, combes, pitfalls, caves deep in Motoporoporo Forest, so dense no dogs scent you there.' I fancy I fell into one such secret place.)

A year later he was recaptured, but Moriori slaves were now too scarce to be indiscriminately slaughtered. The lower Maori were obliged to labour alongside the serfs, much to their disgust. ('We forsook our ancestors' land in Aotearoa for this miserable rock?' they complained.) Autua escaped again & during his second spell of freedom he was granted secret asylum by Mr D'Arnoq for some months, at no little risk to the latter. During this sojourn Autua was baptised & turned to the Lord.

Kupaka's men caught up with the fugitive after a year & sixmonth, but this time the mercurial chieftain evinced a respect for Autua's spirit. After a retributive lashing, Kupaka appointed his slave as fisherman for his own table. Thus employed, the Moriori let another year go by until, one afternoon, he found a rare *moeeka* fish flapping in his net. He told Kupaka's wife this king of fish could be eaten only by a king of men & showed her how to prepare it for her husband. ('Bad bad poison this *moeeka* fish, Missa Ewing, one bite, aye, you sleep, you never wake no mo'.') During that night's feasting, Autua snuck from the encampment, stole his master's canoe & rowed across the current-prone, choppy, moonless sea to deserted Pitt Island, two leagues to the south of Chatham Isle (known as 'Rangiauria' in Moriori & revered as mankind's birthplace).

Luck favoured the stowaway, for he arrived safe at dawn as a squall blew up & no canoes made the crossing after him. Autua subsisted in his Polynesian Eden on wild celery, watercress, eggs, berries, an occasional young boar (he risked fires only under cover of darkness or mist) & the knowledge that Kupaka, at least, had met a condign punishment. Was his solitude not unbearable? 'Nights, ancestors visited. Days, I yarned tales of Maui to birds, & birds yarned sea-tales to I.'

The fugitive lived thus for many a season until last September when a winter gale wrecked the whaler *Eliza* from Nantucket on Pitt Island Reef. All hands drowned, but our Mr Walker, zealous in his pursuit of easy guineas, crossed the straits seeking salvage. When he found signs of habitation & saw Kupaka's old canoe (each is storiated with unique carvings) he knew he had found treasure of interest to his Maori neighbours. Two days later a large hunting party rowed to Pitt Island from the mainland. Autua sat on the beach & watched them arrive, surprised only to see his old enemy, Kupaka, grizzled but very much alive & shouting war-chants.

My uninvited cabin-mate concluded his tale. 'That b—'s greedy dog stole *moeeka* from kitchen & died, not the Maori. Aye, Kupaka flogged me, but he's old & far from home & his *mana* is hollow & starved. Maori thrive on wars & revenge & feudin', but peace kills 'em off. Many go back to Zealand. Kupaka cannot, his land is no mo'. Then last week, Missa Ewing, I see you & I know, you save I, I know it.'

The morning watch smote four bells & my port-hole betrayed a rainy dawn. I had slept a little, but my prayers that the dawn would dissolve the Moriori were unheeded. I bid him to play-act *he had only just revealed himself* & make no mention of our night's conversation. He signalled comprehension, but I feared the worst: an Indian's wit was no match for a Boerhaave.

Along the gangway I stepped (*Prophetess* was bucking like a young bronco) to the officers' mess, knocked & entered. Mr Roderick & Mr Boerhaave were listening to Cpt. Molyneux. I cleared my throat & bade all good morning, at which our amicable captain swore, 'You can better my morning, by b—ing off, instanter!'

Coolly, I asked *when* the captain might find time to hear news of an Indian stowaway who had just emerged from the coils of hawser taking up 'my so-called cabin'. During the ensuing silence

33

Cpt. Molyneux's pale, horny-toad complexion turned roast beef pink. Ere his blast was launched, I added the stowaway claimed to be an able-seaman & begged to work his passage.

Mr Boerhaave forestalled his captain with the predicted accusations & exclaimed, 'On Dutch merchantmen those who abet stowaways share their fate!' I reminded the Hollander we sailed under an English flag & put it to him why, if *I* had hid the stowaway under the coils of hawser, had I asked & asked *again* since Thursday night for the unwonted hawser to be removed, thereby begging for my putative 'conspiracy' to be uncovered? Hitting that bull's-eye fired my mettle & I assured Cpt. Molyneux that the baptized stowaway had resorted to this extreme measure lest his Maori master, who had vowed to eat his slave's warm liver (I sprinkled a little 'seasoning' on my version of events), directed his ungodly wrath towards his rescuer.

Mr Boerhaave swore, 'So this d—d blackamoor wants us to be *grateful* to him?' No, I replied, the Moriori asks for a chance to prove his value to *Prophetess*. Mr Boerhaave spat out, 'A stowaway is a stowaway even if he sh—s silver nuggets! What's his name?' I did not know, I replied, for I had not conducted an interview with the man but come to the captain expeditiously.

Cpt. Molyneux spoke at last. 'Able seaman *first* class, you say?' His wrath had cooled at the prospect of earning a valuable pair of hands he would not have to pay. 'An Indian? Where did he salt his burns?' I repeated, two minutes was insufficient to learn his history, but my instinct considered the Indian an honest fellow.

The captain wiped his beard. 'Mr Roderick, accompany our passenger & his instinct & fetch their pet savage afoot the mizzen.' He tossed a key to his first mate. 'Mr Boerhaave, my fowling-piece, if you please.'

The second mate & I did as bid. 'A risky business,' Mr Roderick warned me. 'The only statute book on *Prophetess* is the Old Man's Whim.' Another statute book named 'Conscience' is observed *lex loci* wherever God sees, I responded. Autua was awaiting his trial in the cotton trowzers I purchased in Port Jackson (he had climbed aboard from Mr D'Arnoq's boat in naught but his savage's loin-cloth & a shark-tooth necklace). His back was exposed. His lacerations, I hoped, would pay testimony to his resilience & bestir sympathy in the observers' breasts.

Rats behind the arras spread tidings of the sport & most hands were gathered on deck. (My ally, Henry, was still abed, unaware of my jeopardy.) Cpt. Molyneux sized the Moriori up as if inspecting a mule & addressed him thus: 'Mr Ewing, who knows *nothing* about how you boarded my vessel, says you regard yourself a seaman.'

Autua replied with courage & dignity. 'Aye, Cap'n, sir, two years on whaler *Mississippi* of Le Havre under Cpt. Maspero, & four years on *Cornucopia* of Philadelphia under Cpt. Caton, three years on an Indiaman—'

Cpt. Molyneux interrupted & indicated Autua's trowzers. 'Did you pilfer this garment from below?' Autua was sensible that I, too, was on trial. 'That Christian gent'man gave, sir.' The crew followed the stowaway's finger to myself, & Mr Boerhaave thrust at the chink in my armour. 'He did? *When* was this gift awarded?' (I recalled my father-in-law's aphorism, 'To fool a judge, feign fascination, but to bamboozle the whole court, feign boredom,' & I pretended to extract a speck from my eye.) Autua answered with primed percipience. 'Ten minutes past, sir, I, no clothes, that gent'man say, naked no good, dress this.'

'If you are a seaman,' our captain jerked his thumb aloft, 'let's see you lower this mid-mast's royal.' At this, the stowaway grew hesitant & confused & I felt the lunatick's wager I had placed on this Indian's word swing against me, but Autua had merely spotted a trap. 'Sir, this mast ain't mid-mast, this mast the mizzen, aye?' Impassive Cpt. Molyneux nodded. 'Then kindly lower the *mizzen* royal.'

Autua fairly ran up the mast & I began to hope all was not lost. The newly-risen sun shone low over the water & caused us to squint. 'Ready & aim my piece,' the captain instructed Mr Boerhaave, once the stowaway was past the spanker gaff, 'fire on my command!'

Now I protested with the utmost vigour, the Indian had received holy sacrament, but Cpt. Molyneux ordered me to shut up or swim back to the Chathams. No American captain would cut a man down, not even a nigger, so odiously! Autua reached the topmost yard & walked it with simian dexterity despite the rough seas. Watching the sail unfurl, one of the 'saltest' aboard, a dour Icelander & a sober, obliging & hardworking fellow, spoke his admiration for all to hear. 'The darkie's salt as I am, aye, he's got fish-hooks for toes!' Such was my gratitude, I could have kissed his boots. Soon Autua had the sail down – a difficult operation even for a team of four men. Cpt. Molyneux grunted approval & ordered Mr Boerhaave to replace his gun, 'But d— me if I pay a stowaway a single cent. He'll work his passage to O-hawaii. If he's no shirker he may sign articles there in the regular fashion. Mr Roderick, he can share the dead Spaniard's bunk.'

I have worn away a nib in narrating the day's excitements. It is grown too dark to see.

Wednesday, 20th November —

Strong easterly breeze, very salty & oppressive. Henry has conducted his examination & has grave news, yet not the gravest. My Ailment is a parasite, *Gusano Coco Cervello*. This Worm is endemic throughout both Melanesia & Polynesia, but has been known to science only these last ten years. It breeds in the stinking canals of Batavia, doubtless the port of my own infection. Ingested, it voyages through the host's blood-vessels to the brain's *cerebellum anterior*. (Hence my migraines & dizziness.) Ensconced in the brain, it enters a gestation phase. 'You are a realist, Adam,' Henry told me, 'so your pills shall be unsugared. Once the Parasite's larvae hatch, the victim's brain becomes a maggoty cauliflower. Putrescent gases cause the ear-drums & eye-balls to protrude until they pop, releasing a cloud of *Gusano Coco* spores.'

Thus reads my death-sentence, but now comes my stay of execution & appeal. An admixture of urussium alkali & orinoco manganese will calcify my Parasite & laphrydictic myrrh will disintegrate it. Henry's 'apothecary' holds these compounds, but a precise dosage is paramount. Less than half a drachm leaves *Gusano Coco* unpurged, but more kills the patient with the cure. My doctor warns me that as the Parasite dies, its poison-sacs split & secrete their cargo, so I shall feel worse before my recovery is compleat.

Henry enjoined me not to breathe a word about my condition, for hyenas like Boerhaave prey on the vulnerable, & ignorant sailors can show hostility to maladies they know not. ('I once heard of a sailor who showed the touch of leprosy a week out of Macao on the long haul back to Lisbon,' recalled Henry, 'and the whole company prodded the wretch overboard without a hearing.') During my convalescence, Henry shall inform the 'scuttlebutt' that Mr Ewing has a low fever caused by the clime & nurse me himself. Henry bridled when I mentioned his fee. 'Fee? You are no valetudinarian viscount with bank-notes padding his pillows! Providence steered you to my ministrations, for I doubt five men in this blue Pacific can cure you! So a fie on "Fee"! All I ask, dear Adam, is that you are an obedient patient! Kindly take my powders & withdraw to your cabin. I shall look in after the last dog.'

My doctor is an uncut diamond of the first water. Even as I write these words, I am tearful with gratitude.

Saturday, 30th November —

Henry's powders are indeed a wondrous medicament. I inhale the precious grains into my nostrils from an ivory spoon & on the instant an incandescent joy burns my being. My senses grow alert, yet my limbs grow Lethean. My Parasite still writhes at night, like a new babe's finger, igniting spasms of pain & dreams obscene & monstrous visit me. 'A sure sign,' Henry consoles me, 'your Worm has reacted to our vermicide & seeks shelter in the recesses of your cerebral canals whence visions spring. In vain *Gusano Coco* hides, dear Adam, in vain. We shall winkle 'im out!'

Monday, 2nd December —

By day, my coffin is hot as an oven & my sweat dampens these pages. The tropic sun fattens & fills the noon sky. The men work semi-naked with sun-blacked torsos & straw hats. The planking oozes scorching tar that sticks to one's soles. Rain squalls blow up from nowhere & vanish with the same rapidity & the deck hisses itself dry in a minute. Portuguese man-o'-wars pulsate in the quicksilver sea, flying fish bewitch the beholder & ochre shadows of hammerheads circle the *Prophetess*. Earlier, I stepped on a squid that had propelled itself over the bulwarks! (Its eyes & beak reminded me of my father-in-law.) The water we took on at Chatham Isle is now brackish &, without a dash of brandy in it, my stomach rebels. When not playing chess in Henry's cabin or the mess-room, I rest in my coffin until Homer lulls me into dreams a-billow with sails of Athenians.

Autua knocked on my coffin door yesterday to thank me for saving his neck. He said he was in my debt (true enough) until the day he saves *my* life (may it never dawn!). I asked how he was finding his new duties. 'Better'n slaving for Kupaka, Missa Ewing.' Anyhow, growing sensible of my fear someone would witness our congress & report to Cpt. Molyneux, the Moriori returned to the fo'c'sle & has not since sought me out. As Henry warns me, 'It's one thing to throw a blackie a bone, but quite another to take him on for life! Friendships between races, Ewing, can never surpass the affection between a loyal gun-dog & its master.'

Nightly, my doctor & I enjoy a stroll on the deck before retiring. It is pleasant merely to breathe the cooler air. One loses one's eye in lanes of sea-phosphorence & the Mississippi of stars streaming across the heavens. Last night, the men were gathered on the foredeck laying up grass into sinnet for ropes by lantern-light & the prohibition on 'supernuminaries' on the foredeck seemed not to apply. (Since the 'Autua Incident' that contempt directed at 'Mr Quillcock' is in recess, as is the epithet.) Bentnail sang ten verses on the world's brothels foul enough to put the most wanton satyr to flight. Henry volunteered an eleventh verse (about Mary O'Hairy of Inverary) that turned the air yet bluer. Rafael was next coerced to take his turn. He sat on the 'widow-maker' & sang these lines in a voice unschooled yet honest & true:–

> *Oh, Shenandoah, I long to see you,*
>   *Hurrah, you rolling river.*
> *Oh, Shenandoah, I'll not deceive you,*
> *We're bound way 'cross the wide Missouri.*
>   *Oh, Shenandoah, I love your daughter,*
>   *I love the place across the water.*
> *The ship sails free, the wind is blowing,*
> *The braces taut, the sheets a-flowing.*
>   *Missouri, she's a mighty river,*
> *We'll brace her up till her topsails shiver.*
>   *Oh, Shenandoah, I'll leave you never,*
>   *Till the day I die, I'll love you ever.*

Silence from rude mariners is a grander accolade than any erudite eulogy. Why should Rafael, an Australian-born lad, have an American song by heart? 'I din't know 'twas a Yankee 'un,' he replied awkwardly. 'My mam teached it me before she died. It's the only thing of hers I got still. It stuck in me.' He turned to his work, an awkward curtness in his manner. Henry & I sensed anew the hostility that workers emanate at the bystanding idler & so we left the toilers to their industry.

Reading my entry for 15th October, when first I met Rafael

Letters from Zedelghem

Sixsmith,

Dreamt I stood in a china shop so crowded from floor to far-off ceiling with shelves of porcelain antiquities etc. that moving a muscle would cause several to fall and smash to bits. Exactly what happened, but instead of a crashing noise, an august chord rang out, half-cello, half-celeste, D-major(?), held for four beats. My wrist knocked a Ming vase affair off its pedestal – E-flat, whole string section, glorious, transcendent, angels wept. Deliberately now, smashed a figurine of an ox for the next note, then a milkmaid, then Saturday's Child – orgy of shrapnel filled the air, divine harmonies my head. Ah, such music! Glimpsed my father totting up the smashed items' value, nib flashing, but *had* to keep the music coming. Knew I'd become the greatest composer of the century if I could only make this music mine. A monstrous Laughing Cavalier flung against the wall set off a thumping battery of percussion.

Woke in my Imperial Western suite, Tam Brewer's collectors nearly knocking my door down and much commotion from corridor. Hadn't even waited until I'd shaved – breathtaking vulgarity of these ruffians. Had no choice but to exit swiftly via the bathroom window before the brouhaha summoned the manager to discover that the young gentleman in Room 237 had no means of settling his now-hefty balance. Escape was not hitchless, sorry to report. Drain-pipe ripped free of its mounting with the noise of a brutalized violin, and down, down, down tumbled your old chum. Right buttock one hellish bruise. Minor miracle I didn't shatter my spine or impale myself on railings. Learn from this, Sixsmith. When insolvent, pack minimally, with a valise tough enough to be thrown on to a London pavement from a 1st or 2nd-floor window. Insist on hotel rooms no higher.

Hid in a tea-room tucked into a sooty nook of Victoria Station, trying to transcribe the music from the china shop of dreams – couldn't get beyond a measly two bars. Would have walked into Tam Brewer's arms just to have that music back again. Miserable spirits. Labouring types surrounded me with bad teeth, parrot voices and unfounded optimism. Sobering to think how one accursed night of baccarat can alter a man's social standing so irreversibly. Those shopworkers, cabbies and tradesmen had more ½ crowns and threepenny bits squirrelled away in their sour Stepney mattresses than I, Son of an Ecclesiastical Somebody, can claim. Had a view of an alley: downtrodden scriveners hurtling by like demisemiquavers in a Beethovian *allegro*. Afraid of 'em? No, I'm afraid of *being* one. What value are education, breeding and talent if one doesn't have a pot to piss in?

Still can't believe it. I, a Caius Man, teetering on the brink of destitution. Decent hotels won't let me taint their lobbies now. Indecent hotels demand cash on the nail. Am barred from any reputable gaming table this side of the Pyrenees. Anyway, I summarized my options: –

(i) Use paltry funds to obtain a dirty room in some lodging house, beg a few guineas from Uncle Cecil Ltd, teach prissy missies their scales and bitter spinsters their technique. Come now. If I could fake courtesy to dunces I'd still be swabbing Professor Mackerras's arse with my ex-fellow undergrads. No, before you say it, I *can't* go running back to Pater with yet another *cri de cœur*. Would validate every poisonous word he said about me. Would rather jump off Waterloo bridge and let Old Father Thames humble me. Mean it.

(ii) Hunt down Caius people, butter 'em up and invite myself to stay for the summer. Problematic, for same reasons as (i). How long could I conceal my starving pocket book? How long could I stave off their pity, their talons?

(iii) Visit turf accountant – but if I lost?

You'd remind me I brought it all upon myself, Sixsmith,

but shrug off that middle-class chip on your shoulder and stick with me a little longer. Across a crowded platform, a guard announced that the Dover-bound train for the ship to Ostend was delayed by thirty minutes. That guard was my croupier, inviting me to double or quits. If one will just be still, shut up and *listen* – lo, behold, the world'll sift through one's ideas for one, esp. in a grimy London railway station. Downed my soapy tea and strode across the concourse to the ticket office. A return ticket to Ostend was too costly – so parlous has my position become – so a single it had to be. Boarded my carriage just as the locomotive's whistle blasted forth a swarm of piccolo Furies. We were under way.

Now to reveal my plan, inspired by a piece in *The Times* and a long soak's daydream in my Savoy suite. In the Belgian backwaters, south of Bruges, there lives a reclusive English composer, named Vyvyan Ayrs. You won't have heard of him because you're a musical oaf, but he's one of the greats. The only Briton of his generation to reject pomp, circumstance, rusticity and charm. Hasn't produced any new work since the early twenties due to illness – he's ½ blind and can hardly hold a pen – but the *Times* review of his *Secular Magnificat* (performed last week at St Martin's) referred to a drawerful of unfinished works. My daydream had me travelling to Belgium, persuading Vyvyan Ayrs he needed to employ me as an amanuensis, accepting his offer to tutor me, shooting through the musical firmament, winning fame and fortune commensurate to my gifts, obliging Pater to admit that, yes, the son he disinherited is *the* Robert Frobisher, greatest British composer of his time.

Why not? Had no better plan. You groan and shake your head, Sixsmith, I know, but you smile too, which is why I love you. Uneventful journey to the Channel . . . cancerous suburbs, tedious farmland, soiled Sussex. Dover an utter fright staffed by Bolsheviks, versified cliffs as Romantic as my arse and a similar hue. Changed last shillings into francs at the port and took my cabin aboard the *Kentish Queen*, a rusty tub that looks old enough to have seen service in Crimea. Spud-faced young steward and I disagreed his burgundy uniform and unconvincing beard were worth a tip. Sneered at my valise and manuscript folder – 'Wise of you to travel light, sir' – and left me to muck for myself. Suited me fine.

Dinner was balsawood chicken, powdery potatoes and a bastard claret. My dining-table companion was Mr Victor Bryant, cutlery lordling of Sheffield. Not a musical bone in his body. He expounded on the subject of spoons for most of the meal, mistook my civil deportment for interest and offered me a job in his sales department on the spot! Can you believe it? Thanked him (keeping straight face) and confessed I'd rather swallow cutlery than ever have to sell the stuff. Three mighty blasts on the fog-horn, engines changed timbre, felt the ship cast off, went on deck to watch Albion withdraw into drizzly murk. No going back now; consequences of what I'd done struck home. R.V.W. conducted *Sea Symphony* in the Orchestra of the Mind, *Sail forth, steer for the deep waters only, Reckless, O Soul, exploring, I with thee, and thou with me.* (Don't much care for this work but it was perfectly programmed.) North Sea wind had me shivering, spray licked me from toe to crown. Glossy black waters invited me to jump. Ignored 'em. Turned in early, leafed through Noyes' *Contrapuntals*, listened to the distant brass of the engine room and sketched a repetitive passage for trombone based on the ship's rhythms, but was rather rubbish, and then guess who came a-knocking at my door? The spud-faced steward, his shift over. Gave him rather more than a tip. No Adonis, scrawny but inventive for his class. Turfed him out afterwards and sank into the sleep of the dead. One part of me wanted that voyage never to end.

But end it did. *Kentish Queen* slid into Dover's snaggletoothed twin sister over the mucky water, Ostend, the Lady of Dubious Virtue. Early, early morning, Europe's snoring rumbled deep below bass tubas. Saw my 1st aboriginal Belgians, hauling crates, arguing, and *thinking* in Flemish, Dutch, whatever. Packed my valise sharpish, afraid the ship might sail back to England with me still aboard; or, rather, afraid of my letting this happen. Grabbed a bite from the 1st class galley's fruit-bowl and dashed down the gangplank before anyone with braiding on his uniform caught up with me. Set foot on Continental macadam and asked a Customs man where I might find the railway station. He pointed towards a groaning tram packed with malnourished workmen, rickets and penury. Preferred Shanks's Pony, drizzle or no drizzle. Followed tram-lines down coffinesque streets. Ostend is all tapioca greys and stained browns. Will admit, I was thinking Belgium was a b. stupid country to run away to. Bought a ticket for Bruges and hauled myself aboard the next train – no platforms, can you believe it? – a decrepit, empty train. Moved compartment because mine smelt unpleasant, but all compartments had same pong. Smoked cigarettes cadged off Victor Bryant to purify the air. The stationmaster's whistle blew on time, the locomotive strained like a gouty proctor on the pot before heaving itself into motion. Soon steaming through a foggy landscape of unkempt dykes and blasted copses at a fair old clip.

If my plan bears fruit, Sixsmith, you may come to Bruges before v. long. When you do, arrive in that six o'clock in the morning *gnossiennesque* hour. Lose yourself in the city's rickety streets, blind canals, wrought-iron gates, uninhabited courtyards – may I go on? Why, thank you – leery Gothic carapaces, Ararat roofs, shrubbery-tufted brick spires, medieval overhangs, laundry sagging from windows, cobbled whirlpools that suck your eye in, clockwork princes and chipped princesses striking their hours, sooty doves and three or four octaves of bells, some sober, some bright.

Aroma of fresh bread led me to a bakery where a deformed woman with no nose sold me a dozen crescent-moon pastries. Only wanted one, but thought she had enough problems. A rag-and-bone cart clattered out of the mist and its toothless driver spoke companionably to me, but I could only reply, 'Excusez-moi, je ne parle pas le Flamand,' which made him laugh like the Goblin King. Gave him a pastry. His filthy hand was a scabby claw. In a poor quarter (alleys stank of effluence), children helped their mothers at the pumps, filling broken jugs with brown water. Finally, the excitement all caught up with me, sat on the steps of a dying windmill for a breather, wrapped myself against the damp, fell asleep.

Next thing, a witch was poking me awake with her broomstick, screeching something like, 'Zie gie doad misschien?' but don't quote me. Blue sky, warm sun, not a wisp of fog to be seen. Resurrected and blinking, I offered her a pastry. She accepted with distrust, put it in her apron for later, and got back to her sweeping, growling an ancient ditty. Lucky I wasn't robbed, I suppose. Shared another pastry with five thousand pigeons, to the envy of a beggar, so I had to give him one too. Walked back the way I might have come. In an odd pentagonal window a creamy maiden was arranging St Paulia in a cut-glass bowl. Girls fascinate in different ways. Try 'em one day. Tapped on the pane, and asked in French if she'd save my life by falling in love with me. Shook her head but got an amused smile. Asked where I could find a police-station. She pointed over a crossroads.

One can spot a fellow musician in any context, even amongst policemen. The craziest-eyed, unruliest-haired one, either hungry-skinny or jovial-portly. This French-speaking, cor anglais-playing, local operatic society-belonging inspector had heard of Vyvyan Ayrs and kindly drew me a map to Neerbeke. Paid him two pastries for this intelligence. He asked if I had shipped over my British car – his son was mad keen about Austins. Said I had no car. This worried him. How would I get to Neerbeke? No bus, no train-line, and twenty-five miles was the devil of a walk. Asked if I could borrow a policeman's bicycle for an indefinite period. Told me that was most irregular. Assured him *I* was most irregular, and outlined the nature of my mission to Ayrs, Belgium's most famous adopted son (must be so few that might even be true), in the service of European music. Repeated my request. Implausible truth can serve one better than plausible fiction, and now was such a time. The honest sergeant took me to a compound where lost items await rightful owners for a few months (before finding their way to the black market) – but 1st, he wanted my opinion on his baritone. He gave me a burst of 'Recitar! . . . Vesti la giubba!' from *I Pagliacci*. (Pleasant enough voice in lower registers but his breathing needed work and his vibrato quivered like a back-stage thunderboard.) Gave a few musical pointers; received the loan of a Victorian Enfield plus cord to secure valise and folder to the saddle and rear mud-guard. He wished me *bon voyage* and fair weather.

Adrian would never have marched along the road I bicycled out of Bruges (too deep in Hun territory) but nonetheless felt an affinity with my brother by virtue of breathing the same air of the same land. The Plain is flat as the Fens but in a bad shape. Along the way I fuelled myself with the last pastries, and stopped at impoverished cottages for cups of water. Nobody said much but nobody said, 'No.' Thanks to a head-wind and a chain that kept slipping off, the afternoon was growing old before I finally reached Ayrs's home village of Neerbeke. A silent blacksmith showed me how to get to Château Zedelghem by elaborating my map with a pencil stub. A lane with harebells and toadflax growing in the middle led me past a deserted lodge-house to a once-stately avenue of mature Italian poplars.

Zedelghem is grander than our rectory, some crumbly turrets adorn its west wing, but it couldn't hold a candle to Audley End or Capon-Tench's country seat. Spied a girl riding a horse over a low hill crowned by a shipwrecked beech tree. Passed a gardener spreading soot against the slugs in a vegetable garden. In the forecourt, a musclebound valet was decoking a Cowley Flat-nose. Seeing my approach, he rose and waited for me. In a terraced corner of this frieze, a man in a wheel-chair sat under foamy wisteria listening to the wireless. Vyvyan Ayrs, I presumed. The easy part of my daydream was over.

Leant the bicycle against the wall, told the valet I had business with his master. He was civil enough, and led me around to Ayrs's terrace, and announced my arrival in German. Ayrs a husk of a man, as if his illness has sucked all juice out of him, but stopped myself kneeling on the cinder-path like Sir Percival before King Arthur. Our overture proceeded more or less like this. 'Good afternoon, Mr Ayrs.'

'Who in hell are *you*?'

'It's a great honour to—'

'I said, "Who in hell *are* you?"'

'Robert Frobisher, sir, from Saffron Walden. I am – I was – a student of Sir Trevor Mackerras at Caius College, and I've come all the way from London to—'

'All the way from London on a bicycle?'

'No. I borrowed the bicycle from a policeman in Bruges.'

'Did you?' Pause for thought. 'Must have taken hours.'

'A labour of love, sir. Like pilgrims climbing hills on their knees.'

'What balderdash is this?'

'I wished to prove I'm a serious applicant.'

'Serious applicant for what?'

'The post of your amanuensis.'

'Are you mad?'

Always a trickier question than it looks. 'I doubt it.'

'Look here, I've not advertised for an amanuensis!'

'I know, sir, but you need one, even if you don't know it yet. The *Times* piece said that you're unable to compose new works because of your illness. I can't allow your music to be lost. It's far, far too precious. So I'm here to offer you my services.'

Well, he didn't dismiss me out of hand. 'What did you say your name was?' I told him. 'One of Mackerras's shooting stars, are you?'

'Frankly, sir, he loathed me.'

As you've learned to your cost, I can be intriguing when I put my mind to it.

'He did, did he? Why might that be?'

'I called his 6th Concerto for Flute,' I cleared my throat, '"a slave of pre-pubescent Saint-Saëns at his most florid" in the college magazine. He took it personally.'

'You wrote *that* about Mackerras?' Ayrs wheezed as if his ribs were being sawed. 'I'll *bet* he took it personally.'

The sequel is short. The valet showed me into a drawing room decorated in eggshell-green, a dull Farquharson of sheep and cornstooks and a not-very-good Dutch landscape. Ayrs summoned his wife, Mrs van Outryve de Crommelynck. She kept her own name, and with a name like that who can blame her? The lady of the house was coolly courteous and enquired into my background. Answered truthfully, though I veiled my expulsion from Caius behind an obscure malady. Of my present financial straits I breathed not a word – the more desperate the case, the more reluctant the donor. Charmed 'em sufficiently. It was agreed I could at least stay the night at Zedelghem. Ayrs would put me through my musical paces in the morning, permitting a decision on my proposal.

Ayrs did not appear at dinner, however. My arrival coincided with the start of a fortnightly migraine, which confines him to his rooms for a day or two. My audition is postponed until he is better, so my fate still hangs in the balance. On the credit side, the Piesporter and lobster *à l'américaine* were the equal to anything at the Imperial. Encouraged my hostess to talk – think she was flattered at how much I know about her illustrious husband, and sensed my genuine love of his music. Oh, we ate with Ayrs's daughter, too, the young equestrian I'd glimpsed earlier. Mlle Ayrs is a horsy creature of seventeen with her mama's retroussé nose. Couldn't get a civil word out of her all evening. Might she see in me a louche English freeloader down on his luck, here to lure her sickly father into a glorious Indian summer where she can't follow and isn't welcome?

People are complicated.

Gone midnight. The château is sleeping, so must I.

Sincerely,
R.F.

— ◆ —

Zedelghem.

3rd – vii – 1931.

A telegram, Sixsmith? You *ass.*

Don't send any more, I beg you – telegrams attract attention! Yes, I'm still Abroad, yes, safe from Brewer's knuckle-men. Shred my parents' request for information on my whereabouts and drop it in the Cam. Pater's only 'concerned' because my creditors are shaking him to see if any bank-notes drop from the family tree. Debts of a disinherited son, however, are nobody's business but the son's – believe me, I've looked into the legalities. Mater is not 'frantic'. Only the prospect of the decanter running dry could make Mater frantic.

My audition took place in Ayrs's music room, after lunch, the day before yesterday. Not an overwhelming success, putting it mildly – no knowing how many days I'll be here, or how few. Admit to a certain *frisson* sitting on Vyvyan Ayrs's own piano stool beforehand. This Oriental rug, battered divan, Breton cupboards crammed with music-stands, Bösendorfer grand, carillon, all witnessed the conception and birth of *Matruschka Doll Variations* and his song cycle *Society Islands*. Stroked the same 'cello who 1st vibrated to *Untergehen Violinkonzert*. Hearing Hendrick wheeling his master this way, I stopped snooping and faced the doorway. Ayrs ignored my 'I do hope you're recovered, Mr Ayrs,' and had his valet leave him facing the garden window. 'Well?' he asked, after we'd been alone ½ a minute. 'Go on. Impress me.' Asked what he wanted to hear. 'I must select the programme, too? Well, have you mastered *Three Blind Mice?*'

So I sat at the Bösendorfer and played the syphilitic crank *Three Blind Mice*, after the fashion of a mordant Prokofiev. Ayrs did not comment. Continued in a subtler vein with Chopin's Nocturne in F Major. He interrupted with a whine, 'Trying to slip my petticoats off my ankles, Frobisher?' Played V.A.'s own *Digressions on a Theme of Lodovico Roncalli*, but before the

1st two bars were out, he'd uttered a six-birch expletive, banged on the floor with his cane, and said, 'Self-gratification makes you go blind, didn't they teach you that at Caius?' Ignored him and finished the piece *note perfect*. For a finale of fireworks, gambled on Scarlatti's 212th in A major, a *bête noire* of arpeggios and acrobatics. Came unstuck once or twice, but I wasn't being auditioned as a concert soloist. After I'd finished, V.A. kept swinging his head to the rhythm of the disappeared *sonata*; or maybe he was conducting the blurry, swaying poplars. 'Execrable, Frobisher, get out of my house this instant!' would have aggrieved, but not much surprised me. Instead, he admitted, 'You *may* have the makings of a musician. It's a nice day. Amble over to the lake and see the ducks. I need, oh, a little *time* to decide whether or not I can find a use for your . . . gifts.'

Left without a word. The old goat wants me, it seems, but only if I'm pathetic with gratitude. If my pocket book had allowed me to go, I'd have hired a cab back to Bruges and renounced the whole errant idea. He called after me, 'Some advice, Frobisher, *gratis*. Scarlatti was a harpsichordist, not a pianist. Don't drench him in colour so, and don't use the pedal to sustain notes you can't sustain with the fingers.' I called back that I needed, oh, a little *time* to decide whether or not I could find a use for Ayrs's . . . gift.

Crossed the courtyard where a beetroot-faced gardener was clearing a weed-choked fountain. Made him understand I wanted to speak to his mistress and *pronto* – he is not the sharpest tool in the shed – and he waved vaguely towards Neerbeke, miming a steering-wheel. Wonderful. What now? See the ducks, why not? Could strangle a brace and leave 'em hanging in V.A.'s wardrobe. Mood was that black. So I mimed ducks and asked the gardener, 'Where?' He pointed at the beech tree, and his gesture said, Walk that way, just on the other side. I set off, jumped a neglected ha-ha, but before reaching the crest, the noise of galloping bore down on me, and Miss Eva van Outryve de Crommelynck – from now plain old Crommelynck shall have to do or I'll run out of ink – rode up on her black pony.

I greeted her. She cantered around me like Queen Boadicea, pointedly unresponsive. 'How humid the air is today,' I small-talked sarcastically. 'I rather think we shall have rain later, wouldn't you agree?' She said nothing. 'Your dressage is more polished than your manners,' I told her. Nothing. Shooting guns crackled across the fields, and Eva reassured her mount. Her mount is a beaut – one can't blame the horse. I asked Eva for the pony's name. She stroked back some black, corkscrew locks from her cheeks. 'J'ai appelé le poney Nefertiti, d'après cette reine d'Egypte qui m'est si chère,' and turned away. 'It speaks!' I cried, and watched the girl gallop off until she was a miniature in the Van Dyck pastoral. Fired artillery shells after her in elegant parabolas. Turned my guns on Château Zedelghem, and pounded Ayrs's wing to smoking rubble. Remembered what country we are in and stopped.

Past the sundered beech, the meadow falls away to an ornamental lake, ringing with frogs. Seen better days. A precarious foot-bridge connects an island to the shore and flamingo-lilies bloom in vast numbers. Now and then goldfish splish and gleam like new pennies dropped in water. Whiskered mandarin ducks honk for bread, exquisitely-tailored beggars – rather like myself. Martins nest in a boat-house of tarred boards. Under a row of pear trees – once an orchard? – I laid me down and idled, an art perfected during my long convalescence. An idler and a sluggard are as different as a gourmand and a glutton. Watched the aerial bliss of coupled dragonflies. Even heard their wings, an ecstatic sound like paper-flaps in bicycle spokes. Gazed on a slow-worm exploring a miniature Amazonia around the roots where I lay. Silent? Not altogether, no. Was woken much later, by first spots of rain. Cumulo-nimbi were reaching critical mass. Sprinted back to Zedelghem as fast as I'll ever run again, just to hear the rushing roar in my ear-canals and feel the 1st fat droplets pound my face like xylophone hammers.

Just had time to change into my one clean shirt before the dinner gong. Mrs Crommelynck apologized, her husband's appetite was still feeble and *demoiselle* preferred to eat alone. Nothing suited me better. Stewed eel, chervil sauce, the rain skittering on terrace. Unlike the Frobishery and most English homes I have known, meals at the château are not conducted in silence and Mme C. told me a little about her family. Crommelyncks have lived at Zedelghem since far-off days when Bruges was Europe's busiest sea-port (so she told me, hard to credit) making Eva the crowning glory of six centuries' breeding. Warmed to the woman somewhat, I admit it. She holds forth like a man and smokes myrrhy cigarettes through a rhino-horn holder. She'd notice pretty sharpish if any valuables were spirited away, however. They've suffered from thieving servants in the past, she happened to mention, even one or two impoverished house-guests, if I could believe people could behave so dishonourably. Assured her my parents had suffered the same way, and put out feelers re: my audition. 'He *did* describe your Scarlatti as "salvageable". Vyvyan spurns praise, both giving and receiving it. He says, "If people praise you, you're not walking your own path."' Asked directly if she thought he'd agree to take me on. 'I do hope so, Robert.' (In other words, wait and see.) 'You must understand, he resigned himself never to compose another note. Doing so caused him great pain. Resurrecting hope that he might compose again – well, that's not a risk to be undertaken lightly.' Subject closed. I mentioned my earlier encounter with Eva, and Mme C. pronounced, 'My daughter was uncivil.'

'Reserved,' was my perfect reply.

My hostess topped up my glass. 'Eva has a disagreeable nature. My husband has taken very little interest in rearing her like a young lady. He never wanted children. Fathers and daughters are reputed to dote on each other, are they not? Not here. Her teachers say Eva is studious, but secretive, and she's never tried to develop herself musically. I often feel I don't know her at all.' I filled Mme C.'s glass and she seemed to cheer up. 'Listen to me, lamenting. Your sisters are immaculately-mannered English roses, I am sure, Monsieur?' Rather doubt her interest in the Frobishery's memsahibs was genuine, but the woman likes to watch me talk, so I painted witty caricatures of my estranged clan for my hostess's amusement. Made us all sound so gay, almost felt homesick.

This morning, a Monday, Eva deigned to share breakfast – Bradenham ham, eggs, bread, all-sorts – but the girl spouted petty complaints to her mother and snuffed my interjections out with a flat '*oui*' or a sharp '*non*'. Ayrs was feeling better so ate with us. Hendrick then drove the daughter off to Bruges for another week at school – Eva boards in the city with a family whose daughters also attend her school, the Van Eels or some such. Whole château breathed a relieved sigh when the Cowley had cleared the poplar avenue (known as the Monk's Walk). Eva does so poison the air of the place. At nine, Ayrs and I adjourned to the music room. 'I've got a little melody for viola rattling about my head, Frobisher. Let's see if you can get it down.' Was delighted to hear it, as I'd expected to start at the shallow-end – tidying up sketchy MSS into best copy and so forth. If I proved my worth as V.A.'s sentient fountain-pen on my first day, my tenure would be well-nigh assured. Sat at his desk, sharpened 2B at the ready, clean MS, waiting for him to name the notes, one by one. Suddenly, the man bellowed: ' "Tar, tar! Tar-tar-tar tattytattytatty, tar!" Got that? "Tar! Tatty-tar! Quiet part – tar-tar-tar-tttt-TAR! TARTARTAR!!!" ' Got that? Old ass obviously thought this was amusing – one could no more notate his shouted garble than one could score the braying of a dozen donkeys – but after another thirty seconds, it dawned on me this was no joke. Tried to interrupt, but the man was so engrossed in his music-making that he didn't notice. Sunk into deepest misery while Ayrs carried on, and on, and on . . . My scheme was hopeless. What had I been thinking about at Victoria Station? Dejected, I let him work through his piece in the lean hope that having it complete in his head might make it easier to duplicate later. 'There, finished!' he proclaimed. 'Got it? Hum it back, Frobisher, and then let's see how it sounds.'

Asked what key we were in. 'B-flat, *of course!*' Time signature? Ayrs pinched the bridge of his nose. 'Are you saying you've lost my melody?'

Struggled to remind myself he was being totally unreasonable. I asked him to repeat the melody, *much* more slowly, and to label his notes, one by one. There was an acute pause that felt about three hours long while Ayrs decided whether or not to throw a tantrum. In the end, he released a martyred sigh. 'Four-*eight*, changing to *eight*-eight after the 12th bar, if you can count that far.' Pause. Remembered my monetary difficulties and bit my lip. 'Let's go all the way back, then.' Patronizing pause. 'Ready now? *Slowly* . . . Tar! What note is that?' Got through a hideous ½-hour with me guessing every single note, one by one. Ayrs verified or rejected my guess with a weary nod or shake of the head. Mme C. carried in a vase of flowers and I made an S.O.S. face, but V.A. himself declared that we call it a day. As I fled, I heard Ayrs pronounce (for my benefit?), 'It is desperate, Jocasta, the boy cannot take down a simple tune. I might as well join the avant-garde and throw darts at pieces of paper with notes written on 'em.'

Down the passageway Mrs Willems – housekeeper – laments the damp, blustery weather and her wet laundry to some unseen underling. She's better off than I am. I've manipulated people for advancement, lust or loans, but never for the roof over my head. This rotting château stinks of mushrooms and mould. Should never have come here.

Sincerely,
R.F.

P.S. Financial 'embarrassment', what an apposite phrase. No wonder the poor are all socialists. Look, must ask you for a loan. The regime at Zedelghem is the laxest I ever saw (thankfully! My father's butler's wardrobe is better supplied than my own at present) but one needs to set some standards. Can't even tip the servants. If I had any wealthy friends left, I'd ask 'em, but truth is I don't. Don't know how you wire money or telegram it or send it in packets or whatever, but you're the scientist, you find a way. If Ayrs asks me to leave, I'll be scuppered. The news would seep back to Cambridge that Robert Frobisher had to beg money from his erstwhile hosts when they threw him out for not being up to the job. The shame would kill me, Sixsmith, it truly would. For God's sake send whatever you can immediately.

— ◆ —

Château Zedelghem.
14th – vii – 1931.

Sixsmith,

All praise Rufus the Blessed, Patron Saint of Needy Composers, Praise in the Highest, *Amen*. Your postal order arrived safe and sound this morning – I painted you to my hosts as a doting uncle who'd forgotten my birthday. Mrs Crommelynck confirms a bank in Bruges will cash it. Will write a motet in your honour and pay your money back soon as I can. Might be sooner than you expect. The deep freeze on my prospects is thawing. After my humiliating 1st attempt at collaboration with Ayrs, I returned to my room in abject wretchedness. That afternoon I spent writing my snivelling lament to you – burn it, by the way, if you haven't already – feeling v. anxious about the future. Braved the rain in wellington boots and a cape and walked to the post office in the village, wondering, frankly, where I might be a month from now. Mrs Willems bonged the gong for dinner shortly after my return, but when I got to the dining-hall, Ayrs was waiting, alone. 'That you, Frobisher?' he asked, with the gruffness habitual to older men trying to do delicacy. 'Ah, Frobisher, glad we can have this little chat alone. Look, I was rotten to you this morning. My illness makes me more . . . direct than is sometimes appropriate. I apologize. Give this cantankerous so-and-so another chance tomorrow, what d'you say?'

Had his wife told him what state she'd found me in? Had Lucille mentioned my ½-packed valise? Waited until I was sure my voice was purged of relief, and told him, nobly, nothing was wrong in speaking his mind.

'I've been far too negative about your proposal, Frobisher. It won't be easy extracting music out of my noddle, but our partnership stands as good a chance as any. Your musicianship and character seem more than up to the job. My wife tells me you even try your hand at composition? Plainly, music is oxygen for us both. With the right will, we'll muddle along until we hit upon the right method.' At this, Mme Crommelynck knocked, peered in, sensed the room's weather in a trice the way some women do, and asked if a celebratory drink was called for. Ayrs turned to me. 'That depends on young Frobisher here. What d'you say? Will you stay for a few weeks, with a view to a few months, if all goes well? Maybe longer, who knows? But you must accept a small salary.'

Let my relief show as pleasure, told him I'd be honoured, and did not out-of-hand reject the offer of a salary.

'Then, Jocasta, tell Mrs Willems to fetch a Pinot Rouge 1908!' We toasted Bacchus and the Muses, and drank a wine rich as unicorn's blood. Ayrs's cellar, some six hundred bottles, is one of the finest in Belgium, and worth a brief digression. It survived the war unlooted by the Hun officers who used Zedelghem as a command post, all thanks to a false wall Hendrick's father built over its entrance before the family's flight to Gothenburg. The library, and various other bulky treasures, also spent the war down there (used to be the vaults of a monastery), sealed up in crates. The Prussians ransacked the building before Armistice, but they never rumbled the cellar.

A work routine is developing. Ayrs and I are in the music room by nine o'clock every morning his various ailments and pains let him. I sit at the piano, Ayrs on the divan, smoking his vile Turkish cigarettes, and we adopt one of our three *modi operandi*. 'Revisionals' – he asks me to run through the previous morning's work. I hum, sing or play, depending on the instrument, and Ayrs modifies the score. 'Reconstitutionals' have me sifting through old scores, notebooks and compositions, some written before I was born, to locate a passage or cadenza Ayrs dimly remembers and wants to salvage. Great detective work. 'Compositionals' are the most demanding. I sit at the piano and try to keep up with a flow of 'Semi-quaver, B-G; semibreve, A flat – hold it four beats, no, six – crotchets! F-sharp – no no no no F-*sharp* – and . . . B! Tar-tatty-tatty-tarrr!' (*Il maestro* will at least name his notes now.) Or, if he's feeling more poetic, it might be, 'Now, Frobisher, the clarinet is the concubine, the violas are yew-trees in the cemetery, the clavichord is the moon, so . . . let the east wind blow that A minor chord, 16th bar onwards.'

Like a good butler (although you can be sure, I am better than good) my job is ⁹⁄₁₀ths anticipation. Sometimes Ayrs will ask for an artistic judgement, something like, 'D'you think this chord works, Frobisher?' or 'Is this passage in keeping with the whole?' If I say no, Ayrs asks me what I'd suggest as a substitute, and once or twice he's even used my amendment. Quite sobering. People in the future will be studying this music.

By one o'clock Ayrs is spent. Hendrick carries him down to the dining-room where Mrs Crommelynck joins us for luncheon, and the dreaded E., if she's back for the w/end or a ½-holiday. Ayrs naps through the afternoon heat. I continue to sift the library for treasure, compose in the music-room, read manuscripts in the garden (Madonna lilies, crowns imperial, red-hot pokers, hollyhocks, all blooming bright), navigate lanes around Neerbeke on the bicycle, or ramble across local fields. Am firm friends with the village dogs. They gallop after me like the Pied Piper's rats or brats. The locals return my '*Goede morgen*' and '*Goede middag*' – I'm now known as the long-term guest up at the '*kasteel*'.

After supper, the three of us might listen to the wireless if there is a broadcast that passes muster, otherwise it will be recordings on the gramophone (an His Master's Voice table model in an oak box), usually of Ayrs's own major works conducted by Sir Thomas Beecham. When we have visitors, there will be conversation or a little chamber music. Other nights, Ayrs likes me to read him poetry, especially his beloved Keats.

He whispers the verses as I recite, as if his voice is leaning on mine. At breakfast, he has me read from *The Times*. Old, blind and sick as Ayrs is, he could hold his own in a college debating society, though I notice he rarely proposes alternatives for the systems he ridicules. 'Liberality? Timidity in the rich!'; 'Socialism? The younger brother of a decrepit despotism, which it wants to succeed'; 'Conservatives? Adventitious liars, whose doctrine of free will is their greatest deception.' What sort of state *does* he want? 'None! The better organized the state, the duller its humanity.'

Irascible as Ayrs is, he's one of few men in Europe whose influence I want my own creativity informed by. Musicologically, he's Janus-headed. One Ayrs looks back to Romanticism's deathbed, the other looks to the future. This is the Ayrs whose gaze I follow. Watching him use counterpoint and mix colours refines my own language in exciting ways. Already, my short time at Zedelghem has taught me more than three years at the throne of Mackerras the Jackass with his Merry Band of Onanists.

Friends of Ayrs and Mrs Crommelynck regularly visit. On an average week, we can expect visitor/s two or three nights. Soloists returning from Brussels, Berlin, Amsterdam or beyond; acquaintances from Ayrs's salad days in Florida or Paris; and good old Morty Dhondt and Wife. Dhondt owns a diamond workshop in both Bruges and Antwerp, speaks a hazy but high number of languages, concocts elaborate multi-lingual puns requiring lengthy explanations, sponsors festivals and kicks metaphysical footballs around with Ayrs. Mrs Dhondt is like Mrs Crommelynck but ten times more so – in truth, a dreadful creation who heads the Belgian Equestrian Society, drives the Dhondt Bugatti herself, and cossets a powder-puff Pekinese called Wei-wei. You'll meet her again in future letters, no doubt.

Relatives thin on the ground: Ayrs was an only child, and the once-influential Crommelynck family evinced a perverse genius for backing the wrong side at decisive moments throughout the war. Those who didn't die in action were mostly pauperized and diseased out of existence by the time Ayrs and his wife returned from Scandinavia. Others died after running away overseas. Mrs Crommelynck's old governess and a couple of frail aunts sometimes pay a call, but they stay quietly in the corner like old hat-stands.

Last week the conductor Tadeusz Augustowski, a great champion of Ayrs in his native Cracow, dropped by unannounced on a 2nd Day of Migraine. Mrs Crommelynck was not at home, and Mrs Willems came to me all of a lather, begging me to entertain the illustrious visitor. I could not disappoint. Augustowski's French is as good as my own, and we spent the afternoon fishing and arguing over the dodecaphonists. He thinks they are all charlatans, I do not. He told me orchestral war-stories, and one indescribably smutty joke that involves hand gestures, so it must wait until we meet again. I caught an eleven-inch trout and Augustowski bagged a monster dace. Ayrs was up when we got back at twilight, and the Pole told him he was lucky to have engaged me. Ayrs grunted something like, 'Quite.' Enchanting flattery, Ayrs. Mrs Willems was less than *enchantée* with our finny trophies, but she gutted 'em, cooked 'em in salt and butter and they melted on the fish-fork. Augustowski gave me his visiting card when he departed the next morning. He keeps a suite at the Langham Court for his London visits, and invited me to stay with him for next year's festival. Cock-a-doodle-doo!

Château Zedelghem isn't the labyrinthine House of Usher it seems at first. True, its west wing, shuttered and dust-sheeted to pay for modernization and upkeep of the east, is in a woebegone state, and will need the demolishers before v. long I fear. Explored its chambers one wet afternoon. Damp disastrous; fallen plaster hangs in nets of cobwebs; mouse, bat droppings crunch on the worn stones; plaster escutcheons above fireplaces sanded over by time. Same story outside – brick walls need new pointing, roof-tiles missing, crenellations toppled to the ground and lying in piles, rainwater runnelling medieval sandstone. The CrommeLyncks did well from Congo investments, but not one male sibling survived the war, and Zedelghem's Boche 'lodgers' selectively gutted whatever was worth looting.

The east wing, however, is a comfortable little warren, though its roof timbers creak like a ship when the wind's up. There's a moody central-heating system and rudimentary electricity that gives one crackling electric shocks from the light switches. Mrs Crommelynck's father had enough foresight to teach his daughter the estate business, and now she leases her land to neighbouring farmers and just about makes the place pay, so I gather. Not an achievement to be sniffed at in this day and age.

Eva still a prissy missy, as hateful as my sisters, but with an intelligence to match her enmity. Apart from her precious Nefertiti, her hobbies are pouting and looking martyred. She likes to reduce vulnerable domestics to tears, then flounces in, announcing, 'She's having *another* weeping fit, Mama, can't you break her in properly?' She has established I am no soft target, and embarked on a war of attrition: 'Papa, how long is Mr Frobisher to stay in our house?'; 'Papa, do you pay Mr Frobisher as much as you pay Hendrick?'; 'Oh, I was only asking, Mama, I didn't know Mr Frobisher's tenure was a delicate subject.' She rattles me, hate to hand it to her, but there it is. Had another encounter – 'confrontation' more the word – on Saturday just gone. I'd taken Ayrs's Bible, *Thus Spake Zarathustra*, to the stone slab bridge over the lake to the willow-tree island. A scorching hot afternoon; even in the shade I was sweating like a pig. After ten pages I felt Nietzsche was reading me, not I him, so I watched the water-boatmen and newts while my mind-orchestra performed Fred Delius's *Air and Dance*. Syrupy florentine of a piece, but its drowsy flute is rather successful.

Next thing I knew, found myself in a trench so deep the sky was a strip high above, lit by flashes brighter than day. Savages patrolled the trench a-straddle giant, evil-toothed, brown rats that sniffed out working-class people and dismembered 'em. Strolled, trying to look well-to-do and stop myself breaking into a panicky run, when I met Eva. I said, 'What in hell are *you* doing down here?'

Eva replied with fury! 'Ce lac appartient à ma famille depuis cinq siècles! Vous êtes ici depuis combien de temps exactement? Bien trois semaines! Alors vous voyez, je vais où bon me semble!' Eva's anger was almost physical, a kick in your humble correspondent's face. Fair enough, I had accused her of trespassing on her mother's estate. Wide awake, I stumbled to my feet, all apologies, explaining I had spoken whilst dreaming.

Quite forgot about the lake. Plunged right in like a b. fool! Soaked! Luckily the pond was only navel-high, and God had saved Ayrs's precious Nietzsche from joining me in the drink. When Eva eventually reined in her laughter, I said I was pleased to see her do something other than pout. I had duckweed in my hair, she answered, in English. Was reduced to patronising her by praising her language skills. She batted back, 'It does not take much to impress an Englishman.' Walked off. Couldn't think of a snappy response until later, so the girl won the set.

Now, pay attention while I talk books and lucre. Poking through an alcove of books in my room I came across a curious dismembered volume, and I want you to track down a complete copy for me. It begins on the 99th page, its covers are gone, its binding unstitched. From what little I can glean, it's the edited journal of a voyage from Sydney to California by a notary of San Francisco named Adam Ewing. Mention is made of the gold rush, so I suppose we are in 1849 or 1850. The journal seems to be published posthumously, by Ewing's son (?). Ewing puts me in mind of Melville's bumbler Cpt. Delano in *Benito Cereno*, blind to all conspirators – he hasn't spotted his trusty Doctor Henry Goose (*sic*) is a vampire, fuelling his hypochondria in order to poison him, slowly, for his money. Something shifty about the journal's authenticity – seems too structured for a genuine diary, and its language doesn't ring quite true – but who would bother forging such a journal, and why?

To my great annoyance, the pages cease, mid-sentence, some forty pages later, where the binding is worn through. Searched high and low in the library for the rest of the damn thing. No luck. Hardly in our interests to draw Ayrs's or Mrs Crommelynck's attention to their unindexed bibliographic wealth, so I'm up a gum tree. Would you ask Otto Jansch on Caithness Street if he knows anything about this Adam Ewing? A half-read book is a half-finished love affair.

Find enclosed an inventory of the oldest editions I can find in Zedelghem's library. As you see, some items are *v*. early, early 17th C., so send me Jansch's best prices as soon as ever, and keep the tight-wad on his toes by letting it slip you've got the Parisian dealers interested.

Sincerely,
R.F.

— ◆ —

Château Zedelghem.
28th – vii – 1931.

Sixsmith,
Cause for minor celebration. Two days ago, Ayrs and I completed our 1st collaboration, a short tone-poem, 'Der Todtenvogel'. When I unearthed the piece, it was a tame arrangement of an old Teutonic anthem, left high and very dry by Ayrs's retreating eyesight. Our new version is an intriguing animal. It borrows resonances from Wagner's *Ring*, then disintegrates the theme into a Stravinskyesque nightmare policed by Sibelian wraiths. Horrible, delectable, wish you could hear it. Ends in a flute solo, no flutterbying flautism this, but the death-bird of the title, cursing the first-born and last-born alike.

Augustowski visited again on his way back from Paris yesterday. He read the score and shovelled praise upon it like a boilerman shovelling coals. So he should! It's the most accomplished tone poem *I* know of written since the War; and I tell you, Sixsmith, that more than a few of its best ideas are mine. Suppose an amanuensis must reconcile himself to renouncing his share in authorship, but buttoning one's lip is never easy. But best is yet to come – Augustowski wants to première the work under his own baton three weeks from now at the Cracow festival!

Got up at crack of dawn yesterday, spent all day transcribing a clean copy. Suddenly it didn't seem so short. My writing hand came unscrewed and staves imprinted themselves in my eyelids, but finished by supper. We drank five bottles of wine between the four of us to celebrate. Dessert was the best muscatels.

Am now Zedelghem's golden boy. Been a v. long time since I was anyone's golden boy and I rather like it. Jocasta suggested that I move out of my guest room into one of the larger unused bedrooms on the 2nd floor, furnished as I pleased with whatever catches my eye from elsewhere in Zedelghem. Ayrs seconded the motion, so I said I would. To my delight Prissy Missy lost her *sangfroid* and mewled, 'Oh, why don't you just write him into the will as well, Mama? Why not give him ½ the estate?'

She got down from the table without being excused. Ayrs croaked, 'First good idea the girl's had in seventeen years!' loud enough for her to hear. 'At least Frobisher earns his damn keep!'

My hosts wouldn't hear my apologies, they said Eva should be apologizing to me, that she has to lose her pre-Copernican view of a universe revolving around herself. Music to my ears. Also re: Eva, she and twenty classmates are bound for Switzerland v. soon to study at a sister-school for a couple of months. More music! It'll be like having a rotten tooth fall out. My new room is big enough for badminton doubles; has a four-poster bed from whose curtains I had to shake last year's moths; centuries-old Cordova peel off the walls like dragons' scales, but it's attractive in its way; indigo witch-ball; armoire inlaid with burr walnut; six ministerial arm-chairs and a sycamore escritoire at which I write this letter. Honeysuckle laces abundant light. To the south one looks over the grizzled topiary. To the west, cows graze in the meadow and the church tower rises above the wood beyond. Its bells are my own clock. (In truth, Zedelghem boasts a good many antique clocks whose chimes go off some early, some late, like a Bruges in miniature.) All in all, a notch or two grander than our chambers in Whyman's Lane, a notch or two less grand than the Savoy or the Imperial, but spacious and secure. Unless I do something clumsy or indiscreet.

Which brings me to Madame Jocasta Crommelynck. Damn my eyes, Sixsmith, if the woman hasn't begun, *subtly*, to flirt with me. The ambiguity of her words, eyes and hand-brushes is too consummate to be chance. See what you think. Yesterday afternoon, I was studying rare Balakirev juvenilia in my room when Mrs Crommelynck knocked. She wore her riding jacket and her hair pinned up to reveal a rather tempting neck. 'My husband wants to give you a present,' she said, moving in as I gave way. 'Here. To mark the completion of "Todtenvogel". You know, Robert,' her tongue lingers on the T of 'Robert', 'Vyvyan's so very happy to be working again. He hasn't been this spry for years. This is just a token. Put it on.' She handed me an exquisite waist-coat, an Ottoman-style silken affair, too remarkable in pattern to be ever in fashion or out. 'I bought it on our honeymoon in Cairo, when he was your age now. He won't be wearing it again.'

Said I was flattered, but protested that I couldn't possibly accept a garment of such sentimental value. 'That's precisely why we want you to wear it. Our memories are in its weave. Put it on.' Did as urged, and she stroked it, on the pretext (?) of removing fluff. 'Come to the mirror!' Did so. The woman stood just inches behind me. 'Too fine for moths' eggs, don't you agree?' Yes, I agreed. Her smile was double-bladed. If we were in one of Emily's breathy novels, the seductress's hands would have encircled the innocent's torso, but Jocasta is a more canny operator. 'You have *exactly* the same physique Vyvyan had at your age. Bizarre, isn't it?' Yes, I agreed again. Her fingernails freed a strand of my hair that had got caught in the waistcoat.

Neither rebuffed nor encouraged her. These things shouldn't be rushed. Mrs Crommelynck left without another word.

At luncheon, Hendrick reported that Doctor Egret's house in Neerbeke had been burgled. Luckily no-one was hurt, but the police have issued a warning to be on the look-out for gypsies and ruffians. Houses should be secured at night. Jocasta shuddered and said she was glad I was at Zedelghem to protect her. Admitted I'd held my own as a pugilist at Eton, but doubted whether I could see off a whole gang of ruffians. Perhaps I could hold Hendrick's towel whilst *he* gave 'em all a sound drubbing? Ayrs didn't comment, but that evening he unwrapped a Luger from his napkin. Jocasta chastised Ayrs for showing his pistol at the dinner-table, but he ignored her. 'On our return from Gothenburg, I found this beastie hidden under a loose floorboard in the master-bedroom, with its bullets,' he explained. 'The Prussian captain either left in a hurry or got himself killed. He stowed it there perhaps as an insurance policy against mutineers, or undesirables. I keep it beside my bed for the same reason.'

Asked if I could hold it, as I'd only ever touched hunting rifles before. 'By all means,' replied Ayrs, handing it over. Every hair on my body rose. That snug iron fellow has killed at least once, I'd wager my inheritance on it, if I still had any. 'So you see,' Ayrs had a crooked laugh, 'I may be an elderly, blind cripple, but I still have a tooth or two left to bite with. One blind man with a gun and *v.* little left to lose. Imagine the *mess* I could make!' Can't decide if I only imagined the menace in his voice.

Excellent news from Jansch, but don't tell him I said so. Will post the three referred volumes to you from Bruges next time I go – the post-master here in Neerbeke has an inquisitive streak I don't trust. Take usual precautions. Remit my lucre to the 1st Bank of Belgium, Head Branch, Bruges – Dhondt snapped his fingers and had the manager open me an account. Only one Robert Frobisher on their lists, I'm quite sure.

Best news of all: started composing on my own account again.

Sincerely,
R.F.

— ◆ —

Zedelghem.
16th – viii – 1931.

Sixsmith,
Summer has taken a sensuous turn: Ayrs's wife and I are lovers. Don't alarm yourself! Only in the carnal sense. One night last week she came to my room, locked the door behind her and, without a word passing between us, disrobed. Don't wish to brag, but her visit didn't take me by surprise. In fact, I'd left the door ajar for her. Really, Sixsmith, you should try to enjoy love-making in total silence. All that ballyhooing transmutes into bliss if you'll only seal your lips.

When one unlocks a woman's body, her box of confidences also spills. (You should try 'em yourself one time, women I mean.) Might this be connected to their hopelessness at cards? After the Act, I am happier just lying still, but Jocasta talked, impulsively, as if to bury our big black secret under littler grey ones. Learnt Ayrs contracted his syphilis at a bordello in Copenhagen in 1915 during an extended separation and has not pleasured his wife since that year; after Eva's birth, the doctor told Jocasta she could never conceive another child. She is v. selective about her occasional affairs, but unapologetic about her right to conduct same. She insisted that she still loves Ayrs. I grunted, dubiously. That love loves fidelity, she riposted, is a myth woven by men from their insecurities.

Talked about Eva too. She worries that she was so busy instilling a sense of propriety into her daughter, they never became friends, and now, it seems, that horse has bolted. Dozed through these trivial tragedies, but shall be more careful around Danes in future and Danish bordellos in particular.

J. wanted a 2nd bout, as if to glue herself to me. Did not object. She has an equestrienne's body, more spring than you normally get in a mature woman, and more technique than many a ten-shilling mount I've ridden. One suspects there stretches back a long line of youthful stallions invited to forage in her manger. Indeed, just as I nodded off for the last time she said, 'Debussy once spent a week at Zedelghem, before the War. He slept in this very bed, if I'm not mistaken.' A minor chord in her tone suggested she was with him. Not impossible. Anything in a skirt, that's what I heard about Claude, and he *was* a Frenchman.

When Lucille knocked in the morning with my shaving water, I was quite alone. J.'s performance over breakfast was as nonchalant as my own, happy to note. Was even slightly caustic with me when I spilt a blob of jam on the place-mat, prompting V.A. to reprimand her, 'Don't be such a stickle-back, Jocasta! *Your* pretty hands won't have to scrub the stain out.' Adultery is a tricky duet to pull off, Sixsmith – as in contract bridge, eschew partners clumsier than oneself or one winds up in a ghastly mess.

Guilt? None. A cuckolder's triumph? Not specially, no. Still rather miffed at Ayrs, if anything. The other evening, the Dhondts came to dinner and Mrs D. asked for some piano music to help the food go down, so I played that 'Angel of Mons' piece I wrote on holiday with you in the Scilly Isles two summers ago, though disclaimed its authorship by saying 'a friend' had composed it. I've been rewriting it. It's better and more fluid and subtle than those sherbety Schubertian pastiches V.A. spewed out in *his* twenties. J. and the Dhondts loved it so much they insisted on an encore. Was only six bars in when V.A. exercised a hitherto unknown veto. 'I'd advise your friend to master the Ancients before he frolics with the Moderns.' Sounds like innocuous enough advice? However, he pronounced 'friend' in a precise semi-tone that told me he was quite aware of my friend's true identity. Perhaps he used the same ruse himself, at Grieg's in Oslo? 'Without a thorough mastery of counterpoint and harmonics,' V.A. puffed, 'this fellow'll never amount to anything but a hawker of fatuous gimmickry. Tell your *friend* that from me.' I fumed in silence. V.A. told J. to put on a gramophone recording of his own 'Scirocco Wind Quintet'. She obeyed the truculent old bully. To console myself, I remembered how J.'s body is under her crêpe-de-Chine summer dress, and how hungrily she slips into my bed. V. well, I shall gloat a little over my employer's cuckold's horns. Serves him right. An old sick prig is still a prig.

Augustowski sent this enigmatic telegram after the performance in Cracow. To translate from the French: FIRST TODTEN-VOGEL MYSTIFIED STOP SECOND PERFORMANCE FISTICUFFS STOP THIRD ADORED STOP FOURTH TALK OF TOWN STOP. We weren't sure what to think until newspaper clippings followed, hot on the telegram's heels, translated by Augustowski on the back of a concert programme. Well, our 'Todtenvogel' has become a *cause célèbre*! So far as we can see, the critics interpreted its disintegration of the Wagnerian themes as a frontal assault on the German Republic. A band of nationalist parliamentarians strong-armed the festival authorities into a 5th performance. The theatre, eyeing receipts, complied with pleasure. The German ambassador made an official complaint, so a 6th was sold out within another twenty-four hours. The effect of all this is to raise the value of Ayrs's stock through the roof everywhere but Germany where, apparently, he is denounced as a Jewish devil. National newspapers across the continent have written to request interviews. I have the pleasure of despatching a polite but firm *pro forma* rejection to each. 'I'm too busy composing,' grumbles Ayrs. 'If they want to know "what I mean" they should listen to my bloody music.' He's thriving on the attention, though. Even Mrs Willems admits, since my arrival the Master is invigorated.

Hostilities continue on the Eva front. Of concern is how she sniffs something rotten between my father and me. She wonders, publicly, why I never receive letters from my family, or why I don't have some clothes of my own sent over. She asked if one of my sisters would like to be her pen-friend. To win time I had to promise to put her proposal to 'em, and I might need you to do another forgery. Make it very good. The devious vixen is almost a female Me.

August in Belgium is blistering this year. The meadow is turning yellow, the gardener is anxious about fires, farmers are worried about the harvest, but show me a placid farmer and I'll show you a sane conductor. Will seal this envelope now and walk to the village post-office through the woods behind the lake. It wouldn't do to leave *these* pages lying around for a certain seventeen-year-old snoop to come across.

The important matter. Yes, I will meet Otto Jansch in Bruges to hand over the illuminated manuscripts in person, but you must broker all the arrangements. Don't want Jansch knowing whose hospitality I'm enjoying. Like all dealers, Jansch is a gluttonous, glabrous grasper, only more so. He wouldn't hesitate to try blackmail to lower our price – or even dispense with a price altogether. Tell him I'll expect payment on the nail in crisp bank-notes, none of his funny credit arrangements with me. Then I'll forward a postal order to you, including the sum you loaned me. This way, you won't be incriminated if any monkey business takes place. I am already disgraced and thus have no reputation to lose by blowing the whistle on him. Tell Jansch that, too.

Sincerely,
R.F.

— ◆ —

Zedelghem.
Evening, 16th – viii – 1931.

Sixsmith,
Your tedious letter from my father's 'solicitor' was an Ace of Diamonds. Bravo. Read it aloud over breakfast – excited only passing interest. Saffron Walden postmark also a masterly touch. Did you actually drag yourself away from your lab into the sunny Essex afternoon to post it yourself? Ayrs invited our 'Mr

Cummings' to see me at Zedelghem, but you'd written time was v. tight, so Mrs Crommelynck said Hendrick'll drive me into town to sign the documents there. Ayrs grumbled about losing a day's work, but he's only happy when he's grumbling.

Hendrick and I set off this dewy morning down the same roads I cycled from Bruges ½ a summertime ago. Wore a smart jacket of Ayrs's – much of his wardrobe is gravitating into mine, now my few items rescued from the Imperial's grasp are beginning to wear out. The Enfield was roped to the rear fender so I could honour my promise to return said bicycle to the good constable. Our vellum-bound loot I had camouflaged in MS paper, which everyone at Zedelghem knows I am never without, and stowed out of casual sight in a mucky satchel I've appropriated. Hendrick had the Cowley's top down so there was too much wind for conversation. Taciturn chap, as is appropriate to his station. Peculiar to admit it, but since I've started servicing Mrs Crommelynck I feel edgier with the husband's valet than I do with the husband. (Jocasta continues to bestow her favour on me, every 3rd or 4th night, though never when Eva is at home, which is v. wise. Anyway, one mustn't gobble one's birthday chocolates all at once.) My unease stems from the probability that Hendrick knows. Oh, we above the stairs like to congratulate ourselves on our cleverness, but there are no secrets to those who strip the sheets. Not too worried. Don't place unreasonable demands on the servants, and Hendrick is canny enough to lay his bets on a strident mistress with many years ahead of her, not on an invalid master of Ayrs's prospects. Hendrick's an odd one, really. Hard to guess his tastes. Would make an excellent croupier.

He dropped me outside the Guild Hall, untied the Enfield and left me to run various errands and pay his respects, he said, to an ailing great-aunt. Rode my two wheels through crowds of sightseers, schoolchildren and burghers and only got lost a few times. At the police-station, the musical inspector made a great fuss of me and sent out for coffee and pastries. He was delighted my position with Ayrs has worked out so well. By the time I got away it was ten o'clock and time for my appointment. Didn't hurry. Good form to let tradesmen wait a little.

Jansch was propping up the bar of Le Royal and greeted me with an 'Aha, as I live and breathe, the Invisible Man, back by popular demand!' I swear, Sixsmith, that warty old Shylock looks more repulsive every time I clap eyes on him. Has he got a magical portrait of himself stashed in his attic, getting more beautiful by the year? Couldn't fathom why he seemed so pleased to see me. Looked around the lounge for tipped-off creditors – one beetly glare and I would have bolted. Jansch read my mind. 'So suspicious, Roberto? *I'*m hardly going to make trouble for a naughty goose who lays such illuminated eggs, am I? Come now,' he indicated the bar, 'what's your poison?'

Replied that sharing a building with Jansch, even such a large one, was poisonous enough, so I'd rather get down to business straight away. He chuckled, clapped me on the shoulder and led me up to the room he'd reserved for our transaction. Nobody followed us, but that didn't guarantee anything. Was now wishing I'd had you arrange a more public rendezvous, so Tam Brewer's thugs couldn't clap a sack over my head, throw me in a trunk and haul me back to London. Got the books out of the satchel and he got his *pince-nez* out of his jacket pocket. Jansch examined 'em at a desk by the window. He tried to knock the price down, claiming the condition of the volumes was more 'fair' than 'good'. Calmly, I wrapped the books up, put 'em in my satchel, and made the stingy Jew chase me down the corridor until he admitted the volumes were indeed 'good'. Let him woo me back to the room, where we counted the bank-notes, slowly, until the sum agreed was paid in full. Business over, he sighed, claimed I'd beggared him, smiled that smile and put his hairy paw on my knee. Said it was books I'd come to sell. He asked why let business preclude pleasure? Surely a young buck abroad could find a use for a little pocket money?

Left Jansch asleep an hour later and his wallet starved. Proceeded directly to the bank across the square and was seen to by the manager's own secretary. Sweet bird of solvency. As Pater is fond of saying, 'One's own sweat is one's best reward!' (not that *he* ever sweated in his sinecured pulpit overly much). Next stop was the city's music shop, Flagstad's, where I bought a brick of MS paper to replace the missing bulk from my satchel for benefit of watchful eyes. Coming out, I saw a pair of drab spats in a shoe-maker's window. Went in, bought 'em. Saw a shagreen cigarette box in a tobacconist's. Bought it.

Two hours remained to kill. Had a cold beer in a café, and another, and another, and smoked a whole packet of delicious French cigarettes. The Jansch money is no dragon's hoard, but God knows it feels like one. Next I found a backstreet church (avoided the tourist places to avoid disgruntled book dealers) of candles, shadows, doleful martyrs, incense. Haven't been to church since the morning Pater cast me out. Street door kept banging shut. Wiry crones came, lit candles, went. Padlock on the votive box was of the best. People knelt in prayer, some moving their lips. Envy 'em, really I do. I envy God, too, privy to their secrets. Faith, the least exclusive club on Earth, has the craftiest doorman. Every time I've stepped through its wide-open doorway, I find myself stepping out on the street again. Did my best to think beatific thoughts, but my mind kept running its fingers over Jocasta. Even the stained-glass saints and martyrs were mildly arousing. Don't suppose such thoughts get me closer to Heaven. In the end, it was a Bach motet that shooed me away – choristers weren't damnably bad, but the organist's only hope for salvation was a bullet through the brain. Told him so, too – tact and restraint all well and good in small-talk, but one mustn't beat around any bush where music is concerned.

At a prim and proper park named Minnewater Gardens, courting couples ambled arm-in-arm between willows, Banksia roses and chaperones. Blind, emaciated fiddler performed for coins. Now he *could* play. Requested 'Bonsoir, Paris!', and he performed with such *élan* I pressed a crisp five-franc note into his hand. He removed his dark glasses, checked the watermark, invoked his pet saint's name, gathered his coppers and scarpered through the flower-beds, laughing like a madcap. Whoever opined, 'Money can't buy you happiness,' obviously had far too much of the stuff.

Sat down on an iron bench. One o'clock bells chimed, nearby, far-off, interspersed. Clerks crawled out from the law and merchants' offices to eat sandwiches in the park and feel the green breeze. Was wondering whether to be late for Hendrick, when guess who waltzed into the park, unchaperoned, in the company of a dandified stick-insect of a man twice her age, a vulgar gold wedding ring on his finger as bold as brass. Right 1st time. Eva. Hid behind a newspaper a clerk had left on the bench. Eva wasn't in physical contact with her companion, but they strolled right by me with an air of easy intimacy that she never, ever wears at Zedelghem. I jumped to the obvious conclusion.

Eva was stacking her chips on a doubtful card. He crowed, in order to be overheard by strangers and impress them. 'A time is one's own, Eva, when oneself and one's peers take the same things for granted, without thinking about it. Likewise, a man is ruined when the times change, but he does not. Permit me to add, empires fall for the same reason.' This jackdaw philosophizer flummoxed me. A girl of E.'s looks could do better for herself, surely? E.'s behaviour likewise flummoxed me. In broad daylight, in her own city! Does she *want* to ruin herself? Is she one of these libertarian suffragette Rossetti types? I followed the couple at a safe distance to a town-house on a well-heeled road. The man gave the street a shifty once-over before putting his key in the latch. I ducked into a mews.

Picture Frobisher rubbing his hands with glee!

Eva returned as usual late on Friday afternoon. In the vestibule between her room and the door to the stables is an oaken throne. In this I planted myself. Unfortunately I became lost in the chords in the chroma of old glass, and didn't notice E., riding crop in her hand, not even aware she was being ambushed. 'S'agit-il d'un guet-apens? Si vous voulez discuter avec moi d'un problème personnel, vous pourriez me prévenir?'

Being caught by surprise like that made me speak my thought aloud. Eva caught the word. '"Sneak", you call me? "Une moucharde"? Ce n'est pas un mot aimable, Mr Frobisher. Si vous dîtes que je suis une moucharde, vous allez nuire à ma réputation. Et si vous nuisez à ma réputation, eh bien, il faudra que je ruine la vôtre!'

Belatedly, I opened fire. Yes, her reputation was precisely what I had to warn her about. If even a visiting foreigner to Bruges had seen her consorting in Minnewater Park during school hours with a scrofulous toad, it was only a matter of time before all the rumour-mongers in the city had turned the name of Crommelynck-Ayrs to Mudd!

One moment I expected a slap, the next, she reddened and lowered her face. Meekly, she enquired, 'Avez-vous dit à ma mère ce que vous avez vu?' I replied that, no, I had not told anyone, yet. E. took careful aim: 'Stupid of you, Monsieur Frobisher, because Mama could have told you that mysterious "consort" was Monsieur van de Velde, the gentleman with whose family I lodge during my school-week. His father owns the largest munitions factory in Belgium, and he is a respectable family-man. Wednesday was a half-holiday, so Monsieur van de Velde was kind enough to accompany me from his office back to his house. His own daughters had a choir rehearsal to attend. The school does not like its girls to walk out alone, even during daylight. Sneaks live in parks, you see, dirty-minded sneaks, waiting to damage a girl's reputation, or perhaps prowling for opportunities to blackmail her.'

Bluff or back-fire? I hedged my bets. '*Blackmail?* I have three sisters of my own, and I was concerned for your reputation! That is all.'

She relished her advantage. 'Ah oui? Comme c'est délicat de votre part! Tell me, Mr Frobisher, what exactly did you think Monsieur van de Velde was going to do to me? Were you *frightfully* jealous?'

Her awful directness – for a girl – quite knocked the bails off my wicket. 'I am relieved that this simple misunderstanding has been cleared up,' I chose my most insincere smile, 'and offer my sincerest apologies.'

'I accept your sincerest apologies in the precise same spirit they are offered.' E. walked off to the stables, her whip swishing the air like a lioness's tail. Went off to the music room to forget my dismal performance in some devilish Liszt. Can normally rattle off an excellent 'La Prédication aux Oiseaux' but not last Friday. Thank God E.'s leaving for Switzerland tomorrow. If she ever found out about her mother's night-time visits – well, doesn't bear thinking about. Why is it I never met a boy I couldn't twist round my finger (not only my finger) but the women of Zedelghem seem to best me every time?

Sincerely,
R. F.

— ◆ —

Zedelghem.
29th – viii – 1931.

Sixsmith,
Sitting at my escritoire in my dressing-gown. The church bell chimes five. Another thirsty dawn. My candle is burnt away. A tiring night turned inside-out. J. came to my bed at midnight, and during our athletics, my door was barged. Farcical horror! Thank God J. had locked it on her way in. The door-knob rattled, insistent knocking began. Fear can clear the mind as well as cloud it, and, remembering my *Don Juan*, I hid J. in a nest of coverlets and sheets in my sagging bed, and left the curtain ½ open to show I had nothing to hide. I fumbled across the room, not believing this was happening to me, deliberately knocking into things to buy time, and, reaching the door, called out, 'What in hell is the matter? Are we on fire?'

'Open up, Robert!' Ayrs! You can imagine, I was ready to duck bullets. Desperate, I asked what time it was, just to win another moment.

'Who cares? I don't know! I've got a melody, boy, for violin, it's a gift, and it won't let me sleep, so I need you to take it down, now!'

Could I trust him? 'Can't it wait until the morning?'

'No, it bloody can't, Frobisher! I might lose it!'

Shouldn't we go to the music room?

'It'll wake up the house and, no, every note is in place, in my head!'

So I told him to wait while I lit a candle. Unlocked my door and there stood Ayrs, a cane in each hand, mummified in his moonlit night-shirt. Hendrick stood behind him, silent and watchful as an Indian totem. 'Make way, make way!' Ayrs pushed past me. 'Find a pen, grab some blank score-paper, turn on your lamp, quickly. Why the deuce do you lock your door if you sleep with the windows open? The Prussians are gone, the ghosts'll just drift through the door.' Garbled some balderdash about not being able to fall asleep in an unlocked room, but he wasn't listening. 'Have you got manuscript paper in here or should I have Hendrick go and get some?'

Relief that V.A. hadn't come to catch me tupping his wife made his imposition seem less preposterous than it actually was, so, fine, I said, yes, I have paper, I have pens, let's start. Ayrs's sight was too poor to see anything suspicious in the foot-hills of my bed, but Hendrick still posed a possible danger. One should avoid relying on servants' discretion. After Hendrick had helped his master to a chair and wrapped a rug round his shoulders, I told him I'd ring for him when we were done. Ayrs didn't contradict me – he was already humming. A conspiratorial flicker in H.'s eyes? Room too dim to be sure. The servant gave a near-imperceptible bow and glided away as if on well-oiled coasters, softly shutting the door behind him.

Splashed a little water on my face at the wash-bowl and sat opposite Ayrs, worrying J. might forget the creaking floorboards and try to tiptoe out. 'Ready.'

Ayrs hummed his sonata, bar by bar, then named his notes. The oddity of the miniature soon absorbed me, despite the circumstances. It's a see-sawing, cyclical, crystalline thing. He finished after the 96th bar and told me to mark the MS *triste*. Then he asked me, 'So what d'you think?'

'Not sure,' I told him. 'It's not at all like you. Not much like anyone. But it hypnotizes.'

Ayrs was now slumped, *à la* a Pre-Raphaelist oil painting entitled *Behold the Sated Muse Discards Her Puppet*. Birdsong foamed in the hour-before-dawn garden. Thought about J.'s curves in the bed, just a few yards away, even felt a dangerous throb of impatience for her. V.A. was unsure of himself for once. 'I dreamt of a . . . nightmarish café, brilliantly lit, but underground, with no way out. I'd been dead a long, long time. The waitresses all had the same face. The food was soap, the only drink was cups of lather. The music in the café was,' he wagged an exhausted finger at the MS, 'this.'

Rang for H. Wanted Ayrs out of my room before daylight found his wife in my bed. After a minute H. knocked. Ayrs got to his feet and limped over – he hates anyone seeing him assisted. 'Good work, Frobisher.' His voice found me from down the corridor. I shut the door and breathed that big sigh of relief. Climbed back to bed where my swampy-sheeted alligator sank her little teeth into her young prey.

We'd begun a luxuriant farewell kiss when, damn me, the door creaked opened again. 'Something else, Frobisher!' Mother of All Profanities, I hadn't locked the door! Ayrs drifted bedward like the wreck of the *Hesperus*. J. slid back under the sheets while I made dishevelling, surprised noises. Thank God, Hendrick was waiting outside – accident or tact? V.A. found the end of my bed, and sat there, just inches from the bump that was J. If J. sneezed or coughed now, even blind old Ayrs would catch on. 'A tricky subject, so I'll just spit it out. Jocasta. She isn't a very faithful woman. Maritally, I mean. Friends hint at her indiscretions, enemies inform me of affairs. Has she ever . . . towards you . . . y' know my meaning?'

Let my voice stiffen, masterfully. 'No, sir, I don't believe I do know your meaning.'

'Spare me your bashfulness, boy!' Ayrs leant nearer. 'Has my wife ever made advances? I have a right to know!'

Avoided a nervous giggle, by a whisker. 'I find your question distasteful in the extreme.' Jocasta's breath dampened my thigh. She must have been roasting alive under the covers. '*I* wouldn't call any "friend" who spread such muck around by that name. In Mrs Crommelynck's case, frankly, I find the notion as unthinkable as it is unpalatable. If, *if*, through some, I don't know, nervous collapse, she *were* to behave so inappropriately, well, to be honest, Ayrs, I'd probably ask for Dhondt's advice, or speak to Dr Egret.' Sophistry makes a fine smoke-screen.

'So you're not going to give me a one-word answer?'

'You shall have a two-word answer. "Emphatically, no!" And I very much hope the subject is now closed.'

Ayrs let long moments fall away. 'You're young, Frobisher, you're rich, you've got a brain, and by all accounts you're not wholly repugnant. I'm not sure why you stay on here.'

Good. He was getting mawkish. 'You're my Verlaine.'

'Am I, young Rimbaud? Then where is your "*saison en enfer*"?'

'In sketches, in my skull, in my gut, Ayrs. In my future.'

Couldn't say if Ayrs felt humour, pity, nostalgia or scorn. He left. Locked the door and climbed into bed for the 3rd time that night. Bedroom farce, when it actually happens, is intensely sad. Jocasta seemed angry with me. 'What?' I hissed.

'My husband loves you,' said the wife, dressing.

Zedelghem's a-stirring. Plumbing makes noises like elderly aunts. Been thinking of my grandfather, whose wayward brilliance skipped my father's generation. Once, he showed me an aquatint of a certain Siamese temple. Don't recall its name, but ever since a disciple of the Buddha preached on the spot centuries ago, every bandit king, tyrant and monarch of that kingdom has enhanced it with marble towers, scented arboretums, gold-leafed domes, lavished murals on its vaulted ceilings, set emeralds into the eyes of its statuettes. When the temple finally equals its counterpart in the Pure Land, so the story goes, that day human- ity shall have fulfilled its purpose, and Time itself shall come to an end.

To men like Ayrs, it occurs to me, this temple is civilization. The masses, slaves, peasants and foot-soldiers exist in the cracks of its flagstones, ignorant even of their ignorance. Not so the great statesmen, scientists, artists and, most of all, the composers of the age, any age, who are civilization's architects, masons and priests. Ayrs sees our role is to make civilization ever more resplendent. My employer's profoundest, or only, wish is to create a minaret that inheritors of Progress a thousand years from now will point to and say, 'Look, there is Vyvyan Ayrs!'

How vulgar, this hankering after immortality, how vain, how false. Composers are merely scribblers of cave paintings. One writes music because winter is eternal and because if one didn't, the wolves and blizzards would be at one's throat all the sooner.

Sincerely,
R.F.

— ◆ —

Zedelghem.
14th – ix – 1931.

Sixsmith,
Sir Edward Elgar came to tea this afternoon. Even you've heard of *him*, you ignoramus. Now, usually, if one asks Ayrs what he thinks of English music he'll say, '*What* English music? There is none! Not since Purcell!' and sulk all day, as if the Reformation were one's own doing. This hostility was forgotten in a trice when Sir Edward telephoned from his hotel in Bruges this morn- ing, wondering if Ayrs might be able to spare him an hour or two. Ayrs made a show of curmudgeonliness, but I could tell by the way he badgered Mrs Willems about the arrangements

for tea, he was pleased as the cat who got the cream. Our celebrated guest arrived at ½ past two dressed in a dark green Inverness cape despite the clement weather. The man's state of health isn't much better than V.A.'s. J. & I welcomed him on the steps of Zedelghem. 'So *you're* Vyv's new pair of eyes, are you?' he said to me, as we shook hands. Said I'd seen him conduct a dozen times at the festival, which pleased him. Guided the composer into the Scarlet Room where Ayrs was waiting. They greeted each other warmly, but as if wary of bruises. Elgar's sciatic pain bothers him greatly, and even on good days, V.A. looks pretty frightful at 1st sight, still worse at the 2nd. Tea was served and they talked shop, mostly ignoring J. & I, but it was fascinating to be a fly on the wall. Sir E. glanced at us now and then to make sure he was not wearing out his host. 'Not at all.' We smiled back. They fenced over such topics as saxophones in orchestras, whether Webern is Fraudster or Messiah, the patronage and politics of music. Sir E. announced he is at work on a 3rd Symphony after a long hibernation: – he even played us sketches of a *molto maestoso* and an *allegretto* on the upright. Ayrs most eager to prove that he isn't ready for his coffin, either, and had me run through some recently completed piano sketches – rather lovely. Several dead bottles of Trappist beer later, I asked Elgar about the *Pomp & Circumstance Marches*. 'Oh, I needed the money, dear boy. But don't tell anyone. The King might want my baronetcy back.' Ayrs went into laughter-spasms at this! 'I always say, Ted, to get the crowd to cry Hosanna, you must first ride into town on an ass. Backwards, ideally, whilst telling the masses the tall stories they want to hear.'

Sir E. had heard about 'Todtenvogel''s reception in Cracow (all London has, it would seem), so V.A. sent me off to fetch a score. Back in the Scarlet Room, our guest took our Death-bird to the window-seat and read it with the aid of a monocle while Ayrs and I pretended to busy ourselves. 'A man at our time of life, Ayrs,' E. spoke at last, 'has no right to such daring ideas. Where are you getting 'em from?'

V.A. puffed up like a smug hornyback. 'I suppose I've won

a rearguard action or two in my war against decrepitude. My boy Robert here is proving a valuable aide-de-camp.'

Aide-de-camp? I'm his bloody general and *he*'s the fat old Turk reigning on the memory of faded glories! Smiled sweetly as I could (as if the roof over my head depended on it. Moreover, Sir E. might be useful one day so it won't do to create an obstreperous impression.) During tea, Elgar contrasted my position at Zedelghem favourably with his 1st job as a musical director at a lunatic asylum in Worcestershire. 'Excellent prep for conducting the London Philharmonic, what?' quipped V.A. We laughed and I half forgave the ratty old selfish crank for being himself. Put another log or two in the hearth. In the smoky firelight the two old men nodded off like a pair of ancient kings passing the aeons in their tumuli. Made a musical notation of their snores. Elgar is to be played by a bass tuba, Ayrs a bassoon. I'll do the same with Fred Delius and John Mackerras and publish 'em all together in a work entitled *The Backstreet Museum of Stuffed Edwardians*.

Three days later.

Just back from a *lento* walk with V.A. down Monk's Walk to the gatekeeper's lodge. I pushed his chair. Landscape v. atmospheric this evening; autumn leaves gusted around in urgent spirals, as if V.A. was the sorcerer and I his apprentice. Poplars' long shadows barred the mown meadow. Ayrs wanted to unveil his concepts for a final, symphonic major work, to be named *Eternal Recurrence* in honour of his beloved Nietzsche. Some music will be drawn from an abortive opera based on *The Island of Doctor Moreau* whose Viennese production was cancelled by the War, some music V.A. believes will 'come' to him, and its backbone will be the 'dream music' piece that he dictated in my room that hairy night last month, I wrote to you about that. V.A. wants four movements, a female choir, and a large ensemble heavy in Ayrsesque woodwind. Truly, a behemoth of the deeps. Wants my services for another ½ year. Said I'd think about it. He said he'd up my salary, both vulgar and crafty of him. Repeated, I needed time. V.A. most upset I didn't give him a breathy 'Yes!' on the spot – but I want the old bugger to admit to himself that he needs me more than I him.

Sincerely,
R.F.

— ♦ —

Zedelghem.
28th – ix – 1931.

Sixsmith,
J. growing v. tiresome. After our love-making, she spreads over my bed like a mooing moon-calf and demands to know about other women whose strings I've quivered. Now she's teased names out of me, she says things like, 'Oh, I suppose Frederica taught you that?' (She plays with that birthmark in the hollow of my shoulder, the one you said resembles a comet – can't *abide* the woman dabbling with my skin.) J. starts petty rows in order to undergo tedious reconciliations and, worryingly, has started to let our moonlight dramas slip into our daylight lives. Ayrs can't see further than *Eternal Recurrence*, but Eva is due back in ten days and that hawk-eyed creature will sniff out a decomposing secret in a jiffy.

J. thinks our arrangement lets her fasten my future more tightly to Zedelghem – she says, ½ playful, ½ darkly, she's not going to let me 'abandon' either her or her husband, not in 'their' hour of need. The devil, Sixsmith, is in the pronouns. Worst of all, she's started to use the L-word on me, and wants to hear it back. What's *wrong* with the woman? She's nearly twice my age! What's she after? Assured her I've never loved anyone except myself and have no intention of starting now, especially with another man's wife, and especially when that man could poison my name in European musical society by writing half a dozen letters. So, of course, the female plies her customary ploys, sobs in my pillow, accuses me of 'using' her. I agree, of course I've 'used' her; just as she's 'used' me too. That's the arrangement. If she's no longer happy with it, she's not my prisoner. So off she storms to pout for a couple of days and nights until the old ewe gets hungry for a young ram, then she's back, calling me her darling boy, thanking me for 'giving Vyvyan his music back', and the stupid cycle begins all over again. I wonder if she's resorted to Hendrick in the past? Wouldn't put anything past the woman. If one of Renwick's Austrian doctors opened up her head, a whole bee-hive of neuroses would swarm out. Had I known she was this unstable, I'd never have let her in my bed that first night. There's a joylessness in her love-making. No, a savagery.

Have agreed to V.A.'s proposal that I stay on here until next summer, at least. No cosmic resonance entered my decision – just artistic advantage, financial practicalities, and because J. might have some sort of collapse if I went. The consequences of *that* would not come out in the wash.

Later, same day

Gardener made a bonfire of fallen leaves – just came in from it. The heat on one's face and hands, the sad smoke, the crackling and wheezing fire. Reminds me of the groundsman's hut at Gresham. Anyway, got a gorgeous passage from the fire – percussion for crackling, alto bassoon for the wood, and a restless flute for the flames. Finished transcribing it this very minute. Air in the château clammy like laundry that won't dry. Door-banging draughts down the passageways. Autumn is leaving its mellowness behind for its spiky, rotted stage. Don't remember summer even saying goodbye.

Sincerely,
R.F.

— ◆ —

Half-Lives
The First Luisa Rey
Mystery

1

Rufus Sixsmith leans over the balcony and estimates his body's velocity when it hits the sidewalk and lays his dilemmas to rest. A telephone rings in the unlit room. Sixsmith dares not answer. Disco music booms from the next apartment, where a party is in full swing, and Sixsmith feels older than his sixty-six years. Smog obscures the stars, but north and south along the coastal strip, Buenas Yerbas' billion lights simmer. West, the Pacific eternity. East, our denuded, heroic, pernicious, enshrined, thirsty, berserking American continent.

A young woman emerges from the next-door party and leans over the neighbouring balcony. Her hair is shorn, her violet dress is elegant, but she looks incurably sad and alone. *Propose a suicide pact, why don't you?* Sixsmith isn't serious, and he isn't going to jump either, not if an ember of humour still glows. *Besides, a quiet accident is precisely what Grimaldi, Napier and those sharp-suited hoodlums are praying for.* An ambulance siren slices through the traffic's incessant rumble. Sixsmith shuffles inside, where the telephone abruptly dies. He pours himself another generous vermouth from his absent host's minibar, dips his hands in the icebox, then wipes his face. *Go out somewhere and phone Megan, she's your only friend left.* He knows he won't. *You can't drag her into this lethal mess.* The disco thump seems to pulse in his temples, but it's a borrowed apartment and he judges it unwise to complain. *Buenas Yerbas isn't Cambridge. Anyway, you're in hiding.* The breeze slams the balcony door, and in fear Sixsmith spills half his vermouth. *No, you old fool, it wasn't a gunshot.*

He mops up the spillage with a kitchen towel, turns on the TV with the sound down low and trawls the channels for M*A*S*H. *It's on somewhere. Just have to keep looking.*

2

Luisa Rey hears a clunk from the neighboring balcony. 'Hello?' *Nobody.* Her stomach warns her to set down her tonic water. *It was the bathroom you needed, not fresh air,* but she can't face weaving back through the party *and, anyway, there's no time* – down the side of the building she heaves: once, twice, a vision of greasy chicken, and a third time. *That,* she wipes her eyes, *is the third foulest thing you've ever done.* She slooshes her mouth out, spits residue into a flower-pot behind a screen. *You are wasting your life.* Luisa dabs her lips with a tissue and finds a mint in her handbag. *Go home and just dream up your crappy three hundred words for once. People only look at the pictures, anyhow.*

A man too old for his leather trousers, bare torso and zebra waistcoat steps on to the balcony. 'Luis*aaa*!' A crafted golden beard and a moonstone and jade ankh around his neck. 'Hiya!'

Luisa wonders if her smell might put him off, but he's too high to notice. 'Richard,' she says.

'Come out for a little star-gazing, huh? Dig. Bix brought eight *ounces* of snow with him, man. One *wild* cat. Hey, did I say in the interview? I'm trying on the name "Ganja" at the moment. Maharaj Aja says "Richard" is outa sync with my Iovedic Self.'

'Who?'

'My guru, Luis*aaa*, my guru! He's on his last reincarnation before—' Richard's fingers go *pufff*! Nirvanawards. 'Come to an audience. His waiting-list normally takes, like, *for ever*, but jade-ankh disciples get personal audiences on the same afternoon. Like, *why* go through college and shit when Maharaj Aja can, like, teach you everything about . . . *It*.' He frames the moon in his fingers. '*Words* are so . . . up*tight* . . . Space . . . it's so . . . y' know, like, *total*. Smoke some weed? Acapulco Gold. Got it off of Bix.' He edges nearer in a certain manner understood by women. 'Say, Lu, let's get high after the party. Alone together, my place, dig? You could get a *very* exclusive interview. I may even write you a song and put it on my next LP.'

'I'll pass.'

The minor-league rock musician narrows his eyes. 'Unlucky time of the month, huh? How's next week? I thought all you media chicks are on the Pill, like, forever.'

'Does Bix sell you your pick-up lines, too?'

He sniggers. 'Hey, has Bix been telling you things?'

'Richard, just so there's no uncertainty, I'd rather jump off this balcony than sleep with you, any time of any month. I really would.'

'Whoah!' His hand jerks back as if stung. 'Pick-*ky*! Who d'you think you are, like, Joni fucking Mitchell? You're only a fucking *gossip columnist* in a magazine that like *no-one ever reads*!'

3

The elevator doors close just as Luisa Rey reaches them, but the unseen occupant jams them with his cane. 'Thank you,' says Luisa to the old man. 'Glad the age of chivalry isn't totally dead.'

He gives a grave nod of acknowledgment.

Hell, Luisa thinks, *he looks like he's been given a week to live.*

Luisa presses G for ground. The old elevator begins its descent. A leisurely needle counts off the stories. Its motor whines, its cables grind, but between the tenth and ninth stories a *gatta-gatta-gatta* detonates then dies with a *phzzz-zzz-zz-z*. Luisa and Sixsmith thump to the floor. The light stutters on and off before settling on a buzzing sepia.

'You okay? Can you get up?'

The sprawled old man recovers himself a little. 'No bones broken, I think, but I'll stay seated, thank you.' His old-school English accent reminds Luisa of the tiger in *The Jungle Book*. 'The power might restart suddenly.'

'Christ,' mutters Luisa. 'A power-outage. Perfect end to a perfect day.' She presses the emergency button. Nothing. She presses the intercom button, and hollers: 'Hey! Anyone there?' Static hiss. 'We have a situation here! Can anyone hear us?'

Luisa and the old man regard each other, sideways, listening.

No reply. Just vague submarine noises.

Luisa inspects the ceiling. 'Got to be an access hatch . . .' There isn't. She peels up the carpet – a steel floor. 'Only in movies, I guess.'

'Are you still glad,' asks the old man, 'the age of chivalry isn't dead?'

Luisa manages a smile, just. 'We might be here some time. Last month's brown-out lasted seven hours.' *Well, at least I'm not confined with a psychopath, a claustrophobe, or Richard Ganga.*

4

Rufus Sixsmith sits propped in a corner sixty minutes later, dabbing his forehead with his handkerchief. 'I subscribed to *Illustrated Planet* in 1967 to read your father's dispatches from Vietnam. Many thousands did. Lester Rey was one of only four or five journalists who grasped the war from the Asian perspective, so I'm fascinated to hear how a policeman became one of the best correspondents of his generation.'

'You asked for it.' The story is polished with each retelling. 'Dad joined the BYPD just weeks before Pearl Harbor, which is why he spent the war here and not in the Pacific like his brother Howie who landed on a Japanese landmine playing beach volleyball in the Solomons. Pretty soon, it became apparent Dad was a 10th Precinct case and that's where he wound up. There's such a precinct in every city in the country – a sort of pen where they transfer all the straight cops who won't go on the take and who won't turn a blind eye. So anyway, on VJ night, Buenas Yerbas was one city-wide party and, you can imagine, the police were thinly stretched. Dad got a call through reporting looting down on Silvaplana Wharf, a sort of no man's land between 10th Precinct, the BY Port Authority and Spinoza Precinct. Whoever alerted the station and why – genuine tip-off, inside betrayal, mistake, malicious joke gone terribly wrong – was never known, but Dad and his partner, a man named Nat Wakefield, drove down to take a look. They park between a pair of cargo containers, kill the engine, proceed on foot and see maybe two dozen men loading crates from a warehouse into an armored truck. The light was dim, but they didn't seem to be dockworkers and they weren't in military uniform. Wakefield tells Dad to go and radio for back-up. Just as Dad gets to the radio, a call comes through saying the original order to investigate looting has been countermanded. Dad reports what he'd seen, but the order is repeated, so Dad runs back to the warehouse just in time to see his partner accept a light from one of the men and get shot six times in the back. Dad somehow keeps his nerve, sprints back to his squad car and manages to radio out a Code 8 – a Mayday – before his car shivers with bullets. He's surrounded on all sides except the dockside, so over the edge he dives, into a cocktail of diesel, trash, sewage and sea. He swims underneath the quay – in those days Silvaplana Wharf was a steel structure like a giant boardwalk, not the concrete peninsula it is today – and hauls himself up a service ladder, soaked, one shoe missing, with his non-functioning revolver. All he can do is observe the men, who are just finishing up when a couple of Spinoza precinct squad cars arrive on the scene. Before Dad can circle around the yard to warn the officers, a hopelessly uneven gunfight breaks out – the gunmen pepper the two squad cars with *sub-machine guns*, the first is taken out. The truck starts up, the gunmen jump aboard, they pull out of the yard and lob a couple of hand-grenades from out the back. Whether they were intended to maim or just to discourage heroics, who knows?, but one caught Dad and made a human pin-cushion of him. He woke up two days later in hospital minus his left eye. The papers described the incident as an opportunistic raid by a gang of thieves who got lucky. The 10th Precinct men reckoned a syndicate who'd been syphoning off arms throughout the war decided to shift their stock, now the war was over and accounting would get tightened up. There was pressure for a wider investigation into the Silvaplana Shootings – three dead cops meant something in 1945 – but the Mayor's office blocked it. Draw your own conclusions. Dad did, and they jaded his faith in law-enforcement. By the time he was out of hospital eight months later he'd completed a correspondence course on journalism.'

'Good grief,' says Sixsmith.

'The rest you may know. Covered Korea for *Illustrated Planet*, then became *West Coast Herald*'s Latin America man. He was in Vietnam for the battle of Ap Bac and stayed based in Saigon until his first collapse back in March. It's a miracle my parents' marriage lasted the years it did – y' know, the longest I spent with him was April to July, this year, in the hospice.' Luisa is quiet. 'I miss him, Rufus, chronically. I keep forgetting he's dead. I keep thinking he's away on assignment, somewhere, and he'll be flying in any day soon.'

'He must have been proud of you, following in his footsteps.'

'Oh, Luisa Rey is no Lester Rey. I wasted years being rebellious and liberated, posing as a poet and working in a bookstore on Engels Street. My posturing convinced no-one, my poetry was "so vacuous it isn't even bad" – so said Lawrence Ferlinghetti – and the bookstore went bust. So I'm still only a columnist.' Luisa rubs her tired eyes, thinking of Richard Ganga's parting shot. 'No award-winning copy from war zones. I had high hopes when I moved to *Spyglass*, but simpering gossip on celebrity parties seems to be the closest I've gotten so far to Dad's vocation.'

'Ah, but is it well-written simpering gossip?'

'Oh, it's *excellently* written simpering gossip.'

'Then don't bemoan your misspent life quite yet. Forgive me for flaunting my experience, but you have no *conception* of what a misspent life constitutes.'

5

'Hitchcock loves the limelight,' says Luisa, the pressure on her bladder now growing uncomfortable, 'but hates interviews. He didn't answer my questions because he didn't really hear them. His best works, he said, are rollercoasters that scare the riders out of their wits, but let them get off at the end, giggling and eager for another ride. I put it to the great man, the key to fictitious terror is partition or containment: so long as the Bates Motel is sealed off from our world, we want to peer in, like at a scorpion enclosure. But a film that shows the world *is* a Bates Motel, well, that's . . . the stuff of Buchloe, dystopia, depression. We'll dip our toes in a predatory, amoral, godless universe – but only our toes. Hitchcock's response was' – Luisa does an above-average impersonation – ' "I'm a director in Hollywood, young lady, not an Oracle at Thebes." I asked why Buenas Yerbas had never featured in his films. Hitchcock answered, "This town marries the worst of San Francisco with the worst of Los Angeles. Buenas Yerbas is a city of nowhere." He spoke in *bons mots* like that, not to you, but into the ear of posterity, for dinner-party guests of the future to say, "That's one of Hitchcock's, you know." '

Sixsmith wrings sweat from his handkerchief. 'I saw *Charade* with my niece at an art-house cinema last year. She strong-arms me into seeing these things, to prevent me from growing "square". I rather enjoyed it, but my niece said Audrey Hepburn was a "bubblehead". Delicious word.'

'*Charade*'s the one where the plot swings on the stamps?'

'A contrived puzzle, yes, but all thrillers would wither without contrivance. Hitchcock's Buenas Yerbas remark puts me in mind of John F. Kennedy's observation about New York. Do you know it? "Most cities are nouns, but New York is a verb." What might Buenas Yerbas be, I wonder?'

'A string of adjectives and conjunctions?'

'Or an expletive?'

6

'Megan, my treasured niece.' Rufus Sixsmith shows Luisa a photograph of a bronzed young woman and a fitter, healthier self taken at a sunny marina. The photographer said something funny just before the shutter clicked. Their legs dangle over the stern of a small yacht named *Starfish*. 'That's my old tub, a relic from more dynamic days.'

Luisa makes polite noises about not being old.

'Truly. If I went on a serious voyage now I'd need to hire a small crew. I still spend a lot of weekends on her, pottering about the marina and doing a little thinking, a little work. Megan likes the sea, too. She's a born physicist with a better head for mathematics than I ever had, rather to her mother's chagrin. My brother didn't marry Megan's mother for her brain, I'm sorry to say. She buys into *feng shui* or *I Ching* or whatever instant-enlightenment mumbo-jumbo is top of the charts on any given week. She misquotes Hamlet's Horatio at me, every single time we meet, you know, the line about there being more things in heaven and earth. But Megan possesses a superb mind. She spent a year of her Ph.D. at my old college at Cambridge. A woman, at Caius!' Sixsmith's sigh is amused. 'Now she's finishing her radioastronomy research at the big dishes on Hawaii. While her mother and her stepfather crisp themselves to toast on the beach in the name of Leisure, Megan and I knock around equations in the bar.'

'Any children of your own, Dr Sixsmith?'

'I've been married to science all my life.' Sixsmith changes the subject. 'A hypothetical question, Miss Rey. What price would you pay, as a journalist I mean, to protect a source?'

Luisa doesn't consider the question. 'If I believed in the issue? Any.'

'Prison, for example, for contempt of court?'

'If it came to it, yes.'

'Would you be prepared to . . . compromise your own safety?'

'Well . . .' Luisa does consider this 'I . . . guess I'd have to.'

'Have to? How so?'

'My father braved booby-trapped marshes and the wrath of generals for the sake of *his* journalistic integrity. What kind of a mockery of his life would it be if his daughter bailed when things got a little tough?'

Tell her. Sixsmith opens his mouth to tell her everything – the whitewashing at Seaboard, the blackmailing, the corruption – but without warning the elevator lurches, rumbles, and resumes its steady descent. Its occupants squint in the restored light and Sixsmith finds his resolve has crumbled away. The needle swings round to '1F.'

The air in the lobby feels as fresh as mountain water. The building reverberates with reanimated appliances.

'I'll telephone you, Miss Rey,' says Sixsmith, as Luisa hands him his stick, 'soon.' *Will I break this promise or keep it?* 'Do you know?' he says. 'I feel I've known you for *years*, not ninety minutes.'

7

The flat world is curved in the boy's eye. Javier Moses leafs through a stamp album under an Anglepoise lamp. A team of huskies barks on an Alaskan stamp, a Hawaiian *nene* honks and waddles on a fifty-cents special edition, a paddle-steamer churns up an inky Congo. A key turns in the lock, and Luisa Rey stumbles in, kicking off her shoes in the kitchenette. She is exasperated to find him here. 'Javier!'

'Oh, hi.'

'Don't "Oh, hi" me. You promised not to jump across the balconies *ever* again! Suppose someone reports a burglar to the cops? Suppose you slipped and fell?'

'Then just give me a key.'

Luisa strangles an invisible neck. 'I can't rest easy knowing an eleven-year-old can waltz into my living space whenever . . .'

your mom's out all night, Luisa replaces with '. . . there's a slow night on TV.'

'So why leave the bathroom window off its latch?'

'Because if there's one thing worse than you jumping the gap once, it'd be you jumping the gap again when you couldn't get in.'

'I'll be eleven in January.'

'No key.'

'Friends give each other keys.'

'Not when one is twenty-six and the other is still in the fifth grade.'

'So why are you back so late? Meet anyone *interesting*?'

Luisa glares, but isn't capable of staying mad at the boy for very long. 'Trapped by the brown-out in an elevator. None of your business, anyhow, mister.' She switches on the main light and flinches when she sees the mean red welt on Javier's face. 'What the – what happened?'

All humor leaves the boy. He glances at the apartment wall, then returns to his stamps.

'Wolfman?'

Javier shakes his head, folds a tiny paper strip, and licks both sides. 'That Clark guy came back. Mom's working the graveyard shift at the hotel all this week, and he's waiting for her. He asked me stuff about Wolfman, and I told him it wasn't any of his business.' Javier attaches the hinge to the stamp. 'It doesn't hurt. I already dabbed stuff on it.' Luisa's hand is already on the telephone. 'Don't phone Mom! She'll rush back, there'll be a massive fight and the hotel'll fire her like last time and the time before.' Luisa considers this, replaces the receiver and starts for the door. 'Don't go round there! He's sick in the head! He'll get angry and wreck our stuff and punch your lights out and then we'll probably get evicted or something! *Please*.'

'Christ.' Luisa looks away. She takes a deep breath. 'Cocoa?'

'Yes, please.' The boy is determined not to cry, but his jaw aches with the effort. He wipes his eyes on his wrists. 'Luisa?'

'Yes, Javi, you're sleeping on my sofa tonight, it's okay.'

8

Dom Grelsch's office is a study in ordered chaos. The view across 3rd Avenue shows a wall of offices much like his own. An *Incredible Hulk* punch-bag hangs from a metal gallows in the corner. The editor-in-chief of *Spyglass* magazine declares the Monday a.m. features meeting open by stabbing a stubby digit at Roland Jakes, a grizzled prune-like man in an Aloha shirt, flared Wranglers and dying sandals. 'Jakes.'

'I, uh, wanna follow up my *Terror in Sewerland* series, to tie in with *Jaws*-fever. Dirk Melon, he can be a freelance hack, is found under 50th East Street on a routine maintenance inspection. Or rather his, uh, remains are. Dental records and tattered press pass ID him. Flesh torn from corpse in manner consistent with *Serasalmus scapularis* – I thank you – queen bitch of all piranhas, imported by fish freaks, then flushed down toilets when the meat bill gets too big. I'll phone Captain Vermin at City Hall and have him deny a spate of attacks on sewage workers. Taking notes, Luisa? Believe nothing till it's officially denied. So c'mon, Grelsch. Time you gave me that raise?'

'Just be grateful your last paycheck didn't *boing*. On my desk by eleven tomorrow, with a pic of one those snappers. And don't forget you're on horoscope detail this week. A question, Luisa?'

'Yes. Is there a new editorial policy no-one's told me about that excludes articles containing truth?'

'Hey, metaphysics seminar is on the roof. Just take the elevator up and keep walking until you hit the sidewalk. Anything is true if enough people believe it is. Nancy, what've you for me?'

Nancy O'Hagan has conservative clothes, a pickled complexion and giraffe-sized eyelashes that often come unstuck. 'My trusty mole in the Betty Ford Clinic got a picture of the bar on the President's airplane. How about "Wing-dings and Gin-slings on Air Force One"? The dumb money says the last drop's been squeezed out of the old soak, but Auntie Nance thinks not.'

Grelsch thinks for a moment. Telephones ringing and type-writers clacking texture the background. 'Okay, if nothing fresher comes up. Oh, and interview that ventriloquist puppet guy who lost his arms for *It Never Rains* . . . Nussbaum. You're up.'

Jerry Nussbaum wipes dewdrops of choco-popsicle from his beard, puts on his mirrored sunglasses by mistake, changes to his reading glasses, leans back and triggers a landslide of papers. 'The cops are chasing their own asses on the St Christopher case, so how about a "Are *You* St Christopher's Next Slaying?" piece? Profiles of all the snuffs to date and reconstructions of the victims' last minutes. Where they were going, who they were meeting, what thoughts were going through their heads . . .'

'When St Chris's bullet went through their heads,' laughs Roland Jakes.

'Yeah, Jakes, let's hope he's attracted to flashy Hawaiian colours. Then later I'm seeing the coloured streetcar driver the cops had on the rack last week. He's suing the police department for wrongful arrest under the Civil Rights Act.'

'Could be a cover story. Luisa?'

'I met an atomic engineer.' Luisa ignores the indifference chilling the room. 'An inspector at Seaboard Incorporated.' Nancy O'Hagan is doing her fingernails, driving Luisa to present her suspicions as facts. 'He believes the new HYDRA nuclear reactor at Swannekke Island isn't as safe as the official line. Isn't safe at all, in fact. Its launch ceremony is this afternoon, so I want to drive out and see if I can turn anything up.'

'Hot shit, a technical launch ceremony,' exclaims Nussbaum. 'What's that rumbling sound, everyone? A Pulitzer Prize, rolling this way?'

'Oh, kiss my ass, Nussbaum.'

Jerry Nussbaum sighs. 'In my wettest dreams . . .'

Luisa is torn between retaliation, *Yeah, and letting the worm know how much he riles you*; and ignoring him, *Yeah, and letting the worm get away with saying what the heck he wants.*

Dom Grelsch breaks her impasse. 'Marketeers prove,' he twirls a pencil, 'every scientific term you use represents two thousand readers putting down the magazine and turning on a rerun of *I Love Lucy*.'

'Okay,' says Luisa. 'How about "Seaboard Atom Bomb to Blow Buenas Yerbas to Kingdom Come!"?'

'Terrific, but you'll need to prove it.'

'Like Jakes can prove his story?'

'Hey.' Grelsch's pencil stops twirling. 'Fictitious people eaten by fictitious fish can't flay every last dollar off you in the courts or lean on your bank to pull the plug. A coast-to-coast operation like Seaboard Power Inc. has lawyers who can and, sweet Mother of God, you put a foot wrong, they *will*.'

9

Luisa's rust-orange VW Beetle travels a flat road towards a kilometer-long bridge connecting Yerbas Cape to Swannekke Island, whose power station dominates the lonely estuary. The bridge checkpoint is not quiet today. A hundred-strong demonstration lines the last stretch, chanting, 'Swannekke C Over Our Dead Bodies!' A wall of police keeps them back from the queue of nine or ten vehicles. Luisa reads the placards while she waits. YOU ARE NOW ENTERING CANCER ISLAND, warns one, another, HELL, NO! WE WON'T GO! and, enigmatically, WHERE OH WHERE IS MARGO ROKER?

A guard taps on the window; Luisa winds it down and sees her face in the guard's sunglasses. 'Luisa Rey, *Spyglass* magazine.'

'Press pass, ma'am.'

Luisa gets it from her purse. 'Expecting trouble today?'

'Nah.' He consults a clipboard and hands back her pass. 'Only our regular tree-huggers from the trailer park. The college boys are vacationing where the surf's better.'

Crossing the long, long bridge, the Swannekke B plant emerges from behind the older, greyer cooling towers of Swannekke A. Once again, she wonders about Rufus Sixsmith. *Why didn't he give me a contact number when I asked? Scientists can't be telephobic. Why did no-one in the super's office in his apartment building even recognize his name? Scientists can't have aliases.*

The island-side checkpoint guard directs her along the island's one road to Seaboard Village. Signs would then lead her to the Public Center in the R&D block.

The road hugs the coastline. Out at sea, gulls hover above fishing boats. Dune grass sways. Ten minutes later Luisa arrives at a colony of some two hundred luxurious homes overlooking a sheltered bay. A hotel and golf-course share the semi-wooded slope below the power station. She leaves her Beetle in the R&D parking lot, and looks at the abstract buildings half hidden by the brow of the hill. An orderly row of palm trees rustles in the Pacific wind.

'Hi, there!' A Chinese-American strides up. 'You look lost. Here for the launch?' Her stylish oxblood suit, flawless makeup and sheer poise make Luisa feel shabby in her blueberry suede jacket. 'Fay Li,' the woman offers her hand, 'Seaboard PR.'

'Luisa Rey, *Spyglass* magazine.'

Fay Li's handshake is powerful. '*Spyglass*? I didn't realize –'

'– our editorial scope includes energy policy?'

Fay Li smiles. 'Don't get me wrong, it's a feisty magazine.'

Luisa invokes Dom Grelsch's reliable deity. 'Market research identifies a growing public who demand more substance. I was hired as *Spyglass*'s high-brow face.'

'Very glad you've come, Luisa, whatever your brow. Let me sign you in at Reception. Security insists on bag searches and the rest, but it's no good having our guests treated like saboteurs. That's why *I* was hired.'

10

Joe Napier watches a bank of CCTV screens covering a lecture theater, its adjacent corridors and the Public Center grounds. He stands, reflumphs up his special cushion, and sits on it. *Is it my imagination, or are my old wounds aching more of late?* His gaze flits from screen to screen to screen. One shows a technician doing a sound check; another, a TV crew discussing angles and light; Fay Li crossing the parking lot with a visitor; waitresses pouring wine into hundreds of glasses; a row of chairs beneath a banner reading SWANNEKKE B – AN AMERICAN MIRACLE.

The real miracle, Joseph Napier ruminates, *was getting eleven out of twelve scientists to forget the existence of a nine-month inquiry.* A screen shows these very scientists drifting onstage, chatting amicably. *Like Grimaldi says, every conscience has an off-switch hidden somewhere.* Napier's thoughts segue through memorable lines from the interviews that achieved the collective amnesia. '*Between us, Dr Franklin, the Pentagon's lawyers are itching to try out their shiny new Security Act. The whistle-blower is to be blacklisted in every salaried position in the land.*'

A janitor adds another chair to the row on stage.

'*The choice is simple, Dr Moses. If you want Soviet technology to burn ahead of ours, leak this report to your Union of Concerned Scientists, fly to Moscow to collect your medal, but the CIA have told me to tell you, you won't be needing a two-way ticket.*'

The audience of dignitaries, scientists, think-tank members and opinion-formers take their seats. A screen shows William Wiley, vice-president of Seaboard Inc., joke with those VIPs to be honored with a seat on stage.

'*Professor Keene, the Defense Department brass are a little curious. Why voice your doubts now? Are you saying your work on the prototype was . . . somehow . . . slip-shod?*'

A slide-projector beams a fish-eye aerial shot of Swannekke B. *Eleven out of twelve. Only Rufus Sixsmith gets away.*

Napier speaks into his walkie-talkie. 'Fay? Show starts in ten minutes.'

Static. 'Copy that, Joe. I'm escorting a visitor to the lecture theater.'

'Report to Security when you're through, please.'

Static. 'Copy. Over and out.'

Napier weighs the set in his hand. *And Joe Napier? Has his conscience got an off-switch?* He sips his bitter black coffee. *Hey, buddy, get off my case. I'm only following orders. Eighteen months till I retire, then it's off to fish in sweet rushing rivers until I turn into a goddamn heron.*

Milly, his deceased wife, watches her husband from the photograph on his console desk.

11

'Our great nation suffers from a debilitating addiction.' Albert Grimaldi, Seaboard CEO and *Newsweek* Man of the Year, is king of the dramatic pause. 'Its name is Oil.' He is gilded by the podium lights. 'Geologists tell us, just seventy-four billion gallons of this Jurassic ocean scum remains in the Persian Gulf. Enough, maybe, to see out our century? Probably not. The most imperative question facing the USA, ladies and gentlemen, is "Then what?"'

Albert Grimaldi scans his audience. *In the palm of my hand.* 'Some bury their heads in the sand. Some fantasize about windturbines, reservoirs and –' wry half-smile '– pig-gas.' Appreciative chuckle. 'At Seaboard we deal in realities.' Voice up. 'I am here today to tell you that the cure for oil is *right* here, *right* now, on Swannekke Island!'

He smiles as the cheers subside. 'As of today, domestic, abundant, and *safe* atomic energy has come of age! Friends, I am *so* very, *very* proud to present one of the major engineering innovations *in history* . . . the HYDRA-Zero reactor!' The slidescreen changes to show a cross-section diagram, and a primed section of the audience applauds wildly, prompting most of the theater to follow suit.

'But hey, now, enough of me, I'm only the CEO.' Affectionate laughter. 'Here to unveil our viewing gallery and flick that switch to connect Swannekke B to the national grid, the Seaboard family is *deeply* honored to welcome a very special visitor. Known on

Capitol Hill as the President's "Energy Guru"' – full smile – 'it gives me profound pleasure to welcome a man who needs no introduction. Energy Secretary Lloyd Hooks!'

An immaculately groomed man strides onstage to great applause. Lloyd Hooks and Albert Grimaldi grasp each other's forearms in a gesture of fraternal love and trust. 'Your scriptwriters are getting better,' Lloyd Hooks murmurs, as both men grin broadly for the audience, 'but you're still Greed on Two Legs.'

Albert Grimaldi backslaps Lloyd Hooks and replies in kind, 'You'll only wrangle your way on to this company's board over my dead body, you venal sonofabitch!'

Lloyd Hooks beams out at the audience. 'So you *can* still come up with creative solutions, Alberto.'

A cannonade of flashes opens fire.

A young woman in a blueberry jacket slips out of a rear exit.

12

'The ladies' rest-room, please?'

A guard speaking on his walkie-talkie waves her down a corridor.

Luisa Rey glances back. The guard's back is turned, so she carries on past the doorway, round a corner and into a grid of repeated corridors, chilled and muffled by humming air coolers. She passes a pair of hurrying technicians in overalls who eye her breasts from under their caps but who do not challenge her. Doors bear cryptic signs. W212 DEMI-OUTLETS, Y009 SUB-PASSES [AC], V770 HAZARDLESS [EXEMPTED]. Periodic higher-security doors have key-pad entry systems. At a stairwell she examines a floor-plan, but finds no trace of any 'Sixsmith'.

'You lost, lady?'

Luisa does her best to recover her poise. A silver-haired black janitor stares at her.

'Yes, I'm looking for Dr Sixsmith's room.'

'Uh-huh. English guy. Third floor, C105.'

'Thank you.'

'He ain't been around a week or two.'

'Is that a fact? Can you tell me why?'

'Uh-huh. Went to Vegas on vacation.'

'Dr Sixsmith? Vegas?'

'Uh-huh. So I was told.'

Room C105's door is ajar. A recent attempt to erase 'Dr Sixsmith' from the name-plate ended in messy failure. Through the gap Luisa Rey watches a young man sitting on the table, bent over a pile of a notebooks, and looking for something. The contents of the room are in several shipping crates. Luisa remembers her father saying, *Acting like an insider can be enough to be one.*

'Well,' says Luisa, strolling in. '*You*'re not Dr Sixsmith, are you?'

The man drops the notebook guiltily, and Luisa knows she's bought a few moments. 'Oh, my God,' he stares back, 'you must be Megan.'

Why be contradictory? 'And you are?'

'Isaac Sachs. Theoretical engineer.' He gets to his feet and aborts a premature handshake. 'I worked with your uncle on his report.' Brisk footsteps echo up the stairwell. Isaac Sachs closes the door. His voice is low and nervy: 'Where's Rufus hiding, Megan? I've been worried sick. Have *you* heard from him?'

'I was hoping you could tell me what's happened.'

Fay Li strides in with the unimpressed security man. 'Luisa. Still looking for the ladies' room?'

Act stupid. 'No. I'm all finished with the ladies' room – it was spotlessly clean – but I'm late for my appointment with Dr Sixsmith. Only . . . well, it seems he's moved out.'

Isaac Sachs makes a 'Hah?' noise. 'You're not Sixsmith's niece?'

'Excuse me, whoever you are, but *I* never said I was.' Luisa produces a pre-prepared grey lie for Fay Li. 'I met Dr Sixsmith at Nantucket last spring. We found we were both from Buenas Yerbas, so he gave me his card. I dug it out three weeks ago, called him up, and we arranged to meet today to discuss a science feature for *Spyglass*.' She consults her watch. 'Ten minutes ago. The launch speeches went on longer than I'd expected, so I slipped quietly away. I hope I haven't caused any trouble?'

Fay Li acts convinced. 'We can't have unauthorized people wandering around a sensitive research institute like ours.'

Luisa acts contrite. 'I thought signing in and having my bag checked *was* the security procedure, but I guess that was naïve. Dr Sixsmith will vouch for me, though. Just ask him.'

Sachs and the guard both glance at Fay Li, who does not miss a beat. 'That isn't going to be possible. One of our Canadian projects needed Dr Sixsmith's attention. I can only imagine his secretary didn't have your contact details when she cleared his appointments diary.'

Luisa looks at the boxes. 'Looks like he's going to be away for while.'

'Yes, so we're shipping him his resources. His consultancy here at Swannekke was winding up. Dr Sachs here has done a gallant job of tying up the loose ends.'

'Well, bang goes my first interview with a great scientist,' says Luisa.

Fay Li holds the door open for her. 'Maybe we can find you another.'

13

'Operator?' Rufus Sixsmith cradles the receiver in an anonymous suburban motel outside Buenas Yerbas. 'I'm having trouble placing a call to Hawaii . . . yes. I'm trying to call . . .' He reads out Megan's telephone number. 'Yes, please. Yes, I'll stay by the phone.'

On a TV with no yellow or green, Lloyd Hooks backslaps

Alberto Grimaldi at the inauguration of the new HYDRA reactor at Swannekke Island. They salute the lecture theater like conquering sportsmen, and silver confetti falls from the roof. 'No stranger to controversy,' says a reporter, 'Seaboard CEO Alberto Grimaldi today announced the go-ahead of Swannekke C. Fifty million federal dollars will be poured into the second HYDRA-Zero reactor, and thousands of new jobs will be created. Fears that the mass arrests seen earlier this summer at Three Mile Island would be repeated in the Golden State did not materialize.'

Frustrated and weary, Rufus Sixsmith addresses the TV. 'And when the hydrogen build-up blows the roof off the containment chamber? When prevailing winds shower radiation over California?' He turns the set off and squeezes the bridge of his nose. *I proved it. I proved it. You couldn't buy me, so you tried intimidation. I let you, Lord forgive me, but no longer. I'm not sitting on my conscience any longer.*

The telephone rings. Sixsmith snatches it up. 'Megan?'

A brusque male voice. 'They're coming.'

'Who is this?'

'They traced your last call to the Talbot Motel, 1046 Olympia Boulevard. Get to the airport *now*, get on the next flight for England, and conduct your exposé from over there, if you must. But go.'

'Why should I believe—'

'Use logic. If I'm lying, you're still back in England safe and sound – with your report. If I'm not lying, you're dead.'

'I demand to know—'

'You've got twenty minutes to get away, max. *Go!*'

Dial tone, a droning eternity.

14

Jerry Nussbaum rotates his office chair, straddles it, places his folded arms on its back and rests his chin on them. 'Picture the scene, me and six dreadlocked freaks of the negroid persuasion, a hand-gun tickling my tonsils. Not talking dead-of-night Harlem here, I'm talking Greenwich goddamn Village in broad goddamn daylight after a sixteen-pound steak with Norman goddamn Mailer. So there we were, this black bro' frisks me down with his bitonal paw and relieves me of my wallet. "Wassis? *Alligator* skin?"' Nussbaum does a Richard Pryor accent. '"No fuckin' *class*, Whitey!" Class? Those bums made me turn out my pockets for my every last cent – *literally*. But Nussbaum had the last laugh, you bet he did. In the cab back to Times Square, I wrote my now-classic "New Tribes" editorial – no point in false modesty – and got it syndicated *thirty* times by the end of the week! My muggers turned me into a household name. So Luey-Luey, what say you take me to dinner and I teach *you* how to extract a little gold from the Fang of Fate?'

Luisa's typewriter pings. 'If the muggers took your every last cent – *literally* – what were you doing in a *cab* from Greenwich Village to Times Square? Sell your body for the fare?'

'You,' Nussbaum shifts his mass, 'have a genius for missing the point.'

Roland Jakes drips candle-wax on to a photograph. 'Definition of the Week. What's a conservative?'

The joke is old by summer 1975. 'A mugged liberal.'

Jakes, stung, goes back to his picture-doctoring.

Luisa crosses the office to Dom Grelsch's door. Her boss is speaking on the phone in a low, irate voice. Luisa waits outside, but overhears. 'No – no, no, Mr Frum, it *is* black-and-white, tell me – hey, *I'm* talking now – tell me a *more* black-and-white "condition" than leukemia? Know what I think? I think my wife is just one piece of paperwork between you and your three o'clock golf slot, isn't she? Then prove it to me. Do you have a wife, Mr Frum? Do you? You do. Can you imagine *your* wife lying in a hospital ward with her hair falling out? . . . What? *What* did you say? "Getting emotional won't help"? Is that all you can offer, Mr Frum? Yeah, buddy, you're damn right I'll be seeking legal counsel!' Grelsch slams the receiver down, lays into his punch-bag gasping 'Frum!' with each blow, collapses into his chair, lights a cigarette and catches sight of Luisa hesitating in his doorway. 'Life. A force ten shit-storm. You hear any of that?'

'The gist. I can come back later.'

'No. Come in, sit down. Are you young, healthy and strong, Luisa?'

'Yes.' Luisa sits on boxes. 'Why?'

'Because what I gotta say about your article on this unsubstantiated cover-up at Seaboard will, frankly, leave you old, sick and weak.'

15

At Buenas Yerbas International Airport, Dr Rufus Sixsmith places a vanilla binder into locker No909, glances around the crowded concourse, feeds the slot with coins, turns the key and slips this into a padded khaki envelope addressed to Luisa Rey at *Spyglass, Klugh Bldg 12F, 3rd Avenue, BY*. Sixsmith's pulse rises as he nears the postal desk. *What if they get me before I reach it?* His pulse rockets. Businessmen, families with luggage carts, snakes of elderly tourists all seem intent on thwarting his progress. The mailbox slot looms closer. Just yards away now, just inches.

The khaki envelope is swallowed and gone. *God speed.*

Sixsmith lines up for a ticket. News of delays lull him like a litany. He keeps a nervous eye out for signs of Seaboard's agents coming to pick him up at this late hour. Finally, a ticket clerk waves him over.

'I have to get to London. Any destination in the United Kingdom, in fact. Any seat, any airline. I'll pay in cash.'

'Not a *prayer*, sir.' The clerk's tiredness shows through her makeup. 'Earliest I can manage . . .' she consults a teleprinted sheet '. . . London Heathrow . . . tomorrow, fifteen fifteen departure, Laker Skytrains, change at JFK.'

'It's terribly important that I leave sooner.'

'I'm sure it is, sir, but we got air-traffic-control strikes and acres of stranded passengers.'

Sixsmith tells himself that not even Seaboard could arrange aviation strikes to detain his escape. 'Then tomorrow it shall have to be. One-way, business class, please, non-smoking. Is there overnight accommodation anywhere in the airport?'

'Yes, sir, third level. Hotel Bon Voyage. You'll be comfortable there. If I can just see your passport, please, so I can process your ticketing?'

16

A stained-glass sunset illuminates the velveteen Hemingway in Luisa's apartment. Luisa is buried in *Harnessing the Sun: Two Decades of Peacetime Atomic Power*, chewing a pen. Javier is at her desk doing a sheet of long-division problems. Carole King's *Tapestry* LP is playing at a low volume. Drifting through the windows comes the dim roar of automobiles heading home through landscaped suburbs and a clarinettist rehearsing nearby. The telephone rings, but Luisa lets it. Javier studies the answering-machine as it clunks into action. 'Hi, Luisa Rey can't come to the phone right now, but if you leave your name and number, I'll get back to you.'

'I *loathe* these contraptions,' complains the caller. 'Cookie, it's your mother. I just heard from Beatty Griffin who told me you split up with Hal – *last month*? I was dumbstruck! You didn't breathe a word at your father's funeral, or at Alphonse's. This bottling-up worries me so much. Dougie and I are having a fund-raiser for the American Cancer Society and it'd mean the sun, the moon and the stars to us if you'd abandon your poky little nest just for one weekend and come stay, Cookie? The Henderson triplets will be here, that's Damien the cardiologist, Lance the gynecologist and Jesse the ... Doug? Doug! Jesse Henderson, what does he do? A lobotomist? Oh, *funny*. Anyway, daughter of mine, Beatty tells me by some freak of planetary alignment all *three* brothers are unattached. On the hoof, Cookie, on the hoof! So *call* the moment you get this. All my love now.' She ends with a suction kiss, 'Mmmmchw*aaa*!'

'She sounds like the witchy mother on *Bewitched*.' Javier lets a little time go by. 'What's "dumbstruck"?'

Luisa doesn't look up. 'When you're so amazed you can't speak.'

'She didn't sound very dumbstruck, did she?'

Luisa is engrossed in her work.

' "Cookie"?'

Luisa flings a slipper at the boy.

17

In his hotel room at the Bon Voyage, Dr Rufus Sixsmith reads a sheaf of letters written to him nearly half a century ago by his friend Robert Frobisher. Sixsmith knows them by heart, but their texture, rustle and his friend's faded handwriting calm his nerves. These letters are what he would save from a burning building. At seven o'clock precisely, he washes, changes his shirt, and sandwiches the nine read letters in the Gideon's Bible – this he replaces in the bedside cabinet. Sixsmith slips the unread letters into his jacket pocket for the restaurant. Frobisher's letters are not the stuff of blackmail, but Sixsmith has a prudent, tidy mind.

Dinner is a minute steak and strips of fried egg-plant, with a poorly washed salad. It deadens rather than satisfies Sixsmith's appetite. He leaves half on his plate and sips carbonated water as he reads Frobisher's last eight letters. He witnesses himself through Robert's words searching Bruges for his unstable friend, first love and *if I'm honest, my last.*

Sixsmith pays the bill and returns to his hotel room. In the elevator he considers the responsibility he put on Luisa Rey's shoulders, wondering if he's done the right thing. The curtains of his room blow in as he opens the door. He calls out, 'Who's in here?'

No-one. No-one knows where you are. His imagination has been playing tricks on him for weeks now. Sleep deprivation. 'Look,' he tells himself, 'in forty-eight hours you'll be back in Cambridge on your rainy, *safe*, narrow island. You'll have your facilities, your allies, your contacts, and you can plan your broadside on Seaboard from there.'

18

Bill Smoke watches Rufus Sixsmith leave his hotel room, waits five minutes, then lets himself in. He sits on the rim of the bathtub and flexes his gloved fists. *No drug, no religious experience touches you like turning a man into a corpse. You need a brain, though. Without discipline and expertise, you'll find yourself strapped into an electric chair.* The assassin strokes a krugerrand in his pocket. It accompanies him on all his special projects. Smoke is wary of being a slave to superstition, but he isn't about to mess with a lucky keepsake just to prove the point. *A tragedy for loved ones, a big fat nothing to everyone else, and a problem solved for my clients. I'm just the instrument of my clients' will. If it wasn't me it'd be the next fixer in the* Yellow Pages. *Blame its owner, blame its maker, but don't blame the gun.* Bill Smoke hears the lock. *Breathe.* The pills he took earlier clarify his perception, terribly, and when Sixsmith shuffles into the bedroom, humming 'Leaving On A Jet-plane', the hitman could swear he can feel his victim's pulse, slower than his own.

Smoke sights his prey through the door crack. Sixsmith flumps on to the bed. The assassin visualizes the required motions: *Three steps out, fire from the side, through the temple, up close.* Smoke darts from the doorway; Sixsmith utters a guttural syllable and tries to rise, but the silenced bullet is already boring through the scientist's skull and into the mattress. The body of Rufus Sixsmith falls back, as if he has curled up for a post-prandial nap.

Blood soaks into the thirsty eiderdown.

Fulfilment throbs in Bill Smoke's brain. *Look what I did.*

19

Wednesday morning is smog-scorched and heat-hammered, like the last hundred mornings and the next fifty. Luisa Rey drinks black coffee in the steamy cool of the Snow White Diner on the corner of 2nd Avenue and 16th Street, a two-minute walk from the *Spyglass* offices, reading about a Baptist ex-naval nuclear engineer from Atlanta called James Carter, who plans to run for the Democratic nomination. 16th Street traffic moves in frustrated inches and headlong stampedes. The side-walks blur with hurrying people and blurred skateboarders. 'Nothin' for breakfast this mornin', Luisa?' asks Bart, the fry cook.

'Only news,' replies his very regular customer.

Roland Jakes trips over the doorway and makes his way over to Luisa. 'Uh, this seat free? Didn't eat a bite this morning. Shirl's left me. Again.'

'Features meeting in fifteen minutes.'

'Bags of time.' Jakes sits down and orders eggs-over-easy. 'Page nine,' he says to Luisa. 'Right-hand bottom corner. Something you should see.'

Luisa turns to page nine and reaches for her coffee. Her hand freezes.

Scientist Suicide at BY Int'l Airport Hotel

Eminent British scientist Dr Rufus Sixsmith was found dead Tuesday morning in his room at Buenas Yerbas International Airport's Bon Voyage Hotel, having taken his own life. Dr Sixsmith, former head of the Global Atomic Commission, had been employed as a consultant for Seaboard Corporation at the blue-chip utility's Swannekke Island installation outside Buenas Yerbas City for ten months. He was known to have a life-long battle with clinical depression, and for the week prior to his death had been incommunicado. Ms Fay Li, spokewoman for Seaboard, said, 'Dr Sixsmith's untimely death is a tragedy for the entire international scientific community. We at Seaboard Village on Swannekke Island feel we've lost not just a greatly respected colleague, but a very dear friend. Our heartfelt condolences go to his own family and his many friends. He shall be greatly missed.' Dr Sixsmith's body, discovered with a single gun-wound to the head by hotel maids, is being flown home for burial in his native England. A medical examiner at BYPD confirmed there are no suspicious circumstances surrounding the incident.

'So,' grins Jakes, 'is your exposé of the century screwed up now?'

Luisa's skin prickles and her eardrums hurt.

'Whoops.' Jakes lights up a cigarette. 'Were you close?'

'He couldn't . . .' Luisa fumbles her words '. . . wouldn't have done it.'

Jakes approximates gentleness. 'Kinda looks like he did, Luisa.'

'You don't kill yourself if you have a mission.'

'You might if your mission makes you crazy.'

'He was murdered, Jakes.'

Jakes represses a *here-we-go-again* face. 'Who by?'

'Seaboard Corporation. Of course.'

'Ah. His employer. Of course. Motive?'

Luisa forces herself to speak calmly and ignore Jakes's mock conviction. 'He'd written a report on a reactor type developed at Swannekke B, the HYDRA. Plans for Site C are waiting for

Energy Department approval. When it's approved, Seaboard can license the design for the domestic and overseas market – the government contracts alone would mean a stream of revenue in the high tens of millions, annually. Sixsmith's role was to give the project his imprimatur, but he hadn't read the script and identified lethal design flaws. In response, Seaboard buried the report and denied its existence. Can't prove it yet, but I will.'

'And your Dr Sixsmith did what?'

'He was getting ready to go public.' Luisa slaps the newspaper. 'This is what the truth cost him.'

Jakes pierces a wobbly dome of yolk with a toast soldier. 'You, uh, know what Grelsch is going to say?'

'"Hard evidence",' says Luisa, like a doctor diagnosing a disease. She looks at her watch. 'Look, Jakes, will you tell Grelsch . . . just tell him I had to go somewhere.'

20

The manager at the Bon Voyage Hotel is having a bad day. 'No, you may *not* see his room! The specialized carpet cleaner has removed all traces of the incident. Whom, I add, we had to pay from our own pocket! What kind of ghoul are you, anyway? A reporter? A ghost-hunter? A novelist?'

'I'm . . .' Luisa Rey buckles with sobs from nowhere '. . . his niece, Megan Sixsmith.'

A stony matriarch enfolds the weeping Luisa in her mountainous bust. Random bystanders shoot the manager foul looks. The manager goes pale and leaves his post to effect damage control. 'Please, come through to the back, I'll get you a—'

'Glass of water!' snaps the matriarch, knocking the man's hand away.

'Wendy! Water! No, now! Please, through here, why don't you—'

'A chair, for goodness' sake!' The matriarch supports Luisa into the shady side-office.

'Wendy! A chair! This instant!'

Luisa's ally clasps her hands firmly. 'Let it out, honey, let it out, Jesus is listening, I'm listening. I'm Janice from Esphigmenou, Utah, and here is my story. When I was your age, I was alone in my house, coming downstairs from my daughter's nursery, and there on the half-way landing stood my mother. "Go check the baby, Janice," she said. I told my mother, I'd checked her one minute ago, she was sleeping fine. My mother's voice turned to ice. "Don't argue with me, young lady, go check the baby, *now*!" Sounds crazy, but only then I remembered my mother had died the Thanksgiving before. But I ran upstairs and found my daughter choking on the cord from the blind, wound round her neck. Thirty seconds and that would have been it. So you see?'

Luisa blinks tearfully.

'You see, honey? They pass over, but they ain't gone.'

The chastened manager returns with a shoebox. 'Your uncle's room is occupied, I'm afraid, but the maid found these letters inside the Gideon's Bible. His name is on the envelope. Naturally, I was going to have them forwarded to your family, but since you're here . . .'

Respectfully, he hands her a sheaf of nine time-browned envelopes, each addressed to 'Rufus Sixsmith, Esq. c/o Caius College, Cambridge, England.' One is stained by a very recent tea-bag. All are badly crumpled and hastily smoothed out.

'Thank you . . .' says Luisa, vaguely, then more firmly. 'Uncle Rufus valued his correspondence and now it's all I have left of him. I won't take up any more of your time. I'm sorry I fell to pieces out there.'

The manager's relief is palpable.

'You're a very special person, Megan,' Janice from Esphigmenou, Utah, assures Luisa, as they part in the hotel lobby.

'*You*'re a very special person, Janice,' Luisa replies, and returns to the parking level, passing within ten yards of locker No909.

21

Luisa Rey has been back at *Spyglass*'s offices for under a minute before Dom Grelsch roars over the newsroom chatter, '*Miss Rey!*'

Jerry Nussbaum and Roland Jakes look up from their desks, at Luisa, at each other, and mouth, '*Ouch!*' Luisa puts the Frobisher letters into a drawer, locks it, and walks into Grelsch's office. 'Dom, sorry I couldn't make the meeting, I—'

'Spare me the woman's-trouble excuse. Shut the door.'

'I'm not in the habit of making any excuses.'

'Are you in the habit of making meetings? You're paid to be.'

'I'm also paid to follow up stories.'

'So you flew off to the crime scene. D'you find hard evidence missed by the cops? A message, in blood, on the tiles? "Alberto Grimaldi did it"?'

'Hard evidence isn't hard evidence if you don't break your back digging for it. An editor named Dom Grelsch told me that.'

Grelsch glares at her.

'I got a lead, Dom.'

'You got a lead.'

I can't batter you, I can't fool you, I can only hook your curiosity. 'I phoned the precinct where Sixsmith's case was processed.'

'There is no case! It was suicide! Unless we're talking Marilyn Monroe, suicides don't sell magazines. Too depressing.'

'Listen to me. Why did Sixsmith buy an airplane ticket if he was going to put a bullet through his head later that day?'

Grelsch extends his arms to show the size of his disbelief that he is even having this conversation. 'A snap decision.'

'Then why would he have a *typed* suicide note – and no typewriter – ready and waiting for this snap decision?'

'I don't know! I don't care! I got a publication deadline Thursday night, a dispute with the printers, a deliveryman's strike in the offing, and Ogilvy holding the Sword of Whatsisname over my head. Hold a séance and ask Sixsmith yourself! Sixsmith was a scientist. Scientists are unstable.'

'We were trapped in an elevator for ninety minutes. Cool as a cucumber. Unstable just isn't a word that sticks to the man. Another thing. He shot himself – supposedly – with just about the quietest gun on the market. A Roachford .34 with fitted silencer. Catalog order only. Why would he go to the trouble?'

'So. The cops got it wrong, the ME got it wrong, everyone got it wrong except Luisa Rey, ace cub reporter, whose penetrating insight concludes the world-famous number-cruncher was assassinated just because he'd pointed out few hitches in some report, a report nobody agrees exists. Am I right?'

'Half right. More likely, the cops were encouraged to arrive at conclusions convenient for Seaboard.'

'Sure, a utility company buys the law-enforcement system. Stupid me.'

'Count in their subsidiaries, Seaboard Corporation is the tenth biggest corporation in the country. They could buy Alaska if they wanted. Give me until Monday.'

'No! You got this week's reviews and, yes, the food feature.'

'If Bob Woodward had told you he suspected President Nixon had ordered a burglary of his political rival's offices *and* recorded himself issuing the order, would you have said, "Forget it, Bob, honey, I need eight hundred words on salad dressings?"'

'Don't dare give me the I'm-an-outraged-feminist act.'

'Then don't give *me* the listen-I've-been-in-the-business-thirty-years act! One Jerry Nussbaum in the building is bad enough.'

'You're squeezing size eighteen reality into a size eleven supposition. The undoing of many a fine newspaperman. Many a fine anyone.'

'Monday! I'll get a copy of the Sixsmith Report.'

'Promises you can't keep are *not* a sound currency.'

'Apart from getting on my knees and begging you, I don't have any other currency. C'mon. Dom Grelsch doesn't snuff out solid investigative journalism just because it doesn't turn up the goods in one morning. Dad told me you were just about the most daring reporter working *anywhere* in the mid-sixties.'

Grelsch swivels and looks over 3rd Avenue. 'Did he *bullshit*.'

'He did too bullshit! That exposé on Ross Zinn's campaign funds in '64. You took a bone-chilling white supremacist out of politics for good. Dad called you dogged, cussed and indefatigable. Ross Zinn took nerve, sweat and time. I'll do the nerve and sweat, all I want from you is a little time.'

'Roping your pa into this was a dirty trick.'

'Journalism calls for dirty tricks.'

Grelsch stubs his cigarette and lights another. 'Monday, *with* Sixsmith's inquiry, and it's got to be hurricane proof, Luisa, with names, sources, facts. Who squashed this report, and *why*, and *how* Swannekke B will turn Southern California into Hiroshima. Something else. If you get *evidence* Sixsmith was murdered, we're going to the cops before we print. I don't want dynamite under my car-seat.'

' "All the news without fear or favor." '

'Beat it.'

Nancy O'Hagan makes a not-bad face as Luisa sits at her desk and takes out Sixsmith's rescued letters.

In his office, Grelsch lays into his punching bag. 'Dogged!' Wham! 'Cussed!' Wham! 'Indefatigable!' The editor catches his reflection, mocking him.

22

A Sephardic romance, composed before the expulsion of the Jews from Spain, fills the Lost Chord Music Store on the north-west corner of Spinoza Square and 6th Avenue. The well-dressed man on the telephone, pallid for this tanned city, repeats the inquiry: '*Cloud Atlas Sextet* . . . Robert Frobisher . . . As a matter of fact I *have* heard of it, though I've never laid my sticky paws on an actual pressing . . . Frobisher was a *wünderkind*, he died just as he got going . . . Let me see here, I've got a list from a dealer in San Fran who specializes in rareties . . . Franck, Fitzroy, *Frobisher* . . . Here we go, even a little footnote . . . Only five hundred recordings pressed . . . in Holland, before the war, my, no wonder it's rare . . . The dealer has a copy of an acetate, made in the fifties . . . by a liquidated French outfit. *Cloud Atlas Sextet* must bring the kiss of death to all who take it on . . . I'll try, he had one as of a month ago, but no promises on the sound quality, and I must warn you, cheap it *ain't* . . . It's quoted here at . . . one hundred twenty dollars . . . plus our commission at ten per cent, that makes . . . It is? Okay, I'll take your name down . . . Ray who? Oh, Miss R-E-Y, so sorry. Normally we ask for a deposit, but you've got an honest voice. A few days. You're welcome now.'

The store clerk scribbles himself a to-do note, and lifts the stylus back to the start of 'Por qué llorax blanca niña', lowers the needle on to shimmering black vinyl, and dreams of Jewish shepherd boys plucking their lyres on starlit Iberian hillsides.

23

Luisa Rey doesn't see the dusty black Chevy coasting by as she enters her apartment building. She has not taken much notice of anything since she read the first long letter found in Rufus Sixsmith's possession. Bill Smoke, driving the Chevy, mentally records the name of her apartment: 108, Pacific Eden Apartments.

Luisa has reread Sixsmith's letters a dozen times or more in the last day and a half. They disturb her deeply. A university friend of Sixsmith's, Robert Frobisher, wrote the series in the summer of 1931 during a prolonged stay at a chateau in Belgium. It is not the unflattering light they shed on a pliable young Rufus Sixsmith that bothers Luisa, but the dizzying vividness of the images of places and people that the letters have unlocked. Images so vivid she can only call them memories. The pragmatic journalist's daughter would, and did, explain away these 'memories' by an imagination hypersensitized by her father's recent death, but a detail in one letter freezes this explanation in its tracks. Robert Frobisher mentions a comet-shaped birthmark between his shoulder-blade and collar-bone.

I just don't believe in this crap. I just don't believe it. I don't.

Builders are remodeling the lobby of Pacific Eden Apartments. Sheets are on the floor, an electrician is prodding a light fitting, an unseen hammerer hammers. Malcolm the super glimpses Luisa, and calls out, 'Hey, Luisa! An uninvited guest ran up to your apartment twenty minutes ago!' But the noise of a drill drowns him out, he has a man from City Hall on the phone about permits and building codes and, anyway, Luisa has already stepped into the elevator.

24

'Surprise,' says Hal Brodie, drily, caught in the act of taking books and records from Luisa's shelves and putting them into his gym bag. 'Hey,' he says, to hide a jab of guilt, 'you've had your hair cut short.'

Luisa isn't very surprised. 'Isn't that what all dumped women do?'

Hal clicks in the back of his throat.

Luisa is angry with herself. 'So. Reclamation Day.'

'Just about done.' Hal brushes imaginary dust off his hands. 'Is the selected Wallace Stevens yours or mine?'

'It was a Christmas present from Phoebe to us. Phone Phoebe. Let her decide. Or else rip out the odd pages and leave me the even. This is like a no-knock raid. You could've phoned and warned me you'd be here.'

'I did. All I got was your machine. Junk it, if you never listen to it.'

'Don't be stupid, it cost a fortune. So what brings you up to town, apart from your love of modernist poetry?'

'Location-scouting for *Starsky and Hutch*.'

'I thought Starsky and Hutch lived in New York.'

'Starsky gets kidnapped. There's a gunfight on Buenas Yerbas Bay Bridge, and we've got a chase scene scripted with David and Paul running over car-roofs at rush-hour. It'll be a headache to okay it with the traffic cops, but we need to do it on location or we'll lose any semblance of artistic integrity.'

'Hey. You're not taking *Blood on the Tracks*.'

'It's mine.'

'Not any more.' Luisa is not joking.

With ironic deference, Brodie takes out the record from the gym bag. 'Look, I was sorry to hear about your dad.'

Luisa nods, feels grief rise and her defences stiffen. 'Yeah.'

'I guess it was . . . a release, of sorts.'

True, but only the bereaved can actually say so. Luisa resists the temptation to say something acidic. She remembers her father ribbing Hal, 'The TV Kid'. They look at the gaps and depletions in the shelves. *I am not going to start crying.* 'So, you're doing okay?'

'I'm doing fine. And you?'

'Fine.'

'Work's good?'

'Work's fine.' *Put us both of us out of our misery.* 'I believe you have a key that belongs to me.'

Hal zips up his gym bag, fishes in his pocket, and drops the door-key on to her palm. With a flourish, to underline the symbolism of the act. Luisa smells an alien aftershave, and imagines *Her* splashing it on him this morning. *He didn't own that shirt eight weeks ago, either.* The cowboy boots they'd bought together the day of the Segovia concert. Hal steps over a pair of Javier's filthy sneakers, and Luisa watches him think better of making a funny about her new man. Instead, he just says, 'So long, then.'

Shake hands? Hug him? 'Yeah.'

The door closes.

Luisa puts the chain on and replays the encounter. She turns on the shower and undresses. Her bathroom mirror is half hidden by a shelf of shampoos, conditioners, a box of sanitary towels, skin creams and gift-soaps. Luisa shunts these aside to get a clearer view of a birthmark between her shoulder-blade and collar-bone. Her recent encounter with Hal is displaced. *Coincidences happen all the time.* But it is undeniably shaped like a comet. The mirror mists over. *Facts are* your *bread and butter. Birthmarks can look like anything you choose, not only comets. You're still upset by Dad's death, that's all.* The journalist steps into the shower, but her mind walks the passageways of Zedelghem chateau.

25

The Swannekke Island protestors' camp lies on the mainland between a sandy beach and a marshy lagoon stranded by the sea. Behind the lagoon, acres of citrus orchards rise inland to arid hills. Tatty tents, rainbow-sprayed camper-vans, and trailer-homes look like unwanted gifts the Pacific dumped here. A strung banner declares: PLANET AGAINST SEABOARD. On the far side of the bridge sits Swannekke A, quivering like Utopia in a noon mirage. White toddlers tanned brown as leather paddle in the lazy shallows; a bearded apostle washes clothes in a tub; a couple of snaky teenagers kiss in the dune grass.

Luisa locks her VW and crosses the scrub to the encampment. Seagulls float in the joyless heat. Agricultural machinery drones in the far-off distance. Several inhabitants approach but not in a friendly manner. 'Yeah?' challenges a man, with a hawkish Native American complexion.

'I presumed this was a public park.'

'You presumed wrong. It's private.'

'I'm a journalist. I was hoping to interview a few of you.'

'Who do you work for?'

'*Spyglass* magazine.'

The bad weather lightens a little. 'Shouldn't you be writing about the latest adventures of Barbra Streisand's nose?' says the Native American, adding a sardonic, 'No disrespect.'

'Well, sorry, I'm not the *Herald Tribune*, but why not give me a chance? You could use a little positive coverage, unless you're seriously planning to dismantle that atomic time-bomb across the water by waving placards and strumming protest songs. No disrespect.'

A southerner growls: 'Lady, you're *full* of it.'

'The interview's over,' says the Native American. 'Get off this land.'

'Don't worry, Milton,' an elderly white-haired russet-faced woman stands on her trailer's step, 'I'll see this one.' An aristocratic mongrel watches from beside his mistress. Clearly, her word carries weight, for the crowd disperses with no further protest.

Luisa approaches the trailer. 'The love and peace generation?'

'1975 is nowhere *near* 1968. Seaboard and the police have informers in our network. Last weekend the authorities wanted to clear the site for the VIPs, and blood was spilled. That gave the cops an excuse for a round of arrests. I'm afraid paranoia pays. Come in. I'm Hester Van Zandt.'

'I was very much hoping to meet you, Doctor,' says Luisa.

26

An hour later Luisa feeds her apple core to Hester Van Zandt's genteel dog. Van Zandt's bookshelf-lined office is as neat as Grelsch's is chaotic. Luisa's host is finishing up. 'The conflict between corporations and activists is that of narcolepsy versus remembrance. The corporations have money, power and influence. Our sole weapon is public outrage. Outrage blocked the Yuccan Dam, ousted Nixon and, in part, terminated the monstrosities in Vietnam. But outrage is unwieldy to manufacture and handle. First, you need scrutiny; second, widespread awareness; only when this reaches a critical mass does public outrage explode into being. Any stage may be sabotaged. The world's Alberto Grimaldis can fight scrutiny by burying truth in committees, dullness and misinformation, or by intimidating the scrutinizers. They can extinguish awareness by blinkering education, owning TV stations, paying "guest fees" to leader writers or just buying the media up. The media – and not just the *Washington Post* – is where democracies conduct their civil wars.'

'That's why you rescued me from Milton and his compatriots.'

'I wanted to give you the truth as we see it, so you can at least make an informed choice about which side you'll back. Write a satire about GreenFront New Waldenites in their mini-Woodstock and you'll confirm every Republican Party prejudice and bury truth a little deeper. Write about radiation levels in seafood, "safe" pollution limits set by pollutors, government policy auctioned for campaign donations and Seaboard's *ex juris* police force, and you'll raise the temperature of public awareness, fractionally, towards its ignition point.'

Luisa is just leaving when she asks, 'Did you know Rufus Sixsmith?'

'I certainly did, may God rest his soul.'

'I'd have put you on opposing sides . . . or no?'

Van Zandt nods at Luisa's tactics. 'I met Rufus in the early sixties at a think-tank in DC, connected with the Energy Department. I was a little in awe of him! Nobel laureate, veteran of the Manhattan Project. He wasn't exactly what you'd call a ladies' man.'

Luisa got the same impression from Robert Frobisher's letters. 'Might you know anything about a report he wrote condemning the HYDRA Zero and demanding Swannekke B be taken off-line?'

'Dr Sixsmith? Are you totally sure?'

'"Totally sure"? No. "Pretty damn sure"? Yes.'

Van Zandt looks edgy. 'My God, if GreenFront could get its hands on a copy . . .' Her face clouds over. 'If *the* Dr Rufus Sixsmith wrote a hatchet job on the HYDRA Zero, and *if* he threatened to go public, well, I no longer believe he shot himself.'

Luisa notices they are both whispering. She asks the question she imagines Grelsch asking: 'Doesn't it smack of paranoia to believe Seaboard would assassinate a Nobel laureate, just to avoid negative publicity?'

Van Zandt removes a photograph of a woman in her seventies from a corkboard. 'A name for you. Margo Roker.'

'I saw her name on a placard the other day.'

'Margo's been a GreenFront activist since Seaboard bought Swannekke Island. She owns this land and lets us operate here as an embarrassing thorn in Seaboard's side. Six weeks ago her bungalow – two miles up the coast – was burgled. Margo has no money, just a few scraps of land, land she's refused to part with, whatever inducements Seaboard dangled. Well. The burglars beat her senseless, left her for dead, but took nothing. It's not actually a murder case, because Margo's still in a coma, so the police line is that it was a poorly planned heist with an unfortunate end.'

'Unfortunate for Margo.'

'And pretty damn fortunate for Seaboard. The medical bills are burying her family. A few days after the assault, an LA real estate company, Open Vista, steps up and makes an offer to Margo's cousin for these acres of coastland scrub at quadruple its market value. To make a private nature reserve. So I ask GreenFront to do some research on Open Vista. It was registered just eight weeks ago, and guess whose name heads the list of corporate donors?' Van Zandt nods in the direction of Swannekke Island.

Luisa weighs all this. 'You'll be hearing from me, Hester.'

'I hope I will.'

27

Alberto Grimaldi enjoys his Extracurricular Security Briefings with Bill Smoke and Joe Napier in his Swannekke office. He likes the no-nonsense demeanor of both men, in contrast to the retinue of courtiers and petitioners. He likes sending his secretary into the reception area where company heads, union leaders and government men are made to wait, ideally for hours, and hear her say, 'Frank, Joe, Mr Grimaldi has a slot for you now.' Smoke and Napier let Grimaldi indulge the J. Edgar Hoover sides of his character. He thinks of Napier as a steadfast bulldog whose New Jersey childhood is unsoftened by thirty-five years of Californian living; Bill Smoke is his familiar, who passes through walls, ethics and legality to execute his master's will.

Today's meeting is enhanced by Fay Li, summoned by Napier for the last item on their unwritten agenda: a journalist visiting Swannekke this weekend, Luisa Rey, who may or may not pose a security risk. 'So, Fay,' asks Grimaldi, balancing on the edge of his desk, 'what do we know about her?'

Fay Li speaks as if from a mental checklist. 'Reporter at *Spyglass* – I presume we all know it? Twenty-six, ambitious, more liberal than radical. Daughter of *the* Lester Rey, foreign correspondent, recently died. Mother remarried an architect after a dull divorce seven years ago, lives in uptown Ewingsville, BY. No siblings. History and economics at Berkeley, first class. Started on the *LA Recorder*, political pieces in the *Tribune* and *Herald*. Single, lives alone, pays her bills on time.'

'Dull as ditchwater,' comments Napier.

'Then remind me why we're discussing her,' says Smoke.

Fay Li addresses Grimaldi: 'We caught her wandering around Research on Tuesday, during the launch. She claimed to have an appointment with Dr Sixsmith.'

'About?'

'A commissioned piece for *Spyglass*, but I think she was fishing.'

The CEO checks with Napier, who shrugs: 'Difficult to read, Mr Grimaldi. If she was fishing, we should assume she knows what sort of fish she was after.'

Grimaldi has a weakness for spelling out the obvious. 'The report.'

'Journalists have feverish imaginations,' says Li, 'especially hungry young ones looking for their first big scoop. I suppose she *might* think Dr Sixsmith's death could be . . . How can I put this?'

Alberto Grimaldi makes a puzzled face.

'Mr Grimaldi,' fills in Smoke, 'what I believe Fay has too much tact to spit out and say is this: the Rey woman might be imagining we rubbed out Dr Sixsmith.'

'"Rubbed out"? Good God. Really? Joe? What do you think?'

Napier spreads his palms. 'Fay might be right, Mr Grimaldi. *Spyglass* isn't known for keeping its feet firmly rooted in fact.'

'Do we have any leverage with the magazine?' asks Grimaldi.

Napier shakes his head. 'I'll get on it.'

'She phoned,' continues Li, 'asking if she could interview a few of our people for a Day-in-the-Life-of-a-Scientist piece. So I invited her to the hotel for tonight's banquet, and promised to make a few introductions over the weekend. In fact,' she glances at her watch, 'I'm meeting her there in an hour.'

'I okayed it, Mr Grimaldi,' says Napier. 'I'd rather have her snooping under our noses where we can watch her.'

'Quite right, Joe. Quite right. Assess how much of a threat she poses. And lay to rest any morbid suspicions about poor Rufus at the same time.' Slight smiles all round. 'Well, Fay, Joe, that's a wrap, thanks for your time. Bill, a word on some matters in Toronto.'

The CEO and his fixer are left alone.

'Our friend,' begins Grimaldi, 'Lloyd Hooks. He worries me.'

Bill Smoke considers this. 'Any angles?'

'He's got a spring like he's holding four aces. I don't like it. Watch him.'

Bill Smoke inclines his head.

'And you'd better have an accident up your sleeve for Luisa Rey. Your work at the airport was exemplary, but Sixsmith was a distinguished foreign national and we don't want this woman to dig out any rumors of foul-play.' He nods after Napier and Li. 'Do those two suspect anything about Sixsmith?'

'Li isn't thinking anything. She's a PR woman, period. Napier's not looking. There's the blind, Mr Grimaldi, there's the wilfully blind, and then there's the soon-to-be-retired.'

28

Isaac Sachs sits hunched in the bay window of the Swannekke Hotel bar and watches the yachts in the creamy evening blues. A beer stands untouched on the table. The scientist's thoughts run from Rufus Sixsmith's death to the fear that his secreted-away copy of the Sixsmith Report might be found, to Napier's warning about confidentiality. *The deal is, Dr Sachs, your ideas are the property of Seaboard Corporation. You don't want to welch on a deal with a man like Mr Grimaldi, do you?* Clumsy but effective.

Sachs tries to remember how it felt not to walk around with this knot in his gut. He longs for his old lab in Connecticut, where the world was made of mathematics, energy and atomic cascades, and he was its explorer. He has no business in these political orders of magnitude, where erroneous loyalties can get your brain spattered over hotel bedrooms. *You'll shred that report, Sachs, page by goddamn page.*

Then his thoughts slide to a hydrogen build-up, an explosion, packed hospitals, the first deaths by radiation poisoning. The official inquiry. The scapegoats. Sachs bangs his knuckles together. So far, his betrayal of Seaboard is a thought-crime, not one of action. *Dare I cross that line?* He rubs his tired eyes. The hotel manager leads a bevy of florists into the banquet hall. A woman saunters downstairs, looks for someone who hasn't yet arrived, and drifts into the lively bar. Sachs admires her well-chosen suede suit, her svelte figure, her quiet pearls. The barman pours her a glass of white wine, and makes a joke that earns an acknowledgment but not a smile. She turns his way and he recognizes the woman he mistook for Megan Sixsmith five days ago: the knot of fear yanks tight, and Sachs hurries out via the veranda, keeping his face averted.

Luisa wanders over to the bay window. An untouched beer sits on the table, but there's no sign of its owner, so she sits down on the warmed seat. It's the best seat in the house. She watches the yachts in the creamy evening blues.

29

Alberto Grimaldi's gaze wanders the candlelit banquet hall. The room bubbles with sentences more spoken than listened to. His own speech got more and longer laughs than that of Lloyd Hooks, who now sits in sober consultation with Grimaldi's vice-president, William Wiley. *Now, what are that pair discussing so intently?* Grimaldi jots another mental note for Bill Smoke. The head of the Environmental Protection Agency is telling him an interminable story about Henry Kissinger's schooldays, so Grimaldi addresses an imaginary audience on the subject of power.

'*"Power." What do we mean? "The ability to determine another man's luck." You men of science, building tycoons and opinion formers: my jet could take off from La Guardia, and before I touched down in BY you'd be a nobody. You Wall Street moguls, elected officials, judges, I might need more time to knock you off your perches, but your eventual downfall would be just as total.*' Grimaldi checks with the head of the EPA to ensure his attention isn't being missed – it isn't. '*Yet how is it some men attain mastery over others while the vast majority live and die as minions, as livestock? The answer is a holy trinity. First: God-given gifts of charisma. Second: the discipline to nurture these gifts to maturity, for though humanity's topsoil is fertile with talent, only one seed in ten thousand will ever flower – for want of discipline.*' Grimaldi glimpses Fay Li steer the troublesome Luisa Rey to a circle where Spiro Agnew holds court. The reporter is prettier in the flesh than her photograph: *So that's how she noosed Sixsmith.* He catches Bill Smoke's eye. '*Third: the* will *to power. This is the enigma at the core of the various destinies of men. What drives some to accrue power where the majority of their compatriots lose, mishandle, or eschew power? Is it addiction? Wealth? Survival? Natural selection? I propose these are all pretexts and results, not the root cause. The only answer can be, "There is no 'Why'. This is our nature." "Who" and "What" run deeper than "Why."'*

The head of the Environmental Protection Agency quakes with mirth at his own punchline. Grimaldi chuckles through his teeth. 'A killer, Tom, an absolute *killer*.'

30

Luisa Rey plays the ditzy reporter on her best behavior to assure Fay Li she poses no threat. Only then might she be given a free enough rein to sniff out Sixsmith's fellow dissidents. Joe Napier, the head of Security, reminds Luisa of her father – quiet, sober, similar age and hair loss. Once or twice during the sumptuous ten-course meal she caught him watching her: not lecherously, but thoughtfully. 'And Fay, you never feel confined on Swannekke Island, at all?'

'Swannekke? It's paradise!' enthuses the publicist. 'Buenas Yerbas only an hour away, LA down the coast, my family up in San Francisco, it's ideal. Subsidized stores and utilities, free clinic, clean air, zero crime, sea views. Even the men,' she confides, *sotto voce*, 'come ready-vetted – in fact I can access their personnel files – so you know there won't be any total freaks in the dating pool. Speaking of which – Isaac! Isaac! You're being conscripted.' Fay Li grabs Isaac Sachs's elbow. 'You'll remember bumping into Luisa Rey the other day?'

'I'm one lucky conscript – hi, Luisa, again.'

Luisa feels an edginess in his handshake.

'Miss Rey is here,' says Fay Li, 'to write an article on Swannekke anthropology.'

'Oh? We're a dull tribe. I hope you'll meet your word-count.'

Fay Li turns her beam on full. 'I'm sure Isaac could find a

little time to answer any of your questions, Luisa, right, Isaac?'

'I'm the very dullest of the dull.'

'Don't believe him, Luisa,' Fay Li warns her. 'It's just a part of Isaac's strategy. Once your defences are down, he pounces.'

The alleged lady-killer rocks on his heels, smiling at his toes uncomfortably.

31

'Isaac Sachs's tragic flaw,' analyzes Isaac Sachs, slumped in the bay window across from Luisa Rey two hours later, 'is this. Too cowardly to be a warrior, but not *enough* of a coward to lie down and roll over like a good doggy.' His words slip like Bambi on ice. A mostly empty wine bottle stands on the table. The bar is deserted. Sachs can't remember when he was last this drunk, or this tense and relaxed at the same time: relaxed, because an intelligent young woman is enjoying his company; tense, because he is ready to lance the boil on his conscience. To Sachs's wry surprise, he is attracted to Luisa Rey, and sorely regrets they met in these circumstances. The woman and the reporter keep blurring into one another. 'Let's change the sub-ject,' Sachs says. 'Your car, your,' he does a Hollywood SS officer accent, '"*Volkswagen*". What's its name?'

'How do you know my Beetle has a name?'

'All Beetle owners give their cars names. But please don't tell me it's John, George, Paul or Ringo.' *God, Luisa Rey, you're beautiful.*

She says, 'You'll laugh.'

'I won't.'

'You will.'

'I, Isaac Caspar Sachs, solemnly vow not to laugh.'

'You'd better not with a middle name like "Caspar". It's "Garcia".'

They both shake, noiselessly, until they burst into laughter. *Maybe she likes me too, maybe she's not just doing her job.*

Luisa lassos her laughter in. 'Is that all your vows are worth?'

Sachs makes a *mea culpa* gesture and dabs his eyes. 'They normally last longer. I don't know why it's so funny, I mean, Garcia' – he snorts – 'isn't such a funny name. I once dated a girl who called her car Rocinante, for Chrissakes.'

'An ex-Berserkeley Beatnik boyfriend named it. After Jerry Garcia, y' know, the Grateful Dead man. He abandoned it at my dorm when its engine sent a gasket through the hood around the time he dumped me for a cheerleader. Cheesy, but true.'

'And you didn't take a blowtorch to it?'

'It's not Garcia's fault his ex-owner was a swindling sperm-gun.'

'The guy must have been mad.' Sachs didn't plan to say so, but he's not ashamed he did.

Luisa Rey nods in gracious acknowledgment. 'Anyway, Garcia suits the car. Never stays tuned, prone to flashes of speed, falling to bits, its trunk won't lock, it leaks oil, but never seems to give up the ghost.'

Invite her back, Sachs thinks. *Don't be stupid, you're not a pair of kids.*

They watch the breakers crash in the moonlight.

Say it. 'The other day,' his voice is a murmur and he feels sick, 'you were looking for something in Sixsmith's room.' The shadows seem to prick up their ears. 'Weren't you?'

Luisa also checks for eavesdroppers, and speaks very quietly indeed. 'I understand Dr Sixsmith wrote a certain report.'

'Rufus had to work closely with the team who designed and built the thing. That meant me.'

'Then you know what his conclusions were? About the HYDRA reactor?'

'We all do! Jessops, Moses, Keene . . . they all know.'

'About a critical design flaw?'

Sachs shudders. 'Yes.' *Nothing has changed, except every-thing.*

'How bad would an accident be?'

'If Dr Sixsmith is right, it'll be much, much worse than bad.'

'Why isn't Swannekke B just shut down pending further inquiry?'

'Money, power, usual suspects.'

'Do you agree with Sixsmith's findings?'

Carefully. 'I agree a substantial theoretical risk is present.'

'Were you put under any pressure to keep your doubts to yourselves?'

'Every scientist was. Every scientist agreed to. Except for Sixsmith.'

'*Who*, Isaac? Alberto Grimaldi? Does it go up to the top?'

Coral tree moonshadows disturb the silvery lawn. 'Luisa, what'd you *do* with a copy of the report, *if* one found its way into your hands?'

'Go public as fast as I possibly could.'

'Are you *aware* of . . .' *I can't say it.*

'Aware that people in the upper echelons would rather see me dead than see HYDRA discredited? Right now it's all I'm aware of.'

'I can't make any promises.' *Christ, how feeble.* 'I became a scientist because . . . it's like panning for gold in a muddy torrent. Truth is the gold. I – I don't know what I want to do . . .'

'Journalists work in torrents just as muddy.'

The moon is over the water.

'Do,' says Luisa finally, 'whatever you can't *not* do.'

32

In blustery early sunshine Luisa Rey watches golfers traverse the lush course, wondering what might have happened last night if she'd invited Isaac Sachs up. He's due to meet her for breakfast.

She wonders if she should have phoned Javier. *You're not his mother, you're not his guardian, you're just a neighbor.* She's not convinced, but just as she didn't know how to ignore the boy she found sobbing by the garbage chute, just as she couldn't *not* go down to the super's, borrow his keys and pick through a skip of garbage for his precious stamp albums, now she doesn't know how to extricate herself. He hasn't got anyone else, and eleven-year-olds don't do subtlety. *Anyway, who else have you got?*

'You look like you got the weight of the world,' says Joe Napier.

'Joe. Have a seat.'

'Don't mind if I do. I'm the bearer of bad news. Isaac Sachs sends his sincere apologies, but he's got to stand you up.'

'Oh?'

'Alberto Grimaldi flew out to our Three Mile Island site this morning – wooing a group of Germans. Sidney Jessops was going along as the technical support, but Sid's father had a heart-attack, and Isaac was the next choice.'

'Oh. Has he left already?'

'Afraid so. He's –' Napier checks his watch '– over the Colorado Rockies. Breastfeeding a hangover, shouldn't wonder.'

Don't let your disappointment show. 'When's he due back?'

'Tomorrow morning.'

'Oh.' *Damn, damn, damn.*

'I'm twice Isaac's age and three times uglier, but Fay's asked me to be show you around the site. She's scheduled a few interviews with some people she thought might interest you.'

'Joe, it's too kind of you all to give me such generous slices of your weekends,' says Luisa. *Did you know Sachs was on the verge of defection? How? Unless Sachs was a plant? I'm out of my depth here.*

'I'm a lonely old man with too much time on my hands.'

33

'So R&D is called the Chicken Coop because the egg-heads live there,' Luisa jots in her notebook, laughing, as Joe Napier holds open the control-room door two hours later. 'What do you call the reactor building?'

A gum-chewing technician calls out: 'Home of the Brave.'

Joe's expression says *funny*. 'That's *definitely* off the record.'

'Has Joe told you what we call the security wing?' grins the controller.

Luisa shakes her head.

'Planet of the Apes.' He turns to Napier. 'Introduce your guest, Joe.'

'Carlo Böhn, Luisa Rey. Luisa's a reporter, Carlo's a chief technician. Stick around and you'll hear plenty of other names for him.'

'Let me show you around, if Joe'll give you up for five minutes.'

Napier watches Luisa as Böhn shows her around the florescent-lit chamber of panels and gauges. Underlings check printouts, frown at dials, tick clipboards. Böhn flirts with her and catches Napier's eye, when Luisa's back is turned, and mimes melon-breasts; Napier shakes his sober head. *Milly would have clucked over you*, he thinks. *Had you over for dinner, fed you way too much and nagged you on what you need to be nagged about.* He recalls Luisa as a precocious little six-year-old. *Must be two decades since I saw you at the last 10th Precinct Station reunion. Of all the professions that lippy little girl could have entered, of all the reporters who could have caught the scent of Sixsmith's death, why Lester Rey's daughter? Why so soon before I retire? Who dreamt up this sick joke? The city?*

Napier could cry.

34

Fay Li searches Luisa Rey's room swiftly and adeptly as the sun sets. She checks inside the toilet cistern; under the mattress for slits; the carpets, for loose flaps; inside the minibar; in the closet. The original might have been Xeroxed down to a quarter of its bulk. Li's tame receptionist reported Sachs and Luisa talking until the early hours. Sachs was removed this morning, but he's no idiot, he could have deposited it for her. She unscrews the telephone mouthpiece, and finds Napier's favoured transmitter, one disguised as a resistor. She probes the recesses of Luisa's overnight bag, but finds no printed matter except *Zen and the Art of Motorcycle Maintenance*. She flicks through the reporter's notepad on the desk, but Luisa's encrypted shorthand doesn't reveal much.

Fay Li wonders if she's wasting her time. *Wasting your time? Mexxon Oil upped their offer to one hundred thousand dollars for the Sixsmith Report. And if they're serious about a hundred thousand, they'll be serious about a million. For discrediting the entire atomic energy program into an adolescent grave, a million is a snip. So keep searching.*

The phone buzzes four times: a warning that Luisa Rey is in the lobby, waiting for the elevator. Li ensures nothing is amiss and leaves, taking the stairs down to the lobby. After ten minutes she rings up to Luisa from the front desk. 'Hi, Luisa, it's Fay. Been back long?'

'Just long enough for a quick shower.'

'Productive afternoon, I hope?'

'Very much so. I've got enough material for two or three pieces.'

'Terrific. Listen, unless you've got other plans, how about dinner at the golf club? Swannekke lobster is the best this side of anywhere.'

'Quite a claim.'

'I'm not asking you to take *my* word for it.'

35

Crustacean shrapnel is piled high. Luisa and Fay Li dab their fingers in pots of lemon-scented water, and Li's eyebrow tells the waiter to remove the plates. 'What a *mess* I've made.' Luisa drops her napkin. 'I'm the slob of the class, Fay. You should open a finishing school for young ladies in Switzerland.'

'That's not how most people in Seaboard Village see me. Did anyone tell you my nickname? No? "Mr Li".'

Luisa isn't sure what response is expected. 'A little context might help.'

'My first week on the job, I'm up in the canteen, fixing myself a coffee. This engineer comes up, tells me he's got a problem of a mechanical nature and asks if I can help. His buddies are sniggering in the background. I say, "I doubt it." The guy says, "Sure you can help," he wants me to oil his bolt and relieve the excess pressure on his nuts.'

'This engineer was how old? Thirteen?'

'Forty, married, two kids. So his buddies are snorting with laughter now. What would you do? Dash off some witty put-down line, let 'em know you're riled? Slap him, get labeled hysterical? Besides, creeps like that enjoy being slapped. Do nothing? So any man on site can say shit like that to you with impunity?'

'An official complaint?'

'Prove that women run to senior men when the going gets tough?'

'So what did you do?'

'Had him transferred to our Kansas plant. Middle of nowhere, middle of January. I pity his wife, but she married him. Word gets round, I get dubbed "Mr Li". A real woman wouldn't have treated the poor guy so cruelly, no, a real woman would have taken his joke as a compliment.' Fay Li smooths wrinkles in the tablecloth. 'You run up against this crap in your work?'

Luisa thinks of Nussbaum and Jakes. 'All the time.'

'Maybe our daughters'll live in a liberated world, but us, forget it. We've got to help ourselves, Luisa. Men won't do it for us.'

The journalist senses a shifting of the agenda.

Fay Li leans in. 'I hope you'll consider me your own insider here on Swannekke Island.'

Luisa probes with caution. 'Journalists need insiders, Fay, so I'll certainly bear it mind. I have to warn you, though, *Spyglass* doesn't have the resources for the kind of remuneration you may be—'

'Men invented money. Women invented mutual aid.'

It's a wise soul, thinks Luisa, *who can distinguish traps from opportunities.* 'I'm not sure . . . how a small-time reporter could "aid" a woman of your standing, Fay.'

'Don't underestimate yourself. Friendly journalists make valuable allies. Sleep on it. If there comes a time when you want to discuss any matters weightier than how many French fries the Swannekke engineers consume per annum,' her voice sinks to a whisper far below the clinking of cutlery, cocktail-bar piano music and background laughter, 'such as data on the HYDRA reactor as compiled by Dr Sixsmith, purely for example, I guarantee you'll find me *much* more cooperative than you think.'

Fay Li clicks her fingers and the dessert trolley is already on its way. 'Now, the lemon and melon sherbet, *very* low in calories, it cleanses the palate, ideal before coffee. Trust me on this?'

The transformation is so total, Luisa almost wonders if she just heard what she just heard. 'I'll trust you on this.'

'Glad we understand each other.'

Luisa wonders: *What level of deceit is permissible in journalism?* She remembers her father's answer, one afternoon in the hospital garden: *Did I ever lie to get my story? Ten-mile-high whoppers every day before breakfast, if it got me one* inch *closer to the truth.*

36

A ringing phone flips Luisa's dreams over and she lands in the moonlit room. She grabs the lamp, the clock-radio and finally the receiver. For a moment she cannot remember her name or what bed she is in. 'Luisa?' offers a voice from the black gulf.

'Yeah, Luisa Rey.'

'Luisa, it's me, Isaac, Isaac Sachs, calling long-distance.'

'Isaac! Where are you? What time is it? Why —'

'Shush, shush, sorry I woke you, and sorry I was dragged away at the crack of dawn yesterday. Listen, I'm in Boston. It's seven-thirty eastern, it'll be getting light soon in California. You still there, Luisa? I haven't lost you?'

He's afraid. 'Yeah, Isaac, I'm listening.'

'Before I left Swannekke, I gave Garcia a present to give to you, just a *dolce per niente*.' He tries to make the sentence sound casual. 'Understand?'

What in God's name is he talking about?

'You hear me, Luisa? Garcia has a present for you.'

A more alert quarter of Luisa's brain muscles in. *Isaac Sachs left the Sixsmith Report in your VW. You mentioned the hood didn't lock. He assumes this hotel is not safe and that we are being eavesdropped.* 'That's very kind of you, Isaac. Hope it didn't cost you too much.'

'Worth every cent. Sorry to disturb your beauty sleep.'

'No worries. Mustn't OD on beauty sleep. Have a safe flight, and see you soon. Dinner, maybe?'

'I'd love that. Well, got a plane to catch.'

'Safe flight.' Luisa hangs up.

Leave later, in an orderly fashion? Or get off Swannekke right now?

37

A quarter of a mile across the science village, Joe Napier is also awake. His window frames the hour-before-dawn night sky. A console of electronic monitoring equipment occupies half the room. From a loudspeaker the sound of a dead phone line purrs. Napier rewinds a squawking reel-to-reel. '"Before I left Swannekke, I gave Garcia a present to give to you, just a *dolce per niente* . . . understand? . . . You hear me, Luisa? Garcia has a present for you."'

Garcia? Garcia?

Napier grimaces at his cold coffee and opens a folder labeled 'LR#2'. Colleagues, friends, contacts . . . no Garcia in the index. *Better warn Bill Smoke not to approach Luisa until I've had the chance to speak with her.* He flicks his lighter into life. *Bill Smoke is a difficult man to find, let alone warn.* Napier draws acrid smoke down into his lungs. His telephone rings: it's Bill Smoke. 'So, who the fuck's this Garcia?'

'Don't know, nothing on file. Listen, I don't want you to—'

'It's your fucking job to know, Napier.'

So, you're addressing me like that now? 'Hey! Hold your—'

'Hey yourself.' Bill Smoke hangs up.

Bad, bad, very bad. Joe grabs his jacket, snuffs his cigarette, leaves his quarters and strides across the site to Luisa's hotel. A five-minute walk. He recalls the menace in Bill Smoke's tone, and breaks into a run.

38

A swarm of *déjà vu* haunts Luisa as she stuffs her belongings into her overnight bag. *Robert Frobisher doing a dine and dash from another hotel.* She takes the stairs down to the empty lobby. The carpet is silent as snow. A radio whispers sweet nothings in the back office. Luisa creeps to the main doors, hoping to leave with no explanation required. The doors are locked to keep people out, not in, and soon Luisa is striding across the hotel lawn to the parking lot. A pre-dawn ocean breeze makes vague promises. The night sky inland is turning dark rose. Nobody else is about, but as she nears her car, Luisa forces herself not to break into a run. *Stay calm, unhurried, and you can say you're driving along the cape for the sunrise.*

At first glance the trunk is empty, but the carpet covers a bulge. Under the flap Luisa finds a package wrapped in a black plastic trash-bag. She removes a vanilla binder. She reads its cover in the semi-light: *THE HYDRA-ZERO REACTOR – AN OPERATIONAL ASSESSMENT MODEL – PROJECT HEAD DR RUFUS SIXSMITH – UNAUTHORIZED POSSESSION IS A FEDERAL CRIME UNDER THE MILITARY & INDUSTRIAL ESPIONAGE ACT 1971.* Some five hundred pages of tables, flowcharts, mathematics, and evidence. A sense of elation booms and echoes. *Steady, this is only the end of the beginning.*

Motion in the middle-distance catches Luisa's eye. A man. Luisa ducks behind Garcia. 'Hey! Luisa! Hold it!' *Joe Napier!* As if in a dream of keys and locks and doors, Luisa stows the vanilla binder in its black trash-bag under the passenger seat – Napier is running now, his flashlight beam swishing the half-darkness. The engine makes a lazy, leonine roar – the VW reverses too fast. Joe Napier thumps into the back, yells, and Luisa glimpses him hopping like a slapstick actor.

She does not stop to apologize.

39

Bill Smoke's dusty black Chevy skids to a stop by the island checkpoint of Swannekke Bridge. A string of lights dots the mainland across the straits. The guard recognizes the car and is already by its driver's window. 'Good morning, sir!'

'Looking that way. Richter, isn't it?'

'Yes, Mr Smoke.'

'I'm guessing Joe Napier has just called you and ordered you not to let an orange VW pass the checkpoint.'

'That's correct, Mr Smoke.'

'I'm here to countermand that order, on Mr Grimaldi's personal authority. You *will* raise the barrier for the VW and let me follow. You'll phone your buddy on the mainland checkpoint now, and tell him not to let anything through until he sees my car. When Mr Napier gets here, about fifteen minutes from now, you will tell him Alberto Grimaldi says, "Go back to bed." Understand, Richter?'

'Understood, Mr Smoke.'

'You got married this spring, if memory serves?'

'You have an excellent memory, sir.'

'I do. Hoping to start a family?'

'My wife's four months pregnant, Mr Smoke.'

'A piece of advice, Richter, on how to succeed in the security business. Would you like to hear this piece of advice, son?'

'I would, sir.'

'The dumbest dog can sit and watch. What takes brains is knowing when to look away. Am I making sense to you, Richter?'

'You're making absolute sense, Mr Smoke.'

'Then your young family's future is secure, son.'

Smoke reverses his car alongside the guard-house and slumps low. Sixty seconds later, a choking VW swerves round the headland. Luisa halts, rolls down her window, Richter appears, and Smoke catches the words 'family emergency'. Richter tells her to have a safe trip, and the barrier rises.

Bill Smoke puts his car into first, second. The sonic texture of the road surface changes as the Chevy reaches the bridge. Third gear, fourth, pedal down. The clapped-out Beetle's tail-lights zoom up, fifty yards, thirty yards, ten . . . Smoke hasn't switched his lights on. He swerves into the empty oncoming lane, shifts into fifth gear and draws alongside. Smoke smiles. *She thinks I'm Joe Napier.* He yanks the wheel sharply and metal screams as the Beetle is sandwiched against his car and the bridge railing until the railing unzips from its concrete and the Beetle lurches out into space.

Smoke slams the brakes. He gets out into the cool air and smells hot rubber. Back aways, sixty–seventy feet down, a VW's front bumper vanishes beneath broken ovals of foamy wavelets into the hollow sea. *If her back didn't snap, she'll have drowned in three minutes.* Bill Smoke inspects the damage to his car's bodywork and feels deflation. *Anonymous, faceless homicides,* he decides, *lack the thrill of human contact.*

The American sun, cranked up to full volume, proclaims a new dawn.

The Ghastly Ordeal of
Timothy Cavendish

One bright dusk, four, five, no, my God, *six* summers ago, I strolled along a Greenwich avenue of mature chestnuts and mock-oranges in a state of grace. Those Regency residences number among London's costliest properties, but should you ever inherit one, dear reader, sell it, don't live in it. Houses like these secrete some dark sorcery that transform their owners into fruitcakes. One such victim, an ex-chief of Rhodesian police, had, on the evening in question, written me a cheque as rotund as himself to edit and print his autobiography. My state of grace was thanks in part to this cheque, and in part to a 1983 Chablis from the Duruzoi vineyard, a magic potion that dissolves our myriad tragedies into mere misunderstandings.

A trio of teenettes, dressed like Prostitute Barbie, approached, drift-netting the width of the pavement. I stepped into the road to avoid collision. But as we drew level they tore wrappers off their lurid ice-lollies and just dropped them. My sense of well-being was utterly V-2'd. I mean, we were level with a bin! Tim Cavendish the Disgusted Citizen exclaimed to the offenders: 'You know, you should pick those up.'

A snorted 'What*chyoo* gonna do'bou' it?' glanced off my back.

Ruddy she-apes. 'I have no intention of *doing* anything about it,' I remarked, over my shoulder, 'I merely said that you—'

My knees buckled and the pavement cracked my cheek, shaking loose an early memory of a tricycle accident before pain erased everything but pain. A sharp knee squashed my face into leaf-mould. I tasted blood. My sixtysomething wrist was winched back through ninety degrees of agony, and my Ingersoll Solar was unclasped. I recall a pick'n'mix of obscenities ancient and modern, but before my muggers could filch my wallet, the chimes of an ice-cream van playing 'The Girl from Ipanema' scattered my assailants, like vampiresses the minute before dawn.

'And you didn't report them? You dolt!' Madame X sprinkled synthetic sugar over her breakfast bran the next morning. 'Phone the police for Christ's sake. What are you waiting for? The trail'll go cold.' Alas, I had already amplified the truth and told her my muggers were five louts with swastikas shaved on to their skulls. How could I now file a report saying three pre-pubescent lollipop girls had bested me so effortlessly? The boys in blue would have choked on their Penguin biscuits. No, my assault was not added to our nation's wishfully fulfilled crime statistics. Had my purloined Ingersoll not been a love-present from a sunnier era of our now-Arctic marriage, I would have kept mum about the entire incident.

Where was I?

Odd how the wrong stories pop into one's head at my age.

It's not odd, no, it's ruddy scary. I meant to begin this narrative with Dermot Hoggins. That's the problem with inking one's memoirs in longhand. You can't go changing what you've already set down, not without botching things up even more.

* * *

Look, I was Dermot 'Duster' Hoggins's *editor*, not his shrink or his ruddy astrologer, so how *could* I have known what lay in store for Sir Felix Finch on that infamous night? Sir Felix Finch, Minister of Culture and El Supremo at the *Trafalgar Review of Books*, how he blazed across the media sky, how visible he remains to the naked eye even now, twelve months later. Tabloidoids read all about it across the front page; broadsheeters spilt their granola when Radio 4 reported who had fallen and how. That aviary of vultures and tits, 'the columnists', eulogized the Lost King of Arts in tribute after twittering tribute.

I, on the other hand, have maintained a dignified counsel until now. I should warn the busy reader, however, that the after-dinner mint of Felix Finch is merely the *apéritif* of my own peripatetic tribulations. The Ghastly Ordeal of Timothy Cavendish, if you will. Now *that* is a snappy title.

'Twas the Night of the Lemon Prize Awards, held in Jake's Starlight Bar, grandly reopened atop a Bayswater edifice with a rooftop garden thrown in for good measure. The whole ruddy publishing food chain had taken to the air and roosted at Jake's. The haunted writers, the celebrity chefs, the suits, the goateed buyers, the malnourished booksellers, packs of hacks and photographers who take 'Drop dead!' to mean 'Why, I'd love to!' Let me scotch that insidious little rumour implying Dermot's invitation was *my* doing, that, oh, yes, Timothy Cavendish knew his author was lusting for a high-profile revenge, *QED*, the entire tragedy was a publicity stunt. Tosh dreamt up by jealous rivals! No-one ever owned up to sending Dermot Hoggins's invitation, and she is hardly likely to step forward now.

Anyway, the winner was announced and we all know who got the fifty-K prize money. I got sloshed. Guy the Guy introduced me to a cocktail called 'Ground Control to Major Tom'. Time's Arrow became Time's Boomerang and I lost count of all my majors. A jazz sextet kicked off a rumba. I went on to the balcony for a breather, and surveyed the hubbub from without. Literary London at play put me in mind of Gibbon on the Age of the Antonines. *A cloud of critics, of compilers, of commentators darkened the face of learning, and the decline of genius was soon followed by the corruption of taste.*

Dermot found me; bad news inexorably does. Let me reiterate, bumping into Pope Pius XIII would have surprised me less. In fact, His Infallibility would have blended in better – my malcontent author wore a banana suit over a chocolate shirt and a Ribena tie. I hardly need remind the curious reader that *Knuckle Sandwich* was yet to take the book world by storm. It was yet to enter a bookshop, in fact, except the sage John Sandoe's of Chelsea, and those hapless newsagents, once Jewish, then Sikh, now Eritrean, located in the Hoggins Bros' East End parish. Indeed, it was matters of publicity and distribution that Dermot wished to discuss on the roof-garden.

I explained to him for the hundredth time how an author–partnership set-up like Cavendish Publishing simply cannot fritter away money on fancy catalogues and team-building go-karting weekends for sales forces. I explained, yet again, that my authors derived fulfilment from presenting their handsomely bound volumes to friends, to family, to posterity. I explained, yet again, that the gangster-chic market was saturated; and that even *Moby Dick* bombed in Melville's lifetime, though I did not deploy that particular verb. 'It *is* a truly fabulous memoir,' I assured him. 'Give it time.'

Dermot, drunk, doleful and deaf, looked over the railings. 'All them chimneys. Long way down.'

The menace, I trusted, was imaginary. 'Quite.'

'Mum took me to *Mary Poppins* when I was a nipper. Chimney sweeps dancing on rooftops. She watched it on video, too. Over and over. In her nursing home.'

'I remember when it came out. That dates me.'

'Here.' Dermot frowned and pointed into the bar through the french windows. 'Who's that?'

'Who's who?'

'Him in the bow-tie chatting up the tiara in the bin-liner.'

'The presenter fellow, Felix . . . oh, Felix whatizzit?'

'Felix f*****g Finch! That c*** who *shat* on my book in his poncy f*****g mag?'

'It wasn't your best review, but—'

'It was my only f*****g review!'

'It really didn't read so badly—'

'Yeah? "*None-hit wonders like Mr Hoggins are the road-kills of modern letters.*" Notice how people insert the "Mr" before sinking the blade in? "*Mr Hoggins should apologize to the trees felled for his bloated 'auto-bio-novel'. Four hundred vainglorious pages expire in an ending flat and inane quite beyond belief.*"'

'Steady now, Dermot, nobody actually reads the *Trafalgar*.'

''Scuse!' My author collared a waiter. 'Heard of the *Trafalgar Review of Books*?'

'Why, sure,' the East European waiter replied. 'My entire faculty swears by the *TRB*, they've got the smartest reviewers.'

Dermot flung his glass over the railing.

'Come now, what's a reviewer?' I reasoned. 'One who reads quickly, arrogantly, but never wisely . . .'

The jazz sextet finished their number and Dermot left my sentence dangling. I was drunk enough to justify a taxi, and was about to leave when a Cockney town crier soundalike silenced the entire gathering: 'Ladies and gentlemen of the jury! Your attention, please!'

Saints preserve us, Dermot was clanging a couple of trays together. 'We have an additional award tonight, fellow book fairies!' he bellowed. Ignoring arch chuckles and 'Oooooo!'s he produced an envelope from his jacket pocket, slit it open and pretended to read: 'Award for Most Eminent Literary Critic.' His audience looked on, cockatooed, booed, or turned away in embarrassment. 'Competition was fierce, but the panel was unanimous in choosing His Imperial Majesty of the *Trafalgar Review of Books*, Mr – beg pudding, *Sir* – Felix Finch O, B and E, come – on – darn!'

Stirrers crowed. 'Bravo, Felix! Bravo!' Finch wouldn't have been a critic if he didn't love unearned attention. Doubtless he was already composing copy in his head for his *Sunday Times* column, 'A Finch About Town'. For his part, Dermot was all sincerity and smiles. 'What might my prize be, I wonder?' smirked Finch, as the applause subsided. 'A signed copy of an unpulped *Knuckle Sandwich*? Can't be many of those left!' Finch's coterie chorused hooty laughter, spurring on their *kommissar*. 'Or do I win a free flight to a South American country with leaky extradition treaties?'

'Yeah, lovie,' Dermot winked, 'a free flight is *exactly* what you won.'

My author grabbed Finch's lapels, rolled backwards, sank his feet into Finch's girth, and judo-propelled the shorter-than-generally-realized media personality high into the night air! High above the pansies lining the balcony railing.

Finch's shriek – his life – ended in crumpled metal, twelve floors down.

Someone's drink poured on to the carpet.

Dermot 'Duster' Hoggins brushed his lapels, leant over the balcony, and yelled: 'SO WHO'S EXPIRED IN AN ENDING FLAT AND INANE QUITE BEYOND BELIEF *NOW*?'

The dumbstruck crowd parted as the murderer made his way to the nibblies table. Several witnesses later recalled a dark halo. He selected a Belgian cracker adorned with Biscay anchovies and parsley drizzled with sesame oil.

The crowd's senses flooded back. Gagging noises, oh-my-Gods and a stampede for the stairs. The most frightful hulla-baloo! My thoughts? Honestly? Horror. Assuredly. Shock? You bet. Disbelief? Naturally. Fear? Not really.

I will not deny a nascent sense of a silver lining to this tragic turn. My Haymarket office suite housed ninety-five unsold shrinkwraps of Dermot Hoggins's *Knuckle Sandwich*, im-passioned memoir of Britain's soon-to-be most famous mur-derer. Frank Sprat – my stalwart printer in Sevenoaks to whom I owed so much money I had the poor man over a barrel – still had the plates and was ready to roll at a moment's notice.

Hardcovers, ladies and gentlemen.

Fourteen pounds ninety-nine pence a shot.

A taste of honey!

As an experienced editor I disapprove of backflashes, fore-shadowings and tricksy devices, they belong in the 1980s with MAs in Postmodernism and Chaos Theory. I make no apology, however, for (re)starting my own narrative with my version of that shocking affair. You see, it paved my first good intention on the road to Hull, or rather Hull's hinterland, where my ghastly ordeal is fated to unfold. My fortune took the glorious turn I had foreseen after Felix Finch's Final Fling. On the wings of sweet, free publicity, my *Knuckle Sandwich* turkey soared up the bestseller charts where it roosted until poor Dermot was sentenced to fifteen of the best in Wormwood Scrubs. The trial made the *Nine o'Clock News* at every turn. In death Sir Felix changed from a smug-scented pomposity with a Stalinist grip on Arts Council money into, oh, Britain's best-loved arts guru since the last one.

On the steps of the Old Bailey, his widow told reporters fifteen years was 'disgustingly lenient', and the very next day a 'Duster Hoggins, Rot in Hell!' campaign was launched. Dermot's family counterattacked on chat-shows, Finch's offending review was pored over, BBC2 commissioned a special documentary in which the lesbian who interviewed me edited my witticisms wholly out of context. Who cared? The money pot bubbled away – no, it boiled over and set the entire ruddy kitchen alight. Cavendish Publishing – Mrs Latham and I, that is – didn't know what had hit us. We had to take on two of her nieces (part-time, of course, I wasn't getting clobbered for National Insurance). The original *Knuckle Sandwich* shrinkwraps vanished within thirty-six hours, and Frank Sprat was reprinting on a near-monthly basis. Nothing in my four decades in the publishing game had geared us for such success. Running costs had always been recouped from author donations – not from actual ruddy sales! It seemed almost unethical. Yet here I was with a bestseller of one-in-a-decade proportions on my lists. People ask me, 'Tim, how do you account for its runaway success?'

Knuckle Sandwich was actually a well-written gutsy fictional memoir. Culture-vultures discussed its socio-political subtexts first on late-night shows, then on breakfast TV. Neo-Nazis bought it for its generous lashings of violence. Worcestershire housewives bought it because it was a damn fine read. Homosexuals bought it out of tribal loyalty. It shifted ninety thousand, yes, *ninety thousand* copies in four months, and yes, I am *still* talking hardcover. The feature film should be in production as I write. At the Frankfurt Book love-in I was fêted by people who until then had never so much as paused to scrape me off their shoes. That odious label 'Vanity Publisher' became 'Creative Financier'. Translation rights fell like territories in the final round of *Risk*. The American publishers, glory glory

Hallelujah, they *loved* the Limey-Aristo-Gets-Comeuppance-from-Downtrodden-Gaelic-Son hook, and a transatlantic auction skyrocketed the advance to giddy heights. I, yes, I, had exclusive rights to this platinum goose with a bad case of the trots! Money entered my cavernously empty accounts like the North Sea through a Dutch dyke. My 'personal banking consultant', a spiv named Elliot McCluskie, sent me a Christmas card photo of his Midwich Cuckoo offspring. The primates on the Groucho Club door greeted me with a 'Pleasant evening, Mr Cavendish,' instead of an 'Oy, you got to be signed in by a member!' When I announced that I would be handling the paperback release myself, the Sundays' book pages ran pieces depicting Cavendish Publishing as a dynamic white-hot player in a cloud of decrepit gas giants. I even made the *FT*.

Was it any wonder Mrs Latham and I were overstretched – just a smidge – on the bookkeeping front?

Success intoxicates rookies in the blink of an eye. I got business cards printed up: Cavendish-Redux, Publishers of Cutting-edge Fiction. Well, I thought, why *not* sell publications instead of publication? Why *not* become the serious publisher that the world lauded me as?

Alackaday! Those dinky little cards were the red flag waved at the Bull of Fate. At the first rumour that Tim Cavendish was flush, my sabre-toothed meerkat creditors bounded into my office. As ever, I left the gnostic algebra of what to pay whom and when to my priceless Mrs Latham. So it was, I was mentally *and* financially under-prepared when my midnight callers visited, nearly a year after the Felix Finch Night. I confess that since Madame X left me (my cuckold was a dentist, I shall reveal the truth no matter how painful) Housekeeping Anarchy had reigned o'er my Putney domicile (oh, very well, the bastard was a German), so my porcelain throne has long been my *de facto* office seat. A decent Cognac sits under the ballgowned lavatory-roll cover, and I leave the door open so I can hear the kitchen radio.

The night in question, I had put aside my perpetual lavatory read, *The Decline and Fall of the Roman Empire*, because of all the manuscripts (inedible green tomatoes) submitted to Cavendish-Redux, my new stable of champions. I suppose it was about eleven o'clock when I heard my front door being interfered with. Skinhead munchkins mug-or-treating?

Cherry-knockers? The wind?

Next thing I knew, the door flew in off its ruddy hinges! I was thinking al-Qaeda, I was thinking ball lightning, but no. Down the hallway tramped what seemed like an entire rugby team, though my intruders numbered only three. (You'll notice, I am always attacked in threes.) 'Timothy,' pronounced the gargoyliest, 'Cavendish, I presume. Caught with your cacks down.'

'My business hours are eleven to two, gentlemen,' Bogart would have said, 'with a three-hour break for lunch. Kindly leave.' All I could do was blurt, 'Oy! My door! My ruddy door!'

Thug Two lit a cigarette. 'We visited Dermot today. He's a bit frustrated. Who wouldn't be?'

The pieces fell into place. I fell into pieces. 'Dermot's brothers!' (I'd read all about them in Dermot's book. Eddie, Mozza, Jarvis.)

Hot ash burnt my thigh, and I lost track of which face uttered what. It was a Francis Bacon triptych come to life. '*Knuckle Sandwich* is doing nicely, by the looks of things.'

'Piles of it in the airport bookshops.'

'You must at least of *suspected* we'd come calling.'

'A man of your business acumen.'

The London Irish unnerve me at the best of times. 'Boys, boys. Dermot signed a copyright-transfer contract. Look, look, it's industry standard, I have a copy in my briefcase here . . .' I did indeed have the document to hand. 'Clause eighteen, about copyright . . . means *Knuckle Sandwich*, legally, is . . . er . . .' It wasn't easy to tell them this with my briefs around my ankles. 'Er, legally the property of Cavendish Publishing.'

Jarvis Hoggins scanned the contract for a moment but tore it up when it proved longer than his concentration span. 'Dermot signed this f*****g pants when his book was just a f*****g hobby.'

'A present to our sick old mam, God rest her soul.'

'A souvenir of Dad's heyday.'

'Dermot never signed no f*****g contract for the event of the f*****g season.'

'We paid your printer, Mr Sprat, a little visit. He went through the economics for us.'

Contract confetti showered. Mozza was close enough for me to smell his dinner. 'Quite a hill of Hoggins Bros' cash you've raked in, it seems.'

'I'm sure we can agree on a, um, um, funds flowchart, which will—'

Eddie cut in: 'Let's make it three.'

I feigned a wince. 'Three thousand pounds? Boys, I don't think—'

'Don't be a silly-billy.' Mozza pinched my cheek. 'Three – o' – clock. Tomorrow afternoon. Your office.'

I had no choice. 'Perhaps we might . . . er . . . moot a pro-visional sum to conclude this meeting, as a basis for . . . ongoing negotiation.'

'Okeydokey. What sum did we *moot* earlier, Mozza?'

'Fifty K sounded reasonable.'

My cry of pain was unfeigned. 'Fifty thousand *pounds*?'

'For starters.'

My intestines bubbled, toiled and troubled. 'Do you really think I keep that kind of money lying around in shoeboxes?' I pitched my voice for Dirty Harry but it was more Lisping Baggins.

'I hope you keep it lying around somewhere, Grandpops.'

'Cash.'

'No bollocks. No cheques.'

'No promises. No deferments.'

'Old-fashioned money. A shoebox will do fine.'

'Gentlemen, I'm happy to pay a negotiated consideration, but the law—'

Jarvis whistled through his teeth. 'Will the law help a man of your years bounce back from multiple spinal fractures, Timothy?'

Eddie: 'Men of your age don't bounce. They splat.'

I fought with all my might, but my sphincter was no longer my own and a cannonade fired off. Amusement or condescension I could have borne, but my tormentors' pity signified my abject defeat. The toilet chain was pulled.

'Three o'clock.' Cavendish-Redux went down the pan. Out trooped the thugs, over my prostrate door. Eddie turned for a last word. 'Dermot did a nice little paragraph in his book. On loan defaulters.'

I refer the curious reader to page 244 of *Knuckle Sandwich*, available from your local bookshop. Not on a full stomach.

Outside my Haymarket office suite taxis inched and sprinted. Inside my inner sanctum, Mrs Latham's Nefertiti earrings (a gift from me to mark her tenth year with Cavendish Publishing, I found them in a British Museum Gift Shop bargain bin) jingled as she shook her head, no, no, no. 'And I am telling *you*, Mr Cavendish, that I cannot find you fifty thousand pounds by three o'clock this afternoon. I cannot find you five thousand pounds. Every *Knuckle Sandwich* penny has already been Hoovered up by long-standing debts.'

'Doesn't anybody owe *us* money?'

'I always keep on top of the invoicing, Mr Cavendish, do I not?'

Desperation makes me wheedle. 'This is the age of ready .credit!'

'This is the age of credit *limits*, Mr Cavendish.'

I retired to my office, poured myself a whisky and slooshed down my dicky-ticker pills before tracing Captain Cook's last voyage on my antique globe. Mrs Latham brought in the mail and left without a word. Bills, junk, moral muggings from charity fundraisers and a package addressed 'FAO The Visionary Editor of "Knuckle Sandwich"' containing a MS titled

Half-lives – lousy name for a work of fiction – and subtitled *The First Luisa Rey Mystery*. Lousier and lousier. Its lady author, one dubiously named Hilary V. Hush, began her covering letter with the following: 'When I was nine my mom took me to Lourdes to pray for my bedwetting to be cured. Imagine my surprise when not St Bernadette but Alain-Fournier appeared in a vision that night.'

Nutcase ahoy. I threw the letter away into my 'Urgent Business' tray and switched on my spanking new fat-gigabyte computer for a game of Minesweeper. After getting blown up twice I telephoned Sotheby's to offer Charles Dickens's own, original, authentic writing-desk for auction with a reserve price of sixty thousand. A charming evaluator named Kirpal Singh commiserated that the novelist's desk was already accounted for by the Dickens' House museum, and hoped I'd not been fleeced too painfully. I confess, I do lose track of my little elaborations. Next I called Elliot McCluskie and asked after his delightful kiddies. 'Fine, thank you.' He asked after my delightful business. I asked for a loan of eighty thousand pounds. He began with a thoughtful 'Right . . .' I lowered my ceiling to sixty. Elliot pointed out that my performance-linked credit stream still had a twelve-month flow-horizon before resizing could be feasibly optioned. Oh, I miss the days when they'd laugh like a hyena, tell you to go to hell and hang up. I traced Magellan's voyage across my globe and longed for a century when a fresh beginning was no further than the next clipper out of Deptford. My pride already in tatters, I gave Madame X a bell. She was having her a.m. soak. I explained the gravity of my situation. She laughed like a hyena, told me to go to hell and hung up. I spun my globe. I spun my globe.

Mrs Latham eyeballed me like a hawk watching a bunny as I stepped outside. 'No, not a loan shark, Mr Cavendish. It just isn't worth it.'

'Never fear, Mrs Latham, I'm just going to pay a call on the one man in this world who believes in me, fair weather or foul.' In the lift I reminded my reflection, 'Blood is thicker than water,' before spiking my palm on the spoke of my telescopic umbrella.

'Oh, Satan's gonads, not you. Look, just get lost and leave us in peace.' My brother glared across his swimming-pool as I stepped down his patio. Denholme's never swum in his pool, as far as I know, but he does all the chlorinating and whatnot every week just the same, even in blustery drizzle. He trawled for leaves with a big net on a pole. 'I'm not lending you a ruddy farthing until you pay back the last lot. Why must *I* forever be giving *you* hand-outs? No. Don't answer.' Denholme scooped a fistful of soggy leaves from the net. 'Just get back in your taxi and bugger off. I'll only ask you nicely once.'

'How's Georgette?' I brushed aphids off his shrivelled rose petals.

'Georgette's going bonkers surely and steadily, not that you ever evince an ounce of genuine interest when you don't want money.'

I watched a worm return to soil and wished I was it. 'Denny, I've had a minor run-in with the wrong sort. If I can't get my hands on sixty thousand pounds I'm going to take an awful beating.'

'Get them to video it for us.'

'I'm not joking, Denholme.'

'Nor am I! So, you're shoddy at being duplicitous. What of it? Why is this my problem?'

'We're brothers! Don't you have a conscience?'

'I sat on the board of a merchant bank for thirty years.'

An amputated sycamore tree shed once-green foliage like desperate men shed once-steadfast resolutions. 'Help, Denny. Please. Thirty grand would be a start.'

I had pushed too hard. 'Damn it to hell, Tim, my bank *crashed*! We were bled dry by those bloodsuckers at Lloyds! The days when I had that kind of spondulicks at my beck and call are gone, gone, gone! Our house is mortgaged, twice over! I'm the mighty fallen, you're the minuscule fallen. Anyway, you've got this ruddy book flying out of every bookshop in the known world!'

My face said what I had no words for.

'Oh, Christ, you idiot. What's the repayment schedule?'

I looked at my watch. 'Three o'clock this afternoon.'

'Forget it.' Denholme put down his net. 'File for bankruptcy. Reynard'll do the papers for you, he's a good man. A hard bullet to bite, I should know, but it'll get your creditors off your back. The law is clear—'

'Law? The only experience *my* creditors have of the law is squatting over a can in an overcrowded cell.'

'Then go to ground.'

'These people are very, *very* well connected with the ground.'

'Not beyond the M25 they aren't, I bet. Stay with friends.'

Friends? I crossed off those to whom I owed money, the dead, the disappeared-down-time's-rabbit-hole, and I was left with . . .

Denholme made his final offer. 'I can't lend you money. I don't have any. But I'm owed a favour or two by a comfortable place where you could possibly lie low for a while.'

*   *   *

Temple of the Rat King. Ark of the Soot God. Sphincter of Hades. Yes, King's Cross Station where, according to *Knuckle Sandwich*, a blowjob costs only five quid – any of the furthest-left three cubicles in the men's lavvy downstairs, twenty-four hours a day. I called Mrs Latham to explain I would be in Prague for a three-week meeting with Vaclav Havel, a lie whose consequences stuck with me like herpes. Mrs Latham wished me *bon voyage*. She could handle the Hogginses. Mrs Latham could handle the Ten Plagues of Egypt. I don't deserve her, I know it. I often wonder why she's stayed at Cavendish Publishing. It isn't for what I pay her.

I navigated the array of ticket types on the ticket machine: Day Return With Railcard Off Peak, Cheap Day Single Without Railcard On Peak, and on, and on, but which, oh, which do I need? A menacing finger tapped my shoulder and I jumped a mile – it was only a little old lady advising me that Returns are Cheaper than Singles. I assumed she was doo-lally but, stone the ruddy crows, 'twas so. I slid in a bank-note with our monarch's head up, then down, then front-first, then back-first, but each time the machine spat it out.

So I joined the queue for a human ticket-seller. Thirty-one people were ahead of me, yes, I counted every one. The ticket-sellers drifted in and out from their counters much as the fancy took them. A looped advertisement on a screen urged me to invest in a stair-lift. Finally, *finally*, my turn was up: 'Hello, I need a ticket to Hull.'

The ticket woman toyed with her chunky ethnic rings. 'Leaving when?'

'As soon as possible.'

'As in "today"?'

'"Today" usually means "as soon as possible", yes.'

'I ain't sellin' you a ticket for today. That's them winders over there. This winder is advance tickets only.'

'But the red flashing sign told me to come to your counter.'

'Couldn't have done. Move along, now. You're holding up the queue.'

'No, that sign ruddy well *did* send me to this counter! I've been queuing for twenty minutes!'

She looked interested for the first time. 'You want me to change the rules for your benefit?'

Anger sparked in Timothy Cavendish like forks in microwaves. 'I want you to evolve problem-solving intelligence and sell me a ticket to Hull!'

'I ain't standing for being addressed in that tone.'

'*I'm* the ruddy customer! *I* won't be addressed like that! Get me your ruddy supervisor!'

'I *am* my supervisor.'

Snarling an oath from an Icelandic saga, I reclaimed my place at the head of the queue.

'Oy!' yelled a punk-rocker, with studs in his cranium. 'There's a fackin' queue!'

Never apologize, advises Lloyd-George. Say it again, only this time, ruder. 'I know there's a "fackin' queue"! I already queued in it once and I am *not* going to queue again just because Nina Simone over there won't sell me a ruddy ticket!'

A coloured yeti in a clip-on uniform swooped. 'Wassa bovver?'

'This old man here reckons his colostomy bag entitles him to jump the queue,' said the skinhead, '*and* make racist slurs about the lady of Afro-Caribbean extraction in the advance-travel window.'

I couldn't believe I was hearing this.

'Look, matey,' the yeti addressed me with condescension reserved for the handicapped or elderly, 'we got queues in this country to keep things fair, see, and if you don't like it you should go back to where you come from, gettit?'

'Do I *look* like a ruddy Egyptian? Do I? I *know* there's a queue! How? Because I already queued in this queue, so—'

'This gentleman claims you ain't.'

'*Him*? Will he still be a "gentleman" when he daubs *Asylum-scrounger* on your housing-association flat?'

His eyeballs swelled, they really did. 'The Transport Police can boot you off the premises, or you can join this queue like a member of a civilized society. Whichever is fine by me. Jumping queues is *not* fine by me.'

'But if I queue all over again I'll miss my connections!'

'Tough,' he enunciated, 'titty!'

I appealed to the people behind that Sid Rotten lookalike. Maybe they had seen me in the queue, maybe they hadn't, but nobody met my eye. England has gone to the dogs, oh, the dogs, the ruddy dogs.

Over an hour later London shunted itself southwards, taking the Curse of the Brothers Hoggins with it. Commuters, these hapless souls who enter a lottery of death twice daily on Britain's decrepit railways, packed the dirty train. Aeroplanes circled in holding patterns over Heathrow, densely as gnats over a summer puddle. Too much matter in this ruddy city.

Still. I felt the exhilaration of a journey begun, and I let my guard drop. A volume I once published, *True Recollections of a Northern Territories Magistrate*, claims that shark victims experience an anaesthetic vision of floating away, all danger gone, into the Pacific blue, at the very moment they are being minced in that funnel of teeth. I, Timothy Cavendish, was that swimmer, watching London roll away, yes, you, you sly, toupéed quizmaster of a city, you and your tenements of Somalians; viaducts of Kingdom Brunel; malls of casualized labour; strata of soot-blitzed bricks and muddy bones of doctors Dee, Crippen *et al.*; hot glass office buildings where the blooms of youth harden into aged cacti like my pennypinching brother.

Essex raised its ugly head. When I was a scholarship boy at the local grammar, son of a city-hall toiler on the make, this county was synonymous with liberty, success and Cambridge. Now look at it. Shopping malls and housing estates pursue their creeping invasion of our ancient land. A North Sea wind snatched frilly clouds in its teeth and scarpered off to the Midlands. The countryside proper began at last. My mother had a cousin out here, her family had a big house, I think they moved to Winnipeg for a better life. There! There, in the shadow of that DIY warehouse, once stood a row of walnut trees where me and Pip Oakes – a childhood chum who died aged thirteen under the wheels of an oil tanker – varnished a canoe one summer and sailed it along the Say. Sticklebacks in jars. There, right there, around that bend we lit a fire and cooked beans and potatoes wrapped in silver foil! Come back, oh, come back! Is one glimpse all I get? Hedgeless, featureless fields. Essex *is* Winnipeg, now. Stubble was burnt and the air tasted of crisp bacon sarnies. My thoughts flew off with other fairies, and we were past Saffron Walden when the train juddered to a halt. 'Um . . .' said the intercom. 'John, is this on? John, what button do I press?' Cough. 'SouthNet Trains regrets that this service will make an unscheduled stop at the next station due to . . . a missing driver. This unscheduled stop will continue for the duration that it takes to locate an appropriate driver. SouthNet

Trains assures you we are striving hard –' I clearly discerned a background snigger! '– to restore our normal excellent standard of service.' Rail rage chain-reactioned down the compartments, though in our age crimes are not committed by criminals conveniently at hand but by executive pens far beyond the mob's reach, back in London's postmodern HQs of glass and steel. Half the mob owns shares in what it would pound to atoms, anyway.

So there we sat. I wished I had brought something to read. At least I had a seat, and I wouldn't have given it up for Helen Keller. The evening was lemon blue. Trackside shadows grew monolithic. Commuters sent calls to families on mobile phones. I wondered how that dodgy Australian magistrate knew what flashed through the minds of the shark-eaten. Lucky express trains with non-missing drivers shot past. I needed the loo, but it didn't bear imagining. I opened my briefcase for a bag of Werner's toffees but came up with *Half-lives – The First Luisa Rey Mystery*. I leafed through its first few pages. It would be a better book if Hilary V. Hush weren't so artsily-fartsily Clever. She had written it in neat little chapteroids, doubtless with one eye on the Hollywood screenplay. Static squealed in the speakers. 'This is a passenger announcement. SouthNet Trains regrets that as a suitable driver for this train cannot be located we will proceed to Little Chesterford station where a complimentary coach will transport passengers on to Cambridge. Those able to are recommended to make alternative travel arrangements, as the coach will not reach Little Chesterford station [how that name chimed in my memory!] for . . . an unknown duration. Further details can be found on our website.' The train crawled a mile of twilight. Bats and windborne rubbish overtook us. Who was driving now if there wasn't a driver?

Stop, shudder, doors open. The abler-bodied streamed off the train, over the footbridge, leaving me and a couple of taxidermist's cast-offs to limp in their wake at quarter speed. I heaved myself up the steps, and paused for breath. There I was. Standing on the footbridge of Little Chesterford station. Ye gods, of all the rural stations for a marooning. The bridlepath to Ursula's old house still skirted the cornfield. Not much else did I recognize. The Sacred Barn of the Longest Snog was now Essex's Premier Fitness Club. Ursula had met me in her froggy Citroën that night during reading week in our first term, right . . . on this triangle of gravel, here. How Bohemian, Young Tim had thought, to be met by a woman in a car. I was Tutankhamun IV in my royal barge, rowed by Nubian slaves to the Temple of Sacrifice. Ursula drove me the few hundred yards to Dockery House, commissioned in art-nouveau times by a Scandiwegian consul. We had the place to ourselves, while Mater and Pater were in Greece holidaying with Lawrence Durrell, if memory serves. ('Memory Serves.' Duplicitous couplet.)

Four decades later the beams of headlights from saloon cars in the station car-park lit up a freak plague of daddy long-legs, and one fugitive publishing gentleman in a flapping raincoat striding around a field now lying fallow for EU subsidies. You would think a place the size of England could easily hold all the happenings in one humble lifetime without much overlap, I mean, it's not ruddy Luxembourg we live in, but no, we cross, criss-cross and recross our old tracks like figure skaters. Dockery House was still standing, isolated from its neighbours by a privet fence. How opulent the house had felt after my own parents' bland box of suburbia – *One day*, I promised, *I'm going to live in a house like this.* Another promise I've broken; at least that one was only to myself.

I skirted the edge of the property, down an access road to a building site. A sign read: *Hazle Close – Highly Prized Executive Homes in the Heart of England.* Upstairs at Dockery, lights were on. I imagined a childless couple listening to a wireless. The old stained-glass door had been replaced by something more burglar-proof. That reading week I'd entered Dockery ready to peel off my shameful virginity, but I'd been so in awe of my Divine Cleopatra, so nervous, so eyeballed-up on her father's whisky, so floppy with green sap that, well, I'd rather draw a veil over the embarrassment of that night, even at forty years' remove. Very well, forty-seven years' remove. That same white-leafed oak had scratted at Ursula's window as I attempted to perform, long after I could decently pretend I was still warming up. Ursula had a gramophone record of Rachmaninov's second piano concerto in her bedroom, that room there, where the electric candle glows in the window.

To this day I cannot hear Rachmaninov without flinching.

The odds of Ursula still living at Dockery House were zilch, I knew. Last I heard she was running a PR office in Los Angeles. None the less, I squeezed myself through the evergreen hedge and I pressed my nose up against the unlit, uncurtained dining-room window trying to peer in. That autumn night long ago Ursula had served a blob of grilled cheese on a slice of ham on a breast of chicken. Right there – right here. I could still taste it. I can still taste it as I write these words.

Flash!

The room was lit electric marigold, and in waltzed – backwards, luckily for me – a little witch with red corkscrew curls. 'Mummy!' I half heard, half lipread through the glass. 'Mummy!' and in came Mummy, with the same corkscrew curls. This being proof enough for me that Ursula's family had long vacated the house, I backtracked into the shrubbery – but I turned once more and resumed my spying because . . . well, because, ahem, *je suis un homme solitaire.* Mummy was repairing a broken broomstick while the girl sat on the table swinging her legs. An adult werewolf came in and removed his mask, and, oddly, though not so oddly I suppose, I recognized him – that current-affairs TV presenter, one of Felix Finch's tribe. Jeremy Someone, Heathcliff eyebrows, terrier manners, you know the chap. He took some insulation tape from the Welsh-dresser drawer and muscled in on the broomstick-repair job. Then Grandma entered this domestic frieze and damn me once, damn me twice, damn me always make it nice, 'twas Ursula. The Ursula. My Ursula.

Behold that spry, elderly lady! In my memory she hadn't aged a day – what makeup artist had savaged her dewy youth? (The same one who savaged yours, Timbo.) She spoke, and her daugh-

ter and granddaughter giggled, yes, giggled, and I giggled too
. . . What? What did she say? Tell me the joke! She stuffed a red
stocking with newspaper balls. A devil's tail. She attached it to
her posterior with a safety-pin, and a memory from a university
Hallowe'en Ball cracked on the hard rim of my heart and the yolk
dribbled out – she'd dressed like a devilette then, too, she'd put
on red face-paint, we'd kissed all night, just kissed, and in the
morning we found a builders' café that sold dirty mugs of strong,
milky tea and enough eggs to fill, to kill, the Swiss Army. Toast
and hot canned tomatoes. HP Sauce. Be honest, Cavendish, was
any other breakfast in your life *ever* so delectable?

So drunk was I on nostalgia, I ordered myself to leave before
I did anything stupid. A nasty voice just a few feet away said
this – 'Don't move a muscle or I'll mackasser you and put you
in a *stew*!'

Shocked? Jet-assisted Vertical Ruddy Take-off! Luckily my
would-be butcherer was not a day older than ten and his chainsaw's teeth were cardboard, but his bloodied bandages were
rather effective. In a low voice, I told him so. He wrinkled his
face at me: 'Are you Grandma Ursula's friend?'

'Once upon a time, yes, I was.'

'What have you come to the party as? Where's your costume?'

Time to leave. I edged back into the evergreen. 'This *is* my
costume.'

He picked his nose. 'A dead man digged up from the
churchyard?'

'Charmed, but no. I've come as the Ghost of Christmas Past.'

'But it's Hallowe'en, not Christmas.'

'No!' I slapped my forehead. 'Really?'

'Yeah . . .'

'Then I'm ten months late! This is terrible! I'd better get back
before my absence is noticed – and remarked upon!'

The boy did a cartoon kung-fu pose and waved his chainsaw
at me. 'Not so fast, Green Goblin! You're a trespasser! I'm telling
the police of you!'

War. 'Tell-tale-tit, are you? Two can play at *that* game. If you tell on me, I'll tell my friend the Ghost of Christmas Future where your house is, and do you know what he'll do to you?'

The wide-eyed shitletto shook his head, shaken and stirred.

'When your family is all tucked up asleep in your snug little beds, he'll slide into your house through the crack under the door and *eat – your – puppy*!' The venom in my bile duct pumped fast. 'He'll leave its curly tail under your pillow and you'll get blamed. Your little friends will all scream, "Puppy-slayer!" whenever they see you coming. You'll grow old and friendless and die, alone, miserably, on Christmas morning half a century from now. So if I were you, I wouldn't breathe a word to *anyone* about seeing me.'

I pushed myself through the hedge before he could take it all in. Heading back to the station along the pavement, the wind carried his sob: 'But I don't even *have* a puppy . . .'

I hid behind *Private Eye* in the health centre's Wellness Café, which was doing a fine trade with us maroonees. I half expected a furious Ursula to turn up with her grandchild and a local bobby. Private lifeboats came to rescue the stockbrokers. Old Father Timothy offers this advice to his younger readers, included for free in the price of this memoir: conduct your life in such a way that, when your train breaks down in the eve of your years, you have a warm, dry car driven by a loved one – or a hired one, it matters not – to take you home.

A venerable coach arrived three Scotches later. Venerable? Ruddy Edwardian. I had to endure chatty students all the way to Cambridge. Boyfriend worries, sadistic lecturers, demonic housemates, reality TV, strewth, I had no idea children of their age were so hyperactive. When I finally reached Cambridge station I looked for a telephone box to tell Aurora House not to expect me until the following day, but the first two telephones were vandalized (in Cambridge, I ask you!) and only when I got to the third did I look at the address and see that Denholme had neglected to write the number. I found a hotel for commercial travellers next to a launderette. I forget its name, but I knew from its Reception that the place was a crock of cat-crap, and as usual my first impression was spot on. I was too ruddy whacked to shop around for something nicer, however, and my wallet was too starved. My room had high windows with blinds I couldn't lower because I am not twelve feet tall. The khaki pellets in the bathtub were indeed mouse droppings, the shower knob came off in my hand, and the hot water was tepid. I fumigated the room with cigar smoke and lay on my bed trying to recall the bedrooms of all my lovers, in order, looking down the mucky telescope of time. Prince Rupert and the Boys failed to stir. I felt strangely unconcerned with the idea of the Hoggins Bros plundering my flat back in Putney. Must be lean pickings compared to most of their heists, if *Knuckle Sandwich* is anything to go by. A few nice first editions, but little else of value. My television died the night George Bush II snatched the throne and I haven't dared replace it. Madame X took back her antiques and heirlooms. I ordered a triple Scotch from Room Service – damn me if I'd share a bar with a cabal of salesmen boasting about boobs and bonuses. When my treble whisky finally came it was actually a stingy double so I said so. The ferrety adolescent just shrugged. No apology, just a shrug. I asked him to lower my blind, but he took one look and huffed, 'Can't reach that!' I gave him a frosty 'That will be all, then,' instead of a tip. He broke wind as he left, poisonously. I read more of *Half-lives* but fell asleep just after Rufus Sixsmith was found murdered. In a lucid dream I was looking after a little asylum-seeker boy who begged for a go in one of those rides in the corners of supermarkets you put 50p into. I said, 'Oh, all right,' but when the child climbed out he had turned into Nancy Reagan. How could I explain that to his mother?

I woke up in darkness with a mouth like Superglue. The Mighty Gibbon's assessment of history – *little more than the register of the crimes, follies and misfortunes of mankind* – ticker-taped by for no apparent reason. Timothy Cavendish's time on Earth, in thirteen words. I refought old arguments, then fought arguments that have never even existed. I smoked a cigar until the high windows showed streaks of a watery dawn. I shaved my jowls. A pinched Ulsterwoman downstairs served a choice of burnt or frozen toast with sachets of lipstick-coloured jam and unsalted butter. I remembered Jake Balokowsky's quip about Normandy: Cornwall with something to eat.

Back at the station my woes began afresh when I tried to get a refund on yesterday's disrupted journey. The ticket-wallah, whose pimples bubbled as I watched, was as intractably dense as his counterpart in King's Cross. The corporation breeds them from the same stem cell. My blood pressure neared its record. 'What do you *mean*, yesterday's ticket is now invalid? It's not my fault my ruddy train broke down!'

'Not our fault neither. SouthNet run the trains. We're TicketLords, see.'

'Then to whom do I complain?'

'Well, SouthNet Loco are owned by a holding company in Düsseldorf who are owned by that mobile-phone company in Finland, so you'd be best off trying someone in Helsinki. You should thank your lucky stars it wasn't a derailment. Get a lot of those, these days.'

Sometimes the fluffy bunny of incredulity zooms round the bend so rapidly that the greyhound of language is left, agog, in the starting cage. A feisty stagger was needed to reach the next train before it left – only to find it had been cancelled! But, 'luckily', the train before mine was so late that it still hadn't departed. All the seats were taken, and I had to squeeze into a three-inch slot. I lost my balance when the train pulled away, but a human crumple zone buffered my fall. We stayed like that, half fallen. The Diagonal People.

Cambridge outskirts are all science parks now. Ursula and I went punting below that quaint bridge, where those Biotech Space Age cuboids now sit cloning humans for shady Koreans. Oh, ageing is ruddy unbearable! The I's we were yearn to breathe the world's air again, but can they ever break out from these calcified cocoons? Oh, can they hell.

*

Witchy trees bent before the enormous sky. Our train had made an unscheduled and unexplained stop on a blasted heath, for how long, I do not recall. My watch was stuck in the middle of last night. (I miss my Ingersoll, even today.) My fellow passengers' features melted into forms that were half familiar: an estate agent behind me, yacking on his mobile telephone, I could *swear* he was my sixth-form hockey captain; the grim woman two seats ahead, reading *A Moveable Feast*, isn't she that Inland Revenue gorgon who gave me such a grilling a few years ago?

Finally the couplings whimpered and the train limped off at a slow haul to another country station whose flaky nameboard read 'Adlestrop'. A voice with a bad cold announced: 'Centrallo Trains regrets that due to a braking-systems failure this train will make a brief stop at this –' sneeze '– station. Passengers are directed to alight here . . . and wait for a substitute train.' My fellow travellers gasped, groaned, swore, shook their heads. 'Centrallo Trains apologizes for any –' sneeze '– inconvenience this may cause, and assures you we are working hard to restore our normal excellent standard of –' huge sneeze '– service. Gi'us a tissue, John.'

Fact: rolling stock in this country is built in Hamburg or somewhere, and when the German engineers test British-bound trains, they use imported lengths of our buggered, privatised tracks because the decently maintained European rails won't provide accurate testing conditions. Who really won the ruddy war? I should have fled the Hogginses up the Great North Road on a ruddy pogo stick.

I elbowed my way into the grubby café, bought a pie that tasted of shoe-polish and a pot of tea with cork crumbs floating in it, and eavesdropped on a pair of Shetland-pony breeders. Despondency makes one hanker after lives one never led. Why have you given your life to books, TC? Dull, dull, dull! The memoirs are bad enough, but all that ruddy fiction! Hero goes on a journey, stranger comes to town, somebody wants something, they get it or they don't, will is pitted against will. 'Admire me, for I am a metaphor.'

I groped my way to the ammonia-smelling gents' where a joker had stolen the bulb. I had just unzipped myself when a voice arose from the shadows. 'Hey, mistah, got a light or sumfink?' Steadying my cardiac arrest, I fumbled for my lighter. The flame conjured a Rastafarian in Holbein embers, just a few inches away, a cigar held in his thick lips. 'Fanks,' whispered my black Virgil, inclining his head to bring the tip into the flame.

'You're, erm, most welcome, quite,' I said.

His wide flat nose twitched. 'So, where you heading, man?'

My hand checked my wallet was still there. 'Hull . . .' A witless fib ran wild. 'To return a novel. To a librarian who works there. A very famous poet. At the university. It's in my bag. It's called *Half-lives*.' The Rastafarian's cigar smelt of compost. I can never guess what they're really thinking. Not that I've ever really known any. I'm not a racialist, but I do believe the ingredients in so-called melting pots take generations to melt. 'Mistah,' the Rastafarian told me, 'you need . . .' and I flinched '. . . some o' this.' I obeyed his offer and sucked on his turd-thick cigar.

Ruddy hell! 'What *is* this stuff?'

He made a noise like a didgeridoo at the root of his throat. 'That don't grow in Marlboro Country.' My head enlarged itself by a magnitude of many hundreds, *Alice*-style, and became a multi-storey car park wherein dwelt a thousand-and-one operatic Citroëns. 'My word, you can say that again,' mouthed the Man Formerly Known As Tim Cavendish.

Next thing I remember, I was on the train again, wondering who had walled up my compartment with moss-stained bricks. 'We're ready for you now, Mr Cavendish,' a bald, spectacled coot told me. Nobody was there, or anywhere. Only a cleaner, making his way down the vacant train, putting litter into a sack. I lowered myself on to the platform. The cold sank its fangs into my exposed neck and frisked me for uninsulated patches. Back in King's Cross? No, this was wintriest Gdansk. In a panic I realized I didn't have my bag and umbrella. I climbed aboard and retrieved them from the luggage rack. My muscles seemed to have atrophied in my sleep. Outside, a baggage cart passed, driven by a Modigliani. Where in hell *was* this place?

'Yurrin Hulpal,' the Modigliani answered.

Arabic? My brain proposed the following: a Eurostar train had stopped at Adlestrop, I had boarded and slept all the way to Istanbul Central. Addled brain. I needed a clear sign, in English. WELCOME TO HULL.

Praise be, my journey was nearly over. When had I last been this far north? Never, that's when. I gulped cold air to stub out a sudden urge to throw up, that's right, Tim, drink it down. The offended stomach supplies pictures of the cause of its discomfort, and the Rastafarian's cigar flashed before me. The station was painted in all-blacks. I rounded a corner and found two luminous clock-faces hung above the exit, but clocks in disagreement are worse than no clock at all. No watcher at the gates wanted to see my exorbitantly priced ticket, and I felt cheated. Out front a kerb-crawler prowled here, a window blinked there, music waxed and waned from a pub across the bypass. 'Spare change?' asked, no, demanded, no, accused, a miserable dog in a blanket. His master's nose, eyebrows and lips were so pierced with ironmongery that a powerful electro-magnet would have shredded his face in a single pass. What do these people do at airport metal detectors? 'Got any change?' I saw myself as he saw me, a frail old giffer in a friendless late city. The dog rose, scenting vulnerability. An invisible guardian took my elbow and led me to a taxi rank.

The taxi seemed to have been going round the same roundabout for a miniature eternity. A howling singer on the radio strummed a song about how everything that dies some day comes back. (Heaven forfend – remember the Monkey's Paw!) The driver's head was far, far too big for his shoulders, he must have that Elephant Man disease, but when he turned round I made out his turban. He was bemoaning his clientele. '*Always* they say, "Bet it ain't this cold where you're from, eh?" and always I say, "Dead wrong, mate. You've obviously never visited Manchester in February."'

'You do know the way to Aurora House, don't you?' I asked, and the Sikh said, 'Look, we've arrived already.' The narrow driveway ended at an imposing Edwardian residence of indeterminate size. 'Sick teen-squid Zachary.'

'I don't know anyone of that name.'

He looked at me, puzzled, then repeated, 'Sixteen – quid – exactly.'

'Oh. Yes.' My wallet was not in my trouser pockets, or my jacket pocket. Or my shirt pocket. Nor did it reappear in my trouser pockets. The awful truth smached my face. 'I've been ruddy robbed!'

'I resent the insinuation. My taxi has a municipal meter.'

'No, you don't understand, my wallet's been stolen.'

'Oh, then I understand.' Good, he understands. 'I understand very well!' The wrath of the sub-continent swarmed in the dark. 'You're thinking, "That curry-muncher knows whose side the fuzz'll take."'

'Nonsense!' I protested. 'Look, I've got coins, change, yes, a pocketful of change . . . here . . . yes, thank God! Yes, I think I've got it . . .'

He counted his ducats: 'Tip?'

'Take it . . .' I had emptied all the shrapnel into his other hand and scrambled outside, straight into a ditch. From my accident-victim's eye-view I saw the taxi speed away and I suffered a disagreeable backflash to my Greenwich mugging. It wasn't the watch or even the bruises or the shock that had scarred me so. It was that I was a man who had once faced down and bested a quartet of Arab ragamuffins in Aden, but in the girls' eyes I was . . . old, merely old. Not behaving the way an old man should – invisible, silent and scared – was, itself, sufficient provocation.

I scaled the ramp up to the imposing glass doors. The reception area glowed grail gold. I knocked, and a woman who could have been cast for the stage musical of *Florence Nightingale* smiled at me. I felt like someone had waved a magic wand and said, 'Cavendish, all your troubles are over!'

Florence let me in. 'Welcome to Aurora House, Mr Cavendish!'

'Oh, thank you, thank you. Today has been too ruddy awful for words.'

An angel incarnate. 'The main thing is you've arrived safely now.'

'Look, there is a slight fiscal embarrassment I should mention at this time. You see, on my way here—'

'All you need to worry about now is getting a good night's sleep. Everything is taken care of. Just sign here and I can show you to your room. It's a nice quiet one overlooking the garden. You'll love it.'

Moist-eyed with gratitude, I followed her to my sanctuary. The hotel was modern, spotless, with very soft lighting in the sleepy corridors. I recognized aromas from my childhood, but couldn't quite identify them. Up the wooden hill to Bedfordshire. My room was simple, its sheets crisp and clean, with towels ready on the heated rail. 'Will you be all right from now, Mr Cavendish?'

'Bliss, my dear.'

'Sweet dreams, then.' I knew they would be. I took a quick shower, slipped into my jim-jams, and cleaned my teeth. My bed was firm but comfy as beaches in Tahiti. The Hoggins Horrors were east of the Horn, I was Scot Free, and Denny, dearest Denholme, was footing my bill. Brother in need, brother indeed. Sirens sang in my marshmallow pillows. In the morning life would begin afresh, afresh, afresh. This time round I would do everything right.

'In the morning'. Fate is fond of booby-trapping those three little words. I awoke to discover a not-so-young woman with a pageboy haircut rifling through my personal effects like a bargain hunter. 'What the *ruddy hell* are you doing in my room, you pilfering warty sow?' I half roared, half wheezed.

The female put down my jacket without guilt. 'Because you are new I will not have you eat soap powder. This time. Be warned. I do not stand for offensive language in Aurora House.

Not from anyone. And I never make idle threats, Mr Cavendish. Never.'

A robber reprimanding his victim for bad language! 'I'll ruddy well talk to you how I ruddy well like, you stinking ruddy thief! Make me eat soap powder? I'd like to see you try! Let's call Hotel Security! Let's call the police! You ask about offensive language, and I'll ask about breaking, entry and theft!'

She came over to my bed and slapped me hard across the chops.

I was so shocked I just fell back on to my pillow.

'A disappointing start. I am Mrs Noakes. You do not wish to cross me.'

Was this some sort of a kinky S&M hotel? Had a madwoman broken into my room after learning my name from the hotel register?

'Smoking is discouraged here. I will have to confiscate these cigars. The lighter is far too dangerous for you to play with. And what, pray, are these?' She dangled my keys.

'Keys. What do you think they are?'

'Keys go walkies! Let's give them to Mrs Judd for safekeeping, shall we?'

'Let's not to give them to anyone, you crazy dragon! You *strike* me! You *rob* me! What kind of ruddy hotel hires *thieves* for chambermaids?'

The creature stuffed her booty into a little burglar's bag. 'No more valuables to be taken care of?'

'Put those items back! Now! Or I'll have your job, I swear it!'

'I'll take that as a "no". Breakfast is eight *sharp*. Boiled eggs with toast soldiers today. None for the tardy.'

I got dressed the moment she was gone, and looked for the phone. There wasn't one. After a very quick wash – my bathroom had been designed for disabled people, it was all rounded edges and fitted with handrails – I hurried to Reception, determined to have due justice. I had acquired a limp but was unsure how. I was lost. Baroque music lilted in identical chair-lined corridors. A leprous gnome gripped my wrist and showed me a jar of hazelnut butter. 'If you want to take this home, I'll jolly well tell you why I *don't*.'

'You've mistaken me for someone else.' I scraped the creature's hand off mine, and passed through a dining-room area where the guests were seated in rows and waitresses were bringing bowls in from the kitchen.

What was so odd?

The youngest guests were in their seventies. The oldest guests were three hundred plus. Was it the week after the schools went back?

I had it. You probably spotted it pages ago, dear Reader.

Aurora House was a nursing home for the elderly.

That ruddy brother of mine! This was his idea of a joke!

Mrs Judd and her Oil of Olay smile were manning Reception. 'Hello, Mr Cavendish. Feeling super this morning?'

'Yes. No. An absurd misunderstanding has occurred.'

'Is that a fact?'

'It most certainly is a fact. I checked in last night believing Aurora House was a *hotel*. My brother made the booking, you see. But . . . oh, it's his idea of a practical joke. Not in the least bit funny. His contemptible ruse that only "worked" because a Rastafarian gave me a puff of a sinister cigar in Adlestrop, and also, the ruddy stem-cell twins who sold me my ticket here, they wore me out so. But listen. You have a bigger problem closer to home – some demented bitch called Noakes is running about the place impersonating a chambermaid. She's probably riddled with Alzheimer's but, yowie, she's got a slap on her. She stole my keys! Now, in a go-go bar in Phuket, that'd be par for the course, but in an old wrecks' home in Hull? You'd get closed down if I was an inspector, you know.'

Mrs Judd's smile was now battery acid.

'I want my keys back,' she made me say. 'Right away.'

'Aurora House is your home now, Mr Cavendish. Your signature authorizes us to apply compliancy. And I'd get out of the habit of referring to my sister in those tones.'

'Compliancy? Signature? *Sister*?'

'The custody document you signed last night. Your residency papers.'

'No, no, no. That was the hotel registry! Never mind, it's all academic. I'll be on my way after breakfast. Make that before breakfast, I smelt the slops! My, this will make a heck of a dinner-party story. Once I've strangled my brother. Bill him, by the way. Only I must insist on having my keys returned. And you'd better call me a cab.'

'Most of our guests get cold feet on their first mornings.'

'My feet are quite warm, but I haven't made myself clear. If you don't—'

'Mr Cavendish, why don't you eat your breakfast first and—'

'Keys!'

'We have your written permission to hold your valuables in the office safe.'

'Then I must speak with the management.'

'That would be my sister, Nurse Noakes.'

'Noakes? Management?'

'Nurse Noakes.'

'Then I must speak with the board of governors, or the owner.'

'They would be me.'

'Look.' Gulliver and Lilliputians. 'You're breaking the ruddy . . . Anti-incarceration Act, or whatever it is.'

'You'll find temper tantrums won't help you at Aurora House.'

'Your telephone, please. I wish to call the police.'

'Residents aren't permitted to—'

'I am *not* a ruddy resident! And since you won't give me back my keys, I'll be back later this morning with one very pissed-off officer of the law.' I shoved the main door but it shoved back harder. Some ruddy security lock. I tried the fire door across the porch. Locked. Over Mrs Judd's protests I smashed a release catch with a little hammer, the door opened, and I was a free man. Ruddy hell, the cold smacked my face with an iron spade! Now I knew why northerners go in for beards, woad and body grease. I marched down the curving driveway through worm-blasted rhododendrons, resisting a strong temptation to break into a run. I haven't run since the mid-seventies. I was level with a lawnmower contraption when a shaggy giant in groundsman's overalls rose from the Earth like Ye Greene Knycht. He was removing the remains of a hedgehog from its blades with his bloody hands. 'Off somewhere?'

'You bet I am! To the land of the living.' I strode on. Leaves turned to soil beneath my feet. Thus it is, trees eat themselves. I was disorientated to discover how the drive wound back to the dining-room annexe. I had taken a bad turn. The Undead of Aurora House watched me through the wall of glass. 'Soylent Green is people!' I mocked their hollow stares, 'Soylent Green is made of people!' They looked puzzled – I am, alas, the Last of my Tribe. One of the wrinklies tapped on the window and pointed behind me. I turned and the ogre slung me over his shoulder. My breath was squeezed out with his every stride. He *stank* of fertilizer. 'I've better things to do than this . . .'

'Then go and do them!' I struggled in vain to get him in a neck-lock, but I don't think he even noticed. So I used my superior powers of language to chain the villain: 'You cruddy ruddy rugger-bugger yob! This is GBH! This is illegal confinement!'

He bear-hugged me several degrees tighter to silence me, and I am afraid I bit his ear. A strategic mistake. In one powerful yank my trousers were pulled from my waist – was he going to bugger me? What he did was even less pleasant. He laid me on the body of his mowing machine, pinned me down with one hand, and caned me with a bamboo cane in the other. The pain cracked across my unfleshy shanks, once, twice, again-again, again-again, again-again!

Christ, such pain!

I shouted, then cried, then whimpered for him to stop. Whack! Whack! Whack! Nurse Noakes finally ordered the giant to desist. My buttocks were two giant wasp stings! The woman's voice hissed in my ear: 'The world outside has no place for you.

Aurora House is where you live now. Is reality sinking in? Or shall I ask Mr Withers here to go over things one more time?'

'Tell her to go to hell,' warned my spirit, 'or you'll regret it later.'

'Tell her what she wants to hear,' shrieked my nervous system, 'or you'll regret it *now*.'

The spirit was willing but the flesh was weak.

I was sent to my room without breakfast. I plotted vengeance, litigation and torture. I inspected my cell. Door, locked from outside, no keyhole. Window that opened only six inches. Heavy-duty sheets made of egg-carton fibres with plastic under-sheet. Armchair, washable seat-cover. Moppable carpet. 'Easy-wipe' wallpaper. 'En-suite' bathroom: soap, shampoo, flannel, ratty towel, no window. Picture of cottage captioned: *A House is Made by Hands, but a Home is Made by Hearts.* Prospects for break-out: piss-poor.

Still, I believed my confinement would not last until noon. One of several exits must open up. The management would realize its mistake, apologize profusely, sack the Offending Noakes and beg me to take compensation in cash. Or, Denholme would learn his gag had backfired and command my release. Or, the accountant would realize nobody was paying my bills and boot me out. Or, Mrs Latham would report me missing, my disappearance would feature on *Crimewatch UK* and the police would trace my whereabouts.

Around eleven the door was unlocked. I readied myself to reject apologies and go for the jugular. A once-stately woman sailed in. Seventy years old, eighty, eighty-five, who knows when they're that old? A rickety greyhound in a blazer followed his mistress. 'Good morning,' began the woman. I stood, and did not offer my visitors a seat.

'I beg to differ.'

'My name is Gwendolin Bendincks.'

'Don't blame me.'

Nonplussed, she took the armchair. 'This . . .' she indicated the greyhound '. . . is Gordon Warlock-Williams. Why don't you take a seat? We head the Residents' Committee.'

'Very nice for you, but since I am not a—'

'I had intended to introduce myself at breakfast, but the morning's unpleasantness occurred before we could take you under our wing.'

'All water under the bridge, now, Cavendish,' gruffed Gordon Warlock-Williams. 'No-one'll mention it again, boyo, rest assured.' Welsh, yes, he would have to be Welsh.

Mrs Bendincks leant forward. 'But understand this, Mr Cavendish: boat-rockers are not welcome here.'

'Then expel me! I beg you!'

'Aurora House does not expel,' said the sanctimonious moo, 'but you will be medicated, if your behaviour warrants it, for your own protection.'

Ominous, no? I had seen *One Flew Over the Cuckoo's Nest* with an extraordinarily talentless but wealthy and widowed poetess whose collected works, *Verses Wild & Wayward*, I was annotating, but who transpired to be less widowed than initially claimed. 'Look, I'm sure you're a reasonable woman.' The oxymoron passed without comment. 'So read my lips. I am *not supposed to be here.* I checked into Aurora House believing it to be a hotel.'

'Ah, but we *do* understand, Mr Cavendish!' Gwendolin Bendincks nodded.

'No you don't!'

'Everyone's visited by the Glum Family at first, but you'll soon cheer up when you see how your loved ones have acted in your best interests.'

'All my "loved ones" are dead or bonkers or at the BBC, except my prankster brother!' You can see it, can't you, dear Reader? I was a man in a horror B-movie asylum. The more I ranted and raged, the more I proved that I was exactly where I should be.

'*This* is the best hotel you'll ever stay in, boyo!' His teeth were biscuit-coloured. Were he a horse, you couldn't have given him away. 'A five-star one, look you. Meals get provided, all your laundry is done. Activities laid on, from crochet to croquet. No confusing bills, no youngsters joy-riding in your motor. Aurora House is a ball! Just obey the regulations and stop rubbing Nurse Noakes up the wrong way. She's not a cruel woman.'

'"Unlimited power in the hands of limited people *always* leads to cruelty."' Warlock-Williams looked at me as if I had spoken in tongues. 'Solzhenitsyn.'

'Betws-y-coed was always good enough for Marjorie and me. But look here! I felt just like you in my first week. Barely spoke to a soul, eh, Mrs Bendincks, a major sourpuss, eh?'

'A maximus sourpuss, Mr Warlock-Williams!'

'But now I'm happy as a pig in clover! Eh?'

Mrs Bendincks smiled, 'twas a ghastly sight. 'We're here to help you reorientate. Now, I understand you were in publishing. Sadly,' she tapped her head, 'Mrs Birkin is less able to record Residents' Committee meetings minutes than she once was. A fine opportunity for *you* to jolly well get *involved*!'

'I still *am* in publishing! Do I *look* like I should be here?' The silence was intolerable. 'Oh, get out!'

'Disappointed.' She gazed at the leaf-littered lawn, dotted with wormcasts. 'Aurora House is your world now, Mr Cavendish.' My head was cork and the corkscrew was Gwendolin Bendincks. 'Yes, you are in a Rest Home. The day has come. Your stay can be miserable or pleasant. But your stay is permanent. Think on, Mr Cavendish.' She knocked on the door. Unseen forces let my tormentors exit but slammed it shut in my face.

I noticed that for the duration of the interview my flies had been wide open.

Behold your future, Cavendish the Younger. You will not apply for membership, but the tribe of the elderly will claim you. Your present will not keep pace with the world's. This slippage will stretch your skin, sag your skeleton, erode your hair and memory, make your skin turn opaque so your twitching organs and blue-cheese veins will be semi-visible. You will venture out only in daylight, avoiding weekends and school holidays. Language, too, will leave you behind, betraying your tribal affiliations whenever you speak. On escalators, on trunk roads, in supermarket aisles, the living will overtake you, incessantly. Elegant women will not see you. Store detectives will not see you. Salespeople will not see you, unless they sell stair-lifts or fraudulent insurance policies. Only babies, cats and drug addicts will acknowledge your existence. So do not fritter away your days. Sooner than you fear, you will stand before a mirror in a care home, look at your body, and think, ET, locked in a ruddy cupboard for a fortnight.

A sexless automaton brought lunch on a tray. I'm not being insulting, but I truly couldn't tell if she or he was a he or a she. It had a slight moustache but tiny breasts too. I thought about knocking it out cold and making a Steve McQueen dash for liberty, but I had no weapon except a bar of soap and nothing to tie it up with except my belt.

Lunch was a tepid lamb chop. The potatoes were starch-grenades. The canned carrots were revolting because that is their nature. 'Look,' I begged the automaton, 'at least bring me some Dijon mustard.' It showed no evidence of understanding. 'Coarse grain, or medium. I'm not fussy.' She turned to go. 'Wait! You – speak-ee – English?' She was gone. My dinner outstared me.

My strategy had been wrong from square one. I had tried to shout my way out of this absurdity, but the institutionalized cannot do this. Slavers welcome the odd rebel to dress down before the others. In all the prison literature I've read, from *Gulag Archipelago* to *An Evil Cradling* to *Knuckle Sandwich*, rights must be horse-traded and accrued with cunning. Prisoner resistance merely justifies an ever-fiercer imprisonment in the minds of the imprisoners.

Now was the season for subterfuge. I should take copious notes for my eventual compensation settlement. I should be courteous to the Black Noakes. But as I pushed cold peas on to my plastic fork a chain of firecrackers exploded in my skull and the old world came to an abrupt end.

An Orison of Sonmi~451

Historians still unborn will appreciate your cooperation in the future, Sonmi~451. We archivists thank you in the present. Our gratitude may not mean much, but I'll endeavour to grant any last request you may have, if it lies within my ministry's influence. Now, this silver egg-shaped device is called an orison. It records both an image of your face and your words. Once we're finished, the orison will be archived at the Ministry of Testaments. This isn't an interrogation, remember, or a trial. Your version of the truth is what matters.

No other version of the truth has ever mattered to me.

Let's begin. Usually, I start by asking interviewees to recall their very earliest memories. You look uncertain.

I have no earliest memories, Archivist. Every day of my life in Papa Song's was as uniform as the fries we vended.

Then would you please describe that world.

It was a sealed dome about eighty metres across, a dinery owned by Papa Song Corp. Servers spend twelve working years without venturing outside this space, ever. The décor is starred and striped in reds, yellows and the rising sun. Its celsius is adjusted to Outside; warmer in winter, cooler in summer. Our dinery was on the minus ninth floor under Chongmyo Plaza. Instead of windows, AdVs decorated the walls. Set into the eastern wall was the dinery elevator; the sole entrance and exit. North was the Seer's office; west, his Aides' room; south, the servers' dormroom. Consumers' hygieners were ingressed at north-east, south-east, south-west and north-west. The Hub sat in the centre. Here the diners ordered their meals; we input their orders, debited their Souls on the tellers, then trayed their meals. Rising from the Hub is Papa Song's Plinth. Here He performs antics for the amusement of the diners.

Antics?

Various 3D conjuring tricks; drinking styros of guavaberry with a finger; juggling fiery burgers; sneezing moths. Children love His gentle demeanor; of course His servers love Him too. We knew no mother or father but Papa Song, our corp Logoman.

How many staff worked in the dinery?

Fourteen, approx. A standard Papa Song dinery employs one human Seer, two or three Aides and houses twelve servers; usually three members of four stem-types. During my freshfaced year, we had three Hwa-Soons, three Yoonas, three Ma-Leu-Das, and three Sonmis; this complement was enough to cope with hours of peak demand. Four hundred consumers could be seated, but on Ninth Nites and Tenth Days such large crowds came in from the Corpocracy Sports Stadium that consumers dined standing up.

Can you describe a server's schedule?

Hour four thirty is yellow-up. Stimulin enters the airflow to rouse us from our cots. We file into the hygiener; then we steam-clean. Back in our dormroom we dress in a fresh uniform; then gather around the Hub with our Seer and his Aides. Papa Song appears on His Plinth for Matins, and we recite the Six Catechisms together. Our Logoman then delivers His Sermon. At a minute before hour five we go to our positions around the Hub.

The elevator brings the day's first consumers. For nineteen hours we greet diners, input orders, tray food, vend drinks, upstock condiments, wipe tables, bin garbage, clean consumers' hygieners and pray our honorable diners to debit their Souls on our Hub tellers.

You have no rests?

'Rests' constitute time-theft, Archivist! Hour zero is curfew, of course, so all consumers are gone by then. We clean every centimeter in the dinery by zero thirty, then assemble around the Plinth for Vespers, then file to the dormroom where we imbibe our sacs of Soap. By zero forty-five the soporifix take effect. In under four hours, the solars yellow-up for a new working shift, and another day begins.

Is it true, fabricants really dream, just like us?
Yes, Archivist, we really dream. I used to dream often about seeing Hawaii over the turquoise waves; of life in Xultation; of praise from Papa Song; of my sisters, consumers, Seer Rhee and the Aides. We have nitemares, too; of angry diners, foodtube blockages, lost collars and shameful destarrings.

What have your dreams been about here in prison?
Strange cities; pursuit across black-and-white lands; my future xecution in the Lighthouse; I was dreaming of Hae-Joo Im just before the guard woke me to show you in. Both in Papa Song's and in this cube, my dreams are the single unpredictable factor in my zoned days and nights. Nobody allots them, or censors them. Dreams are all I have ever truly owned.

Do servers never wonder about the bigger world outside the dome, or did you believe your dinery *was* the whole cosmos?
Our cosmology is not so crude, or our intelligence so limited. We saw Outside on AdV; Papa Song showed us scenes of Xultation; and we knew the consumers and the food that we served them must come from somewhere.

However, Soap deadens curiosity; we preferred not to wonder.

It's difficult to imagine, living with so many . . . imponderables.
When you were three or four, Archivist, your father vanished daily to a realm called 'Work', did he not? He stayed at 'Work' until curfew, but you didn't worry yourself over the dimensions, location or nature of that realm because your concerns lay xclusively in your foreground. This is how indoor fabricants view that place known as 'Outside'.

So you never wanted to step in the elevator and just . . . y'know, go see?
How pureblooded are your questions, Archivist! No elevator functions without a Soul aboard.

Fair point. Did you have a sense of time? Of the future?

Yes: as governed by Catechism Six.

Which states?

One Year, One Star, Twelve Stars to Xultation! At the Star Sermon on New Year's morning, our twelvestarred sisters made the sign of the dollar, genuflected, then left by the Exit for the voyage aboard Papa Song's golden Ark. On 3D we saw them again as they embarked for Hawaii; later, their arrival at Xultation; soon after, their transformation into busy, well-dressed consumers. Their collars were gone; they showed us their topaz Souls in their fingers; they waved from a world beyond our lexicon. Boutiques, hairdressers, dineries; green seas, rose skies; wildflowers, rainbows, lace, ponies, cottages, footpaths, butterflies. How we marvelled! How happy our sisters looked. They xhorted us to work hard; earn our stars with diligence; repay the Investment; and join them on Xultation as soon as possible.

'As soon as possible'? I thought your working life was set at twelve years?

If a server reports a sister's deviance, she is awarded one star from the deviant's badge, and Xultation comes a year nearer. Destarring is an efficient deterrent. I only ever saw one.

Ah, yes, the notorious Yoona~939. Can you remember meeting her?

I can. My first impression was negative. Ma-Leu-Das tend to awe freshfaceds; Hwa-Soons boss us; Yoonas seem aloof and sullen, and Yoona~939 was no xception. I wished to be partnered with another Sonmi, but Seer Rhee divided his stem-types evenly around the Hub tellers. Yoona~939 and I worked side by side; our dormroom cots, too, were side by side.

My opinion of her changed by my first Tenth Day. She was not aloof, but watchful; her ivory eyes were not sullen, but eloquent. Her inner character had colors that attracted me; she reciprocated my desire for friendship; she warned me when Seer Rhee's inspections were due; she decifered drunk diners' orders. It is thanks to the intended and unintended lessons she taught me that I survived my time at Papa Song's.

These 'colors' you mention, were they a result of her ascension?

Student Boom-Sook's research notes were so chaotic I could not ascertain when the xperiment on Yoona~939 was triggered; but from my own xperience, I believe ascension only frees what was suppressed by Soap. Ascension doesn't implant traits that were never present. Despite what purebloods strive so hard to convince themselves, fabricants' minds differ greatly, even if their features and bodies do not.

'Despite what purebloods strive so hard to convince themselves'? Why do you say that?

To enslave an individual distresses the conscience, but to enslave a clone is merely like owning the latest mass-produced six-wheeled ford. In fact, all fabricants, even same-stem fabricants, are singular as snowflakes. Pureblood naked eyes cannot discern these differences, but they exist.

When did Yoona~939's deviances become apparent to you?

Questions of 'when' are problematic in a world with no calendar or windows. The first outward sign of Yoona's ascension was her speech. This began around Month Six. First, she spoke more. Catechism does not decree silence in the dormroom or hygiener, but Seer Rhee rebuked us if we spoke without cause. Yoona began speaking during quiet periods at the Hub, or during cleaning; about consumers, manners and dress; gossip about the Seer and Aides. Even in the hygiener, and as we imbibed our Soap. It amused all of us, at first, even the Ma-Leu-Das.

Yoona's language then grew more complex; she became difficult to understand. Orientation teaches us the vocabulary we need for our work, but the amnesiads in our Soap erase subsequently learnt words. Yoona's speech was filled with blanks the rest of us could not register. She sounded pureblood.

What other deviances showed themselves?

Yoona~939 mimicked the consumers. When we mopped the diners' hygiener, Yoona pretended to be an ill-mannered pureblood. She yawned, chewed, sneezed, burped and acted drunk.

She hummed Papa Song's Psalm in absurd deviations. She took pleasure in making me laugh. Laughter is an anarchic blasphemy. Tyrants are wise to fear it.

And when did Yoona~939 actually violate a Catechism in public?

During Month Eight Yoona broke Catechism Five. This forbids a server to address a diner uninvited. A mother consumer and her young son ordered seaweed doodlemoos, but the chute was peakjammed so Yoona prayed them to wait. The bored boy asked why some servers look xactly alike. His mother xplained we were grown in the same wombtank, like radishes in his biology class. The boy then asked what wombtank *he* had been grown in. Two straws, queried his mother, blushing slitely, or three? The boy persisted: who looked after the fabricants' babies while we worked here? Fabricants don't have babies, replied Mother, because they don't want them. The boy considered this, then asked if Aunt Ae-Sook was fabricant too?

Mother said fabricants don't worry about dollars, tests, insurance, rising upstrata or sinking downstrata, sickness or birth quotas. She waved her hand at Yoona and me; these lucky clones, she said, labour for a mere twelve years before they retire to paradise in Hawaii. That is why servers always smile.

Yoona said, 'Trash, madam.'

She said *that* to a consumer! What did the woman do?

Her amazement equalled your own, Archivist. Flabbergasted, she verified that Yoona was addressing her.

'I am.' Yoona did not stop. '*You* work on this Hub for nineteen hours, ten days a week, twelve years a life; *you* serve abusive consumers; *you* abase yourself to a Seer, Aides and a Logoman; *you* obey our Catechisms; do all these, then tell me fabricants are the happiest stratum in the State. We smile because we are genomed to do so. "Happy", you call us? I would end my life now, but all the knives in this prison are plastic. Madam.'

The boy stared at Yoona~939, wide-eyed, then sobbed.

The mother grabbed her son and fled to the exit.

Why didn't the mother report Yoona~939's deviance, then or afterwards?
Maybe the woman was numb with shock; maybe she was a covert Abolitionist; maybe she did file a complaint, but Unanimity buried it to protect their xperiment. I shall never know for sure.

There were no other witnesses to the transgression?
Ma-Leu-Da~801 was the third sister serving west. She 'hated' Yoona~939 for befriending the freshface and because she was a hateful Ma-Leu-Da. She let Yoona's outburst go unreported, but I glimpsed cunning in her xpression. I begged Yoona to be more cautious, but my friend was indifferent.

In my experience, servers have trouble threading a sentence of five words. How did Yoona develop her verbal skills in that hermetic world?
Ascension absorbs language as dry soil absorbs water. Words you don't even know you own fly out of your mouth. Remember, Archivist, Yoona was no ordinary server and no dinery is truly hermetic. Every prison has jailers and jailers are ducts. During my own ascension I, too, collected new words, grammar and idioms from our Seer and his Aides, Papa Song, AdVs, the diners and their sonys.

A more general question. Were you happy in those days?
Is happiness the absence of deprivation? If so, servers are, as purebloods like to believe, the happiest stratum in the corpocracy. But if happiness is the conquest of adversity, or the sensation of being valued and fulfilled, then of all Nea So Copros' slaves we are surely the most miserable.

There are no slaves in Nea So Copros! The very word is abolished!
Archivist: is your youth genuine or dewdrugged? Why were you assigned to my 'unprecedented' case? I don't mean to offend you.

You're not offending me. My presence here is a compromise. Unanimity insisted that a heretic had nothing to offer the state archives but sedition. Genomicists pulled levers on the Juche to get Rule 54.iii enforced against

Unanimity's wishes, but had not reckoned on senior archivists watching your trial and judging your case too hazardous to risk their reputations on. I am only an eighth-stratum archivist at our uninfluential Ministry, but when I petitioned to be assigned your case, approval was granted before I could change my mind. There. Your 'confessor' has confessed.

So you are gambling your entire career on my Testimony?

. . . That is more or less the truth of the matter, yes.

I learned to xpect only duplicity from my interrogators, but your frankness is refreshing.

A duplicitious archivist wouldn't be much use to anyone! Could you tell me a little about Seer Rhee? He played a major part in your life at Papa Song's, and testified against you at your trial. What manner of man was he?

Seer Rhee was a corp man, to the bone. His ultimate goal in life was to attain the strata of xec in the Papa Song Corp; a vain hope. He had long passed the age when Seers are promoted to strata of real power. Rhee clung to the belief that hard work and a blemishless record were enough to achieve what he craved. He curfewed most nights in his office; was respectful to all diners; sycofantic to superiors; a whipman to his fabricants; and courteous to his many cuckolds, whom he hoped would pluck him from obscurity as they moved upstrata.

Did you say, 'his many *cuckolds*'?

Seer Rhee must be understood in the context of his wife. Mrs Rhee used her husband as a dollar-udder. She had sold her male-child quota years before, made shrewd investments of her own and spent her husband's salary on dewdrugs and facescaping so that her seventy years passed for thirty. Mrs Rhee visited the dinery to inspect the latest male Aides. She must have had some influence in the Papa Song hierarchy; Yoona~939 told me that Aides who obliged her could xpect promotion to a more prestigious dinery. Bleakest Manchuria awaited the hapless young men who didn't.

How come she never used this influence on her own husband's behalf?

I don't know the inner mechanics of their marriage, Archivist, and cannot speculate. You will have to ask Mrs Rhee that question.

But why did Seer Rhee tolerate such . . . ongoing humiliation?
First: his wife xuded glamour at corp functions, compensating for his own deficit. Second: no Boardman was ever a divorcee. Third: because he had to.

Did Yoona~939 threaten Seer Rhee's blemishless record, do you think?
I am certain she did. A server acting pureblood is trouble; trouble attracts blame; blame rises to the top. So when Seer Rhee noticed Yoona~939's deviations, he bypassed destarring and summoned a corp Medic to have her reorientated. This was a tactical mistake of the type that xplains Seer Rhee's lacklustre career. Yoona~939 passed the xamination with a perfect score, and the Medic announced she was working as genomed. He prescribed an xtra five milligrams of amnesiads in her Soap; nothing more. Seer Rhee could not now discipline Yoona further without implying criticism of a senior corp Medic.

At what point did Yoona~939 make you complicit in her crimes?
Yoona attempted to xplain the meaning of a newfound word, *secret*. The concept of knowing something no-one else knew, not even Papa Song, was unthinkable. So Yoona, one night after the shift, as we sat steam-cleaning, promised to show me a secret.

When I woke it was not to brash yellow-up lites, but to Yoona, shaking me in the pale light of the curfew lamp. Our sisters lay in their cots immobile xcept for minute spasms.

'Follow me,' Yoona ordered, like a Seer.

'It's curfew,' I told her. 'I'm afraid.'

'Don't be. Follow me.'

'Where are we going?'

'To a secret.' She led me from the dormroom into the dome. Its awful silence fritened me. Reds and yellows were greys and browns. Papa Song's Plinth was a dead slab. Dim lite leaked thru Seer Rhee's door. Yoona opened it; I learnt then, fear of discovery waits inside every secret.

Our Seer lay slumped with his head on his desk. Drool glued his chin to his sony; his eyelids remmed and a gurgle was trapped in his throat. Every Tenth Nite, Yoona told me, our Honorable Seer stays in the dinery thru curfew. He tells his Aides he must catch up on office-work, but really he imbibes Soap and sleeps until yellow-up. 'Soap affects purebloods like a drug.' She kicked his gut as hard as she could; my consternation amused her. 'You can do anything you like, he never wakes up. He has lived with fabricants for so long, he is one of us, almost.'

Yoona opened Seer Rhee's desk, xtracted a tiny silver key and led me across the dome to the wall between the entrance and the north-east hygiener. 'What do you see?' asked Yoona. I saw nothing, I said. 'Look again, look properly.' Then I saw a fine line and a speck. I touched the speck; it was a hole. Yoona gave me the key. I inserted it. The line became a rectangle, and a door swung open. The dark room beyond gave no clue of what lay within. Yoona took my hand.

I hesitated. If roaming the dinery during curfew was not destarrable, climbing into unknown rooms must surely be. But Yoona didn't let go. I genuflected to the dollar three times and let her pull me thru. The door clicked shut behind me. The blackness smelt of dust, decay and old detergent. Yoona whispered, 'Now, Sonmi, you are inside a secret.' A blade of lite cut the black; I saw a narrow storeroom crammed with forgotten objects: stacked seats; plastic plants; coats, hats, fans; a burnt-out sun; many umbrellas. Yoona's face; my eyes. The lite hurt. 'Is lite alive?' I asked.

'Lite *is* life,' answered Yoona. She had found the torch left under a table, so she hid it in our Hub and brought it to the secret room later. This shocked me most of all.

Why so?

Catechism Three teaches that for servers to own anything, even thoughts, denies the love Papa Song shows us by His Investment. I wondered, did Yoona still observe *any* Catechism? She showed me a metal box of unpaired earrings, bracelets and necklaces.

She slid an emerald tiara thru her braids, strung blueberry pearls around my neck. I asked how Yoona had found the secret room.

'Curiosity,' she said.

I didn't know the word. 'Is curiosity a torch, or a key?'

Yoona said it was both. Then she showed me the finest treasure of all. 'This book,' she said, with reverence, 'shows Outside, as it really is.'

Could Yoona read like a pureblood as well as talk like one?

I asked the same question; her reply was a rueful no. But we read the pictures. One showed a candelit chamber of purebloods dressed in glorious robes and shimmering dresses. I was mesmerized. Why didn't the pictures move like the pictures on diners' sonys? Yoona speculated the book was broken; this xplained why its owner had abandoned it.

The book had many pictures: a grimy server serving three ugly sisters; a white witch showering her with stars, turning her into a lady like Mrs Rhee; a handsome pureblood clearing a way thru a thorny forest with a sword; seven half-sized fabricants carrying strange cutlery behind a girl in a white skirt; a house built from candy; a seahorse combing a mermaid's hair; castles, mirrors, dragons. Of course, we couldn't identify most of these objects then. Most of the words in this interview I could not have employed when I was a server.

So many strangenesses in one curfew toxed my head. Yoona shone the torch on a rolex, and said we must be getting back to dormroom before yellow-up. Next time, she promised, she would show me more.

There was a next time?

Certainly. Ten Tenth Nites, or fifteen, Yoona woke me and took me to her secret. Each time I vowed would be my last. Each time, I marvelled at new treasures. By winter, it was only during our clandestine visits to the treasure room that my friend became her animated self. Pondering over the Book of Outside, she voiced doubts that shook my faith in every aspect of what I held to be true.

What shapes did these doubts take?

Doubts about the sureties of the fabricant world. How could Papa Song stand on a plinth in Chongmyo Plaza Papa Song's *and* walk the Xultation's beaches at the same time? Why were fabricants born into debt but purebloods not? Who decided Papa Song's Investment took twelve years to repay? Why not eleven? Six? One?

How did you respond?

I begged Yoona to stop voicing crimes of blasphemy. I was scared she would be reorientated. I was scared of being destarred for not judasing her. You see, her doubts accused Papa Song of terrible lies. Yoona admitted she had done xactly that one nite, before she showed me her secret. She had stood before His Plinth and said it: *Liar.* Just to see what happened.

'Nothing happened,' said Yoona, 'nothing at all. So I wonder, is our Logoman even there?'

I recited my Catechisms harder than ever; prayed to Papa Song to heal my friend; begged Yoona to fake normalcy. All in vain: her behavior grew more pureblood with every passing day. Soon even Seer Rhee would be prompted to take decisive action. Yoona watched AdVs as she cleared and wiped the tables. Our sister fabricants avoided her. Yoona~939 didn't care. One nite in the secret room she confided that she wanted to leave the dinery; and for me to go with her. Purebloods force us to work trapped underground, Yoona said, so they can enjoy the beautiful places on the surface without sharing them.

I could never commit such a wicked deviance, I told her. I recited Catechism Six. Yoona~939 reacted angrily. She called me a fool and a coward like my sisters.

But two Inside servers fleeing their corp, unaided, that would be . . . sheerest folly. Unanimity would round you up in five minutes.

How could Yoona~939 know that? Her Book of Outside promised a world of beauty, space and hiding-places.

Winter of my firststarred year arrived. Consumers brushed snow off their nikes by the entrance and we had to mop the floors regularly. Yoona deteriorated into a supine malaise. Ascension creates a hunger so sharp, it eventually consumes one's mind.

Did anything trigger the Yoona~939 deviancy, or did it just . . . appear from out of the blue?

The deviancy was an inevitability awaiting a trigger. During the New Year Sextet, when every day was busy with holiday crowds, Seer Rhee came to the Hub and reprimanded Yoona for lackluster greetings. He ordered her to recite the Papa Song Welcome fifty times: 'Hi! I'm Yoona! See our menu, place your order! Mouthwatering, magical, *Papa Song's!*'

Seer Rhee let Yoona reach forty-five times before telling her to start over. 'Being a Soulless, hatched clone doesn't xcuse attitude defects. If you break Catechism Four again, I'll have you reorientated into fertilizer products!'

I was afraid Yoona would commit a destarrable crime, but she recited the greeting fifty times to Seer Rhee's satisfaction; only I knew the effort it cost her. Our seer returned to his office, well pleased with the authoritative impression he had made on the queuing diners.

'Better a Soulless clone,' Yoona spoke coldly to his back, 'than a Souled roach.'

I prayed to Papa Song that nobody had heard; my prayers knew no other address. But why should He help my ingrate sister? Then I saw Ma-Leu-Da~108 whisper to Aide Cho. The Aide took Ma-Leu-Da~108 to Seer Rhee's office.

Something very bad was going to happen.

Did you tell Yoona~939 your fears?

My sister had ascended so far, she no longer felt downstrata from Seer Rhee. That night, after Last Catechism, our Seer circummed the Hub moodily. One of us had disgraced her uniform, he announced. Did she have the courage to confess her crime?

Seer Rhee stopped in front of Yoona.

'But you must be a roach,' Yoona began. 'Think about it. It xplains why you eat Soap: roaches eat anything. It xplains why you revolt your Aides and your wife: roaches are repulsive. It xplains the way you scuttle and your skin shines: roaches scuttle and are shiny.'

We servers could not believe our ears.

Seer Rhee clicked open his briefcase. 'I see.' He produced the Book of Outside. One by one he ripped out the pictures. 'See what damage,' rip, 'a *roach* can do,' rip, 'to your secrets,' *rip*, 'your treasures,' *rip*, 'your future.'

Yoona~939 grabbed the book; Seer Rhee was a heavy man. He locked my friend's head under her arm and battered it against the Plinth, repeatedly, until she was limp and senseless. Rhee kicked her until he was maroon with xertion. Yoona was now crushed, bloodied, and nearly unrecognizable. '*Look at her,*' he snarled, to us cowering fabricants. 'This is what happens to clones with ideas above their strata. That *deviant*'ll be sent away for reorientation, first thing tomorrow.' Seer Rhee bent over, planted his nike on her face, and ripped her collar off. The barcode stayed implanted in her windpipe. Rhee's fingers were wet with membrane and blood. The Seer inserted a single smeared star into Ma-Leu-Da's collar, saying nothing. Then he ground nine years of Yoona~939's labour under his nike's heel.

Ma-Leu-Da did not look happy with her prize. How unlike the cheerful Star Ceremony it was. Aide Cho ordered two Hwan-Soons to drag my unconscious friend into the dormroom. I was assigned to mop up her blood.

Can Seers inflict that kind of damage on corp property with impunity?
Seers manage the fabricants as they see fit, in theory. In practice, disfiguring a server worsened Rhee's standing in the hierarchy. Yoona~939 was incapacitated during the busiest period of the year. Medics were not available. Transport to Reorientation could not be arranged during the New Year Sextet. She was kept unconscious on her cot and drip-fed Soap.

But the Yoona~939 deviancy on New Year's Eve went far beyond this. Can you describe the event from your vantage-point?
I was wiping tables at the raised rim of my quarter; my view was clear. Aide Cho was serving at the Hub to replace our

damaged sister. A children's party was in progress in the east. Balloons, paper streamers and party hats filled the space near the elevator. Popsongs and the noise of hundreds of diners filled the dome. Papa Song boomeranged 3D eclairs over the children's heads; they passed thru their clutches and returned to our Logoman's snaky tongue. I was thinking of Yoona; I feared she thought I judased her. The dormroom opened, and a bruised, swollen Yoona~939 appeared.

She limped towards the party in the east. I knew what she was doing. Despite her disturbing condition, few diners looked up from their meals, sonys or AdV; those consumers who did pointed, rather than raised any alarm. When Yoona scooped up a kindergarten boy in a sailor suit, bystanders assumed she was one more fabricant maid to have fallen foul of her mistress.

Media reported that Yoona stole the child to use as a human shield.
Media reported what Unanimity told them to report. The Book of Outside was a collection of fairy tales, not a terrorists' manual. You see, Archivist, Yoona truly believed the elevator led to the magic kingdom of those illustrations. Once on the surface, she meant to disappear into hidden glades and velvet hills. She took the child only because the elevator would not ascend for a Soulless fabricant. She would have put him back in the elevator; not ransom him or use him as a shield or eat him and spit out his bones.

She didn't discuss her escape attempt with you?
Yoona had stopped discussing anything with me. Acting alone, she carried the fritened boy into the escalator. She didn't see me. The boy's mother, however, saw Yoona, just as the doors closed; her scream punctured the dinery noise. Hysteria xploded; dropped trays, spilt shakes, panicking purebloods; an off-duty enforcer unholstered his colt; he waded into the turmoil, shouting for calm.

Seer Rhee appeared in his office door, slipped on a spilt drink, and vanished under the swell of panicky consumers. All the while Papa Song surfed noodle waves on His Plinth.

Aide Cho yelled into his handsony.

Rumours multiplied xponentially; a Yoona kidnapped a boy; no, a baby; no, a pureblood kidnapped a Yoona; an enforcer shot a boy; no, a fabricant shot an enforcer; a Yoona hit the Seer, see, his nose is bleeding.

'The elevator!' someone shouted. 'It's coming!'

Quietness chilled the pandemonium.

The enforcer shouted for space, crouched, aimed at the doors.

The diners scrambled clear.

The elevator doors opened. The boy was balled up in one corner, quivering; his sailor suit was no longer white, but he seemed to be unhurt. Yoona~939's body was already a pulp of gun holes.

I saw that image too, Sonmi. When I got home from the ministry that nite, my dormmates were glued to the sony. Most of Nea So Copros was watching. The story was repeated over and over, with footage from a Chongmyo Plaza nikon showing the enforcer eliminating the deviant Yoona. We couldn't believe it. We were sure a Union terrorist had facescaped herself to *look* like a server. When Unanimity confirmed Yoona~939 was a *genuine* fabricant . . .

You felt the world would never be the same. You vowed never to trust a fabricant. You knew Abolitionism preached as insidious and dangerous a dogma as Union.

. . . Yes, I felt all that, and worse. What happened down in your dome?

The two other Yoonas were escorted into the dormroom before enraged consumers tore them to pieces. The dinery was evacuated quarter by quarter in an orderly manner. Unanimity arrived to interview witnesses. We cleaned the dome and, for the first time in our lives, ate Soap without a Vespers.

At yellow-up, we conducted our morning rituals. It was quiet without Yoona~939; none of us said a word. Papa Song delivered His Anti-Union Sermon at Matins.

I was amazed that a Logoman told his fabricants about Union's xistence.

Such was the level of panic. His Sermon may have been for Media consumption. Papa Song's head filled half the dome; we stood inside his mind. His face was heavy with grief and rage. The Hwan-Soons trembled; even the Aides looked awed. Seer Rhee looked pasty and sick.

Can you recount for the archives what Papa Song actually said?

He said that New Year's Day was normally a joyous occasion, when the twelvestarreds finished repaying His Investment and were free to embark for Xultation. This year, however, he had terrible news.

A gas called evil xists in the world, Papa Song said. When purebloods breathe in this gas, they change. They become terrorists. Terrorists hate everything that is good: Unanimity, Papa Song, hardworking fabricants, even the Beloved Chairman of Nea So Copros and his Juche. Terrorists have a corp named Union. Union wants to become the most powerful corp in plutocracy by changing consumers into terrorists; by killing consumers who oppose them.

At Papa Song's in Chongmyo Plaza, our Logoman narrated how a Union terrorist had released evil, and Yoona~939 had breathed it in. His voice rang with despair; his eyes were hollow with mourning. Had Yoona~939 reported the terrorist to her Seer or an Aide? No, Yoona~939 had not: she had breathed in the evil gas; and yesterday, this server had committed such criminal deviance that, had it not been for the skill of the Unanimity enforcer who was passing in Chongmyo Plaza, a consumer's innocent son would now be dead. The child survived, but purebloods' trust in fabricants had died; and with it, consumers' faith in Papa Song dineries. In the difficult year ahead, Papa Song concluded, we must work together and work hard to earn back that trust.

If ever a pureblood mentioned the name 'Union' to us, *no matter how long our queues*, we must tell our Seer without delay. This was a new Catechism, stronger than all the others. If we obeyed, Papa Song would love us. If we failed to do so, we would never get to Xultation: we would stay freshfaceds for ever, and never receive a single work star.

Did we understand?

Mutters of 'Yes, Papa Song' were voiced around the Hub.

'I cannot hear you!' our Logoman xhorted us.

'Yes, Papa Song!' Every fabricant shouted. 'YES, PAPA SONG!'

Wasn't Yoona~939 a Union member, as stated by the Corpocratic Court?
How and when could Union recruit her? Why would a Unionman risk the xposure? Of what worth was a genomed server to a terrorist ring?

So after the Sermon . . . New Year's Day was business as usual?
Business: not quite as usual. The two twelvestarreds, Hwa-Soon and another Sonmi, were escorted Outside by Seer Rhee. He returned with two freshfaced new stem-type servers, Kyelim~889, Kyelim~689 and a new Yoona. The rest of us received our yearly stars, which Aide Ahn inserted into our collars.

When the first elevator opened, a pack of Media streamed in, flashing nikons and besieging Seer Rhee's office. He had spent all curfew being interrogated at Papa Song's echelon. He only persuaded them to leave after sticking a ~939 ID over another Yoona's collar and allowing them to sony her. A few ghoulish consumers came to nikon each other pretending to be dead in the elevator. Around hour sixteen a platoon of Papa Song Medics arrived. Each of the servers was given an xhaustive xamination. We were questioned about Union, but none of us had heard of it before that morning's Sermon. I was afraid my visits to the secret room with Yoona~939 would endanger me, but apparently these were not known about. Only my birthmark attracted any passing comment.

I didn't know fabricants had birthmarks.
We don't: they are genomed out. Every Medic who ever saw it xpressed bewilderment. My birthmark always caused me embarrassment when xposed. Ma-Leu-Da~108 called it 'Sonmi~451's stain'. You can see it, Archivist, between my collar-bone and shoulder-blade: here.

Please show it to the orison. Xtraordinary. It resembles a comet.

Hae-Joo Im made the same observation.

So, I assume you passed the Medic's xamination?

Yes. At Vespers, no mention was made of Union or Yoona ~ 939. Amnesiads and soporifix in our Soap were boosted. By the second yellow-up of the new year Ma-Leu-Da ~ 108 could not have said where her xtra work star had come from, nor even that it was an xtra star. Only I remembered everything.

Did Seer Rhee retain his position?

Yes. Hae-Joo Im researched the results of the shooting for me. Rhee survived the Yoona deviancy by telling the inquiry how he had asked for an urgent Medic's report on Yoona ~ 939 months before. But profits fell across the Papa Song Corp; diners' numbers at the Chongmyo Plaza dinery dipped. Purebloods like quoting the aphorism about lightning never striking the same place twice; tho they often act as if the opposite is true.

Purebloods also have short memories; they soon forget that lightning ever struck, especially if their stomachs are involved. By Second Month, diners' numbers were back to average levels. The Kyelims were a new attraction; genomed with zoescope eyes and rabbit teeth, they drew long queues of nikoning fabricant-spotters. The Ma-Leu-Das were envious.

Servers' memories are genomed weak, and you say xtra amnesiads were added to your Soap. How can you recall events in the dinery with such precision?

A simple question with a simple answer: my own ascension had begun. I recognized it from Yoona ~ 939's symptoms. I anticipate your next question, Archivist: you want me to describe the xperience.

Go on.

First, a voice began speaking inside my head. It alarmed me greatly, until I learnt nobody else heard it; the voice of sentience. Ascension was an alarming xperience, especially in the aftermath of Yoona ~ 939. All over Nea So Copros, purebloods were scrutinizing fabricants' behavior for signs of unwarranted intelligence and reporting them for reorientation at the rate of hundreds per week.

Second, my language evolved, much as Yoona~939's had. When I meant to say 'good', my mouth uttered *favorable, pleasing* or *correct*. I learnt to edit and modify every single word I used.

Third, my own curiosity about Outside increased. I eavesdropped on diners' sonys, conversations, AdVs, weather reports, Boardmen's speeches.

Fourth, I suffered alienation: other servers avoided me, just as they had done with Yoona~939 – one's sisters know, even if they don't know they know; monotony decelerated time; I grew to hate the waves of consumers disgorged from the elevator's mouth; Yoona's doubts about our world haunted me, incessantly. Suppose Papa Song was not our father but an AdV?

How I envied my uncritical, unworried sisters! I dared not mention my metamorphosis to any of them.

You knew what not to do. What did you intend to do?
What could I do but wait and endure?

Two ascensions, side by side, suggested a program with a purpose. I had to avoid reorientation or a fate like Yoona~939's to learn what this purpose might be. So I studied the other fabricants to mimic their blankness, desperately. I obeyed all Catechisms, especially when Seer Rhee was present. It was not easy. Fear hardens caution, but boredom erodes it. I dared not visit Yoona's secret room, for it was no secret, but a trap.

And how long did you have to endure your secret ascension?
On Fourth Month, Last Week, Ninth Nite, I woke up during curfew. I dared not leave our dormroom to pass the time. All I could do was wait for yellow-up or more sleep. But coming from the dome, I heard a faint, definite sound: glass, tinkling.

I strained to hear more: nothing.

My sisters were asleep on their cots. Who else was in the dome? Only Seer Rhee.

Silently, I got up, and padded to the dormroom door. I turned the handle and peered into the curfewed dinery. White lite escaped from Seer Rhee's office. Thru his open door I saw him, immobile; his face flattened against the floor; his chair upended. I crossed the dome, crouching in the shadows until I was sure Seer Rhee was unconscious. His pupils had vanished into his pureblood irises. A line of blood was traveling over the contours of his worn face from his ear and nostrils. Around him, glass shards shone in the lite.

Rhee was dead?

I smelt lethe, a soporifix added to Soap. The usual dosage for a fabricant server is three drops, but Rhee had drunk a half-liter bottle. If I had called a Medic immediately, maybe his life could have been saved. But how to xplain my intervention? The whole of corpocracy was watching for another ascended fabricant; for evidence of a Union plot. Save a defeated man from a painless suicide or protect myself from an agonizing reorientation and begin my working life again as a zerostarred?

I returned to my cot.

Did that decision cause you any guilt?

No. I felt only foreboding that the nite was not yet over. I don't know how much time passed, but I heard the elevator arrive. Then footsteps. I felt they had come for me; but I didn't stir. Yellow-up came, but sisters stayed asleep in their cots. No scent of stimulin was in the air. Yoona's Book showed a palace of bluebloods and servants who had fallen asleep in the middle of eating, sewing, cooking. I thought of that picture.

There was a tiny rip in the silence. A match? Then I heard the tap-tap-tap of a sony. I got to my feet, crept to the door, and peered out of the dormroom. The dome lites were half on, but there were no consumers; no Aides had reported to work; no Papa Song on His Plinth, reciting Vespers.

Only a man in a dark suit, nursing a coffee and writing in the strange lite. We watched each other; finally, he wished me a good morning, and hoped that I was feeling better than poor Seer Rhee.

An enforcer?

He was a chauffeur, he told me. His name was Mr Chang. I apologized; I did not know 'chauffeur'.

The quiet visitor xplained, chauffeurs drive fords for Boardmen and xecs. Chauffeurs sometimes serve as messengers. Mr Chang had a message for me, for Sonmi~451, from his own Seer. The message was a choice: I could leave the dinery that morning, go Outside and repay my Investment in a new way; or I could remain in Papa Song's, wait for Aide Cho to discover Seer Rhee, summon enforcers and their DNA sniffers; and wait for my ascension to be brought to lite and to suffer its consequences.

Not much of a choice.

It was the first choice of my life, and simpler than most since. Mr Chang folded his sony, put his coffee cup in the trash-chute, and we walked to the elevator; a smaller room even than the servers' hygiener, but a mighty gateway for me. I thought of Yoona~939 lying prostrate in this corner after her shooting. I looked across the empty dome to the Hub. Mr Chang instructed me which button to press to ascend. The doors closed on my old life.

My torso squashed my suddenly feeble legs and I fell over. Mr Chang caught me. Yoona must have fallen and dropped the boy when she underwent this same ascension. Mr Chang reassured me that every underground fabricant xperienced an identical discomfort on the first elevator ride. I recalled scenes from the Book of Outside to dam my nausea. Its cobweb streams, oceanous forests, caverns, gnarled towers. When the elevator slowed, my torso seemed to rise into the air.

'Ground level,' announced Mr Chang.

The doors opened on Outside.

I almost envy you. Please, describe xactly what you saw.

Chongmyo Plaza on a Fourth Month pre-dawn. How vast it seemed! My head whirled, after my life in the dome, tho the plaza is not five hundred meters across. Around the eternal feet of the Beloved Chairman, consumers hurried; walkway sweepers droned; taxis buzzed riders; fords fumed; trashtrucks crawled along the kerb; thruways, eight lanes wide, lined by suns on poles, roofed by canopies, canyoned by concrete, glass; AdVs dazzling, blaring; words, logos; neonized, amped; sirens, engines, machinery, circuitry; underfoot ducts rumbling; lite of every intensity at every angle.

I didn't have enough names for what I saw.

My question got no further than 'What . . . ?'

It must have been overwhelming.

Overwhelming: the apposite word. Outside's many-flavored air; fumes, kim-chee, sewage, consumers' bodies. A running consumer missed me by an inch, *Watch out, clone!* She had gone before I could apologize. My hair was mussed by the breath of a giant, invisible aircon.

'The streets funnel the wind,' xplained Mr Chang, steering me across the walkway to a mirrored ford. A trio of students were admiring the vehicle; they returned to the stream of consumers upon Mr Chang's approach. The rear door hissed open. The chauffeur ushered me in.

A bearded passenger slouched in the roomy interior, working on his sony. He xuded authority, like a Logoman, but much more so. I crouched by the door, watching his flexing knuckles, his aged face, waiting for his order. Mr Chang started the engine and the ford edged into the traffic. From the rear window the golden arches of Papa Song's receded into a hundred other corp logos. Some logos I knew from AdV; most not. I marveled at the city of new symbols sliding by. Fords sped by and slowed up alongside ours. What Seer prevented a thousand fatal collisions per minute? The ford braked and I lost my balance. The bearded man mumbled that no-one would object if I sat down.

Uncertain if he had issued an order or even set a trap, I apologized for not knowing the right Catechism.

'My collar is Sonmi ~451,' I said, but he ignored me, rubbed raw eyes and asked Mr Chang for a weather report. Warm, clear and breezy, replied the chauffeur, adding that the fordjams were bad and our journey would take approx ninety minutes. The bearded man looked at his rolex and swore.

We hadn't gone far before a roaring bore down on us; I felt a boiling dread that Papa Song had come to punish me for leaving his service. But the roar inched away, and thru the rear window, I saw the underbelly of a hovering black machine. The passenger called forward to Mr Chang: did he suppose the airo was Enforcement, Unanimity or just a Boardman wanting all the downstrata citizens to know in whose fleeting shadows they must queue? Mr Chang judged it was the latter.

Didn't you ask where you were being taken?
Why ask a question whose answer would demand a dozen more questions? Remember, Archivist, I had never even seen a building's exterior, nor even xperienced conveyance; yet here I was, thruwaying Nea So Copros' second biggest conurb in a mirrored ford. I was less a cross-zone tourist, more a time-traveler from a bygone century. The ford cleared the urban canopy near Moon Tower and I saw my first Outside dawn over the Kangwon-Do mountains. The sight mesmerized me as it dazzled; the Immanent Prime Chairman's True Sun, its molten lite, petro-clouds, and His dome of sky, higher than high, wider than wide! I looked for my own awe reflected in my fellow passenger's reaction, but he was dozing. I couldn't understand how the conurb didn't grind to a halt in the presence of such beauty.

What else caught your eye?
Back below the canopy, the buildings squattened and we passed a dew garden. Feathery, fronded, mossdrenched green; pondwater green; lawn green. Acres of it, set around dervishing fountains. In Papa Song's the only green was lettuce squares and chlorophyl shakes; we servers assumed green was as precious as gold. Rainbows sleeved alongside the ford windows. Dormblocks lined the thruway, each one adorned by a stiff Nea So Copros flag. Waysides fell away and we passed over a wide, winding, ordure-brown strip. I summoned up my courage to ask Mr Chang what it was.

'Han river,' the driver told me, 'Sōngsu Bridge.'

I could only ask, what were these things?

This time, the passenger muttered an answer, 'A thruway made of water.' Disappointment flattened his voice. 'A bridge is a road over a river.'

The water in the river and the clear liquid that gushed from drink nozzles in the dome couldn't have been more different, but I had no time to stay confused. Mr Chang pointed at a low peak ahead. 'Mount Taemosan.'

So you were taken to Taemosan University straight from Papa Song's?

To reduce xperimental contamination, yes. The road zigged up thru woodland. Trees, their incremental gymnastics and noisy silence, are another wonder of Outside to me. Ten minutes later we arrived on the plateau campus. Cuboid buildings competed for space. Students and auxils walked along narrow walkways. The ford coasted to a halt under a rainstained, suncracked overhang. Mr Chang opened the door for me but the bearded passenger dozed on. Litter drifted and lichen yeasted between slabs. Mount Taemosan's air tasted cleaner than down in the conurb, but the overhang's lobby was grimed and unlit.

We paused at the foot of a double-helix staircase. This is an old-style elevator, Mr Chang xplained. 'The university xercises students' bodies as well as their minds.' So I fought gravity for the first time, step by step, grasping the handrail. Two students descended the down-helix, laughing at my clumsiness; one commented, 'That's one specimen which won't be making a dash for freedom any time soon.' Mr Chang warned me not to look over my shoulder; I did so, and vertigo tipped me over. If my guide had not caught me I would have tumbled down to the lobby.

It took several minutes to ascend to the sixth floor, the topmost. Here, a slitted corridor ended at a door, slitely ajar, nameplated *Boom-Sook Kim*. Mr Chang knocked, but no answer came.

'Wait in here for Mr Kim,' the chauffeur told me. 'Honour

and obey him as you would your Seer.' Entering, I asked Mr Chang what work I should do, but the chauffeur had gone. I was quite alone for the first time in my life.

What did you make of your new home?

I was struck by its dirt, unfavorably. Our dinery was always spotless, for cleanliness is one of the Catechisms. Boom-Sook Kim's lab was, in contrast, a long gallery, dusty and rancid with pureblood males' odor. Bins overflowed; a crossbow target hung by the door; the walls were lined with lab-benches, buried desks, obsolete sonys and sagging bookshelves. A framed kodak of a boy beaming over a bloodied snow-leopard hung over the only desk to show much evidence of use. A dirty window overlooked a neglected courtyard where a mottled figure stood on a Plinth. I hoped he was my new Logoman, but he never stirred.

In a cramped anteroom I found a cot, a hygiener and sort of portable steam-cleaner. When was I to use it? Was I missing Vespers? What Catechisms governed my life in this place?

The air was hot and brite with dust. My genome-sealed pores prickled. A housefly buzzed in lazy figures of eight. I gazed, entranced.

Had you never seen insects before?

Only rogue-gened roaches; Papa Song's aircon inflows insecticide, so if any insects enter via the elevator, they die instantly to be swept up later. The fly hit the window, over and over. I did not then know windows open. It rested on the ceiling. Why didn't it fall off?

I heard off-key singing; a popsong about Pnom Pnem Girls. Moments later a student in beach-shorts, sandals and silk weighed down by shoulderbags kickboxed the door open. He saw me and groaned; 'What in the name of Holy Corpocracy are *you* doing here?'

I bared my collar. 'Sonmi~451, Sir. Papa Song's server from—'

'Shut up, shut up, I know *what* you are!' The young man had the froggish mouth and hurt eyes then in vogue. 'But you're not supposed to be here until *Fifth* Day! If those registry *dildoes* xpect me to cancel a five-star Taiwanese conference just because they can't read calendars, well, sorry, they can suck *maggots* in an *ebola* pit. I only came in to pick up my worksony and discs. I'm not babysitting an xperimental clone still in uniform when I could be sinning myself sticky in Taipei.'

The fly hit the window again; the student picked up a pamphlet and pushed past me. The whack made me jump. He inspected the smear with a laugh of triumph and a crooked, jocular voice: 'Let that be a warning to you!' I didn't know if that 'you' meant me or the fly. 'Nobody doublecrosses Boom-Sook Kim and gets away with it!' He turned to me. 'Don't touch anything, don't go anywhere. Soap's in the boxfridge – thank Chairman they delivered your feed early. I'll be back on Fifth Day. If I don't leave for the airport *now* I'll miss my flite.'

I was left alone.

He reappeared in the doorway. 'Hey. You *do* speak, don't you?'

I nodded.

Boom-Sook Kim xhaled, histrionically: 'Thank *Chairman*! Fact – for every moronity, there's a registry clone-bone somewhere commiting it as we speak.'

What . . . were you supposed to do for the next three days?

I had no idea. I watched the rolex hand erode the hours. We are genomed to stand for nineteen hours on end, remember. I thought about Mrs Rhee. Was she a grieving widow, or a glad one? Would Aide Ahn or Aide Cho be promoted to Chongmyo Plaza Seer? How distant my old life seemed. How mystifying my new life was.

From the courtyard I heard pins and needles of sound. They came from the shrubs below the Plinth. I looked closer, and saw real birds for the first time; swallows and martins. I had seen birds on 3D, but no mob of birds so random and rampant as these. An airo overflew close, and many hundreds poured upwards. Why did they sing? For whose benefit?

I watched the birds all day until the sky curfewed and the room grew dark. My first nite in Outside. Windows across the courtyard yellowed-up. I saw labs like Boom-Sook's, housing young purebloods; neater offices, occupied by professors; busy corridors, quiet ones. But not a single fabricant did I see.

At midnite I imbibed a sac of Soap, lay in the cot and wished Yoona~939 was there to make sense of the day's legion mysteries.

When you woke, did you remember where you were?

The Soap had less amnesiads but more soporifix than in Papa Song's, so I slept for longer but awoke with a clearer mind. The first surprise of my second day Outside stood across the anteroom. A towering figure, over three meters tall and dressed in an orange zipsuit, was studying the bookshelves. The xposed skin on his face and neck was scalded red, burned black and patched pale, but he seemed quite at ease. His collar confirmed he was no pureblood, but I'd never seen a fabricant of his stem-type or stature.

'No stimulin here.' He spoke as if from a deep hole. His lips were genomed out, and his ears were protected by valves of nail-like substance. 'You wake when you wake, especially if your postgrad is as lazy as Boom-Sook Kim. Xec postgrads are the worst. They have their asses wiped for them from kindergarten to euthanasium. They lack discipline; never think about others' needs. A waste of space.' With a giant, two-thumbed hand he indicated a blue zipsuit half the size of his own. 'For you, little sister.' As I changed from my Papa Song's uniform into my new garment I asked if he had been sent by Seer or Aide to orientate me. 'No,' said the burnt giant. 'Your postgrad and mine are friends, sort of. Boom-Sook called by yesterday to complain about your unxpected delivery. I would have visited you before curfew, but the Faculty of Genome Surgery postgrads work late, unlike the slackers in the Faculty of Psychogenomics. I'm Wing~027. Let's find out why you're here.'

The rolex on the lab wall gave me my second surprise: I had slept for six whole hours. Wing~027 sat on Boom-Sook's desk and switched on the sony, ignoring my protests that my postgrad had forbidden me to touch it. Wing clicked the screenboard:

Yoona ~ 939 appeared. Wing trailed his finger along the rows of words. 'Let's pray to the Immanent Chairman that Boom-Sook won't make *that* error again . . .'

I asked Wing, could he read?

Wing told me that any randomly thrown together pureblood can read, so a carefully designed fabricant should learn with ease. A Sonmi appeared on the sony. Wing read: '*In-Dormroom Cerebral Upsizing the Service Fabricant: A Feasibility Case Study on Sonmi ~451* by Boom-Sook Kim. Now why,' Wing wondered, 'is such a no-brainer xec postgrad aiming so high?'

What sort of fabricant was Wing~O27? A militiaman?

A disasterman, he boasted. 'We operate in deadlands so infected or radioactive that purebloods perish there like bacteria in bleach. Our brains have only minor genomic refinements: we need to think for ourselves. Our orientation teaches us more than pureblood universities. And show me a pureblood who can survive this.' He bared his hideously burnt forearm. 'My postgrad's Ph.D. is tissue flameproofing.'

I didn't even know what a deadland was. Wing ~ o27 xplained how these irradiated or toxic swathes force the Consumer and Production Zones to retrench, mile by mile. His description appaled me, but the disasterman saw them in another lite. The day when all Nea So Copros is deadlanded, he told me, will be the day of the fabricants.

This sounded deviant. If these deadlands were so widespread in the world, I asked, why had I not seen them from the ford?

Wing ~ o27 switched off the sony and asked me how big I believed the world to be. I was unsure, but said I had been driven all the way from Chongmyo Plaza to this mountain, so I must have seen most of it.

The giant told me to follow and strode to the door. I hesitated: Boom-Sook had ordered me not to go anywhere. Wing ~ o27 beckoned me, sternly: 'To survive for long, Sonmi ~ 451, you must create Catechisms of your own.' He slung me over his charred shoulder, carried me along the slitted corridor, around a tite corner, up a dusty spiral staircase where he fisted open a rusty door. The morning sunlite blinded me; the wind slapped my face and pulled my hair.

The roof of the Psychogenomics Faculty, Wing~027 informed me, setting me down on the ledge beside him. I gripped the railing: six levels down was a cactus garden, birds hunting insects in the needles; eight levels down the hillside, a ford park, half full; ten levels down, a sports track, circummed by a regiment of uni- formed students; below that, a consumer plaza; beyond that, woods, sloping down to the spilled, charred-and-neon conurb, hi- rises, dorm-blocks, the Han river, finally mountains lining the airoscored sunrise. Wing spoke in his soft, burnt voice: 'Held against the whole world, Sonmi~451, all you see here is this chip of stone.'

My mind fumbled with this enormity and dropped it; I didn't even know what I needed in order to understand such a limitless place.

Wing replied, I needed intelligence: ascension would provide this. I needed time: Boom-Sook Kim's own idleness would give me time. But I also needed knowledge.

I asked, how is knowledge found?

'You must learn how to read, little sister,' he said.

So Wing~027, not Hae-Joo Im or Boardman Mephi, mentored you first?
Wing~027 could have mentored me further, but our second meeting was our final one. He returned to Boom-Sook's lab an hour before curfew on my first day to give me an 'unlost' sony: one preloaded with every single autodidact module in corpocracy schooling. The disasterman showed me its operation, then warned me never to let a pureblood catch me gathering know- ledge, for the sight scares them, and there is nothing a scared pureblood will not do.

By Boom-Sook's return from Taiwan on Fifth Day I had mastered the sony's usage and graduated from elementary school. By Sixth Month I completed xec secondary school. You look sceptical, Archivist, but remember, I was a starving servant at a banquet. My appetite deepened as I dined. The sony's pathways led me thru university and corpocracy libraries. We are only what we know.

I didn't mean to look skeptical, Sonmi. Your mind, speech, your . . . self prove your dedication to learning, amply. What confuses me is, why did Boom-Sook Kim give you so much time to study? An xec heir, surely, was no covert Abolitionist? What about his Ph.D. xperiments on you?

Boom-Sook Kim cared not for xperiments, but for drinking, gambling, his crossbow. His father was an echelon xec at Kwangju Genomics; he was even lobbying for Juche board-manship until his son soiled the Kim family's market value.

Then how was Boom-Sook planning to obtain his Ph.D.?

By paying an academic agent to collate his paper from the agent's own sources; a beloved route to success for xec-stratum post-grads. The chemicals responsible for ascending Yoona~939 and I were pre-formulated, together with yields and conclusions. Boom-Sook could not have named the bio-molecular properties of toothpaste. In nine months he set me no 'xperiment' more arduous than cleaning his lab and preparing his tea. Fresh data might cloud those he had bought; and risk xposing him as a fraud. My presence was required to give his stolen research a fig-leaf of credibility.

These, I learnt, were the terms of my new life, and they suited me well; contrast them with Papa Song's dinery. During my postgrad's absences I could study without risk of discovery. Every other day, Boom-Sook came to his office at around hour fourteen to copy another tranche of culled data into his sony.

Was Boom-Sook Kim's academic mentor aware of this plagiarism?

Professors value tenure too much to muckrake the sons of future Boardmen.

Did Boom-Sook never talk to you . . . interact with you, in any way?

He addressed me like purebloods speak to a cat. It amused him to toss questions at me, ones he fancied were incomprehensible to me: *So, should I tell my father to stick his head up his democracy-*

hole, Sonmi? Or, *Hey, Sonmi, is it worth azuring my teeth, d'you reckon, or is sapphire just a passing fad?* He didn't xpect cogent answers; I didn't disabuse him. My reply became so habitual that Boom-Sook nicknamed me, 'I-Don't-Know-Sir~451.'

So for nine months nobody observed your skyrocketing sentience?

Boom-Sook Kim's only regular visitors were Min-Sic and Fang. Fang's real name was never used in my hearing. They bragged about their new fords and suzukis and played poker. There is no point describing their features: they underwent facescaping monthly. The three postgrads were not the sort of purebloods who noticed fabricants, outside a Huamdonggil comfort-hive. Gil-Su Noon, Boom-Sook's neighbor, a downstrata postgrad on scholarship aid, banged on the wall to complain about the noise from time to time, but the three xecs banged back louder. I only saw him once or twice.

What is 'poker'?

A card game played by xploitative liars who pretend to be friends. Fang won thousands of dollars from Boom-Sook and Min-Sic's Souls during their poker sessions. Other times, Boom-Sook told me to get out while they used xec drugs; when toxed, he said I made him nervous. I would go to the faculty roof, sit in the shade of the watertank, and watch the swifts trawl for giant gnats until dark, when the three postgrads would be gone.

Why was it that you never met Wing~027 again?

One humid afternoon, three weeks after my arrival at Taemosan, a knock on the door distracted Boom-Sook from his facescaper catalog. Unxpected visitors were rare, as I have said. 'Enter!' said Boom-Sook, hiding his catalog under a volume entitled *Practical Genomics*. He had never read it; unlike me.

A wiry student poked the door open with his toe. 'Boom-Boom,' he called Boom-Sook. My postgrad sprang to attention; sat down again; then slouched. 'Hey, Hae-Joo,' he faked a casual manner, 'what's up?'

The visitor said he was just passing to say hi, and accepted

Boom-Sook's offered chair. Listening in, I learnt Hae-Joo Im was Boom-Sook's classmate from high school, now studying in Taemosan's Unanimity faculty. I was told to fetch Hae-Joo Im a glass of tea while they discussed topics of no importance. The visitor then mentioned, 'You'll know about your friend Min-Sic's appaling day by now?'

Boom-Sook denied Min-Sic was necessarily a 'friend' before asking why his day was appalling. 'His specimen, Wing~027, was burnt to bacon.' Apparently, Min-Sic mistook a minus for a plus on the label of a bottle of inflammable alkali.

My own postgrad smirked, giggled, then laughed. Hae-Joo next did an unusual action: he looked at me.

Why is that unusual?
Purebloods always see us but rarely look at us. Much later, Hae-Joo admitted he was curious about my response. Boom-Sook noticed nothing: he speculated about compensation claims by the corp sponsoring Min-Sic's research. In his own, solo, research, Boom-Sook gloated, no-one cared if you dropped an xperimental fabricant or two along the way.

Did you feel . . . well, what did you feel? Resentment? Grief?
Fury. I retreated to the anteroom. We fabricants lack both the means and the rights to xpress emotion, but the notion we cannot xperience it is a widespread myth. Wing~027 was worth twenty Min-Sics, by any measure; because of an xec's arrogant carelessness, my only friend on Mount Taemosan was dead; and Boom-Sook had pronounced this *hysterical*.

Fury forges a steel will. I see now, that day was the first step to my *Declarations*; to this prison cube, and to the Lighthouse.

What happened to you over summer recess?
According to regulations, Boom-Sook should have deposited me into a holding dormroom to avoid contamination. Luckily, my postgrad was so eager to go hunt fabricant elk on Hokkaido in eastern Korea that he forgot to do so; or else assumed a lesser-stratum oddsbody would do it for him.

So one summer morning, I woke to find the whole building deserted. No echoes from the busier corridors; no time bell; no announcements; even the aircons were turned off. From the roof, the conurb fumed and trafficked, and swarming airos left vapor streaks across the sky, but the campus was much quieter than usual. Its fordparks were semi-vacant. Builders were resurfacing the oval square in the hot sun. Then I thought to check on the sony's calendar, and learnt today was the beginning of recess. I bolted the lab's door and hid myself in the anteroom.

So you never set foot outside Boom-Sook's lab in five weeks? Not once?
Not once: I dreaded being separated from my sony, you see. A security guard tested the lab door every Ninth Day. Sometimes I heard Gil-Su Noon at work in the adjacent lab. I lowered the blind and kept the solars off at nite; I had enough Soap to last the duration.

But that's fifty days of unbroken solitude.
My mind traveled the length, breadth and depth of our culture in those fifty days. I devoured the twelve seminal texts: Jong-Il's *Seven Dialects*; Prime Chairman's *Founding of Nea So Copros*; Admiral Yeng's *History of the Skirmishes*; you know the list. Indices in an uncensored *Commentaries* led me to pre-Skirmish thinkers. The library refused many requests, of course, but I succeeded with two Optimists translated from the Late English, Orwell and Huxley; and Washington's *Satires on Democracy*.

Were you still Boom-Sook's thesis specimen – putatively – when he returned for the second semester?
I was. My first autumn arrived; I made a secret collection of the flame-colored leaves that drifted on the faculty roof. Autumn itself aged, and my leaves lost their colors. Nites became icy; then even daylite hours frosted up. Coldness was another intriguing sensation after the everwarm dinery. Boom-Sook dozed on the heated *ondul* most afternoons, watching 3D. He had lost a lot of dollars in dubious investments over the summer, and as his father was refusing to pay his debts, my postgrad

was in a foul mood. My only defense against his tantrums was to act void.

What was your reaction to snow?

It is beautiful. The first snows fell very late last year; the last First Nite of Twelfth Month. I woke before lite and watched, entranced, the flakes halo the New Year fairies decorating the courtyard windows. The undergrowth beneath the neglected statue drooped under the weight of snow; the statue assumed a comic majesty. Snow's whites are bruised lilacs in half-lite.

And it must have been around then that Dr Mephi enters the story?

Yes, on Sextet Eve. Boom-Sook, Min-Sic and Fang burst in late on, toxflushed and bent with laughter. I was in the anteroom, and barely had time to hide my sony. Boom-Sook wore a mortar-board hat, and Min-Sic hugged a basket of mint-scented orchids as big as himself. He threw them at me, saying, 'Petals for Spoony, Sponny, Sonmi, whatever its name is . . .'

Fang rifled the cupboard where Boom-Sook kept his *soju* and tossed three bottles over his shoulder. 'The brands are all dog-piss!' he barked. Min-Sic caught two but one smashed on the floor, triggering relapses of laughter. 'Clean it up, Cind'rella!' Boom-Sook clapped his hands at me, then pacified Fang by saying he'd open a bottle of the best stuff being as how the Sextet Recess came only once a year.

By the time I had swept up every glass shard, Min-Sic had found a pornslash disney on 3D. They watched it with relish, bickering over its merits and realism and drinking the fine *soju*. Their drunkenness had a recklessness that nite, especially Fang's, that unnerved me. I retreated to the anteroom; from there I heard Gil-Su Noon at the lab door, asking the revelers to be quieter. I spied.

Min-Sic mocked Gil-Su's glasses, asking why his family couldn't find the dollars to correct his myopia. Boom-Sook suggested that his neighbor shove his head up his own ass if he wanted peace and quiet on the last day of the Old Year's Semester. Fang spoke about getting his father to order a tax inspection on the Noon clan. Gil-Su Noon fumed in the doorway until the three xecs pelted him away with plums and further derision.

Fang seems to be the ringleader.

He was: he could chisel open the faultlines of personality and so xploit people. Doubtless he is currently practicing law in one of the twelve capitals with great success. That nite he decided to rile Boom-Sook, by wagging the *soju* bottle at the kodak of the dead snow-leopard. How dopey, asked Fang, were these predators genomed down to make them safe for the tourists to hunt?

Boom-Sook's pride was pricked: he retorted that he only hunted animals whose viciousness was genomed *up*. He and his brother had stalked the snow-leopard for hours in a Kathmandu Valley reserve before the cornered animal leapt for his brother's throat. Boom-Sook had a single shot. The bolt entered the beast's eye in mid-air.

Fang and Min-Sic faked awe for a moment, then fired a fresh barrage of laughter. Min-Sic thumped the floor, saying, 'You are *so* full of shit, Kim!' Fang peered closer at the kodak and remarked that it looked dijied.

Boom-Sook inked a face on a synthetic melon, solemnly, wrote 'Fang' on its brow and balanced the fruit on a stack of journals by the door. He took his crossbow from his desk, walked to the far-end window, and took aim.

Fang called out a 'No-no-no-no-no-no-no!' and waved his arms, objecting that melons don't rip out a hunter's throat in the event of a miss. Boom-Sook was not under sufficient pressure. He beckoned me over to stand by the door.

I saw his intention and began to appeal to my postgrad, but Fang cut me off, warning that if I didn't do his bidding he'd put Min-Sic here in charge of my Soap. Min-Sic's smile wilted: I understood Fang's threat. He sank his nails into my arm, led me over, put the mortar-board hat on my head, drew a cat's face on the melon, and placed the fruit on the hat. 'So, Boom-Sook,' he teased, 'd'you still reckon your marksmanship is so unerring?'

Boom-Sook's friendship with Fang was, in fact, a compound of rivalry and loathing. 'Of course,' he said.

I asked my postgrad to please stop.

Boom-Sook raised his crossbow and ordered me not to move a muscle.

The bolt's steel tip glinted. Dying in one of these boys' dares was a futile, stupid death, but fabricants cannot dictate terms. A twang, an airwhoosh and the crossbolt crisped into melon pulp; the fruit rolled off the hat. Min-Sic applauded warmly, hoping to thaw the situation.

My relief flushed out my indignity.

'You hardly need laser-guided marksmanship to hit a huge great melon.' Fang sniffed. 'Anyway, look,' he held up the melon, 'you missed Pussy's eye.' Surely, he went on, a mango was a worthier target for a hunter of Boom-Sook's alleged credentials?

Boom-Sook held out his crossbow to Fang, daring him to match his own skill; hit the mango from fifteen paces.

'Done.' Fang took the crossbow, ordering me to stay where I was.

'Sir —' I began, despairingly.

'Shut up,' Boom-Sook growled at me, drawing an eye on the mango. Fang counted his paces and loaded the bolt.

Min-Sic, uneasily, warned his friends that the paperwork on a dead xperimental specimen was hell.

Fang aimed for a long time. His hand vibrated. The mango exploded and juiced the walls. I knew I should not assume my ordeal was over. Fang blew on the crossbow. 'Melon at thirty paces, mango at fifteen . . . I'll raise you a . . . *plum*, at ten.' He noted a plum was still bigger than a snow-leopard's eye, but added that if Boom-Sook wanted to admit he was full of shit, and decline the challenge, Min-Sic and he would consider the chapter closed, for a whole ten minutes.

Boom-Sook weighed my safety against his honor. He balanced the plum on my head and told me to hold very, *very* still. He counted his ten steps, turned, loaded and took aim.

My feelings approached the murderous.

Gil-Su banged on the door again. *Go away*, I thought at him. *No distractions now . . .*

Boom-Sook's jaw twitched as he drew back the bow.

The banging grew insistent. Fang blasted back obscenities about Gil-Su's genitals and his mother.

Boom-Sook's eyes bored the plum on my head. His knuckles whitened.

My head was whipcracked around; pain sank teeth into my ear; the door flew open behind me. I looked up; Boom-Sook, Min-Sic and Fang all wore xpressions of sudden doom. Curiosity numbed my massing pain for a moment. There, in the doorway, was a bearded man, out of breath, thunderously angry. His cape was crusted with snow and ice.

Boardman Mephi?

Unanimity Professor, architect of the Californian Boat-people Solution, holder of a Nea So Copros Medal for Eminence, monographist on Tu-Fu and Li-Po; Boardman Mephi. I didn't recognize him at first. Liquid trickled down my neck and spine. I dabbed my ear and pain bit deep; my fingers were shiny and scarlet.

Boom-Sook's voice wobbled: 'Boardman, we—' No help was offered from Fang or Min-Sic. The Boardman pressed a crisp silk handkerchief against my ear, and told me to keep the pressure steady. He took a handsony from an inner pocket. 'Mr Chang,' he said into it, and now I recognized the sleepy passenger who had accompanied me from Chongmyo Plaza eight months before. He requested immediate first aid.

Now he turned back to the postgrads and told them they had made an ominously ill-starred beginning to the year of the snake. Min-Sic and Fang would be notified by the disciplinary board of their debits, he said, then dismissed them. Both bowed and hurried out. Min-Sic left his cloak on the *ondul*, but he didn't come back. Boom-Sook looked inconsolably sorry for himself. My rescuer let the postgrad suffer for some seconds before asking, 'Are you planning to shoot at *me* with that thing, too?'

Boom-Sook Kim saw he still held the incriminating crossbow, and dropped it as if it were a hundred celsius hot. Boardman Mephi inspected the lab, sniffing at the neck of the *soju* bottle. The octopoid rapine on 3D distracted him. Boom-Sook fumbled with the remo, dropped it, picked it up, pressed STOP, aimed it the right way, pressed STOP. The Boardman's patience was profoundly menacing; he was curious to hear Boom-Sook's xplanation of why he was using his faculty's xperimental fabricant for crossbow practice.

I'm curious to hear that, too.
Boom-Sook tried everything. He was inxcusably drunk for Sextet Eve; he had misprioritized; ignored stress symptoms; chosen friends unwisely; got carried away while disciplining his specimen for arrogance; it was all Fang's fault. His lack of conviction in any one of these betrayed him as an inept liar.

Mr Chang arrived with a medicube, sprayed my ear, dabbed coag and applied a patch. My postgrad asked if my ear would heal. Boardman Mephi's answer was that Boom-Sook's doctorate was terminated. The x-postgrad blanked and whitened as he saw the consequences.

Mr Chang pressed my blood-soaked hand, kindly, and told me my ear-lobe was torn off. A Medic would replace it in the morning. I already foresaw recriminations from Boom-Sook once we were alone, but Mr Chang said that he and Boardman Mephi would accompany me to a new home. I was to leave with them.

That must have come as very good news.
Yes, xcept for my sony. How could I bring that along? No plan came to mind, so I nodded meekly, hoping I could maybe retrieve it during Sextet Recess.

What reason did the Boardman give for your timely rescue?
I didn't ask; my rescuer offered no xplanation until later. The helix stairs down to the lobby consumed my concentration; descents are harder than ascents. In the lobby, eddies and

wavelets of snow broke against the glass. Mr Chang produced a hooded cloak for me and a pair of icenikes.

Boardman Mephi complimented Mr Chang, drolly, on his choice of zebraskin design. Mr Chang responded that zebraskin was *de rigueur* in Lhasa's chicest streets this winter.

I was being transferred to the Unanimity Faculty on the western lip of campus, Boardman Mephi said, apologizing for letting 'those three xec mice' play games with my life. The weather had prevented a timelier intervention. Unsure how to respond, I gave a meek, well-orientated, 'Yes, sir.'

The campus walkways and cloisters were festive with Sextet Eve crowds. Mr Chang taught me how to shuffle thru the more granular ice to gain traction. Snowflakes settled on my eyelashes and nostrils. If I looked at the sky, I felt I was falling upwards. Snowfights ceasefired as Professor Mephi approached; combatants bowed. Hidden in my hood, the sensation of anonymity was delicious.

Passing thru a courtyard, I heard music. Not AdV or popsong, but a sound naked and echoing. Boardman Mephi noted my fascination and told me it was a human choir. We halted for a minute, the better to hear the music.

Two enforcers guarding the Unanimity Faculty lobby saluted and took our cloaks. The building's opulence was entirely new; its furnishings were as sumptuous as the Psychogenomics Faculty's had been Spartan. Carpeted corridors were lined with Iljongian mirrors, urns of Kings of Scilla, 3Ds of Unanimity heroes. Boardman Mephi recited their names. The elevator had a chandelier; its voice recited Unanimity Catechisms, but Boardman Mephi told it to shut up.

The elevator opened on to a spacious, low-lit, sunken apartment from one of those upstrata lifestyle AdVs. A 3D fire flickered in the central hearth, surrounded by hovering maglev furniture. Two one-way glass walls afforded a dizzying view of the conurb, obscured by the haze-brite snowfall. Paintings took up the inner walls. I asked the Boardman, was this his office?

'My office is one storey up,' he replied. 'These are your new quarters.'

Mr Chang nodded confirmation, and suggested I invite my guest to sit down. I begged Boardman Mephi's pardon; I had never had a guest before, so my manners lacked polish.

The maglev sofa swung slitely under the Boardman's weight; he told me his daughter-in-law had redesigned my quarters with me in mind. She had chosen the Rothko canvases in the hope I would find them meditative. 'Molecule-for-molecule copies of the originals,' he assured me, though I had no idea what 'Rothko' meant, 'though one may argue no originals remain in our world. The artist's style seems resonant of your own position, Sonmi~ 451; he painted how the blind must see.'

A bewildering evening – crossbolts one moment, art history the next . . .
Certainly, and it wasn't over. The professor chastized himself for overlooking my potential when he rode with me in his ford from Chongmyo Plaza. 'I assumed you were yet another semi-ascended xperiment, doomed to mental disintegration in a few weeks. If memory serves, I even dozed off – Mr Chang, did I? The truth now.'

From his post near the elevator, Mr Chang recalled that his master had rested his eyes during the journey. Boardman Mephi shrugged. 'You're more than likely wondering what you did to bring yourself to my attention, Sonmi?'

His statement felt like a handshake; *come out, I know you're in there*. Or a trap. I feigned polite incomprehension.

Mephi's xpression of complicity told me he didn't blame me for being cautious. He said that Taemosan has thirteen thousand nine hundred students who generate in xcess of two million library download requests per semester. Most are course-texts and related articles – the remainder is anything from real estate to stock prices, sportsfords to steinways, yoga to caged birds. 'The point is, Sonmi, it takes a reader of *truly* eclectic habits for the head librarian to bother alerting me.' The professor switched on his handsony and read from my list of download requests. Sixth Month 18th, *Epic of Gilgamesh*; Seventh Month 2nd, Ireneo Funes' *Remembrances*. Ninth Month 1st, Gibbon's

Decline and Fall. The Boardman, bathed in mauve sonyglow, looked almost proud; 'Tenth Month 11th, a brazen-as-you-please cross-search for references to that cancer in our beloved body corpocratic, Union.'

As a Unanimityman, he continued, such a hunger for alternative times, places and ideas alerts him to the presence of an inner *émigré*. Such *émigrés* are *very* promising raw material for Unanimity agents.

My 'guest' xplained how he had identified the sony's inquisitive owner as Nun Hel-Kwon, a geothermist from blizzard-prone Onsōng who had died two winters ago in a skiing accident. Boardman Mephi assigned a gifted graduate the old-fashioned detective's task of tracing the thief. E-wave surveillance located the sony's receptor in Boom-Sook Kim's lab; but the notion of Boom-Sook absorbed by Wittgenstein defied belief. So Mephi's student had implanted a microeye in every sony in the room, during curfew six weeks ago. 'Next day, we found our dissident-*manqué* was no pureblood, but, apparently, science's first stabilized ascendant and sister-server of the notorious Yoona~939. My work, Sonmi, can be taxing and hazardous, but dull? Never.'

Denial was plainly pointless.
Indeed. Mephi was no Rhee. I listened to Mephi's account of the interdepartmental squabbles that broke out when he reported his findings. Old-school corpocrats wanted me euthanazed as a deviant; psychogenomicists wanted me to undergo cerebral vivisection; Marketing wanted to go public and claim me as Taemosan University's own xperimental breakthru.

Obviously none of them got their way.
No. Unanimity won a stop-gap compromise: I was permitted to continue my self-education, observed from a distance in my illusory free-will, until a consensus of opinion could be reached. Boom-Sook's crossbow, however, forced Unanimity's hand.

So . . . what did Boardman Mephi intend to do with you now?
Frame a new compromise between those interests competing for

a slice of me; then enforce it. Billions of research dollars had been spent in private labs by corps, unsuccessfully, to achieve what, simply, I was, what I am. To keep the genomicists happy, an array of vetted scientists would conduct cross-disciplinary tests on me. I remember Mephi, dipping his hands into the heart of the 3D flames, assuring me these would not be onerous or painful, nor xceed three hours per day, five days out of ten. To win over the Taemosan Board, research access would be auctioned; I would raise a lot of dollars for my new masters. To keep the orthodox corpocrats quiet, the ascended fabricant would be described as yet another unstable xperiment nearing mental entropy; thereby denying the Abolitionists and Union a Trojan Horse, an icon, a martyr.

Did Sonmi~451's interests enter this simultaneous equation?
The University would enrol me as a foundation student. I would also have a Soul implanted in my collar so I could come and go on campus as I pleased. Boardman Mephi even promised to mentor me when he was on campus. He withdrew his hand from the fire and inspected his fingers. 'All lite, no heat. Youngsters nowadays wouldn't know a real flame if it burned down their dorms.' He told me to call him 'professor' instead of 'sir'.

One thing I can't work out. If Boom-Sook Kim was such an idle buffoon, how had he attained this holy grail of psychogenomics – stable ascension?
Hae-Joo Im's xplanation was this. The agent Boom-Sook had hired to produce his Ph.D. had struck lucky with his sources. A refugee at Baikal Institute, Yusouf Suleiman, had written Boom-Sook's thesis fifteen years ago. Xtremist Abolitionists were killing genomicists in Siberia at that time, and Suleiman and three of his professors were blown up by a car bomb. Baikal being Baikal and Suleiman being a Production Zone immigrant, his research languished in obscurity until it found its way to Boom-Sook's thesis jockey. The agent liaised with Papa Song Corp to add the ascension formula in our Soap. Yoona~939 was the principal specimen; I was the modified back-up. If that sounds unlikely, Hae-Joo said, I should remember that many major

events in the history of science were the results of similar serendipitous accidents.

And Boom-Sook Kim stayed unaware of the furore his Ph.D. had triggered?
Only a fool who had never squeezed a pipette or handled a petri-dish in his life could have remained unaware, but Boom-Sook Kim was such a fool. Maybe that was no accident.

How did you find your new regime in the Unanimity Faculty?
You will recall I was moved on Sextet Eve, so I had six quiet days before the new regime began in earnest. Last Sextet was the coldest since the forties. I walked around the icy campus only once; I am genomed to be comfortable in hot eateries. Xposure to the Han Valley winter on Mount Taemosan burnt my skin and lungs, so I spent the six days inside, studying.

On New Year's Day I awoke from curfew to discover three gifts. A star for my collar, my third; the battered old sony Wing~027 had given me, retrieved from Boom-Sook's x-lab; and a book whose title I could now read: *Fairy Tales of Hans Christian Andersen*. I opened its covers and recognized Yoona's Book of Outside. I read it from start to finish, and thought of my sisters all over Nea So Copros enjoying their Star Ceremonies. The lucky twelvestarreds would be departing for Xultation on Hawaii this very morning, their Investment repaid.

How I wished Yoona~939 could attend my first lecture on Second Day with me. I missed her, sorely; I still do.

What was your first lecture?
Swanti's 'Biomathematics'; but its real lesson was humiliation. I walked to the lecture theater across dirty slush hooded and unnoticed. But when I took off my cloak in the corridor my Sonmi features provoked surprise, then unease. In the lecture theater, my entry detonated resentful silence.

It didn't last. 'Oy!' a boy yelled. 'One hot ginseng, two dogburgers!' and the room laughed. I am not genomed to blush, but my pulse rose. I took a second row seat, occupied by girls. Their leader had emeralded teeth: 'This is *our* row. Go to the back.

You stink of mayo.' I obeyed. A paper dart hit my face. 'I don't vend burgers in your dinery, fabricant: why are you taking up space in my lecture theater?' I was about to leave, when spidery Dr Chu'an tripped on to the stage and dropped her notes, marking the start of the lecture. I did my best to concentrate; I was familiar with Swanti's theories, but not their applications. After about fifteen minutes, Dr Chu'an's eyes roamed her audience, saw me; she stopped midsentence. The audience realized why. Dr Chu'an forced herself to continue. I forced myself to stay where I was. I lacked the courage to ask questions at the end. Outside a barrage of snideries was waiting for me.

Did Professor Mephi know about the students' unfriendliness?
Yes. The professor asked if my lecture had been fruitful; I chose the word 'informative', and asked why the students despised me so when I had given them no cause for offense?

He asked why any dominator fears their dominated gaining knowledge.

I dared not utter the word 'insurrection' and chose a circumspect route. 'What if the differences between social strata stem not from genomics or inherent xcellence or even dollars, but differences in knowledge?'

The professor asked, would this not mean that the whole Pyramid is built on shifting sands?

I speculated such a suggestion could be ruled a serious deviancy.

Mephi seemed delited. 'Try this: fabricants are mirrors held up to purebloods' consciences; what purebloods see therein sickens them. So they blame the mirrors.'

I asked when purebloods might start blaming themselves.

Mephi replied, 'History suggests not until they are *made* to.'

I realized I was sick of the winter. 'When will that happen?'

The professor spun his antique globe. 'Dr Chu'an's lecture continues tomorrow.'

It must have taken courage to return.
An enforcer escorted me. This time no-one flung insults at me. The enforcer addressed the second-row girls with courteous

malice: 'This is *our* row; you might find some room at the back.'
The girls melted away, but I was uncomfortable: it was the girls'
fear of Unanimity, not their acceptance of me, that had prevailed.
Dr Chu'an was so flustered by the enforcer that she mumbled
thru her entire lecture without once looking at her audience.

Prejudice is permafrost.

Did you brave any more lectures?

One, on Lööw's *Fundaments*. I went unescorted, preferring
insults to xternal armour. I arrived early, took a side seat and
kept a vizor on as the theatre filled. The students regarded me
with mistrust but no paper missiles were launched. Two boys
in front turned round. They had honest, concerned faces. One
asked if I really was some sort of artificial genius.

'"Genius" is not a word to bandy so casually,' I suggested.

Hearing a server talk made the pair marvel. 'It must be hell,'
the other asked me, 'to have an intelligent mind trapped in such
an inferior body genomed for service?'

I said I had grown attached to my body.

This time, when I departed from the lecture theater, a fifty-
headed hydra of questions, miked walkmans and flash nikons
pounced. What Papa Song's had I come from? Who had enrolled
me on Taemosan? Had I really been 'ascended'? How? Were
there more of me? Had I heard of Sonmi~939? How many
weeks did I have before my ascension degenerated? Was I an
Abolitionist? Did I have a boyfriend?

Media had been allowed into a state-funded university?

No, but Media was offering rewards for features on the Sonmi
of Taemosan. I hooded and tried to elbow my way back to the
Unanimity Faculty, but the crush was so thick, my vizor was
knocked off and I was floored and badly bruised before two
plainclothes enforcers could evacuate the corridor. Professor
Mephi met me in the Unanimity lobby, muttering that I was too
valuable to xpose myself to the prurient mob. He rotated his
rainstone ring, vigorously; his unconscious indicator of stress.

We agreed my lectures should be dijied to my sony.

How were the morning xperiments you underwent?
A daily reminder of my true status. Looking back, I recognize the alienation Yoona ~ 939 suffered when she withdrew into herself. What was all this knowledge for, I would ask myself, if I could not use it to better my xistence? I saw the bleakness of the bigger picture. How would I fit in on Xultation nine years and nine stars later with my superior knowledge? Could amnesiads erase the knowledge I had acquired? Did I want that to happen?

I sat for hours without scrolling a page of my sony. All I read one week was a tale called 'The Little Mermaid' in Yoona's Book of Outside, a dark treatise on unbelonging. Fourth Month arrived, bringing my first anniversary as a specimen freak on Taemosan, but the spring did not make me glad.

My curiosity is dying, I told Professor Mephi during our seminar on Thomas Paine. It was a brite First Day, and noise from a baseball game drifted thru his open window.

My mentor said we had to identify the source of this illness, urgently.

I said something about reading not being true knowledge, that true knowledge without xperience is food without sustenance.

'You need to get out more,' remarked the professor.

Back to lectures? Out on the campus? Or out in the conurb?
Ninth Nite brought a young Unanimity postgrad named Hae-Joo Im to my quarters. Addressing me as Miss Sonmi, he xplained that Professor Mephi had asked him to 'cheer you up'. Professor Mephi held the power of life and death over his future, so here he was. 'That was a joke,' he added. Then he asked if I remembered him.

I did. His black hair was crewcut maroon now and his eyebrows were zigged where they had been unadorned; but he was Boom-Sook's wiry onetime classmate who had brought the news of Wing ~ 027's death at the idiot hands of Min-Sic.

He looked around my living space. 'Well, this beats Boom-Sook Kim's pokyhole. It could swallow my family's entire apartment.'

I agreed: the apartment was very spacious.

A silence inflated. Hae-Joo Im offered to stay inside the elevator until I wanted him to leave.

Once again, I apologized for my lack of social grace and invited him in.

He took his nikes off, saying, '*I* apologize for *my* lack of social grace. I talk too much when I get nervous, and say stupid things. Here I go again. Can I try out your maglev *chaise-longue*?'

Yes, I said; and asked why I made him nervous.

The obvious thing, he told me, was that I looked like any Sonmi in any old dinery but when I opened my mouth I turned into a doctor of philosophy. The postgrad crosslegged on the *chaise-longue* and swayed, passing his hand through the magnetic field. He confessed, 'A little voice in my head is saying, "Remember, this girl is a landmark in the history of science. The first stable ascended fabricant! Watch what you say! Make it profound!"' So of course, he said, he just spouts rubbishy nothings.

I assured him I felt more like a specimen than a landmark.

Hae-Joo shrugged, and told me the professor had said I could use a nite out downtown, and waved a Soul Ring, smiling, 'Unanimity xpenses. Way-hay. Sky's the limit. What's your idea of fun?'

I had no idea of fun, I apologized.

Well, Hae-Joo probed, what did I do to relax?

'I play Go against my sony,' I said.

'To *relax*?' he responded, incredulous. 'Who wins, you or the sony?'

'The sony,' I answered, 'or how would I ever improve?'

'So winners,' Hae-Joo proposed, 'are the real losers because they learn nothing?' What, then, were losers? Winners?

I didn't know if he was being serious. I said, 'If losers can xploit what their adversaries teach them, yes, losers can become winners in the long term.'

'Sweet Corpocracy,' Hae-Joo Im puffed, 'let's go downtown.'

Didn't he irritate you a little?

At first, he irritated me a lot; but I reminded myself that this postgrad was Professor Mephi's prescription for my malaise. Also, Hae-Joo had paid me the compliment of referring to me as a 'person', and not even Yoona~939 had spoken with me so spontaneously. I asked my visitor what he normally did on Ninth Nites, when not coerced into looking after prize specimens?

Hae-Joo used a diplomatic lowered smile, and told me how men of Mephi's stratum don't need to coerce; they just suggest. He said on Ninth Nites he might go to a dinery or bar with classmates, or, if he got lucky, go clubbing with a girl.

I was not a classmate and not xactly a girl.

He suggested a galleria, to 'sample the fruits of Nea So Copros'.

Would he not be embarrassed, I asked, to be seen with a Sonmi? I could wear a hat and wraprounds.

Hae-Joo Im looked dubious and proposed a stick-on wizardly beard and a pair of reindeer antlers.

'I don't have any,' I said.

Hae-Joo laughed and told me to wear whatever I felt comfortable in, assuring me that I'd blend in much better downtown than in a lecture theater. A taxi was downstairs, and he'd be waiting for me in the lobby.

Were you nervous about leaving Taemosan?

Slitely, yes. Hae-Joo distracted me by siteseeing talk. He directed the taxi via the Memorial to the Fallen Plutocrats, around Kyōngbokkung Palace, down the Avenue of Ten Thousand AdVs. The driver was a pureblood Bangladeshi with a sharp nose for a fat fare from a corp xpense account. 'An ideal nite for Moon Tower, sir,' he happened to mention, and Hae-Joo agreed on the spot. The helterway ascended the gigantic pyramid, high, high above the canopies, high above everything xcept the corp monoliths. Have you ever been up the Moon Tower by nite, Archivist?

No, nor even by day. Us citizens leave the Tower for the tourists, mostly.
Go. From the two-hundred-and-thirty-fourth story, the conurb
was a fog of xenon and neon and motion and carbdiox and
canopies. But for the glass dome, Hae-Joo told me, the wind at
this altitude would launch us away like runaway kites. He indicated various humpbacks and landmarks, some of which I had
heard of or seen on AdV and 3D. Chongmyo Plaza was hidden
behind a monolith, but its stadium was visible: an open dayblue
eye. SeedCorp was the lunar sponsor that nite. The immense
lunar projector on far-off Fuji beamed AdV after AdV on to the
moon's face; tomatoes big as babies; creamy cauliflower cubes;
holeless lotus roots; speech bubbles ballooned from the Seed-
Corp Logoman's juicy mouth.

Descending, the elderly taxi driver spoke of his boyhood in a
distant conurb called Mumbai, now flooded, when the moon
was always naked. Hae-Joo said an AdVless moon would freak
him out.

Which galleria did you go to?
Wangshimni Orchard. The galleria made me think of an encyclo-
pedia, constructed not of words but objects. For hours, I pointed
at items, and Hae-Joo answered: bronze masks, instant birds'
nest soup, fabricant servants, golden suzukis, air-filters, acid-
proof skeins, oracular models of the Beloved Chairman and
statuettes of the Immanent Prime Chairman, jewel-powder per-
fumes, pearlsilk scarves, realtime maps, deadland artefacts, pro-
gramable violins. Hae-Joo showed me a pharmacy: its packets
of pills for cancer, aids, alzheimer's, lead-tox; for corpulence,
anorexia, baldness, hairiness, xuberance, glumness, dewdrugs
for aging; drugs for overindulgence in dewdrugs.

Hour twenty-one chimed, yet we had covered less than a tenth
of a single precinct. How the consumers seethed to buy, buy,
buy; a many-celled sponge of demand that sucked goods and
services from every vendor, dinery, bar, shop and nook as it
spilled dollars.

Hae-Joo led me to a stylish café platform. He bought a styro of starbuck for himself and an aqua for me. He xplained that under the Enrichment Laws, consumers have to spend a fixed quota of dollars each month, depending on their strata. Hoarding is an anti-corpocratic crime. I knew this already but didn't interrupt. He said his mom feels intimidated by modern galleries, so Hae-Joo usually works through the quota.

I asked him to tell me how it feels to be in a family.

The postgrad smiled and frowned at the same time. 'A necessary drag,' he confided. 'Mom's hobby is collecting minor ailments and drugs to cure them. Dad works at the Ministry of Statistics, and sleeps in front of 3D with his head in a bucket.' Both parents were only natural conceptions, he confessed, who sold their second child quota and spent the dollars on having Hae-Joo genomed properly, which let him aim for his cherished career in Unanimity. He'd wanted to be a Unanimityman since he saw enforcer dramas on 3D. Kicking down doors for money looked like a fine life.

His parents must love him very much to make such a sacrifice, I suggested. Hae-Joo noted that their pension will come out of his salary. Then he asked, had it not been a seismic shock to be uprooted from Papa Song's and transplanted into Boom-Sook's lab? Didn't I miss the world I had been genomed for?

I answered, 'Fabricants are orientated not to miss things.'

He probed: hadn't I ascended above my orientation?

I said I would have to think about it.

Did you xperience any negative reactions from consumers in the galleria? As a Sonmi outside Papa Song's, I mean.

Many fabricants could be seen there: porters, domestics and cleaners. I didn't really stand out so much. I received another clue why no-one xpressed the outrage of the campus students a little while later, when Hae-Joo had gone to the hygiener. A ruby-freckled woman with a teenage complexion but tell-tale older eyes apologized for disturbing me. 'Look, I'm a media fashion-scout,' she said, 'call me Lily. I've been spying on you!' and she giggled. 'But that's what a woman of your courage, your flair, but most of all your *prescience*, my dear, must xpect, wouldn't you say?'

I was very confused.

She said I was the first consumer she'd seen to go the whole way and facescape like a well-known service fabricant. 'Lesser strata,' she said, solemnly, 'may call it brave, I call it genius.' Then she asked, how would I like to model for 'an abhorrently chic 3D magazine'? I'd be paid *stratospherically*, she assured me, and my boyfriend's friends would be *crawling* with jealousy, and for women jealousy in our men is as good as dollars in the Soul.

I thanked her, but declined, adding that fabricants don't have boyfriends. She smiled indulgently, xamining every contour on my face, and begged to know which facescaper had done me. 'A craftsman like this I have *got* to know. Such a miniaturist!'

After my seedtank and orientation, I said, my life had been spent behind a counter at Papa Song's, and so I had never met my facescaper.

The fashion editor's laugh was droll but vexed.

Oh, now I get it – she couldn't believe you weren't a pureblood?
She gave me her card, urging me to reconsider and *call*. 'Opportunities like me don't come trotting along ten days a week.'

When the taxi dropped me at Unanimity, Hae-Joo Im asked me to use his given name from then on. 'Mr Im' made him feel like he was in a seminar. Lastly, he asked if I might be free next Ninth Day.

I said I didn't want him to spend his valuable time on a professorial obligation.

Hae-Joo admitted he hadn't known what to xpect, but insisted he'd enjoyed himself. 'So let's have a return match.'

I said, 'Well, okay.'

So the xcursion helped dislodge your . . . sense of *ennui*?
I understood that one's environment is a key to one's identity, but that my environment, Papa Song's, was a key I had lost. I

realized I wanted to revisit my x-dinery under Chongmyo Plaza. I'm not sure I can xplain why, but an impulse can be both vaguely understood and strong.

. . . It could hardly be wise for an ascended server to visit a dinery?

I am not saying it was wise; only that it was necessary. Hae-Joo was also dubious, ten days later, worrying that it might 'unearth buried things'.

That, xactly, was my point. I had buried too much of myself.

He agreed, and showed me how to upswirl my hair and apply cosmetics. A flamboyant silk neck-scarf hid my collar, and in the elevator down to the taxi he fitted his jade shades over my face.

On a Fourth Month Ninth Nite, Chongmyo Plaza was not the litterswarming wind-tunnel I remembered: it was a seething kaleidoscope of AdVs, consumers, xecs and popsongs. Beloved Chairman's monumental statue surveyed his teeming peoples with an xpression wise and benign. From the Plaza's south-east rim, Papa Song's arches drew into focus. Hae-Joo held my hand and reminded me we could turn back at any time. We queued for the elevator; he slipped a Soul Ring on to my finger.

Why?

For good luck: Hae-Joo had a superstitious streak. We entered the elevator's crush and the box descended; how different it had been with Mr Chang!

Suddenly, the doors were opening and hungry consumers riptided me into the dinery; I stood, stunned, at how misleading my memories had been.

In what ways?

That spacious dome: so poky. Its glorious reds and yellows: stark and vulgar. The wholesome air: its greasy stench gagged me. After the silence on Taemosan, the dinery noise was like neverending gunfire. Papa Song stood on His Plinth; greeting us. I tried to swallow but my throat was dry. Surely, our Logoman would condemn his prodigal daughter?

No. He winked at us, tugged himself skywards by his own nikestraps, sneezed, oopsied, and plummeted down to His Plinth. Children screamed with laughter. How had an inane hologram inspired such awe in us?

Hae-Joo went to find a table while I circummed the Hub. My sisters smiled under sweet toplites. How unflaggingly they worked! Here were Yoonas, here was Ma-Leu-Da~108, her collar still boasting my dead friend's star. My planned revenges seemed so puny now. What fate could I concoct worse then twelve years in Papa Song's? At my old counter on west was a freshfaced Sonmi. Here was Kyelim~889, Yoona's replacement. I queued at her teller, my nervousness growing acute as my turn approached. 'I'm Kyelim~889! Mouthwatering, magical *Papa Song's*! Yes, madam? Your pleasure today?'

I asked her if she knew me.

Kyelim~889 smiled xtra to dilute her confusion.

I asked, soft and slow, if she remembered Sonmi~451, a server who worked beside her, who disappeared one morning?

A blank smile. The verb 'remember' was outside her lexicon. 'Hi! I'm Kyelim~889! Mouthwatering, magical *Papa Song's*!'

I asked, 'Are you happy, Kyelim~889?'

Enthusiasm lit her smile as she nodded.

'"Happy" is a word in the Second Catechism. I can still quote them. "Proviso I obey the Catechisms, Papa Song loves me; proviso Papa Song loves me, I am happy."'

A cruel compulsion brushed me. I asked the Kyelim, didn't she want to live how purebloods live? Sit at dinery tables instead of wiping them?

Kyelim~889 wanted so badly to please, telling me 'Servers eat Soap!'

Yes, I persisted, but didn't she want to see Outside?

The server's xpression could have been my own when Yoona~939 uttered her deviancies. She said, 'Servers don't go Outside until twelvestarred.'

A consumer girl with zinc-ringlets and plectrum nails jabbed me. 'If you've *got* to taunt dumb fabricants, do it on First Day mornings, not Ninth Nites. I need to get to the gallerias *this* side of curfew, yeah?'

Hastily, I ordered rosejuice and sharkgums from Kyelim~889. I wished Hae-Joo was still with me: I was jumpy in case the Ring Soul malfunctioned, and xposed me as an escaped fabricant.

The Ring Soul worked, but my questions had marked me as a troublemaker. 'Upstratum your *own* fabricants!' the consumer's boyfriend glowered, as I pushed by with my tray. '*Abolitionist.*' Other purebloods in the queue glanced at me as I passed, worried, as if I carried a disease.

Hae-Joo had found a free table in the west quarter. How many tens of thousands of times had I wiped this surface? Hae-Joo asked, gently, if I had discovered anything valuable.

I whispered, 'We are just *slaves* here for twelve years.'

The Unanimity postgrad scratched his ear and checked no-one was eavesdropping. He sipped his rosejuice, nodding. We watched AdV for ten minutes, not speaking.

So your visit to Papa Song's was an ... anticlimax? Did you find the 'key' to your ascended self?

I suppose the key was, there was no key. In Papa Song's I had been a slave; at Taemosan I was a slitely more privileged slave. One more thing occurred, however, as we headed back to the elevator. I recognized an xec wife, working at her sony. I spoke her name out loud: 'Mrs Rhee.'

The immaculately dewdrugged woman looked up with a puzzled smile formed by luscious, remodeled lips. 'I *was* Mrs Rhee, but I'm Mrs Ahn now. My late husband drowned in a fishing-boat accident last year.'

'Oh,' I said. 'That's just awful.'

Mrs Ahn asked if I had known her late husband well.

Lying is harder than purebloods make it look.

Mrs Ahn repeated her question.

'My wife was a qualities standardizer for the Corp before our marriage,' Hae-Joo xplained quickly, adding that Chongmyo

Plaza was in her area and that Seer Rhee had been an xemplary corpman.

Mrs Ahn's suspicions were aroused. She asked xactly when I had worked under her late husband.

Now I knew what to say. 'When his Aide was a consumer named Cho.'

Her smile stayed firm but changed quality. 'Ah, yes, Aide Cho was sent north, somewhere, to learn team spirit.'

Hae-Joo took my arm, saying, 'Well, "All for Papa Song, Papa Song for All." The gallerias beckon, darling. Mrs Ahn is obviously a woman who wastes no time.' We wished each other good fortune.

Later, back in my quiet apartment, Hae-Joo paid me this compliment. 'If *I* had ascended from server to prodigy in twelve straight months, my current address wouldn't be a guest quarter in the Unanimity Faculty, it'd be deep in the heart of La-la-la Land. You say you're "depressed" – all I see is resilience. You are *allowed* to feel messed up and inside out. It doesn't mean you're defective – it just means you're human.'

We played Go until curfew. Hae-Joo won the first game; I, the second.

How many of these xcursions took place?

Every Ninth Nite until Corpocracy Day. Familiarity bred regard for Hae-Joo. I came to share Boardman Mephi's high opinion of him. The professor didn't discuss our outings during our seminars; his *protégé* may have filed reports, but Mephi wanted me to savour a sense of privacy. Board business demanded more of his time and I saw him less regularly. The morning tests continued, with courteous but unmemorable scientists.

Hae-Joo's fondness for campus intrigue was informative. I learnt how Taemosan was no united organism but a hillock of warring tribes and interest groups, much like the Juche. The Unanimity Faculty maintained a despised dominance. 'Secrets are magic bullets,' Hae-Joo quoted his professor. But this dominance also xplains why trainee enforcers have few friends outside the faculty. Girls looking for husbands, Hae-Joo admitted, were attracted to his future status, but males his own age upwards didn't want to get drunk in his company.

Archivist, time is passing. Can we segue to my final nite on campus?

As you wish.
A keen passion of Hae-Joo's was disneys, and one perq of Professor Mephi's mentorship was access to forbidden items in the security archives.

You mean Union samizdat from the Production Zones?
No. I mean that zone even more forbidden: the past. Disneys from before the Skirmishes. They were called 'movies' in those days. Hae-Joo said the ancients had an artistry that 3D and corpocracy had long obsolesced. I had to believe him: the only disneys I had ever seen were Boom-Sook's pornsplatters. On Six Month's last Ninth Nite, Hae-Joo came dangling a key to a viewing auditorium on campus, saying by way of xplanation that a Media student owed him a favour. He spoke in a theatrical whisper: 'I've got a disc of, seriously, one of the greatest movies ever made by any director, from any age.'

Namely?
A picaresque entitled *The Ghastly Ordeal of Timothy Cavendish*, made before the foundation of Nea So Copros in a long-deadlanded province of the abortive European democracy. Have you ever seen film from the early twenty-first century, Archivist?

An eighthstratum archivist can't dream of getting such security clearance! I'm amazed a mere postgrad was entrusted with such inflammatory fiction, even a Unanimity one.
Why our corpocratic state outlaws *any* historical discourse is a perplexing question. Is it that history provides a bank of human xperience that rivals Media's? If so, why preserve archives like your ministry's, whose very xistence is a state secret?

I'm sure I couldn't say. What was your own opinion of this *Ghastly Ordeal*?

Its world intrigued me; its differences from our own were indescribable. Purebloods did all the menial work then; the only fabricants were sickly sheep. People sagged and uglified as they aged; no dewdrugs. Elderly people waited to die in prisons for the senile and incontinent; no fixed-term lifespans, no euthanasium.

It all sounds grimly dystopian.

Then, as now, dystopia was a function of poverty, not state policy. The deserted auditorium was a haunting frame for its rainy landscapes of the old disney. Giants strode across the screen, lit by sunlite captured thru a lens when your grandfather's grandfather, Archivist, was kicking inside his mother's womb.

Time is what stops history happening at once; time is the speed at which the past disappears. Film gives those lost worlds a brief resurrection. Those since-fallen buildings, those long-decayed faces, they engrossed me. *We were as you are*, they said. *The present doesn't matter.* My fifty minutes in front of the cinema screen with Hae-Joo were an xercise in happiness.

Only fifty minutes?

Hae-Joo's handsony purred at a key scene, when the film's eponymous book thief suffered some sort of seizure; his face, contorted above a plate of peas, froze. A panicky voice buzzed from Hae-Joo's handsony: 'It's Xi-Li! I'm outside! Let me in! The worst has happened!' Hae-Joo pressed the remo-key and the auditorium door opened; a wedge of yellow lite slid over the empty seats. A student ran over, his face shiny with sweat, saluted to Hae-Joo, and broke news that would unravel my life. Again. Forty or fifty enforcers had stormed the Unanimity Faculty, arrested Professor Mephi, and were searching for us. Their orders were to capture Hae-Joo for interrogation, and kill me on sight. The campus checkpoints were manned.

What did you think on hearing that?

I couldn't think.

My companion now xuded a grim authority that I realized

had always been there. He glanced at his rolex and asked if Mr Chang was still free. Xi-Li, the messenger, reported that Mr Chang had headed for the fordpark in the basement.

The man I had known as Postgrad Hae-Joo Im, backdropped by a long-dead actor playing a character conceived a century ago, looked into my eyes and said my name. 'I am not xactly who I said I am.'

Sloosha's Crossin' an' Ev'rythin' After

Old Georgie's path an' mine crossed more times'n I'm comfy mem'ryin', an' after I'm died, no sayin' what that fangy devil won't try an' do to me . . . so gimme some mutton an' I'll tell you 'bout our first meetin'. A fat joocesome slice, nay, none o'your burnt wafery off'rin's . . .

Adam, my bro, an' Pa'n'me was trekkin' back from Honokaa Market on miry roads with a busted cart-axle in draggly clothesies. Evenin' catched us up early so we tented on the southly bank o' Sloosha's Crossin', 'cos Waipio river was furyin' with days o' hard rain an' swollen by a spring tide. Sloosha's was friendsome ground tho' marshy, no'un lived in the Waipio Valley 'cept for a mil'yun birds, that's why we din't camo our tent or pull-cart or nothin'. Pa sent me huntin' for tinder'n' firewood while he'n'Adam tented up.

Now, I'd got diresome hole-spew that day 'cos I'd ate a gammy dog-leg in Honokaa, an' I was squattin' in a thicket o' ironwood trees upgulch when sudd'nwise eyes on me, I felt 'em. 'Who's there?' I called, an' the mufflin' ferny swallowed my voice.

Oh, a darky spot you're in, boy, murmed the mufflin' ferny.

'Name y'self!' shouted I, tho' not so loud. 'I got my blade, I have!'

Right 'bove my head some'un whisped, *Name y'self, boy, is it Zachry the Brave or Zachry the Cowardy?* Up I looked an' sure 'nuff there was Old Georgie crossleggin' on a rottin' ironwood tree, a slywise grinnin' in his hungry eyes.

'I ain't 'fraid o' *you!*' I told him, tho' tell-it-true my voice was jus' a duck-fart in a hurrycane. Quakin' inside I was when Old Georgie jumped off his branch an' then what happened?

He dis'peared in a blurry flurryin', yay, b'hind me. Nothin' there...'cept for a plump lardbird snufflyin' for grubs, jus' askin' for a pluckin'n'a spit! Well, I reck'ned Zachry the Brave'd faced down Old Georgie, yay, he'd gone off huntin' cowardier vic'tries'n me. I wanted to tell Pa'n'Adam 'bout my eery adventurin' but a yarnin' is more delish with broke-de-mouth grinds, so hushly-hushly up I hoicked my leggin's an' I crept up on that meatsome feathery buggah . . . an' I dived.

Mister Lardbird he slipped thru my fingers an' skipped off but I wasn't givin' up, nay, I chased him upstream thru bumpy 'n'thorny thickets, spring-heelin' dead branches'n'all, thorns scratched my face diresome, but see I'd got the chasin' fever so I din't notice the trees thinnin' nor the Hiilawe Falls roarin' nearer, not till I ran schnock into the pool clearin' an' giddied up a bunch o' horses. Nay, not wild horses, these was horses decked in studded leather armour an' on the Big Isle that means one' thing only, yay, the Kona.

Ten–twelve of them painted savages was 'ready risin'n' reachin' for their whips'n'blades, yellin' war-cries at me! O, now I legged it back downgulch the way I'd come, yay, the hunter was the hunted. The nearest Kona was runnin' after me, others was leapin' on their horses an' laughin' with the sport. Now panickin' wings your foot but it muddies your thinkin' too, so I rabbited back to Pa. I was only a niner so I jus' followed my instinct without thinkin' thru what'd happen.

I never got back to our tentin' tho', or I'd not be sittin' here yarnin' to you. Over a ropy root – Georgie's foot maybe – I tripped'n'tumblied into a pit o' dead leaves what hid me from the Kona hoofs thunderin' over me. I stayed there, hearin' them jagged shouts goin' by, jus' yards away runnin' thru' them trees . . . straight t'ward Sloosha's. To Pa'n'Adam.

I creeped slywise'n'speedy but late I was, yay, way too late. The Kona was circlin' our camp, their bullwhips crackin'. Pa he'd got his axe swingin' an' my bro'd got his spiker, but the Kona was jus' toyin' with 'em. I stayed at the lip o' the clearin', see fear was pissin' in my blood an' I cdn't go on. *Crack!* went a whip, an' Pa'n'Adam was topsied an' lay wrigglyin' like eels on the sand. The Kona chief, one sharky buggah, he got off his horse an' walked splishin' thru the shallows to Pa, smilin' back at his painted bros, got out his blade an' opened Pa's throat ear to ear.

Nothin' so ruby as Pa's ribbonin' blood I ever seen. The chief licked Pa's blood off the steel.

Adam'd got the dead shock, his spunk was drained off. A painted buggah binded his heels'n'wrists an' tossed my oldest bro over his saddle like a sack o' taro, an' others sivvied our camp for ironware'n'all an' busted what they din't take. The chief got back on his horse an' turned'n'looked right at me . . . them eyes was Old Georgie's eyes. *Zachry the Cowardy*, they said, *you was born to be mine, see, why even fight me?*

Did I prove him wrong? Stay put an' sink my blade into a Kona neck? Follow 'em back to their camp an' try'n free Adam? Nay, Zachry the Brave Niner he snakysnuck up a leafy hideynick to snivel'n'pray to Sonmi he'd not be catched'n'slaved too. Yay, that's all I did. O, if I'd been Sonmi list'nin', I'd o' shooked my head digustly an' crushed me like a strawbug.

Pa was still lyin'n'bobbin' in the salt shallows when I sneaked back after night'd fallen; see, the river was calmin' down now an' the weather clearin'. Pa, who'd micked'n'biffed'n'loved me. Slipp'ry as cavefish, heavy as a cow, cold as stones, ev'ry drop o'blood sucked off by the river. I cudn't grief prop'ly yet nor nothin', ev'rythin' was jus' too shock'n'horrorsome, see. Now Sloosha's was six–seven up'n'down miles from Bony Shore, so I built a mound for Pa where he was. I cudn't mem'ry the Abbess's holy words 'cept *Dear Sonmi, Who Art Amongst Us, Return this Beloved Soul to a Valley Womb, We Beseech Thee.* So I said 'em, forded the Waipio, an' trogged up the switchblade thru the night forest.

An elf-owl screeched at me, *Well fought, Zachry the Brave!* I yelled at the bird to shut up, but it screeched back, *Or else? You'll bust me like you bust them Kona? O, for the sake o'my chicky-chick-chicks do have mercy!* Up in the Kohala Mountains, dingos was howlin', *Cowardyyy-yy-y Zachryyy-yy-y*. Lastly the moon she raised her face, but that cold lady din't say nothin' nay she din't have to, I knowed what she thinked o' me. Adam was lookin' at that same moon, only two-three-four miles away, but for all I could help him, that could'o been b'yonder Far Honolulu. I bust open an' sobbed'n'sobbed'n'sobbed, yay, like a wind-knotted babbit.

An uphill mile later I got to Abel's dwellin' an' I hollered 'em up. Abel's eldest Isaak let me in an' I telled 'em what'd happened at Sloosha's Crossin', but ... did I tell the hole true? Nay, wrapped in Abel's blankies, warmed by their fire'n'grinds, the boy Zachry lied. I din't 'fess how I'd leaded the Kona to Pa's camp, see, I said I'd just gone huntin' a lardbird into the thicket, an' when I got back ... Pa was killed, Adam taken an' Kona hoofs in the mud ev'rywhere. Cudn't do nothin', not then, not now. Ten Kona bruisers could'o'slayed Abel's kin jus'as easy as slayin' Pa.

Your faces are askin' me. Why'd I lie?

In my new tellin', see, I wasn't Zachry the Stoopit nor Zachry the Cowardy, I was jus' Zachry the Unlucky'n'Lucky. Lies are Old Georgie's vultures what circle on high lookin' down for a runty'n'weedy soul to plummet'n'sink their talons in, an' that night at Abel's dwellin', that runty'n'weedy soul, yay, it was me.

Now you people're lookin' at a wrinkly buggah, mukelung's nibblin' my breath away, an' I won't be seein' many more winters out, nay, nay, I know it. I'm shoutin' back more'n forty long years at myself, yay, at Zachry the Niner, *Oy, list'n! Times are you're weak 'gainst the world! Times are you can't do nothin'! That ain't your fault, it's this busted world's fault is all!* But no matter how loud I shout, Boy Zachry, he don't hear me nor never will.

Goat tongue is a gift, you got it from the day you're borned or you ain't got it. If you got it, goats'll heed your say-so, if you ain't, they'll jus' trample you into the mud and stand there laughin'n'scornin'. I'd got my goat tongue from Pa, an' sum-times, when I was herdin'em I reck'ned I heard him playin' his flute not so far off, tho' Abbess said he'd been reborned at Kashinski Dwellin' over in Mormon Valley. Anyway, ev'ry dawnin' I'd milk the nannies an' most days take the hole herd up the throat o'Elepaio Valley, thru Vert'bry Pass to pasturin' in the Kohala Peaks. I herded Aunt Bees' goats too, they'd got fifteen–twenty goats so all-telled I'd got fifty–sixty to mind'n' help their birthin' an' watch for sick'uns. A lot o' goats to minder is that many, but I loved them dumb beasts more'n I loved myself, 'spesh'ly after Pa was killed'n Adam was slaved. Ev'ry last'un had a name what I gived 'em. When rain thundered I'd get soaked pluckin' off their leeches, when sun burnt I'd crispen 'n'brown, an' if we was high up in the Kohalas times was I'd not go back down for three–four nights runnin', nay. You'd got to keep your eyes beetlin'. Dingos scavved in the mountains an' they'd try to pick off a wibbly newborn if you wasn't mindin' with your spiker. When my pa was a boy, savages from Mookini'd wander up from Leeward an' rustler away a goat or two, but then the Kona slaved the Mookini all southly an' their old dwellin's in Hawi went to moss'n'ants. We goaters we knowed the Kohala Mountains like no'un else, the crannies'n' streams'n'haunted places, steel trees what the oldtime scavvers'd missed, an' one-two-three old'un buildin's what no'un knowed but us.

Goaters had a spesh rep'tation for hornyin' up the girls. See, if a girl got a throb for a goater she could just follow our whistlin' to where no'un was, an' we'd just do it under the sky an' no'un see 'cept the goats, an' goats never say nothin' to Old Ma Yibber. I planted my first babbit up Jayjo from Cutter Foot Dwellin' this way, under a lemon tree one a-sunny day. Leastways hers was the first what I knowed. Girls get so slywise 'bout who'n'when'n'all. I was twelve, Jayjo'd got a firm'n'eager body an' laughed, twirly an' crazy with love we both was, yay, jus' like you two sittin' here, so when Jayjo plummed up ripe we was talkin'bout marryin' so she'd come'n'live at Bailey's

Dwellin'. We'd got a lot o' empty rooms, see. But then Jayjo's waters busted moons too soon an' Banjo fetched me to Cutter Foot where she was labourin'. The babbit came out jus' a few beats after I'd got there.

This ain't a smilesome yarnie, but you asked 'bout my life on Big Island, an' these is the mem'ries what are minnowin' out. The babbit'd got no mouth, nay, no nose-holes neither, so it cudn't breath an' was dyin' from when Jayjo's ma skissored the cord, poor little buggah. Its eyes never opened, it just felt the warm of its pa's hands on its back, turned bad colors, stopped kickin' an' died.

Jayjo she was clammy'n'tallow an' looked like dyin' too. The women told me to clear out an' make space for the herb'list.

I took the died babbit wrapped in a woolsack to the Bony Shore. So lornsome I was, wond'rin' if Jayjo's seed was rotted or my seed was rotted or jus' my luck was rotted. Slack mornin' it was under the bloodflower bushes, waves lurched up the beach like sickly cows an' fell over. Buildin' the babbit's mound din't take as long as Pa's. Bony Shore had the air o' kelp an' flesh'n' rottin', old bones was lyin'mongst the pebbles, an' you din't hang 'bout longer'n you needed to, 'cept you was borned a fly or a raven.

Jayjo she din't die, nay, but she never laughed twirly like b'fore an' we din't marry, nay, you got to know your seeds'll grow a purebirth or sumthin' close, yay? Or who'll scrape the moss off your roof an' oil your icon 'gainst termites when you're gone? So if I met Jayjo at a gath'rin' or bart'rin' she'd say, *Rainy mornin' ain't it?* an' I'd answer, *Yay, rain till nightfall it will I reck'n*, an' we'd pass by. She married a leather-maker from Kane Valley three years after, but I din't go to their marryin' feast.

It was a boy. Our died no-name babbit. A boy.

Valleysmen only had one god an' her name it was Sonmi. Savages on Big I norm'ly had more gods'n you could wave a spiker at. Down in Hilo they prayed to Sonmi if they'd the moodin' but they'd got other gods too, shark gods, volcano gods, corn gods, sneeze gods, hairy-wart gods, O, you name it, the Hilo'd birth a god for it. The Kona'd got a hole tribe o' war gods an' horse gods'n all. But for Valleysmen savage gods weren't worth knowin', nay, only Sonmi was real.

She lived 'mongst us, minderin' the Nine Folded Valleys. Most times we cudn't see her, times was she was seen, an old crone with a stick, tho' I sumtimes seen her as a shimm'rin' girl. Sonmi helped sick'uns, fixed busted luck, an' when a truesome 'n'civ'lized Valleysman died she'd take his soul an' lead it back into a womb somewhere in the Valleys. Time was we mem'ried our gone lifes, times was we cudn't, times was Sonmi telled Abbess who was who in a dreamin', times was she din't . . . but we knew we'd always be reborned as Valleysmen, an' so death weren't so scarysome for us, nay.

Unless Old Georgie got your soul, that is. See, if you b'haved savage-like an' selfy an' spurned the civ'lize, or if Georgie tempted you into barb'rism an' all, then your soul got heavy'n' jagged an' weighed with stones. Sonmi cudn't fit you into no womb then. Such crookit selfy people was called 'stoned' an' no fate was more dreadsome for a Valleysman.

Now the candle o' civ'lize is burnt away, does any o' this matter? Well, I can't say yay an' I can't say nay. I jus' place my soul in Sonmi's hands an' pray she'll lead my soul to a good place in the next life 'cos she saved my soul in this 'un an' by 'n'by, if the fire don't dozy you to sleep, I'll be tellin' you how.

The Icon'ry was the only buildin' on Bony Shore 'tween Kane Valley an' Honokea Valley. There was no say-so 'bout keepin' out, but no'un went in idlesome 'cos it'd rot your luck if you din't have no good reason to 'sturb that roofed night. Our icons, what we carved'n'polished'n'wrote words on durin' our lifes, was stored there after we died. Thousands of 'em there was shelfed in my time, yay, each 'un a Valleysman like me borned 'n'lived'n'reborned since the Flotilla what bringed our ancestors got to Big I to 'scape the Fall.

First time I went inside the Icon'ry was with Pa'n'Adam'n'

Jonas when I was a sevener. Ma'd got a leakin' malady birthin' Catkin, an' Pa took us to pray to Sonmi to fix her, 'cos the Icon'ry was a spesh holy place an' Sonmi was norm'ly list'nin' there. Watery dark it was inside. Wax'n'teak-oil'n'time was its smell. The icons lived in shelfs from floor to roof, how many there was I cudn't tell, nay, you don't go countin'em like goats, but the gone-lifes outnumber the now-lifes like leafs outnumber trees. Pa's voice spoke in the shadows, fam'liar it was but eery too, askin' Sonmi to halt Ma's dyin' an' let her soul stay in that body for longer, an' in my head I prayed the same, tho' I knowed I been marked by Old Georgie at Sloosha's Crossin'. An' then we heard a sort o' roaring underneath the silence, made o' mil'yuns o' whisp'rin's like the ocean, only it wasn't the ocean, nay, it was the icons, an' we knew Sonmi was in there list'nin' to us.

Ma din't die. Sonmi's got mercy, see.

My second time in the Icon'ry was Dreamin' Night. When fourteen notches on our icons said we was a growed Valleysman, we'd sleep 'lone in the Icon'ry an' Sonmi'd give us a spesh dreamin'. Some girls seen who they'd marry, some boys seen a way o' livin', other times we'd see stuff what we'd take to Abbess for an augurin'. When we left the Icon'ry in the mornin' we'd be men an' women.

So gone sunset I lay under my pa's blanky in the Icon'ry with my own uncarved icon as a pillow. Outside Bony Shore was rattlin'n'clackin' an' breakers was churnin'n'boilin' an' a whip-poorwill I heard. But it weren't no whippoorwill, nay, it was a trapdoor openin' right by me, an' a rope swingin' down into the underworld sky. *Climb down*, Sonmi told me, so I did, but the rope was made o' human fingers'n'wrists weaved together. I looked up an' seen fire comin' down from the Icon'ry floor. *Cut the rope*, said a crookit man, but I was scared to 'cos I'd o' fallen, yay?

Next dream, I was holdin' my freakbirth babbit boy in Jayjo's room. He was kickin'n'wrigglyin' like he'd done that day. *Quick, Zachry*, said the man, *cut your babbit a mouth so he can breathe!*

I'd got my blade in my hand so I carved my boy a smily slit, like cuttin' cheese it was. Words frothed out, *Why'd you kill me, Pa?*

My last dream had me walkin' long Waipio river. On the far side I seen Adam, fishin' happ'ly! I waved but he din't see me, so I ran to a bridge what ain't there in wakin' life, nay, a gold 'n' bronze bridge. When fin'ly I got to Adam's side tho', I sobbed griefsome 'cos nothin' was left but mouldrin' bones an' a little silver eel flippy-flappin' in the dust.

The eel was dawnlight crackin' under the Icon'ry door. I mem'ried the three dreams an' walked thru the drizzly surf to Abbess without meetin' not a body. Abbess was feedin' her chicklin's b'hind the school'ry. She list'ned close to my dreamin's, then told me they was slywise augurin's an' say-soed me to wait inside the school'ry while she prayed to Sonmi for their true meanin's.

The school'ry room was touched with the holy mist'ry o' the Civ'lized Days. Ev'ry book in the Valleys sat on them shelfs, saggy'n'wormy they was gettin' but, yay, they was books an' words o' knowin'! A ball o'the world there was too. If hole world is a giant big ball, I din't und'stand why people don't fall off it an' I still don't. See, I'd not much smart in school'ry learnin', not like Catkin who could o' been the next Abbess if all things happened diff'rent. School'ry windows was glass still unbusted since the Fall. The greatest of 'mazements tho' was the clock, yay, the only workin' clock in the Valleys an' in hole Big I, hole Ha-Why, far as I know. See, it din't need batt'ries it was a wind-up. When I was a schooler I was 'fraid of that tick-tockin' spider watchin'n'judgin' us. Abbess'd teached us Clock Tongue but I'd forgot it, 'cept for *O'Clock* an' *Half Past.* I mem'ry Abbess sayin', *Civ'lize needs time, an' if we let this clock die, time'll die too, an' then how can we bring back the Civ'lized Days as it was b'fore the Fall?*

I watched the clock's tickers that mornin' too till Abbess came back from her augurin' an' sat 'cross from me. She told me Old Georgie was hungerin' for my soul, so he'd put a cuss on my dreamin's to fog their meanin'. But luck'ly Sonmi'd spoke her what the true augurin's was. An' you too you got to mem'ry these augurin's well 'cos they'll change the path o'this yarnin' more 'in once.

One: *Hands are burnin', let that rope be not cut.*

Two: *Enemy's sleeping, let his throat be not slit.*

Three: *Bronze is burnin', let that bridge be not crossed.*

I 'fessed I din't und'stand. Abbess said she din't und'stand neither, but it din't matter 'cos *I'd* und'stand the augurin's when the true beat come, an' she made me nail her words fast to my mem'ry. Then she gave me a hen's egg for brekker, still spitty 'n'warm from the bird, an' showed me how to suck out its yolk thru a straw.

So you want to hear about the Great Ship o'the Prescients?

Nay, the Ship ain't no mythy yarnin', it was real as I am an' you are. These here very eyes they seen it ooh, twenty times or more. The Ship'd call at Flotilla Bay twice a year, near the spring an' autumn half'n'halfs when night'n'day got the same long. Notice it never called at no savage town, not Honokaa, not Hilo, not Leeward. An' why? 'Cos only us Valleysmen got 'nuff civ'lize for the Prescients, yay. They din't want no barter with no barb'rians what thinked the Ship was a mighty white bird god or sumthin'! The Ship was the sky's colour was so you cudn't see it till it was jus' offshore. It'd got no oars, nay, no sails, it din't need wind nor currents neither, 'cos it was driven by the smart o' Old'uns. Long as a big islet was the Ship, high as a low hill, it carried two-three-four hundred people, a mil'yun maybe.

Old'un Smart brings queries'n'mys'tries mozzyin' round, don't it? The Ship was no diff'rent. How did it move? Where'd its journeyin's take it? How'd it s'vived all the flashbangin' an' the Fall? Well, I never knowed many o' the answers, an' unlike most storymen, Zachry's yarns ain't made up. The tribe what lived on the Ship was called Prescients, an' they came from an isle named Prescience I. Prescience was bigger'n Maui, smaller'n

Big I, an' far-far in the northly blue, more'n that I ain't knowin' or ain't sayin'.

So the Ship'd anchor 'bout ten throws off School'ry Head an' a pair o' littler hornety boats'd come out the Ship's prow an' fly over the surf to the beach. Each'd got six–eight men'n' women, all dressed in smart clothesies what din't stay wet when they was wet. O, ev'rythin'bout 'em was wondersome. Ship-women too was mansome, see, their hair was sheared, not braided like Valleyswomen, an' they was wirier'n'strong. Their skins was healthy'n'smooth without a speck o'the scabbin', but brewy-brown'n'black they was all of 'em, an' they looked more alike'n other people what you see on Big I. An' Prescients din't speak much, nay. Two guards stayed by the shored boats an' if we asked 'em, *What's your name, sir?* or *Where you headed, miss?* they'd just shake their heads, like sayin', *I won't answer nothin', nay, so don't ask no more.* A mys'trous Smart stopped us goin' close up. The air got thicker till you cudn't go no nearer. A dizzyin' pain it gave you too so you din't donkey 'bout with it, nay.

The barterin' took place in the Commons. Prescients spoke in a strange way, not lazy'n'spotty like the Hilo but salted'n' coldsome. By the time they'd landed, the yibber'd been busy an' most dwellin's was 'ready rushin' baskets o' fruits'n'veggies'n' meats'n'all to the Commons. Also the Prescients filled spesh casks with fresh water from the stream. In return, Prescients bartered ironware what was better'n any made on Big I. They bartered fair an' never spoke knuckly like savages at Honokaa, but politesome speakin' it draws a line b'tween you what says, *I respect you well 'nuff but you an' I ain't kin, so don't you step over this line, yay?* An' so the Prescients never asked us our names an' they never told us theirs, tho' us young'uns we nicknamed 'em *Short Chief* an' *Hammerhead* an' *Ugly Sis* an' our mas'n'pas used our nicknames when the visitors'd gone back to their Ship.

Yay, the Prescients'd whoah strict rules 'bout barterin' with us. They'd not barter gear Smarter'n anythin' ready on Big I.

259

For 'zample, after Pa was killed, a gath'rin' agreed to build a garrison by Abel's dwellin' to protect the Muliwai Trail what was our main track from Sloosha's Crossin' into our Nine Valleys. Abbess asked the Prescients for spesh weapons to defend us from Kona. The Prescients said nay. Abbess begged 'em, more-less. They still said nay an' that was that.

'Nother rule was not to tell us nothin'bout what lay b'yonder the ocean, not even Prescience Isle, 'cept for its name. Napes of Inoyue Dwellin' asked to earn passage on the Ship, an' that was nearest I seen the Prescients all laugh. Their chief said nay an' no'un was s'prised. We never pushed these rules to bendin' point, 'cos we reck'ned they did our civ'lize an honor by barterin' with us. Abbess'd always invite 'em to stay for a feastin', but the chief'd always naysay politesome. Back to their boats they'd lug their bartered gear. An hour later the Ship'd be gone, eastly in spring, northly in fall.

So the visits was, ev'ry year, since any'un could mem'ry. Season come, season go, Ship come, Ship go. Until my sixteenth year when a Prescient woman called Meronym visited my dwellin' for a spell o' time, an' nothin'd be the same, not in my life, not in the Valleys, nay, not never. Of all my yarnin's, the only'uns I reck'n are truesome mine an' not'uns I scavved off other Storymen, they're my yarnin's 'bout her, 'bout Meronym.

Way back up b'hind Vert'bry Pass was a ridge called Moon's Nest what'd got the best view o' Windward from the Kohala pastures. One glitt'ry spring aft'noon I was herdin' up on Moon's Nest when I spied the Ship 'proachin' Flotilla Bay an' a whoah beautsome sight she was too, blue same as the ocean an' if you wasn't lookin' right at her you'd not see her, nay. Now I knowed I should' o' gone quicksharp to the barterin' but, see, I'd the goats to minder'n all an' by the time I got to the Commons the Prescients'd prob'ly be leavin' anyhow, so I stayed put an' lolled, gazin' on that wondersome Ship o' Smart what came'n'went with the wild gooses an' whales.

Well, that's my reason for stayin', what I told myself, tho' the true reason was a girl called Roses who'd been gatherin' *palila* leafs for her ma's med'sun-makin'. We'd got a feverish hornyin' for each other, see, an' in that druggy skylarkin' aft'noon I was slurpyin' her lustsome mangoes an' moistly fig an' the true is I din't want to go nowhere else, an' Roses din't gather many *palila* leafs that day neither, nay. O, you're laughin' you blushin' young'uns, but time was, yay, I was jus' as you are now.

Come evenin' when I herded my goats home, Ma was flappin' n'anxin' like a one-wing gander an' cussin' me so crazy it was Sussy what I got the hole yibber off. After barterin' at the Commons, instead o' signallin' ev'ry'un back to the Ship how he norm'ly did, the Prescient chief asked to speak to Abbess in private. After a long beat, Abbess'd come out o' the meet an' called a gath'rin'. Valleysmen from the nearby dwellin's was there, 'cept Bailey's our dwellin'. See Ma'd not gone to the Commons neither. So the gath'rin' kicked off there'n'then. *The Prescient chief wants to make a spesh bart'rin' this year*, said Abbess. *One Ship woman wishes to live'n'work in a dwellin' for half a year, to learn our ways an' und'stand us Valleysmen. In return, the chief'll pay us double ev'rythin' we bartered today. Nets, pots, pans, ironware, ev'rythin' double. Now think what an honor this is, an' think o' what we can get for all the gear at the next Honokaa Barter.* Well, it din't take long for one great *Yay!* to gather speed round the gath'rin', an' Abbess had to shout her next question over the rowdy. *Who's to host our Prescient guest?* O, that *Yay!* stopped cold. Folks sudd'nwise had hole bags o'scuses. *We ain't got 'nuff space. We got two babbits comin', our guest cudn't sleep well. The mozzies round our dwellin'd bite her to shreds.* Rusty Volvo that greasy buggah it was who first speaked it. *What 'bout Bailey's dwellin'?* See, Ma nor me wasn't there to coldwater the plan, an' it fired hot pretty quick. *Yay, they got empty rooms since Pa Bailey was killed! Baileys taked more out o' Commons'n they put in last harvest, yay, it's their duty! Yay, they got need o' workin' hands at Bailey's, Ma Bailey'll be* glad *o'the help!* An' so the gath'rin's say-so was settled.

Well, the one-wing gander now it was me, yay. What do Prescients eat'n'drink? Do they sleep in straw? Do they sleep? Six moons! Ma was cussin' me for not goin' to the Ship Barter, an' even tho', yay, Ma was the real chief o' Bailey's, I was the oldest man o' the dwellin' so I should o' gone fair cop. I said, *Look I'll go to Abbess an' tell her we can't host no Prescient here . . .* when *knock, knock, knock,* said our door.

Yay, it was Abbess bringin' the Prescient to move in, with Mylo the school'ry 'sistant. We all knowed we was lumbered with the Valleys' guest then, like it or not like it, we cudn't say, *Get lost* now, yay? It'd bring shame to our roof an' shame to our icons. The Shipwoman she'd got that vin'gary stink o' Smart an' she spoke first, 'cos me'n'Ma was both tongue-knotted so. *Good evenin',* she said, *I'm Meronym, an' I'm thankin' you kindly for hostin' my stay in the Valleys.* Mylo was grinnin' mocksome'n'toady at my anxin', I could o' killed him.

Sussy mem'ried her hostin' manners first, an' she settled our guests an' sent Jonas to fetch brew'n'grinds'n'all. Meronym speaked, *My people got a custom to give small presents to their hosts at the beginnin' of a visit, so I hope you won't mind . . .* She reached into a bag what she'd bringed an' gived us presents. Ma got a fine pot what'd cost five–six bales o'wool at Honokaa, an' she was left breathy sayin' she cudn't accept such a presh gift 'cos welcomin' strangers was Sonmi's way, yay, welcomin' should be free or not at all, but the Prescient woman answered these gifts wasn't payments, nay, they was jus' thanks b'fore kindnesses, an' Ma din't refuse the pot a second time, nay. Sussy'n'Catkin got necklesses what twinked starry, bug-eyed'n' joysome they was, an' Jonas got a hole square mirror what fass'nated him, brighter'n any busted shard what you still see now'n'again.

Mylo wasn't grinnin' so toadsome now, but I din't like this giftin' not a bit, nay, see this offlander was buyin' my kin sure 'nuff an' I wasn't havin' it. So I jus' said the Shipwoman could stay in our dwellin' but I din't want her gift an' that was that.

I said it ruder'n I meant, an' Ma looked spikers at me but Meronym jus' said, *Sure I und'stand*, like I'd speaked ord'nary 'n'norm'ly.

Now a herd o' visitors bleated to our dwellin' that night an' some nights after, from up'n'down the Nine Valleys, kin'n'bros 'n'lastlife fam'ly'n'half-strangers what we only met at bart'rin's, yay, ev'ryun' from Mauka to Mormon came knockin' to see if Old Ma Yibber spoke it true, that a real'n'livin' Prescient was stayin' at Bailey's. We'd got to invite ev'ry last visitor inside o' course an' they gaped in wonderment like Sonmi herself was sittin' in our kitchen, tho' their 'mazement weren't so great they cudn't chomp our grinds'n'down our brew no worries, an' as they drank years o' questions 'bout Prescience an' their whoah-some Ship came pourin' thick'n'fast.

But the wyrd thing was this. Meronym seemed to answer the questions, but her answers didn't quench your curio none, nay, not a flea. So my cuz Spensa o' Cluny Dwellin' asked, *What makes your Ship move?* The Prescient answered, *Fusion engines.* Ev'ryun' nodded wise as Sonmi, O, *fusion engines it is, yay*, no'un asked what 'fusion engine' was 'cos they din't want to look barb'ric or stoopit in front o'the gath'rin'. Abbess asked Meronym to show us Prescience Isle on a map o' the world, but Meronym jus' pointed to a spot an' said, *Here.*

Where? we asked. See, there weren't nothin' but blue sea an' I for one thought she was mickin' us mocksome.

Prescient I weren't on any map made jus' b'fore the Fall, Meronym said, 'cos Prescience's founders kept it secret. It was on older maps, yay, but not the Abbess's.

I'd got a bit o' the brave by now an' I asked our visitor why Prescients with all their high Smart'n'all want to learn 'bout us Valleysmen? What could we poss'bly teach her what she din't know? *The learnin' mind is the livin' mind*, Meronym said, *an' any sort o' Smart is truesome Smart, old Smart or new, high*

Smart or low. No'un but me seen the arrows o'flatt'ry them words fired, or how this crafty spyer was usin' our ign'rance to fog her true 'tentions, so I follered my first question with this pokerer. *But you Prescients got more greatsome'n'mighty Smart'n this hole world, yay?* O, so slywise she picked her words! *We got more'n the tribes o'Ha-Why, less'n Old'uns b'fore the Fall.* See? Don't say a hole lot does it, nay?

I mem'ry jus' three honest answers she gived us. Ruby o' Potter's asked why Prescients'd all got dark skins like cokeynuts, nay, we'd never seen a pale'un or pink'un come off of their Ship. Meronym said her ancestors b'fore the Fall changed their seeds to make dark-skinned babbits to give 'em protection 'gainst the redscab sickness, an' so them babbits' babbits also got it, like father like son, yay, like rabbits'n'cukes.

Napes o' Inouye Dwellin' asked, was she married, 'cos he was single an' had a macadnut orchard an' fig'n'lemon plantation all his own. Ev'ry 'un laughed even, yay, Meronym smiled. She said she'd been married once, yay, an' had a son named Anafi livin' on Prescience I, but her husband'd been killed by savages years ago. She sorried losin' the chance o' them lemons'n'figs but she was too old for the husband market, an' Napes shaked his head in dis'pointment an' said, *O, Shipwoman, you breaked my heart yay you do.*

Last up, my cuz Kobbery asked, *So how old are you?* Yay, that was what we was all wond'rin'. No'un was ready for her answer tho'. *Fifty.* Yay, that's she said an' we was 'mazed as you are now. *Fifty.* The air in our kitchen changed like the cold wind suddenwise comin'. Livin' to fifty ain't wondersome, nay, livin' to fifty is eery an' ain't nat'ral, yay? *How old do Prescients live, then?* asked Melvil o' Black Ox. Meronym shrugged. *Sixty, seventy . . .* O, we all got the gaspin' shock! Norm'ly by forty we're prayin' Sonmi to put us out o' misery an' reborn us quick in a new body, like bladin' a dog's throat what you loved what was sick'n'agonyin'. The only Valleysman who'd ever lived to fifty an weren't flakin' with redscab or dyin' of mukelung was Truman Third, an' ev'ry'un knowed how he'd done a deal with

Old Georgie one hurrycanin' night, yay, that fool'd sold his soul for some extra years. Well, the yarnin' was busted prop'ly after that, an' folks left in gaggles to yibber what'd been said an' answered, ev'ry'un whispin', *Thank Sonmi she's not stoppin' in our dwellin'*.

I was pleased our dammit crookit guest'd teached ev'ry'un to step slywise an' not trust her, nay, not a flea, but I din't sleep none that night, 'cos o' the mozzies an' nightbirds an' toads ringin' an' a myst'rous some'un what was hushly clatt'rin' thru our dwellin' pickin' up stuff here an' puttin' it down there an' the name o'this myst'rous some'un was Change.

First, second, third days the Prescient woman was wormyin' into my dwellin'. Got to 'fess she din't b'have like no queeny-bee, nay, she never lazed a beat. She helped Sussy with dairyin' an' Ma with twinin'n'spinnin' an' Jonas took her bird-eggin' an' she list'ned to Catkin's yippin'bout school'ry, an' she fetched water'n'chopped wood an' she was a quicksome learner. Course the yibber was keepin' a close eye on her an' visitors kept callin' to see the wondersome fifty-year-old woman what jus' looked twenty-five years. Folks what s'pected her to be doin' tricks'n' whizzies was dis'pointed very soon 'cos she din't, nay. Ma she lost her anxin'bout the Shipwoman in a day or two, yay, she started gettin' friendsome with her an' crowy too. *Our visitor Meronym this* an' *Our visitor Meronym that*, it was cockadood-lydooin' morn till night, an' Sussy was ten times badder. Meronym she jus' got on with her work, tho' at night she'd sit at our table an' write on spesh paper, O so finer'n ours. A whoah fast writer she was, but she din't write in our tongue, nay, she wrote in some other speakin'. See, there was other tongues spoken in the Old Countries, not just ours. *What you writin 'bout, Aunt Meronym?* asked Catkin, but the Prescient jus' answered, *My days, pretty one, I'm writin'bout my days.*

I hated her *pretty one* stuff in my fam'ly an' I din't like the way old folks came creepin' up askin' her for lowdown on how to live long. But her writin'bout the Valleys what no Valleysman could read, that anxed me most. Was it Smart or was it spyin' or was it the touch o' Old Georgie?

One steamin' dawn I'd done the milkin'cos Sussy was sluggybeddin' sick when our guest asked to come herdin' the goats with me. Ma said yay, o' course. I din' say yay, I said, coolsome'n' stony, *Grazin' goats ain't int'restin' for folks with so much Smart as you.* Meronym said politesome, *Ev'rythin' Valleysmen do is int'restin' for me, Host Zachry, but course if you jus' don't want me to watch your work, that's fine, jus' come out an' say-so.* See? Her words was slipp'ry wrestlers, they jus' flipped your *nay* into a *yay*. Ma was hawkeyein' me so, *Sure, fine, yay, come*, I'd got to say.

Herdin' my goats up Elepaio Track, I din' say nothin' else. Past Cluny's Dwellin' a bro o' mine, Gubboh Hogboy, shouted, *Howzit, Zachry!* for a discussin' but when he seen Meronym he awked an' jus' said, *Go careful, Zachry.* O, I wished I could shruck that woman off my back, so I say-soed, *Stop draggin', you slugger-buggahs*, to my goats an' hiked harder, hopin' to wear her out, see, upstream thru Vert'bry Pass we went but she din't quit, nay, not even on the rocky trail to Moon's Nest. Prescient tuff it's a match for goater tuff, I learnt it then. I reck'ned she knowed my thinkin' an' was laughin' at me, inward, so I din't speak nothin' more to her.

What did she do when we reached Moon's Nest? She sat on Thumb Rock an' got out a writin' book an' sketched that whoahsome view. O, Meronym'd got whoahsome drawin'-Smart I got to 'fess. On that paper the Nine Folded Valleys appeared an' the coast'n'headlands, an' highlands'n'lowgrounds, jus' as real as the real'uns. I din't want to give her no int'rest but I cudn't stop me. I named ev'rythin' she'd marked, an' she wrote the names until it was half picturin' half writin', I said. *'Zactly so*, said Meronym, *it's a map we done here.*

Now. I heard a twig snappin' in a fringe o' firs b'hind us. Not the fluky wind it weren't, nay, it was a leg done it sure 'nuff, but a foot or hoof or claw I cudn't tell. Kona up the

Windward Kohalas weren't knowed but so weren't Kona at Sloosha's Crossin', nay, so into that thicket I went for a look-see. Meronym wanted to come with me but I told her to stay put. Could it be Old Georgie come back to stone my soul some more? Or jus' a hermity Mookini wand'rin' for grinds? I'd got my spiker an' I crept nearer the firs, nearer the firs . . .

Roses sat straddlin' a mossy fat stump. *See you got fresh comp'ny*, she said politesome, but there was a furyin' dingo bitch in her eyes.

Her? I pointed back at Meronym, who sat watchin' us talk. *Ain't yibber telled you, the Shipwoman's older'n my granny was when Sonmi reborned her! Don't be jealous o' her! She ain't like you, Roses. She's got so much Smart in her head she's got a busted neck.*

Roses weren't politesome now. *So I ain't got no Smart?*

Women, O, women! They'll find the baddest meanin' in your words an' hold it up, sayin', *Look what you attacked me with!* Lust-bonered hothead what I was, a bit o' knuckly talkin'd cure Roses' senses, so I reck'ned. *You know that ain't what I'm sayin' you dumb vamoosin' bint—*

I din't finish speakin' my cure 'cos Roses schnockoed my face so hard the ground dived forward an' I crashed on my jaxy. So shocked I was I jus' sat there like a dropped babbit, I dabbed my nose an' my fingers was red. *Oh*, said Roses, then *Ha!* then, *You can bitchmouth your nanny goats all you wants, herder, but not me, so Old Georgie stone your soul!* The baddest cuss Valleysmen knowed was that. Our lovin'n'throbbin' for each other was smashed to a mil'yun ittybitties an' off Roses went then, swingin' her basket.

Mis'ry'n'barrassment are hungersome for blame, an' what I blamed for losin' Roses was the dammit Prescient. That mornin' on Moon's Nest I got up an' hollered my goats an' droved 'em to Thumb Pasture without even sayin' goodbye to Meronym. She'd got 'nuff Smart to leave me be, mem'ry she'd got a son o'her own back on Prescience I.

When I got home that evenin', Ma'n'Sussy'n'Jonas was sittin' round. They seen my nose an' looked slywise at each other. *What happened to your conker there, bro?* Jonas asked, all la-di-da. *This? O, I slipped'n'schnockoed it on Moon's Nest*, I telled him quicksharp.

Sussy sort o' snigged. *You don't mean you schnockoed it on Roses' Nest there, bro Zachry?* an' all three of 'em cackled like a danglin o' screechbats an' I redded diresome'n'steamin'. Sissy telled me she'd got the yibber off Roses' cuz Wolt what'd telled Bejesus what'd met Sissy, but I wasn't really list'nin', nay, *I* was cussin' Meronym to Old Georgie, an' I din't stop, an' it's a bless she weren't at Bailey's that night, nay, she was learnin' loomin' at Aunt Bees'.

So down I went to the ocean an' watched Lady Moon to cool my fiery mis'ry. A greenbill came draggin' itself up the beach to lay eggs I mem'ry, an' I nearly spikered the turtle there'n'then out o'spite, see, if my life weren't fair why should an animal's be? But I seen its eyes, so ancient was his eyes they seen the future, yay, an' I let it go. Gubboh'n'Kobbery came troopin' with their boards an' started surfin' in the starry water, a whoah beautsome surfer was Kobbery, an' they called me to join 'em but I weren't in no surfin' mood, nay, I'd got more soberin' bis'ness to push at.

A schooler from Last Valley who boarded'n'served at the school'ry showed me into his hostess's house, got me some brew an' went to fetch Abbess from the Commons. Jus' the fire was cracklin' an' the ocean boomin' b'low in Flotilla Cape. Abbess came in, she'd been slaughterin' a chicklin', *The yibber says you're doin' fine hostin' for our spesh visitor*, what s'prised me some.

Is that so? Well, it's our spesh visitor what's anxin' me so, said I.

Is it now? said Abbess. *How so?*

Yay, you know she's been makin' secret maps o' our Valleys? said I.

O, you mean one o' these? said Abbess, holdin' me up the

selfsame map Meronym'd done up on Moon's Nest that mornin'. *She gave the school'ry this'un for our schoolers to know our lands' shapes'n'sizes.*

Well, that pissed on my cukes, but on I pushed anyhow. *She's scribblin' what she's learnin'bout Valleysmen in a book, but it ain't a real tongue she's writin', nay, it's a spyin' tongue what no'un 'cept her can read.*

This din't anx Abbess none neither. *B'fore the Fall there was dozens o' diff'rent tongues speaked thru' Ha-Why, an' hun'erds more speaked thru' the Hole World. See, Zachry,* Abbess telled me, *if Prescience Isle was hostin' me, I'd write my mem'ries in my tongue, so why shudn't our guest write in her tongue here on Big I?*

Abbess, speaked I back fin'ly, *ain't you suspishin' the Prescients o' trouble? Makin' maps may be part one o' invadin' us. S'posin' they want to drive us from our land? S'posin' they got a secret pax with the Kona? I mean, we don't know nothin 'bout 'em, nay, not really.*

Abbess she list'ned but she din't b'lief me none, nay, she thinked I was jus' wrigglyin' out o' hostin' Meronym. *You seen the Ship, an' you seen their ironware, an' you seen the bit o'the Smart they'll show us. If Prescients was plannin' on invadin' Nine Valleys, d'you truesome reck'n we'd be sittin' here discussin' it? Bring me ev'dence Meronym's plannin' to murder us all in our beds, I'll summon a gath'rin'. If you ain't got ev'dence, well, hold your counsel. Makin'cusations 'gainst a spesh guest, it jus' ain't politesome, Zachry, an' your pa'd not o' been pleased.*

Our Abbess never stamped her say-soes on no'un, but you knew when the discussin' was over. That was it, then, I was on my own, yay. Zachry 'gainst the Prescients.

Days rose'n'fell an' summer hotted up green'n'foamy. I watched Meronym wormy her way 'round all the Valleys, meetin' folk 'n'learnin' how we lived, what we owned, how many of us could fight, an' mappin' passes into the Valleys thru the Kohalas. One or two o' the older'n'cunninger men, I tried to suss out if they'd got any doubts or anxin's 'bout the Prescient, but when I said *invade* or *attack* they looked shocked'n'sp'rised spikers at me'n'my accusin's so I got shamed an' I shut up, see, I didn't want yibber smearin' me. I should fake a bit o' manners to Meronym so she may get lazy an' let her friendsome mask slip a littl' an' show me her true plannin's b'hind that mask, yay, give me some ev'dence I could show to Abbess an' summon a gath'rin'.

I didn't have no choice to wait'n'see. Meronym was truesome pop'lar. Women 'fessed stuff to her 'cos she was an outsider an' she'd not tell Old Ma Yibber no secrets. A no-name black dog what nuisanced Elepaio Valley started trottin'round after her what she named Pythag'ras or sumthin' tricksy, we jus' called him Py an' fed him slops an' he guarded the goats at night. See? Even Valley stray dogs took a shinin' to that dammit Prescient. Abbess asked our guest to teach numbers at the school'ry an' Meronym said yay. Catkin said she was a good teacher, but din't teach 'em nothin' b'yonder Abbess's own Smart tho' Catkin knowed she could o' done if she'd' o'wanted. Some schoolers even started inkin' their faces blacker to look like a Prescient but Meronym told 'em to clean up or she'd not teach 'em nothin', 'cos Smart'n'civ'lize ain't nothin' to do with the color o' the skin, nay.

Now one evenin' on our v'randa, Meronym was questionin'bout icons. *Is icons a home for the soul? Or a common mem'ry o' faces'n'kin'n'age'n'all? Or a prayer to Sonmi? Or a tombstone wrote in this-life with messages for next-life?* See it was always whys'n'whats with Prescients, it weren't never 'nuff sumthin' just *was* an' leave it be. Duophysite was the same here on Maui, nay? Unc'Bees was tryin' to answer but foggin' out, he 'fessed he knowed 'zactly what Icons is until the beat he'd to explain 'em. The Icon'ry, Aunt Bees said, held Valleysmen's past an' present all t'gether. Now it didn't often happ'n I could read any'un's thinkin's, but that beat I seen the Shipwoman wond'rin', *Oho, then this Icon'ry I got to go visit it, yay.* Nay, I didn't say nothin', but the f'llowin' sun-up I strolled down to

Bony Shore an' hid up on Sooside Rock. See, I reck'ned if I could catch the offlander bein' dis'spectful to our icons or better still cockaroachin' one, I could pit the older Valleysmen 'gainst her, an' so wise up my people'n'kin to the Prescient's truesome plannin's'n'all.

So I sat'n'waited on Sooside Rock, thinkin' o'the folks Georgie'd pushed off of there into the gnashin' foamin' b'low. Windy mornin' it was, yay, I mem'ry well, sand'n'dunegrass whippin' an' bloodflower bushes threshin' an' surf flyin' off scuddin' breakers. I ate some fungusdo' what I'd bringed for brekker, but b'fore I'd finished who do I spy trompin' long to the Icon'ry but Meronym, yay, *an'* Napes of Inouye. Clusterin' n'talkin' thick as thiefs! O, my thinkin' giddyupped now! Was Napes settin' himself up as the offlander's right arm? S'pose he was plannin' on replacin' Abbess as chief o' Nine Valleys once the Prescients'd run us all over the Kohalas an' into the sea with their snaky judasin' Smart?

Now Napes'd got the charm he had, yay, ev'ry'un loved him, his jokey yarnin's'n'smile'n all. If I got the goat tongue, well, Napes'd sort o' got the people tongue. You can't go trustin' folks what lassoop words so skillsome as him. Into the Icon'ry Napes'n'Meronym went, bold as a pair o'cockadoodlies. The dog Py waited outside where Meronym told him.

Quiet as breezes I crept in after 'em. Py watched me, sayin', *I got my eye on you, Zachry* but he din't bark. Napes'd 'ready jammed the door open for seein'-light an' so it din't squeak none when I tippied in b'hind 'em. From the dim'n'shadowy shelves what the oldest icons was kept on I heard Napes murmin'. Plans'n'conspiries, I jus' knowed it! I crept nearer to hear what I'd hear.

But Napes was braggin'bout his gran'pa's pa named Truman, yay, the self-same Truman Third what still walks thru stories on Big I an' here on Maui too. Seems Meronym'd got the curio, so Napes was showin' Truman Third's icon an' braggin'bout his oldtime kin's climb up Mauna Kea. Yay, *that* snuffed yarn! Well, if you young'uns don't know the story o' Truman

Napes time you did, so sit still, be patient an' pass me the dammit weed.

Truman Napes was a scavver back when Old'un gear was still junkifyin' in craters here'n'there. One mornin' an idea rooted in his mind what said the Old'uns may o'stashed presh gear up on Mauna Kea for safekeepin'. This idea growed'n'growed till by evenin' Truman'd settled to climb that scaresome mountain an' see what he'd see, yay, an' leave the very next day. His wife told him, *You're crazy, there ain't nothin' on Mauna Kea but Old Georgie an' his temples hid in his 'closure walls. He'll not let you in unless you're 'ready died an' your soul is his.* Truman jus' said, *Go to sleep, you crazy old bint, there ain't no truth in them crookit supe'stitions*, so he sleeps'n'wakes an' thru the crack o'dawn up Waipio Valley off he stomps.

Brave Truman trekked'n'climbed for three solid days an' had varyin' adventurin's what I ain't time to tell you now, but he s'vived 'em all till he was up that feary'n'ghostsome summit in the clouds what you can see from anywhere on Big I an' so high up he cudn't see the world b'low. Ashy it was, yay, no speck o' green an' a mil'yun winds tore here'n'there like rabies' dingos. Now Truman's steps was stopped by a wondersome ironstone wall, higher'n redwoods, what circled the hole peak for miles 'n'miles. Truman walked daylong 'round it searchin' for a breach, 'cos there wasn't no scalin' it nor diggin' under, but guess what he finded in the hour b'fore dark? A man o' Hawi, yay, hooded tight 'gainst the wind, crossleggin' behind a rock an' smokin' a pipe. The Hawi was a scavver too up on Mauna Kea for the selfsame reason o' Truman, can you b'lieve it? So lornsome was that place, Truman an' the man o' Hawi settled to team up'n'divvy any gear what they finded t'gether, fifty-fifty.

Well, Truman's luck changed the very next beat, yay. Them thick'nin' clouds got watery'n'thin an' them archin' steely gates in the 'closure wall shook free an'groaned thundersome an' budged open all o' itself. Thru that gate, Smart or magic Truman din't know, our hero spied a cluster o'eerysome temples, jus' like the old yarns say there was, but Truman din't get feary, nay, he got joocey thinkin'bout all the presh old'un gear'n' makin's what must be inside 'em. He slapped the Hawi Man's back, sayin', *Yo ho ho, we're richer'n kings'n'senators b'fore the Fall, Bro Hawi!* Tho' if Truman Napes was like his great-gran'son, he was prob'ly plottin' how to keep that scavved loot all for himself.

But that Hawi Man weren't smilesome, nay, he speaked grim from under his hood. *Bro Valleysman, my sleepin' hour is come at last.*

Truman Napes din't und'stand. *It ain't sundown yet, what's your meanin'? I ain't so sleepy so why are you now?*

But thru that mournsome gate the Hawi Man treaded. Truman was puzzlin' now, an' called out, *It ain't no time for sleepin', Bro Hawi! It's time for scavvin' whoah presh gear o' the Old'uns!* Into that silent 'closure Truman followed his part-ner-scavver. Black'n'twisted rocks was lyin' ev'rywhere an' the sky it was black'n'busted. The Hawi Man sank to his knees, prayin'. Truman's heart was struck chillsome, see, a cold hand o' wind unhooded that kneelin' Hawi Man. Truman seen his partner was a long-died corpse, half skellyton'n'half maggoty meat, an' that cold hand o' wind was Old Georgie's hand, yay, the devil what was standin' there wavin' a crookit spoon. *Wasn't you achin'n'lornsome outside, my presh,* speaked that king o' devils to the Man o' Hawi, *wand'rin' the lands o' the livin' with a stony soul an'ready died? Why din't you obey my summ'nin' sooner, you foolsome man?* Then Old Georgie sunk his crookit spoon thru' the Hawi Man's sockets, yay, an' dug out the soul, drippin' in smeary brain, an' crunched it, yay, it cracked 'tween his horsy teeth. The man o' Hawi folded over an' was suddenwise jus' one more black'n'twisted rock litt'rin' the 'closure.

Old Georgie swallered the Hawi Man's soul, wiped his mouth, ass-belched an' started hickin'. *Bar'brian's souls, delish an' fine,* that devil rhymed, dancin' up to Truman, *walnuts pickled, sourest wine.* Truman cudn't move one limb, nay, so scarysome was that sight, see. *But Valleys' souls are pure'n'strong, an' melt like honey on my tongue.* The devil's breath stunk fishy'n'farty. *Fifty-fifty your deal it said.* Old Georgie licked his own crookit 'n'warty spoon. *D'you want your half now, or when you're dead, Truman Napes Third o' Mormon Valley?*

Well, now, Truman got his limbs back an' rabbited'n'ran'n' fell out o' the mournsome gate, an' slid down that screesome mountain for his life never lookin' b'hind him not once. When he got back to the Valleys ev'ry'un stared in 'mazement even b'fore he voiced his 'ventures. Truman's hair'd been black as crows b'fore, but now it was whiter'n surf. Ev'ry single hair.

You'll mem'ry I, Zachry, was curled in my hideynick in the Icon'ry, list'nin' to Napes tellin' that mildewy yarn to my unwelcome dwellin'-guest an' showin' Meronym his fam'ly icons o' dead lifes. He teached her their meanin's an' usin's for a fair few beats, then Napes said he'd got to go fix nets, an' off he went leavin' Meronym 'lone. Now he'd not been gone hardly any time b'fore the Prescient called out in the dark, *So what d'you reck'n'bout Truman, Zachry?*

O, I'd got the shock, I din't dream she knowed I was there eavesdroppin'! But she faked her voice like weren't her plan to 'barrass nor shame me, nay, she faked her voice like we'd both gone into the Icon'ry t'gether. *D'you reck'n Truman's jus' an old woman's stoopit yarner? Or d'you reck'n it's got some true in it?*

No point me fakin' I weren't there neither, nay, 'cos she knowed I was there, no frettin'. Up I stood an' walked thru the shelfs to where the Prescient sat sketchin' the icon. My eyes'd got owlier in the dim an' I could see Meronym's face prop'ly now. *This place it's got the holy o' holies,* I told her. *This is Sonmi's dwellin' you're in.* My voice'd got my strongest say-so, tho' my eavesdroppin' made it weaker. *No offlander's got no bis'ness trespyin' thru' our icons.*

Meronym was politesome as I weren't. *I asked Abbess's p'mission to enter. She say-soed I could. I ain't touchin' no icon but*

Napes's fam'ly's. He say-soed I could. *Please s'plain why you're frettin' so, Zachry. I want to und'stand but I can't.*

See? That dammit Prescient thinked o' your attacks b'fore you thinked of 'em yourself! *You may be stoopidin' our Abbess,* I told her, coolsome'n'mean now, *an' you may be stoopidin' Ma'n'my fam'ly an' the hole dammit Nine Valleys but you ain't stoopidin' me nay not for one beat! I know it you ain't sayin' the hole true!* Now I'd s'prised her for once, an' a pleasin' feelin' it was to stop my skulkin' an' show my thinkin's to the open day.

Meronym sort o' frowned. *I ain't sayin' the hole true 'bout what?* Yay, I'd got Queen Smart cornered proper.

'Bout why you're here sussin' our lands! Sussin' our ways! Sussin' us!

Meronym sighed'n put Napes's icon back in its shelf. *What matters here ain't part-true or hole true, Zachry, but harm or not harmin', yay.* What she said next was a spiker thru' my guts. *Ain't you yourself got a secret what you're hidin' this "hole true" to ev'ryun, Zachry?*

My thinkin' went blurry. How could she know 'bout Sloosha's Crossin'? That was years ago! Was Prescients workin' with the Kona? Did they have some Smart what dug deep'n'dark lookin' for buried shames in minds? I din't say nothin'.

I swear it, Zachry, she said, *I vow on Sonmi—*

O, I shouted at her, offlanders'n'savages don't even *b'lief* in Sonmi so she'd got no bis'ness dirtyin' Sonmi's name with her tongue!

Meronym speaked calm'n'quietsome like always. I was way wrong, she said, she b'liefed in Sonmi, yay, even more'n I did, but if I pr'ferred it she'd lay her vowin' on her son, Anafi. On his luck'n'life, she vowed, no Prescient planned no harm to any Valleysman, nor ever, an' Prescients r'spected my tribe way way *way* more'n I knowed. She vowed when she could tell me the hole true she'd do it.

An' she left, takin' her vic'try with her.

I stayed a whiles an' visited Pa's icon, an' seein' his face carved in the grain I seen his face lyin' in Elepaio river. O, hot tears o' shame'n'sorryin' brimmed out. Head o' Bailey's dwellin' I was s'posed to be, but I'd got no stronger say-so'n a frighty lambkin an' no springier wit'n a coney in a trap.

Bring me ev'dence, Valleysman, Abbess'd said, *or hold your counsel*, so now I thinked ev'ry moment how to get my ev'dence, an' if I cudn't get grasp of it honor'bly well, so-be-it, I'd have to sneak my ev'dence. A bunch o' days later my fam'ly was over at Aunt Bees', with Meronym, 'cos she was learnin' honeyin'. I came back from herdin' early, yay, with the sun still 'bove the Kohalas an' I crept into our vis'tors' room an' searched for her gearbag. Din't take long, the Shipwoman'd stowed it under the plankin'. Inside was littl' gifts like what she'd gived us when she first come, but some Smart gear too. Sev'ral boxes what din't rattley but'd got no lid neither so I cudn't open 'em, an eery tool what I din't know shaped'n'smooth as a goat's shin-bone but gray'n'heavy like lava-stone, two pairs o'well-crafted boots, three–four books o'sketchin's'n'writin's in secret Prescient tongue. I don't know where them sketchin's was drawn but it weren't on Big Isle, nay, there was plants'n'birds what I'd not even seen in dreamin's, nay. Last was most wondersome.

One big silv'ry egg it was, sized a babbit's head, with dents 'n'markin's on it what fingers rested in. Its fat weight was eery an' it wouldn't roll. I know that don't sound senseful, but yarns 'bout Old'un Smart an' flyin' dwellin's an'growin' babbits in bottles an' pictures zoomin' cross the Hole World ain't senseful neither but that's how it was, so storymen an' old books tell it. So I cupped that silv'ry egg in my own hands, an' it started purrin' an' glowin' some, yay, like it was livin'. Quicksharp I let go the egg, an' it died dull. Was my hands' warmness makin' it stir?

So hungrysome was my curio, I held it again, an' the egg vibed warm till a ghost-girl flickered'n'appeared there! Yay, a ghost-girl, right 'bove the egg, as truesome as I'm sittin' here, her head'n'neck was jus' floatin' there, like 'flection in moonwater an' she was *talkin'*! Now I got scared an' took my hands off the sil'vry egg but the ghost-girl stayed, yay.

What did she do? Nothin' but talk'n'talk, like I am to you. But not a norm'ly storyman she weren't, nay, she was talkin' in Old'un tongue, an' not p'formin' none, jus' answerin' questions what a man's hushly voice asked, tho' he never showed his face. For ev'ry word I und'standed 'bout five–six followed what I din't. The ghost-girl's lips was fixed in a bitter smile but her creamy eyes was sad so sad but proud'n'strong too. When I got 'nuff spunk I speaked up, I murmed, *Sis, are you a lost soul?* Ignored me she did, so I asked, *Sis, can you see me?* Fin'ly I cogged the ghost-girl weren't talkin' to me an' cudn't see me.

I tried strokin' her cloudy skin'n'bristly hair but, I vow it, my fingers passed right thru, yay, jus' like a water 'flection. Papery moths blowed thru her shimm'rin' eyes'n'mouth too, to'n'fro, yay, to'n'fro.

O, eery'n'so beautsome'n'blue she was, my soul was achin'.

Suddenwise the ghost-girl vanished back into that egg an' a man took her place. A ghost-Prescient he was, this'un *could* see me an' fiercesome he speaked at me. *Who are you, boy, an' where is Meronym?*

The Prescient leant nearer'n'his face growed. Growly'n'fangy his voice was. *I asked you two questions, boy, answer'em now or I'll cuss your fam'ly so diresome no babbit'll live past one moon old now nor never!*

I sweated'n'gulped dry. *Zachry, sir,* I said, *an' Meronym's howzittin' fine, yay, she's at Aunt Bees' learnin' honeyin'.*

The Prescient shootered my soul with his eyes, yay, settlin' whether or nay to b'lief me. *An' does Meronym know her host sivvies his guest's gear when she's out? Answer truesome now 'cos I can tell a liar.*

I was flinchin' for pain as I shaked my head.

List'n close. That man had as much say-so as any Abbess. *You'll put this orison, this 'egg' you're holdin' now, back where you finded it. You'll tell* no'un *but* no'un *'bout it. Or else d'you know what I'll do?*

Yay, answered I. *Cuss my fam'ly so diresome no babbit'll ever live.*

Yay, you cogged it, answered that thund'ry man. *I'll be watchin', Zachry o' Bailey's Dwellin'*, that ghost-Prescient speaked, see he even knowed my dwellin' like Old Georgie. He vanished an' the silv'ry egg simmered quiet then died. Quick-sharp I packed Meronym's b'longin's back in her gearbag an' stowed it back under the plankin', wishin' I'd never gone nose-yin'. See, what I'd found weren't ev'dence for my doubtin's to show Abbess, nay, what I'd finded was a Smart cuss on my stoned luck an', I 'fessed it to me myself, a grimy smear on my honour as a host.

But I cudn't forget that ghost-girl neither, nay, she haunted my dreams wakin'n'sleepin'. So many feelin's I'd got I din't have room 'nuff for 'em. O, bein' young ain't easy 'cos ev'rythin' you're puzzlin'n'anxin' you're puzzlin'n'anxin' it for the first time.

Lady Moon growed fat, her daughter growed thin, an' sud-denwise three o' the six moons b'fore the Prescient Ship was due back for Meronym'd 'ready gone by. A sort o' truce was laid b'tween me'n'our guest now. I din't trust the Shipwoman but I tol'rated her 'round my dwellin' politesome 'nuff so I could spy her better. Then one squally aft'noon the first o' sev'ral happ'nin's fell, yay, happ'nin's what changed that truce into sumthin' where her fates'n'mine was binded t'gether like two twines o' vine-cord.

One rainy mornin' Bro Munro's littlest F'kugly came screein' upgulch to find me huddlin'neath 'brella leaves on Ranch Rise, fetchin' direst news to me he was. My sis Catkin'd been line-fishin' on Dog Rock Shore an'd trod on a scorpionfish an' now she was dyin' o' shakes'n'heats at Munro's Dwellin'. The herb'list, Wimoway, yay, Roses' ma, was tendin' her an' Leary the Hilo healer was doin' his inchanties too, but Catkin's life was fadin', yay. Strappin' musclers don't usually s'vive a scorpionfish, nay, an' poor littl' Catkin was dyin'n'd got two hours maybe three.

F'kugly mindered the goats an' I slid down thru the dogwood trees to Munro's Dwellin' an', yay, there it was jus' like F'kugly'd said it. Catkin was burnin' an' breathin' chokely an' she din't know no'un's face. Wimoway'd tweezed out the poison fins an' bathed the stingin' in *noni* pulp an' Sussy was pressin' cool sops to calm her head. Jonas was gone prayin' to Sonmi at the Icon'ry. Beardy Leary was mumblin' his Hilo spells an' shakin' his magic tufty spikers to drive off evil spirits. Din't seem Leary was helpin' much, nay, Catkin was dyin', the air smelt of it, but Ma wanted Leary there, see you'll b'lief in a mil'yun diff'rent b'liefin's if you reck'n jus' *one* of 'em may aid you. So what could I do, 'cept sit there an' hold b'loved Catkin's burnin' hands an' mem'ry my stock-still useless self watchin' Kona bullwhippin'n'circlin' Pa'n'Adam? Now maybe the voice was Pa's or maybe Sonmi's or maybe no'un's but mine but a hushly voice popped a bubble jus' inside my ear: *Meronym*, it said.

Yibber told me Meronym was up Gusjaw's Gulch so there I ran an', yay, there she was fillin' littl'Smart jars o' water up Gusjaw's Gulch in the steamin' rain, see Wolt'd passed by her earlier'n told the yibber. The Prescient'd got her spesh gearbag with her an' I thanked Sonmi for that. *Good aft'noon*, called the Shipwoman when she seen me splashin' upstream.

No, it ain't, I shouted back. *Catkin's dyin'!* Meronym list'ned griefsome 'nuff as I told her 'bout the scorpionfish but she sorried, nay, she din't have no healin' Smart an' anyway Wimoway's herb'lin's an' Leary's 'cantations was Big Isle healin' an' that was best for Big Isle sick folks, wasn't it, nay?

Dingo shit, said I.

She shaked her head so sad. *We Prescients vow not to interfere in no nat'ral order o' things.*

Slywise I speaked now, *Catkin calls you 'Auntie' an' she b'lieves you're kin. You surefire b'have in our dwellin' like you're kin. Is that jus'nother fake for you to study us some more? 'Nother part o'your 'not the hole true'?*

Meronym flinched. *No, Zachry, it ain't.*

Well, then, I gambled some luck, *I say you got spesh Smart what'll help your kin.*

Meronym threw a spiker in her words. *Why don't you sivvy thru my gear again an' thief my spesh Prescient Smart yourself?*

Yay, she knowed 'bout me'n'the silv'ry egg. She'd been fakin' she din't but she knowed. No point naysayin' so I din't. *My sis is dyin' while we're standin' here knucklyin'.*

So much rivers'n'rain in the world it flowed by us. Fin'ly Meronym said yay, she'd come'n'see Catkin but scorpionfish poison was quick'n'thick an' she prob'ly cudn't do nothin' to save my littl'sis an' I'd best und'stand that truth now. I din't say yay nor nay I jus' leaded her quicksharp down to Munro's Dwellin'. When the Prescient walked in Wimoway s'plained what she'd done tho' Beardy Leary said, *Ooo . . . a devil's drawn near . . . ooo, I sense her with my spesh powers . . .*

Catkin'd gone under now, yay, she lay still'n'stiff as an icon, jus' a whispin'breathin' scratched in her throat. Meronym's griefsome face jus' said *Nay, she's too far gone I can't do nothin'*, an' she kissed my sis' forehead g'bye, walked back sadsome into the rain. *O, see the Prescient*, Leary crowed, *their Smart can move magicky ships o' steel but only the Holy Chant o'Angel Laz'rus can tempt back the girl's soul from them despairin' marshes b'tween life'n'death.* Despair I felt, my sis was dyin', rain was drummin' but that same voice din't shut up in my ear. *Meronym.*

I din't know why but I followed her out. Shelt'rin' in Munro's pott'ry doorway she was starin' at the rods o' rain. *I ain't got no right to ask you for favors, I ain't been a good host, nay I been a pisspoor bad'un, but . . .* I'd ran out o' words.

The Prescient din't move nor look at me, nay. *The life o' your tribe's got a nat'ral order. Catkin'd o' treaded on that scorpionfish if I'd been here or not.*

Rainbirds spilt their galoshin'-galishin' song. *I'm jus' a stoopit goat-herder, but I reck'n jus' by bein' here you're bustin' this nat'ral order. I reck'n you're killin' Catkin by not actin'. An' I reck'n if it was your son Anafi lyin' there with scorpionfish* poison meltin' his heart'n'lungs, this nat'ral order'd not be so important to you, yay?

She din't answer but I knowed she was list'nin'.

Why's a Prescient's life worth more'n Valleysman's?

She lost her calm. *I ain't here to play Lady Sonmi ev'ry time sumthin' bad happ'ns an' click my fingers'n make it right! I'm jus' human, Zachry, like you like any'un!*

I promised, *It won't be ev'ry time sumthin' bad happens, it's jus' now.*

Tears was in her eyes. *That ain't no promise you can keep or break.*

Sudd'nwise I finded myself tellin' her ev'ry flea o' true 'bout Sloosha's Crossin', yay, ev'rythin'. How I'd leaded the Kona to kill Pa an' slave Adam an'd never 'fessed to no'un till that very beat. I din't know why I was spillin' this corked secret to my enemy, not till the very end, when I cogged its meanin' an' telled her too. *What I jus' teached you 'bout me'n'my soul is a spiker 'gainst my throat an' a gag over my mouth. You can tell Old Ma Yibber what I telled you, an' ruin me, any time you want. She'll b'lief you an' so she should 'cos it's true ev'ry word an' folks'll b'lief you 'cos they sense my Soul is stoned. Now if you got any Smart, yay, anythin' what may help Catkin now, give it me, tell it me, do it. No'un'll ever, ever know, nay, I vow it jus' you an' me.*

Meronym placed her hands on her head like it boomed up with woe an' she mumbed to herself sumthin' like, *If my pres'dent ever finded out, my hole faculty'd be disbandied,* yay, times was she used hole flocks o' words what I din't know. From a lidless jar in her gearbag she got out a tiny small-as-an-ant-egg turquoise stone an' telled me to sneak it into Catkin's mouth so slywise no'un seen, nay, nor even *thinked* they seen. *An' for Sonmi's sake,* Meronym warned me, *if Catkin lives, an' I ain't promisin' she will, make sure the herb'list gets the hooray-hooray for healin' her, not that voodoo snakeoilster from Hilo, yay?*

So I took that turquoise med'sun an' thanked her jus' once.

Meronym said, *Don't mention no words, not now an' never while I'm livin'*, an' that promise I kept tight. Into my presh sis's mouth I dropped it as I changed her sop-cloth, like Meronym'd told me, so no'un saw nothin'. An' what happ'ned?

Three days later Catkin was back learnin' the school'ry, yay.

Three days! Well, I stopped lookin' for ev'dence that Prescients was spyin' to slave us. Leary from Hilo crowed to the toads on the roads an' the hole wide world, no healer was greater'n he, not even the Prescients, tho' folks mostly b'liefed Wimoway'd done it, yay, not him.

Coneys'n'roasted taro we was eatin' one supper 'bout a moon after Catkin's sick when Meronym made a s'prisin'nouncement. She meant to climb up Mauna Kea b'fore the Ship returned, she said, for to see what she'd see. Ma speaked first, 'ready worrysome. *What for, Sis Meronym? Ain't nothin' up Mauna Kea but never-endin' winter an' a big heap o' rocks.*

Now Ma'd not said what we was all thinkin' cos she din't want to look barb'ric'n'savage, but Sussy din't hold back none. *Aunt Mero, if you go up there Old Georgie'll freeze you an' dig out your soul with a cruel'n'crookit spoony an' eat it so you'll never even be reborned an' your body'll be turned into a frostbited boulder. You want to stay here in the Valleys where it's safe.*

Meronym din't mick Sussy none, she jus' said Prescients'd got Smart what'd ward Old Georgie away. Climbin' Mauna Kea was ness'ary to map Windward, she said, an' anyhow, Valleysmen needed more low-down on Kona movements over Leeward'n'Waimea Town. Now time was, such words'd o' roused my s'picions buzzin', but I din't think that now, nay, tho' I was diresome worried for our guest. Well, the yibber was busy for days when this news jumped out. *The Shipwoman's climbin' Mauna Kea!* Folks dropped by warnin' Meronym not to go pokin' her nose into OG's 'closure, or she'd never come back down. Even Napes visited, sayin' climbin' Mauna Kea in a story was one thing, doin' it for real was cracked'n'crazed. Abbess said Meronym could come'n'go where she pleased, but she'd not say-so no'un to guide Meronym up, jus' too unknowed'n' risky that summit was, three days up'n'three more down, an' dingos'n'Kona'n'Sonmi knows what on the way, an' anyhow prep'ration for the Honokaa barterin' was needin' all hands in the dwellin's.

Now I s'prised ev'ry'un, yay, me too, when I settled to go with her. I weren't known as the bravest-balled bullock in the barn. So why'd I done it? Simple 'nuff. One, I owed Meronym for Catkin. Two, my soul was 'ready half stoned, yay, surefire I'd not get rebirthed, so what'd I got to lose? Better if Old Georgie ate my soul'n some'un else's who'd get rebirthed else, yay? That ain't brave, nay, it's jus' sense. Ma din't act pleased, a busy 'nuff time in the Valleys 'cos o' harvest comin'n'all, but come the dawn Meronym'n'me set off she gived me journey-grinds what she'd smoked'n'brined an' said Pa'd o' prouded to see me so growed'n'gutsy. Jonas gived me a spesh sharp'n'fine rockfish spiker, an' Sussy gived amulets o' pearlshell to dazzle 'n'blind Georgie's eye if he chased us. Kobbery my cuz was over to minder my goats, he gived a bag o'raisins from his fam'ly's vines. Catkin was last, she gived me a kiss an' Meronym too, an' made us both promise we'd be back in six days.

Eastly o' Sloosha's we din't climb the Kukuihaele track, nay, we trekked inland southly up Waiulili stream an' I cogged the clearin' by Hiilawe Falls where I'd s'prised the Kona what killed Pa five–six years b'fore. Overgrown now it was, jus' traces o' bygone campfires scorchin' the middle. In Hiilawe Pool's shallows I spikered a couple o' rockfish with Jonas's gift, to last out our grinds. Rain fell so the Waiulili stream gushed too fierce for footin', so we bushwhacked up thru sugar cane, yay, a hard half-day's goin' it was till we cleared the Kohala Ridge; the windy open made us gasp an' thru riftin' clouds we seen Mauna Kea higher'n the sky, yay. Now I seen Mauna Kea from Honokaa b'fore, o' course, but a mountain you're plannin' on climbin' ain't the same as the one you ain't. It ain't so pretty, nay. Hush 'nuff an' you'll *hear* it. The cane thinned to tind'ry pines an' we got to Old'uns' Waimea Track. Sev'ral miles 'long this ancient 'n'cracked road we clopped till we met a fur trapper an' his laughin' doggy restin' by a slopin' pond. Old Yanagi was his name an' he'd got mukelung so bad by'n'by Young Yanagi'd be takin' over the fam'ly bis'ness, I thinked. We said we was herb'lists sivvyin' for presh plants an' maybe Yanagi b'lieved us an' maybe he din't, but he bartered us fungusdo' for rockfish an' warned us Waimea Town weren't so friendsome as it'd been once, nay, Kona say-soed'n'knucklied ficklewise an' you cudn't guess their b'havin's.

A mile or so eastly o' Waimea Town we heard shod hoofs cloppin' an' we dived off the track in the nick b'fore three Kona fighters on black stal'yons an' their horse-boy on a pony galloped by. Hate'n'fear quaked me an' I wanted to kill 'em like prawns on a skewer, but slower'n that. The boy I thought may' o'been Adam but I always thinked that 'bout young Kona, they was wearin' helms so I cudn't see too sure, nay. We din't speak much from then 'cos speakin' can be heard by spyers what you can't spy. Southly thru shrubby heath we tromped now till we got to wideway. Wideway I'd heard o' from storymen an' here it was, an open, long, flat o' roadstone. Saplin's'n'bush was musclin' up but wondersome'n'wild was that windy space. Meronym said it was named 'Air Port' in Old'uns' tongue, where their flyin' boats'd anchor down, yay, like wild geese on the Polulu Marshes. We din't cross wideway, nay, we skirted it, there wasn't no cover see.

By sundown we tented up in a cactusy hollow an' when it was dark 'nuff I lit us a fire. Lornsome I felt to be away from my Valleys'n'kin, but in that no man's land Meronym's mask was slippin' an' I was seein' her more clear'n I'd ever done b'fore. I asked her straight, *What's it like, the Hole World, the offlands over the ocean?*

Her mask'd not slipped right off tho'. *What d'you reck'n?*

So I told her my 'maginin's o' places from old books'n'pics in the school'ry. Lands where the Fall'd never falled, towns bigger'n all o' Big I, an' towers o' stars'n'suns blazin' higher'n Mauna Kea, bays of not jus' one Prescient Ship but a mil'yun, Smart boxes what make delish grinds more'n'any'un can eat, Smart pipes what gush more brew'n'any'un can drink, places where it's always spring an' no sick, no knucklyin' an' no slavin'. Places where ev'ry'un's a beautsome purebirth who lives to be one hun'erd'n'fifty years.

Meronym pulled her blanky tighter. *My parents an' their gen- 'ration b'lieved, somewhere, hole cities o' Old'uns s'vived the Fall b'yonder the oceans, jus' like you, Zachry. Oldtime names haunted their 'maginin's . . . Melbun, Orkland, Jo'berg, Buenas Yerbs, Mumbay, Sing'pore.* The Shipwoman was teachin' me what no Valleysman'd ever heard an' I list'ned tight'n'wordless. *Fin'ly, five decades after my people's landin' at Prescience, we relaunched the Ship what bringed us there.* Dingos howled in the far-far 'bout folks soon to die, I prayed Sonmi it weren't us. *They finded the cities where the old maps promised, but dead-rubble cities, jungle-choked cities, plague-rotted cities, but never a sign o' them livin' cities o' their yearnin's. We Prescients din't b'lief our weak flame o' Civ'lize was now the brightest in the Hole World, an' further an' further we sailed year by year, but we din't find no flame brighter. So lornsome we felt. Such a presh burden for two thousand pairs o'hands! I vow it, there ain't more'n sev'ral places in Hole World what got the Smart o'the Nine Valleys.*

Anxin'n'proudful at one time hearin' them words made me, like a pa, an' like she an' me weren't so diff'rent as a god an' a worshiper, nay.

Second day fluffsome clouds rabbited westly an' that snaky lee- ward sun was hissin' loud 'n' hot. We drank like whales from icy'n'sooty brooks. Higher to cooler air we climbed till no moz- zie pricked us no more. Stunty'n'dry woods was crossed by swathes o' black'n'razory lava spitted'n'spewed by Mauna Kea. Snailysome goin' was them rockfields, yay, jus' brush that rock light an' your fingers'd bleed fast'n'wetly so I binded my boots 'n'hands in strips o' hidebark an' did the same for Meronym. Blisters scabbed her foots, her soles'd not got my goat tuff see, but that woman weren't no moaner, nay, whatever else she was. We tented up in a forest o' needles'n'thorns an' a waxy mist hid our campfire but it hid any sneaker-uppers too an' I got nervy. Our bodies was busted by tiredness but our minds wasn't sleepy yet so we talked some while eatin'. *You really ain't feary*, said I, jerkin' my thumb upwards, *o' meetin' Georgie when we get to the summit, like Truman Napes did?*

Meronym said the weather was way more scaresome to her.

I spoke my mind: *You don't b'lief he's real, do you?*

Meronym said Old Georgie weren't real for her, nay, but he could still be real for me.

Then who, asked I, *tripped the Fall if it weren't Old Georgie?*

Eery birds I din't knowed yibbered news in the dark for a beat or two. The Prescient answered, *Old'uns tripped their own Fall.*

O, her words was a rope o' smoke. *But Old'uns'd got the Smart!*

I mem'ry she answered, *Yay, Old'uns' Smart mastered sicks, miles, seeds an' made miracles ord'nary, but it din't master one thing, nay, a hunger in the hearts o' humans, yay, a hunger for more.*

More what? I asked. *Old'uns'd got ev'rythin'.*

O, more gear, more food, faster speeds, longer lifes, easier lifes, more power, yay. Now the Hole World is big but it weren't big 'nuff for that hunger what made Old'uns rip out the skies an' boil up the seas an' poison soil with crazed atoms an' donkey 'bout with rotted seeds so new plagues was borned an' babbits was freakbirthed. Fin'ly, bit'ly, then quicksharp, states busted into bar'bric tribes an' the Civ'lize Days ended, 'cept for a few folds'n'pockets here'n'there, where its last embers glimmer.

I asked why Meronym'd never spoke this yarnin' in the Valleys.

Valleysmen'd not want to hear, she answered, *that human hunger birthed the Civ'lize, but human hunger killed it too. I know it from other tribes offland what I stayed with. Times are you say a person's b'liefs ain't true, they think you're sayin' their lifes ain't true an' their truth ain't true.*

Yay, she was prob'ly right.

Third day out was clear'n'blue but Meronym's legs was jelly-fishin' so I lugged ev'ry'thin' on my back 'cept for her gearbag. We'd trekked over the mountain's shoulder to the southly face where the scars of an Old'un track zigzaggered summitwards. Around noon Meronym rested while I gathered 'nuff firewood for two faggots 'cos we was in the last trees now. Lookin' down t'ward Mauna Loa we squinted a troop o' horses on Saddle Road, their Kona metal spicklin' in sunlight. So high up we was, their horses was jus' termite-sized. I wished I could o' crushed them savages b'tween my finger'n'thumb an' wipe the slime off on my pants. I prayed Sonmi no Kona ever turned up this Summit Track 'cos fine places there was for an' ambushin' an' Meronym 'n'me cudn't knuckly hard nor long I reck'ned. I din't see no hoofprints nor tentin' marks anyhow.

The trees ended an' the wind got musclier'n'angrier, bringin' not a sniff o' smoke, no farmin', no dung, no nothin'cept fine, fine dust. Birds was rarer too in them sheer'n'scrubby slopes, jus' buzzards surfin' high. By evenin' we got to a cluster of Old'un buildings what Meronym said'd been a village for s'tron'mers what was priests o' the Smart what read the stars. This village'd not been lived in since the Fall an' no more des'late place I'd ever seen. No water nor soil an' the night fell, O, fangy 'n'cold so we dressed thick an' lit a fire in an empty dwellin'. Flamelights danced with shadows 'round them unloved walls. I was anxin'bout the summit next day, so in part to blind my mind, I asked Meronym if Abbess spoke true when she said the Hole World flies 'round the sun, or if the Men o' Hilo was true sayin' the sun flies 'round the Hole World.

Abbess is quite correct, answered Meronym.

Then the true true is diff'rent to the seemin' true? said I.

Yay, an' it usually is, I mem'ry Meronym sayin', *an' that's*

why true true is presher'n'rarer'n diamonds. By'n'by sleep
hooded her, but my thinkin's kept me awake till a silent woman
came an' sat by the fire, sneezin'n'shiv'rin' hushly. Her necklace
o' cowrie shells said she was a Honomu fisher an' if she'd o'
been living she'd o'been joocesome no frettin'. Into the fire the
woman uncurled her fingers, into the prettiest bronze'n'ruby
petals, but she jus' sighed lornsomer'n a bird in a box in a well,
see, them flames cudn't heat her up none. She'd got pebbles
'stead o'eyeballs an' I wondered if she was climbin' Mauna Kea
to let Old Georgie fin'ly put her soul to stony sleep. Dead folk
hear livin's thinkin's, an' that drowned fisher gazed at me with
them pebbles, noddin' *Yay* an' she took out a pipe for comfort
but I din't ask for no skank. Long beats later I waked, the fire
was dyin' an' the stoned Honomu'd taked her leave. No tracks
that'un left in the dust but I smelt the smoke from her pipe for
a beat or two. *See*, I thought, *Meronym knows a lot 'bout Smart
an' life but Valleysmen know more 'bout death.*

Fourth dawn was a wind not o' this world, nay, it warped that
brutal'n'ringin' light an' hooped the horizon an' ripped words
out o' your mouth an' your body's warmness thru your tarp'n'
furs. Summit trail from the s'tron'mers' village was busted'n'
roded diresome, yay, great mouthfuls landslipped away an' no
leafs nor roots nor mosses even jus' dry'n'freezed dust'n'grit
what scratched our eyes like a crazed woman. Our Valleys boots
was shredded by now so Meronym gived us both a pair o' Smart
Prescient boots made o' I din't know what but whoah warm'n'
soft'n'tuff they was so we could go on. Four–five miles later the
ground flatted out so you din't feel you was on a mountain no
more, nay, more like an ant on a table, jus' a flatness hangin'
in nothin' b'tween worlds. Fin'ly near noon we rounded a bend
an' I gasped shocksome 'cos here was the 'closure, jus' like
Truman'd said it, tho' its walls wasn't as tall as a redwood,
nay, more a spruce high. The track leaded straight to the steely
gates, yay, but its unbusted walls weren't so endless long, nay,
you could o' walked 'round it in a quarter of a mornin'. Now

inside the 'closure on rising ground was the bowls o' temples, yay, the eeriest Old'un buildings in Ha-Why or Hole World, who knows? How could we get to 'em tho'? Meronym stroked that awesome gate an' muttered, *We'd need a dammit diresome flashbang to get these off their hinges, yay.* Out o' her gearbag tho' she got not a flashbang, nay, but a Smart rope, like the Prescients bartered sumtimes, fine'n'light. Two stumps stuck up 'bove the steely gate, an' she tried to lassoop one. The wind was craftier'n her aim but I tried next an' lassooped it first time, an' up Old Georgie's 'closure we scaled hand by hand by hand.

Inside that dreadsome place at the world's top, yay, the wind hushed like a hurrycane's clear eye. The sun was deaf'nin' so high up, yay, it roared an' time streamed from it. No paths there wasn't inside the 'closure just a mil'yun boulders like in Truman Napes's yarn, the bodies o' the stoned'n'unsouled they was, an' I wondered if Meronym or me or both'd be boulders by nightfall. Ten–twelve temples waited here'n'there, white'n'silv'ry an' gold 'n'bronze with squat bodies'n'round crowns an' mostly windowless. The nearest 'un was jus' a hun'erd paces away an' we set off for it first. I asked if this was where Old'uns worshiped their Smart.

Meronym spoke, marv'lin' as much as me, they wasn't temples, nay, but *observ'trees* what Old'uns used to study the planets'n'moon'n'stars, an' the space b'tween, to und'stand where ev'rythin' begins an' where ev'rythin' ends. We stepped caref'ly b'tween them twisted rocks. Round one I seen crushed cowrie shells from Honomu way an' I knowed it was my visitor the night b'fore. The wind bringed my gran'pa's voice whispin' from the far-far . . . *Judas.* Eery, yay, but shockin', nay, 'cos ev'rythin' in that place was eery . . . *Judas.* I din't tell Meronym.

How she got that observ'tree door open, I ain't knowin' so don't mozzie me. A sort of umb'licky cord b'tween the door's dusted 'n'rusty niche an' her orison-egg worked in a beat or two. Now I was busy guardin' us from the dwellers o' that 'closure. My gran'pa's whispin's was now cussin' half-faces what dis'peared when you stared straight. A sharp hiss as the observ'tree door cracked open. Air guffed out stale'n'sour like it was breathed b'fore the Fall an', yay, so it prob'ly was. In we stepped an' what did we find?

Describin' such Smart ain't easy. Gear there was what we ain't mem'ried on Ha-Why so its names ain't mem'ried neither, yay, almost nothin' in there could I cogg. Shimm'rin' floors, white walls'n'roofs, one great chamber, round'n'sunk, filled by a mighty dish wider'n ten men laid end to end what Meronym named a *rad'yo tel'scope* what was, she said, the furthest-seein' eye Old'uns ever made. Ev'rythin' white'n'pure as Sonmi's robes, yay, not one flea o' dirt 'cept what we tromped in. Tables'n' chairs sat 'round waitin' for sitters on balconies made o' steel so our foots gonged. Even the Shipwoman was smacked wondersome by all this perfect Smart. She showed her orison ev'ry'thin' we seed. The orison glowed'n'purred an' windows came'n' went. *It's mem'ryin' the place*, s'plained Meronym, tho' I din't und'stand so good an' I asked what that Smart egg was true-be-telled.

Meronym rested a beat an' drank a mouth o' brew from her flask. *An orison is a brain an' a window an' it's a mem'ry. Its brain lets you do things like unlock observ'tree doors what you jus' seen. Its window lets you speak to other orisons in the far-far. Its mem'ry lets you see what orisons in the past seen'n' heard, an' keep what my orison sees'n'hears safe from f'gettin'.*

Shamed to mem'ry Meronym o'my sivvyin' I was, yay, but if I din't ask then I may not o' got the chance ever, so I asked it, *The shimm'rin'n'beautsome girl what I seen in this . . . orison b'fore . . . was she a mem'ry or a window?*

Meronym hes'tated. *Mem'ry.*

I asked if the girl was livin' still.

Nay, answered Meronym.

I asked, was she a Prescient?

She hes'tated, an' said she wanted to tell me a hole true now, but that other Valleysmen'd not be ready for its hearin'. I vowed on Pa's icon to say nothin', nay, to no'un. *Very well. She was Sonmi, Zachry. Sonmi the freakbirthed human what your ancestors b'liefed was your god.*

Sonmi was a human like you'n'me? I'd never thinked so nor'd Abbess ever speaked such loonsomeness, nay. Sonmi'd been birthed by a god o' Smart named Darwin, that's what we b'liefed. Did Meronym b'lief this Sonmi'd lived on Prescience I or on Big I?

She was borned'n'died hun'erds o' years ago 'cross the ocean west-nor'westly, so Meronym speaked, *on a pen'sula all dead-landed now but its oldtime name was Nea So Copros an' its ancient one Korea. A short'n'judased life Sonmi had, an' only after she'd died did she find say-so over purebloods 'n' freakbirths' thinkin's.*

All this shockin' newness buzzed'n'busted my brain an' I din't know what to b'lief. I asked what Sonmi's mem'ry was doin' in Meronym's orison hun'erds o' years after.

Now I seen Meronym was sorryin' she'd beginned, yay. *Sonmi was killed by Old'un chiefs what feared her, but b'fore she died she spoke to an orison 'bout her acts'n'deedin's. I'd got her mem'ry in my orison 'cos I was studyin' her brief life, to und'stand you Valleysmen better.*

That's why that girl'd haunted me so. *I seen a sort o' Smart ghost?*

Meronym yayed. *Zachry, we got many buildin's to visit b'fore nightfall.*

Now crossin' the 'closure to the second observ'tree, the boulders began speakin'. *O, you was right 'bout the dammit Prescients first time, Bro Zachry! She's fuggin' your b'liefs'n'all up'n'down 'n'in'n'out!* I clamped my ears but, yay, them voices went thru these hands. *This woman only saved Catkin's life to cloudy your thinkin' with debt'n'honor!* Crampsome was them stones' shapes 'n'words, I clamped my jaw shut to stop me answerin'. *She's scavvin'n'sivvyin' Big Isle Smart what truesome b'longs to Valleysmen!* Grit devils got under my eyelids. *Your pa'd not let no lyin' offlander worm into* his *trust, bro, nor use him as a pack-mule!* Them words was so true I cudn't argue back none, an' I stumbled painsome.

Meronym steadied me. I din't 'fess the boulders was yibber-stinkin' her, but she seen sumthin' weren't right. *The air up here is thin'n'watery*, she speaked, *an' your brain'll get diresome hungry an' make this wyrd place wyrdsomer.*

We got to the second buildin' an' I slumped droozy while the Prescient worked the door open. O, that hollerin' sun hollowed my head. *She's a sly'un no frettin', Zachry!* Truman Napes Third was perched on his boulder. Meronym'd not even heard him. *You b'lief her or your own kin?* he called me, mournsome. *Are your truths jus' 'thin'n'watery air'? Am I?* O, I was reliefed the next beat when the observ'tree door open. Them ghosts'n'their spikery truths cudn't follow us inside, see, I s'pose the Smart kept 'em out.

So it went all aft'noon long, yay. Most o' the observ'trees was much like the first. The Prescient opened up, s'plored the place with her orison, an' mostly forgot I was there. Me, I just sat an' breathed that Smart air till she was done. But stompin' b'tween buildin's, twisted boulders'd chorused me, *Judas!* an' *Pack-mule!* an' *Ship-slave!* Ghosts o' Valleysmen pleaded me thru unpartin' frostbitted lips, yay, *She ain't your tribe! Ain't even your color!* an' then'n'there, O, frightsome sense they made I 'fess it here'n'now.

S'picion rotted me.

No Prescient'd ever been straight with no Valleysman an' that day I knowed Meronym was no diff'rent. The boulders'd changed the blue sky to anxin'n'flinty gray by the last buildin'. Meronym teached me weren't no observ'tree but a *gen'rator* what made a Smart magic named *'lectric* what worked the hole place like a heart works the body. She was whoahin' at the machines'n all but I was jus' feelin' stoopit'n'judased for bein' blinded by the Shipwoman since she'd come elbowin' into my dwellin'. I din't know what to do nor how to stop her plans but Georgie'd got his plans, cuss him.

This gen'rator's innards was diff'rent from other buildin's. The Prescient woman glowed with fass'nation as we stepped into the echoey chambers but I din't. See, I knowed we wasn't alone in there. Shipwoman din't b'lieve me, o' course, but in the biggest space where a mighty iron heart stood silent was a sort o' throne s'rounded by tables o' littl'windows an' numbers'n' all, an' on this throne was a died Old'un priest slumpin' under an' arched window. The Prescient swallowed hard an' peered close. *A chief s'tron'mer, I reck'n,* she spoke hushly, *he must o' soosided here when the Fall came, an' the sealed air's saved his body from rottin'.* A priest-king not a chief, I reck'ned, in such a wondersome palace. She got to work mem'ryin' ev'ry inch o' that doomin' place on her orison while I 'proached nearer that priest-king from the world o' perfect Civ'lize. His hair straggled an' his nails was hooky an' the years'd shrunk'n'sagged his face some sure but his Smart sky clothes was spiff'n'fine, sapphires pierced his ear an' he mem'ried me of Unc'Bees, same hooky nose, yay.

List'n to me, Valleysman, the soosided priest-king spoke, *yay, list'n. We Old'uns was sick with Smart an' the Fall was our cure. The Prescient don't know she's sick, but, O, real sick she is.* Thru that arch o' glass waves o' snow was tossin'n'turnin' an' drownin' the sun. *Put her to sleep, Zachry, or she'n'her kind'll bring all their offland sick to your beautsome Valleys. I'll minder her Soul well in this place never fear.* The Shipwoman was movin'bout with her orison, hummin'a Prescient babby-bye what she'd teached Catkin'n'Sussy. Tick-tockin' was my thinkin'. Wasn't killin' her barb'ric'n'savage?

Ain't no right or wrong, the s'tron'mer king teached me, *jus' protectin' your tribe or judasin' your tribe, yay, jus' a strong will or a weak'un. Kill her, bro. She ain't no god, she's only blood'n'tubes like you'n me what apes us Old'uns. You kill it's your duty you know it.*

I said I cudn't, the yibber'd tag me murderer an' Abbess'd call a gath'rin' what'd exile me from the Valleys.

O, think, Zachry, the king micked me. *Think! How'll the*

yibber know? Yibber'll say, 'That knowed-all offlander ignored our yarns'n'ways an' went trespyin' up Mauna Kea an' brave Zachry went 'long to try'n'minder her but it turned out she weren't so Smart what she thinked.'

Beats passed. *All right*, I answered fin'ly'n'grim, *I'll spiker her when we step outside.* The priest-king smiled, pleased, an' din't speak no more. Fin'ly my victim howzitted me. *Fine*, said I, tho' I were nervy, see, the biggest thing I ever killed was goats an' now I'd vowed to kill a Prescient human. She said we should set off 'cos she din't want to get stranded in no blizzard up here, an' leaded us back out the gen'rator.

Outside, the boulders'd falled silent in the ankle-snow. One snowstorm'd gone but another bigger'un was comin' so I reck'ned.

We walked t'wards the steely gates, her in front, me grippin' Jonas's spiker an' testin' its sharp on my thumb.

Do it now! say-soed ev'ry murd'rous stone on Mauna Kea.

Nothin' to be gained by dillyin', nay. Hushly I aimed at the top o' the Prescient's neck an' Sonmi have mercy on my soul I thrust that sharky point home as hard as I could.

Nay, I din't murder her, see in a split-beat b'tween aimin' an' thrustin', Sonmi *had* mercy on my soul, yay, she changed my aim an' that spiker went flyin' high over them steely gates. Meronym din't even cogg she'd nearly had her skull skewered but I cogged sure 'nuff I'd been magicked by the devil o' Mauna Kea, yay, we all know his name, cuss him.

You see sumthin' up there? asked Meronym, after my spiker.

Yay, I lied, *but it weren't no'un, nay, it was jus' the tricks o' this place.*

We're leavin', she said, *we're leavin' now.*

Old Georgie was outwitted, see, there weren't no means I could kill her quicksharp without my spiker, but I knowed he'd not jus' lay down an' watch my vic'try, nay, I knew that slywise buggah of old.

As I climbed up the rope with the gearbag, Mauna Kea took

a lungsome breath an' howled giddyin' snow so I cudn't see the ground clearly an' ten winds tore our faces an' my fingers was stiff with cold an' half-way up I slid half-way down an' that rope burned my hands but fin'ly I hauled myself up top an' bringed up the gearbag with my painful stingin'n'raw palms. Meronym weren't so fast but she weren't far from the top o' the wall when suddenwise time stopped.

Time stopped, yay, you heard right. For Hole-World 'cept me an' a certain cunnin' devil, yay, you know which'un came swagg'rin' along the wall, time was jus' . . . stopped.

Snowflakes hanged specklin' the air. Old Georgie swished 'em aside. *I tried reas'nin' with you, Zachry, you stubbornsome boy, now I got to use warnin's an' augurin's an' say-so. Get out your blade an' cut this rope thru.* His foot touched the rope what was holdin' time-freezed Meronym. Worn face screwed 'gainst the blizzard it was an' her muscles strainin' to climb that rope. Twenty feet o' nothin' below. *Her fall may not kill her when I let time flow again,* Old Georgie seen my thinkin', *but them rocks b'low'll bust her spine'n'legs an' she'll not s'vive the night. I'll let her consider her follyin's.*

I asked him why he din't jus' kill Meronym himself.

Why-why-why? Old Georgie micked. *I want you to do it, an' here's why-why-why. See, if you don't cut that rope, inside o' three moons your dearsome fam'ly be dead, I vow it! I vow it. So you got a choosin'. On one side you got Brave Ma, Strong Sussy, Bright Jonas, Sweet Catkin, all dead. Cowardy Zachry'll live on an' regret'll flay him till his dyin' day. On th'other side you got jus' one dead offlander no'un'll miss. Four you love 'gainst one you don't. I may even magick Adam back from Kona.*

No bolt-hole out o' this. Meronym had to die.

Yay, no bolt-hole, boy. I'm countin' to five . . .

I got my blade. A seed sprouted thru the crust o' my mem'ry, an' that seed was a word Georgie'd speaked jus' then, '*augurin''*.

Quicksharp I chucked my blade down after my spiker an' looked that devil in his terrorsome eyes. He'd got the s'prised curio an' his dyin' smile'd got a bucket o' dark meanin's. I spat at him but my spit boom'ranged back on me. Why? Was I crazed 'n'loonin'?

Old Georgie'd made a diresome mistake, see, he'd mem'ried me o' my augurin's from my Dreamin' Night. *Hands are burnin', let that rope be not cut.* My decidin' was settled, see, my hands was burnin', so this was that rope Sonmi'd say-soed me not to cut.

My blade chimed on the ground an' time started an' the mil'yun hands'n'screams o' that devil's blizzard tore'n'pummeled me but cudn't hurl me off the 'closure wall, nay, somehow I pulled up Meronym an' got us down the other side too with no bones busted. We leaned 'gainst the furyin' white'n'dark snow-storm back to the s'tron'mers' village, we staggered'n'tripped an' got back more freezin'n'livin' but a dry faggot was waitin' by Sonmi's grace an' I somehow got a fire cracklin' an' I vow that fire saved our lifes all over again. We boiled ice to water an' unfroze our bones an' dried our furs best we could. We din't speak none we was too icy'n'drained. Did I regret spurnin' Old Georgie?

Nay, not then, not now. Whatever Meronym's cause was for scalin' this cussed mountain, I din't b'lief she'd ever judas no Valleysman, nay, not in my heart an' the Kona'd' o'done to the Valleys what happened sooner or later anyhow. That was in the future that first night from the summit. My friend gived us both med'sun pills after grinds an' we sleeped the no-dream sleep o' the s'tron'mer king.

Now, gettin' back to the Valleys weren't no summery stroll neither, nay, but tonight ain't the time to yarn them 'ventures. Meronym'n'me din't talk much goin' down, a sort o' trust'n' und'stand'in' tied us now. Mauna Kea'd done its cussed best to kill us but we'd s'vived it t'gether. I cogged she was far-far from her own fam'ly'n'kin an' my heart ached for her lornsomeness. Abel welcomed us in his garrison dwellin' three evenin's later an' sent word to Bailey's we'd come back. Ev'ry'un'd got jus' one question, *What did you see up there?* It was lornsome'n' hushly, I telled 'em, with temples o' lost Smart'n'bones. But I din't breathe a word 'bout the s'tron'mer king nor what Meronym'd telled me 'bout the Fall an' speshly not my knuckly with Old Georgie, nay, not till years'd come'n'gone.

I und'standed why Meronym'd not said the hole true 'bout Prescience Isle an' her tribe too. People b'lief the world is built *so* an' tellin'em it ain't *so* caves the roofs on their heads 'n'maybe yours.

Old Ma Yibber spread the news that the Zachry what came down off Mauna Kea weren't the same Zachry what'd gone up an' true 'nuff I s'pose, there ain't no journey what don't change you some. My cuz Kobbery 'fessed that mas'n'pas thru the Nine Valleys was warnin' their daughters 'gainst frolickin' with Zachry o' Bailey's 'cos they reck'ned I must o' bis'nessed with Old Georgie to 'scape that shrieky place with my soul still in my skull, an' tho' that weren't the hole true, it weren't the hole wrong. Jonas'n'Sussy din't mick with me like they once did. But Ma got weepy to see us home an' hugged me, *My little Zacha-man,* an' my goats was gladsome an' Catkin din't change none. She'n'her bros at the school'ry'd made a new game, *Zachry'n' Meronym on Mauna Kea,* but Abbess say-soed 'em not to 'cos times are pretendin' can bend bein'. A whoah game it was, said Catkin, but I din't want to know its rules nor endin'.

By'n'by Meronym's last moon in Nine Valleys swelled up an' time it was for the Honokaa barterin', the biggest gath'rin' o' Windward peoples, jus' once a year it comed 'round under the harvest moon, so for many days we was hard at work loomin' goatwool blankies what was our dwellin's bestest bart'rin'. Now, since my pa's killin' we'd trekked to Honokaa in groups o' ten or more but that year there was twice that number 'cos o'the spesh Prescient loot we'd got, thanks to us hostin' Meronym. There was hand-carts an' pack-mules for all the dried meat'n'leather'n'cheese'n'wool. Wimoway'n'Roses was goin' to trade herbs what din't grow near the Valleys, tho' Roses'n'

Kobbery was spoonyin' by then an' that was fine by me. I wished my cuz luck 'cos luck he'd need an' a whip'n'iron back'n all.

Crossin' Sloosha's Crossin' I'd to bear watchin' journeyers put fresh stones on Pa's mound, so our custom was my Pa'd got a bucket o' friends'n'bros what loved him truesome. Up on Mauna Kea that devil was sharp'nin' his nails on a whetstone to feast on this cowardy liar, yay. After Sloosha's came the zigzag up to Kukuihaele. One hand-cart busted'n'tipped so slow 'n'thirstsome goin' it was, yay, noon was long gone b'fore we reached the scraggy hamlet sittin' up the far side. Us young'uns shimmed the cokeynut trees for grinds an' ev'ry'un welcomed that milk, no frettin'. Trampin' southly the buckin' Old'un way t'ward Honokaa Town the ocean breeze turned freshly an' our spirits was mended so we told yarnies to shrink the miles, with the yarner sittin' backwards on the leadin' ass so ev'ry'un could hear. Rod'rick yarned the Tale o' Rudolf the Red-ringed Goat Thief an' Iron Billy's Hideous Spiker, an' Wolt sang a spoony song 'O Sally o' the Valleys-o' tho' we pelted him with sticks 'cos his singin' busted that liltsome tune. Then Unc'Bees asked Meronym to teach us a Prescient yarnie. She hes'tated a beat or two an' said Prescience tales was drippin' with regret'n'loss an' not good augurin' for a sunny aft'noon b'fore Barter Day, but she could tell us a yarn what she'd heard from a burntlander in a far-far spot named Panama? We all yaysayed so up she sat on the lead-ass an' a short'n'sweet yarn she spoke what I'll tell you now so all you shut up, sit still an' someun' fetch me a fresh cup o'spiritbrew my throat's gluey'n'parched.

Back when the Fall was fallin', humans f'got the makin' o' fire. O, diresome bad things was gettin', yay. Come night, folks cudn't see nothin', come winter they cudn't warm nothin', come mornin' they cudn't roast nothin'. So the tribe went to Wise Man an' asked, *Wise Man, help us, see we f'got the makin' o' fire, an', O, woe is us an' all.*

So Wise Man summ'ned Crow an' say-soed him these words: *Fly across the crazed'n'jiffyin' ocean to the Mighty Volcano, an' on its foresty slopes, find a long stick. Pick up that stick in your beak an' fly into that Mighty Volcano's mouth an' dip it in the lake o' flames what bubble'n'spit in that fiery place. Then bring the burnin' stick back here to Panama so humans'll mem'ry fire once more an' mem'ry back its makin'.*

Crow obeyed the Wise Man's say-so, an' flew over this crazed 'n'jiffyin' ocean until he saw the Mighty Volcano smokin' in the near-far. He spiralled down on to its foresty slopes, nibbed some gooseb'ries, gulped of a chilly spring, rested his tired wings a beat, then sivvied 'round for a long stick o'pine. A one, a two, a three an' *up* Crow flew, stick in his beak, an' *plop* down the sulf'ry mouth o' the Mighty Volcano that gutsy bird dropped, yay, swoopin' out of his dive at the last beat, draggin' that stick o' pine thru' the melty fire, *whooo-ooo-ooosh*, it flamed! Up'n' out o' that Crow flew from the scorchin' mouth, now flew with that burnin' stick in his mouth, yay, toward home he headed, wings poundin', stick burnin', days passin', hail slingin', clouds black'nin', O, fire lickin' up that stick, eyes smokin', feathers crispin', beak burnin' . . . *It hurts!* Crow crawed. *It hurts!* Now, did he drop that stick or din't he? Do we mem'ry the makin' o' fire or don't we?

See now, said Meronym, riding backwards on that lead-ass, *it ain't 'bout Crows or fire, it's 'bout how we humans got our spirit.*

I don't say that yarn's got a hole sack o' sense but I always mem'ried it an' times are less sense is more sense. Anyhow, the day was dyin' in soddy clouds an' we was still some miles shy o' Honokaa so we tented up for the night an' throwed dice for watch, see, times was bad an' we din't want to risk no ambush. I got a six'n'six so maybe my luck was healin', so I thinked, fool o' fate what I am, yay, what we all are.

Honokaa was the bustlin'est town o' nor-east Windward, see, Old'uns'd builded it high 'nuff to s'vive the risin' ocean, not like half o' Hilo nor Kona neither what was flooded most moons. Honokaa men was traders'n'makers mostly, O, they worshiped

Sonmi but they divvied their chances slywise an' worshiped Hilo gods too so we Valleysmen reck'ned'em half-savages. Their chief was called Senator, he'd got more power'n our Abbess, yay, he'd got an army o' ten–fifteen knuckly men with whoah spikers whose job was to force Senator's say-so, an' no'un chose Senator, nay, it was a barb'ric pa-to-son bis'ness. Honokaa was a fair midway for Hilo'n'Honomu folks, an' Valleysmen'n' Mookini b'fore they was slaved, an' the hill-tribes upcountry. The town's Old'un walls was rebuilded fresh an' blown-off roofs mended over'n'over but you could still strolly 'round its narrow 'n'windy streets an'magin' flyin' kayaks an' no-horse carts wheelyin' here'n'there. Last there was the bart'rin' hall, a whoah spacy buildin' what Abbess said was once named *church* where an ancient god was worshiped but the knowin' of that god was lost in the Fall. Church'd got strong walls an' beautsome colored glass an' sat in a lushly green space with lots o' stone slabs for pennin' sheep'n'goats'n'pigs'n'all. Durin' the barter, Senator's guards manned the town gates an' storehouses an' they'd got a lock-up too with iron bars. No armyman never knucklied no trader tho' not unless he thiefed or busted peace or law. Honokaa'd got more law'n anyplace else on Big Isle 'cept the Nine Folded Valleys I s'pose, tho' law an' Civ'lize ain't always the same, nay, see Kona got Kona law but they ain't got one flea o' Civ'lize.

That bart'rin', we Valleysmen did a whoah good trade for ourselves an' the Commons. Twenty sacks o' rice from the hill-tribes we got for the Prescient tarps, yay, an' cows'n'hides from Parker's Ranch for the metalwork. We telled no'un 'bout Meronym bein' an' offlander, nay, we named her Ottery o' Hermit Dwellin' from upgulch Pololu Valley, Ottery was a herb'list an' a lucky freakbirth, we said, to s'plain her black skin an' white tooths. The Prescients' gear we said was new salvage we'd finded in a stashed hideynick, tho' no'un ever asks, *So where'd you get this gear?* an' s'pects to hear a truesome answer. Old Ma Yibber keeps her slurryful mouth corked outside Nine Valleys, so when a storyman named Lyons asked me if I was the same Zachry o' Elepaio Valley what'd climbed Mauna Kea last moon I was diresome s'prised. *Yay*, said I, *I'm Zachry o' that Valley but I don't hate this life so much I'd go anywhere near the roof o' that mountain, nay.* I said I'd gone huntin' presh leafs'n'roots with my last-life Aunt Ottery but we din't go no higher'n where the trees stopped, nay, an' if he'd heard diff'rent, well, I were here tellin' him he'd heard wrong. Lyons's words was friendsome 'nuff but when my bro Harrit told me he'd seen Lyons'n'Beardy Leary mutt'rin' down a smoky dead-end I reck'ned I'd tell-tale him to Abbess when we got home an' see what she thinked. A rat's ass tang I'd always smelt comin' off Leary, an' I'd be findin' in jus' a bunch o' hours how, O, how right I was.

Meronym'n'me bartered off our goatwool spinnin's'n'blank-ies'n'all pretty soon on, yay, I got a sack o' fine Manuka coffee, some plastic pipin' in fine nick, fat oats an' bags o' raisins from a dark Kolekole girl, an' more gear too what I don't mem'ry now. Kolekole folk ain't so savage I reck'n tho' they bury their dead'uns b'neath them same long-houses where the livin' dwell 'cos they b'lief they'll be less lonesome there. Then I helped with our Commons barter for a beat or two then strolled here'n' there, howzittin' with some traders from round'bouts, savages ain't always bad folks, nay. I learned the Mackenzymen'd dreamed up a shark god an' was sac'ficin' bladed'n'footless sheeps into their bay. Usual tales I heard too 'bout Kona rowdy-in's eastly o' their normal huntin' grounds what shadowed all our hearts'n'minds. A crowd o' watchers I finded gatherin'round some'un, nustlied nearer an' seen Meronym, or Ottery, sittin' on a stool an' sketchin' people's faces, yay! She bartered her sketchin's for trinklety doodahs or a bite o' grinds an' folks was gleesomer'n anythin', watchin' with 'mazement as their faces 'ppeared from nowhere on to paper an' more folks clustered sayin', *Do me next! Do me next!* Folks asked her where she'd got that learnin' an' her answer was always, *It ain't learnin', bro, jus' practice is all.* Uglies she gived more beautsome'n their faces'd got, but artists'd done so all down hist'ry so Ottery the

Sketchin' Herb'list said, Yay, when it came to faces, pretty lies was better'n scabbin' true.

Night fell an' we tromped back to our stores an' drawed lots for sentryin', then partyin' began in spesh dwellin's named bars. I did my sentryin' early on then showed Meronym some places with Wolt an' Unc'Bees b'fore the musickers drawed us back to Church. A squeezywheezy an' banjos an' catfish fiddlers an' a presh rare steel guitar there was, an' barrels o' liquor what each tribe bringed to show their richness an' sacks o' blissweed 'cos where there's Hilo, O, there's blissweed. I skanked deep on Wolt's pipe an' four days' march from our free Windward to Kona Leeward seemed like four mil'yun, yay, babbybies o' blissweed cradled me that night, then the drummin' started up, see ev'ry tribe had its own drums. Foday o' Lotus Pond Dwellin' an' two-three Valleysmen played goatskin'n'pingwood tom-toms an' Hilo beardies thumped their flumfy-flumfy drums an' a Honokaa fam'ly beat their sash-krrangers an' Honomu folk got their shell-shakers an' this whoah feastin' o' drums twanged the young'uns' joystrings an' mine too, yay, an' blissweed'll lead you b'tween the whack-crack an' boom-doom an' pan-pin-pon till we dancers was hoofs thuddin' an' blood pumpin' an' years passin' an' ev'ry drumbeat one more life shedded off of me, yay, I glimpsed all the lifes my soul ever was till far-far back b'fore the Fall, yay, glimpsed from a gallopin' horse in a hurrycane but I cudn't describe 'em 'cos there ain't the words no more but well I mem'ry that dark Kolekole girl with her tribe's tattoo, yay, she was a saplin' bendin' an' I was that hurrycane, I blowed her she bent, I blowed harder she bent harder an' closer, then I was Crow's wings beatin' an' she was the flames lickin' an' when the Kolekole saplin' wrapped her willowy fingers around my neck her eyes was quartzin' and she murmed in my ear, *Yay, I will, again, an' yay, we will, again.*

Get up now, boy, my pa biffed me anxsome, *this ain't no mornin' for sluggybeddin' cuss you.* That bubbly dream popped an' I waked proper under itchy Kolekole blankies. The dark girl'n' me was twined, yay, like a pair o' oily lizards swallowin' each other. She smelt o' vines'n'lava ash an' her olive breasts rose'n' fell an' watchin' her I got the tenderlies like she was my own babbit slumb'rin' by me. Blissweed was foggin' me still an' I heard near-far shouts o' wild partyin' tho' a misty dawn was 'ready up, yay, it happens so at harvest barterin's, times are. So I yawned'n'stretched, yay, achin'n'feelin' all good'n'scooped, y'know how it is when you shoot up a beautsome girl. Smoky brekkers was bein' cooked nearby so I put on my pants'n'jacket 'n'all an' the Kolekole girl's eyes opened fawny an' she murmed, *Mornin', goatman*, an' I laughed an' said, *I'll be back with grinds*, an' she din't b'lieve me so I settled I'd prove her wrong an' see her smile when I bringed her brekker. Outside the Kolekole storehouse was a cobbly track runnin' by the Town Wall, but northly or southly I din't cogg so I was puzzlin' my path there when a Honokaa guard dropped from the rampart an' missed killin' me by inches.

My guts shot half up an' half down.

A crossbolt shaft stuck out his nose an' its point thru the back o' his head. Its iron point jolted that mornin' an' ev'rythin' into, O, its horrorsome place.

That near-far wild partyin' were battlin'n'fightin', yay! That smokin' brekker was thatch burnin', yay! Now my first thinkin' was my people so I backrabbited t'ward the Valleysmen's store in the town hub shoutin', *KONA! KONA!* Yay, the dark wings o' that dreadsome word beat furyin' thru Honokaa an' I heard a thund'ry splint'rin' an' a diresome shout kicked up an' I cogged the town gate was busted down. Now I got to the square but whackaboom panickin' blocked my way an' fear, yay, fear an' its hot stink turned me back. I roundybouted the narrow roads but nearer'n'nearer Kona roars an' horses an' bullwhips came fillin' them misty'n'burnin' alleys like a tsunami an' I din't know what way I'd come nor was goin' an' *ker-bam!* I got shoved into the gutter by a milkeyed old ma clubbin' thin air with a roller pin bansheein', *You'll never lay your filthsome hands on me*, but when I got up again she was still'n'pale, see, she'd got

303

a crossbolt blossomin' her bosom an' suddenwise *whoah* a whip binded my legs t'gether an' *whoah* up I flew an' *whoah* down my head dropped an' *aieee* the pavestones smashed my skull, yay, fiercer'n a chop from a cold dammit chisel.

When I waked next my young body was an' old bucket o'pain, yay, my knees was busted an' one elbow stiff'n'bruised an' my ribs chipped an' two teeth gone an' my jaws din't fit no more an' that lump on my head was like a second head. I was hooded like a goat b'fore slaught'rin' an' my hands'n'feet binded cruelsome an' laid flat on'n'under other sorrysome bodies, yay, I *hurt* like I'd never knowed b'fore nor since, nay! Cartwheels was groanin' an' iron-shoes clip-cloppin' an' with each sway pain sloshed 'round my skull.

Well, there weren't no myst'ry. We was bein' slaved an' carted back to Kona jus' like my lost bro Adam. I weren't speshly gladsome at livin' still, I weren't nothin' jus' achin' an' helpless as a strung-up lardbird bein' bled from a hook. A squirmin' foot squashed my balls so I murmed, *Any'un else awake here?* See, I thinked I may yet manage to rabbit out o' that hole, but a rook-raw Kona voice yelled jus' inches away, *Shut your mouths, my strappin' lads, or I vow on my blade I'll slit the tongues from ev'ry last dingo-shat one o' you!* A warm wet quilted my arm, as some'un lyin' on me pissed, what cooled to a chill wet as beats went by. I counted five Kona speakin', three horses an' a cage o' chicklin's. Our slavers was discussin' the girls what they'd torn open'n'shooted up durin' the Honokaa raid, so I knowed I'd been hooded half the day or more. I din't have no hungry but, O, I was thirsty as hot ash. One o'the Kona voices I cogged but I din't see how. Ev'ry long beat'd bring a thund'rin'o'war hoofs 'long the road an' there'd be a *Howzit, Captain!* an' a *Yay, sir* an' *The battlin' goes well!* an' so I learned the Kona'd not made jus' a reccyin' raid on Honokaa but was seizin' the hole o' northly Big I, yay, an' that meant the Valleys. My Nine Folded Valleys. *Sonmi,* I prayed, *Mercysome Sonmi, minder my fam'ly'n'kin.*

Fin'ly sleep dragged me off an' I dreamed o' the Kolekole girl but her breasts'n'flank was made o'snow'n'lava rock an' when I waked in that cart again I found a died slave under me was suckin' all the warmness out o' me. I shouted, *Hey, Kona, you got a died'un here an' maybe your cart-horse'd thank you to lose some draggin' heavy.* A boy on top o' me yelped as the Kona driver whipflicked him to reward him for my O-so-kindly consid'ration, he was the pisser maybe. I knowed by the birds' lilts evenin' was near, yay, an' all day we'd been carted.

A long beat later we stopped an' off that cart I was hauled an' pricked by a spiker. I yelled an' wrigglied, heard a Kona say, *This un's still livin' anyhow,* an' was lifted off'n'leaned 'gainst a hut-sized rock an' after a beat my hood was taken off. I sat up an' squinted in the mournsome dim. We was on the drizzly Waimea Way an' I cogged 'zactly where, yay, see it was by the slopin' pond an' that hut-sized rock we was leaned against was the selfsame rock where Meronym'n'me'd meeted Old Yanagi jus' a moon ago.

Now I watched the Kona sling away three died slaves for the dingos'n'ravens an' I knowed why I'd cogged a fam'liar voice b'fore, see one of our capturers was Lyons the storyman bro o'Leary. Storyman an' spyer, may Old Georgie cuss his bones. There was no Valleysmen 'cept me in the s'vivin' ten, nay, mostly Honomu'n'Hawi I reck'ned. I prayed one o' the slinged three wasn't Kobbery my cuz. All of us was young men, yay, so they'd killed the older'uns back in Honokaa, I s'posed, Meronym too, I reck'ned, 'cos I knowed she cudn't s'vive nor 'scape such a furyin' attack. One o' the Kona poured a slug o' pondwater on our faces, we opened our mouths for ev'ry brackish drop but it weren't 'nuff to damp our parchin'. The chief say-soed their horse-boy to tent up an' then spoke to his trembly catches. *Since this mornin'*, said the painted buggah, *your lifes, yay, your bodies are Kona b'longin's, an' the sooner you accept this, the likelier you'll s'vive as a slave o' the true inheritors o' Big I an' one day Hole Ha-Why.* Chief told us our new lifes'd got new rules, but luck'ly the rules was easy learnin'. *First rule is, slaves do your Kona masters' say-so, quicksharp an' no but-whyin'. Bust this rule an' your master'll bust you a bit, or a lot, d'pends on his will, till you learn better obeyin'. Second rule is, slaves don't speak 'cept when your master asks 'em. Bust this rule an' your master'll slit your tongue an' I will too. Third rule is, you don't waste no time plottin'scapes. When you're sold next moon you'll be branded on your cheeks with your master's mark. You'll never pass for pureblood Kona 'cos you ain't, true-be-telled all Windwards are freakbirthed shits. Bust this rule an' I vow it, when you're catched your master'll blade off your hands an' feet, blade off your cock to gag your mouth, an' leave you by the wayside for the flies 'n'rats' feastin'. Sounds like a quick death you may think but I done it sev'ral times an' s'prisin' slowsome it is, b'lief me.* Chief said all good masters kill a bad or idlin' slave now'n'then to mem'ry the others what happens to slackers. Last, he asked if there was any complainers.

No complainers there weren't, nay. Us peacesome Windward men was busted in body by wounds'n'thirst'n'hunger an' busted in spirit by the killin' we'd seen an' the slaved future we seen b'fore us. No fam'ly, no freeness, no nothin' but work an' pain' an' work an' pain till we died, an' where'd our souls be rebirthed then? I wondered if I may meet Adam or if he was died 'ready or what. An elfy Hawi boy started blubbin' some but he was jus' a niner or a tenner so no'un hissed him to shuttup, in fact he shedded tears for all of us, yay. Jonas'd be slaved most prob'ly, an' Sussy'n'Catkin too, but they was grim thinkin's, see, both was pretty 'nuff girls. Ma was an agein' woman, tho' ... What use'd the Kona find for her? I din't want to think 'bout the roller pin woman in Honokaa who'd whocked me into the ditch but I cudn't stop myself. Lyons came over, said, *Boo!* to the elfy boy so he blubbed badder an' Lyons laughed, then yanked off my Prescient boots. He admired 'em on his own feet. *No more scavvin' up Mauna Kea for Zachry Goatboy,* that judaser speaked, *so he won't be needin' these no more, nay.*

I din't say nothin' but Lyons din't like the *way* I din't say nothin' so he kicked my head'n'groin with my own boots. I weren't sure but I reck'n he was second-in-charge after chief, leastways no'un challenged him for my boots.

Night dripped an' the Kona roasted chicklin's over the fire an' any of us'd o' bartered our souls for a drip o'that chicklin' grease on our tongues. We was gettin' chill now, an' tho' the Kona din't want us too busted b'fore the slave market, they wanted us kept puny'n'frail 'cos we was ten but they was only five. They opened a cask o' liquor an' drank an' drank some more an' tore them delish-smellin' chicklin's an' drank some more. They murmed a bit an' looked at us, then a Kona was sent over to us with a torchin' stick. He held it by each of us while his tribesmen crowed *Yay!* or *Nay!* Fin'ly he unbinded the elfy Hawi's feet an' s'ported him hobblin' over to the campfire. There they warmed him an' fed him some chicklin' an' liquor. Us f'gotten slaves was bein' drained by hunger'n'pain an' the mozzies from the slopin' pond now an' we was envyin' that Hawi boy diresome, till at a nod from Lyons they ripped down Elfy's pants an' held him an' busted that boy's ring, oilin' his hole up with lardbird fat b'tween turns.

Lyons was porkerin' the sorrysome child when I heard a *kssssss* noise an' he jus' keeled over. The other four bust laughin' see they b'lieved Lyons was bladdered with liquor but then *ksss-ksss* an' two red spots grew b'tween another Kona's eyes an' he dropped stone dead too. A helmeted'n'caped Kona strided into the clearin' holdin' a sort o'shin-bone what he pointed at our last three catchers. Another *kssss* an' the boy Kona was felled. Now the chief grabbed his spiker an' hurled it at the helmeted killer, who dived'n'sort o' rolled cross the clearin' so the spiker tore his cloak but missed his body. A *ksssSSSsss* tore a slopin' gash cross the chief's torso an' he sort o' slid into two halfs. Hope creeped up on my shock but *crack!* The last Kona's bullwhip wrapped 'round that lethal killin' shin-bone an' *crack!* That shooter quicksharped out o' the rescuer's hands an' into our catcher's hands like a magicky. Now the last Kona swivvied the weapon at our rescuer an' 'proached close so he cudn't miss an' I seen his hands squeeze its trigger an' *KSSSS!* The last

Kona's head was missin' an' the breadfruit tree what'd stood b'hind him was a *whooosh* o' cindery flamin's cracklin'n' steamin' in the rain.

His body stood lonesome for a beat like a babbit learnin' to walk, then . . . *dumm-fff*! See, he'd errored the shooter's mouth for its ass and flashbanged his own head off. Our mist'ry Kona rescuer sat up, rubbin' elbows tendersome, plucked off his helmet an' stared mis'rably at the five died'uns.

I'm too old for this, Meronym said, grim'n'frownin'.

We unbinded the other slaves an' let 'em have the Kona's grinds, Meronym'd got 'nuff for us in her horse's saddlebags an' them unslaved buggahs needed all the help they could get. All we took from the died five was my boots back off Lyons's foots. *In war*, Meronym teached me, *first you anx 'bout your boots, only second you anx 'bout grinds 'n'all*. My rescuer giced me her full yarn a long beat later in this Old'un ruin in trackless bush on the Leeward Kohalas what we found an' lit a small fire.

It ain't long in the yarnin', nay. Meronym weren't in the Valleysmen's store when the Kona attacked Honokaa, nay, she was up on the town walls sketchin' the sea till a torchin' crossbolt kicked that sketchbook out o' her hands. She got back to the Valleysmen's store b'fore the town gate was down, but Unc'Bees shouted her I was missin' so she went off lookin' an' that was the last she seen o' my kin. Her horse'n'helmet she'd got from a Kona chief who'd charged down an alley an' din't charge out no more. In Kona gear an' riotsome annacky, Meronym bluffed a way out o' the bloodshot'n'torchin' town. There weren't no battlin', nay, it was jus' more a round-up, see, the Senator's army s'rendered faster'n any'un. Meronym first rided northly Valleywards but Kona was gath'rin' thick 'round Kuikuihaele for their swarm into the Valleys so she'd turned inland 'long the Waimea Way, but that road was thickly sentried tho' an' she cudn't pass for Kona if stopped. Meronym turned southly reck'nin' to reach Hilo'n'see if it was still in freesome hands. But Sonmi stayed her for long 'nuff to glance a cart trundlin' by, an' stickin' out o' that cart was two feet, an' on those two feet was Prescient boots, an' only one Windwardsman she knowed what weared Prescient boots. She daren't try to rescue me in daylight an' one time she lost the cart 'cos she'd roundy-bouted a platoon o' horses, an' if it weren't for the Kona's bladdery chorusin' as they gewgawed the Hawi boy she might've missed us in the dark an' ridden by. O, the risk she'd taked to rescue me! *Why din't you hide an' save your skin proper?* asked I.

She made a *stoopit question* face.

Yay, but what'd we do? My thinkin' was stormin'n'fearin'. *The Valleys is raided'n'burnin', prob'ly ... an' if Hilo ain't fallen yet, it'll fall soon ...*

My friend jus' tended my wounds'n'hurtin's with bandagin's 'n'stuff then raised a cup'n'med'sun stone to my lips. *This'll help fix your busted body, Zachry. Shut up your yibberin' an' sleep now.*

A murmin' man woked me in a leaky Old'un shelter with leafs bustin' thru' the window holes. I was achin' in a dozen places but not painin' so sharply. Mornin' was brisk'n'leeward-smellin', but I mem'ried the desp'rate new age what was shadowin' Windward an', O, in my head I groaned to be wakin'. 'Cross the room Meronym was speakin' thru' her orison to that sternsome Prescient what'd catched me sivvyin' thru Meronym's gear that first time. I gazed on for a beat marv'lin' once more, see, colours are spicier'n'brighter in orison windows. Soon he seen me risin' an' cogged me with a raise o' his head. Meronym turned too an' howzitted.

Better'n yesterday, I stepped over to see that spesh Smart. My joints'n'bones groaned some. Meronym said I'd 'ready met this Prescient what she said was named Duophysite, an' I said I'd not f'gotten 'cos he'd been so scarysome. The windowed Prescient was list'nin' to us an' his skel'tony face soft'ned jus' one shade. *O, I wish we wasn't meetin' in such dark times, Zachry,* said Duophysite, *but I'm askin' you to guide Meronym on one last trek, to Ikat's Finger. You know it?*

Yay, I knowed it, northly from the Last Valley over Pololu Bridge, a long spit o' land what pointed nor'eastly. Was the Ship anchorin' for Meronym at Ikat's Finger?

The two Prescients bartered a glance an' Duophysite spoked after a beat. *We got bad news of our own to teach you, sorry-some to say. The orisons on Prescience an' the Ship ain't answered no transmission for days'n'days.*

What's a transmission? I asked.

A message, said Meronym, *a window, an orison gath'rin' like we was discussin' with Duophysite now.*

I asked, *Are the orisons busted?*

Way worser it may be, speaked the windowed'un, *see in recent moons a plague's neared Prescience Isle, westly from Ank'ridge, yay, a terrorsome sick what our Smart can't cure. Jus' one in two hundred what catch this plague s'vive it, yay. Us Prescients on Ha-Why we got to act like we're on our own now 'cos the Ship prob'ly ain't comin'.*

But what 'bout Anafi, Meronym's son? Meronym's face made me wish I'd bit my tongue off b'fore I'd asked.

I got to live with not knowin', said my friend, so bleaksome I could o' blubbed. *I ain't the first'un who lived so an' I ain't the last neither.*

Well, that yibber busted a hope in me what I'd not cogged I'd got. I asked Duophysite how many Prescients was there on Hole Ha-Why.

Five, answered the man.

Five hun'erd? I asked.

Duophysite seen my dismay an' knowed it too. *Nay jus' five. One on each main I o' the chain. Our hole true is simply telled an' it's time now you knowed it. We anxed this plague'd reach Prescience an' snuff out Civ'lize's last bright light. We was searchin' for good earth to plant more Civ'lize in Ha-Why, an' we din't want to scare you islandsmen by big numbers of offlanders.*

So you see, spoked Meronym now, *your fears 'bout my true aims'n'all wasn't total wrong.*

I din't care 'bout that no more. I said, if Prescients was like Meronym, yay, five thousand of 'em'd o'been welcomed in the Valleys.

Duophysite darked, thinkin' how few Prescients might be livin' now. *The boss o'my tribe here on Maui where I'm speakin' to you from is a friendsome leader same as your Abbess. He's say-soed two war kayaks to 'cross the Maui Straits what'll be at Ikat's Finger come noon the day after 'morrow.*

I vowed him I'd get Meronym safe there by then.

Then I can thank you for helpin' her in person. Duophysite plussed there'd be space on them kayaks if I wanted to 'scape off Big I with her.

That settled my mind. *Thank you*, I told the stranded Prescient, *but I got to stay an' find my fam'ly.*

We stayed hid in that ruin one more night for my muscles to knit'n'my bruisin' to heal. Heartbuggahin' it was not rushin' back to the Valleys for battlin' or reccyin' but Meronym seen the Kona horses'n'crossbowmen pourin' t'ward the Valleys via Kukuihaele an' she 'ssured me, there'd not' o' been no dragged battlin' for Nine Valleys yay it'd all o' been over in hours not days, nay.

Bleaksome'n'haunted day it was. Meronym teached me how to use that spesh shin-boney shooter. We practiced on pineapples then giant burrs then acorns till my aim was sharp. I sentried while Meronym sleeped, then she sentried while I sleeped some more. Soon our fire was dirtyin' twilight mist again an' we dined on Kona rations o' salt-mutton'n'seaweed an' lilikoi fruits what growed in that ruin. I filled the horse's oatbag an' petted him an' named him Wolt 'cos he was ugly as my cuz, then gloomed hurtsome, wond'rin' who o' my kin was still livin'. True-betelled, not knowin' the worst is badder'n knowin' the worst.

A flutterby-thinkin' touched me an' I asked Meronym why a Shipwoman rode horses as good as any Kona. She 'fessed most Prescients cudn't ride no animal but she'd lived with a tribe called the Swannekke what lived way past Ank'ridge an' way past Far Couver. The Swannekke bred horses like Valleysmen bred goats, yay, an' their littl'uns could ride b'fore they could walk, an' she'd learnt durin' her seasons with them. Meronym teached me lots 'bout the tribes she'd lived 'mongst but I ain't got time for those yarns now, nay, it's gettin' late. We speaked 'bout the 'morrow's route to Ikat's Finger, see, one way was to follow the Kohalas' razorback over Nine Valleys, but 'nother way was to follow Waipio river down to Abel's Garrison first an' spy what we'd spy. We din't know see if the Kona'd slashed 'n'burned then emptied the Valleys like they'd done the Mookini or if they was aimin' to conquer'n'settle our dwellin's an' slave us in our own dwellin's. Now I'd vowed to get Meronym to Ikat's Finger safe'n'sound an' reccyin'bout Kona horsemen weren't safe nor sound, but Meronym say-soed we'd spy the Valleys first an' so the 'morrow's way was settled.

Dawn fogged waxy'n'silty. It weren't easy gettin' the horse over the Kohala ridge'n'thickets to Waipio spring, not knowin' if a Kona platoon was waitin' thru the walls o' cane we was noise-somely hackin'. Mostly we'd to walk'n'lead the beast but we reached the spring fin'ly by noon an' tethered him in a hollow upgulch an' creeped the mile to Abel's 'long the spruce spur. Fog turned ev'ry tree stump into a huddled Kona sentry, but still I was thanksome to Sonmi for the camo. We peered over the overlookin' lip an' lookin' down on the garrison. Grim viewin', yay. Only Abel's gates stood shut, see, the walls'n' outbuildin's was all charred'n'busted. A naked man was hanged off the gatebar, yay, by his ankles in the Kona way, maybe it were Abel'n'maybe it weren't but crows was 'ready minin' his guts an' a pair o'ballsy dingos scavvin' dropped slops.

Now as we watched, a thirty–forty head round-up o' slaved Valleysmen was bein' shunted out to Kuikuihaele. I'll mem'ry that sight till my dyin' day an' longer. Some was mulin' carts o' loot'n'gear. Kona shouts'n'say-soes ruckused'n'whips crackled. The fog was too swampy for me to make out my tribesmen's faces but, O, sorrysome was their figures dragglin' out t'ward

Sloosha's Crossin'. Ghosts. Livin' ghosts. *Watch the fate o' the last civ'lized tribe o' the Big I*, thinked I, *yay, the result of our schoolry'n'Icon'ry, jus' slaved for Kona fields an' dwellin's an' stables an' beds an' holes in Leeward ground.*

What could I do? Rush 'em? Some twenty Kona horsemen was convoyin' em off the Leeward. Even with Meronym's shooter I could maybe take out five o' the twenty sentries, maybe more if I got lucky, but then what? The Kona'd spiker ev'ry Valleysman to death at the first whisp o' knucklyin'. This weren't Zachry the Cowardy knucklyin' Zachry the Brave, nay, it was Zachry the Soosider knucklyin' Zachry the S'viver an' I ain't got no shame to say which Zachry vic'tried. To Meronym I signalled we was retreatin' back to the horse tho' tears was in my eyes.

Short-ass, get me a roasted taro. Mem'ryin' that despair is hollowin' me out.

Now backtrackin' up to the Kohala grazin' pastures the mist slid b'low us an' southly rose Mauna Kea from that ocean o' cloud, clear'n'close 'nuff to spit at so it seemed so I did, yay, I spitted hard. My soul may be stoned an' my luck may be rotted but I can still cuss a cuss. From each o' the Nine Folded Valleys black cobras o' smoke was risin' an' ev'ry carrion winger'n' legger on Big I was crawkin'n'feastin' in our Valleys that mornin' I reck'ned. Up in the pastures we finded goats scattered, some o' mine, some from Kaima, but we din't see not one goatherd, nay. I milked some an' we drank the last free Valleysman's goat-milk. Thru' Vert'bry Pass we downed t'ward Thumb Rock where Meronym'd sketched her map five moons b'fore, yay, over the heathery turf what'd cupped Roses under me six moons b'fore. Sun steamed the mist'n'dew away an' thru a fine-weaved rainbow I seen the school'ry was razed, yay, jus' a black shell now, the last books an' the last clock. Down we rode to Elepaio stream where I got off an' Meronym helmeted up an' loosely roped my hands so if we was spied it'd look like she'd slaved a 'scaped run'way an' maybe win us a lethal beat. Down the track we walked this way to Cluny's what was the highest dwellin' upgulch. Meronym dismounted an' gripped her shooter as we creeped hushly as mouses thru the buildin's but my heart weren't hushly, nay. A big knuckly'd happened there an' gear was crashed 'n'busted, but no bodies was lyin'round, nay. We taked some fresh grinds for the journey ahead, I knowed Cluny'd not o' minded. Leavin' Cluny's front gate I spied a cokeynut spikered on a stained pole with flies buzzin' what was wyrd'n'unnat'ral so we peered closer an' it weren't no cokeynut, nay, it was Macca Cluny's head, yay, with his pipe still poked in his mouth.

Such barb'ric buggahs are them painted Kona, bros. You trust one once you're a dead man, b'lief me. Macca's head gived me furyin' nervies as we trekked further down to Bailey's Dwellin'.

A pail o'curdlin' goats' milk stood in the milk'ry an' I cudn't stop 'maginin' Sussy bein' dragged away from that upbusted milkin' stool an' what'd been done to her, O, my poor'n'sweet 'n'dear sis. A possy o'hoofs stamped the yard mud. Goats was all shooed away, our chicklin's thiefed. So hush. No loom clackin', no Catkin singin', no Jonas makin' nothin'. The stream an' a laughin'-thrush in the eaves an' nothin' else. No horror-some sight on the gatepost, I thanked Sonmi for that much. Inside, eggs'n'apricocks was spilled from the upturned table. Ev'ry room I was dreadin' what I'd find but, nay, by the grace o' Sonmi it seemed my fam'ly'd not been slayed yet . . .

Guilt an' sorrow whacked me.

Guilt 'cos I always s'vived an'scaped despite my dirtsome'n' stony soul. Sorrow 'cos the ruins o'my busted old life was strewed here'n'there'n'ev'rywhere. Jonas's toys what Pa'd whittled years ago. Ma's loomwork hangin' in the doorways, swayin' in the last o'summer's soft breathin'. Burnt fish an' blissweed hanged in the air. Catkin's writin' work for school'ry still lied on the table where she was workin'. Din't know what to think or say or what. *What do I do?* I asked my friend as I asked me. *What do I do?*

Meronym sat on a woodbox Jonas'd made, what Ma'd called

his first masterwork. *A bleaksome'n'dark choice to settle, Zachry*, she replied. *Stay in the Valleys till you're slaved. 'Scape an' stay till the Kona attack an' be killed or slaved. Live in backwilds as a hermit bandit till you're catched. Cross the straits to Maui with me an' prob'ly never return to Big I no more.* Yay, that was my all choices, no frettin', but I cudn't settle one, all I knowed was that I din't want to run away from Big I without vengeancin' what'd happened here.

This ain't the safest place to sit'n'think, Zachry, said Meronym, so tendersome that fin'ly my tears oozed out.

Mountin' the horse to leave back upgulch I mem'ried my fam'ly's icons in our shrine. Now, if I left 'em there to be axed by'n'by for firewood there'd be nothin' to proof the Bailey's Dwellin' kin'd ever existed. So back I ran alone to get 'em. Comin' back down the passage I heard crock'ry fall off the pantry shelf. I freezed.

Slowsome I turned an' looked.

A fat rat strutted there, stink-eyein' me an' twitchin' its whisk'ry nose. *Bet you're sorryin' you din't jus' cut that rope on the wall o' my 'closure now Zachry, yay? All this woe'n' grief you could o'voided.*

I din't list'n to that liar's liar. The Kona'd o'attacked anyhow, yay, it weren't nothin' to do with me defyin' that Dev'lish Buggah. I picked up a pot to hurl at Old Georgie but when I taked aim the fat rat'd dis'peared, yay, an' from the empty room to my left came a breezy sighin' from the bed where I din't see b'fore. I should' o' jus' rabbited, yay, I knowed it but I din't, I tippytoed in an' seen a Kona sentry lyin' there in a soft nest o'blankies an' skankin' deep on Mormon Valley blissweed. See, he'd been so sure us Valleysmen was all rolled over'n'slaved that he'd blissed out, on duty.

So here was the fearsome en'my. Nineteen–twenty maybe he was. A vein pulsed in his Adam's apple what was left white b'tween two lizardy tattoos. *You found me, yay, so slit me*, whisped that throat. *Blade me.*

My second augurin', you'll be mem'ryin' an', yay, so was I. *En'my's sleeping, let his throat be not slit.* This was the beat that augurin'd foreseen, no frettin'. I say-soed my hand'n'arm to do it but they was locked'n'springed somehow. I'd been in knucklies 'nuff, who ain't?, but I'd never killed no'un b'fore. See, murderin' was forbidded by Valleysmen law, yay, if you stole another's life no'un barter nothin' with you nor see you nor nothin'cos your soul was so poisoned you may give 'em a sickness. Anyhow I stood there, by my own bed, my blade inches from that soft pale throat.

That laughin'-thrush was yarnin' fast'n'loud. Bird-lilts sound like blades bein' sharp'ned, I cogged for the first time there'n' then. I knowed why I shudn't kill this Kona. It'd not give the Valleys back to the Valleysmen. It'd stony my cussed soul. If I'd been rebirthed a Kona in this life he could be me an' I'd be killin' myself. If Adam'd been, say, adopted an' made Kona, this'd be my brother I was killin'. Old Georgie *wanted* me to kill him. Weren't these reasons 'nuff jus' to leave him be an' hushly creep away?

Nay, I answered my en'my, an' I stroked my blade thru his throat. Magicky ruby welled'n'pumped an' frothed on the fleece an' puddled on the stone floor. I wiped my blade clean on the dead'un's shirt. I knowed I'd be payin' for it by'n'by but, like I said a while back, in our busted world the right thing ain't always possible.

Goin' out I bumped Meronym rushin' in, *Kona!* she hissed. There weren't no time to s'plain what I'd done in there an' why. Hurryin', I stuffed my fam'ly's icons in the saddlebags an' she hoicked me on the horse. Comin' up the track from Aunt Bees' was three–four horses cloppin'. O, we speeded out o' Bailey's for the final time like Old Georgie was bitin' our asses. I heard men's voices b'hind an' glanced back an' even saw their armour glintin' thru the fig orchards but by Mercysome Sonmi, they din't see us vanishin'. One beat later we heard a shrill conchin's echo up the Valley, yay, three blasts it was, an' I knowed the

Kona must o' found that sentry I'd slayed an' was sendin' an alarm out, *Valleysmen ain't all slaved or mass'kered.* I knowed I'd be payin' for ignorin' the second augurin' sooner'n I'd gambled, yay, an' Meronym too.

But our luck din't yet wilt. Other conchin's answered the first, yay, but they was downgulch an' we galloped back thru Vert'bry Pass anxin' but we wasn't ambushed. One whoah narrow escape it was, yay, one more beat at my dwellin' an' them Kona horsemen'd o'seen an' chased us. Avoidin' the open Kohala ridge'n'pastures we skirted the forest for camo an' only then did I 'fess to Meronym what I'd done back to that sleepin' sentry. I don't know why it is but secrets jus' rot you like teeth if you don't yank 'em out. She just list'ned, yay, an' she din't judge me none.

I knowed a hid cave by Mauka waterfall an' to here it was I took us for what'd be Meronym's final night on Big Isle if ev'rythin' worked as planned. I'd hoped Wolt or Kobbery or 'nother goatherd may o' scaped an' be hidin' there but, nay, it was empty, jus' some blankies what we goatherds stashed for sleepin'. The trade wind was giddyuppin' an' I feared for the kayakers who'd be settin' out from Maui at dawn but it weren't so chillsome so I din't risk no fire, not so near the en'my, nay. I bathed my wounds in the pool an' Meronyn bathed an' we ate the grinds I'd got from Cluny's an' fig-loaf what I grabbed from my own dwellin' when I'd gone back for the icons.

I cudn't stop mem'ryin'n'yarnin' while we ate, nay, 'bout my fam'ly an' Pa'n'Adam too, it was like if they lived in words they cudn't die in body. I knowed I'd miss Meronym diresome when she was gone, see I din't have no other bro on Big I who weren't 'ready slaved. Lady Moon rose an' gazed o'er my busted'n' beautsome Valleys with silv'ry'n'sorryin' eyes an' the dingos mourned for the died'uns. I wondered where'd my tribesmen's souls be reborned now Valleyswomen'd not be bearin' babbits here. I wished Abbess was there to teach me 'cos I cudn't say an' nor could Meronym. *We Prescients*, she answered, after a beat, *b'lief when you die you die an' there ain't no comin' back.*

But what 'bout your Soul? I asked.

Prescients don't b'lief Souls exist.

But ain't dyin' terrorsome cold if there ain't nothin' after?

Yay, she sort o' laughed but not smilin', nay, *our truth is terrorsome cold.*

Jus' that once I sorried for her. Souls cross the skies o' time, Abbess'd say, like clouds crossin' skies o'the world. Sonmi's the east'n'west, Sonmi's the map an' the edges o'the map an' b'yonder the edges. The stars was lit an' I sentried first but I knowed Meronym weren't sleepin', nay, she was thinkin'n'tossin' under her blanky till she gived up an' sat by me watchin' the moonlighted waterfall. Questions was mozzyin' me plaguesome. The fires o' Valleysmen an' Prescients both are snuffed tonight, I speaked, so don't that proof savages are stronger'n civ'lized people?

It ain't savages what are stronger'n civ'lizeds, Meronym reck'ned, *it's big numbers what're stronger'n small numbers. Smart gived us a plus for many years, like my shooter gived me a plus back at Slopin' Pond, but with 'nuff hands'n'minds that plus'll be zeroed one day.*

So is it better to be savage'n to be civ'lized?

What's the naked meanin' b'hind them two words?

Savages ain't got no laws, I said, but Civ'lizeds got laws.

Deeper'n that it's this. The savage sat'fies his needs now. He's hungry, he'll eat. He's angry, he'll knuckly. He's swellin', he'll shoot up a woman. His master is his will an' if his will say-soes 'Kill' he'll kill. Like fangy animals.

Yay, that was the Kona.

Now the Civ'lized got the same needs too, but he sees further. He'll eat half his food now, yay, but plant half so he won't go hungry 'morrow. He's angry, he'll stop'n'think why so he won't get angry next time. He's swellin', well, he's got sisses an' daughters what need respectin' so he'll respect his bros' sisses an' daughters. His will is his slave an' if his will say-soes, 'Don't!' he won't, nay.

So, I asked 'gain, is it better to be savage'n to be Civ'lized?

List'n, savages an' Civilizeds ain't divvied by tribes or b'liefs or mountain ranges nay, ev'ry human is both, yay. Old'uns'd got the Smart o' gods but the savagery o' jackals an' that's what tripped the Fall. Some savages what I knowed got a beautsome Civ'lized heart beatin' in their ribs. Maybe some Kona. Not 'nuff to say-so their hole tribe, but who knows one day? One day.

'One day' was only a flea o' hope for us.

Yay, I mem'ry Meronym sayin', but fleas ain't easy to rid.

Lady Moon lit a whoahsome wyrd birthmark jus' b'low my friend's shoulder blade as she sleeped fin'ly. A sort o' tiny hand-mark it were, yay, a head o' six streaks strandin' off, pale 'gainst her dark skin, an' I curioed why I'd never seen it b'fore. I covered it over with the blanky so she din' catch cold.

Now Mauka Stream falled snaky'n'goshin' down dark Mauka Valley, yay, it watered only five–six dwellin's in the hole valley 'cos it weren't no friendsome'n'summery place, nay. No Mauka dwellin' did goatin' so the track was strangled by creepers'n'thornbushes what'd whelk your eye out if you din't watch close an' hard-goin' it was for the horse. I got clawed fierce after a quart'mile even shelt'rin' b'hind Meronym. The last dwellin' upvalley an' the first we comed to was Saint-Sonmi's Dwellin' whose chief was a one-eye named Silvestri who farmed taro'n'oats. The yibber reck'ned Silvestri was too fond o' his many daughters'n was nat'ral an' skankmouthed him for not payin' no fairshare to Commons. Laundry was scattered 'round the yard an' the daughters'd been taken, but Silvestri'd not gone nowhere, his bladed head was up on the pole watchin' us as we rided up. Some time he'd been there, see, he'd gotten maggoty an' a fat rat'd scamped up the pole an'd eaten thru' one eyeball as we rided up. Yay, the whiskery devil twitched his sharp nose at me, *Howzit, Zachry, don't you reck'n Silvestri looks handsomer now'n b'fore?* but I din' pay him no mind. A cocklydoo 'rupted from the chimney-pot an' nearly shocked me off the horse, see, I thinked it was an ambush yell.

Now we'd a choice o' sorts, to farewell the horse an' spider up the crumbly ridge over to Pololu Valley, or to follow the Mauka trail down to the shore an' risk runnin' into stray Kona moppin' up their attackin'. Dwindlin' time choosed for us to stay on the horse, see, we'd to get to Ikat's Finger by noon what was still ten miles far from Silvestri's. We missed Blue Cole Dwellin' an' Last Trout too, see, we wasn't reccyin' no more. A tide o' rain skirted us downvalley from the Kohalas but we got to the shore without no ambush tho' we seen fresh Kona prints b'neath the knife-finger palms. The ocean was no pond that day, nay, but nor so hilly a craft'ly-oared kayak'd overtoss. A Kona conch churned in the near-far an' vibed me uneasy. I heard my name in its churnin'. The air was drummed tight an' I'd ignored my second augurin', I'd knowed I'd be payin' for that life I taked what weren't ness'ary to take.

Where the rucky beach rocked up into Medusa Cliffs we had to wind inland thru banana groves to the Pololu Track what leaded out o' the northliest valley into No'un's Land an' fin'ly Ikat's Finger. The track squeezed thru two fat black rocks an' we heard a whistlin' what was more human'n bird. Meronym reached in her cloak but b'fore she'd got the shin-boney two sharky Kona sentries'd leapt down both sides on both rocks. That was four cock'n'primed crossbows aimed right at our heads from inches. Thru rubbery trees I spied a hole dammit Kona platoon! A dozen horsemen or more was sittin' round a tentment an' I knowed we was finished so near the end an' all.

Pass code, horseman? barked one sentry.

What's this, soldier, an' why? another jiggered his crossbow at my nips. *A Valleysboy's ass smearin' a good Kona horse? Who's your gen'ral, horseman?*

I was fearin' diresome an' I knowed I looked it.

Meronym did an eery'n'angry yarlin' growl an' looked thru

her helmet at the four, then 'rupted a shout out so blastsome, birds skimmed off krawlin' an' her tongue-slant was buried under furyin' noise. *HOW DARE YOU DAMMIT RAT-SHAT HOG-SLITS ADDRESS A GEN'RAL IN THAT MANNER! MY SLAVE'S ASS'LL SMEAR WHEREVER AN'WHATEVER I SAY-SO! WHO'S MY GEN'RAL? MY GEN'RAL IS ME YOU DAMMIT WORMS' BLADDERS! OFF THAT ROCK THIS SPLIT BEAT AN' BRING ME YOUR CAPTAIN NOW OR I VOW BY ALL THE WAR GODS I'LL HAVE YOU PEELED'N'NAILED TO THE NEAREST HORNET TREE!*

A desp'rate an' freakbirthed plan, yay.

Meronym's bluff vic'tried jus' one beat an' one beat was nearly 'nuff. Two sentries paled an' lowered their crossbows an' jumped down in our path. Two more dis'ppeared the back way. *Ksss! Ksss!* Them two Kona b'fore us din't get up no more, Meronym suddenwise heeldigged an' our horse whinnied an' reared an' bolted an' my balance was busted. Sonmi's hand stayed me on the saddle, yay, 'cos if hers din't whose did? Shouts an' *Stops!* an' conches ruckused b'hind us an' the horse galloped an' a *fisssssssss*-kwangggggggggg as the first crossbolt bedded into a bough I ducked under then a crackle o'pain flamed in my left calf jus' here an' I got that sick'n'calm shock you get when your body knows sumthin's way too busted for an easy mendin'. Look, I'll roll my trousers an' you can see the scar where the crossbolt tip bedded . . . yay, it hurt as much as it looks it hurt an' more.

We was gallopin' down Pololu Way now over knotty'n'rooty ground, faster'n surfin' inside a roller an' as hard to stay balanced an' there was nothin' I could do 'bout that seizin' agonyin'cept grip Meronym's waist tighter'n'tighter an' try'n ride the horse's rhythmin' with my right leg or I'd be tossed right off, yay, an' there'd not be no time to mount me on again b'fore the Kona 'n'their bone-drillin' crossbolts catched us up.

The track leaded thru the scalp-brushin' tunnel o' trees to the Old'un's bridge over the Pololu river's sea-mouth what marked the Valley's northly bound'ry. Now we was jus' a hun'erd paces shy o' this bridge when the sun unclouded an' I looked ahead an' its worn plankin' burned bright'n'gold, an' its rusted struts was shaded bronze. My pain shaked loose a mem'ry, yay, my third augurin'. *Bronze is burnin', let that bridge be not crossed.* I cudn't s'plain to Meronym on a gallopin' horse so I jus' yelled in her ear, *I'm hit!*

She pulled up the horse a yard shy o' the bridge. *Where?*

My left calf, I telled her.

Meronym looked back anxin' diresome. Weren't no sign of our chasers yet so she swung down to the ground an' peered at the pain. She touched my wound an' I groaned. *Right now the shaft's pluggin' the wound, yay, we got to get to friendsome ground first then I'll—*

Drummin' o' vengesome hoofs was nearin' up Pololu Way.

I telled her then, we cudn't cross that bridge. *What?* She twisted to fix my eyes. *Zachry, are you sayin' that bridge ain't safe?*

Now so far's I knowed the bridge was strong 'nuff, see, I often taked Jonas gull-eggin' northly when he was littler an' McAulyff o' Last Trout went seal-huntin' over it with his hand-cart most moons, but an' Icon'ry dreamin' din't lie, nay, not never an' Abbess'd made me mem'ry my augurin's for a spesh day an' that day was now. *I'm sayin'*, I said, *Sonmi telled me not cross to it.*

Fear made Meronym sarky, see, she was jus' human like you 'n'me. *An' did Sonmi know we got a furyin' swarm o' Kona on our tail?*

Pololu river is wide at its sea-mouth, I teached her, so it ain't whooshin' deep nor its current so sinewy. The track forked b'fore the bridge right where we was, yay, an' it leaded down jus' a stretch away where we could ford the river. The hoofs drummed closer'n'closer an' soon the Kona'd be seein' us.

Well, Meronym b'liefed my loonsome say-so, I cudn't say why but she did, an' soon the bright'n'cold Pololu was up numbin' my wound but the horse was slippin' diresome on the shingly riverbed. *Padddooom padddooom*, three Kona galloped on to the bridge an' seen us an' the air 'round us quavered'n'slit with one crossbolt, two, the third hit the water an' sprayed us. Three new Kona catched up the first three an' din't stop to shoot, nay, they was padddooomin'cross Pololu Bridge to cut us off on the far bank. Desp'rate I was, cussin' myself, *Yay, we're died lard-birds no frettin'*, I was thinkin'.

Now you know when you adze down a tree for lumber? The noise after the last stroke, o' fibres shriekin' an' the hole trunk groanin' slowsome as it falls? That's what I heard. See one or two Valleysmen crossin' hushly with a hand-cart was one thing, but a gallopin' horse was another an' six–seven–eight gallopin' Kona armored war-horses was too much. That bridge busted like it was made o' spit'n'straw, yay, struts snapped an' plankin' split an' worn cables pinged.

It weren't no little drop, nay. It was fifteen men high or more was Pololu Bridge. Down fell the horses, spinnin' belly-up, the riders catched in their stirrups an' all, an' like I said the Pololu river weren't a safe deep pool what'd catch 'em an' buoy'em up, nay, it was a crowded river o' fat tabley'n'pointy rocks what busted their falls bad, diresome bad. None o'the Kona got up nay jus' two–three sorrysome horses lay writhin'n'kickin' but it weren't no time for animal doctorin', nay.

Well, my yarn's nearly done'n'telled now. Meronym'n'me forded the far side an' I prayed my thanks to Sonmi tho' there weren't no Valleys Civ'lize to save no more, she'd saved my skin one last time. I s'pose the rest o' the Kona platoon was too busy with their died'n'drowned to come trackin' us two, yay. We crossed the Lornsome Dunes an' fin'ly reached Ikat's Finger with no ax'dents. No kayaks was waitin' yet but we dismounted an' Meronym used her Smart on that crossbolt-mauled calf o' mine. When she pulled the bolt out the pain travelled up my body an' hooded my senses so true-be-telled I din't see the Maui kayaks arrivin' with Duophysite. Now my friend had a choice to settle, yay, see, either she loaded me in that kayak or left me on Big

Isle not able to walk nor nothin' jus' a short ride off from Kona ground. Well, here I am yarnin' to you so you know what Meronym settled an' times are I regret her choosin', yay, an' times are I don't. The chanty o'my new tribe's rowers waked me half-way 'cross the Straits. Meronym was changin' my bleeded bindin', she'd used some Smart med'sun to numb its pain a hole lot.

I watched clouds awobbly from the floor o'that kayak. Souls cross ages like clouds cross skies, an' tho' a cloud's shape nor hue nor size don't stay the same it's still a cloud an' so is a soul. Who can say where the cloud's blowed from or who the soul'll be 'morrow? Only Sonmi the east an' the west an' the compass an' the atlas, yay, only the atlas o' clouds.

Duophysite saw my eyes was open an' pointed me Big Isle, purple in the sou'eastly blue an' Mauna Kea hidin' its head like a shy bride.

Yay, my Hole World an' hole life was shrinked 'nuff to fit in the O o' my finger'n'thumb.

*　*　*　*

Zachry my old pa was a wyrd buggah, I won't naysay it now he's died. O, most o' Pa's yarnin's was jus' musey duck-fartin' an' in his loonsome old age he even b'liefed Meronym the Prescient was his presh b'loved Sonmi, yay, he 'sisted it, he said he knowed it all by birthmarks an' comets'n'all.

Do I b'lief his yarn 'bout the Kona an' his fleein' from Big I? Most yarnin's got a bit o' true, some yarnin's got some true, an' a few yarnin's got a lot o' true. The stuff 'bout Meronym the Prescient was mostly true, I reck'n. See, after Pa died my sis 'n'me sivvied his gear an' I finded his silv'ry egg what he named 'orison' in his yarns. Like Pa yarned, if you warm the egg in your hands a beautsome ghost-girl appears in the air an' speaks in an' Old'un tongue what no'un alive und'stands nor never will, nay. It ain't Smart you can use 'cos it don't kill Kona pirates nor fill empty guts, but some dusks my kin'n'bros'll wake up the ghost-girl jus' to watch her hov'rin'n'shimm'rin'. She's beautsome and she 'mazes the litt'luns an' her murmin's bab-bybye our babbits.

Sit down a beat or two.

*

Hold out your hands.

*

Look.

An Orison of Sonmi~451

Then who *was* Hae-Joo Im, if he was 'not xactly who he said he was'?

I surprised myself by answering that question myself: 'Union.'

Hae-Joo said, 'That honour is mine to bear, yes.'

The student Xi-Li was xtremely agitated.

Hae-Joo told me if I didn't place myself in his trust, I would be dead in a matter of minutes.

I nodded okay, I would trust him.

But he had already lied to you about his ID – why believe him this time? How did you know for sure he wasn't abducting you?

I didn't know for sure. My decision was based on character. I could only hope time would prove it well-founded. We abandoned Timothy Cavendish to his unknown fate and hurried to our own fates down steps and stairs; elevators read Souls and could be controlled to trap us. Corridors rolled by, firedoors swung, passages faded into black. Hae-Joo half carried me down many stairs; we could not wait for me to negotiate them unaided.

In a sub-basement Mr Chang waited in a plain-looking ford. We had no time for greetings. The vehicle accelerated through a sequence of tunnels and ford parks. Mr Chang glanced at his sony, reporting that the north and east approach roads were blocked, but the slipway still looked free and that their people should be waiting for us there.

Hae-Joo gave the order to try the slipway. Then he got a flickknife from his pouch and sliced off the tip of his left index, gouged and xtracted a tiny metallic egg. Throwing this from the window, he ordered me to discard my Soul Ring similarly. Xi-Li also cut out his Soul.

Unionmen *really* cut out their own Juche-given eternal Souls?

How else can a resistance movement elude Unanimity? They would otherwise risk detection whenever they passed a traffic lite. The ford rounded a ramp and a blizzard of phosphate burst the windows in; metal groaned; the ford scraped along walls, jarring to an abrupt stop.

From my crouch I heard more coltfire.

The ford juddered and sped into motion; I heard a body thump off the vehicle. A wailing continued: it was Xi-Li. Hae-Joo held a handcolt against Xi-Li's head and fired.

What? *Why?*

Unanimity dumdums combine kalodoxalyn and giga-stimulin, I learnt later. The former is a poison that fries the victim in agony, so his screams give his position away; the latter prevents him losing consciousness. Xi-Li slumped over into a foetal position. Hae-Joo lowered the colt. The cheerful postgrad I had known was gone; I wondered if he had ever been there.

Rain and wind blew through the shot-out windows. Mr Chang drove down a narrow garbage alley, ripping out drainpipes, until the perimeter road. Ahead were red-and-blue flashes at the campus gates. A hovering airo thrashed the trees; imperious loudspeakers gave incoherent orders to who knew whom? Mr Chang warned us to brace, killed the engine and swerved off the road. The ford bucked; its roof whacked my head; somehow Hae-Joo wedged me under him. The ford gathered speed, weight and weightlessness.

I remember the drop: it shook free an earlier memory of blackness, inertia, gravity, of being trapped in another ford; I could not find its source in my own memories.

Bamboo splintered, metal crumpled, my ribs slammed the floor. Chaos and noise blurred.

The ford was dead. I heard insect songs and rain on leaves, then urgent whispers. I was crushed under Hae-Joo, who stirred, groaning. A torch cut into my eyes; its owner asked if anyone was conscious. I heard Mr Chang ask for the door to be opened.

Soon hands xtricated Hae-Joo, Mr Chang and myself from the wrecked ford; I was bruised but unbroken. Xi-Li's body was left where it lay. Anxious faces, resolute faces, faces that rarely slept: Unionmen. I was lowered down a manhole. My hands gripped rungs; my knees scraped along a short tunnel. More arms lifted me into what registered later was a mechanic's shop. I was put into a smart two-seater xec ford. Orders were issued; messages dispatched. The driver's door opened and Hae-Joo Im swung in and started the engine. Garage doors jerked open.

We drove down suburban backlanes before veering on to a jammed artery. The fords around us held lonely commuters, couples on dates, small families, some placid, some rowdy. Mr Chang, I noticed, had vanished without saying goodbye, again. When Hae-Joo finally spoke his voice was racked. He said if a dumdum ever scratched him, I was to euthanaze him as quickly as he had Xi-Li. I didn't know how to respond.

The Unionman begged my patience a little longer, saying that if we were captured now, the less I knew the better. We had a busy nite ahead, he added. First, we were bound for Huamdonggil. Have you ever visited that zone, Archivist?

No. My ministry would xpel me if I were ever Eyed in an *untermensch* slum. What did you find there?
Huamdonggil is a noxious maze of crookeds, ramshacks, flophouses, pawnshops, drug-bars and comfort hives belonging to a more benited world. Hae-Joo left the ford in a lockup, warning me to keep my eyes and head hooded, as stolen fabricants end up in the slum's brothels – made serviceable after clumsy surgery.

Zigzagging alleys and conduits reeked of sewerage. Purebloods slumped in doorways, their skins inflamed by prolonged xposure to the city's scalding rain. Children lapped water from puddles. I asked who lived here; Hae-Joo told me how hospitals drain the Souls of migrants with enceph or leadlung until only enough dollars remain for a euthanazing jab – or a ride to Huamdonggil.

I could not understand why migrants fled their Production Zones for a fate such as this. Hae-Joo listed malaria, flooding, drought, rogue crop-genomes, parasites, encroaching deadlands, and a simple desire to better the lives of their children. Papa Song Corp, he assured me, is a humane employer compared to the factories many of those migrants ran away from. Traffickers promise them it *rains* dollars in the Twelve Conurbs – migrants yearn to believe it, and only discover the truth when they have become *untermensch*. Traffickers only operate one-way. Hae-Joo steered me away from a miaowing two-headed rat, warning me that they bite.

I asked why the City Board tolerated such squalor.

Hae-Joo told me how Huamdonggil is viewed as a chemical toilet where unwanted human waste disintegrates, discreetly; yet not quite invisibly. *Untermensch* slums motivate downstrata consumers by showing them what befalls those who fail to spend and work like good citizens. Entrepreneurs take advantage of the legal vacuum to erect ghoulish pleasurezones within the slums, so Huamdonggil pays its way in taxes and bribes to the upstrata. MediCorp open a weekly clinic for dying *untermensch* to xchange healthy body-parts for euthanazing; OrganiCorp has a lucrative contract with the conurb to send in a daily platoon of immune-genomed fabricants – not unlike disastermen – to mop up the dead before the flies hatch. My guide then told me to stay silent, as we had arrived at our destination.

Which was what, xactly?

I recall an overhanging mah-jong house with a high whitewashed lintel to keep the drainwater out; but I wouldn't be able to recognize the building again. Huamdonggil is not gridnumbered or charted. Hae-Joo knocked, an eyehole blinked, bolts unclacked, and a doorman opened up. His bodyarmour was stained, his iron bar lethal, and he grunted at us to wait there for Ma Arak Na. I wondered if he wore a fabricant's collar under his neckplate.

A smoky corridor bent out of view, walled with paper screens.

I heard mah-jong tiles; smelt feet; watched xotically-clad pure-blood servers carry trays of drinks. Their hassled xpressions morphed to girly delite every time they slid open a paper screen. I copied Hae-Joo's xample and removed my nikes, dirtied by the Huamdonggil alleyways.

'You wouldn't be here if the news wasn't bad,' I heard a discordant voice. Its owner addressed us from a ceiling hatch. Whether her webbed lips, crescent eyes and disconnected speech were genomed or mutated I could not be sure. Her gem-warted fingers gripped the hatch-ridge.

Hae-Joo moved directly beneath the square and addressed Ma Arak Na, whom I took to be the madam of the establishment. The Unionman told her that a cell had turned cancerous, Mephi and his cell were under arrest and Xi-Li dead.

Ma Arak Na's tongue was double the normal length; she used it to swat away a fly. Her eyes glinted in the attic darkness. She asked how far the cancer had spread. Hae-Joo answered that he had come to ascertain that very question. The madam of the establishment told us to proceed to the parlor.

The parlor?

A gaproom behind a roaring kitchen and a false wall, lit by a weak solar. A cup of ruby lime waited on the rim of a cast-iron brazier that predated the building if not the city. We sat on well-worn floor cushions. Hae-Joo sipped the drink and told me I could unhood. The planked ceiling thumped and creaked, a hatch flipped open and Ma Arak Na's face appeared. She saw my face but didn't voice any surprise.

The ancient brazier hummed with xtremely modern circuitry. A spherical field of darkness and silence ebbed out until the parlor was consumed, slurring the kitchen noises. A piebald light above the brazier morphed into a carp.

A carp? As in the fish?

A numinous, pearl-and-tangerine, fungus-blotted, mandarin-whiskered, half-meter-long carp. One lazy slap of its tail propelled the fish toward me. Roots of water-lilies parted as it moved. Its ancient eyes read mine; its lateral fins rippled, hovering it still. The carp sank a few inches to read my collar, and I heard my name spoken by an old man. I looked at Hae-Joo, but he was barely visible through the murky underwater air.

'I am as profoundly thankful to see you,' the 3D's transceived voice was cultured but splintered, 'as I am honored to meet you.' The carp introduced himself as An-Kor Apis of Union, and apologized for the visual dramatics; camouflage was prudent, for Unanimity were combing all frequencies that nite.

I responded that I understood, hesitantly.

An-Kor Apis promised I would soon understand much more, and begged me to be patient a little longer. The carp swung toward Hae-Joo, addressing my companion as Commander Im.

Hae-Joo reported that he had euthanazed Xi-Li.

Apis said that he knew, and that no anaesthetic xisted for Hae-Joo's pain. He reminded Hae-Joo that Unanimity killed Xi-Li; Hae-Joo had released him; and he exhorted Hae-Joo to ensure Xi-Li's sacrifice was not in vain. A briefing followed: six cells had been xposed, and twelve more firebreaked. Boardman Mephi had managed to kill himself before his torture started. Then the carp ordered Hae-Joo to xit me from the conurb thru West Gate One, to proceed north in a convoy; and to reflect well upon what he had told him.

The carp circled, vanishing into the parlor wall, before re-appearing through my chest. 'You have chosen your friends wisely, Sonmi,' Apis told me. 'We may achieve changes together, great changes, historic changes to transform our society.' He promised we would meet again soon.

The sphere shrank back into the brazier as the parlor restored itself. The carp became a streak of lite, a dot; then nothing.

How was Hae-Joo planning to pass through a conurb exit without Souls in your indexes?
The Soul implanter was ushered in minutes later. A slite, anony-mous-looking man, he xamined Hae-Joo's torn finger with pro-

fessional disdain; tweezered a minute speck from a jelpack; bedded it into fresh tissue and sprayed cutane over the digit. I wondered at how such an insignificant-looking dot confers the rights of consumerdom on its bearers yet condemns those lacking one to an xistence of abject servitude or worse. 'Your new name is Ok-Kyun Pyo,' the implanter told Hae-Joo, adding that any sony would download his history.

The implanter turned to me, talking as he produced a pair of laser pliers. The laser, he xplained, cut steel but didn't even scratch living tissue, so all I would feel was a slite tickling sensation. I heard a click. 'Now for the subcutaneous barcode.' The Soulman swabbed anesthetic over my throat, warning me that the next stage *would* hurt, but that the blade's damping field would stop the barcode xploding on contact with air and severing my head from my body.

'Ingenious,' muttered Hae-Joo. He held my hand.

'Of course it's ingenious,' retorted the implanter. 'I designed it myself.' He regretted being unable to patent it and told Hae-Joo to be ready with a cloth to soak up the blood. A jagged pain tore at my throat. Hae-Joo stanched the bleeding; the implanter showed me the barcode of Sonmi~451 with a pair of tweezers and told me he'd dispose of it himself, carefully. He sprayed healant over my wound and applied a skin-tone dressing, telling me to change the bandage before I slept. 'And now,' he continued, 'I commit a crime so novel it doesn't even have a name. The Souling of a fabricant. But instead of a brass band, a nobel of outstanding scientific achievement and a university sinecure, all I earn is a guaranteed bench in the Lighthouse.'

And, Hae-Joo noted, a paragraph in the history of the struggle against corpocracy.

The implanter replied, 'Thanks, brother. A whole paragraph.' The surgery was swift. He laid my right palm on a cloth, applied anesthetic, incised the fingerpad of my index, dabbed coag to stem the blood, tweezered my Soul into the cut, and sprayed cutane to hide all evidence of my sudden ascension into the pureblood stratum. This time his sarcasm betrayed a core of sincerity. 'May your Soul bring you much fortune in the promised land, Sister Yun-Ah Yoo.'

I thanked him. I had all but forgotten Ma Arak Na watching from her ceiling hatch. 'Sister Yoo best get a new face for her new Soul,' she observed, 'or some awkward questions will arise between here and the promised land.'

So I guess your next destination was the facescaper.

Yes. The doorman escorted us as far as T'oegyero Street, Huam-donggil's northern boundary. We metroed to a once-fashionable galleria in Shinch'on and escalatored thru chandeliers chiming the psalms of the Immanent Chairman, to a warren-like pre-cinct in the canopy level frequented only by consumers sure of their destination. Hae-Joo led me through twists and turns lined with discreet entrances and cryptic nameplates to a plain door. A tiger-lily bloomed in a niche. 'Don't speak to the madam,' he warned me, as he rang the bell. 'Her prickles need cosseting.'

The tiger-lily striped brite and asked us our business.

Hae-Joo answered that we had an appointment with Madam Ovid.

The flower flexed to peer at us and told us to wait.

The door opened: '*I* am Madam Ovid,' announced a bone-white woman, 'and no such appointment xists.' Dewdrugs had frozen her harsh beauty in its mid-twenties, long ago, but her voice was rough as a saw. 'Our biocosmeticians only accept personal recommendations. Try a "face-maker" on one of the lower floors.'

The door shut in our faces.

Hae-Joo cleared his throat and spoke into the tiger-lily. 'Kindly inform the estimable Madam Ovid,' he said, 'that Lady Heem-Young sends cordial regards.'

A pause ensued. The tiger-lily blushed and inquired if we had traveled far. I recognized a series of passwords.

Hae-Joo completed the code. 'Travel far enough, you meet yourself.'

Madam Ovid opened the door but didn't dilute her contempt. 'Who can argue with Lady Heem-Young?' She told us to follow her, no dawdling. The interior of curtained passageways was designed for maximum discretion. The solars were dark and dampeners absorbed voices and footsteps. After a minute of latticed corridors, Madam Ovid clicked her fingers and a silent assistant joined us. A door opened into a briter studio and our voices returned. Tools of the facescaper's trade gleamed in the sterile solar. Madam Ovid asked me to unhood. She didn't act surprised by my server's features. I doubt she ever set foot in a Papa Song's. She asked how much time we had for the treatment.

When Hae-Joo replied that we had to leave in ninety minutes, Madam Ovid lost her needle-sharp *sangfroid*. 'Why bother coming to an artist?' she demanded. 'Why not do the job yourself with wrigley and lipstick? Does Lady Heem-Young take Tiger-Lily for a discount troweler's with before-and-after kodaks in the window?'

Hae-Joo hastened to xplain he was not xpecting the full morph – only cosmetic adapts to fool an Eye or a casual glance. Ninety minutes *is* a ludicrously short time, he admitted, which was why Lady Heem-Young needed the best of the best.

The proud facescaper diagnosed flattery but was not immune. 'Nobody,' she boasted, 'sees the face inside the face like I do.' Madam Ovid angled my jaw, saying that she could alter my skin, color, hair, lids and brows. She would dye my irises a pureblood color. Dimples could be punched in, and my tell-tale fabricant cheekbones removed. She decided that we would make the best of our eighty-nine precious minutes.

So what happened to Madam Ovid's artistry? You look like a Sonmi fresh from the wombtank, to me.

Unanimity refaced me for my peaktime courtroom appearances. The star actress had to look the part. But when I xited the Tiger-Lily, buzzing with face-ache, not even Seer Rhee would have known me. My ivory irises were hazeled, my eyes lengthened, my follicles ebonized. You may consult the kodaks taken at my arrest if you are curious, Archivist.

A golden boy with a red balloon waited by the escalator. We followed him at twenty paces to a busy fordpark below the galleria. He had disappeared, but the balloon was strung on the wiper of a cross-country vehicle. We took Thruway One for the East Gate One.

East Gate One? The Union general – Apis – had ordered you through West Gate One.

The leader suffixed his orders with 'Reflect well upon what I have told you.' This crypto signified, 'Invert these orders.' West meant east, north meant south, 'travel in a convoy' meant 'travel alone'.

That's a dangerously simple crypto.

Meticulous brains often overlook the simple. As we sped along the thruway, I asked if 'Hae-Joo Im' was a real name. The Unionman responded that no names were real for men of his calling. The xit downcurved to the tollgates. We slowed to a queuing crawl. At the xit each driver reached through the ford window to Eye his Soul. Enforcers stopped fords for random questioning. 'One in thirty, approx,' Hae-Joo muttered, 'pretty good odds.' Our turn at the scanner came. Hae-Joo placed his index on the scanner and an alarm sounded.

The barrier shot down.

The Unionman hissed at me: keep smiling, act vapid.

An enforcer strode up, jerking his thumb. 'Out.'

Hae-Joo obeyed, grinning boyishly.

The enforcer demanded a name and destination.

My escort's performance was masterly. 'Oh, uh, Ok-Kyun Pyo. Officer. We're, uh, driving to a motel in an outer conurb.' Hae-Joo glanced around and did a hand gesture whose lewd meaning I had learnt from Boom-Sook and Fang. His rubbish about his mother's cat license was interrupted in short order. How far was this motel, the enforcer demanded; didn't he know it was already gone hour twenty-three?

'The BangBangYou'reDead in Yōju,' replied Hae-Joo, conspiratorially. 'Comfy, clean, reasonable rates, though they'd probably let an enforcer like you sample the facilities *gratis*. Only thirty minutes in the fast lane, eastbound xit ten.' We'd be there before curfew with time to spare, he promised.

The enforcer asked how Hae-Joo had injured his index finger.

'Oh, is *that* why the Eye tripped?' Hae-Joo did a stage-groan, and described how he had cut it destoning a natural avocado, at his girlfriend's mother's house. Blood everywhere, *so* embarrassing, only stoneless avocados for *him* from now on, nature was more trouble than it was worth.

The enforcer peered into the ford and ordered me to unhood. I hoped my fear came over as coyness.

The enforcer asked if my boyfriend talked this much all the time.

I nodded, shyly.

Was that why I didn't speak at all?

'Yes, sir,' I said. 'Yes, Officer.'

The enforcer told Hae-Joo girls are obedient and demure until their wedding day, after which they start yacking and never stop. 'Get going,' he said.

Where did you curfew that nite? The outer motel?

No. We xited the overway at xit two, then forked on to an unlit country lane. A dike of thorned pines hid an industrial field of a hundred plus units. So close to curfew, our ford was the only vehicle around. We parked and crossed a windy forecourt to a concrete bloc signed: HYDRA NURSERY CORP. Hae-Joo's Soul blinked the rollerdoor open.

Inside was not a horticulture unit but a redlit ark, roofing giant tanks. The air was uncomfortably warm and moist. The tangled, stringy broth I saw through the tanks' viewing windows concealed their contents, for a moment. Then individual limbs and hands came into focus; the nascent faces, every one identical.

Wombtanks?

We had entered a genomics unit, yes. I watched the clusters

of embryo fabricants suspended in uterine jel. Some slept, motionless, some sucked thumbs, some scurried a hand or foot as if digging or running. I asked Hae-Joo, had I been cultivated here?

Hae-Joo said no: Papa Song's nursery in Kwangju is five times bigger than that place. He peered into the wombtank and told me those nascents were destined for uranium tunnels under the Yellow Sea; their eyes were bowl-like. Insanity would ensue if xposed to unfiltered daylight for too long.

The unit's temperature had Hae-Joo glistening with sweat. 'You must need Soap, Sonmi,' he said. 'Our six-star penthouse is this way.'

A penthouse? In a fabricant nursery?
The Unionman was fond of irony. Our 'penthouse' was a niteman's room: a concrete space containing only a water-shower, a single cot, a desk, a stack of chairs, a choking aircon and a broken pingpong table. Fat pipes throbbed hot. A sony-panel monitored the wombtanks and a window overlooked the nursery. Hae-Joo suggested I take a shower now as he could not guarantee one tomorrow nite; he strung up a tarp for privacy and built a bed from chairs for himself while I washed my body. A sac of Soap was waiting on the cot when I emerged, with a set of new clothes.

You didn't feel vulnerable, sleeping in the middle of nowhere without even knowing Hae-Joo Im's true name?
No. Fabricants stay awake for over twenty hours because of the stimulin in Soap; but when fatigue hits us, we drop, almost without warning.

I woke three hours later, alert; the embryo miners' Soap was oxygenated richly. Hae-Joo slept on his cloak. I studied a scab of clotted blood on his cheek, scratched during our escape from Taemosan. Pureblood skin is so delicate. His eyeballs gyred behind their lids; nothing else in the room moved. He may have said Xi-Li's name, or perhaps it was just noise. I wondered which 'I' he became when he dreamed.

I blinked my Soul on Hae-Joo's handsony to learn about my own alias, Yun-Ah Yoo. I was a student genomicist, born Second Month 30th in Naju during the Year of the Horse. Father was a Papa Song's Aide; mother a housewife; no siblings . . . the data onscrolled for tens of pages, hundreds. The curfew faded away. Hae-Joo massaged his temples. 'Ok-Kyun Pyo would like a cup of starbuck.'

I chose that moment to put my question to him; why had Union paid such a crippling price to protect an xperimental fabricant?

'Ah.' Hae-Joo picked sleep from his eyes. 'Long answer, long journey.'

More evasion?

No: he gave me an xhaustive reply as he drove us deeper into the countryside. I shall précis it for your orison now, Archivist. Nea So Copros is poisoning itself to death. Its soil is polluted, its rivers lifeless, its air toxloaded, its food supplies riddled with rogue genes. The downstrata can't buy the drugs necessary to counter these privations. Melanoma and malaria belts advance northwards at forty kilometers per year. Those Production Zones of Africa and Indonesia that supply Consumer Zones' demands are sixty per cent uninhabitable. Plutocracy's legitimacy, its wealth, is drying up; the Juche's Enrichment Laws are mere sticking plasters on haemorrhages and amputations. Its only other response is that strategy beloved of all bankrupt ideologues: denial. Downstrata purebloods fall into the *untermensch* sinks; xecs parrot Catechism Seven, 'A Soul's Value is the Dollars Therein.'

But where's the logic in allowing downstrata purebloods to die in places like Huamdonggil? What will replace their valuable labor?

Us. Fabricants cost very little to cultivate, Archivist, and have no awkward hankerings for a better, freer life. As a fabricant xpires after forty-eight hours without a highly genomed Soap whose manufacture and supply is the Corp's monopoly, 'it' will not run away. Myself xcepted, fabricants are the ultimate organic machinery. Archivist, do you still maintain there are no slaves in Nea So Copros?

And how did Union aim to xpunge these . . . alleged 'ills' from our state?
Revolution.

Pre-Skirmish East Asia was a chaos of sickly democracies, democidal auto-cracies and nascent deadlands! If the Board had not unified and cordonized the region we would have backslid to barbarism. How can *any* organization embrace such . . . terrorism?
Corpocracy smells of corruption and senility. The sun sets.

You seem to have embraced Union propaganda wholeheartedly, Sonmi.
I might observe that you have embraced Nea So Copros propaganda wholeheartedly, Archivist.

Did Hae-Joo mention xactly *how* Union plans to overthrow a state with a standing army of two million?
He did. Union intended to engineer the ascension of six million fabricants.

I don't understand how you didn't recognize this as sheerest fantasy?
All revolutions are the sheerest fantasy until they happen; then they become historical inevitabilities.

How could Union possibly achieve this 'simultaneous ascension'?
The battlefield was at the molecular level. A few hundred Union-men working in nodal installations such as Soap manufacturing plants and wombtank nurseries could trigger several million ascensions by adding Dr Suleiman's catalyst into key supply streams.

What damage could even six million ascended fabricants inflict on the most stable state Pyramid in the history of civilization?
Who would work factory lines? Process sewage? Feed fishfarms? Xtract oil and coal? Stoke reactors? Construct buildings? Serve in dineries? Xtinguish fires? Man the cordon? Fill exxon tanks? Lift, dig, pull, push? Sow, harvest?

Purebloods have lost the skills that build societies. The true question is, what damage could six million ascensions *not* inflict, in combination with cordonland militia, and downstrata purebloods on the brink of the *untermensch*.

Unanimity would maintain order. The police agencies aren't entirely composed of Union double-agents.

What weapons of intimidation would Unanimity possess? Wave colts at the ascendants? Even Yoona~939, a fabricant server, chose death over slavery.

Wait, wait, wait . . . Unanimity were already alert to the conspiracy by the time of your escape – they had tried to round you up. Security firewalls would spring up around the Soap manufacturing plants.

Unanimity were alerted to Union spies at Taemosan, and an ascended fabricant server. Nothing more.

And your role in this . . . *über*plan?

My first role was to provide proof that Suleiman's ascension catalyst worked. My mind had done so, simply by not degenerating. The catalyst was being synthesized in mass quantities in several underground factories.

'Your second role,' Hae-Joo informed me that morning, 'would be ambassadorial.' General Apis – the carp in the mahjong parlor – hoped I would act as an emissary, an interlocutor between Union and the ascending fabricants; to help them mobilize as revolutionary citizens.

How did you feel about such a role in a terrorist organization?

The greatest trepidation: I was not genomed to alter history, I told the Unionman, who responded that no-one ever was. Think it over, he urged. Apis was hoping I would reach a decision by the time we met. All Union was asking for the present was that I didn't reject the proposal out of hand.

Weren't you curious about Union's blueprint for the briter tomorrow? How could you know the new order would not give birth to a worse tyranny? Think of the Bolshevik, the Saudi Arabian, the Pentecostal Revolutions of

North America. If great change becomes necessary, surely a program of incremental reforms, of cautious steps, is the wisest way to proceed?
Your study base is curiously broad for an eighthstratum archivist. Have you encountered this dictum in your early twentieth-century reading? 'An abyss cannot be crossed in two steps'?

We're circling a contentious core, Sonmi. Let's return to your journey.
We reached Suanbo Plain around hour eleven, via minor routes. Cropdusters stewed clouds of saffron fertilizer, blanking the horizons. Xposure to EyeSats worried Hae-Joo, so we took a TimberCorp plantation track. It had rained during the nite, so pools bogged the dirt track and progress was slow, but we saw no other vehicle. The Norfolk pine–rubberwood hybrids were planted in unerring rank-and-file and created the illusion that the forest was marching past our stationary ford; a regiment of millions. I got out only once, when Hae-Joo refilled the exxon tank from a can. It had been a brite morning on the plain, but inside the plantation every daylite hour was dank dusk. The only sound was the sterile wind swishing blunted needles. The pollenless trees were genomed to repel bugs and birds; the stagnant air reeked of insecticide.

The forest left as abruptly as it had arrived; the land grew hillier. The track turned east with the Woraksan Range to the south; Ch'ungju Lake spread to the north. Now it was the lakewater that smelt bad, Hae-Joo xplained; effluence from salmon netponds. Crosswater hills displayed mighty corp logos; a malachite statue of Prophet Malthus surveyed a dustbowl. The track passed under the Ch'ungju–Taegu–Pusan xpressway. Hae-Joo said we could be in Pusan within two hours if he dared join it; but he preferred slow caution. Our pot-holed road switchbladed up into the Sobaeksan Mountains.

Hae-Joo Im wasn't trying to get to Pusan in one day?
No. At about hour seventeen he hid the ford in an abandoned lumberyard and we hiked up a mountain path. The xperience fascinated me, as the conurb once had: limestone bulges oozed lichen; rowan saplings and mountain ash grew from clefts.

The breeze was fragrant with pollen and sap; clouds scrolled. Once-genomed moths spun around our heads, electron-like; their wings' logos had mutated over generations into a chance syllabary.

I felt reborn into another element as alien to fabricant servers as Alpine meadows are unknown to the nautilus.

On an xposed shelf, Hae-Joo pointed across a gulf and asked if I saw him.

Who? I saw only a rockface.

Keep looking, my guide ordered, and from the rock emerged the carved features of a giant sitting in the lotus position. One slender hand was raised in a graceful gesture gravid with meaning. Weaponry and elements had strafed, ravaged and cracked his features, but his outline was still discernible once you glimpsed the whole. I needed some seconds to recollect whom the huge carving reminded me of: it was Timothy Cavendish.

Hae-Joo was much amused by my saying so. He had once assumed the giant was some ancient democrat or bandit-king with a penchant for self-advertisement; but in fact, the pre-consumers actually worshiped him as a deity who offered salvation from a perpetuity of birth and rebirth. Indeed, the weather-cracked giant from another age still boasted a lingering divinity. Only the inanimate may be so alive. The Abbess, Hae-Joo went on, could tell me more. I suppose QuarryCorp will destroy him when they get around to processing those mountains.

What was the purpose of this xpedition into the middle of nowhere?

Every nowhere is somewhere. Over the ridge we came upon a modest grainbed in a clearing, clothes drying on bushes, vegetable plots, a crude irrigation system of bamboo, a cemetery. I heard a thirsty cataract. Hae-Joo led me thru a narrow cleft into a courtyard, walled by ornate buildings unlike any I had seen. A very recent xplosion had cratered the flagstones, blown away timbers and collapsed a tiled roof. One pagoda had succumbed to a typhoon and fallen on its twin. Ivy more than joinery kept the latter upright.

Hae-Joo told me that an abbey had stood in that place for fifteen centuries, until corpocracy dissolved the pre-consumer religions after the Skirmishes. Now it serves as shelter for a colony of dispossessed purebloods who prefer scraping a life out of the mountains to the *untermensch* sinks.

So Union hid its interlocutor, its . . . 'messiah', in a colony of recidivists?
'Messiah'. What a grand title for a Papa Song server.

I heard a scratching on the flagstones behind us: a creased, sunscorched peasant woman limped into the courtyard, leaning on an enceph-scarred boy; a mute. The boy smiled shyly at Hae-Joo; the woman hugged Hae-Joo as affectionately as, I imagine, a mother would. I was introduced to the Abbess as 'Ms Yoo'. One eye was milkblind; the other brite and watchful; together they gave the impression of being observed by two xaminers. She clasped my hands in hers; the gesture charmed me. Her face was as aged as a senior from Cavendish's time. 'You are welcome here,' she told me, 'most welcome.'

Hae-Joo asked about the bomb crater.

The Abbess replied that the airborne zealots were teething; a chinook had appeared the previous month and launched a shell without warning, causing serious injuries and one death. An act of malice, the Abbess speculated; or a bored pilot; or maybe a developer had seen potential in the site as a healthspa hotel for xecs and wanted us gone. 'Who knows?' She sighed.

My companion promised to try to find out.

So who were these squatters xactly? *Untermensch*? Terrorists? Union?
Each colonist had a different story. I met Uyghur dissidents; dustbowled farmers from Ho Chi Minh delta; once-respectable conurbdwellers who had fallen foul of Corp politics; unemployable deviants; those undollared by mental illness. Of the seventy-five colonists, the youngest was nine weeks old; the oldest, the Abbess, was sixty-eight, though if she'd said three hundred, I would have believed her.

But ... how could they survive without franchises and gallerias? What did they eat? Drink? How about electricity? Entertainment? How could a micro-society function without enforcers and hierarchy?

Their food came from the forest and garden; water from the cataract. Scavenge-trips to landfills yielded plastics and metals for tools. Their 'school' sony was powered by a water-turbine. Solar nitelamps recharged during daylite hours. Their entertainment was themselves; consumers cannot xist without 3D and AdV, but humans used to and still can. Enforcement? I am sure problems arose, but the colonists treasured their independence and were resolved to protect it from slackers within or xploiters without.

What about the mountain winters?

They survived as fifteen centuries of nuns had before them: by planning, thrift and fortitude. The colony was built over a cave, xtended by bandits during the Japanese annexation. These tunnels offered shelter from winter and Unanimity airos.

It was no bucolic Utopia. Yes, winters are severe; rainy seasons are relentless; crops are prey to disease; the caves are susceptible to vermin, and few colonists live as long as upstrata consumers. Yes, the colonists bicker and grieve as people will. But they do it in a community. Nea So Copros has no communities; it only has the state.

So what was Union's interest in the monastery?

Union provides hardware such as solars; the colony provides a safe-house, kilometers from the nearest Eye. I woke in my dorm-tunnel just before dawn, and crept to the cave's mouth. A guard nursed a stimulin brew; she lifted the mosquito net for me, but warned me about coyotes scavenging below the old abbey walls. I promised not to go out of earshot, skirted the courtyard and squeezed between the narrow rocks to the balcony of blacks and grays.

The mountain dropped away; an updraft rose from the valley, carrying animal cries, calls, growls and snuffles; not one could I identify. Mountain stars are not these apologetic pinpricks over urban skies: mountain stars hang plump and drip lite. A boulder stirred, just a meter away. 'Ah, Ms Yoo,' came the Abbess's voice, 'another early riser.'

I gave an appropriate greeting.

The colonists, she told me, didn't like her wandering about before sun-up in case she wandered over the edge of the gulf. She produced a pipe from her sleeve, stuffed its bowl and lit up; she wouldn't offer me any on account of my youthful lungs, she said, but at her age it no longer mattered. The tobacco smoke smelt of aromatic leather.

I asked about the figure in the escarpment across the gulf.

That old rogue, she nodded. Siddhartha had other names, all lost now. The Abbess's predecessors could have recited all his names and sermons, but the old Abbess and senior nuns were Lighthoused when the abbeys were criminalized fifty years ago. The woman speaking to me had been a novice in the abbey then, so Unanimity judged her young enough to be re-educated and sent her to grow up in an orphans' bloc in Pearl City Conurbation.

I asked, was Siddhartha a sort of god?

'A sort of god' is an apt description, the Abbess told me. Siddhartha doesn't bolster our luck, inflict punishment, change the weather or protect us from the pain of life. He did teach about overcoming pain, however, and how to earn a higher reincarnation in future lifetimes. She still prayed to him so early in the morning, 'to show him I'm still serious', though few of the colonists were believers.

I said I hoped that Siddhartha would reincarnate me in her colony.

Lite from the coming day defined the world more clearly now. The Abbess asked me why I hoped so.

It took a little time to xpress my feelings in sentences, but the Abbess was not the sort of person to hurry thought. Finally I articulated my reason: the only purebloods whose eyes lack the hunger in consumers' eyes were colonists.

The Abbess understood. If consumers are satisfied with their lives at any meaningful level, she xtemporized, plutocracy is finished. That is why the colony offends the state so. Media compares them to tapeworms; castigates them for stealing rain from WaterCorp; royalties from VegCorp patent holders; oxygen from AirCorp. 'The day may come,' the Abbess speculated, 'when the Board decides we are a rival model for life outside corpocratic ideology.' That day, she feared, the 'tapeworms' would be renamed 'terrorists', smart-bombs would rain and the old abbey tunnels flood with fire.

I remarked that their community must be made of the destitute, but invisibly.

'Xactly.' Her voice hushed so I had to lean in to hear. 'A balancing-act as demanding as impersonating a pureblood, I imagine.'

How did she know?

I didn't ask: maybe a spyhole in our quarters had captured me imbibing my Soap. My host said that xperience had taught them to keep an Eye on their guests, even Unionmen and their friends. 'It violates the old abbey's code of hospitality,' the Abbess apologized, 'but our younger colonists are adamant we stay vigilant, especially in a world when anyone can become anyone else after a day at the facescaper.'

Why did she show her hand?

To xpress solidarity, possibly; I don't know. Of the Juche's numerous crimes, the Abbess said, the creation of a 'substrata of slaves' was the most heinous.

Was she speaking in general terms or specific?

I didn't learn that until the following nite. By now pans were banging in the courtyard: the breakfast detail was starting work. The Abbess looked at the cleft to the courtyard and changed her tone. 'And who might this young coyote be?'

The mute boy padded over and sat by the Abbess's feet, smiling. Sunlite bent around the world from the east, restoring fragile colour to the wildflowers.

So Day Two as a fugitive got under way.

Hae-Joo breakfasted on potato cakes and fig-honey; unlike the previous nite, no-one pressed me to eat the pureblood food. We said our farewells; two or three of the teenage girls were tearful to see Hae-Joo depart; these shot me hateful glances, much to his amusement. In some ways Hae-Joo was a hard-bitten revolutionary; in others he was a boy. The Abbess whispered, 'I shall pray to the old rogue for you.' Under her god's gaze we left that rarefied height and hiked down through the noisy forest. The ford was where Hae-Joo had hidden it, untouched.

Progress towards Yōngju was fair; we passed upbound timber rigs driven, I noticed, by burly fabricants all of the same stemcell. The rice-plains north of Andongho Lake have fast but xposed roads, so we stayed inside the ford, hidden from EyeSats until hour fifteen or so.

Crossing an old suspension bridge, high above an angry Chuwangsan river, we got out to stretch our legs. Hae-Joo apologized for his pureblood bladder and pissed into the trees a hundred meters below. I watched monochrome parrots roost on the guano-stained chasm face; their flapping and honking reminded me of Boom-Sook Kim and his xec friends. A ravine wound upstream; downstream, the river was directed thru leveled hills until disappearing under Ūlsōng's canopy. Airos clustered over the conurb; dots.

The bridge cables groaned under the strain of a streamed xec ford; an xpensive auto to encounter on such a rustic road. Hae-Joo reached into our ford for his colt. He returned, hand in his jacket pocket, warning me to let him do any talking, and get ready to dive for cover behind our ford if the driver showed a colt.

The xec ford slowed to a stop. A stocky man with a facescaped sheen swivelled out from the driver's seat with a friendly nod. 'Beautiful afternoon.'

Hae-Joo nodded back, observing it was not too sultry.

A pureblood woman genomed for sex appeal unfolded her

legs from the passenger door. She wore thick wraparounds so that only her pixie nose and sensual lips showed. She leaned on the opposite railing, with her back to us, and lit a sulky marlboro. Her male companion had meanwhile opened the ford boot and was lifting out an airbox, one suitable for a medium-sized dog. He unlocked its clickers and lifted out a striking, perfectly formed but tiny girl, about thirty centimeters in height.

She mewled in terror and tried to wriggle free; she saw us; her miniature scream was wordless but imploring.

The man tossed her off the bridge by her hair. He watched her fall, and made a plopping noise with his tongue. 'Cheap riddance,' he grinned at us, 'to *very* xpensive trash.'

I forced myself to stay motionless and silent: hatred and fury tore at my heart. Hae-Joo touched my arm. I forced my mind elsewhere, anywhere; a scene from *The Ghastly Ordeal of Timothy Cavendish*, when an innocent pureblood is thrown off a balcony by a criminal, emerged unbidden from my memory.

I presume the man had discarded a fabricant living doll.
The xec was keen to tell us all about it. 'The Zizzi Hikaru Doll was the *must-have* the Sextet before last. My daughter didn't give me a *moment*'s rest. Of course, my official wife,' he nodded at the woman on the other side of the bridge, 'put *her* all in, morning, noon and nite. "How am I supposed to look our neighbours in their faces if our daughter is the *only* girl in our carousel *not* to have a Zizzi?" she asked.' The xec admitted to a sneaking admiration for the marketers of these things. Take one junky toy fabricant, he said, genome it like an ancient glitzy idol, then up its price by *fifty thousand* and watch 'em fly off the shelves. 'That's *before* you shell out for designerware, doll-house, accessories. So what did I do? I paid for the damn thing, just to shut the women up! Four months later, what happens? Teencool surfs on and Marilyn Monroe dethrones poor *passé* Zizzi.' With disgust, he told us that a registered fabricant xpirer set one back nine hundred dollars. Cheering up,

he noted with a jerk of his thumb over the railing that an accidental plunge comes for free; so why chuck good dollars after bad? 'Pity,' the male winked at Hae-Joo, 'divorces aren't as hitchless.'

'I heard that, Lardass!' His wife faced us. 'You should have taken the Zizzi back to the franchise and had your Soul redollared when I told you. It was defective from the start. It couldn't even sing. The damn thing bit me.'

Lardass was all sweetness: 'Can't imagine why *that* didn't kill it, darlingest.' His wife muttered a casual obscenity. The man now uncled Hae-Joo, running his eyes over my genomed-out breasts, and asked if we were vacationing or passing thru that remote spot on business.

'Ok-Kyun Pyo, sir, at your service.' Hae-Joo bowed, IDing himself as a fifthstratum aide in Eagle Accountancy Franchise; a minor corp division.

The xec's weak curiosity died. He managed the Golf Coast between P'yŏnghae and Yŏngdōk, he told us. 'You are a golfer, Pyo? *No?* Golf isn't just a game, y' know, golf is a career advantage.' The Paegam course, the manager promised, had a vacancy or two coming up; an all-weather fifty-four holer, lickable greens, lake features and fountains as glorious as the Beloved Chairman's water-gardens. His chuckle nauseated me. 'We outbid the local downstrata mob for aquifer access. Just mention my name to our membership people: Seer Kwon.'

Ok-Kyun Pyo gushed gratitude.

Pleased, Seer Kwon began telling his xec life-story, but his wife tossed her marlboro after the Zizzi Hikaru, climbed into the ford and kept her hand on the horn while black and white parrots cannonaded skywards. The xec gave Hae-Joo a rueful grin and advised him to pay the xtra dollars to conceive a son when he got married. As he drove off I prayed to Siddhartha for the ford to smash through the barrier.

You considered him a murderer?
One so shallow he didn't even know it.

But hate men like Seer Kwon, and you hate the whole world.
Not the whole world, Archivist: only the Juche and the Corpocratic Pyramid.

When did you finally reach Pusan?
Nitefall. Hae-Joo pointed at exxon clouds from Pusan refinery,
turning melon pink to anthracite gray. 'We're here,' he said.

We entered Pusan's northern rim on an unEyed farmtrack.
Hae-Joo deposited the ford at a lock-up in Sōmyōn suburb and
we took the metro to Ch'oryang Square Galleria; its franchises
were the same as Wangshimi Orchard's. Fabricant nannies
scooted after their xec charges; swanning couples assessed
couples swanning; corp-sponsored 3Ds competed to outdazzle
all the others. In an older back galleria an old-style festival was
taking place where hawkers sold palm-size curios, 'friends for
life': toothless crocs, monkey-headed chicklets, jonahwhales in
jars. Hae-Joo told me they die forty-eight hours after you get
them home. A circusman was touting for business through a
megaphone: 'Marvel at the Two-Headed Schizoid Man! Gaze
upon Madame Matryoshka and Her Pregnant Embryo!' Pureblood sailors from all over Nea So Copros sat in bars, flirting
with comforters, under the scrutiny of PimpCorp men. I saw
leathery Himalayans, Han Chinese, pale-hued hairy Baikalese,
bearded Uzbeks, wiry Aleutians, coppery Viets and Thais. Comfort houses' AdVs promised satisfaction for every peccadillo a
pureblood could imagine. 'If Seoul is a Boardman's faithful
spouse,' said Hae-Joo, 'Pusan is his no-pantied mistress.'

The backstreets grew narrower; a funneled wind bowled
bottles and cans; hooded figures hurried by. Hae-Joo took my
arm and led me through a surreptitious doorway, up a glimlit
tunnel to a portcullised entrance; KUKJE MANSIONS was
inscribed over a side-window. Hae-Joo pressed a buzzer. Dogs
barked; the blind upzipped and a pair of identical sabretooths
slavered at the glass, making me jump. An unshaven woman
hauled them aside and peered at us; her face lit with recognition
at Hae-Joo. 'Nun-Hel Han!' she xclaimed. 'It's been nearly

twelve months! Little wonder, if the rumours about your brawls were even half true! How were the Philippines?'

Hae-Joo's accent was now hardscoured; in fact, I glanced to check it was still him at my side. 'Sinking, Mrs Lim, sinking fast.' Only half joking, he asked if she had sublet his dormroom.

'Oh, I keep a reliable house!' She faked offense, checking an account book, but warning him that she'd need a fresh blip of dollars if his next voyage was as long as his last. The portcullis rose and she glanced at me: 'Say, Nun-Hel, if your fluffball stays over a week, single apartments are charged as doubles. House rules. Like it, lump it, all the same to me.'

Nun-Hel Han the sailor said I would only be with him a nite or two.

'One in every port,' leered the landlady with ill-intent. 'What they've always said is true, then.'

Was she Union?

No. Drop-house landladies will judas their own mothers for a dollar; they could make much more judasing Unionmen. But drop-house landladies also discourage the inquisitive, Hae-Joo told me, and provide xcellent camouflage. A stained stairwell echoed with arguments and the noise of 3Ds; I was, at last, getting used to stairs. On the ninth floor we walked down a wormwood corridor. Hae-Joo retrieved a surreptitiously placed toothpick-stump from the hinge, noting that the management had succumbed to a nasty rash of honesty.

The room had a sour mattress, a tidy kitchenette, a closet of clothes for varying climates, a dijied kodak of white whores straddling Nun-Hel Han and two companions, souvenirs from the Twelve Conurbs and minor ports and, of course, a framed kodak of the Beloved Chairman. A lipsticked marlboro was left teetered on a beer can. The window was shuttered.

Hae-Joo showered and changed for an all-nite cell meeting, warning me to keep the shutter down and not to answer the door or fone unless it was him or Apis with this code-line: he wrote the words THESE ARE THE TEARS OF THINGS on a scrap of paper, which he then burnt in the ashtray. My Soap was in the fridge, he said, and promised to be back shortly after curfew on the following morning.

Surely such a distinguished defector deserved a grander reception?
Grand receptions draw attention. I studied Pusan's geography on the sony, imbibed my nite's Soap, showered, then slept until hour six thirty when Hae-Joo returned with a pungent bag of take-out *ttōkbukgi* looking xhausted. I made him a cup of starbuck; one useful trick from my server days. He drank it gratefully. Then he asked me to stand by the window and cover my eyes.

I obeyed. The shutter uprolled, squeaking with disuse. 'Don't look . . .' Hae-Joo commanded. 'Now, open your eyes.'

A sunny swarm of roofs, thruways, commuter hives, AdVs, concrete . . . and there, in the background, the sky's sediment had sunk to a place where all the woe of the words 'I am' dissolved into blue peace.

He said it. 'The ocean.'

You'd never seen it before?
Only on sony, Papa Song's 3Ds of life in Xultation, and Yoona's book; never the real thing, never with my own eyes. I yearned to go and touch it and walk by it. Hae-Joo thought it safest to stay hidden during daylite until we were requartered somewhere more remote. Then he lay on the mattress and within a minute had begun snoring.

Hours passed; in ocean slots between buildings, I watched freighters and naval vessels. Downstrata women aired worn linen on nearby rooftops. Later the weather grew more overcast; airos rumbled thru armored clouds. I studied. It rained. Hae-Joo rolled over, still sleeping, slurred, 'No, only a friend of a friend,' and fell silent again. Drool slid from his mouth, wetting his pillow. I thought about Professor Mephi: in our last seminar he had spoken of his estrangement from his family, and confessed he spent more time educating me than his own daughter.

Hae-Joo woke midafternoon, showered and brewed ginseng

tea. I envy purebloods their cuisine; before my ascension, Soap seemed the most delicious substance imaginable, but now it tastes drab and bland. I get sick if I eat purebloods' food. The Unionman shuttered the window. 'Time to liaise.' He then unhooked the Beloved Chairman's kodak and placed it face down on the low table. Hae-Joo plugged his sony into a socket concealed in the frame.

An illegal transceiver? Hidden in a kodak of Nea's architect?
The sacred is a fine hiding-place for the profane: they are always so similar. A 3D of a man clarified britely; he appeared to be an inxpensively healed serious-burn victim. His lips were slitely out of synch with his words. He congratulated me on my safe arrival, and asked who had the prettier face, he or the carp.

I replied honestly: the carp.

An-Kor Apis's laugh became a cough. 'This is my true face, whatever that means.' He said that his sickly appearance suited him well, as enforcers worried about contagion. Then he inquired if I had enjoyed my trip across our beloved motherland.

Hae-Joo Im had looked after me well, I said.

General Apis asked if I understood the role Union wished me to xecute. I said, yes, I understood, but my unwillingness to declare my indecision was pre-empted. 'We want to xpose you to a . . . sight, a formative xperience in Pusan, before you decide, Sonmi,' Apis began. He warned me it would not be pleasant, but it was imperative. 'To give you the chance to make an informed decision about your future with us.' If I was agreeable, Commander Im could escort me to the place now.

Pleased to win more time, I said I would go.

'Then we'll speak very soon,' promised Apis, disconnecting his imager. Hae-Joo produced a pair of technic uniforms and semi-vizors from his closet; we dressed in these, then wore our cloaks over the uniforms for the landlady's benefit. Outside was cold for the season, and I was glad of the double garments. We rode the metro to the port terminal, and took a conveyor down to the waterfront berths, passing vast ocean-going vessels. The nite sea was oily black; one vessel, however, pulsed golden arches and resembled an undersea palace. I had seen it before, in a previous life. 'Papa Song's golden ark,' I xclaimed, telling Hae-Joo this was the ship that carried twelvestarred servers to Xultation in Hawaii.

Hae-Joo knew; we were going aboard the golden ark.

Security on the gangway was minimal; a bleary-eyed pure-blood with his feet on the desk, watching fabricant gladiators in the Shanghai Colosseum on 3D. 'And you are?'

Hae-Joo blinked his Soul: 'Fifth Stratum Technic Man-Shik Gang.' He checked his handsony and read out he had been sent to recalibrate thermostats on deck seven.

'Seven?' The guard smirked. 'Hope you haven't just eaten.' After confirming the work-order the man regarded me. I looked at the floor. 'Who's this verbal marathonette, Technic Gang?'

'My new Aide,' said Hae-Joo. 'Technic Aide Yoo.'

'That so? Is tonite your maiden visit to our pleasuredome?'

I nodded, yes, it was.

The guard said there was no time like the first time. He waved us aboard with a lazy twitch of his foot.

Gaining access to a corp ship was so straitforward?

Papa Song's golden ark is not xactly a magnet for illegal boarders, Archivist. Crew and Aides bustled in the gangways, too intent on their own business to notice us. The service shafts were empty; we descended unquestioned to the ark's underbelly. Our nikes clanged on the metal stairs. A giant motor drummed. I thought I heard singing. Hae-Joo consulted his deckplan, unlatched an access hatch, and paused to tell me something.

He changed his mind, clambered in, helped me thru, then locked the hatch behind us.

I found myself on a hangway suspended from the roof of a sizeable holding chamber; its far end was concealed by flaps, and lacked the headroom for us to stand. Thru the hangway's gridded floor I saw some two hundred twelvestarred Papa Song servers, being processed thru turnstiles; the only direction was

357

onwards. Yoonas, Hwa-Soons, Ma-Leu-Das, Sonmis, some older stem-sisters I didn't recognize. How dreamlike it was to see my x-sisters outside a Papa Song's dome. They sang Papa Song's Psalm, over and over. Their music interwove with background hydraulics. How jubilant they sounded. Their Investment was paid off; the voyage to Hawaii was under way; their new life on Xultation would shortly begin.

Did you envy them?
I envied their certainty about the future.

At intervals of about fifty seconds, an Aide at the front ushered the next server thru golden arches. The sisters clapped each time; the lucky twelvestarred turned around, waved her hands, and passed thru to be shown to her cabin. The turnstiles rotated the fabricants one turn nearer. Finally, Hae-Joo tapped my foot, and signaled for me to crawl onwards thru the flap dividing the hangway from the next chamber.

Weren't you in danger of being seen?
Brite droplites underswung our hangway; from below, we were invisible. Anyway, we were not intruders but technics conducting maintenance work.

The next chamber was in fact a confined cell. A plastic chair stood on a dais; a bulky helmet mechanism, suspended from a ceiling monorail, hung just above it. Three smiling Aides dressed in Papa Song scarlet guided the server on to the chair. One Aide xplained that the helmet would remove their collar, as promised in Catechism Ten. 'Thank you, Aide,' burbled the xcited server. 'Oh, thank you!'

The helmet was fitted over the Sonmi's head and neck; at this moment I noticed the number of doors into the cell. The conclusions chilled me.

What was so odd about that?
There was one door: the entrance from the holding pen. One door only. How had all the previous servers left? A sharp 'clack' from the helmet refocused my attention on the dais

directly below; the server slumped, her eyeballs rolled backwards; the cabled spine connecting the helmet mechanism to the monorail stiffened; the helmet rose; the server sat upright; was lifted off her feet into the air. Her corpse tapdanced; the xcited smile frozen in death tautened as her facial skin took some of the load. One worker hoovered bloodloss from the plastic chair; another wiped it clean. The monorailed-helmet conveyored its cargo parallel to our hangway, through a flap and into the next chamber. A new helmet lowered itself over the plastic stool, where the three Aides were already seating the next xcited server.

Hae-Joo whispered in my ear, 'Those ones you can't save, Sonmi. They were doomed when they boarded.' He was nearly correct; in fact, they were doomed from their wombtanks.

Another helmet clacked its bolt home. This server was a Yoona.

The horror of that room cannot be adequately described or imagined; it can only be lived thru.

We crawled onwards through a soundlock. The helmets conveyed the cadavers into a violet-lit vault; as we passed thru the flap, the celsius fell sharply and the roar of machinery burst our ears.

A slaughterhouse production line opened out below us, manned by figures wielding scissors, swordsaws, tools I don't know the names of . . . blood-soaked, from head to toe, like sadistic visions of hell. The devils down there snipped off collars, stripped clothes, shaved follicles, peeled skin, offcut hands and legs, sliced off meat, spooned organs . . . Drains hoovered the blood . . . the noise was colossal.

But . . . why would – what would the purpose be of such . . . carnage?
The genomics industry demands huge quantities of liquefied biomatter for wombtanks but, most of all, for Soap. What more economic way to supply this protein than by recycling fabricants who have reached the end of their working lives? Additionally, leftover 'reclaimed proteins' are used to produce Papa Song food

products, eaten by consumers in the corp's dineries all over Nea So Copros.

No. Murdering servers to supply dineries with food and Soap . . . no. The charge is . . . preposterous. I'm not denying you saw what you saw, but it must, *must* have been a Union . . . set, created to brainwash you. No such . . . 'slaughtership' could possibly be permitted to exist. Neither the Beloved Chairman nor the Juche would permit such depravity! If fabricants weren't paid for their labor in retirement communities, the whole Pyramid would be . . . the foulest perfidy.

Business is business.

But . . . why didn't this emerge during your trial?

I must reiterate, Archivist: my 'trial' was no such thing, but an xercise in opinion-forming.

Yes, but what you allege is . . . nitemarish!

It is, but the nitemarish is not necessarily impossible. Do you, personally, know anyone who has visited Xultation? Where *do* servers go after retirement? Not just servers: the hundreds of thousands of fabricants who end their serviceable lives every year. Where are their conurbs?

What about the 2Ds of Hawaii? You saw them in the Papa Song's at Chongmyo Plaza yourself. There's your proof.

Xultation is a sony-generated simulacrum dijied in Neo Edo. In the real Hawaiian archipelago, there is no such location. You know, during my final weeks at Papa Song's, it seemed that scenes of life in Xultation were repeating themselves. The same Hwa-Soon ran down the same sandy path to the same rockpool. My unascended sisters didn't notice, and I doubted myself at the time; but now I had my xplanation.

No, I cannot accept — I do not see how — such evil could take root in our civilized state. Nea So Copros law is founded on equitable commerce.

My fifth *Declaration* proposes how the law was subverted. It is a cycle as old as tribalism. In the beginning there is ignorance. Ignorance engenders fear. Fear engenders hatred, and hatred engenders violence. Violence breeds further violence until the only law is whatever is *willed* by the most powerful. What is willed by the Juche is the creation, subjugation and tidy xtermination of a vast tribe of duped slaves.

Your Testimony will stand as you speak it. I – we must progress . . . How long did you watch the slaughter you describe?
I don't recall. My next memory is of Hae-Joo leading me through the dining area. Purebloods played cards, ate noodles, smoked, sent mail, joked, engaged in ordinary life. How could they know what happened in the underbelly and just . . . sit there, as if their vessel was a sardine-processor? The bearded security guard beamed at me, telling me to come back soon, honeysuckle.

In the metro, the commuters swayed; I 'saw' cadavers on the monorail. Ascending the stairwell, I 'saw' cadavers hoisted from the xecution room. In his room, Hae-Joo didn't switch on the solar; he just raised the shutter a few inches to let the city lites dilute the darkness. He poured himself a glass of *soju*. Not a word had passed between us since the slaughtership.

I alone, of all my sisters, had seen the true Xultation and lived.

Our sex was joyless, graceless and necessarily improvised; but it was an act of the living. Stars of sweat on Hae-Joo's back were his gifts to me; these I harvested on my tongue.

The young man smoked a nervy marlboro in silence and studied my birthmark, curiously. He fell asleep on my arm, squashing it. I didn't wake him; the pain turned to numbness; the numbness to pins and needles; then I squirmed from under him. I spread a blanket: purebloods catch colds, even in warm weather. Pusan readied itself for curfew. Its smeary glow dimmed as AdVs and lites were switched off. The final server of the final queue would be dead by now. The carnage line would be cleaned and silent; the slaughtermen, if they were fabricants, would be in their cots. The golden ark would sail away tomorrow to a new port where the recycling would begin afresh.

At hour zero I imbibed my Soap and joined Hae-Joo under

the blanket. His body was warm, living and young, despite the horror we had witnessed. Because of the horror, we numbed the memory of the slaughtership, the way a woman and a man may.

But weren't you angry with him and Apis for xposing you to the golden ark without trying to prepare you for the xtreme shock?
No. What words could they have used?

Morning brought a sweaty haze. Hae-Joo showered, then devoured a huge bowl of rice, pickled cabbage, eggs and seaweed soup. I washed up; my pureblood lover sat across the table from me.

I spoke for the first time since seeing that protein-xtraction line. I said, 'The ship must be destroyed; every slaughtership in Nea So Copros like it must be sunk.'

Hae-Joo said, 'Yes.'

I said, 'The shipyards that build them must be demolished; the systems that facilitated them must be dismantled; the laws permitting the systems must be rescinded.'

Hae-Joo said, 'Yes.'

I said, 'Every consumer, xec and Boardman in Nea So Copros must be persuaded that fabricants *are* purebloods; if persuasion does not work, ascended fabricants must fight with Union to achieve this end, using whatever force is necessary.'

Hae-Joo said, 'Yes.'

I said, 'Ascended fabricants need a Catechism: to teach them rights; to harness their anger; to channel their energies.' I was the fabricant to write these words. I asked if Union could – would – seedbed such a declaration of rights?

Hae-Joo said, 'You damn well bet we will.'

Many xpert witnesses at your trial denied *Declarations* was the work of a fabricant, ascended or otherwise, and maintained it was ghosted by a pure-blood Abolitionist.
How lazily 'xperts' dismiss what they don't understand!

I wrote *Declarations* in Ūlsukdo Ceo, outside Pusan, in an isolated xec villa overlooking the Nakdong estuary. During its composition I consulted a judge, genomicist, syntaxist and

An-Kor Apis; but the Ascended Catechisms of *Declarations*, their logic and ethics, denounced at my trial as 'the foulest wickedness in the history of social deviancy', were the fruits of *my* mind, Archivist. My *Declarations* were germinated when Seer Rhee maimed Yoona~939; nurtured by Boom-Sook and Fang; strengthened by Mephi and the Abbess; birthed in Papa Song's slaughtership.

And your capture came shortly after completing your text?
The same afternoon. Once my function was fulfiled it was hazardous to let me run free. My arrest was dramatized for Media. I handed my *Declarations* on sony to Hae-Joo. We looked at each other for the last time; nothing we could say was as eloquent as nothing. I knew we would never meet again; maybe he knew that I knew.

At the edge of the property a small colony of wild ducks survived the pollution; rogue genomes give them a resilience lacking in their pureblood ancestors. I fed them bread, watched waterwalkers dimple the chromebrite surface, then returned to the house to watch the show from inside. Unanimity didn't keep me waiting long.

Six airos sharked over the water; one landed in the back garden. Agents jumped out, priming their colts, and bellysnaked towards my window with much hand-signing and fearless bravado. I had left the doors and windows open for them, but my captors contrived a spectacular siege with snipers and megaphones.

You are implying that you xpected the raid, Sonmi?
Once I had finished my manifesto, the next stage could only be my arrest.

What do you mean? What 'next stage' of what?
Of the theatrical production, set up while I was still a server in Papa Song's.

Wait, wait, wait. What about . . . well, everything? Are you saying your whole . . . confession is composed of . . . scripted events?

Its key events, yes. Some actors were unwitting: Boom-Sook and the Abbess, for xample, but the major players were provocateurs. Hae-Joo Im and Boardman Mephi certainly were. Didn't you spot the hairline cracks?

Such as?
Wing~027 was as stable an ascendant as me; was I really so unique? Would Union really risk their secret weapon on a cross-country dash? Didn't Seer Kwon's murder of the Zizzi Hikaru fabricant on the suspension bridge underline the purebloods' brutality a little too neatly; was its timing not a little too fortuitous?

But what about Xi-Li, the young pureblood killed on the nite of your flight from Taemosan? His blood was not . . . tomato ketchup!
That poor idealist was an xpendable xtra in Unanimity's disney.

But . . . Union? Are you saying even Union was fictioned for your script?
No: Union pre-xists me, but its *raisons d'être* are not to foment revolution. First, it attracts social malcontents like Xi-Li and keeps them where Unanimity can watch them; second, it provides Nea So Copros with the enemy required by any hierarchical state for social cohesion.

I still can't understand why Unanimity would go to the xpense and trouble of staging this fake . . . adventure story?
To generate a show-trial, Archivist! To make every last pureblood in Nea So Copros mistrustful of every last fabricant. To manufacture consent for the Fabricant Containment Act being presented to the Juche. To discredit Abolitionism. The whole conspiracy was a resounding success.

But if you knew about this . . . conspiracy, why did you cooperate with it?
Why does any martyr cooperate with his judases? He sees a further endgame.

What is yours?
The *Declarations*. Media have flooded Nea So Copros with my Catechisms. Every schoolchild in Nea So Copros knows my

twelve 'blasphemies' now. My guards tell me there is even talk of a State-wide 'Vigilance Day' against fabricants who show signs of the *Declarations*. My ideas have been reproduced a billionfold.

But to what end? Some . . . future revolution?
To Corpocracy, to Unanimity, to the Ministry of Testaments, to the Juche and to the Chairman, I quote Seneca's warning to Nero: No matter how many of us you kill, you will never kill your successor.

Two brief last questions. Do you regret the course of your life?
How can I? 'Regret' implies a freely chosen, but erroneous, action; free will plays no part in my story.

Did you love Hae-Joo Im?
Tell the Chairman of Narcissism he'll have to consult future historians on that. My narrative is over. You can switch off your silver orison now, Archivist. My time is short and I claim my last request.

Very well . . . name it.
The use of your sony and access codes.

What do you wish to download?
I wish to finish viewing a film I began watching when, for an hour in my life, I knew happiness.

The Ghastly Ordeal of
Timothy Cavendish

'Mr Cavendish? Are we awake?' A liquorice snake on a field of cream wriggles into focus. The number five. November 5th. Why does my old John Thomas hurt so? A prank? My God, I have a tube stuck up my willy! I fight to free myself, but my muscles ignore me. A bottle up there feeds a tube. The tube feeds a needle in my arm. The needle feeds me. A woman's stiff face framed with a pageboy haircut. 'Tut *tut*. Lucky you were here when you fell over, Mr Cavendish. Very lucky indeed. If we *had* let you go wandering over heaths, you'd be dead in a ditch by now!'

Cavendish, a familiar name, Cavendish, who is this 'Cavendish'? Where am I? I try to ask her, but I can only squeal, like Peter Rabbit tossed off Salisbury Cathedral's spire. Blackness embraces me. Thank God.

A number six. November 6th. I've woken here before. A picture of a thatched cottage. Text in Cornish or Druidic. The willy tube is gone. Something stinks. Of what? My calves are raised and my arse is wiped with a brisk cold wet cloth. Excrement, faeces, cloying, clogging, smearing . . . poo. Did I sit on a tube of the stuff? Oh. No. How did I come to this? I try to fight the cloth away, but my body only trembles. A sullen automaton looks into my eyes. A discarded lover? I'm afraid she is going to kiss me. She suffers from vitamin deficiencies. She should eat more fruit and veg, her breath stinks. But at least she controls her motor functions. At least she can use a lavatory. Sleep, sleep, sleep, come free me.

Speak, Memory. No, not a word. My neck moves. Hallelujah. Timothy Langland Cavendish can command his neck and his name has come home. November 7th. I recall a yesterday and see a tomorrow. Time, no arrow, no boomerang, but a concertina. Bedsores. How many days have I lain here? Pass. How old is Tim Cavendish? Fifty? Seventy? A hundred? How can you forget your age?

'Mr Cavendish?' A face rises to the muddy surface.

'Ursula?'

The woman peers in. 'Was Ursula your lady wife, Mr Cavendish?' Don't trust her. 'No, I'm Mrs Judd. You've had a stroke, Mr Cavendish. Do you understand? A teeny-weeny stroke.'

When did it happen? I tried to say. 'Airn-dit-hpn' came out.

She crooned. 'That's why everything's so topsy-turvy. But don't worry, Dr Upward says we're making super progress. No horrid hospital for us!' A stroke? Two-stroker? Stroke me? Margo Roker had a stroke. Margo Roker?

Who *are* all you people? *Memory, you old sod.*

I offer that trio of vignettes for the benefit of lucky readers whose psyches have never been razed to rubble by blood capillaries rupturing in their brains. Putting Timothy Cavendish together again was a Tolstoyan editing job, even for the man who once condensed the nine-volume *Story of Oral Hygiene on the Isle of Wight* to a mere seven hundred pages. Memories refused to fit, or fitted but came unglued. Even months later, how would I know if some major tranche of myself remained lost?

My stroke was relatively light, true, but the month that followed was the most mortifying of my life. I spoke like a spastic. My arms were dead. I couldn't wipe my own arse. My mind shambled in fog, yet was aware of my witlessness, and ashamed. I couldn't bring myself to ask the doctor or Sister Noakes or Mrs Judd, 'Who are you?', 'Have we met before?', 'Where do I go when I leave here?' I kept asking for Mrs Latham.

Basta! A Cavendish is down but never out. When *The Ghastly Ordeal of Timothy Cavendish* is turned into a film, I advise thee, Director dearest, whom I see as an intense, turtlenecked Swede named Lars, to render that November as a 'boxer-in-training-for-the-big-fight' montage. True Grit Cavendish takes his injections without a quiver. Curious Cavendish rediscovers language. Feral Cavendish redomesticated by Dr Upward and Nurse Noakes. John Wayne Cavendish on a zimmerframe (I graduated to a stick, which I still use. Veronica said it lends me a Lloyd-George air). Cavendish *à la* Carl Sagan, caged in a Dandelion Clock. As long as Cavendish was anaesthetized by amnesia, you could say he was content enough.

Then, Lars, strike a chord sinister.

The *Six o'Clock News* on the first day of December (advent calendars were on show) had just begun. I had fed myself mashed banana with evaporated milk without tipping it down my bib. Nurse Noakes passed by and my fellow inmates fell silent, like songbirds under the shadow of a hawk.

All at once, my memory's chastity belt was unlocked and removed.

I rather wished it hadn't been. My 'friends' at Aurora House were senile boors who cheated at Scrabble with stunning ineptitude and who were nice to me solely because in the Kingdom of the Dying the most Enfeebled is the common Maginot Line against the Unconquerable Führer. I had been imprisoned a whole month by my vengeful brother, so plainly no nationwide manhunt was under way. I would have to effect my own escape, but how to outrun that mutant groundsman, Withers, when a fifty-yard dash took a quarter of an hour? How to outwit the Noakes from the Black Lagoon when I couldn't even remember my postcode?

Oh, the horror, the horror. My mashed banana clagged my throat.

*　　*　　*

My senses rethroned, I observed the Decembral rituals of man, nature and beast. The pond iced over in the first week of December and disgusted ducks skated. Aurora House froze in the mornings and boiled in the evenings. The asexual careworker, whose name was Deirdre, unsurprisingly, strung tinsel from the light fittings and failed to electrocute herself. A plastic tree appeared in a bucket wrapped in crêpe paper. Gwendolin Bendincks organized paper-chain drives to which the Undead flocked, both parties oblivious to the irony of the image. The Undead clamoured to be the advent calendar's window-opener, a privilege bestowed by Bendincks like the Queen awarding Maundy money: 'Mrs Birkin has found a cheeky snowman, everyone, isn't that fabulous?' Being Nurse Noakes's sheepdog was her and Warlock-Williams's survival niche. I thought of Primo Levi's *The Drowned and the Saved*.

Dr Upward was one of those Academy Award-winning Asses of Arrogance you find in educational administration, law or medicine. He visited Aurora House twice a week and if, aged fifty-five or so, his career was not living up to the destiny his name foretold, it was down to us damnable obstacles in the way of all Emissars of Healing, *sick people*. I dismissed him as a possible ally the moment I clapped eyes on him. Nor were the part-time botty-wipers, bath-scrubbers and gunk-cookers about to jeopardize their lofty positions in society by springing one of their charges.

No, I was stuck in Aurora House all right. A clock with no hands. 'Freedom!' is the fatuous jingle of our civilization, but only those deprived of it have the barest inkling *re*: what the stuff actually is.

A few days before our Saviour's Birthday, a minibusload of private-school brats came to sing carols. The Undead sang along with wrong verses and death-rattles and the racket drove me out, it wasn't even funny. I limped around Aurora House in search of my lost vigour, needing the lavvy every thirty minutes. (The Organs of Venus are well known to All but, Brothers, the Organ of Saturn is the Bladder.) Hooded doubts dogged my heels. Why was Denholme paying my captors his last precious copecks to infantilize me? Had Georgette, incontinent with senility, told my brother about our brief diversion from the highway of fidelity, so many years ago? Was this trap a cuckold's revenge?

*

Mother used to say escape is never further than the nearest book. Well, Mumsy, no, not really. Your beloved large-print sagas of rags, riches and heartbreak were no camouflage against the miseries trained on you by the tennis-ball launcher of life, were they? But, yes, Mum, there again, you have a point. Books don't offer real escape but they can stop a mind scratching itself raw. God knows, I had bog all else to do at Aurora House except read. The day after my miracle recovery I picked up *Half-lives* and, ye gods, began wondering if Hilary V. Hush might not have written a publishable thriller after all. I had a vision of *The First Luisa Rey Mystery* in stylish black-and-bronze selling at Tesco checkouts; then a *Second Mystery*, then the *Third*. Queen Gwen(dolin Bendincks) exchanged a sharp 2B pencil for a blunt blandishment (missionaries are so malleable if you kid them you're a possible convert) and I set about giving the thing a top-to-bottom edit. One or two things will have to go: the insinuation that Luisa Rey is this Robert Frobisher chap reincarnated, for example. Far too hippie-druggy-new age. (I, too, have a birthmark, below my left armpit, but no lover ever compared it to a comet. Georgette nicknamed it Timbo's Turd.) But, overall, I concluded the young-hack-versus-corporate-corruption-thriller had potential. (The Ghost of Sir Felix Finch whines, 'But it's been done a hundred times before!' – as if there could be anything *not* done a hundred *thousand* times between Aristophanes and Andrew Void-Webber! As if Art is the *What*, not the *How*!)

My editing work on *Half-lives* hit a natural obstacle when Luisa Rey was driven off a bridge and the ruddy manuscript ran out of pages. I tore my hair and beat my breast. Did part two even exist? Was it stuffed in a shoebox in Hilary V.'s Manhattan apartment? Still abed in her creative uterus? For the twentieth time I searched the secret recesses of my briefcase for the covering letter, but I had left it in my Haymarket office suite.

Other literary pickings were lean. Warlock-Williams told me Aurora House had once boasted a little library, now mothballed. ('The Jellyvision's so much more *Real* for ordinary people, that's what it boils down to.') I needed a miner's helmet and a ruddy pick to locate this 'library'. It was down a dead-end blocked off by stacked-up Great War memorial plaques headed *Lest We Forget*. The dust was deep and crisp and even. One shelf of back editions of a magazine called *This England*, a dozen Zane Grey westerns (in large print), a cookbook entitled *No Meat for Me Please!*. That left *All Quiet on the Western Front* (in whose page-corners a creative schoolboy had long ago drawn frames of a cartoon stick-man masturbating with his own nose – where are they now?) and *Jaguars of the Skies*, a yarn of everyday helicopter pilots by 'America's Foremost Military Suspense Writer' (but, I happen to know, ghostwritten at his 'Command Center' – I shall name no names for fear of legal reprisals) and, frankly, bugger all else.

I took the lot. To the starving man, potato peelings are *haute cuisine*.

Ernie Blacksmith and Veronica Costello, come in, your time is up. Ernie and I had our moments, but were it not for these fellow dissidents, Nurse Noakes would still have me drugged up to my ruddy eyeballs today. One overcast afternoon while the Undead were in rehearsal for the Big Sleep, the staff were in a meeting and the only sound troubling Aurora House's slumbers was a WWF contest between Fat One Fauntleroy and the Dispatcher, I noticed, unusually, a careless hand had left the front door ajar. I crept out for a recce, armed with a fib about dizziness and fresh air. Cold singed my lips and I shivered! My convalescence had stripped me of subcutaneous fat; my frame had shrunk from quasi-Falstaffian to John of Gaunt. It was my first venture outside since the day of my stroke, six or seven weeks before. I circumnavigated the inner grounds and found the ruins of an old building, then fought through unkempt shrubberies to the brick perimeter wall to check for holes or breaches. An SAS sapper could have clambered over with a nylon rope but not a stroke victim with a stick. Drifts of brown-paper leaves were eroded and formed by the wind as I passed. I came to the magnificent iron gates, opened and closed by a flash pneumatic stroke electronic gizmo. Ruddy hell, they even had a surveillance camera and a two-way phone thingy! I imagined Nurse Noakes boasting to the children (I nearly wrote 'parents') of prospective residents that they slept safe and secure thanks to these state-of-the-art surveillance arrangements, meaning, of course, 'Pay us on time and you won't hear a dicky-bird.' The view did not bode well. Hull lay to the south, a half-day hike away for a robust stripling down side-roads lined with telegraph poles. Only lost holidaymakers would ever stumble across the institute gates. Walking back down the drive, I heard screeching tyres and a furious beep from a Jupiter-red Range Rover. I stepped aside. The driver was a bullish fellow clad in one of those silvery anoraks beloved of transpolar fundraisers. The Range Rover screeched to a gravelly stop at the front steps and the driver swaggered up to Reception like a flying ace from *Jaguars of the Skies*. Coming back to the main entrance I passed the boiler-room. Ernie Blacksmith poked his head out: 'A dram of firewater, Mr Cavendish?'

I didn't need to be asked twice. The boiler room smelt of fertilizer but was warmed by the boiler's coal furnace. Perched on a sack of coal and making contented baby noises was a long-time resident with the status of institution mascot, Mr Meeks. Ernie Blacksmith was the kind of quiet man you notice at second glance. This observant Scot kept company with a lady named Veronica Costello who had owned the finest hat shop, legend had it, in Edinburgh's history. The couple's demeanour suggested residents at a shabby Chekhovian hotel. Ernie and Veronica respected my wish to be a miserable bugger and I respected that. He now produced a bottle of Irish malt from a coal scuttle. 'You're half rocked if you're thinking of getting out of here without a helicopter.'

No reason to give anything away. 'Me?'

My bluff was dashed to pieces on the Rock of Ernie. 'Take a pew,' he told me, grim and knowing.

I did so. 'Cosy in here.'

'I was a certificated boilerman once upon a time. I service the workings for free, so the management turn a blind eye to one or two little liberties I allow myself.' Ernie poured two generous measures into plastic beakers. 'Down the hatch.'

Rain on the Serengeti! Cacti flowered, cheetahs loped! 'Where do you get it?'

'The coal merchant is not an unreasonable man. Seriously, you want to be careful. Withers goes out to the gate for the second post at a quarter to four daily. You don't want him to catch you plotting your getaway.'

'You sound well informed.'

'I was a locksmith too, that was after the army. You come into contact with the semi-crim, in the security game. Gamekeepers and poachers and all. Not that I ever did anything illegal myself, mind you, I was straight as an arrow. But I learnt that a good three-quarters of prison bust-outs fall flat, because all the grey matter,' he tapped his temple, 'gets spent on the escape itself. Amateurs talk strategy, professionals talk logistics. That fancy electric lock on the gate, for example, I could take it apart blindfolded if I had the mind to, but what about a vehicle on the other side? Money? Bolt-holes? You see, without logistics, where are you? Belly-up is where, and in the back of Withers's van five minutes later.'

Mr Meeks screwed up his gnomish features, and ground out the only two coherent words he had retained: 'I *know*! I *know*!'

Before I could discern whether or not Ernie Blacksmith was warning me or sounding me out, Veronica came in through the interior door wearing a hat of ice-melting scarlet. I just stopped myself from bowing. 'Good afternoon, Mrs Costello.'

'Mr Cavendish, how pleasant. Wandering abroad in this biting cold?'

'Scouting,' Ernie answered, 'for his one-man escape committee.'

'Oh, once you've been initiated into the Elderly, the world doesn't want you back.' Veronica settled herself in a rattan chair and adjusted her hat just so. 'We – by whom I mean anyone over sixty – commit two offences just by existing. One is Lack of Velocity. We drive too slowly, walk too slowly, talk too slowly. The world will do business with dictators, perverts and drug barons of all stripes, but being slowed down, it cannot *abide*. Our second offence is being Everyman's *memento mori*. The world can only get comfy in shiny-eyed denial if we are out of sight.'

'Veronica's parents served life sentences in the intelligentsia,' put in Ernie, with a dash of pride.

She smiled fondly. 'Just look at the people who come here during visiting hours! They need treatment for shock. Why else do they spout that "You're only as old as you feel!" claptrap? Really, who are they hoping to fool? Not us – themselves!'

Ernie concluded, 'Us elderly are the modern lepers. That's the truth of it.'

I objected: 'I'm no outcast! I have my own publishing-house, and I need to get back to work, and I don't expect you to believe me, but I *am* being confined here against my will.'

Ernie and Veronica exchanged a glance in their secret language.

'You *are* a publisher? Or you *were*, Mr Cavendish?'

'Am. My office is in Haymarket.'

'Then what,' queried Ernie reasonably, '*are* you doing here?'

Now, that was the question. I recounted my unlikely yarn to date. Ernie and Veronica listened the way sane attentive adults do. Mr Meeks nodded off. I got as far as my stroke, when a yelling outside interrupted me. I assumed one of the Undead was having a fit, but a look through the crack showed the driver of the Jupiter-red Range Rover shouting into his mobile phone. 'Why bother?' Frustration twisted his face. 'She's in the clouds! She thinks it's 1966! . . . No, she's *not* faking it. Would you wet *your* knickers for kicks? . . . No, she didn't. She thought I was her first husband. She said she didn't *have* any sons . . . You're telling me it's Oedipal . . . Yes, I described it again. Three times . . . In detail, *yes*. Come and have a go yourself if you think you can do better . . . Well, she never cared for me either. But bring perfume . . . No, for *you*. She reeks . . . What else would she reek of? . . . Of *course* they do, but it's hard to keep up, it just . . . trickles out all the time.' He mounted his Range Rover, and roared off down the drive. Sprinting after it and nipping through the gates before they swung shut did cross my mind, then I reminded myself of my age. Anyway, the surveillance camera would spot me and Withers would pick me up before I could flag anyone down.

'Mrs Hotchkiss's son,' Veronica said. 'She was a sweet soul, but her son, ooh, no. You don't own half the hamburger franchises in Leeds and Sheffield by being nice. Not a family short of a bob or two.'

A mini-Denholme. 'Well, at least he visits her.'

'And here's why.' An attractive, wicked gleam illuminated the old lady. 'When Mrs Hotchkiss got wind of his plan to pack her off to Aurora House, she crammed every last family gem into a shoebox and buried it. Now she can't remember where, or she can remember but isn't saying.'

Ernie divided up the last drops of malt. 'What gets my goat about him is how he leaves his keys in the ignition. Every time. He'd never do that out in the real world. But we're so decrepit, so harmless, that he doesn't even have to be careful when he visits.'

I judged it poor form to ask Ernie why he had noticed a thing like that. He had never spoken an unnecessary word in his life.

I visited the boiler room on a daily basis. The whiskey supply was erratic, but not so the company. Mr Meeks's role was that of a black Labrador's in a long-lived marriage, after the kids have left home. Ernie could spin wry observations about his life and times and Aurora House folklore, but his *de facto* spouse could converse on most topics under the sun. Veronica maintained a vast collection of not-quite-stars' autographed photographs. She was widely read enough to appreciate my literary wit, but not so widely read that she knew my sources. I like that in a woman. I could say things to her like, 'The most singular difference between happiness and joy is that happiness is a solid, and joy a liquid,' and, safe in her ignorance of J. D. Salinger, I felt witty, charming and, yes, even youthful. I felt Ernie watching me as I showed off, but what the heck? I thought. A man may flirt.

Veronica and Ernie were survivors. They warned me about the dangers of Aurora House: how its pong of urine and disinfectant, the Undead Shuffle, Noakes's spite, the catering redefine the concept of 'ordinary'. Once any tyranny becomes accepted as ordinary, according to Veronica, its victory is indomitable.

Thanks to her, I ruddy well bucked my ideas up. I clipped my nasal hair and borrowed some shoe polish from Ernie. *Shine your shoes every night*, my old man used to say, *and you're as good as anyone*. Looking back, Ernie tolerated my posturing because he knew Veronica was only humouring me. Ernie had never read a work of fiction in his life, 'Always a radio man, me,' but watching him coax the Victorian boiler system into life one more time, I always felt shallow. It's true, reading too many novels makes you go blind.

I cooked up my first escape plan alone, one so simple it hardly warrants the name. It needed will and a modicum of courage, but not brains. A nocturnal telephone call from the phone in Nurse Noakes's office to the answering machine of Cavendish Publishing. An SOS for Mrs Latham, whose rugger-bugger nephew drives a mighty Ford Capri. They arrive at Aurora House; after threats and remonstrances I get in; nevvie drives off. That's all. On the night of December 15th (I think) I woke myself up in the early hours, put on my dressing-gown and let myself into the dim corridor. (My door had been left unlocked since I began playing possum.) No sound but snores and plumbing. I thought of Hilary V. Hush's Luisa Rey creeping around Swannekke B. (Behold my bifocals.) Reception looked empty, but I crawled below the level of the desk commando-style and hoisted myself back to the vertical – no mean feat. Noakes's office light was off. I tried the door handle and, yes, it gave. In I slipped. Just enough light came in through the crack to see. I picked up the receiver and dialled the number of Cavendish Publishing. I did not get through to my answering-machine.

'You cannot make the call as dialled. Replace the handset, check the number, and try again.'

Desolation. I assumed the worst, that the Hogginses had torched the place so badly that even the telephones had melted. I tried once more, in vain. The only other telephone number I could reconstruct since my stroke was my next, and last, resort. After five or six tense rings Georgette, my sister-in-law, answered in the kittenish pout I knew, Lordy, Lordy, I knew. 'It's gone bedtime, Aston.'

'Georgette, it's me, Timbo. Put Denny on, will you?'

'Aston? What's wrong with you?'

'It isn't Aston, Georgette! It's Timbo!'

'Put Aston back on, then!'

'I don't know Aston! Listen, you *must* get me Denny.'

'Denny can't come to the phone right now.'

Georgette's grip on her rocker was never exactly firm, but she sounded buckarooed over the rainbow. 'Are you drunk?'

'Only if it's a nice wine bar with a good cellar. I can't abide pubs.'

'No, listen, it's Timbo, your brother-in-law! I've got to speak to Denholme.'

'You sound like Timbo. Timbo? Is that you?'

'Yes, Georgette, it's me, and if this is a—'

'Rather rum of you not to turn up at your own brother's funeral. That's what the whole family thought.'

The floor spun. '*What?*'

'We knew about your various tiffs, *but* I *mean*—'

I fell. 'Georgette, you just said Denny is dead. Did you mean to say it?'

'Of course I did! D'you think I'm bloody doo-lally?'

'Tell me once more.' I lost my voice. 'Is – Denny – dead?'

'D'you think I'd make something like this up?'

Nurse Noakes's chair creaked with treachery and torture. 'How, Georgette, for Chrissakes, how?'

'Who are you? It's the middle of the night! Who is this, anyway? Aston, is this you?'

I had cramp in my throat. 'Timbo.'

'Well, what clammy stone have *you* been hiding under?'

'Look, Georgette. How did Denny,' saying made it more so, 'pass away?'

'Feeding his priceless carp. I was spreading duckling pâté on crackers for supper. When I went to fetch Denny he was floating in the pond, face down. He may have been there a day or so, I wasn't his babysitter, you know. Dixie had told him to cut back on the salt, strokes run in his family. Look, stop hogging this line and put Aston on.'

'Listen, who's there now? With you?'

'Just Denny.'

'But Denny's dead!'

'I know that! He's been in the fish-pond for absolutely . . . weeks, now. How am I supposed to get him out? Listen, Timbo, be a dear, bring me a hamper or something from Fortnum and Mason's, will you? I ate all the crackers and all the thrushes ate the crumbs so now I've got nothing to eat but fish food and Cumberland sauce. Aston hasn't called back since he borrowed Denny's art collection to show his evaluator friend, and that was . . . days ago, weeks rather. The gas people have stopped the supply and . . .'

My eyes stung with light.

The doorway filled with Withers. 'You again.'

I flipped. 'My brother has died! Dead, do you understand? Stone Ruddy Dead! My sister-in-law's *bonkers* and she doesn't know what to do! This is a family emergency! If you have a Christian bone in your ruddy body you'll help me sort this out this godawful ruddy mess!'

Dear Reader, Withers saw only a hysterical inmate making nuisance calls after midnight. He shoved a chair from his path with his foot. I cried into the phone: 'Georgette, listen to me, I'm trapped in a ruddy madhouse hell-hole called Aurora House in Hull, you've got that? *Aurora House* in *Hull*, and for Christ's sake, get anybody there to come up and rescue—'

A giant finger cut my line. Its nail was gammy and bruised.

Nurse Noakes walloped the breakfast gong to declare hostilities open. 'Friends, we have clasped a *thief* to our bosom.' A hush fell over the assembled Undead.

A desiccated walnut banged his spoon. 'The Ay-rabs know what to do with 'em, Nurse! No light-fingered Freddies in Saudi, eh? Friday afternoons in the mosque car parks, *chop*! Eh? Eh?'

'A rotten apple is in our barrel.' I swear, it was Gresham Boys' School again, sixty years on. The same Shredded Wheat disintegrating in the same bowl of milk. 'Cavendish!' Nurse Noakes's voice vibrated like a penny whistle. 'Stand!' The heads of those semi-animate autopsies in mildewed tweeds and colourless blouses swivelled my way. If I responded like a victim I would seal my own sentence.

It was hard to care. I had not slept a wink all night. Denny was dead. Turned to carps, most likely. 'Oh, for God's sake, woman, get some proportion in your life. The Crown Jewels are still safe in the Tower! All I did was make one crucial telephone call. If Aurora House *had* a cyber-café I would willingly have sent an e-mail! I didn't want to wake anyone up, so I used my initiative and borrowed the telephone. My profoundest apologies. I'll pay for the call.'

'Oh, Pay You Shall. Residents, what do we do to Rotten Apples?'

Gwendolin Bendincks rose and pointed her finger. 'Shame on you!'

Warlock-Williams seconded the motion. 'Shame on you!'

One by one those Undead sentient enough to follow the plot joined in. 'Shame on you! Shame on you! Shame on you!' Mr Meeks conducted the chorus like Herbert von Karajan.

I poured my tea, but a wooden ruler knocked the cup from my hands.

Nurse Noakes spat electrical sparks: 'Don't *dare* look away while you're being shamed!'

The chorus died the death, except for one or two stragglers.

My knuckles whimpered. Anger and pain focused my wits like a *Zazen* beating-stick. 'I doubt the kindly Mr Withers told you, but it transpires my brother Denholme is dead. Yes, stone dead. Call him yourself, if you won't believe me. Indeed, I beg you to call him. My sister-in-law is not a well woman and she needs help with funeral arrangements.'

'How could you know your brother had died before you broke into my office?'

A crafty double-Nelson. Her crucifix-toying inspired me. 'St Peter.'

Big Bad Frown. 'What about him?'

'In a dream he told me that Denholme recently passed to the Other Side. "Phone your sister-in-law," he said. "She needs your help." I told him using the telephone was against Aurora House rules, but St Peter assured me that Nurse Noakes was a God-fearing Catholic who wouldn't mock such an explanation.'

La Duca was actually halted in her tracks by this balderdash. (*Know thine Enemy* trumps *Know thyself*.) Noakes ran through the alternatives: was I a dangerous deviant; harmless delusional; realpolitikster; Petrine visionary? 'Our rules in Aurora House are for everyone's benefit.'

Time to consolidate my gains. 'How true that is.'

'I shall have a chat with the Lord. In the meantime,' she addressed the dining-room, 'Mr Cavendish is on probation. This episode is not gone and not forgotten.'

After my modest victory I played patience (the card-game, not the virtue, never that) in the lounge, something I had not done since my ill-starred Tintagel honeymoon with Madame X. (The place was a dive. All crumbling council houses and joss-stick shops.) Patience's design flaw became obvious for the first time in my life: the outcome is decided not during the course of play but when the cards are shuffled before the game even begins. How pointless is that?

The point is that it lets your mind go elsewhere. Elsewhere was not rosy. Denholme had died some time ago, but I was still in Aurora House. I dealt myself a new worst-case scenario, one where Denholme sets up a standing order from one of his tricky-dicky accounts to pay for my residency in Aurora House, out of kindness or malice. Denholme dies. My flight from the Hogginses was classified, so nobody knows I'm here. The standing order survives its maker. Mrs Latham tells the police I was last seen going to a loan shark. Detective Plod conjectures I had been turned down by my lender of the last resort, and had Done a Eurostar. So, five weeks later, nobody is looking for me, not even the Hogginses.

Ernie and Veronica came up to my table. 'I used that telephone to check the cricket scores.' Ernie was in ill-humour. 'Now it'll be locked up at nights.'

'Black ten on red Jack,' advised Veronica. 'Never mind, Ernie.'

Ernie ignored her. 'Noakes'll be looking to lynch you now.'

'What can she do? Take away my Shredded Wheat?'

'She'll Mickey Finn your food! Like the last time.'

'What on earth are you talking about?'

'Remember the last time you crossed her?'

'When?'

'The morning of your conveniently timed stroke was when.'

'Are you saying my stroke was . . . induced?'

Ernie made an extremely irritating 'wakey, wakey!' face.

'Oh, pish and tosh! My father died of a stroke, my brother probably died of one. Print your own reality if you must, Ernest, but leave Veronica and me out of it.'

Ernie glowered. (Lars, lower the lighting.) 'Aye. You think you're so damn clever, but you're nothing but a hoity-toity southern wazzock!'

'Better a wazzock, whatever one of those is, than a quitter.' I knew I was going to regret that.

'A quitter? Me? Call me that just once more. Go on.'

'Quitter.' (Oh, Imp of the Perverse! Why do I let you speak for me?) 'What I think is this. You've given up on the real world outside this prison because it intimidates you. Seeing someone else escape would make you uncomfortable with your taste in deathbeds. That's why you're throwing this tantrum now.'

The Gas Ring of Ernie flared. 'Where I stop isn't for you to pass judgements on, Timothy Cavendish!' (A Scot can turn a perfectly decent name into a head-butt.) '*You* couldn't escape from a garden centre!'

'If you've got a foolproof plan, let's hear it.'

Veronica attempted to mediate. 'Boys!'

Ernie's blood was up. '"Foolproof" depends on the size of the fool.'

'Witty homily, that.' My sarcasm disgusted me. 'You must be a genius in Scotland.'

'No, in Scotland a genius is an Englishman who gets himself *accidentally* imprisoned in a retirement home.'

Veronica gathered my scattered cards. 'Do either of you know clock patience? You have to add cards up fifteen?'

'We're leaving, Veronica,' growled Ernie.

'No,' I snapped, and stood up, wanting to avoid Veronica having to choose between us, for my sake. '*I'm* leaving.'

I vowed not to visit the boiler room until I received an apology. So I didn't go that afternoon, or the next, or the next.

Ernie refused to meet my eye all Christmas week. Veronica gave me sorry smiles in passing, but her loyalties were clear. In hindsight, I am stupefied. What was I thinking? Jeopardizing my only friendships with sulks! I've always been a gifted sulker, which explains a lot. Sulkers binge on lonely fantasies. Fantasies about the Chelsea Hotel in Washington Square, about knocking on a certain door. It opens, and Miss Hilary V. Hush is *very* pleased to see me, her nightshirt hangs loose, she is as innocent as Kylie Minogue but as she-wolfish as Mrs Robinson. 'I've flown round the world to find you,' I say. She pours a whiskey from the mini-bar. 'Mature. Mellow. Malty.' That naughty she-husky then draws me to her unmade bed where I search for the fount of eternal youth.

Half-lives, Part II sits on a shelf above the bed. I read the manuscript, suspended in the post-orgasmic Dead Sea, while Hilary takes a shower. The second half is even better than the first, but the Master will teach his Acolyte how to make it superb. Hilary dedicates the novel to me, wins the Pulitzer and confesses at her acceptance speech that she owes everything to her agent, friend and, in many ways, father.

Sweet fantasy. Cancer for the cure.

Christmas Eve at Aurora House was a lukewarm dish. I strolled out (a privilege bartered through the offices of Gwendolin Bendincks) to the gates for a glimpse of the outside world. I gripped the iron gate and looked through the bars. (Visual irony, Lars. *Casablanca*.) My vision roamed the moor, rested on a burial mound, an abandoned sheep pen, hovered on a Norman church yielding to Druidic elements at last, skipped to a power station, skimmed the ink-stained Sea of the Danes to the Humber bridge, tracked a warplane over corrugated fields. Poor England. Too much history for its acreage. Years grow inwards here, like my toenails. The surveillance camera watched me. It had all the time in the world. I considered ending my sulk with Ernie Blacksmith, if only to hear a civil Merry Christmas from Veronica.

No. To hell with 'em both.

'Reverend Rooney!' He had a sherry in one hand, and I tied up the other with a mince-pie. Behind the Christmas tree, fairy-lights pinkened our complexions. 'I have a teeny-weeny favour to beg.'

'What might that be, Mr Cavendish?' No comedy vicar, him. Reverend Rooney was a Career Cleric, the spitting image of a tax-evading Welsh picture-framer I once crossed swords with in Hereford, but that is another story.

'I'd like you to pop a Christmas card in the post for me, Reverend.'

'Is that all? Surely if you asked Nurse Noakes she'd see to it for you?'

So the hag had got to him, too.

'Nurse Noakes and I don't always see eye to eye regarding communications with the outside world.'

'Christmas is a wonderful time for bridging the spaces between us.'

'Christmas is a wonderful time for letting snoozing dogs snooze, Vicar. But I do so want my sister to know I'm thinking of her over our Lord's Birthday. Nurse Noakes may have mentioned the death of my dear brother-in-law?'

'Terribly sad.' He knew about the St Peter affair all right. 'I'm sorry.'

I produced the card from my jacket pocket. 'I've addressed it to "The Caregiver", just to make sure my Yuletide greetings do get through. She's not all,' I tapped my head, '*there*, I'm sorry to say. Here, let me slip it into your cassock pouch . . .' He squirmed but I had him cornered. 'I'm so blessed, Vicar, to have friends I can trust. Thank you, *thank you*, from the bottom of my heart.'

Simple, effective, subtle, you sly old fox, TC. By New Year's Day, Aurora House would wake to find me gone, like Zorro.

Ursula invites me into the wardrobe. 'You haven't aged a day, Timbo, and neither has *this* snaky fellow!' Her furry fawn rubs up against my Narnian-sized lamp-post and mothballs . . . but then, as ever, I awoke, my swollen appendage as welcome as a swollen appendix, and as useful. Six o'clock. The heating systems composed works in the style of John Cage. Chilblains burned my toe-knuckles. I thought about Christmases gone, so many more gone than lay ahead.

How many more mornings did I have to endure?

'Courage, TC. A spanking red post-office train is taking your letter south to Mother London. Its cluster bombs will be released on impact, to the police, to the social welfare people, to Mrs Latham c/o the old Haymarket address. You'll be out of here in a jiffy.' My imagination described those belated Christmas presents I would celebrate my freedom with. Cigars, vintage whiskey, a dalliance with Little Miss Muffet on her ninety pence per minute line. Why stop there? A return match to Thailand with Guy the Guy and Captain Viagra?

I noticed a misshapen woollen sock hanging from the mantelpiece. It hadn't been there when I had turned out the light. Who could have crept in without waking me? Ernie calling a Christmas truce? Who else? Good old Ernie! Shuddering happily in my flannel pyjamas, I retrieved the stocking and brought it back to bed. It was very light. I turned it inside out, and a blizzard of torn paper came out. My handwriting, my words, my phrases!

My letter!

My salvation, ripped up. I beat my breast, gnashed my hair, tore my teeth, I injured my wrist by pounding my mattress. Reverend Ruddy Rooney Rot in Hell! Nurse Noakes, that bigoted bitch! She had stood over me like the Angel of Death, as I slept! Merry Ruddy Christmas, Mr Cavendish!

I succumbed. Late fifteenth-century verb, Old French *succomber* or Latin *succumbere*, but a basic necessity of the human condition, especially mine. I succumbed to the bovine care-assistants. I succumbed to the gift tag: 'To Mr Cavendish from your new pals – many more Aurora House Christingles to come!' I succumbed to my gift: the Wonders of Nature two-months-to-a-page Calendar. (Date of death not included.) I succumbed to the rubber turkey, the synthetic stuffing, the bitter Brussels sprouts; to the bangless cracker (mustn't induce heart-attacks, bad for business), its midget's paper crown, its snonky bazoo, its clean joke (Barman: 'What'll it be?' Skeleton: 'Pint and a mop, please.') I succumbed to the soap-opera specials, spiced with extra Christmas violence; to Queenie's speech from the grave. Coming back from a pee, I met Nurse Noakes, and succumbed to her triumphal 'Season's greetings, Mr Cavendish!'

A history programme on BBC2 that afternoon showed old footage shot in Ypres in 1919. That hellish mockery of a once-fair town was my own soul.

Three or four times only in my youth did I glimpse the Joyous Isles, before they were lost to fogs, depressions, cold fronts, ill winds and contrary tides ... I mistook them for adulthood. Assuming they were a fixed feature in my life's voyage, I neglected to record their latitude, their longitude, their approach. Young ruddy fool. What wouldn't I give now for a never-changing map of the ever-constant ineffable? To possess, as it were, an atlas of clouds.

I made it to Boxing Day because I was too miserable to hang myself. I lie. I made it to Boxing Day because I was too cowardly to hang myself. Lunch was a turkey broth (with crunchy lentils), enlivened only by a search for Deirdre's (the androgynous automaton) misplaced mobile phone. The zombies enjoyed thinking where it could be (down sides of sofas), places it probably wasn't (the Christmas tree), and places it couldn't possibly be (Mrs Birkin's bedpan). I found myself tapping at the boiler-room door, like a repentant puppy.

Ernie stood over a washing-machine in pieces on newspapers. 'Look who it isn't.'

'Merry Boxing Day, Mr Cavendish,' beamed Veronica, in a Romanov fur hat. She had a fat book of poetry propped on her lap. 'Come in, do.'

'Been a day or two,' I understated, awkwardly.

'I *know!*' gurned Mr Meeks. 'I *know!*'

Ernie still radiated disdain.

'Er ... can I come in, Ernie?'

He hoisted then dropped his chin a few degrees to show it was all the same to him. He was taking apart the boiler again, tiny silver screws in his chunky oily digits. He wasn't making it easy for me. 'Ernie,' I finally said, 'sorry about the other day.'

'Aye.'

'If you don't get me out of here . . . I'll lose my mind.'

He dissassembled a component I couldn't even name. 'Aye.'

Mr Meeks rocked himself to and fro.

'So . . . what do you say?'

He lowered himself on to a bag of fertilizer. 'Oh, don't be soft.'

I don't believe I had smiled since the Frankfurt Book Fair. My face hurt.

Veronica corrected her flirty-flirty hat. 'Tell him about our fee, Ernest.'

'Anything, anything.' I never meant it more. 'What's your price?'

Ernie made me wait until every last screwdriver was back in his toolbag. 'Veronica and I have decided to venture forth to pastures new.' He nodded in the direction of the gate. 'Up north. I've got an old friend who'll see us right. So, you'll be taking us with you.'

I hadn't seen that coming, but who cared? 'Fine, fine. Delighted.'

'Settled, then. D-Day is three days from now.'

'So soon? You've already got a plan?'

The Scot sniffed, unscrewed his Thermos, and poured pungent black tea into its cap. 'You could say as much, aye.'

Ernie's plan was a high-risk sequence of toppling dominoes. 'Any escape strategy,' he lectured, 'must be more ingenious than your guards.' It *was* ingenious, not to say audacious, but if any domino failed to trigger the next, instant exposure would bring dire results, especially if Ernie's macabre theory of enforced medication was in fact true. Looking back, I am amazed at myself for agreeing to go along with it. My gratitude that my friends were talking to me again, and my desperation to get out of Aurora House – alive – muted my natural prudence, I can only suppose.

December 28th was chosen because Ernie had learnt from Deirdre that Mrs Judd was staying in Hull for nieces and panto-mimes. 'Intelligence groundwork.' Ernie tapped his nose. I would have preferred Withers or the Noakes harpy to be off the scene, but Withers only left to visit his mother in Robin Hood's Bay in August, and Ernie considered Mrs Judd was the most level-headed and thus the most dangerous.

D-Day. I reported to Ernie's room thirty minutes after the Undead were put to bed at ten o'clock. 'Last chance to back out if you don't think you can hack it,' the artful Scot told me.

'I've never backed out of anything in my life,' I replied, lying through my decaying teeth. Ernie unscrewed the ventilation unit and removed Deirdre's mobile telephone from its hiding-place. 'You've got the poshest voice,' he had informed me, when allocating our various roles, 'and bullshitting on telephones is how you make your living.' I entered Johns Hotchkiss's number, obtained by Ernie from Mrs Hotchkiss's phone book months earlier.

It was answered with a sleepy 'Whatizzit?'

'Ah, yes, Mr Hotchkiss?'

'Speaking. You are?'

Reader, you would have been proud of me. 'Dr Conway, Aurora House. I'm covering for Dr Upward.'

'Jesus, has something happened to Mother?'

'I'm afraid so, Mr Hotchkiss. You must steel yourself. I don't think she'll make it to the morning.'

'Oh! Oh?'

A woman in the background demanded, 'Who is it, Johns?'

'Jesus! Really?'

'Really.'

'But what's . . . wrong with her?'

'Severe pleurisy.'

'*Pleurisy?*'

Perhaps my empathy with the role outpaced my expertise, by a whisker. 'Healey's pleurisy is *never* impossible in women your mother's age, Mr Hotchkiss. Look, I'll go over my diagnosis once you're here. Your mother is asking for you. I've got her on twenty mgs of, uh, morphadin-50, so she isn't in any pain.

Odd thing is, she keeps talking about jewellery. Over and over, she's saying, "I must tell Johns, I must tell Johns . . ." Does that make any sense to you?'

The moment of truth.

He bit! 'My God. Are you positive? Can she remember where she put it?'

The background woman said, '*What? What?*'

'She seems terribly distressed that these jewels stay in the family.'

'Of course, of course, but where are they, Doctor? Where is she saying she stashed them?'

'Look, I have to get back to her room, Mr Hotchkiss. I'll meet you in Reception at Aurora House . . . When?'

'Ask her where – no, tell her – tell Mummy to – look, Doctor – er—'

'Er . . . Conway! Conway.'

'Dr Conway, can you hold your phone against my mother's mouth?'

'I'm a doctor, not a telephone club. Come yourself. Then she can tell you.'

'Tell her – just hang on till we get there, for God's sake. Tell her – Pipkins loves her very much. I'll be over . . . half an hour.'

The end of the beginning. Ernie zipped his bag. 'Nice work. Keep the phone, in case he calls back.'

Domino two had me standing sentinel in Mr Meeks's room watching through the crack in the door. Due to his advanced state of decay, our loyal boiler-room mascot wasn't in on the great escape, but his room was opposite mine, and he understood 'Shush!'. At a quarter past ten Ernie went to Reception to announce my death to Nurse Noakes. This domino could fall in unwelcome directions. (Our discussions over whom the corpse and whither the messenger had been lengthy: Veronica's death would require a drama beyond Ernie's powers not to arouse our shrew's suspicion; Ernie's death, reported by Veronica, was ruled out by her tendency to lapse into melodrama; both Ernie and

Veronica's rooms were bordered by sentient Undead who might throw a spanner in our works. My room, on the other hand, was in the old school wing, and my only neighbour was Mr Meeks. So I was chosen to play the goner.) The big unknown was Nurse Noakes's obvious loathing for me. Would she rush to see her enemy fallen, to stick a hatpin in my neck to check I was truly dead? Or celebrate in style first?

Footsteps. A knock on my door. Nurse Noakes, sniffing the bait. Domino three was teetering, but already deviations were creeping in. Ernie was supposed to have accompanied her as far as the door of my death-chamber. She must have rushed on ahead. From my hiding-place I saw the predator peering in. She switched on the lights. The classic plot staple of pillows under the blankets, more realistic than you'd think, lured her in. I dashed across the corridor and yanked the door shut. From this point on, the third domino depended on lock mechanisms – the external latch was a stiff, rotary affair and before I had it turned Noakes was hauling the door open again – her foot levered against the door-frame – her demonic strength uprooting my biceps and tearing my wrists. Victory, I knew, would not be mine.

So I took a big risk and abruptly released the handle. The door flew open and the witch soared across the room. Before she could charge at the door again I had it shut and locked. A *Titus Andronicus* catalogue of threats beat at the door. They haunt my nightmares still. Ernie came puffing up with a hammer and some three-inch nails. He nailed the door to its frame and left the huntress snarling in a prison cell of her own invention.

Down in Reception, domino four was bleeping blue murder on the main gate intercom machine. Veronica knew what button to press. 'I've been bloody bleeping this bloody thing for ten bloody minutes while Mother is bloody fading away!' Johns Hotchkiss was upset. 'What the f*** are you people playing at?'

'I had to help Dr Conway restrain your mother, Mr Hotchkiss.'

'Restrain her? For *pleurisy?*'

Veronica pressed the 'open' switch and across the grounds the gate, we hoped, swung wide. (I pre-empt the letter-writing reader who may demand to know why we hadn't used this very switch to make a run for it by explaining that the gate closed automatically after forty seconds; that the reception desk was ordinarily manned; and that wintry miles of moorland lay beyond.) Through the freezing mist, the screech of tyres grew louder. Ernie hid in the back office and I greeted the Range Rover on the outside steps. Johns Hotchkiss's wife was in the driving seat.

'How is she?' demanded Hotchkiss, striding over.

'Still with us, Mr Hotchkiss, still asking for you.'

'Thank Christ. You're this Conway?'

I wanted to head off more medical questions. 'No, the doctor's with your mother, I just work here.'

'I've never seen you.'

'My daughter is an assistant nurse here, actually, but because of the staffing shortage and emergency with your mother I'm out of retirement to man the front desk. Hence the delay in getting the main gate open.'

His wife slammed the car door. '*Johns!* Hello? It's below freezing out her and your mother is dying. Can we sort out lapses in protocol later?'

Veronica had appeared in a spangly nightcap. 'Mr Hotchkiss? We've met on several occasions. Your mother is my dearest friend here. Do hurry to her, please. She's in her own room. The doctor thought it too dangerous to move her.'

Johns Hotchkiss half smelt a rat, but how could he accuse this dear old biddy of deceit and conspiracy? His wife harried and hauled him down the corridor.

I was in a driving seat again. Ernie hoisted his arthritic *cara* and an unreasonable number of hatboxes into the back, then jumped into the passenger seat. I hadn't replaced the car after Madame X left, and the intervening years did not fall away as I had hoped. Ruddy hell, which pedal was which? Accelerator, brake, clutch, mirror, signal, manoeuvre. I reached for the key in the ignition. 'What are you waiting for?' asked Ernie.

My fingers insisted there was no key.

'Hurry, Tim, hurry!'

'No key. No ruddy key.'

'He *always* leaves it in the ignition!'

My fingers insisted there was no key. 'His wife was driving! She took the keys! The ruddy female took the keys in with her! Sweet St Ruddy Jude, what do we do now?'

Ernie looked on the dashboard, in the glove compartment, on the floor.

'Can't you hot-wire it?' My voice was desperate.

'Don't be soft!' he shouted back, scrabbling through the ash-tray.

Domino five was superglued vertical. 'Excuse me . . .' said Veronica.

'Look under the sun-flap!'

'Nothing here but a ruddy ruddy ruddy—'

'Excuse me,' said Veronica. 'Is this a car key?'

Ernie and I turned, howled, 'No-*oooooo*,' in stereo at the Yale key. We howled again as we saw Withers running down the nightlit corridor from the dining-room annex, with two Hotchkisses close behind.

'Oh,' said Veronica. 'This fat one fell out, too . . .'

We watched as Withers reached Reception. He looked through the glass straight at me, transmitting a mental image of a Rottweiler savaging a doll sewn in the shape of Timothy Langland Cavendish, aged 65¾. Ernie locked all the doors, but what good would that do us?

'How about this one?' Was Veronica dangling a car key in front of my nose? With a 'Range Rover' logo on it'.

Ernie and I howled, '*Yeeeeee-sss!*'

Withers flung open the front door and leapt down the steps.

My fingers fumbled and dropped the key.

Withers flew head-over-arse on a frozen puddle.

I banged my head on the steering-wheel and the horn sounded.

Withers was pulling at the locked door. My fingers scrabbled as indoor fireworks of pain flashed in my skull. Johns Hotchkiss was screaming, 'Get your bony carcasses out of my car or I sue – DAMMIT I'LL SUE ANYWAY!' Withers banged my window with a club, no, it was his fist; the wife's gemstone ring scratched the glass; the key somehow slid home into the ignition; the engine roared into life; the dashboard lit up with fairy-lights; Chet Baker was singing 'Let's Get Lost'; Withers was hanging on to the door and banging; the Hotchkisses crouched in my headlamps like El Greco sinners; I put the Range Rover into first but it shunted rather than moved because the handbrake was on; Aurora House lit up like the *Close Encounters* UFO; I flung away the sensation of having lived through this very moment many times before; I released the handbrake, bumped Withers; moved up to second; the Hotchkisses were not drowning but waving and there they went and we had lift-*off*!

I drove round the pond, away from the gates because Mrs Hotchkiss had left the Range Rover pointing that way. I checked the mirror – Withers and the Hotchkisses were sprinting after us like ruddy commandos. 'I'm going to lure them away from the gates,' I blurted to Ernie, 'to give you time to pick the lock. How long will you need? I reckon you'll have forty-five seconds.'

Ernie hadn't heard me.

'How long will you need to pick the lock?'

'You'll have to ram the gates.'

'*What?*'

'Nice big Range Rover at fifty miles per hour should do the trick.'

'*What?* You said you could pick the lock in your sleep!'

'A state-of-the-art electric thing? No way!'

'I wouldn't have locked up Noakes and stolen a car if I'd known you couldn't pick the lock!'

'Aye, exactly, you're nesh, so you needed encouragement.'

'Encouragement?' I yelled, scared, desperate, furious in equal thirds. The car tore through a shrubbery and the shrubbery tore back.

'How terribly *thrilling*!' exclaimed Veronica.

Ernie spoke as if discussing a DIY puzzler. 'So long as the centre pole isn't sunk deep, the gates'll just fly apart on impact.'

'And if it is sunk deep?'

Veronica revealed a manic streak. 'Then *we*'ll fly apart on impact! So, foot to the floor, Mr Cavendish!'

The gates flew at us, ten, eight, six car-lengths away. Dad spoke from my pelvic floor. 'Do you have any *inkling* of the trouble you're in, boy?' So I obeyed my father, yes, I obeyed him and I slammed on the brakes. Mum hissed in my ear: 'Sod it, our Timbo, what have you got to lose?' The thought that I had slammed not the brakes but the accelerator was the last – two car-lengths, one, *wham*!

The vertical bars became diagonal ones.

The gates flew off their hinges.

My heart bungee-jumped from throat to bowel, back again, back again and the Range Rover skidded all over the road, I gripped my intestines shut with all my might, the brakes screeched but I kept her out of the ditches, engine still running, windscreen still intact.

Dead stop.

Fog thickened and thinned in the headlight beams.

'We're proud of you,' Veronica said, 'aren't we, Ernest?'

'Aye, pet, that we are!' Ernie slapped my back. I heard Withers barking doom and ire, close behind. Ernie wound down the window and howled back at Aurora House: 'Waaaaaaazzzzzz-oooooocccccckkk!' I touched the accelerator again. The tyres scuffed gravel, the engine flowered, and Aurora House disappeared into the night. Ruddy hell, when your parents die they move in with you.

*

'Road map?' Ernie was ferreting through the glove compartment. His finds so far included sunglasses and Werner's toffees.

'No need. I memorized our route. I know it like the back of my hand. Any escape is nine-tenths logistics.'

'Better steer clear of the motorways. They have cameras and whatnot nowadays.'

I contemplated my career change from publisher to car rustler. 'I know.'

Veronica impersonated Mr Meeks – brilliantly. *'I know! I know!'*

I told her it was an uncannily accurate impression.

A pause. 'I didn't say anything.'

Ernie turned round and yelled in surprise. When I looked in the mirror and saw Mr Meeks twitching in the rearmost compartment of the vehicle, I nearly drove us off the road. 'How—' I began. 'When – who—'

'Mr Meeks!' cooed Veronica. 'What a nice surprise.'

'A surprise?' I said. 'He's broken the laws of ruddy physics!'

'We can't very well do a U-ey back to Hull,' Ernie stated, 'and it's too cold to drop him off. He'd be an ice block by morning.'

'We've run away from Aurora House, Mr Meeks,' Veronica explained.

'I know,' the sozzled old duffer bleated, 'I know.'

'All for one and one for all, is it?'

Mr Meeks leaked a giggle, sucked toffees and hummed 'The British Grenadiers' as the Range Rover wolfed down the northward miles.

A sign – PLEASE DRIVE CAREFULLY IN THAWICKE CROSS – shone in the headlights. Ernie had ended our route plan here with a big red X and now I saw why. An all-night petrol station servicing an A-road – next door to a pub called the Hanged Greyhound. Midnight was long gone but the lights were still on. 'Park in the pub. I'll go and get us a can of petrol so nobody'll spot us. Then my vote's for a swift pint to celebrate a job well done. Silly Johns left his jacket in the car, and in the jacket – tra-la.' Ernie flashed a wallet the size of my briefcase. 'I'm sure he can stand us a round.'

'*I know!*' enthused Mr Meeks. 'I know!'

'A Drambuie and soda,' Veronica decided, 'would hit the spot.'

Ernie was back in five minutes carrying the can. 'No bother.' He syphoned the petrol into the tank, then the four of us walked across the car park to the Hanged Greyhound. 'A crisp night,' remarked Ernie, offering his arm to Veronica. It was ruddy freezing and I couldn't stop shivering. 'A beautiful moon, Ernest,' added Veronica, looping hers through his. 'What a splendid night for an elopement!' She giggled like a sixteen-year-old. I screwed the lid down on my old demon, Jealousy. Mr Meeks was wobbly, so I supported him as far as the door where a blackboard advertised 'The Massive Match!'. In the warm cave inside, a crowd watched TV soccer in a distant fluorescent time-zone. In the eighty-first minute England was a goal down to Scotland. Nobody even noticed us. England playing Scotland, abroad, in the deep midwinter – is the World Cup back again already? Talk about Rip Van Ruddy Winkle.

I'm no fan of television pubs, but at least there was no thumpy-thumpy-thump acidic music, and that evening freedom was the sweetest commodity. A sheepdog made room for us on a fireside pew. Ernie ordered the drinks because he said my accent was too southern and they might spit in my glass. I had a double Kilmagoon and the most expensive cigar the bar could muster, Veronica ordered her Drambuie and soda, Mr Meeks a ginger beer, and Ernie a pint of Angry Bastard bitter. The barman didn't take his eyes off the TV – he got our drinks by sense of touch alone. Just as we took our seats in an alcove, a cyclone of despair swept through the bar. England had been awarded a penalty. Tribalism electrified the audience.

'I'd like to check my route. Ernie, the map if you will.'

'You had it last.'

'Oh. Must be in . . .' My room. Extreme close-up, Director Lars, of Cavendish realizing his fateful mistake. I had left the map on my bed. For Nurse Noakes. With our route marked out in felt pen. '. . . the car . . . oh, God. I think we had better drink up and move on.'

'But we've only just started this round.'

I swallowed hard. 'About the, er, map . . .' I checked my watch and calculated distances and speeds.

Ernie was catching on. 'What about the map?'

My answer was drowned in a howl of tribal grief. England had equalized. And at that *exact* moment, I fib not, Withers looked in. His Gestapo eyes settled on us. Not a happy man. Johns Hotchkiss appeared beside him, saw us, and he looked very happy indeed. He reached for his mobile phone to summon his angels of vengeance. A third lout with oil-stained overalls completed the posse, but it appeared Nurse Noakes had so far prevailed on Johns Hotchkiss to leave the police out of it. The oily lout's identity I was never to discover, but I knew right then: the game was up.

Veronica sighed a frail sigh. 'I had so hoped to see,' she half sang, 'the wild mountain thyme, all across the blooming heather, and it's go, lassie, go . . .'

A drug-addled semi-life of restraints and daytime programmes lay ahead. Mr Meeks meekly stood up to go with our gaoler.

He let out a Biblical bellow. (Lars: zoom the camera in from the outside car park, across the busy bar, and right down between Mr Meeks's rotted tonsils.) The TV viewers dropped their conversations, spilt their drinks and looked. Even Withers was stopped in his tracks. The octogenarian leapt on to the bar, like Astaire in his prime, and roared this SOS to his universal fraternity, 'Are there nor *trrruuue Scortsmen* in tha *hooossse*?'

A whole sentence! Ernie, Veronica and I were stunned as mullets.

High drama. Nobody stirred.

Mr Meeks pointed at Withers with skeletal forefinger and intoned this ancient curse: 'Those there English gerrr*runts* are trampling o'er ma God-gi'en rrr*aights*! Theeve used me an' ma pals morst *direly* an' we're inneed of a wee *assista*nce!'

Withers growled at us: 'Come quiet and face your punishments.'

Our captor's southern Englishness was out! A rocker rose like Poseidon and flexed his knuckles. A crane-operator stood by him. A sharky-chinned man in a thousand-quid suit. An axewoman with the scars to prove it.

The TV was switched off.

A Highlander spoke softly: 'Aye, laddie. We'll nort let ye doone.'

Withers assessed the stage and went for a *get real!* smirk. 'These men are car thieves.'

'You a copper?' The axewoman advanced.

'Show us your badge then,' the crane-operator advanced.

'Aw, you're full o'shite, man,' spat Poseidon.

Cool-headedness might have lost us the day, but Johns Hotchkiss scored a fatal own goal. Finding his way blocked by a pool cue he prefixed his distress with 'Now you just look here, you *grebo*, you can go shag your bloody sporran if you think—' One of his teeth splashed into my Kilmagoon, fifteen feet away. (I fished the tooth out to keep as proof because otherwise no one will ever believe me.) Withers caught and snapped an incoming wrist, hurled a wee Krankie over the pool table, but the ogre was one and his enraged foes legion. Oh, the ensuing scene was Trafalgaresque. I must admit, the sight of that brute being brutalized was not wholly unpleasant, but when Withers hit the deck and disfiguring blows began to fall, I proposed a tactful exit stage left to our borrowed vehicle. We departed via the back and scuttled over the blustery car park as fast as our legs, whose combined age well exceeded three centuries, could carry us. I drove. North.

Where all this will end, I do not know.

THE END

* * *

Very well, dear Reader, you deserve an epilogue if you've stayed with me this far. My ghastly ordeal touched down in this spotless Edinburgh rooming house, kept by a discreet widow from the Isle of Man. After the brawl at the Hanged Greyhound we four blind mice drove to Glasgow, where Ernie knows a bent copper who can take care of the Hotchkiss vehicle. Here our fellowship parted. Ernie, Veronica and Mr Meeks waved me off at the station. Ernie promised to take the flak if the law were ever to catch up, as he's too old to stand trial, which is ruddy civilized of him. He and Veronica were headed to a Hebridean location where Ernie's handyman-preacher-cousin does up falling-down crofts for Russian mafiosi and German enthusiasts of the Gaelic tongue. I offer my secular prayers for their well-being. Mr Meeks was to be deposited in a public library with a 'Please Look After This Bear' tag, but I suspect Ernie and Veronica will take him with them. After my arrival at Widow Manx's I slept under my goosedown quilt as sound as King Arthur on the Blessed Isle. Why didn't I get on the first train south to London, there and then? I'm still not sure. Maybe I recall Denholme's remark about life beyond the M25. I shall never know what part he played in my incarceration, but he was right – London darkens the map like England's bowel polyp. There is a whole country up here.

I looked up Mrs Latham's home number at the library. Our telephone reunion was a moving moment. Of course, Mrs Latham smothered her emotion by lambasting me, before filling me in on my missing weeks. The Hoggins Hydra had ripped the office apart when I failed to show for my three o'clock castration, but years of financial brinksmanship had stood my redoubtable pit-prop in good stead. She had captured the vandalism on a cunning video camera supplied by her nephew. The Hogginses were thus restrained: steer clear of Timothy Cavendish, Mrs Latham warned, or this footage will appear on the Internet and your various probations shall hatch into prison sentences. Thus they were prevailed upon to accept an equitable proposal cutting them into future royalties. (I suspect they had a sneaking admiration for my lady bulldog's cool nerves.) The building management used my disappearance – and the trashing of my suite – as an excuse to turf us out. Even as I write, my former premises are being turned into a Hard Rock Café for homesick Americans. Cavendish Publishing is currently run from a house owned by my secretary's eldest nephew, who resides in Tangiers. Now for the best news: a Hollywood studio has optioned *Knuckle Sandwich – the Movie* for a figure as senselessly big as the number on a bar code. A lot of the money will go to the Hogginses, but for the first time since I was twenty-two, I am flush.

Mrs Latham sorted out my bank cards, etc., and I am designing the future on beer mats, like Churchill and Stalin at Yalta, and I must say the future is not too shabby. I shall find a hungry ghostwriter to turn these notes you've been reading into a film script of my own. Well, sod it all, if Dermot 'Duster' Hoggins can write a bestseller and have a film made, why the ruddy hell not Timothy 'Lazarus' Cavendish? Put Nurse Noakes in the book, the dock and on the block. The woman was sincere – bigots mostly are – but no less dangerous for that, and she shall be named and shamed. The minor matter of Johns Hotchkiss's vehicle-loan needs to be handled with delicacy, but fouler fish have been fried. Mrs Latham got on the e-mail to Hilary V. Hush to express our interest in *Half-lives*, and the postman delivered part two not an hour ago. A photo was enclosed, and it turns out the 'V' is for 'Vincent'! And what a lard-bucket! I'm no Chippendale myself, but Hilary has the girth to fill not two but three airline economy seats. I'll find out if Luisa Rey is still alive in a corner of the Whistling Thistle, my *de facto* office and a wrecked galleon of a back-alley tavern where Mary, Queen of Scots, summoned the devil to assist her cause. The landlord, whose double-measures would be quadruples in management-consulted Londinium, swears he sees Her ill-starred Majesty, regularly. *In vino veritas.*

That is more or less it. Middle-age is flown, but it is attitude, not years, that condemns one to the ranks of the Undead, or else proffers salvation. In the domain of the young there dwells many an Undead soul. They rush about so, their inner putre-fraction is concealed for a few decades, that is all. Outside, fat snowflakes are falling on slate roofs and granite walls. Like Solzhenitsyn labouring in New York, I shall beaver away in exile, far from the city that knitted my bones.

Like Solzhenitsyn, I shall return, one bright dusk.

Half-lives

The First Luisa Rey
Mystery

40

The black sea roars in. Its coldness shocks Luisa's senses back to life. Her VW's rear struck the water at 45° so the seat saved her spine, but the car now swings upside-down. She is trussed by her seat-belt inches from the windshield. Seawater pounds her head. *Get out, or die here.* Luisa panics, breathes a lungful of water and struggles into a pocket of air, coughing. *Unhook this belt.* She squirms and jackknifes up to the belt-lock. *Release button.* It doesn't click. *Your weight stops it engaging.* The car half somersaults deeper and, with a wrenching noise, a giant squid-shaped air bubble flies away. Her clothes are bloated and heavy and cling to her body. Luisa stabs the button, frantic, and the strap drifts free. *More air.* She finds an air-pocket trapped beneath a windscreen of dark water. The sea's mass jams the door shut. *Roll down the window.* It inches half-way and jams, *right where it always jams.* Luisa shimmies around, squeezes her head, shoulders and torso through the gap. Two words are jolted free.

Sixsmith Report!

She pulls herself back into the sinking vehicle. *Can't see a damn thing. A plastic trash-bag. Wedged under the seat.* She doubles up in the confined space . . . *It's here.* She hauls, like a woman hauling a sack of rocks. She feeds herself feet-first back out the window, but the report is too fat. The sinking car drags Luisa down. Her lungs ache now. The sodden papers have quadrupled their weight. The trash-bag is through the window, but as she kicks and struggles Luisa feels a lightening. Hundreds of pages spin free from the vanilla binder, wheeling wherever the sea will take them, wheeling around her, *playing-cards in* Alice. She kicks off her shoes. Her lungs shriek, curse, beg. Every pulse is a thump in Luisa's ears. *Which way is up?* The water is too murky to guess. *Up is away from the car.* Her lungs will collapse in another moment or two. *Where's the car?* Luisa realizes she has paid for the Sixsmith Report with her life.

41

Isaac Sachs looks down on a brilliant New England morning. Labyrinthine suburbs of ivory mansionettes and silk lawns inset with turquoise swimming-pools. The executive-jet window is cool against his face. Six feet directly beneath his seat is a suitcase in the baggage hold containing enough C-4 to turn an airplane into a meteor. *So,* thinks Sachs, *you obeyed your conscience. Luisa Rey has the Sixsmith Report.* He recollects as many details of her face as he can. *Do you feel doubt? Relief? Fear? Righteousness?*

A premonition I'll never see her again.

Alberto Grimaldi, the man he has double-crossed, is laughing at an aide's remark. The hostess passes with a tray of clinking drinks. Sachs retreats into his notebook where he writes the following sentences.

- *Exposition: the workings of the* actual *past* + *the* virtual *past may be illustrated by an event well known to collective history such as the sinking of the* Titanic. *The disaster as it* actually *occurred descends into obscurity as its eyewitnesses die off, documents perish* + *the wreck of the ship dissolves in its Atlantic grave. Yet a* virtual *sinking of the* Titanic, *created from reworked memories, papers, hearsay, fiction – in short, belief – grows ever 'truer'. The actual past is brittle, ever-dimming* + *ever more problematic to access* + *reconstruct: in contrast, the virtual past is malleable, ever-brightening* + *ever more difficult to circumvent/expose as fraudulent.*
- *The present presses the virtual past into its own service, to lend credence to its mythologies* + *legitimacy to the imposition of*

will. Power seeks + is *the right to 'landscape' the virtual past. (He who pays the historian calls the tune.)*

- *Symmetry demands an actual + virtual future, too. We imagine how next week, next year or 2225 will shape up – a virtual future, constructed by wishes, prophecies + daydreams. This virtual future may influence the actual future, as in a self-fulfilling prophecy, but the actual future will eclipse our virtual one as surely as tomorrow eclipses today. Like Utopia, the actual future + the actual past exist only in the hazy distance, where they are no good to anyone.*

- *Q: Is there a meaningful distinction between one simulacrum of smoke, mirrors + shadows – the actual past – from another such simulacrum – the actual future?*

- *One model of time: an infinite matrioshka doll of painted moments, each 'shell' (the present) encased inside a nest of 'shells' (previous presents) I call the actual past but which we* perceive *as the virtual past. The doll of 'now' likewise encases a nest of presents yet to be, which I call the actual future but which we* perceive *as the virtual future.*

- *Proposition: I have fallen in love with Luisa Rey.*

The detonator is triggered. The C-4 ignites. The jet is engulfed by a fireball. The jet's metals, plastics, circuitry, its passengers, their bones, clothes, notebooks and brains all lose definition in flames exceeding 1200°C. The uncreated and the dead exist solely in our actual and virtual pasts. Now the bifurcation of these two pasts will begin.

42

'Betty and Frank needed to shore up their finances,' Lloyd Hooks tells his breakfast audience, in the Swannekke Hotel. A circle of neophytes and acolytes pay keen attention to the Presidential Energy Guru. 'So they decide Betty'd go on the game to get a little cash in hand. Night comes round, Frank drives Betty over to Whore Lane to ply her new trade. "Hey, Frank," says Betty, from the sidewalk. "How much should I charge?" Frank does his sums, and tells her, "A hundred bucks for the whole shebang." So Betty gets out, and Frank parks down a quiet alley. Pretty soon this guy drives up in his beat-up old Chrysler and propositions Betty: "How much for all night, sugar?" Betty says, "Hundred dollars." The guy says, "I only got thirty dollars. What'll thirty buy me?" So Betty dashes round to Frank and asks him. Frank says, "Tell him thirty dollars buys a handjob." So Betty goes back to the guy—'

Lloyd Hooks notices Bill Smoke in the background. Bill Smoke raises one-two-three fingers; the three fingers become a fist; the fist becomes a slashing gesture. *Alberto Grimaldi, dead; Isaac Sachs, dead; Luisa Rey, dead. Swindler, sneak, snoop.* Hooks's eyes tell Smoke he has understood and a figment from a Greek myth surfaces in his mind. *The sacred grove of Diana was guarded by a Warrior Priest on whom luxury was lavished but whose tenure was earned by slaying his predecessor. When he slept, it was at the peril of his life. Grimaldi, you dozed for too long.*

'So, anyway, Betty goes back to the guy, and says his thirty'll buy a handjob, take it or leave it. The guy says, "Okay, sugar, jump in, I'll take the handjob. Is there a quiet alley round here?" Betty has him drive around the corner to Frank's alley, and the guy unbelts his pants to reveal the most – y'know, gargantuan – schlong. "Wait *up!*" gasps Betty. "I'll be right back." She jumps out of the guy's car and knocks on Frank's window. Frank lowers the window, "What *now?*"' Hooks pauses for the punchline. 'Betty says, "Frank, hey, Frank, lend this guy seventy dollars!"'

The men who would be board members cackle like hyenas. *Whoever said money can't buy you happiness*, Lloyd Hooks basks, *obviously didn't have enough of the stuff.*

43

Through binoculars Hester Van Zandt watches the divers on their launch. An unhappy-looking barefoot teenager in a poncho ambles along the beach and pats Hester's mongrel. 'They found the car yet, Hester? Channel's pretty deep at that point. That's why the fishing's so good there.'

'Hard to be sure at this distance.'

'Kinda ironic to drown in the sea you're polluting. The guard's kinda got the hots for me. Told me it was a drunk driver, a woman, 'bout four in the morning.'

'Swannekke Bridge comes under the same special security remit as the island. Seaboard can say what they like. No-one'll cross-check their story.'

The teenager yawns. 'D'you s'pose she drowned in her car, the woman? Or d'you think she got out and kinda drowned later?'

'Couldn't say.'

'If she was drunk enough to drive through a railing, she couldn't have made it to the shore.'

'Who knows?'

'Gross way to die.' The teenager yawns and walks off. Hester trudges back to her trailer. Milton the Native American sits on its step, drinking from a milk carton. He wipes his mouth and tells her, 'Wonder Woman's awake.'

Hester steps around Milton and asks the woman on the sofa how she is feeling.

'Lucky to be alive,' answers Luisa Rey, 'full of muffins, and drier. Thanks for the loan of your clothes.'

'Lucky we're the same size. Divers are looking for your car.'

'The Sixsmith Report, not my car. My body would be a bonus.'

Milton locks the door. 'So you crashed through a barrier, dropped into the sea, got out of a sinking car, and swam three hundred meters to shore, with no injuries worse than mild bruising.'

'It hurts plenty when I think of my insurance claim.'

Hester sits down. 'What's your next move?'

'Well, first I need to go back to my apartment and get a few things. Then I'll go stay with my mother, on Ewingsville Hill. Then . . . back to square one. I can't get the police or my editor interested in what's happening on Swannekke without the Report.'

'Is it safe at your mother's?'

'As long as Seaboard thinks I'm dead, Joe Napier won't come looking. When they learn I'm not . . .' She shrugs, having gained an armor of fatalism from the events of the last six hours. 'Altogether safe, possibly not. An acceptable degree of risk. I don't do this sort of thing often enough to be an expert.'

Milton digs his thumbs into his pockets. 'I'll drive you back to Buenas Yerbas. Gimme a minute, I'll go call a friend and get him to bring his pick-up over.'

'Good guy,' says Luisa, after he's left.

'I'd trust Milton with my life,' answers Hester.

44

Milton strides over to the flyblown general store that services the campsite, trailer-park, beach-goers, traffic to Swannekke and the isolated houses hereabouts. An Eagles song comes on a radio behind the counter. Milton feeds a dime into the phone, checks the walls for ears, and dials in a number from memory. Water vapor rises from the Swannekke cooling towers like cauliflower genies. Pylons march north to Buenas Yerbas and south to Los Angeles. *Funny*, thinks Milton. *Power, time, gravity, love. The forces that really kick ass are all invisible.* The phone is answered. 'Yeah?'

'Yeah, Napier? It's me. Listen, about a woman called Luisa REY. Well, suppose she isn't? Suppose she's still walking about eating popsicles and paying utility bills? Would her whereabouts be worth anything to you? Yeah? How much? No, *you* name a figure. Okay, double that . . . no? Nice talking with you, Napier, I gotta go and . . .' Milton smirks '. . . the usual account within one working day, if you *please*. Right. What? No, no-one else has seen her, only Crazy Van Zandt. No. She did mention it, but it's in the bottom of the deep blue sea. Quite sure. Fishfood. Course not, my exclusives are for your ears only . . . Uh-huh, I'm driving her back to her apartment, then she's going to her mother's . . . Okay, I'll make it an hour. The usual account. One working day.'

45

Luisa opens her front door to the sounds of a Sunday ball-game and the smell of popcorn. 'Since when did I say you could fry oil?' she calls through to Javier. 'Why are the blinds all down?'

Javier bounces down the hallway, grinning. 'Hi, Luisa! Your uncle Joe made the popcorn. We're watching Giants v. Dodgers. Why are you dressed like an old woman?'

Luisa feels her core sicken. 'Come here. Where is he?'

Javier sniggers. 'On your sofa! What's up?'

'Come here! Your mom wants you.'

'She's working overtime at the hotel.'

'Luisa, it wasn't me, on the bridge, it wasn't me!' Joe Napier appears behind him, holding out his palms as if reassuring a scared animal. 'Listen—'

Luisa's voice judders. 'Javi! Out! Behind me!'

Napier raises his voice. 'Listen to me—'

Yes, I am talking with my own killer. 'Why in hell should I listen to a *word* you say?'

'I'm the only insider at Seaboard who doesn't want you dead!' Napier's calm has deserted him. 'In the parking lot, I was trying to warn you! *Think* about it! If I *was* the hitman would we even be having this conversation? With witnesses around? Don't go, for Chrissakes! It's not safe! Your apartment could be under surveillance still. That's why the blinds are down.'

Javier looks aghast. Luisa holds the boy but doesn't know the least dangerous way to turn. 'Why are you here?'

Napier is quiet again, but tired and troubled. 'I knew your father, when he was a cop. VJ Day on Silvaplana Wharf. Come in, Luisa. Sit down.'

46

Joe Napier calculated that the neighbor's kid would tether Luisa long enough to make her listen. He's not proud that his plan paid off. Napier, more a watcher than a speaker, chisels out his sentences with care. 'In 1945, I'd been a cop for six years at Spinoza District Station. No commendations, no black marks. A regular cop, keeping his nose clean, dating a regular girl in a typing-pool. On fifteenth August, the radio said the Japs had surrendered and Buenas Yerbas danced one almighty hula. Drink flowed, cars revved up, firecrackers were let off, people took a holiday even if their bosses didn't give 'em one. Come nine o'clock or so, my partner and I were called to a hit-and-run in Little Korea. Normally we didn't bother with that end of town, but the victim was a white kid so there'd be relatives and questions. We were *en route* when a code eight comes through from your father, calling all available cars to Silvaplana Wharf. Now, the rule of thumb was, you didn't go snooping round that part of the docks, not if you wanted a career. The mob had their warehouses there, under a City Hall umbrella. What's more, Lester Rey,' Napier decides not to modify his language, 'was known as a 10th Precinct pain-in-the-ass Sunday-school cop. But two officers were down, and that ain't the same ball-game. It could be your buddy bleeding to death on the Tarmac. So we flat-outed and reached the wharf just behind another Spinoza car, Brozman and Harkins. Saw nothing at first. No sign of Lester Rey, no sign of a squad car. The dockside lights were off. We drove between two walls of cargo containers, around the corner into a yard where men were loading up an army truck. I was thinking we were in the wrong zone of the docks, when I noticed how fast, how hard the men were working. That made no sense, not on a national party-night. Then the wall of bullets hit us, and it made plenty of sense. Brozman and Harkins took the first wave – brakes, glass filling the air, our car skidded into theirs, me and my partner rolled out of our car and holed up behind a stack of steel tubes. Brozman's car horn sounds, doesn't stop, and they don't appear. More bullets ack-ack-acking around us, I'm shitting myself – I'd become a cop to *avoid* war-zones. My partner starts firing back. I follow his lead, but our chances of hitting anything are nearly zilch. To be honest with you, I was glad when the truck trundled by. Dumb-ass that I was, I broke cover too soon – to see if I could get a license plate.' The root of Napier's tongue is aching. 'Then all this happens. A yelling man charges me from across the yard. I fire at him. I miss – the luckiest miss of my life, and yours too, Luisa, because if I'd shot your father you wouldn't be here. Lester Rey is pointing behind me as he sprints by, and he kicks an object rolling my way, lobbed from the back of the truck. Then a blinding light fries me, a noise axes my head, and a needle of pain shoots through my butt. I lay where I fell, half conscious, until stretchermen hoisted me into an ambulance.'

Luisa still isn't saying anything.

'I was lucky. A fragment of grenade shrapnel tore through both cheeks of both buttocks. The rest of me was fine. The doctor said it was the first time he'd seen one projectile make four holes. Your dad, of course, was not so fine. Lester was a piece of Swiss cheese. They'd operated but failed to save his eye the day before I left hospital. He wasn't feeling sorry for himself, however; we just shook hands and I left, I didn't know what to say. The most humiliating thing you can do to a man is to save his life. Lester knew it too. But there's not a day, possibly not an hour, that's gone by without my thinking about him. Every time I sit down.'

Luisa says nothing for a while. 'Why didn't you tell me this on Swannekke Island?'

Napier scratches his ear. 'I was afraid you'd use the connection to squeeze me for juice . . .'

'On what really happened to Rufus Sixsmith?'

Napier doesn't say yes, doesn't say no. 'I know how reporters work.'

'*You* are picking holes in *my* integrity?'

She's speaking generally – she can't know about Margo Roker's house. 'If you carry on looking for Rufus Sixsmith's report,' Napier wonders if he should say this in front of the boy, 'you'll be killed, plain and simple. Not by me! But it'll happen. I am begging you. Leave town now. Jettison your old life and job, and go.'

'Alberto Grimaldi sent you to tell me that, did he?'

'No-one knows I'm here – pray God, or I'm in as much trouble as you.'

'One question first.'

'You want to ask if . . .' he wishes the kid was elsewhere '. . . if Sixsmith's "fate" was my work. The answer is no. That sort of . . . job, it wasn't my business. I'm not saying I'm innocent. I'm just saying I'm only guilty of looking the other way. Grimaldi's fixer killed Sixsmith and drove you off the bridge last night. A man by the name of Bill Smoke – one name of many, I suspect. I can't make you believe me but I hope you will.'

'How did you know I'd survived?'

'Vain hope. Look, life is more precious than a damn scoop. I'm begging you, one last time, and it will be the last, to drop this story. Now I've got to leave, and I wish to Christ you'd do the same.' He stands. 'One last thing. Can you use a gun?'

'I have an allergy to guns.'

'How do you mean?'

'Guns make me nauseous. Literally.'

'*Everyone* should learn to use a gun.'

'Yeah, you can see crowds of 'em laid out in morgues. Bill Smoke isn't going to wait politely while I get a gun out of my handbag, is he? My only way out is to get evidence that'll blow this affair so totally, killing me would be a pointless act.'

'You're underestimating man's fondness for petty revenge.'

'Why are you worried about me? You've paid back your debt to Dad. You've salved your conscience.'

Napier gives a morose sigh and knows he can do no more. 'Enjoyed the ballgame, Javi.'

'You're a liar,' says the boy.

'I lied, yes, but that doesn't make me a liar. Lying's wrong, but when the world spins backwards, a small wrong may be a big right.'

'That doesn't make sense.'

'You're damn right it doesn't, but it's still true.'

Joe Napier lets himself out.

Javier is angry with Luisa, too. 'And you act like I'm gambling with my life just because I jump across a couple of balconies?'

47

Luisa and Javier's footsteps reverberate in the stairwell. Javier peers over the handrail. Lower floors recede like the whorls of a shell. A wind of vertigo blows, making him gasp and giddy. It works the same looking upwards. 'If you could see into the future,' he asks, 'would you?'

Luisa slings her bag. 'Depends on if you could change it or not.'

'S'posing you could? So, say you saw you were going to be kidnaped by Communist spies on the second story, you'd take the elevator down to the ground floor.'

'But what if the spies called the elevator, agreeing to kidnap whoever was in it? What if trying to avoid the future is what triggers it all?'

'If you could *see* the future, like you can see the end of 16th Street from the top of Kilroy's department store, that means it's already there. If it's already there, that means it isn't a thing you can change.'

'Yes, but what's at the end of 16th Street isn't made by what *you* do. It's pretty much fixed, by planners, architects, designers, unless you go and blow a building up or something. What happens in a minute's time *is* made by what you do.'

'So what's the answer? Can you change the future or not?'

Maybe the answer is not a function of metaphysics, but one, simply, of power. 'It's a great imponderable, Javi.'

They have reached the ground floor. *The Six Million Dollar Man's* bionic biceps jangle as they flex on Malcolm's TV.

'See you, Luisa.'

'I'm not leaving town for ever, Javi.'

At the boy's initiative they shake hands. The gesture surprises Luisa: it feels formal, final and intimate.

48

A silver carriage clock in Judith Rey's Ewingsville home tinkles one o'clock in the afternoon. Bill Smoke is being talked at by a financier's wife. 'This house never fails to bring out the demon of covetousness in me,' the fifty-something bejeweled woman confides, 'it's a copy of a Frank Lloyd Wright. The original's on the outskirts of Salem, I believe.' She is standing an inch too close. *You look like a witch from the outskirts of Salem gone fucking crazy in Tiffany's*, Bill Smoke thinks, remarking, 'Now is that so?'

Hispanic maids supplied by the caterers carry trays of food between the all-white guests. Swan-shaped linen napkins bear place-cards. 'That white-leafed oak tree on the front lawn would have been here when the Spanish missions were built,' the wife says, 'wouldn't you agree?'

'Without doubt. Oaks live for six hundred years. Two hundred to grow, two hundred to live, two hundred to die.'

He sees Luisa enter the lavish room, accepting a kiss on both cheeks from her stepfather. *What do I want from you, Luisa Rey?* A female guest of Luisa's age hugs her: 'Luisa! It's been three or four years!' Close-up, the guest's charm is cattish and prying. 'But is it true you're not *married* yet?'

'I certainly am not,' is Luisa's crisp reply. 'Are *you?*'

Smoke senses she senses his gaze, and refocuses his attention on the wife and agrees that, yes, there are redwoods not sixty minutes from here that were mature when Nebuchadnezzar was on his throne. Judith Rey stands on a footstool brought specially for the purpose and taps a silver spoon on a bottle of pink champagne until everyone is listening. 'Ladies, gentlemen and young people,' she declaims, 'I am told dinner is served! But before we all begin, I'd like to say a few words about the wonderful work done by the Buenas Yerbas Cancer Society, and how they'll use the monies raised by our fundraiser you are so generously supporting today.'

Bill Smoke amuses a pair of children by producing a shiny gold krugerrand from thin air. *What I want from you, Luisa, is a killing with intimacy.* For a moment Bill Smoke wonders at the powers inside us that are not us.

49

The maids have cleared the dessert course, the air is pungent with coffee fumes, and an overfed Sunday drowsiness settles on the dining room. The eldest guests find nooks to snooze in. Luisa's stepfather rounds up a group of contemporaries to see his collection of 1950s cars, the wives and mothers conduct maneuvers of allusion, the schoolchildren go outside to bicker in the leafy sunshine and around the pool. The Henderson triplets dominate the discourse at the matchmaking table. Each is as blue-eyed and gilded as his brothers, and Luisa doesn't distinguish between them. 'What'd *I* do?' says one triplet, 'if *I* was President? First, I'd aim to *win* the Cold War, not just aim not to lose it.'

Another takes over. 'I *wouldn't* kowtow to Arabs whose ancestors parked camels on lucky patches of sand . . .'

'. . . or to red gooks. I'd establish – I'm not afraid to say it – our country's rightful – corporate – empire. Because if we don't do it . . .'

'. . . the Japs'll steal the march. The corporation is the future. We need to let business run the country and establish a true meritocracy.'

'Not choked by welfare, unions, "affirmative action" for amputee transvestite colored homeless arachnophobes . . .'

'A meritocracy of acumen. A culture that is not ashamed to acknowledge that wealth attracts power . . .'

'. . . and that the wealth*makers* – us – are rewarded. When a man aspires to power, I ask one simple question: "Does he think like a businessman?"'

Luisa rolls her napkin into a compact ball. 'I ask three simple questions. How did he get that power? How is he using it? And how can it be taken off the sonofabitch?'

50

Judith Rey finds Luisa watching an afternoon news report in her husband's den. '"Bulldyke", I heard Anton Henderson say, and if it wasn't about you, Cookie, I don't know – it's not funny! Your . . . rebellion issues are getting *worse*. You complain about being lonely so I introduce you to nice young men, and you "bulldyke" them in your *Spyglass* voice.'

'When did I ever complain about being lonely?'

'Boys like the Hendersons don't grow on trees, you know.'

'Aphids grow on trees.'

There is a knock on the door and Bill Smoke peers in. 'Mrs Rey? Sorry to barge in, but I have to leave soon. Hand on heart, today was the most welcoming, best-organized fundraiser I've ever attended.'

Judith Rey's hand flutters to her ear. 'Most kind of you to say so . . .'

'Herman Howitt, junior partner at Musgrove Wyeland, up from the Malibu office. I didn't get the chance to introduce myself before that superb dinner – I was the last-minute booking this morning. My father passed away over ten years ago, God bless his soul, cancer – I don't know how my mother and I would have gotten through it without the Society's help. When Olly mentioned your fundraiser, just out of the blue, I *had* to call to see if I could replace any last-minute cancellations.'

'We're *very* glad you did, and welcome to Buenas Yerbas.' *A little short,* assesses Judith Rey, *but muscular, well-salaried and probably on Luisa's side of thirty-five. Junior partner sounds promising.* 'I hope Mrs Howitt can join you next time?'

Bill Smoke a.k.a. Herman Howitt does a mousey smile. 'I'm sorry to say, the only Mrs Howitt is my ma. So far.'

'Now is that a fact,' responds Judith Rey.

He peers at Luisa who is not paying attention. 'I admired your daughter's principled stand downstairs. So many of our generation seem to lack a moral compass nowadays.'

'I *so* agree. The sixties threw out the baby with the bathwater. Luisa's departed father and myself separated some years ago, but we always aimed to instil a sense of right and wrong in our daughter. Luisa! Will you tear yourself away from the television set for *just* a moment, please, dear? Herman will be thinking – Luisa? Cookie, what is it?'

The anchorman intones: 'Police confirmed the twelve killed on a Lear jet accident over the Colorado Rockies this morning included Seaboard Power CEO, Alberto Grimaldi, America's highest-paid executive. Preliminary investigations from FAA investigators suggest an explosion triggered by a defect in the fuel system. Wreckage is strewn over several square kilometers . . .'

'Luisa, Cookie?' Judith Rey kneels by her daughter, who stares aghast at pictures of twisted airplane pieces in cornfields.

'How . . . *appalling*!' Bill Smoke savours a complex dish, all of whose ingredients even he, the chef, can't list. 'Did you *know* any of those poor souls, Miss Rey?'

51

Monday morning. The *Spyglass* newsroom swarms with rumors. One has it the magazine is bust; another, that Kenneth P. Ogilvy, its owner, will auction it off; the bank is giving a fresh transfusion; the bank is pulling the plug. Luisa hasn't informed them that she survived a murder attempt twenty-four hours ago. She doesn't want to involve her mother or Grelsch and, except for her bruising, it all feels increasingly unreal.

Luisa feels a painful sense of personal loss at the death of Isaac Sachs, a man she hardly knew. She is also afraid, but she functions by focusing on work. Her father told her how war photographers refer to an immunity from fear bestowed by the camera lens; this morning it makes perfect sense. She jots down pieces of the conspiracy in an unpruned shrub-diagram. *If Bill Smoke knew about Isaac Sachs's defection, his death makes sense – but who wanted Alberto Grimaldi taken down at the same time?* The staff writers gravitate into Dom Grelsch's office as usual for the ten o'clock meeting. Ten fifteen comes around.

'Grelsch wasn't this late even when his first wife gave birth,' says Nancy O'Hagan, polishing her nails. 'Ogilvy's got him screwed into an instrument of torture.'

Roland Jakes gouges wax from his ear with a pencil. 'I met the drummer who'd done the actual drumming on the Monkees' hits. He was banging on about tantric sex – I thank you. His favourite position is, uh, called "The Plumber". You stay in all day but nobody comes.'

Silence.

'Jeez, just trying to lighten the vibes.'

Grelsch arrives. '*Spyglass* is being sold. We'll learn later today who'll survive the sacrificial cull.'

Jerry Nussbaum loops his thumbs through his belt. 'Sudden.'

'Damn sudden. Negotiations began late last week.' Grelsch simmers. 'By this morning it was a done deal.'

'Must have been, uh, one helluvan offer,' angles Jakes.

'Ask KPO that.'

'Who's the buyer?' asks Luisa.

'Press announcement later today.'

'Go on, Dom,' wheedles O'Hagan.

'I said, there'll be a press announcement later today.'

Jakes rolls a cigarette. 'Seems like our mystery buyer, like, *really* wants *Spyglass* and, uh, if it ain't broken, don't fix it.'

Nussbaum snorts. 'Who says our mystery buyer doesn't think we're broken? When Allied News bought *Nouveau* last year they even fired the window-cleaners.'

'So.' O'Hagan clicks her compact shut. 'My cruise up the Nile is off again. Back to my sister-in-law's in Chicago for Christmas. Her brats and the frozen-beef capital of the world. What a difference a day makes.'

52

For months, Joe Napier realizes, looking at the coordinated artwork in vice-CEO William Wiley's anteroom, he has been sidelined. Loyalties snaked out of sight, and power was tapped from the known ducts. *That was fine by me*, Napier thinks, *only a year and a half to go.* He hears footsteps and feels a draft. *But downing an airplane with twelve men on board isn't security, it's multiple homicide. Who gave the order? Was Bill Smoke working for Wiley? Could it just be an aviation accident? They happen. All I understand is that not understanding is dangerous.* Napier berates himself for warning off Luisa Rey yesterday, a stupid risk that achieved a big nothing.

William Wiley's secretary appears at the door. 'Mr Wiley will see you now, Mr Napier.'

Napier is surprised to see Fay Li in the office. The setting demands an exchange of smiles. William Wiley's 'Joe! How are ya?' is as vigorous as his handshake.

'A sad morning, Mr Wiley,' replies Napier, taking the seat but refusing the cigarette. 'I still can't take it in about Mr Grimaldi.' *I never liked you. I never saw what you were for.*

'None sadder. Alberto can be succeeded, but never replaced.'

Napier permits himself one question under the guise of small-talk. 'How long will the board leave it before discussing a new appointment?'

'We're meeting this afternoon. Alberto wouldn't want us to drift without a chief-of-staff for longer than necessary. You know, his respect for you, personally, was . . . well . . .'

'"Devout",' suggests Fay Li.

You have *come up in the world*, Mister *Li.*

'Precisely! Exactly! Devout.'

'Mr Grimaldi was a great guy.'

'He sure was, Joe, he sure was.' Wiley turns to Fay Li. 'Fay. Let's tell Joe about the package we're offering.'

'In recognition of your exemplary record, Mr Wiley is proposing to set you free early. You'll receive full pay for the eighteen months still on your contract, your bonus – then your index-linked pension will kick in.'

Walk the plank! Napier makes a 'wow' expression. *Bill Smoke is behind this.* 'Wow' fits both the retirement offer and Napier's sense of the seismic shift in his role from insider to liability. 'This is . . . unexpected.'

'Must be, Joe,' says Wiley, but adds nothing. The telephone rings. 'No,' frowns Wiley, into the mouthpiece, 'Mr Reagan can wait his turn. I'm busy.'

Napier has decided by the time Wiley hangs up. *A golden chance to exit a blood-stained stage.* He plays an old retainer speechless with gratitude. 'Fay. Mr Wiley. I don't know how to thank you.'

William Wiley peers like a jokey coyote. 'By accepting?'

'Of course I accept!'

Wiley and Fay Li are all congratulations. 'You understand, of course,' Wiley continues, 'with a post as delicate as Security, we need for the change to come into force when you leave this room.'

Jesus, you people don't waste a second, do you?

Fay Li adds, 'I'll have your effects shipped on, plus paperwork. I know you won't be offended by an escort to the mainland. Mr Wiley has to be seen to respect protocol.'

'No offence, Fay,' smiles Napier, cursing her. 'I wrote our protocol.' *Napier, keep your .38 strapped to your calf until you're off Swannekke, and for a long time after.*

53

The music in the Lost Chord Music Store subsumes all thoughts of *Spyglass*, Sixsmith, Sachs and Grimaldi. The sound is pristine, riverlike, spectral, hypnotic . . . *intimately familiar.* Luisa stands, entranced, as if living in a stream of time. 'I *know* this music,' she tells the store clerk, who eventually asks if she's okay. 'What the hell is it?'

'I'm sorry, it's a customer order, not for sale. I shouldn't really be playing it.'

'Oh.' *First things first.* 'I phoned last week. My name's Rey, Luisa Rey. You said you could find an obscure recording for me by Robert Frobisher, called *Cloud Atlas Sextet*. But forget that for a moment. I have to own this music too. I *have* to. You know what it's like. What is it?'

The clerk presents his wrists for imaginary handcuffs. '*Cloud Atlas Sextet* by Robert Frobisher. I listened to it to make sure it's not scratched. Oh, I lie. I listened to it because I'm a slave to curiosity. Not exactly Delius, is it? Why companies won't finance recordings of gems like this, it's criminal. Your record is in the mintest condition, I'm happy to report.'

'Where have I heard it before?'

The young man shrugs. 'Can't be more than a handful in North America.'

'But I know it. I'm telling you I *know* it.'

54

Nancy O'Hagan is speaking excitedly on her phone when Luisa returns to the office. 'Shirl? Shirl! It's Nancy. Listen, we may yet spend Christmas in the shadow of the Sphinx. The new owner is Trans Vision Inc.' – she raises her voice – '*Trans Vision Inc* . . . Me neither, but –' O'Hagan lowers her voice '– I've just seen KPO, yeah, the old boss, he's on the new board. But listen up, what I'm calling to say is, my job's safe!' She gives Luisa a frenetic nod. 'Uh-huh, almost no jobs are being axed, so phone Janine and tell her she's spending Christmas alone with her abominable little snowmen.'

'Luisa,' Grelsch calls from his doorway, 'Mr Ogilvy'll see you now.'

K. P. Ogilvy occupies Dom Grelsch's temperamental chair, exiling the editor to a plastic stacker seat. In the flesh, *Spyglass*'s proprietor reminds Luisa of a steel engraving. Of a Wild West judge. 'There's no nice way to say this,' he begins, 'so I'll just say it the blunt way. You're fired. Orders of the new owner.' He ends.

Luisa watches the news bounce off her. *No, it can't compare to being driven off a bridge into the sea in semi-darkness.* Grelsch can't meet her eye. 'I've got a contract.'

'Who hasn't? You're fired.'

'Am I the only staff writer to incur your new masters' displeasure?'

'So it would seem.' K. P. Ogilvy's jaw flinches once.

'I think it's fair to ask, "Why me?"'

'Owners hire, fire and say what's fair. When a buyer offers a rescue package of the bounty that Trans Vision offered, one doesn't nitpick.'

'"A Picked Nit". Can I have that on my gold watch?'

Dom Grelsch squirms. 'Mr Ogilvy, I think Luisa's entitled to some kind of an explanation.'

'Then she can go ask Trans Vision. Perhaps her face doesn't

fit their vision of *Spyglass*. Too radical. Too feminist. Too dry. Too pushy.'

He's trying to make a smokescreen. 'I'd like to ask Trans Vision a number of things. Where's their head office?'

'Out east somewhere. But I doubt anyone'll see you.'

'Out east somewhere. Who are your new fellow board members?'

'You're being fired, not taking down an affidavit.'

'Just one more question, Mr Ogilvy. For three magical years of unstinting service, just answer this – what's the overlap between Trans Vision and Seaboard Power?'

Dom Grelsch's curiosity is sharp. Ogilvy hesitates a fraction, then blusters, 'I've got a lot of work to get through. You'll be paid until the end of the month, no need to come in. Thank you and goodbye.'

Where there's bluster, thinks Luisa, *there's duplicity.*

55

YOU ARE NOW LEAVING SWANNEKKE COUNTY, HOME OF THE SURF, HOME OF THE ATOM, DON'T STAY AWAY TOO LONG!

Life's okay. Joe Napier shifts his Jeep into cruise control. *Life's good.* Seaboard Power, his working life, Margo Roker and Luisa Rey recede into his past at 80 m.p.h. *Life's great.* Two hours to his log cabin in the Santo Cristo mountains. He could catch catfish for supper if he's not too tired by the drive. He checks his mirror: a silver Chrysler has been sitting a hundred yards behind him for a mile or two, but now it overtakes and vanishes into the distance. *Relax*, Napier tells himself, *you've gotten away.* Something in his Jeep is rattling. The afternoon reaches its three o'clock golden age. The freeway runs alongside the river for mile after mile, slowly climbing. *Upcountry's gotten uglier in the last thirty years, but show me a place that hasn't.* Either side, housing estates colonize the bulldozer-leveled shelves. *Getting out took me all my life.* Buenas Yerbas dwindles to a bristling smudge on the coastal horizon in Napier's rear-view mirror. *You can't stop Lester's daughter playing Wonder-woman. You gave it your best shot. Let her go. She ain't a kid.* He sifts the radiowaves, but it's all men singing like women and women singing like men, until he finds a hokey country station playing 'Everyone's Talkin' At Me'. Milly was the musical half of his marriage. Napier revisits the first evening he saw her: she was playing fiddle for Wild Oakum Hokum and His Cowgirls in the Sand. The glances musicians exchange, when music is effortless, that was what he wanted from Milly, that intimacy, and pretty soon they'd fallen in love. *Luisa Rey is too a kid, and you know it.* Napier turns off at exit eighteen and takes the old gold-miners' road up towards Copperline. *That rattling isn't getting any better.* Fall is licking the mountain woods up here. The road follows a narrowing gorge under ancient pines to where the sun goes down.

He's here, all of a sudden, unable to recall a single thought from the last three-quarters of an hour. Napier pulls over at the Copperline grocery store, kills the engine and swings out of his Jeep. *Hear that rushing? The Lost River.* It reminds him Copperline isn't Buenas Yerbas, and he unlocks his Jeep again. The store-owner greets the visitor by name, delivers six months' gossip in as many minutes, and asks if Napier's on vacation for the whole week.

'I'm on permanent vacation now. I was offered early . . .' he's never used the word on himself before '. . . retirement. Took it like a shot.'

The store-owner's gaze is all-seeing. 'Celebration at Duane's tonight? Or commiseration at Duane's tomorrow?'

'Make it Friday. A bit of both. Celebration mostly. I want to spend my first week of freedom resting in my cabin, not slumped, drunk, under one of Duane's tables.' Napier pays for his groceries and leaves, suddenly eager to be alone in his cabin. The Jeep's tires crunch the stony forest track. Its headlights illuminate the primeval forest in bright sweeping moments.

Here. Once again, Napier hears the Lost River. He remembers the first time he brought Milly up to the cabin he, his brothers and his dad built. Now he's the last one left. They went skinny-dipping that night. It was her idea. The forest dusk fills his lungs and his head. No phones, no CCTV or just TV, no ID clearances, no 'informal' security meetings in the president's soundproofed office. Not ever again. The retired ex-security man checks the padlock on the door for signs of tampering before he opens the shutters. *Relax, for Chrissakes. Seaboard let you go, free, no strings, no comeback.*

None the less his .38 is in his hand as he enters the cabin. *See? Nobody.* Napier gets a fire crackling and fixes himself beans and sausages and sooty baked potatoes. A couple of beers. A long, long piss outdoors. The fizzing Milky Way. A deep, deep sleep.

Awake, again, parched, with a beer-swollen bladder. *Fifth time now or sixth?* The sounds of the forest don't lullaby Napier tonight, but itch his sense of wellbeing. A car's brakes? *An elf-owl.* Twigs snapping? *A rat, a mountain quail, I don't know, you're in a forest, it could be anything. Go to sleep, Napier.* The wind. *Voices under the window?* Napier wakes to find a cougar crouched on a cross-beam over his bed; he wakes up with a yell; the cougar was Bill Smoke, arm poised to stove Napier's head in with a torch; nothing on the cross-beam. *Is it raining this time?* Napier listens.

Only the river, only the river.

He lights another match to see if it's a time worth getting up for: 4:05. No. An inbetween hour. Napier nustles down in folded darkness for holes of sleep, but bright, recent memories of Margo Roker's house follow him. Bill Smoke saying, *Stand guard. My contact says she keeps her documents in her room.* Napier agreeing, glad to reduce his involvement. Bill Smoke switching on his hefty rubber flashlight and going upstairs.

Napier scanning Roker's orchard. The nearest house was over half a mile away. Wondering why solo operator Bill Smoke wanted him along for this simple job.

A frail scream. An abrupt ending.

Napier running upstairs, slipping, a series of empty rooms.

Bill Smoke kneeling on an antique bed, clubbing something on the bed with his flashlight, the beam whipping the walls and ceiling, the near-noiseless thump as it lands on the senseless head of Margo Roker. Her blood on the bedsheets – obscenely scarlet and wet.

Napier, shouting for him to stop.

Bill Smoke turned around, huffing. *Wassup, Joe?*

You said she was out tonight!

No, no, you heard wrong. I said my contact said the old woman was out tonight. Reliable staff, hard to find.

Christ, Christ, Christ, is she dead?

Better safe than sorry, Joe.

A neat little set-up, Joe Napier admits in his sleepless cabin. A shackle of compliance. Party to the clubbing of a defenceless, elderly activist? Any dropout law student with a speech impediment could send him to prison for the rest of his life. A blackbird sings. *I did a great wrong by Margo Roker, but I've left that life.* Four small bullet-scars, two in each cheek of both buttocks, ache. *I went out on a limb to get Luisa Rey wised up.* The window is light enough to discern Milly in her frame. *I'm only one man*, he protests. *I'm not a platoon. All I want out of life is life. And a little fishing.*

Joe Napier sighs, dresses and begins reloading the Jeep.

Milly always won by saying nothing.

56

Judith Rey, barefoot, fastens her kimono-style dressing-gown and crosses a vast Byzantine rug to her marble-floored kitchen. She takes out three ruby grapefruits from a cavernous refrigerator, halves them, then feeds the snow-cold dripping hemispheres into a juicer. The machine buzzes like trapped wasps and a jug fills with pulpy, pearly, candy-colored juice. She pours herself a heavy blue glass, and slooshes it around every recess of her mouth.

On the striped veranda sofa, Luisa scans the paper and chews a croissant. The magnificent view – over Ewingsville's monied roofs and velveteen lawns to downtown Buenas Yerbas, where skyscrapers rear from sea-mist and commuter-smog – has an otherworldliness at this hour.

'Not sleeping in, Cookie?'

'Morning. No, I'm going to collect my stuff from the office, if you don't mind me borrowing one of the cars again.'

'Sure.' Judith Rey reads her daughter. 'You were wasting your talents at *Spyglass*, Cookie. It was a squalid little magazine.'

'True, Mom, but it was *my* squalid little magazine.'

Judith Rey settles on the arm of the sofa and shoos an impertinent fly from her glass. She examines a circled article in the business section.

'Energy Guru' Lloyd Hooks to head Seaboard Inc.

In a joint statement, the White House and electricity giant Seaboard Power Inc. have announced Energy Secretary Lloyd Hooks is to fill the CEO's seat left vacant by Alberto Grimaldi's tragic death in an airplane accident two days ago. Seaboard's share price on Wall Street leapt 40 pts in response to the news. 'We're delighted Lloyd has accepted our offer to come on board,' said Seaboard vice-president William Wiley, 'and while the circumstances behind the appointment couldn't be sadder, the board feels Alberto in heaven joins with us today as we extend the warmest welcome to a visionary new chief executive.' Menzies Graham, Energy Department spokesman, said 'Lloyd Hooks' expertise will obviously be missed here in Washington, but President Ford respects his wishes, and looks forward to an ongoing liaison with one of the finest minds tackling today's energy challenges and keeping our great nation great.' Mr Hooks is to take up his new responsibilities from next week. His successor at the White House is due to be announced later today.

'Is this a project you were working on?' asks Judith.

'Still am.'

'On whose behalf?'

'On behalf of the truth.' Her daughter's irony is sincere. 'I'm freelance.'

'Since when?'

'Since the moment KPO fired me. Firing me was a political decision, Mom. It proves I was on to something big. Mammoth.'

Judith Rey watches the young woman. *Once upon a time, I had a baby daughter. I dressed her in frilly frocks, enrolled her for ballet classes and sent her to horse-riding camp five summers in a row. But look at her. She turned into Lester anyway.* She kisses Luisa's forehead. Luisa frowns, suspiciously, like a teenager. 'What?'

57

Luisa Rey drops into the Snow White Diner for the last coffee of her *Spyglass* days and to say goodbye to Bart. The only free seat is adjacent to a man hidden behind the *San Francisco Chronicle*. Luisa thinks, *A good paper*, and takes the seat. Dom Grelsch says, 'Morning.'

Luisa feels a flare of territorial jealousy. 'What are you doing here?'

'Even editors eat. I've come here every morning since my wife's . . . y'know. Waffles I can make in the toaster but . . .' His gesture at his platter of veal chops implies, *Need I say more?*

'I never saw you in here once.'

'That's 'cos he leaves,' says Bart, performing three tasks at once, 'an hour before you arrive. Usual, Luisa?'

'Please. How come you never told me, Bart?'

'I don't gossip about *your* comings and goings to no-one else either.'

'First one into the office,' Dom Grelsch folds the newspaper, 'last one out at night. Editor's lot. I wanted a word with you, Luisa.'

'I have a distinct memory of having been fired.'

'Can it, willya? I want to say why – how – I'm not resigning over how Ogilvy crapped on you. And since my confessions are rolling out, I knew you were for the ax since last Friday.'

'Nice of you to let me know beforehand.'

The editor lowers his voice to the bare minimum. 'You know about my wife's leukemia. Our insurance situation?'

Luisa decides to grant him a nod.

Grelsch steels himself. 'Last week, during the takeover negotiations . . . it was intimated, if I stayed on at *Spyglass* and agreed I'd never heard . . .' Grelsch isn't happy '. . . of a certain report, strings could be pulled at my insurers'.'

Luisa maintains her composure. 'You trust these people to keep their word?'

'On Sunday morning my claims man, Arnold Frum, phones. Apologies for disturbing us, blah-blah, but he thought we'd want to know Blue Shield have reversed their decision, and will be handling all my wife's medical bills. A reimbursement check for past payments is in the mail. We even get to keep our house. I'm not proud of myself, but I won't be ashamed for putting my family ahead of the truth.'

'The truth is radiation raining on Buenas Yerbas.'

'We all make choices about levels of risk. If I can protect my wife in return for playing a bit part in the *chance* of an accident at Swannekke, well, I'll have to live with that. I sure as hell wish you'd think a little more about the risk you're exposing *your*self to by taking these people on.'

Luisa's memory of sinking under water returns to haunt her and her heart lurches. Bart places a coffee in front of her.

Grelsch slips a typewritten page over the counter. It contains two columns of seven names per column. 'Guess what this list is.' Two names jump out: Lloyd Hooks and William Wiley.

'Board members of Trans Vision Inc.?'

Grelsch nods. 'Almost. Board membership is a matter of public knowledge. This is a list of unlisted corporate advisors who receive money sourced in Trans Vision Inc. The circled names should interest you. Look. Hooks *and* Wiley. Lazy, damning, just plain greedy.'

Luisa folds the list and pockets it. 'I should thank you for this.'

'Nussbaum the Foul did the digging. One last thing. Fran Peacock, at the *Western Messenger*, you know her?'

'Just to say hi at superficial media parties.'

'Fran and me go back a ways. I dropped by her office last night, mentioned your story's salient points. I was noncommital, but once you've got battleworthy evidence she'd like to say more than just hi.'

'Is this in the spirit of your understanding with Trans Vision Inc.?'

Grelsch stands up and folds his newspaper. 'They never said I couldn't share my contacts.'

58

Jerry Nussbaum returns the car-keys to Luisa. 'Dear God in Heaven, let me be reincarnated as your mother's sports car. I don't care which one. That's the last of the boxes?'

'Yep,' says Luisa, 'and thanks.'

Nussbaum shrugs like a modest maestro. 'The place'll sure feel empty without a real woman to crack chauvinist jokes on. Nance is actually a man after so many decades in a newsroom.'

Nancy O'Hagan thumps her jammed typewriter and gives Nussbaum the finger.

'Yeah, like,' Roland Jakes surveys Luisa's empty desk, glumly, 'I still don't believe how, y'know, the new guys'd give you the high jump but keep on a mollusc like Nussbaum.'

Nancy O'Hagan hisses, cobra-like, 'How can *Grelsch*,' she jabs her cigar at his office, 'just roll over waving his feet in the air and let KPO stiff you like that?'

'Wish me luck.'

'Luck?' Jakes scoffs. 'You don't need luck. Don't know why you stayed with this dead shark for so long. The seventies is gonna see satire's dying gasp. It's true what Lehrman said. A world that'll award Henry Kissinger the Nobel Peace Prize throws us *all* out of a job.'

'Oh,' Nussbaum remembers, 'I came back via the mailroom. Something for you.' He hands Luisa a padded khaki envelope. Luisa doesn't recognize the crabbed, looping script. She scrutinizes the smudged postmark, and shows it to Nussbaum. 'Does that say fourth September?'

Nussbaum squints. 'Think so. What's so special about then?'

She doesn't answer and slits open the khaki envelope. Inside is a safety-deposit key, wrapped in a short note. Luisa's expression intensifies as her eyes move down the note. She double-checks the label on the key. 'Third Bank of California, 9th Street. Where's that?'

'Downtown,' answers O'Hagan, 'where 9th crosses Flanders Boulevard.'

'See you all around.' Luisa is going. 'It's a small world.'

'Whoah,' says Jakes, 'like, uh, what's that about?'

59

Waiting for the lights to change, Luisa glances once more at Sixsmith's letter to treble-check she hasn't missed anything. It was written in a hurried script.

> *BY International Airport,*
> *3rd – ix – 1975*

Dear Miss Rey,

Forgive this scribbled note. I have been warned by a well-wisher at Seaboard I am in imminent danger of my life. Exposing the HYDRA-Zero's defects calls for excellent health, so I will act on this tip-off. I will be in touch with you as soon as I can from Cambridge or via the IAEA. In the meantime, I have taken the liberty of depositing my report on Swannekke B in a strongbox

> *at the 3rd Bank of California on 9th Street. You will need it should*
> *anything happen to me.*
> *Be careful.*
> *In haste,*
> *R.S.*

Angry horns blast as Luisa fumbles with the unfamiliar gearbox. After 13th Street the city loses its moneyed Pacific character. Carob trees, watered by the city, give way to buckled street-lights. Joggers do not pant down these side-streets. The neighborhood could be from any manufacturing zone in any rust-belt. Bums doze on benches, weeds crack the sidewalk, skins get darker block by block, flysheets cover barricaded doors, graffiti spreads across every surface below the height of a teenager holding a spray-can. The garbage-collectors are on strike, again, and mounds of rubbish putrefy in the sun. Pawnshops, nameless laundromats and grocers scratch a lean living from threadbare pockets. After more blocks and street-lights the shops give way to anonymous manufacturing units and project housing. Luisa has never even driven through this district and feels unsettled by the unknowability of cities. *Was Sixsmith's logic to hide his report and then hide the hiding-place?* She comes to Flanders Boulevard and sees the 3rd Bank of California dead ahead, with a customer's parking lot around the side. Luisa doesn't notice the battered black Chevy parked across the street.

60

Fay Li, in vizor sunglasses and a sunhat, checks her watch against the bank's clock. The air-conditioning is losing its battle against the mid-morning heat. She dabs perspiration from her face and forearms with a handkerchief, fans herself and assesses recent developments. *Joe Napier, you look dumb but you're deep-down smart, smart enough to know when to bow out.* Luisa Rey should be here any time now, if Bill Smoke was on the money.

Bill Smoke, you look smart but you're deep-down dumb, and your men aren't as loyal as you think. Because you *don't do it for the money, you forgot how easily littler mortals can be bought.*

Two well-dressed Chinese men walk in. A look from one tells her Luisa Rey is coming. The three converge at a desk guarding a side-corridor: SAFETY DEPOSIT BOXES. This facility has had very little traffic all morning. Fay Li considered getting a plant in place, but a minimum-wage rent-a-guard's natural laxness is safer than giving Triad men a sniff of the prize.

'Hi,' Fay Li fires off her most intolerable Chinese accent at the guard, 'brothers and I want get from strong box.' She dangles a deposit-box key. 'Looky we got key.'

The bored wiry youth has a bad skin problem. 'ID?'

'ID here, you looky, ID you looky.'

The Chinese ideograms repel white scrutiny with their ancient tribal magic. The guard nods down the corridor and returns to his *Aliens!* magazine. 'Door's not locked.' *I'd fire your ass on the spot, kid,* thinks Fay Li.

The corridor ends at a reinforced door, left ajar. Beyond is the deposit-box room shaped like a three-pronged fork. One associate joins her up the left prong, and she orders the other down the right. *About six hundred boxes in here. One of them hides a five-million-dollar, ten-thousand-bucks-per-page report.*

Footsteps approach down the corridor. *Clipping, female heels.*

The reinforced door swings open. 'Anyone in here?' calls Luisa Rey.

Silence.

As the door clangs shut the two men rush the woman. Luisa is gripped with a hand over her mouth. 'Thank you.' Fay Li prises the key from the reporter's fingers. Its engraved number is: 36/64. She wastes no words. 'Bad news. This room is sound-proof, unmonitored, and my friends and I are armed. The Sixsmith Report isn't destined for your hands. Good news. I'm acting for clients who want the HYDRA strangled at birth and Seaboard discredited. Sixsmith's findings will hit the news networks within two or three days. Whether they want to pursue the corporate executions is their business. Don't look at me like that, Luisa. Truth doesn't care who discovers it, so why should you? Even better news. Nothing bad will happen to you. My associate will escort you to a holding location in BY. By evening, you'll be a free woman. You won't cause us any trouble between now and then,' Fay Li produces a photo of Javier from Luisa's pinboard and waves it an inch from her face, 'because we'd reciprocate in kind.'

Submission replaces defiance in Luisa's eyes.

'I knew you had a fine head on your shoulders.' Fay Li addresses the man holding Luisa in Cantonese. 'Take her to the lock-up. Nothing dirty before you shoot her. She may be a reporter, but that doesn't make her a total whore. Dispose of the body in the usual way.'

They leave. The second associate remains by the door, holding it ajar.

Fay Li locates strongbox 36/64 at neck-height, at the tip of the middle prong.

The key turns and the door swings open.

Fay Li pulls out a vanilla binder. *THE HYDRA-ZERO REACTOR – AN OPERATIONAL ASSESSMENT MODEL – PROJECT HEAD DR RUFUS SIXSMITH – UNAUTH-ORIZED POSSESSION IS A FEDERAL CRIME UNDER THE MILITARY & INDUSTRIAL ESPIONAGE ACT 1971.* A flame of jubilation whooshes up inside Fay Li and she permits herself a smile. *The land of opportunity.* Then she sees two wires trailing from inside the binder to the back of the strongbox. She peers in. A red diode blinks on a neat 4×2 bundle of taped cylinders, wires, components.

Bill Smoke, you goddamn—

61

The blast picks Luisa Rey and throws her forward, irresistibly, like a Pacific breaker. The corridor rotates through 90° – several times – and pounds into Luisa's ribs and head. Petals of pain unfold across her vision. Masonry groans. Chunks of plaster, tile and glass shower, drizzle, stop.

An ominous peace. *What am I living through?* Calls for help spring up in the dust and smoke, screams from the street, alarm bells drill the burnt air. Luisa's mind reactivates. *A bomb.* The rent-a-guard croaks and moans. Blood from his ear trickles into a delta flooding his shirt collar. Luisa tries to pull herself away but her right leg has been blown off.

She opens her mouth to scream, but the horror passes, her leg is just jammed under her unconscious Chinese escort. She pulls free and crawls, stiff and hurting but otherwise okay, across the lobby, now transformed into a movie set. Luisa finds the reinforced door, blown off its hinges. *Must have missed me by inches.* Broken glass, upended chairs, chunks of wall, cut-and-shocked people. Oily black smoke belches from the ducts and a sprinkler system kicks in – Luisa is drenched and choked, slips on the wet floor, and stumbles, dazed, bent-double, into others.

A friendly hand takes Luisa's wrist. 'I got you, ma'am, I got you, let me help you outside, there may be another explosion.'

Luisa allows herself to be led into congested sunlight where a wall of faces looks on, hungry for horror. The fireman guides her across a road blocked with gridlocked cars and she is reminded of April's war footage from Saigon. Smoke still spills in senseless quantities. 'Get away! Over here! Get back! Over there!' Luisa the journalist is trying to tell Luisa the victim something. She has grit in her mouth. Something urgent. She asks her rescuer, 'How did you get on the scene so soon?'

'It's okay,' he insists, 'you have a concussion.'

A fireman? 'I can make my own way now—'

'No, you'll be safe this way—'

The door of a dusty black Chevy swings open.

'Let go of me!'

His grip is iron. 'In the car now,' he mutters, 'or I'll blow your fucking brains out.'

The bomb was supposed to get me, and now—

Luisa's abductor grunts and falls forwards.

62

Joe Napier grabs Luisa Rey's arm and swings her away from the Chevy. *Christ, that was close!* A baseball bat is in his other hand. 'If you want to live to see the day out you'd better come with me.'

Okay, thinks Luisa. 'Okay,' she says.

Napier pulls her back into the jockeying crowd to block Bill Smoke's line of fire, hands the baseball bat to a bewildered boy, and marches towards 81st Avenue, away from the Chevy. *Walk discreetly; or run for it and break your cover?*

'My car's next to the bank,' says Luisa.

'We'll be sitting ducks in this traffic,' says Napier. 'Bill Smoke's got two more apemen, they'll just fire through the window. Can you walk?'

'I can run, Napier.'

They advance a third of the way down the block but then Napier makes out Bill Smoke's face ahead, his hand hovering around his jacket pocket. Napier checks behind him. A second goon is the second pincer. Across the road is a third. There won't be any cops on the scene for minutes yet, and they have mere seconds. Two killings in broad daylight: risky, but the stakes are high enough for them to chance it, and there's so much chaos here, they'll get away with it. Napier is desperate: they are level with a windowless warehouse. 'Up these steps,' he tells Luisa, praying the door opens.

It does.

A sparse reception area, shady and lit by a single tube, a tomb of flies. Napier bolts the door shut behind them. From behind a desk, a young girl in her Sunday best and an aged poodle in a cardboard box bed watch, unperturbed. Three exits at the far end. The noise of machinery is monolithic.

A black-eyed Mexican woman swoops from nowhere and flutters in his face: 'No 'llegals here! No 'llegals here! Bossaway! Bossaway! Come back 'notherday!'

Luisa Rey addresses her in very battered Spanish. The Mexican woman glares, then jerks a savage thumb at the exits. A blow crunches the outer door. Napier and Luisa run across the echoing chamber. 'Left or right?' demands Napier.

'Don't know!' gasps Luisa.

Napier looks back for guidance from the Mexican, but the street door shudders under one blow, splinters under the next, and flies open with the third. Napier pulls Luisa through the left exit.

63

Bisco and Roper, the two sidemen Bill Smoke recruited for this job, body-charge the door. In the courtroom of his head, Bill Smoke finds William Wiley and Lloyd Hooks guilty of gross stupidity. *I told you! Joe Napier couldn't be trusted to pack up his conscience and pick up his fishing rods.*

The door is in pieces.

A spidery Mexican woman inside is having hysterics. A placid child and a bedecked poodle sit on an office desk as if they, not the Mexican, are the secret brains of the outfit. 'FBI!' Bisco yells, flourishing his driver's license. 'Which way did they go?'

The Mexican woman screeches: 'We care our workers! Very good! Very much pay! No need union!'

Bisco takes out his gun and blasts the poodle against the wall. 'WHICH WAY THEY FUCKING GO?'

Jesus Muhammad Christ, this *is why I work alone.*

The Mexican woman bites her fist, shudders, and launches a rising wail.

'Brilliant, Bisco, like the FBI kill poodles.' Roper leans over the child, who hasn't responded in any way to the death of the dog. 'Which exit did the man and the woman take?'

She gazes back as if he is nothing but a pleasant sunset.

'You speak English?'

A hysteric, a mute, a dead dog, Bill Smoke walks to the three exits, *and a pair of fuck-ups royale.* 'We're losing time! Roper, right door. Bisco, left. I'm the middle.'

64

Rows, aisles and ten-box-high walls of cardboard conceal the true dimensions of the storeroom. Napier wedges the door shut with a trolley. 'Tell me you've got over your gun-allergy since yesterday,' he hisses.

Luisa shakes her head. 'You?'

'Only a popgun. Six shots. C'mon.'

Even as they run, she hears the door being forced. Napier blocks the line of vision with a tower of boxes. Then again, a few yards down. They run, but now they seem to have been running for minutes and still haven't gotten anywhere. A third tower topples ahead of them, however, and dozens of Big Birds – Luisa recognizes the dim-wit yellow emu from the children's program Hal used to watch between jobs – spill free. Napier gestures: *run with your head down.* Luisa hopes the noise of machinery coming through the wall muffled the noise of the toppling boxes.

Five seconds later a bullet rips through cardboard three inches shy of Luisa's head, and Big Bird stuffing poofs into her face. She trips, and collides with Napier; a rod of noise punches the air above them. Napier draws his gun and fires twice around Luisa. The noise makes her curl into a ball. 'Run!' barks Napier, grabbing her upright. Luisa obeys – Napier starts knocking down walls of boxes to impede their pursuer.

Ten meters later Luisa gets to a corner. A plywood door is marked EMERGENCY EXIT.

Locked. Breathless, Joe Napier reaches her. He fails to force the door.

'Give it up, Napier!' they hear. 'It's not you we're after!'

Napier fires point blank at the lock.

The door still won't open. Napier empties three more bullets into the lock: each bang makes Luisa flinch. The fourth bang is an empty click. Napier kicks the door with the sole of his boot.

An underworld sweatshop clattering with five hundred sewing machines. Flakes of textile are suspended in the viscous heat, haloing the naked bulbs hanging over each machinist. Luisa and Napier skirt the outer walkway in a rapid semi-crouch. Limp Donald Ducks and crucified Scooby-Doos have their innards stitched, one by one, row by row, pallet by pallet. Each woman – Hispanic or Chinese only – keeps her eyes fixed on the needle-plates, so Luisa and Napier cause little commotion.

But how do we get out of here?

Napier runs, literally, into the Mexican woman from the makeshift reception. She beckons them down a semi-blocked unlit side-passage. Napier turns to Luisa, yelling over the metallic din, his face saying, *Do we trust her?*

Luisa's face replies, *Any better ideas?* They follow the woman between reams of fabric and wire, split boxes of teddy-bear eyes and assorted sewing-machine body-shells and innards. The passage corners right and stops at an iron door. Day filters in through a grimy grill. The Mexican fumbles with her key-ring. *It's 1875 down here*, thinks Luisa, *not 1975*. One key won't fit. The next fits but won't turn. Even thirty seconds on the factory floor has affected her hearing.

A war-cry from six yards away: 'Hands in the air!' Luisa spins around. 'I said, *Hands in the fuckin' air*!' Luisa's hands obey. The gunman keeps his pistol trained on Napier. 'Turn around, Napier! *Slow!* Drop your gun!'

The *señora* shrills: 'No shoot I! No shoot I, Señor! They force I show door! They say they kill—'

'Shuddup, you crazy fuckin' wetback! Scram! Outa my way!'

The woman creeps around him, pressing herself against the wall, shrieking, '*¡No dispares! ¡No dispares! ¡No quiero morir!*'

Napier shouts, through the funneled factory noise, 'Easy now, Bisco, how much you being paid?'

Bisco hollers back, 'Don't bother, Napier. Last words.'

'I can't hear you! What did you say?'

'WHAT – ARE – YOUR – LAST – WORDS?'

'Last words? Who are you? Dirty Harry?'

Bisco's mouth twitches. 'I got a book of last words, and those were yours. You?' He looks at Luisa, keeping the gun trained on Napier.

A pistol shot punches a hole in the din and Luisa's eyes clench shut. A hard thing touches her toe. She forces her eyes open. It is a handgun, skidded to a stop. Bisco's face is contorted into inexplicable agony. The *señora*'s monkey wrench flashes and crumples the gunman's lower jaw. Ten or more blows of extreme ferocity follow, each one making Luisa flinch, punctuated by the words, '*Yo! Amaba! A! Ese! Perro! Hijo! De! Puta!*'

Luisa checks Joe Napier. He looks on, unhurt, thunderstruck.

The *señora* wipes her mouth and leans over the motionless, pulp-faced Bisco. 'And *don*'t call me "wetback"!' She steps over his clotted head and unlocks the exit.

'You might want to tell the other two *I* did that to him,' Napier tells her, retrieving Bisco's gun.

The *señora* addresses Luisa. '*Quítatelo de encima, cariña. Anda con gentuza y ¡Dios mío! este viejo que podría ser tu padre.*'

Napier sits on the graffiti-frescoed subway train, watching Lester Rey's daughter. She is dazed, disheveled, shaky, and her clothes are still damp from the sprinkler. 'How did you find me?' she asks, finally.

'Big fat guy at your office. Nosboomer, or something.'

'Nussbaum.'

'That's it. Took a heap of persuading.'

A silence lasts from Reunion Square subway to 17th Avenue. Luisa picks at a hole in her jeans. 'I guess you don't work at Seaboard any longer.'

'I was put out to pasture yesterday.'

'Fired?'

'No. Early retirement. Yes. I was put out to pasture.'

'And you came back from the pasture this morning?'

'That's about the size of it.'

The next silence lasts from 17th Avenue to McKnight Park.

'I feel,' Luisa hesitates, 'that I – no, that *you* – broke some sort of decree back there. As if Buenas Yerbas had decided I was to die today. But here I am.'

Napier considers this. 'No. The city doesn't care. And you could say it was your father who just saved your life, when he kicked away that grenade rolling at me, thirty years ago.' Their compartment groans and shudders. 'We've got to go via a gun-store. Empty guns make me nervous.'

The subway emerges into the sunlight.

Luisa squints. 'Where are we going?'

'To see somebody.' Napier checks his watch. 'She's flown in specially.'

Luisa rubs her red eyes. 'Can the somebody give us a copy of the Sixsmith Report? Because it seems to me nothing else matters here.'

'I don't know yet.'

Megan Sixsmith sits on a low bench in the Buenas Yerbas Museum of Modern Art and stares back at a giant portrait of an old lady's ursine face, rendered in interlacing gray and black lines on a canvas otherwise blank. The only figurative in a room of Pollocks, de Koonings and Mirós, the portrait quietly startles. *'Look,' she says,* thinks Megan, *'at your future. Your face, too, will one day be mine.'* Time has knitted her skin into webs of wrinkles. Muscles sag here, tauten there, her eyelids droop. Her pearls are of inferior quality most likely, and her hair is mussed from an afternoon of rounding-up grandchildren. *But she sees things I don't.*

A woman about her own age sits next to her. She could use a wash and a change of clothes. 'Megan Sixsmith?'

Megan glances sidelong. 'Luisa Rey?'

She nods towards the portrait. 'I've always liked her. My dad met her, the real lady, I mean. She was a Holocaust survivor who settled in BY. Ran a boarding-house over in Little Lisbon. She was the artist's landlady, before he was famous.'

Courage grows anywhere, thinks Megan Sixsmith, *like weeds.*

'Joe Napier said you flew in today from Honolulu.'

'Is he here?'

'The guy behind me, in the denim shirt pretending to look at the Warhol. He's watching out for us. I'm afraid his paranoia is amply justified.'

'Yes. I need to know you are who you say you are.'

'I'm happy to hear it. Any ideas?'

'What was my uncle's favorite Hitchcock movie?'

The woman claiming to be Luisa Rey thinks for a while, and smiles. 'We talked about Hitchcock in the elevator – I'm guessing he wrote you about that – but I don't remember him naming a favorite. He admired that wordless passage in *Vertigo*, where Cary Grant trails the mysterious woman to the waterfront with the San Francisco backdrop. He enjoyed *Charade* – it tickled him, you calling Audrey Hepburn a bubblehead.'

Megan reclines into the seat. 'Yes, my uncle referred to you in a card he wrote from the airport hotel. It was agitated, and worrying, and dotted with phrases like "If anything should happen to me" – but it wasn't suicidal. Nothing could make Rufus do what the police said. I know it.' *Ask her, and control your trembling, for God's sake.* 'Miss Rey – do *you* think my uncle was murdered?'

Luisa Rey replies, 'I'm afraid I know he was. I'm sorry.'

The journalist's conviction is cathartic. *So you're not going crazy.* 'I know about his work for Seaboard and the Defense Department. Now, I never saw the whole report, but I checked its mathematics when I visited Rufus back in June. We vetted each other's work.'

'The Defense Department? You don't mean Energy?'

'Defense. A by-product of the HYDRA-Zero reactor is weapons-grade uranium. Highest quality, lots of it.' Megan lets Luisa Rey digest the new implications. 'What do you need?'

'His work. The report, only the report, will bring Seaboard crashing down in public and legal arenas. And, incidentally, save my own skin.'

Trust this stranger or get up and walk away?

A crocodile of schoolchildren clusters around the portrait of the old woman. Megan murmurs, under the curator's short speech, 'Rufus kept academic papers, data, notes, early drafts, et cetera on *Starfish* – his yacht – for future reference. His funeral isn't until next week, probate won't begin until then, so this cache should still be untouched. I would bet a lot he had a copy of his report aboard. Seaboard's people may have already combed the boat, but he had a thing about not mentioning *Starfish* at work . . .'

'Where's *Starfish* moored now?'

67

CAPE YERBAS MARINA ROYALE
PROUD HOME OF *PROPHETESS*
BEST-PRESERVED SCHOONER IN THE WORLD!

Napier parks the hired Ford by the clubhouse, a weatherboarded former boathouse. Its bright windows boast an inviting bar, and nautical flags ruffle stiff in the evening wind. Sounds of laughter and dogs are carried from the dunes as Luisa and Napier cross the clubhouse garden, and descend the steps to the sizeable marina. A three-masted wooden ship is silhouetted against the dying east, towering over the sleek fibreglass yachts around it. Some people mill on the jetties and yachts, but not many. '*Star-fish* is moored on the furthest jetty away from the clubhouse,' Luisa consults Megan Sixsmith's map, 'past the *Prophetess*.'

The nineteenth-century ship is indeed restored beautifully. Despite their mission, Luisa is distracted by a strange gravity that makes her pause for a moment and look at its rigging, listen to its wooden bones creaking.

'What's wrong?' whispers Napier. It's too dark to read her expression well.

What is *wrong?* Luisa's birthmark throbs. She grasps for the ends of this elastic moment, but they disappear into the past and the future. 'Nothing.'

'It's okay to be spooked. I'm spooked myself.'

'Yeah.'

'C'mon. We're almost there.'

Starfish is where Megan's map says. They clamber aboard. Napier inserts a clip into the cabin door and slides a popsicle stick into the gap. Luisa watches for watchers. 'Bet you didn't learn that in the army.'

'You lose your bet. Cat burglars make resourceful soldiers, and the Draft Board wasn't choosy . . .' A click. 'Got it.' The tidy cabin is devoid of books. An inset digital clock blinks from

21:55 to 21:56. Napier's flashlight's pencil-beam rests on a navigation table fitted atop a mini-filing cabinet. 'How about in there?'

Luisa opens a drawer. 'This is it. Shine here.' A mass of folders and binders. One, vanilla in colour, catches her eye. *THE HYDRA-ZERO REACTOR – AN OPERATIONAL ASSESSMENT MODEL – PROJECT HEAD DR RUFUS SIXSMITH*. 'Got it. This is it. Joe? You okay?'

'Yeah. It's just . . . about time something went well, so simply.'

So Joe Napier can *smile.*

A motion in the cabin doorway; a man blocks out the stars. Napier reads Luisa's alarm and whirls around. In the torchlight Luisa sees a tendon in the gunman's wrist twitch, twice, but no gunfire sounds. *Jammed safety catch?*

Joe Napier makes a hiccuping sound, slumps to his knees and cracks his head on the steel foot of the navigation table.

He lies inert.

Luisa loses all but the dimmest sense of being herself. Napier's flashlight rolls in the gentle swell, and its beam rotates to show his shredded torso. His lifeblood spreads obscenely quickly, obscenely scarlet, obscenely shiny. Rigging rings in the wind, untuned bells.

The killer closes the cabin door behind him. 'Put the report on the table, Luisa.' His murmur is kindly. 'I don't want blood on it.' She obeys. His face is hidden. 'Well, you get to make peace with your maker.'

Luisa grips the table. 'You're Bill Smoke. You killed Sixsmith.'

The darkness answers, 'Bigger forces killed all of you. I just dispatched the bullet.'

Focus. 'You followed us, from the bank, in the subway, to the art museum . . .'

'Does death always make you so verbose?'

Luisa's voice trembles. 'What do you mean "always"?'

68

Joe Napier drifts in a torrential silence.

The ghost of Bill Smoke hovers in his dark vision.

More than half of himself has gone already.

Words come bruising the silence again. *He's going to kill her. That .38 in your pocket.*

I've done my duty, I'm dying, for Chrissakes.

Hey. Go tell Lester Rey about duty and dying.

Napier's right hand inches to his buckle. He wonders if he is a baby in his cot or a man dying in his bed. Nights pass, no, lifetimes. Often Napier wants to ebb away but his index finger has a mission that it refuses to forget. The butt of a gun arrives in his palm. His finger enters a loop of steel and a flare of clarity illuminates his purpose. *The trigger, this, yes. Pull her out. Slowly now . . .*

Angle the gun. Bill Smoke is just yards away.

The trigger resists his index finger – then a blaze of incredible noise spins Bill Smoke backwards, his arms flailing like a marionette's.

In the fourth to last moment of his life, Napier fires another bullet into the marionette silhouetted by stars. The word 'Silvaplana' comes to him, unasked for.

In the third to last moment, Bill Smoke's body slides down the cabin door.

Second to last, an inset digital clock blinks from 21:57 to 21:58.

Napier's eyes sink, newborn sunshine slants through ancient oaks and dances on a lost river. *Look, Joe, herons.*

69

In Margo Roker's ward in Swannekke County Hospital, Hester Van Zandt glances at her watch. 21:57. Visiting hours end at eight o'clock. 'One more for the road, Margo?' The visitor glances at her comatose friend, then leafs through her *Anthology of American Poetry*. 'A little Emerson? Ah, yes. Remember this one? You introduced it to me.

> 'If the red slayer thinks he slays,
> Or if the slain think he is slain
> They know not well the subtle ways
> I keep, and pass, and turn again.

> Far or forgot to me is near;
> Shadow and sunlight are the same;
> The vanish'd gods to me appear
> And one to me are shame and fame.

> They reckon ill who leave me out;
> When me they fly, I am the wings;
> I am the doubter and the doubt
> And I the hymn the Brahmin sings.

> The strong gods pine for my abode,
> And pine in vain —'

'Margo? Margo? Margo!' Margo Roker's eyelids vibrate as if in REM. A groan squirms in her larynx. She gulps for air, then her eyes are wide open, blinking in confusion and alarm at the tubes in her nose. Hester Van Zandt is also panicky, but with hope. 'Margo! Can you hear me? Margo!'

The patient's eyes settle on her old friend, and she lets her head sink into her pillow. 'Yes, I can hear you, Hester, you're shouting in my goddamn ear.'

Luisa Rey surveys the 1 October edition of the *Western Messenger* amid the steamy clatter of the Snow White Diner.

Lloyd Hooks skips $250,000 bail
President Ford vows to 'root out crooks who bring ignominy to Corporate America'

A BYPD spokesman confirmed the newly appointed CEO of Seaboard Power Inc. and former Energy 'Guru' Lloyd Hooks has fled the country, forfeiting the quarter-million dollars bail posted Monday. The latest twist to 'Seaboardgate' comes a day after Hooks swore to 'defend my integrity and the integrity of our great American company against this pack of nefarious lies'. President Ford weighed into the fray at a White House press conference, condemning his former advisor and distancing himself from the Nixon appointee. 'My cabinet makes no distinction between lawbreakers. We will root out the crooks who bring ignominy to corporate America and punish them with the utmost severity of the law.'

Lloyd Hooks's disappearance, interpreted by many observers as an admission of guilt, is the latest twist in a serious of revelations triggered by a Sep. 4 incident at Cape Yerbas Marina Royale in which Joe Napier and Bill Smoke, security officers at Seaboard Inc.'s controversial Swannekke Island atomic power stations, shot each other. Eyewitness Luisa Rey, correspondent to this newspaper, summoned police to the crime scene, and the subsequent investigation has already spread to last month's killing of British atomic engineer and Seaboard consultant Dr Rufus Sixsmith, the crash of former CEO Alberto Grimaldi's Lear jet over Colorado two weeks ago and an explosion in 3rd Bank of California downtown BY which claimed the lives of two people. Five directors at Seaboard Power have been charged in connection with the conspiracy and two have committed suicide. Three more, including vice-CEO William Wiley, have agreed to testify against Seaboard Corporation.

The arrest of Lloyd Hooks two days ago was seen as vindication of this newspaper's support for Luisa Rey's exposé of this major scandal, initially dismissed by William Wiley as 'libelous fantasy culled from a spy novel and wholly unworthy of a serious response' ... *Cont. p. 2, Full Story p. 5, Comment p. 11.*

'Front page!' Bart pours Luisa's coffee. 'Lester would be mighty proud.'

'He'd say I'm just a journalist doing my job.'

'Exactly.'

Seaboardgate is no longer Luisa's scoop. Swannekke swarms with reporters, Senate investigators, FBI agents, county police and Hollywood scriptwriters. Swannekke B is in mothballs; C is suspended.

Luisa gets Javier's postcard out again. It shows three UFOs zooming under the Golden Gate Bridge:

Hi Luisa, it's OK here but we live in a house so I can't jump across balconies when I visit my friends. Paul (that's Wolfman but Mom says I mustn't call him that any more though he kind of likes it when I do) is taking me to a stamp fare tommorrow, then I can choose what paint I want for my bedroom and he cooks better than Mom. Saw you again on TV last night and in the papers. Don't forget me just because you're fameous now, OK? Javi

The other item of mail is an airmailed package from Megan Sixsmith, sent in response to Luisa's request. The package contains the final eight letters Robert Frobisher wrote to his friend Rufus Sixsmith. Luisa uses a plastic knife to slit the package open. She removes one of the yellowed envelopes, postmarked 10 October 1931, holds it against her nose, and inhales. *Are molecules of Zedelghem Chateau, of Robert Frobisher's hand, dormant in this paper for forty-four years, swirling in my lungs, now, in my blood?*

Who is to say?

Letters from Zedelghem

Sixsmith,

Ayrs in bed for three days, fogged with morphine, calling out in pain. V. distracting and distressing. Dr Egret warns J. and I not to confuse Ayrs's newfound *joie de vivre* in music with actual health, and forbids V.A. to work from his sickbed. Dr Egret gives me the creeps. Never met a quack whom I didn't half suspect of plotting to do me in as expensively as he could contrive.

Buried in music of my own. Cruel to say it, but when Hendrick arrives at breakfast and tells me, 'Not today, Robert,' I'm almost relieved. Spent last night working on a rumbling 'cello *Allegro* lit by explosive triplets. Silence punctuated by break-neck mousetraps. Remember the church clock chiming three a.m. *I heard a whippoorwill*, Huckleberry Finn says, *and a dog crying about somebody who was going to die*. Always haunted me, that line. Next thing I know, Lucille was ballooning sheets of bright morning by the window. Morty Dhondt was downstairs, she told me, ready for our excursion. Thought I was dreaming but no. My face was crusted over and for a second I couldn't have told you my name. Grunted I didn't want to go anywhere with Morty Dhondt, I wanted sleep, I have work to do. 'But last week you arranged to go motoring today!' objected Lucille.

I remembered. I washed, put on fresh clothes and shaved. Sent Lucille to find the house-boy who'd polished my shoes, etc. Down in the breakfast room, the amiable jewel merchant was smoking a cigar and reading *The Times*. 'Don't hurry,' he told me, when I apologized for my tardiness. 'Where we're going no-one will notice if we're early or late.' Mrs Willems brought me some kedgeree, and J. breezed in. She hadn't forgotten what day it was, and gave me a bunch of white roses, tied with a black ribbon, and smiled, just like her old self.

Dhondt drives a claret 1927 Bugatti Royale Type 41, a real spanker, Sixsmith. Goes like a greased devil – nearly fifty on the metalled highway! – and boasts a klaxon hooter that Dhondt fires off at the least provocation.

Beautiful day for a grim journey. The nearer to the Front one goes, naturally, the more blasted the countryside becomes. Beyond Roeselare, the land grows crater-scarred, criss-crossed with collapsing trenches and pocked with burnt patches where not even weeds take root. The few trees still standing here and there are, when you touch them, lifeless charcoal. The skein of green on the land seems less nature revivified, more nature mildewed. Dhondt shouted over the engine's roar that farmers still daren't plough the land for fear of unexploded ordnance. One cannot pass by without thinking of the density of men in the ground. Any moment, the order to charge would be given, and infantrymen well up from the earth, brushing off the powdery soil. The thirteen years since Armistice seemed only as many hours.

Zonnebeke is a ramshackle village of semi-repaired ruins and the site of a cemetery of the 11th Essex of the 53rd Brigade. The War Graves Commission told me this cemetery has the best chance of being where my brother was laid to rest. Adrian died in the charge of July 31st on Messines Ridge, right in the thick of it. Dhondt dropped me off at the gates and wished me luck. Tactfully, he told me he had business nearby – we must have been fifty miles from the nearest jeweller's – and left me to my quixotic quest. A consumptive ex-soldier guarded the gates when not tending his sorry vegetable plot. He also worked as a groundsman – self-appointed, one suspects – and waved a donation box at me, for 'upkeep'. Parted with a franc, and the fellow asked in tolerable English if I was looking for anyone in particular, as he had committed the entire cemetery to memory. Wrote down my brother's name, but he did that Gallic mouth-droop that indicates, 'My problems are mine, and yours are yours, and this one is yours.'

Always felt I would divine which KNOWN UNTO GOD was

Adrian's. A glowing inscription, a nodding magpie, or just a musical certainty would lead me to the right plot. Utter tripe, of course. The headstones were uncountable, uniform and arrayed as if on parade. Coils of brambles invaded the perimeter. The air was stuffy as if the sky were sealing us in.

Along the aisles and rows I searched the Fs. Long odds, but one never knows. The War Office makes mistakes – if war's 1st victim is truth, its 2nd is clerical efficiency. In the event, no 'Frobisher' was resting in that plot of Flanders. The closest was 'Froames, B.W., Private 2389 18th (Eastern Division)' so I laid J.'s white roses on his stone. Who is to say? Maybe Froames asked Adrian for a light, one tired evening, or cowered with him as bombs rained down, or shared a Bovril. Am a sentimental fool and I know it.

One encounters buffoons like Orford at Balliol, who wear an air of deprivation that the War ended before they had a chance to show their mettle. Others, Figgis springs to mind, confess their relief not to have been of service age before 1918, but a certain shame that they feel this relief. I've often banged on to you about growing up in my legendary brother's shadow – every rebuke began with an 'Adrian never used to . . .' or 'If your brother were here now he'd . . .' Grew to hate the sound of his name. During the run-up to my forcible ejection from the Frobishery, it was all 'You're a disgrace to Adrian's memory!' Never, ever forgive the parents that. Remembered our last send-off one drizzly autumn afternoon at Audley End, Adrian was in uniform, Pater clasping him. Days of bunting and cheering were long over – later heard Military Police were escorting conscripts to Dunkirk to deter mass desertions. All those Adrians jammed like pilchards in cemeteries throughout eastern France, western Belgium, beyond. We cut a pack of cards called historical context – our generation, Sixsmith, cut tens, Jacks and Queens. Adrian's cut threes, fours and fives. That's all.

Of course, 'That's all' is never all. Adrian's letters were hauntingly aural. One can shut one's eyes but not one's ears. Crackle of lice in seams; scutter of rats; snap of bones against bullet;

stutter of machine-guns; thunder of distant explosions, lightning of nearer ones; ping of stones off tin helmets; flies buzzing over no man's land in summer. Later conversations add the scream of horses; cracking of frozen mud; buzz of aircraft; tanks, churning in mud-holes; amputees, surfacing from the ether; belch of flame-throwers; squelch of bayonets in necks. European music is passionately savage, broken by long silences.

Do wonder if my brother liked boys as well as girls too, or if my vice is mine alone. Wonder if he died celibate. Think of these troopers, lying together, cowering, alive; cold, dead. Tidied B. W. Froames's headstone and went back to the gates. Well, my mission was bound to be futile. Groundsman was twiddling with twine, said nothing. Morty Dhondt collected me bang on time and off we hurtled back towards civilization, ha.

Passed through a place called Poelkapelle or some such, down an avenue of elms lasting mile after mile. Dhondt chose this straight to push the Bugatti as fast as she would go. Individual elms blurred into a single tree repeated to infinity, like a spinning top. The needle was nudging top speed when a form like a running madwoman ran out smack in front of us – she hit the windscreen and spun over our heads. Heart popped like a gunshot, I can tell you! Dhondt braked, the road tilted us one way, shrugged us the other, the tyres screamed and singed the air with hot rubber. We had run out of infinity. My teeth had bitten deep into my tongue. If the brakes hadn't locked in such a way that the Bugatti continued its trajectory along the road, we would have finished our day – if not our lives – wrapped around an elm. The car scraped to a halt. Dhondt and I jumped out and ran back – to see a monster pheasant, flapping its broken wings. Dhondt blew out an elaborate oath in Sanskrit or something, and gave a *ha!* of relief that he hadn't killed some*one* that also expressed dismay at having killed some*thing*. Had lost the power of speech, and dabbed my bleeding tongue on my handkerchief. Proposed putting the poor bird out of its misery. Dhondt's answer was a proverb whose idiocy may have been deliberate: 'To Those upon the Menu, the Sauce is no

Concern.' He went back to try to coax the Bugatti back to life. Couldn't fathom his meaning, but walked up to the pheasant, causing it to flap ever more desperately. Its medallion breast feathers were matted with blood and fæcal spewings. It cried, Sixsmith, just like a two-day-old baby. Wished I had a gun. On the roadside was a stone as big as my fist. I smashed it down on the pheasant's head. Unpleasant – not the same as shooting a bird, not at all.

Wiped its blood off the best I could, using dock-leaves plucked from the roadside. Dhondt had the car running, I hopped aboard and we drove as far as the next village. A no-name place, as far as I could see, but it had a miserable café-cum-garage-cum-funeral parlour shared by a gang of silent locals and many flies who wheeled through the air like drugged angels of death. The hard braking had misaligned the Bugatti's front axle, so M.D. stopped here to have it seen to. We sat *al fresco* on the edge of a 'square', in reality a pond of cobbly mud with a plinth plonked in its navel whose original inhabitant had long ago been melted down for bullets. Some dirty children chased the only fat hen in the country across the square – it flew up to the plinth. The children began throwing stones at it. Wondered where the bird's owner might be. I asked the barman who had formerly occupied the plinth. He didn't know, he was born in the south. My glass was dirty so I made the barman change it. He took umbrage and was less talkative from then on.

M.D. asked about my hour in the Zonnebeke cemetery. Didn't really answer. Mangled, bloodied pheasant kept flashing before my eyes. Asked M.D. where he'd spent his War. 'Oh, you know, attending to business.' In Bruges? I asked, surprised, hard put to imagine a Belgian diamond merchant prospering under the Kaiser's occupation. 'Good God, no,' answered M.D., 'Johannesburg. My wife and I got out for the duration.' I complimented his foresight. Modestly, he explained, 'Wars do not combust without warning. They begin as little fires over the horizon. Wars approach. A wise man watches for the smoke, and prepares to vacate the neighbourhood, just like Ayrs and Jocasta. My

461

worry is that the next war will be so big, nowhere with a decent restaurant will be left untouched.'

Was he so sure another war was coming?

'Another war is *always* coming, Robert. They are never properly extinguished. What sparks wars? The will to power, the backbone of human nature. The threat of violence, the fear of violence, or actual violence, is the instrument of this dreadful will. You can see the will to power in bedrooms, kitchens, factories, unions and the borders of states. Listen to this and remember it. The nation state is merely human nature inflated to monstrous proportions. *QED*, nations are entities whose laws are written by violence. Thus it ever was, so ever shall it be. War, Robert, is one of humanity's two eternal companions.'

So, I asked, what was the other?

'Diamonds.' A butcher in a blood-stained apron ran across the square, and the children scattered. Now he had the problem of luring the hen down from its plinth.

The League of Nations? Surely nations knew laws other than warfare? What of diplomacy?

'Oh, diplomacy,' said M.D., in his element, 'it mops up war's spillages; legitimizes its outcomes; gives the strong state the means to impose its will on a weaker one, while saving its fleets and battalions for weightier opponents. Only professional diplomats, inveterate idiots and women view diplomacy as a long-term substitute for war.'

The *reductio ad absurdum* of M.D.'s view, I argued, was that science devises ever bloodier means of war until humanity's powers of destruction overcome our powers of creation and our civilisation drives itself to extinction. M.D. embraced my objection with mordant glee. 'Precisely. Our will to power, our science, and those v. faculties that elevated us from apes, to savages, to modern man, are the same faculties that'll snuff out *Homo sapiens* before this century is out! You'll probably live to see it happen, you fortunate son. What a symphonic crescendo *that*'ll be, eh?'

The butcher came over to ask the barman for a ladder. Got to end here. Can't keep my eyes open any longer.

Sincerely,
R.F.

— ◆ —

Zedelghem.
21st − x − 1931.

Sixsmith,
Ayrs should be up on his feet tomorrow after a bed-bound fortnight. Wouldn't wish syphilis on my worst enemies. Only one or two, anyway. The syphilitic decays in increments, like fruit rotting in orchard verges. Dr Egret calls by every other day, but there's not much left to prescribe except ever-bigger doses of morphine. V.A. loathes using it because it clouds his music.

J. prone to bouts of despondency. Some nights, she just clings to me as if I'm her life-belt and she's drowning. Feel sorry for the woman, but I'm interested in her body, not her problems. Was.

Spent the fortnight gone in the music room, reworking my year's fragments into a 'sextet for overlapping soloists': piano, clarinet, 'cello, flute, oboe and violin, each in its own language of key, scale and colour. In the 1st set, each solo is interrupted by its successor: in the 2nd, each interruption is recontinued, in order. Revolutionary or gimmicky? Shan't know until it's finished, and by then it'll be too late, but it's the 1st thing I think of when I wake, and the last thing I think of before I fall asleep, even if J. is in my bed. She should understand, the artist lives in two worlds.

Next day.
Had the devil of a spat with V.A. He dictated a toccata-like étude during this morning's compositional, it seemed deuced

familiar, then I recognized the refrain from my own 'Angel of Mons'! If Ayrs hoped I'd not notice he was v. much mistaken. I told him straight – this was my music. He changed his tune: 'What d'you mean, *your* music? Frobisher, when you grow up, you'll find that all composers draw inspiration from their environments. You're one of many elements in mine, drawing a fair salary, I might add, enjoying daily masterclasses in composition, and mingling with the greatest musical minds of the age.' Well, a v. different man from the one I'd wheeled down to the lodge-house a few weeks ago when he'd pleaded with me to stay on until next spring. I asked whom he had in mind to replace me. Mrs Willems? The gardener? Eva? Nefertiti? 'Oh, I'm sure Sir Trevor Mackerras could lay his hands on a suitable boy for me. Yes, I shall advertise. You're not as singular as you like to think. Now. Do you want your job or not?'

Couldn't find a way to win back lost ground so I walked out, complaining of agony in my big toe. V.A. fired this warning at my flank: 'If your toe isn't better by the morning, Frobisher, get it fixed in London and don't come back.' Sometimes I want to build a bloody great bonfire and toss the old sod into its roaring heart.

A week later, or so.
Still here, J. visited later, spun me a line about Ayrs's pride, how much he values my work, artistic tempers, etc., but please stay, for her sake if not for his. Accepted this proxy fig-leaf-cum-olive-branch, and our love-making that night was almost affectionate. Winter coming on, and I'm not up to adventuring around Europe on my modest nest-egg. Would need to meet a stupid, wealthy heiress rather smartish if I left now. Anyone spring to mind? Will send another package for Jansch, to boost my emergency fund. If Ayrs won't cut me in for my ideas that went into 'Todtenvogel' – enjoying its twentieth public outing since Warsaw – I'll just have to reimburse myself. Resolve to be much more cautious before showing V.A. my own compositions again. You know, having the roof over one's head dependent

upon the good offices of an employer is a *loathsome* way to live. Christ only knows how the serving classes stand it. Are the Frobishery domestics forever biting *their* tongues as I must, one wonders?

Eva back from her summer in Switzerland. Well, this young woman *says* she's Eva, and the resemblance is certainly striking, but that snotty duckling who left Zedelghem three months ago has returned a most graceful swan. She supports her mother, bathes her father's eyelids with cotton-wool dipped in cold water and reads him Flaubert for hours on end, she's courteous to the servants, and she even asks me about my sextet's progress. Was sure it was some new strategy to oust me, but seven days on I'm beginning to suspect E. the stinker just might be dead and buried.

V. well, there *is* more to E.'s & my pax than meets the eye, but must 1st provide some background. Since my arrival in Neerbeke, Eva's 'landlady' in Bruges, Mme van de Velde, had been on at both E. & J. for me to visit their house, so her five daughters – E.'s schoolfellows – can practise their English on a genuine English gentleman. M. van de Velde, you'll remember, is the alleged rake of Minnewater Gardens who turned out to be a manufacturer of munitions and respected civic pillar etc. Mme van de Velde is one of those tiresome persistent women whose ambitions won't be thwarted by 'He's v. busy at the moment.' Actually, one suspects J. of fixing the *fait accompli* out of spite – as her daughter grows swanlike, the mother is turning into a nasty old rook.

Today was the day appointed for me to dine at the van d. V.s – five evenly-spaced daughters plus Mater and Pater. Needed a new set of strings for the 'cello, and it does Ayrs no harm to see how helpless he is without me, so I put on my brave face and hoped the v.d.V.s employ a chef commensurate to a factory-owner's income. So at eleven o'clock the van de Velde car – a silver Mercedes-Benz, thank you very much – arrived at Zedelghem and their driver, a perspiring snowman with no neck and no French, drove E. and me back to Bruges. In the past we would have ridden in stony silence, but found myself telling E. a little about my Cambridge days. E. warned me that the eldest van de Velde, Marie-Louise, had decided to marry an Englishman at any cost, so I should have to guard my chastity with the utmost care.

How do you like *that*?

At the van de Veldes' town-house, the girls were arranged on the stairway to greet me in ascending order of age – ½ expected 'em to burst into song, and stone the crows, Sixsmith, that's what they did. 'Greensleeves', in English. Syrupy as humbugs. Then Mrs v.d.V. pinched my cheek as if I were a homecoming runaway and said, owlishly, 'How do you *do-ooo*?' Was ushered into 'the salon' – a nursery – and seated on 'the question chair', a toy-box. The v.d.V. daughters, a hydra of heads named Marie-Louise, Stephanie, Zenobe, Alphonsine and I forget the last, ranged from nine years of age to said Marie-Louise, one year Eva's senior. All girls possess a thoroughly unjustified self-confidence. A v. long sofa sagged beneath this family of porkers. The maid brought lemonade while Mme began the questions. 'Eva tells us your family are v. well connected in Cambridge, Mr Frobisher?' Glanced Eva-wards; she pulled a mock-fascinated face. Hid my smile and admitted my family are in the Domesday Book and that Pater is an eminent churchman. All attempts to turn the topic away from my eligibility were yorkered, and after a quarter of an hour the bug-eyed Marie-Louise had sensed her mater's approval and settled I would be her Prince Charming. She asked this: 'Mr Frobisher, are you well acquainted with Sherlock Holmes of Baker Street?' Well, thought I, the day might not be a complete wreck. A girl with a taste for irony must conceal some depths. But Marie-Louise was serious! A congenital dunce.

No, I replied, I didn't know Mr Holmes personally but he and David Copperfield could be seen playing billiards at my club every Wednesday.

Luncheon was served on fine Dresden crocks in a dining-room with a large reproduction of *The Last Supper* over floral wallpaper. Food a disappointment. Dry trout, greens steamed to a sludge, gâteau simply vulgar; thought I was back dining in London. The girls tittered *glissando* at my trivial missteps in French – yet their English rasps on one's ear unbearably. Mme v.d.V., who also summered in Switzerland, gave laborious accounts of how Marie-Louise had been eulogized in Berne as 'the Flower of the Alps' by Countess Slāck-Jawský or the Duchess of Sümdümpstädt. Couldn't even force out a civil 'Comme c'est charmant!'

M. v.d.V. arrived from his office. Asked a hundred questions on cricket to amuse his daughters with this quaint English ritual of 'Ins that are Out' and 'Outs that are In'. A pi-jawed ass of kingly proportions, so busy planning his next boorish interruption that he never listens properly. Pays himself unveiled compliments, beginning, 'Call me old-fashioned but . . .' or 'Some consider me a snob but . . .' Eva sent me a wry look. It said, 'And to think you honestly thought *this* oaf was a threat to my reputation!'

After luncheon, the sun came out and Mme v.d.V. announced we would all go for a walk to show the honoured visitor the sights of Bruges. Tried to say I'd already impinged on their hospitality enough, but wasn't to get away so lightly. The Great Patriarch excused himself – had a pile of chits to sign as high as the Matterhorn. May he die in an avalanche. After the maids had hatted and gloved the girls, the carriage was summoned and I was carted around one church after another. As dear old Kilvert notes, nothing is more tiresome than being told what to admire, and having things pointed at with a stick. Can scarcely recall the name of a single sight. By the itinerary's finale, the great clock-tower, my jaw was hurting from all the yawns I'd suppressed. Mme van de Velde gave the pinnacle one squint and announced that she would let us young things scramble up there by ourselves, and wait in the *pâtisserie* across the piazza. Marie-Louise, who outweighs her mother, remarked that it wouldn't be ladylike to allow Maman to wait alone. Brainbox couldn't go because of her asthma, and if Brainbox wasn't going etc. &

etc., until in the end only Eva and I bought tickets to go up. I paid, to show I wasn't blaming her personally for the hideous waste of a day. Went 1st. The stairway was an ever-narrower spiral. A rope ran at hand-height through iron-rings set into the wall. Feet had to feel their own way. Only source of light was occasional narrow windows. Only sounds were our feet and E.'s feminine breathing, reminding me of my nocturnes with her mother. The van de Veldes are five never-ending, ill-tuned harpsichord *allegretti* and my ears rang with gratitude to be free of 'em. Had forgotten to count the steps, I thought aloud. My voice sounded locked in a closet of blankets. Eva gave me a lazy '*Oui* . . .'

Emerged into an airy chamber housing the cartwheel-sized cogs of the clock mechanism. Ropes and cables disappeared into the ceiling. A dogsbody snoozed in his deck-chair. He was supposed to inspect our tickets – on the continent one must forever be producing a ticket – but we slipped by him up a final flight of wooden stairs to the viewing belvedere.

Tricolour Bruges spread out, far below: rooftile orange; masonry grey; canal brown. Horses, automobiles, cyclists, a crocodile of choirboys, witch-hat roofs, washing on lines across side-streets. Looked for Ostende, found it. Sunlit strip of North Sea turned Polynesian ultramarine. Seagulls wheeled in currents, I got giddy following 'em and thought of Ewing's mollyhawk. Eva declared she had spotted the van de Veldes. Assumed this was a comment on their ampleness, but looked where she said and, sure enough, six little blobs in pastels around a café table. E. folded her ticket into a paper dart and flung it over the parapet. Wind carried it off until the sun burned it up. What would she do if Dogsbody woke and demanded her ticket? 'I'll cry and say the horrible English boy stole it.' So I folded my ticket into a paper dart, too, told E. she had no evidence and launched it. Instead of soaring high, my dart fell out of sight in a moment. E.'s character depends on which angle you're looking from, a quality of superior opals. 'You know, I can't remember seeing Papa so content and alive as he is now,' she said.

The awful v.d.V.s had created a camaraderie. Asked her straight what had happened in Switzerland. Had she fallen in love, worked in an orphanage, had a mystical encounter in a snowy grotto?

She began to say something several times. In the end, she said (blushing!), 'I was missing a certain young man I met this June.'

You're surprised? Imagine *my* feelings! Yet I was every inch the gentleman you know me for. Instead of flirting back, I said, 'And your first impression of this young man? Was it not wholly negative?'

'Partly negative.' I observed her beads of perspiration from the climb, her lips and the fine, fine hairs on her upper lip.

'He's a tall, dark, handsome, musical foreigner?'

She snorted. 'He *is* . . . tall, yes; dark, quite; handsome, not so much as he thinks, but let us say he can catch the eye; musical, prodigiously; a foreigner, to his core. Remarkable that you know so much about him! Are you spying on him too, as he passes through Minnewater Park?' I had to laugh. So did she. 'Robert, I sense . . .' She gazed at me shyly. 'You're experienced. May I call you Robert, by the way?'

I said it was about time she did.

'My words are not . . . entirely appropriate. Are you angry?'

No, I said, no. Surprised, flattered, but angry, not at all.

'I behaved so spitefully to you. But I'm hoping we can start again.' Answered, of course, I'd like that too. 'Since my child-hood,' E. said, looking away, 'I've thought of this balcony as my own belvedere, from *A Thousand and One Nights*. I often come up here at this hour, after school. I'm the empress of Bruges, you see. Its citizens are my subjects. The van de Veldes are my jesters. I shall chop off their heads.' A beguiling creature, she really is. My blood was hot and I was seized by an impulse to give the empress of Bruges a lingering kiss.

Got no further, a party of infernal American tourists swarmed up through the narrow doorway. Fool that I am, I pretended not to be with Eva. Took in view from other side, trying to wind in all unravelled strings of myself. When Dogsbody

469

announced that the viewing balcony was closing shortly, Eva had left. How true to form. Once again forgot to count the steps going down.

At the cake shop Eva was helping littlest v.d.V. at pussy's cradle. Mme van de Velde fanned herself with a menu and ate *boule de l'Yser* with Marie-Louise as they dissected the fashions of passers-by. Eva avoided my eye. Spell was broken. Marie-Louise sought my eye, the spoony-eyed little heifer. Ambled back to the v.d.V.s' house where, hallelujah, Hendrick was waiting with the Cowley. Eva bade me *au revoir* in the doorway – glanced back to see her smile. Bliss! The evening was golden and warm. All the way to Neerbeke, saw Eva's face, strand or two of hair across her face, left there by the wind. Don't be hatefully jealous, Sixsmith. You know how it is.

J. senses the *entente* between Eva and me and doesn't like it one fig. Last night, I imagined E. was under me rather than her mother. Crescendo followed only bars later, a whole movement before J. Can women detect imaginary betrayals? I ask because, with stupendous intuition, she gave me this subtle warning. 'I want you to know something, Robert. If you ever touch Eva, I'll find out, and I'll destroy you.'

'I shouldn't think of it,' I lied.

'I shouldn't even dream of it, if I were you,' she warned.

Couldn't leave it like that. 'Why in hell do you think I'm attracted to your gangly, unpleasant daughter, anyway?' She did the v. same snort Eva had done up on her belvedere.

Sincerely,
R.F.

— ◆ —

Zedelghem.
24th − x − 1931.

Sixsmith,
Where the blazes is your reply? Look here, I'm much obliged to you, but if you think I'll wait around for your letters to appear, I'm afraid you're sorely mistaken. It is all perfectly hateful, hateful as my hypocrite father. I could ruin him. He's ruined me. Anticipating the end of the world is humanity's oldest pastime. Dhondt is right, damn his Belgian eyes, damn all Belgian eyes. Adrian would still be alive if 'plucky little Belgium' never existed. Someone should turn this dwarf-country into a giant boating lake and toss in Belgium's inventor, his feet tied to a Minerva. If he floats, he's guilty. To sink a white-hot poker through my father's damn eyes! Name one. Go on, name me just *one* famous Belgian. He has more money than Rothschild, but will he pay me another farthing? Miserable, so miserable. How Christian is it to cut me off without a single shilling to my name? Drowning is too good for him. Dhondt is right, I'm afraid. Wars are never cured, they just go into remission for a few years. The End is what we want, so I'm afraid the End is what we're damn well going to get. There. Set that to music. Timpani, cymbals and a million trumpets, *if* you would be so kind. Paying the old bastard with my own music. Kills me.

Sincerely,
R.F.

— ◆ —

Zedelghem.
29th – x – 1931.

Sixsmith,

Eva. Because her name is a synonym for temptation: what treads nearer to the core of man? Because her soul swims in her eyes. Because I dream of creeping throught the velvet folds to her room, where I let myself in, hum her a tune so – so – *so* softly, she stands with her naked feet on mine, her ear to my heart and we waltz like string-puppets. After that kiss, she says, 'Vous embrassez comme un poisson rouge!' and in moonlit mirrors we fall in love with our youth and beauty. Because all my life, sophisticated, idiotic women have taken it upon themselves to *understand* me, to *cure* me, but Eva knows I'm *terra incognita*, and explores me unhurriedly, like you did. Because she's lean as a boy. Because her scent is almonds, meadow-grass. Because if I smile at her ambition to be an Egyptologist she kicks my shin under the table. Because she makes me think about something other than myself. Because even when serious she shines. Because she prefers travelogues to Sir Walter Scott, prefers Billy Mayerl to Mozart and couldn't tell C-major from a sergeant-major. Because *I*, only I, see her smile a fraction before it reaches her face. Because Emperor Robert is not a good man – his best part is commandeered by his unperformed music – but she gives me that rarest smile, anyway. Because we listened to nightjars. Because her laughter spurts through a blow-hole in the top of her head and sprays all over the morning. Because a man like me has no business with this substance 'beauty', yet here she is, in these soundproofed chambers of my heart.

Sincerely,
R.F.

— ◆ —

Le Royal Hôtel, Bruges.
6th – xi – 1931.

Sixsmith,

Divorces. V. messy affairs but Ayrs's and mine was over in a single day. Just yesterday morning we were at work on the 2nd movement of his ambitious swan-song. He announced a new approach for our Compositional. 'Frobisher, today I'd like you to come up with some themes for my *Severo* movement. Something eve-of-war-ish in E minor. Once you've got something that catches my eye, I'll take it over and develop its potential. Got that?'

Got that I had. Like it I didn't, not one bit. Scientific papers are co-authored, yes, and a composer might work with a virtuoso musician to explore the boundaries of the playable – like Elgar and W. H. Reed – but a co-authored symphonic work? V. dubious idea, and told V.A. so in no uncertain terms. He tsked. 'I didn't say "co-authored", boy. You gather the raw material, I refine it as I see fit.' This hardly reassured me. He chided me: 'All the Greats have their apprentices do it. How else could a man like Bach churn out new masses every week?'

We were in the twentieth century when I last looked, I retorted. Audiences pay to hear the composer whose name is on the programme notes. They don't pay money for Vyvyan Ayrs only to get Robert Frobisher. V.A. got agitated. 'They won't "get" you! They'll get me! You're not listening, Frobisher. *You* do the block-and-tackle work, *I* orchestrate, *I* arrange, *I* polish.'

'Block-and-tackle' work like my 'Angel of Mons', robbed at gunpoint for the *Adagio* in Ayrs's glorious final monument? One may dress plagiarism up however one wishes, it's still plagiarism. 'Plagiarism?' Ayrs kept his voice low but his knuckles on his cane were whitening. 'In bygone days – when you were grateful for my tutelage – you called me one of the greatest living European composers. Which is to say, the world. Why would such an artist possibly need to "plagiarize" anything from a copyist who, may I remind him, was unable to obtain even a Bachelor's degree for himself from a college for the terminally privileged? You're not hungry enough, boy, that's your problem. You're Mendelssohn aping Mozart.'

The stakes rose like inflation in Germany, but I am constitutionally unable to fold under pressure: – I dig in. 'I'll tell you why you need to plagiarize! Musical sterility!' The finest moments in 'Todtenvogel' are mine, I told him. The contrapuntal ingenuities of the new work's *Allegro non troppo* are mine. I hadn't come to Belgium to be his damn fag.

The old dragon breathed smoke. Ten bars of silence in 6/8. Stubbed out his cigarette. 'Your petulance doesn't deserve serious attention. In fact it deserves dismissal, but that would be acting in the heat of the moment. Instead, I want you to think. Think about reputation.' Ayrs unrolled the word. 'Reputation is everything. Mine, save for a youthful exuberance that earned me the clap, is beyond reproach. Yours, my disinherited, gambling, bankrupt friend, is expired. Leave Zedelghem whenever you wish. But be warned. Leave without my consent and all musical society west of the Urals, east of Lisbon, north of Naples and south of Helsinki will know a scoundrel named Robert Frobisher forced himself upon purblind Vyvyan Ayrs's wife, his beloved wife, yes, the enchanting Mevrouw Crommelynck. She will not deny it. Imagine the scandal! After everything Ayrs had done for Frobisher, too ... well, no wealthy patron, no *impoverished* patron, no festival organizer, no board of governors, no parent whose Little Lucy Lamb wants to learn the piano, will have anything, *anything* to do with you.'

So V.A. knows. For weeks, months, probably. Was badly wrong-footed. Highlighted my impotence by calling Ayrs some v. rude names. 'Oh, flattery!' he crowed. 'Encore, Maestro!' Stopped myself battering the pox-nibbled corpse to a premature death with the bassoon. *Didn't* stop myself hissing that if Ayrs was ½ as good a husband as he was a manipulator and a larcenist of better men's ideas, his wife might not put it about so much. Come to think of it, I added, how much credibility would his campaign to smear my name carry when European society learned what kind of woman Jocasta Crommelynck was in her private life?

Hadn't even scratched him. 'You ignorant ass, Frobisher. Jocasta's numerous affairs are discreet, always have been. Any society's upper-crust is *riddled* with immorality, how else d'you think they keep their power? Reputation is king of the *public* sphere, not *private*. It is dethroned by *public* acts. Disinheritance. Fleeing famous hotels. Defaulting on monies owed to the gentry's lenders of last resort. Jocasta had my blessing when she seduced you, you stuck-up piffler. I required you to finish "Todtenvogel". You fancy yourself a larky buck, but there's alchemy between Jocasta and I you cannot *begin* to fathom. She'll fall out of love with you the *moment* you threaten us. You'll see. No, go away and come back tomorrow with your homework done. We will pretend your little tantrum never happened.'

Was only too pleased to comply. Needed to think.

J. must have played a major part in investigating my recent history. Hendrick doesn't speak English, and V.A. couldn't have done this delving alone. She must like louche men – explains why she married Ayrs. Where E. stands on all of this I couldn't guess, because yesterday was Wednesday so she was at school in Bruges. Eva could not know about my affair with her mother, and still make such open signs of love to me. Surely?

Spent afternoon walking across the bleak fields in solitary rage. Sheltered from hailstones in a bombed-out chapel's lychgate. Thought about E., thought about E., thought about E. Only two things were clear: – hanging myself from Zedelghem's flagpole was preferable to letting its parasite-master plunder my talents a day longer; and never seeing E. again was unthinkable. 'It'll all end in tears, Frobisher!' Yes, possibly, elopements often do, but I love her, I actually love her, and there it is.

Returned to the château just before it got dark, ate cold meats in Mrs Willems's kitchen. Learnt that J. and her Circean caresses were in Brussels on estate business and would not be back that night. Hendrick told me V.A. had retired early with his wireless and instructions not to be disturbed. Perfect. Took a long soak in the tub and a wrote a well-knotted set of scalic bass lines. Crises send me scurrying into music where nothing can harm me. Retired early myself, locked my door, and packed my valise.

Woke myself this morning at four o'clock. Freezing fog outside. Wanted to pay V.A. a final call. Barefoot except for socks, I crept along the wintry corridors to Ayrs's door. Shivering, eased it open, at pains to avoid the slightest noise – Hendrick sleeps in an adjoining room. Lights off, but in the ember-glow from the hearth I saw Ayrs, stretched out like that mummy in the British Museum. His room stank of bitter medicine. Crept to the cabinet by his bed. Drawer was stiff, and as I jerked it open an ether bottle on top wobbled – just caught it. V.A.'s flaunted Luger lay bundled in its chamois cloth wrapped in a string vest, next to a little saucer of bullets. They rattled. Ayrs's fragile skull was only inches away, but he didn't wake. His breathing was wheezy as a ratty old barrel-organ. Felt an impulse to steal a clutch of bullets so I did.

A blue vein throbbed over Ayrs's Adam's apple and I fought off an unaccountably strong urge to open it up with my penknife. Most uncanny. Not quite *déjà vu*, more *jamais vu*. Killing, an experience that comes to few outside wartime. What is the timbre of murder? Don't worry, I'm not writing you a murder confession. Working on my sextet while evading a man-hunt would be far too much trouble, and ending one's career swinging in soiled underwear is hardly dignified. Even worse, murdering Eva's father in cold blood might put the kibosh on her feelings for me. V.A. slumbered on, oblivious to all this, and I pocketed his pistol. I'd stolen the bullets, so taking the Luger too had a sort of logic. Curiously heavy things, guns. It emanated a bass note against my thigh: it's killed people, for sure; this little Luger went to market. Why did I take it, exactly? Couldn't tell you. But place its mouth against your ear and you hear the world in a different way.

Last port of call was Eva's empty room. Lay on her bed,

stroked her clothes, you know how I get sentimental over part-ings. Left the shortest letter of my life on her dressing-table; 'Empress of Bruges. Your belvedere, your hour.' Back to my room. Bade my four-poster bed a fond farewell, raised the stub-born sash-window and effected my flight over the icy roof. Flight was nearly the word – a tile slid out and crashed down to the gravel walk below. Lay prone, expecting shouts and alarums at any second, but no-one had heard. Reached Earth courtesy of the obliging yew tree, and made my way through the frosty herb garden, keeping the topiary between me and the servants' rooms. Rounded the front of the house and walked down Monk's Walk. East wind straight from the Steppes, was glad of Ayrs's sheep-skin. Heard arthritic poplars, nightjars in the fossilized woods, a crazed dog, feet on frozen gravel, rising pulse in my temples, some sorrow too, for myself, for the year. Passed the old lodge, took the Bruges road. Had hoped to hitch a lift on a milk-truck or cart, but there was nothing about. Stars were fading in the frosty pre-dawn. A few cottage candles were lit, glimpsed a fiery face in the smithy, but the road north was nobody's but mine.

So I thought, but the noise of an automobile was following me. Wasn't going to hide, so I stopped and faced it. Headlamps dazzled, the car slowed, the engine stalled, and a familiar voice shrieked at me: 'And where might *you* be creeping off to at such an ungodly hour?'

Mrs Dhondt, none other, wrapped up in a black sealskin coat. Had the Ayrses sent her out to capture the runaway slave? Confusedly, I garbled out, like a total idiot, 'Oh, there's been an accident!'

Cursed myself for this cul-de-sac of a lie, for clearly I was fit as a fiddle, alone, on foot, and with my valise and satchel. 'What terrible luck!' responded Mrs Dhondt, with martial gusto, filling in my blanks for me. 'Friend or family?'

I saw my lifeboat. 'Friend.'

'Bruno did warn Mr Ayrs against buying a Cowley for pre-cisely this reason, you know! Unreliable in a crisis. Silly Jocasta, why didn't she telephone me? Jump in, then! One of my Arabian mares gave birth to two glorious foals just an hour ago and all three are doing splendidly! I was on my way home but I'm far too excited to sleep, so I'll drive you to Ostende if you miss the connection at Bruges. I do so love the roads at this hour. So what is the nature of the accident? Buck up, now, Robert. Never assume the worst until you have all the facts to hand.'

Reached Bruges by dawn by virtue of a few plain untruths. Selected this superior hotel across from St Wenceslas' because its exterior looks like a book-end and its flower-boxes are well planted with miniature firs. My rooms overlook a quiet canal on the west side. Now I've finished this letter, will take forty winks until it's time to go to the belfry. E. might be there. If not, will lurk in an alleyway near her school and waylay her. If she fails to appear there, a call at the van de Veldes' may be necessary. If my name is fouled, shall disguise myself as a chimney-sweep. If I am rumbled, a long letter. If long letter is intercepted, another one is waiting in her dressing-table. I am a determined man.

Sincerely,
R.F.

P.S. – Thanks for your anxious letter dated November 5th, but why the clucking Mother Goose? Yes, of *course* I'm fine – apart from the consequences of described contretemps with V.A. Am more than fine, to tell the truth. My mind is capable of any creative task it can conceive. Composing the best work of my life; of all lives. Have money in my pocket-book and more in the 1st Bank of Belgium. Reminds me. If Otto Jansch won't budge from thirty guineas for the Münthe pair, tell him to skin his mother and roll her in salt. See what the Russian on Greek Street'll cough up.

P.P.S. – One last serendipitous discovery. Back at Zedelghem, whilst packing my valise, checked nothing had rolled under the bed. Found ½ a ripped-in-two volume wedged under one of the legs by a long-since-departed guest to stop the bed wobbling. Prussian officer, maybe, or Debussy, who knows? Thought nothing of it until a minute later, when the title on the spine registered. Grimy job, but I lifted the bed up and extracted the bound pages. Sure enough: – 'The Pacific Journal of Adam Ewing.' From the interrupted page to the end of the 1st volume. Would you believe it? Slipped the ½-book into my valise. Will finish gobbling it down v. soon. Happy, dying Ewing, who never saw the unspeakable forms waiting around history's corner.

— ◆ —

Le Royal Hôtel, Bruges.
Near the endth – xi – 1931.

Sixsmith,
Working nights on *Cloud Atlas Sextet* until I drop, quite literally, no other way to get off to sleep. My head is a Roman Candle of invention. Lifetime's music, arriving all at once. Boundaries between noise and sound are conventions, I see now. All boundaries are conventions, national ones too. One may transcend any convention, if only one can first conceive of doing so. Take this island, midstream between timbre and rhythm, not down in any book of theory, but it's here! Hear the instruments in my head, perfect clarity, anything I wish for. When it's finished, there'll be nothing left in me, I know, but the King's Shilling I hold in my sweaty palm is the Philosopher's Stone! A man like Ayrs spends his allotted portion in dribs and drabs over a dragged-out lifetime. Not I. Heard nothing from V.A. or that adulterous, rubbery, melodramatic wife of his. Suppose they believe I ran home to England. Last night dreamt I fell from the Imperial Western, clutching my drainpipe. Violin note, misplayed, hideously – that's my sextet's final note.

Am perfectly well. Wish I could make you see this brightness. Prophets went blind if they saw Jehovah. Not deaf, but blind, you appreciate the significance. Could still hear him. Talk to myself all day long. Did it absently at first, the human voice soothes me so, but now it takes real effort to stop, so I let it run and run. Take walks when not composing. Could write a Michelin guide to Bruges now, had I but space enough, and time. Round the poorer quarters, not just the groves of the wealthy. Behind a grubby window a grandmother was arranging St Paulia in a bowl. Tapped on the pane and asked her to fall in love with me. Pursed her lips, don't think she spoke French, but I tried again. Cannonball-headed fellow with absolutely no chin appeared at the window, spat out brimstone curses on me and my house.

Eva. Every day I've climbed up the belfry chanting a lucky chant at one syllable per beat, 'To – day – to – day – let – her – be – here – to – day – to – day.' Not yet, though I wait until it's dark. Golden days, bronze days, iron days, watery days, foggy days. Turkish Delight sunsets. Nights drawing in, frosty nip in the air. Eva is guarded in a schoolroom down on Earth, chewing her pencil, dreaming of being with me, I know it, me, looking down from amongst exfoliating apostles, dreaming of being with her. Her damn parents must have found the note in her dressing-table. Wish I'd gone about things more cunningly. Wish I'd shot the damn fraudster when I had the chance. Ayrs'll never find a replacement for Frobisher – *Eternal Recurrence*'ll die with him. Those van de Veldes must have intercepted my second letter to Eva in Bruges. Tried to bluff my way into her school but got chased out by a pair of liveried pigs with whistles and sticks. Followed E. back from school, but the curtains of day are undrawn so briefly, cold and darkling when she leaves her school, cowled in her brown cape, orbited by v.d.V.s, chaperones and class-mates. Peered out between my cap and muffler, waiting for her heart to sense me. Not funny.

Today I brushed Eva's cape as I passed in drizzle, in crowd. E. didn't notice me. As I near her a tonic pedal rises in volume, from groin, resounding in my chest cavity, up to somewhere behind my eyes.

Why so nervous? Tomorrow maybe, yes, tomorrow, for certain. Nothing to be afraid of. She has told me she loves me. Soon, soon.

Sincerely,
R.F.

— ◆ —

Le Royal Hôtel.
25th – xi – 1931.

Sixsmith,
Streaming nose and bad cough since Sunday. Matches my cuts and bruises. Hardly stepped outside, nor do I wish to. Freezing fog crawls out of the canals, it stifles one's lungs and chills one's veins. Send me an india-rubber hot-water bottle, would you? Only earthenware ones here.

Hotel manager dropped by earlier. An earnest penguin with no bottom at all. One presumes it is his patent-leather shoes that squeak so as he walks, but one never knows in the Low Countries. His real reason for calling was to ensure I *am* a wealthy student of architecture, not some dubious Cad the Lad who'll skip town without settling his account. Anyway, promised to show the colour of my money at Reception tomorrow, so a bank visit is unavoidable. This cheered the fellow up, and he hoped my studies were proceeding well. Excellently, I assured him. I don't say I'm a composer because I can no longer face the Moronic Inquisition: 'What kind of music do you write?'; 'Oh, should I have heard of you?'; 'Where do you get your ideas from?'

Not in the mood for letter-writing, after all, not after my recent encounter with E. Lamp-lighter is making his rounds. If I could turn back the clock, Sixsmith. Would that I could.

Next day.

Improved. Eva. Ah. I'd laugh, if it didn't hurt quite so much. Can't remember where I was when last I wrote to you. Time is an *allegrissimo* blur since my Night of Epiphany. Well, it had become pretty clear I wasn't going to be able to catch E. on her own. She never appeared at the belfry at 4 p.m. That my communiqués were being intercepted was the only explanation that occurred to me. (Don't know if V.A. kept his promise to poison my name back in England; maybe you've heard something? Don't overly care, but one would like to know.) ½ hoped J. might track me down to this hotel – in my second letter I wrote my whereabouts. Would even sleep with her if it could open a channel to Eva. Reminded myself I'd not committed any crime – *va bene*, hare(*sic*)splitter, not a crime against the Crommelynck-Ayrs that they know of – and it seems that J. was once again playing under her husband's baton. Probably always was. So I had no choice but to pay a call to the van de Veldes' town-house.

Crossed dear old Minnewater Park in twilit sleet. Cold as the Urals. Ayrs's Luger had wanted to come along, so I'd buttoned my steel friend into my sheepskin's cavernous pocket. Jowly prostitutes smoked in the bandstand. Was not tempted for a moment – only the desperate venture out in this weather. Ayrs's ravages has put me off 'em, possibly for life. Outside the v.d.V. house cabriolets queued, horses snorted cold air, drivers huddled in long coats, smoking, stamping to keep warm. Windows were lit by vanilla lamps, fluttery débutantes, champagne flutes, fizzing chandeliers. A major social event was under way. Perfect, I thought. Camouflage, you see. A happy couple climbed the steps with care, the door opened – Sesame – a gavotte escaped into the frozen air. Followed 'em up the salt-strewn steps, and rapped the golden knocker, trying to remain calm.

The coat-tailed Cerberus recognized me – a surprised butler is never good news. 'Je suis désolé, Monsieur, mais votre nom ne figure pas sur la liste des invités.' Boot already in door. Guest lists, I warned him, don't apply to established family friends. The man smiled an apology – I was dealing with a professional. Sequined gaggle of mantled goslings streamed past me just then and the butler unwisely let 'em pass me. Was ½-way down the glittering hallway before the white-gloved hand clamped my shoulder.

Snapped, must admit, in a most undignified manner – it's been an abysmal time, shan't deny it – and roared Eva's name, over and over, like a spoilt child in a temper tantrum, until the dance music collapsed and the hallway and stairs were packed with shocked revellers. Only the trombonist played on. That's trombonists for you. A beehive of consternation in all major languages opened up and swarmed forth. Through the ominous buzzing came Eva, in an electric blue ballgown, a rivière of green pearls. Think I shouted, 'Why have you been avoiding me?' or something equally dignified.

E. did not glide through the air into my arms, melt into my embrace, and caress me with words of love. Her 1st Movement was Disgust: 'What's *happened* to you, Frobisher?' A mirror hung in the hallway; looked to see what she meant. I'd let myself go, but I become a lax shaver when composing, as you know. 2nd Movement, Surprise: 'Madame Dhondt said you'd gone back to England.' Things went from worse to worst. 3rd Movement, Anger: 'How *dare* you show your face here, after . . . everything?' Her parents had told her nothing but lies about me, I assured her. Why else had they intercepted my letters to her? She had received both my letters, she said, but shredded them 'out of pity'. Now rather shaken. Demanded to speak with her *tête-à-tête*. We had so much to sort out. A superficially handsome young fellow had his arm round her, and he barred my way and told me something in proprietorial Flemish. I told him in French he was pawing the girl I loved, adding that the War should have taught Belgians when to duck in the face of superior force. Eva caught his right arm, cupped his fist in both her hands. An intimate act, I see now. Caught her gallant's name, muttered by a friend warning him not to belt me one: Grigoire. Bubble of jealousy deep in my gut now had a name. I asked of Eva who her fearsome lap-dog was. 'My fiancé,' she said, calmly, 'and he's not Belgian, he's Swiss.'

Your *what*? Bubble popped, veins poisoned.

'I *told* you about him, that afternoon on the belfry! Why I came back from Switzerland, so much happier . . . I *told* you, but then you subjected me to those . . . humiliating letters.' No slip of her tongue or my pen. *Grigoire the Fiancé.* All those cannibals, feasting on my dignity. There we were. My im- passioned love? No such thing. Never was. That unseen trom- bonist was now monkeying about with 'Ode to Joy'. Roared at him with elemental violence – damaged my throat – to play it in the key Beethoven intended or not play it at all. Asked, 'Swiss? Why's he acting so aggressively, then?' Trombonist began a flatulent Beethoven's 5th also in wrong key. E.'s voice was one degree off absolute zero. 'I think you're ill, Robert. You should leave now.' Grigoire the Swiss Fiancé and the butler each clamped one of my unresisting shoulders and marched me back- wards to the doorway through the herd. High, high above, I glimpsed two small v.d.V.s in their nightcaps peering down the stairwell through the landing railings like nightcapped gar- goylettes. Winked at 'em.

Gleam of triumph in my rival's lovely long-lashed eyes and his accented 'Go home to England!' ignited Frobisher the Rotter, sorry to say. Just I was flung over the threshold, I embraced Grigoire in a rugger grip, determined that smug cockatoo was coming with me. Birds-of-paradise in the hallway shrieked, baboons roared. Down the steps we bounced, no, we thudded, slipped, swore, thumped and tore. Grigoire cried in alarm, then pain – the very medicine prescribed by Dr Vengeance! Stone steps and icy pavements bruised my own flesh as black as his, banged my elbows and hips just as hard, but at least mine was not the only ruined evening in Bruges and I yelled, kicking his ribs once for each word, before ½ running ½ hobbling off on my whacked ankle, 'Love hurts!'

Am in better spirits now. Hardly remember what E. even

looks like. Once, her face was burned into my idiotic eyes, saw her everywhere, in everyone. Grigoire has exquisite fingers, long and pliant. Franz Schubert maimed his hands by tying weights to 'em. He thought it'd increase his range at the keyboard. Majestic string quartets but what a bloody fool! Grigoire on the other hand possesses perfect hands by birth, but probably doesn't know a crotchet from crochet.

Six or seven days later.

Forgot about this unfinished letter, well, ½ forgot, it got buried under my piano MS & too busy composing to fish it out. Icy seasonal weather. Half the clocks in Bruges have frozen fast. So, now you know about Eva. The affair hollowed me out, but what, pray, resounds in hollows? Music, Sixsmith, let there be Music and behold. During a six-hour fireside bath last night I scored 102 bars of a funereal march based on 'Ode to Joy' for my clarinettist.

Another visitor this morning; haven't been this popular since that notorious day at the Derby. Woken at noon by a friendly but firm knock-knock-knock. Called out, 'Who's there?'

'Verplancke.'

Couldn't place the name, but when I opened the door, there stood my musical policeman, the one who had lent me the bicycle in my old life. 'May I come in? Je pensais vous rendre une visite de courtoisie.'

'Most certainly,' I replied, adding rather wittily, 'Voilà qui est bien courtois, pour un policier.' Cleared him an armchair & offered to ring for tea, but my visitor declined. Couldn't quite conceal his surprise at the untidiness. Explained how I tip the maids to stay away. Can't abide having my MS touched. M. Verplancke nodded in sympathy, then wondered why a gentle-man might check into his hotel under a pseudonym? An eccen-tricity inherited from my father, I said, a notable in public life who prefers to keep his private one private. Keep my own vocation similarly hush-hush so I'm not put upon to tinkle the ivories during cocktail hour. Refusals cause offence. V. seemed

485

satisfied with my explanation. 'A luxurious home away from home, Le Royal.' He glanced around my sitting-room. 'I did not know amanuenses were so well paid.' Admitted what the tactful fellow doubtless already knew: Ayrs and I had parted company, adding I have my own independent income, which a mere 12 months ago would have been the truth. 'Ah, a bicycling million-aire?' He smiled. Tenacious, isn't he? Not quite a millionaire, I smiled back, but, providentially, of sufficient consequence to afford Le Royal.

He got to the point at last. 'You've made an influential enemy during your short residency in our city, M. Frobisher. A certain manufacturer, I think we both know who, made a complaint to my superior about an incident a few nights ago. His secretary – a very fine harpsichordist in our little group, in fact – recog-nized your name, and deflected the complaint to my desk. So here I am.' Took pains to assure him it was all an absurd misunderstanding over a young lady's affections. Charming fel-low nodded. 'I know, I know. *Cherchez la femme*. In youth, one's heart plays *più fortissimo* than the head. Our difficulty is, the young man's father is banker for several of our city elders, and is making unpleasant noises about charging you with battery and assault.'

Thanked M. Verplancke for his warning and tact, and promised to keep a lower profile from now on. Alas, not so simple. 'Monsieur Frobisher, don't you find our city intolerably cold in winter? Don't you think Mediterranean climes might better inspire your Muse?'

Asked if the banker's anger might be appeased if I gave my word to leave Bruges within seven days, after my sextet's final revision. V. thought yes, such an understanding should defuse the situation. So I gave my word as a gentleman to make the necessary arrangements.

Business concluded, V. asked if he might have a preview of my sextet. Showed him the clarinet cadenza. He was unnerved at first by its spectral and structural peculiarities, but spent a further hour asking perceptive questions about my semi-invented notation and the singular harmonics of the piece. As we shook hands, he gave me his card, urged me to post a published copy of the score for his ensemble, and expressed regret that his public persona had had to impinge upon his private one. Was sorry to see him go. Writing is such a damn lonely sickness.

So you see, I must put my final days to good account. Don't worry about me, Sixsmith, I'm quite well, and far too busy for melancholia! There's a sailor's tavern at the end of the street where I could find companionship if I chose (one catches salty boys going in and out at any hour) but only music matters to me now. Music clatters, music swells, music tosses.

Sincerely,
R.F.

— ◆ —

Hôtel Memling, Bruges.
Quarter past four in the morning, 12th – xii – 1931.

Sixsmith,
Shot myself through the roof of my mouth at 5 a.m. this morning with V.A.'s Luger. But I saw you, my dear, dear fellow! How touched I am that you care so much! On the belfry's look-out, yesterday, at sunset. Sheerest fluke you didn't see me 1st. Had got to that last flight of stairs, when I saw a man in profile leaning on the balcony, gazing at the sea – recognized your natty Gaberdine coat, your one and only Trilby. One more step up, you'd have seen me crouching in the shadows. You strolled to the north side – one turn my way, I would have been rumbled. Watched you for as long as I dared – a minute? – before pulling back and hotfooting it down to Earth. Don't be cross. Thank you *ever* so for trying to find me. Did you come on the *Kentish Queen*?

Questions rather pointless now, aren't they?

Wasn't the sheerest fluke I saw you 1st, not really. World's a shadow-theatre, an opera, and such things writ large in its libretto. Don't be too cross at my role. You couldn't understand, no matter how much I explained. You're a brilliant physicist, your Rutherford chap *et al.* agree you've got a brilliant future, quite sure they're right. But in some fundamentals you're a dunce. The healthy can't understand the emptied, the broken. You'd try to list all the reasons for living, but I left 'em behind at Victoria Station back in early summer. Reason I crept back down from the belvedere was that I can't have you blaming yourself for failing to dissuade me. You may anyway but don't, Sixsmith, don't be such an ass.

Likewise, hope you weren't too disappointed to find me gone from Le Royal. The manager got wind of M. Verplancke's visit. Obliged to ask me to leave, he said, on account of heavy bookings. Piffle, but I took the fig-leaf. Frobisher the Stinker wanted a tantrum, but Frobisher the Composer wanted peace and quiet to finish my sextet. Paid in full – bang went the last Jansch money – and packed my valise. Wandered crooked alleys and crossed icy canals before coming across this deserted-looking caravanserai. Reception a rarely-manned nook under the stairs. Only ornament in my room a monstrous Laughing Cavalier too ugly to steal and sell. From my filthy window, one sees the very same dilapidated old windmill on whose steps I napped on my first morning in Bruges. The very same. Fancy that. Around we go.

Knew I'd never see my 25th birthday. Am early for once. The lovelorn, the cry-for-helpers, all mawkish tragedians who give suicide a bad name are the idiots who rush it, like amateur conductors. A true suicide is a paced, disciplined certainty. People pontificate, 'Suicide is Selfishness.' Career churchmen like Pater go a step further and call it a cowardly assault on the living. Oafs argue this specious line for varying reasons: to evade fingers of blame; to impress one's audience with one's mental fibre; to vent anger; or just because one lacks the necessary suffering to sympathize. Cowardice is nothing to do with it –

suicide takes considerable courage. Japanese have the right idea. No, what's *selfish* is to demand another to endure an intolerable existence, just to spare families, friends and enemies a bit of soul-searching. The only selfishness lies in ruining strangers' days by forcing 'em to witness a grotesqueness. So I'll make a thick turban from several towels to muffle the shot and soak up the blood, and do it in the bath-tub, so it shouldn't stain any carpets. Last night I left a letter under the manager's day-office door – he'll find it at 8 a.m. tomorrow – informing him of the change in my existential status, so with luck an innocent chambermaid will be spared an unpleasant surprise. See, I *do* think of the little people.

Don't let 'em say I killed myself for love, Sixsmith, that would be too ridiculous. Was infatuated by Eva Crommelynck for a blink of an eye, but we both know in our hearts who is the true love of my life.

Along with this letter and the rest of the Ewing book, I've made arrangements for a folder containing my completed manuscript to find you at Le Royal. Use the Jansch money to defray publishing costs, send copies to everyone on the enclosed list. Don't let my family get hold of either of the originals, whatever you do. Pater'll sigh, 'It's no *Eroica*, is it?' and stuff it into a drawer; but it's an incomparable creation. Echoes of Scriabin's *White Mass*, Stravinsky's lost footprints, chromatics of the more lunar Debussy, but truth is I don't know where it came from. Waking dream. Will never write anything one hundredth as good. Wish I were being immodest, but I'm not. *Cloud Atlas Sextet* holds my life, *is* my life, now I'm a spent firework; but at least I've been a firework.

People are obscenities. Would rather be music than be a mass of tubes squeezing semi-solids around itself for a few decades before becoming so dribblesome it'll no longer function.

Luger here. Thirteen minutes to go. Feel trepidation, naturally, but my love of this coda is stronger. An electrical thrill that, like Adrian, I *know* I am to die. Pride, that I shall see it through. Certainties. Strip back the beliefs pasted on by governesses, schools and states, you find indelible truths at one's core. Rome'll decline and fall again, Cortazar'll sail again and, later, Ewing will too, Adrian'll be blown to pieces again, you and I'll sleep under Corsican stars again, I'll come to Bruges again, fall in and out of love with Eva again, you'll read this letter again, the Sun'll grow cold again. Nietzsche's gramophone record. When it ends, the Old One plays it again, for an eternity of eternities.

Time cannot permeate this sabbatical. We do not stay dead long. Once my Luger lets me go, my birth, next time around, will be upon me in a heartbeat. In thirteen years from now we'll meet again at Gresham, ten years later I'll be back in this same room, holding this same gun, composing this same letter, my resolution as perfect as my many-headed sextet. Such elegant certainties comfort me.

Sunt lacrimæ rerum.
R.F.

— ◆ —

The Pacific Journal of
Adam Ewing

during our shared *mal de mer* on the Tasman Sea, I stand amazed at how that sprite lad, aglow with excitement at his maiden voyage & so eager to please, has become this sullen youth in only six weeks. His luminous beauty is chipped away, revealing the timber-muscled seaman he shall become. Already he looks rather given to rum & water. Henry says this 'sloughing off of his cocoon' is inevitable, *bon gré mal gré*, & I suppose he is right. Those smatterings of education & sensibility Rafael received from his patron, Mrs Fry of Brisbane, serve a cabin-boy ill in the harum-scarum world of the fo'c'sle. How I wish *I* could help him! Were it not for the intervention of my Mr & Mrs Channing, my own fate may well have been of a piece with Raf's. I asked Finbar if he thought the boy was 'fitting in well'. Finbar's Delphic reply, 'Fitting *what* in well, Mr Ewing?' left the galley cackling but myself quite in the dark.

Saturday, 7th December —

Petrels are aloft, sooty terns afloat & Mother Carey's Chickens roost on the rigging. Fish similar to borettoes pursued fish similar to sprats. As Henry & I ate supper, a blizzard of purplish moths seemed to issue from the cracks in the moon, smothering lanterns, faces, food & every surface in a twitching sheet of wings. To confirm these portents of nearby islands, the man at the lead shouted a depth of only eighteen fathoms. Mr Boerhaave ordered the anchor to be weighed lest we drift on to a reef in the night.

The whites of my eyes have a lemon-yellow aspect & their rims are reddened & sore. Henry assures me this symptom is welcome, but has obliged my request for an increased dosage of vermicide.

Sunday, 8th December —

Sabbath not being observed on *Prophetess*, this morning Henry & I decided to conduct a short Bible Reading in his cabin in the 'low-church' style of Ocean Bay's congregation, 'astraddle' the fore-noon & morning watches so both starboard & port shifts might join us. I am sorry to write, no man from either shift braved the first mate's displeasure by attending, but we shall persist in our efforts undiscouraged. Rafael was up the mast-head & interrupted our prayers with a treble-cry of 'Land! a-hoyyyyyy!'

We ended our worship early & braved dousings of sea-spray to watch land emerge from the rocking horizon. 'Raiatea,' Mr Roderick told us, 'of the Societies.' (Once again *Prophetess*'s keel crosses the *Endeavour*'s. Cpt. Cook himself named the group.) I asked if we would be putting ashore. Mr Roderick affirmed, 'The captain wants to pay one of the Missions a call.' The Societies loomed larger & after three weeks of oceanic greys & blazing blues, our eyes rejoiced at the moss-drenched mountain faces, aglint with cataracts, daubed with cacophonous jungle. *Prophetess* cleared fifteen fathoms, yet so clear was the water, iridescent corals were visible. I speculated with Henry upon how we might prevail upon Cpt. Molyneux for permission to go ashore, when the very same appeared from the deck-house, his beard trimmed & forelock oiled. Far from ignoring us, as is his custom, he walked over to us with a smile as friendly as a cut-purse's. 'Mr Ewing, Dr Goose, would you care to accompany the first mate & I ashore on yonder isle this morning? A settlement of Methodists lies in a bay on the northern coast, "Nazareth" they've named it. Gentlemen of enquiring minds may find the place diverting.' Henry accepted with enthusiasm, & I did not with-hold my consent, though I mistrusted the old raccoon's motivations. 'Settled,' the captain pronounced.

An hour later *Prophetess* kedged into Bethlehem Bay, a black-sand cove sheltered from trade-winds by Cape Nazareth's crook. Ashore was a stratum of cruder thatched dwellings erected on 'stilts' near the water-line, occupied (I correctly assumed) by the baptized Indians. Above these were a dozen timber buildings crafted by civilized hands, & higher still, below the hill's crown, stood a proud church denoted by a white cruciform. The larger of the skiffs was lowered for our benefit. Its four rowers were Guernsey, Bentnail & a pair of garter-snakes. Mr Boerhaave donned a hat & waist-coat more suitable for a Manhattan salon than a haul across the surf. We beached with no mishap worse than a good soak, but our sole emissary from the colonists was a Polynesian dog panting under golden jasmine & vermilion trumpet-flowers. The shore-line huts & 'Main Street' winding up to the church were devoid of human life. 'Twenty men, twenty muskets,' commented Mr Boerhaave, 'and the place'd be ours by dinner-time. Makes you think, eh, sir?' Cpt. Molyneux instructed the rowers to wait in the shade while we 'Call on the King in his Counting House'. My suspicion that the captain's new graces were skin-deep was confirmed when he found the trading store boarded up & he vented a fanged oath. 'Mayhap,' speculated the Dutchman, 'the niggers unconverted themselves & ate their pastors for pudding?'

A bell rang from the church tower & the captain slapped his fore-head. 'D— my eyes, what am I thinking? It's the Sabbath, by G— & these holy s—s'll be a-braying in their rickety church!' We wound our way up the steep hill at a crawl, our party slowed by Cpt. Molyneux's gout. (I feel a loamy breathlessness when I exert myself. Recalling my vigour on the Chathams, I am worried at how severely the Parasite taxes my constitution.) We reached Nazareth's house of worship just as the congregation was emerging.

The captain removed his hat, boomed a hearty, 'Greetings! Jonathon Molyneux, captain of the *Prophetess*.' He indicated our vessel in the bay with a sweep of his hand. The Nazarenes were less effusive, the men awarding us wary nods, their wives & daughters hiding behind fans. Cries of 'Fetch Preacher Horrox!' echoed into the church recesses as its native occupants now poured out to see the visitors. Upward of sixty adult men &

women I counted, of whom around a third were White, garbed in their Sunday 'Best' (as could be managed two weeks' voyage from the nearest haberdashery). The Blacks watched us with bare curiosity. The native women were decently clothed but more than a few were blighted with goitre. Boys protecting their fair-skinned mistresses from the sun's fierceness with parasols of palm leaves grinned a little. A privileged 'platoon' of Polynesians wore a natty brown shoulder-band embroidered with a white crucifix as a uniform of sorts.

Now bounded out a cannonball of a man whose clerical garb declaimed his calling. 'I,' announced the patriarch, 'am Giles Horrox, preacher of Bethlehem Bay & representative of the London Missionary Society on Raiatea. State your business, sirs, be quick about it.'

Cpt. Molyneux now extended his introductions to include Mr Boerhaave 'of the Dutch Reformist Church', Dr Henry Goose, 'Physician of the London Gentry & late of the Feejee Mission', & Mr Adam Ewing, 'American Notary of Letters & Law'. (*Now* I stood wise to the rogue's game!) 'The name of Preacher Horrox & Bethlehem Bay is spoken of with respect amongst us peripatetic devout of the South Pacific. We had hoped to celebrate the Sabbath before your altar,' the captain looked ruefully at the church, 'but, alas, contrary winds delayed our arrival. At the very least, I pray your collection plate is not yet closed?'

Preacher Horrox scrutinised our captain. 'You command a godly ship, sir?'

Cpt. Molyneux glanced away in an imitation of humility. 'Neither as godly nor as unsinkable as your Church, sir, but yes, Mr Boerhaave & I do what we can for those souls in our care. 'Tis an unceasing struggle, I am sorry to say. Sailors revert to their wanton ways as soon as our backs are turned.'

'Oh, but, Captain,' spoke a lady in a lace collar, 'we have our recidivists in Nazareth too! You will pardon my husband's caution. Experience teaches us most vessels under so-called Christian flags bring us little but disease & drunkards. We must assume guilt until innocence is established.'

The captain bowed again. 'Madam, I can grant no pardon where no offence was given nor any taken.'

'Your prejudices against those "Visigoths of the Sea" are amply warranted, Mrs Horrox,' Mr Boerhaave entered the exchange, 'but *I* won't tolerate a drop of grog aboard our *Prophetess*, however the men holler! & oh, they holler, but I holler back, "The only spirit you need is the Holy Spirit!" & I holler it louder & longer!'

The charade was having its desired effect. Preacher Horrox presented his two daughters & three sons, all of whom were born here in Nazareth. (The girls might have stepped from a Ladies' School, but the boys were tanned as kanakas beneath their starched collars.) Loath as I was to be lassoed into the captain's masquerade, I was curious to learn more of this island theocracy & let the current of events carry me along. Soon our party proceeded to the Horroxes' parsonage, which dwelling would not shame any petty southern hemisphere consul. It included a large drawing room with glass windows & tulipwood furniture, a necessary room, two shacks for servants & a dining room where presently we were served with fresh vegetables & tender pork. The table stood with each leg immersed in a dish of water. Mrs Horrox explained, 'Ants, one bane of Bethlehem. Their drowned bodies must be emptied periodically, lest they build a causeway of themselves.'

I complimented the domicile. 'Preacher Horrox,' the lady of the house told us with pride, 'was trained as a carpenter in the shire of Gloucester. Most of Nazareth was built by his hands. The pagan mind is impressed with material display, you see. He thinks: – "How spick & span are Christians' houses! How dirty our hovels! How generous the White God is! How mean is ours!" In this way, one more convert is brought to the Lord.'

'If I could but live my life over,' opined Mr Boerhaave, without the slightest blush, 'I should chuse the missionary's selfless path. Preacher, we see here a well-established mission with roots struck deep, but how does one *begin* the work of conversion upon a benighted beach where no Christian foot ever trod?'

Preacher Horrox gazed beyond his interrogator to a future lecture-hall. 'Tenacity, sir, compassion & law. Fifteen years ago our reception in this bay was not so cordial as your own, sir. That anvil-shaped island you see to the west, thither? Borabora, the blacks call it, but "Sparta" is an apter name, so warlike were its warriors! On the beach of Bethlehem Cove we fought & some of us fell. Had our pistols not won that first week's battles, well, the Raiatea Mission should have remained a dream. But it was the will of the Lord that we light his beacon here & keep it burning. After a half-year we could bring over our womenfolk from Tahiti. I regret the Native deaths, but once the Indians saw how God protects his flock, why, even the Spartans were begging us to send preachers.'

Mrs Horrox took up the story. 'When the pox began its deadly work, the Polynesians needed succour, both spiritual & material. Our compassion then brought the heathen to the holy font. Now 'tis the turn of Holy Law to keep our flock from Temptation – & marauding seamen. Whalers, particularly, despise us for teaching the women chastity & modesty. Our men must keep our fire-arms well oiled.'

'Yet if shipwrecked,' noted the captain, 'I'll warrant those same spouters beg Fate to wash 'em up on beaches where those same "cursed missionaries" have brought the Gospels, do they not?'

Assent was indignant & universal.

Mrs Horrox answered my query about the enforcement of law & order in this lonesome outpost of Progress. 'Our Church Council – my husband & three wise elders – passes those laws we deem necessary, with guidance of prayer. Our Guards of Christ, certain natives who prove themselves faithful servants of the Church, enforce these laws in return for credit at my husband's store. Vigilance is vital, or by next week . . .' Mrs Horrox shuddered as apostasy's phantoms danced a *hula* on her grave.

The meal over, we adjourned to the parlour where a native boy served us cool tea in pleasing gourd-cups. Cpt. Molyneux asked, 'Sir, how does one fund a Mission as industrious as yours?'

Preacher Horrox felt the breeze change & scrutinized the captain afresh. 'Arrow-root starch & cocoa-nut oil defray costs, Captain. The blacks work on our plantation to pay for the school, Bible study & church. In a week, God will it, we shall have an abundant harvest of copra.'

I asked if the Indians worked of their own free will.

'Of course!' exclaimed Mrs Horrox. 'If they succumb to sloth, they know the Guards of Christ will punish them for it.'

I wished to ask about these punitive incentives, but Cpt. Molyneux snatched back the conversation. 'Your Missionary Society ship carries these perishable commodities back around the Horn to London?'

'Your conjecture is correct, Captain.'

'Have you considered, Preacher Horrox, how more secure your Mission's secular footing – & by extension its *spiritual* one – would be, if you had a reliable market closer to the Societies?'

The preacher told the serving boy to quit the room. 'I have considered this question at length, but where? Mexico's markets are small & prone to banditry, Cape Town is a marriage of corrupt excisemen & greedy Afrikaners. The South China Seas swarm with ruthless, saucy pirates. The Batavian Dutch bleed one dry. No offence, Mr Boerhaave.'

The captain indicated myself. 'Mr Ewing is a denizen of . . .' he paused to unveil his proposal '. . . San Francisco, California. You will know of its growth from a paltry town of seven hundred souls to a metropolis of . . . a quarter million? No census can keep count! Celestials, Chileans, Mexicans, Europeans, foreigners of all colours are flooding in by the day. An egg, Mr Ewing, kindly inform us how much is presently paid for an egg in San Francisco?'

'A dollar, so my wife wrote to me.'

'One Yankee dollar for a common egg.' (Cpt. Molyneux's smile is that of a mummified crocodile I once saw hanging in a Louisiana dry-goods store.) 'Surely, this gives a man of your acumen some pause for thought?'

Mrs Horrox was nobody's fool. 'All the gold will be mined out soon.'

'Aye, madam, but the hungry, clamouring, enriched city of San Francisco – only three weeks away by a trim schooner like my *Prophetess* – will remain & its destiny is clear as crystal. San Francisco shall become the London, the Rotterdam, & the New York of the Pacific Ocean.'

Our *capitán de la casa* picked his teeth with a bluefin bone. 'Do *you* believe, Mr Ewing, commodities grown in our plantations may fetch a fair price in your city' (how strange 'tis hearing our township so appelled!) 'both of the moment & after the gold-rush?'

My truthfulness was a card Cpt. Molyneux had played to his devious advantage, but I would not lie to spite him any more than I would to aid him. 'I do.'

Giles Horrox removed his clergyman's collar. 'Would you care to accompany me to my office, Jonathon? I am rather proud of its roof. I designed it myself to withstand the dreadful *typhoo*.'

'Is that so, Giles?' replied Cpt. Molyneux. 'Lead the way.'

Notwithstanding the name of Dr Henry Goose was unknown in Nazareth until this morning, once the wives of Bethlehem learned a famed English surgeon was ashore, they recalled all manner of ailments & beat a crowded path to the Parsonage. (So odd to be in the presence of the fairer sex again after so many days penned up with the uglier one!) My friend's generosity could not turn away a single caller, so Mrs Horrox's salon was commandeered as his consultation room & draped with linen to provide appropriate screens. Mr Boerhaave returned to the *Prophetess* to see about making more space in the hold.

I begged the Horroxes' leave to explore Bethlehem Bay, but its beach was unbearably hot & its sand-flies pestilential, so I retraced our steps up the 'Main Street' towards the church, whence issued the sound of psalmody. I intended to join in the afternoon worship. Not a soul, not a dog, not even a Native, stirred the Sabbath stillness. I peered into the dim church, & so thick was the smoke within, I feared, erroneously, the building was aflame! The singing was now over & substituted by choruses of coughing. Fifty dark backs faced me & I realized the air was thick with the smoke, not of fire nor incense but raw-cut tobacco! for every man jack of them was puffing on a pipe.

A rotund White stood in the pulpit sermonizing in that hybrid accent, 'Antipodean Cockney'. This shew of informal religiosity did not offend until the content of the 'sermon' became apparent. I quoth: 'So it came to pass, see, St Peter, aye, 'im 'oo Mistah Jesus called Sweeter Peter Piper, he cameth from Rome an' he taughteth them hooky-nosed Jews in Palestine what was what with the Old Baccy, an' this is what I'm teachin' you now, see.' Here he broke off to give guidance to an individual. 'Nah, Tarbaby, you're doing it all wrong, see, you load your baccy in the *fat* end, aye, that one, see, oh, J—s sneezed! how many times I told you, *this* is the *stem*, this is the d—d *bowl*! Do it like Mudfish next to you, nah, let me shew you!'

A sallow, stooping White leant against a cabinet (containing, I later verified, hundreds of Holy Bibles printed in Polynesian – I must request one as a souvenir ere our departure) watching the smoky proceedings. I made myself known to him in whispers so as not to distract the smokers from their sermon. The young man introduced himself as Wagstaff & explained the pulpit's occupant was 'The Head Master of the Nazareth Smoking School'.

I confessed, such an academy was unknown to me.

'An idea of Father Upward's, at the Tahitian Mission. You must understand, sir, your typical Polynesian spurns industry because he's got no reason to value money. "If I hungry," says he, "I go pick me some, or catch me some. If I cold, I tell woman, 'Weave!'" Idle hands, Mr Ewing, & we both know what work the Devil finds for them. But by instilling in the slothful so-an'-sos a gentle craving for this harmless leaf, we give him an incentive to earn money, so he can buy his baccy – not liquor, mind, just baccy – from the Mission trading-post. Ingenious, wouldn't you say?'

How could I disagree?

The light ebbs away. I hear children's voices, exotic avian octaves, the surf pounding the cove. Henry is grumbling at his cuff-links. Mrs Horrox, whose hospitality Henry & I are enjoying tonight, has sent her maid to inform us dinner is served.

Monday, 9th December —

A continuance of yesterday's narrative. After the smoking school was dismissed (several of the students were swaying & nauseous, but their teacher, an itinerant tobacco trader, assured us, 'They'll be hooked like pufferfish in no time!'), the back of the heat was broken, though Cape Nazareth still broiled in glowing sunshine. Mr Wagstaff strolled with me along the wooded arm of land shouldering northwards from Bethlehem Bay. The youngest son of a Gravesend curate, my guide had been drawn to the missionary's vocation since infancy. The Society, by arrangement with Preacher Horrox, sent him hither to wed a widow of Nazareth, Eliza, née Mapple, & be a father to her son, Daniel. He arrived on these shores last May.

What fortune, I declared, to dwell in such an Eden, but my pleasantry punctured the young man's spirits. 'So I believed in my first days, sir, but now I don't rightly know. I mean, Eden's a spick 'n' span place, but every living thing runs wild here, it bites & scratches so. A pagan brought to God is a soul saved, I know it, but the sun never stops *burning* & the waves & stones are always so bright, my eyes ache till dusk comes. Times are, I'd give anything for a North Sea fog. The place puts a straining on *our* souls, to be truthful, Mr Ewing. My wife's been here since she was a small girl, but that doesn't make it easier for her. You'd think the savages'd be grateful, I mean, we school them, heal them, bring employment & eternal life! Oh, they say "Please, sir," an' "Thank you, sir" prettily enough, but you feel *nothing*,' Wagstaff pounded his heart, 'here. Aye, *look* like Eden it might, but Raiatea is a fallen place, same as everywhere, aye, no snakes but the Devil plies his trade here as much as anywhere else. The ants! Ants get everywhere. In your food, your clothes, your nose, even. Until we convert these accursed ants, these islands'll never be truly ours.'

We arrived at his modest dwelling, crafted by his wife's first husband. Mr Wagstaff did not invite me in, but went inside to fetch a flask of water for our walk. I took a turn around the modest front garden, where a black gardener was hoeing. I asked what he was growing.

'David is dumb,' a woman called to me from the doorway dressed in a loosened, grubby pinafore. I am afraid I can only describe her appearance and manner as slovenly. 'You're the English doctor staying at the Horroxes'.'

I explained I was an American notary & asked if I might be addressing Mrs Wagstaff.

'My wedding banns and marriage lines say so, yes.'

I said Dr Goose was holding an *ad hoc* surgery at the Horroxes', if she wished to consult with him. I assured her of Henry's excellence as a physician.

'Excellent enough to spirit me away, restore the years I've wasted here, & set me up in London with a stipend of three hundred pounds per annum?'

Such a request was beyond my friend's powers, I admitted.

'Then your excellent physician can do nothing for me, sir.'

I heard giggles in the bushes beyond me, turned around, & saw a host of little Black boys (I was curious to note so many light-skinned issue of miscegenous unions). I ignored the children & turned back to see a White boy of twelve or thirteen, as grubby as his mother, slip by Mrs Wagstaff, who did not attempt to waylay him. Her son frolicked as *déshabillé* as his native playmates! 'Ho, there, young fellow,' I reprimanded, 'won't you get a sunstroke running about in that state?' The boy's blue eyes held a feral glint & his answer, barked in a Polynesian tongue, baffled me as much as it amused the pickaninnies, who flew off like a flock of greenfinches.

Mr Wagstaff followed in the boy's wake, much agitated.

'Daniel! Come back! *Daniel!* I know you hear me! I'll lash you! Do you hear? I'll lash you!' He turned back to his wife. '*Mrs* Wagstaff! Do you *want* your son to grow up a savage? At the very least make the boy wear clothes! Whatever will Mr Ewing be thinking?'

Mrs Wagstaff's contempt for her young husband, if bottled, could have been vended as rat-poison. 'Mr Ewing will think whatever Mr Ewing will think. Then, tomorrow, he will leave on his handsome schooner, taking his thinkings with him. Unlike you & I, *Mr* Wagstaff, who'll die here. Soon, I pray God.' She turned to me. 'My husband could not compleat his schooling, sir, so it is my sorry lot to explain the obvious, ten times a day.'

Averse to seeing Mr Wagstaff's humiliation at the hands of his wife, I gave a noncommittal bow & withdrew outside the fence. I heard male indignation trampled by female scorn & concentrated my attention on a nearby bird whose refrain, to my ears, sounded thus: – *Toby isn't telling, nooo . . . Toby isn't telling . . .*

My guide joined me, most visibly glum. 'Beg pardon, Mr Ewing, Mrs Wagstaff's nerves are fearful frayed today. She don't sleep much on account of the heat & flies.' I assured him the 'eternal afternoon' of the South Seas taxes the sturdiest physiologies. We walked under slimy fronds, along the tapering headland, noxious with fertility, & furry caterpillars, plump as my thumb, dropped from talons of exquisite heliconica.

The young man narrated how the Mission had assured Mr Wagstaff's family of his intended's impeccable breeding. Preacher Horrox had married them a day after his arrival in Nazareth, while the enchantment of the Tropics still dazzled his eyes. (Why Eliza Mapple had consented to such an arranged union remains uncertain: Henry speculates the latitude & clime 'unhinges' the weaker sex & renders them pliable.) Mr Wagstaff's bride's 'infirmities', true age & Daniel's obstreperous nature came to light scarcely after their signatures on the wedding documents had dried. The step-father had tried beating his new charge but this led to such 'wicked recriminations' from both mother & step-son that he knew not where to turn. Far from helping Mr Wagstaff, Preacher Horrox chastised him for a weakling & the truth is, nine days out of ten he is wretched as Job. (Whatever Mr Wagstaff's misfortunes, could any compare to a parasitic Worm gnawing his cerebral canals?)

Thinking to distract the brooding youth with matters more logistical, I asked why such an abundance of Bibles lay untouched (& read only by book-lice, to tell the truth) in the church. 'Preacher Horrox should by rights tell it but, briefly, the Matavia Bay Mission first translated the Lord's Word into Polynesian & native missionaries using those Bibles achieved so many conversions that Elder Whitlock – one of Nazareth's founders what's dead now – convinced the Mission to repeat the experiment here. He'd once been 'prenticed to a Highgate engraver, see. So with guns & tools the first missionaries brought a printing press, paper, bottles of ink, trays of type & reams of paper. Within ten days of founding Bethlehem Bay three thousand primers was printed for Mission schools, before they'd dug the gardens, even. Nazareth gospels came next & spread the Word from the Societies to the Cooks to Tonga. But now the press is rusted up, we've got thousands of Bibles begging for an owner & why?'

I could not guess.

'Not enough Indians. Ships bring disease-dust here, the Blacks breathe it in & they swell up sick & fall like spinney-tops. We teach the survivors about monogamy & marriage, but their unions aren't fruitful.' I found myself wondering how many months have passed since last Mr Wagstaff smiled. 'To kill what you'd cherish & cure,' he opined, 'that seems to be the way of things.'

The path ended down by the sea at a crumbling 'ingot' of black coral, twenty yards in length & in height two men. 'A *marae*, this is called,' Mr Wagstaff informed me. 'All over the South Seas you see 'em, I'm told.' We scrambled up & I had a fine view of the *Prophetess*, an easy 'dip' away for a lusty swimmer. (Finbar emptied a vat over the side & I spied Autua's black silhouette atop the mizzen, furling the fore-skysail-lifts.)

I enquired after the origins & purpose of the *marae* & Mr
Wagstaff obliged, with brevity, 'Just one generation ago, the
Indians did their screaming & bloodletting & sacrificing to their
false idols right on these stones where we're standing.' My
thoughts went back to the Banquet Beach on Chatham Isle. 'The
Christ Guards gives any Black who sets foot here now a hefty
flogging. Or would do. The native children don't even know the
names of the old idols no more. It's all rats' nests & rubble
now. That's what all beliefs turn to one day. Rats' nests &
rubble.'

Plumeria petals and scent enwrapped me.

My neighbour at the dinner table was Mrs Derbyshire, a widow
well into her sixth decade, as bitter & hard as green acorns. 'I
confess to a disrelish for Americans,' she told me. 'They killed
my treasured uncle Samuel, a colonel in His Majesty's Artillery,
in the War of 1812.' I gave my (unwanted) condolences, but
added that notwithstanding my own treasured father was killed
by Englishmen in the same conflict, some of my closest friends
were Britons. The doctor laughed too loudly & ejaculated,
'Hurrah, Ewing!'

Mrs Horrox seized the rudder of conversation ere we ran on
to reefs. 'Your employers evince great faith in your talents, Mr
Ewing, to entrust you with business necessitating such a long
& arduous voyage.' I replied that, yes, I was a senior enough
notary to be entrusted with my present assignment, but a junior
enough scrivener to be obligated to accept the same. Knowing
clucks rewarded my humility.

After Preacher Horrox had said grace over the bowls of turtle-
soup & invoked God's blessing on his new business venture
with Cpt. Molyneux, he sermonized upon a much-beloved topic
as we ate. 'I have always unswervingly held, that God, in our
Civilizing World, manifests himself not in the Miracles of the
Biblical Age, but in Progress. It is Progress that leads Humanity
up the ladder towards the God-head. No Jacob's Ladder this,
no, but rather "Civilization's Ladder", if you will. Highest of

all the races on this ladder stands the Anglo-Saxon. The Latins are a rung or two below. Lower still are Asiatics – a hardworking race, none can deny, yet lacking our Aryan bravery. Sinologists insist they once aspired to greatness, but where is your yellow-hued Shakespeare, eh, or your almond-eyed da Vinci? Point made, point taken. Lower down, we have the Negro. Good-tempered ones may be trained to work profitably, though a rumbunctious one is the devil incarnate! The American Indian, too, is capable of useful chores on the Californian *barrios*, is that not so, Mr Ewing?'

I said 'tis so.

'Now, our Polynesian. The visitor to Tahiti, O-hawaii, or Bethlehem for that matter, will concur that the Pacific Islander may, with careful instruction, acquire the "A–B–C" of literacy, numeracy & piety, thereby ascending past the Negroes to rival Asiatics in industriousness.'

Henry interrupted to note that the Maori have risen to the 'D–E–F' of mercantilism, diplomacy & colonialism.

'Proves my point. Last, lowest & least come those "Irreclaimable Races", the Australian Aboriginals, Patagonians, various African peoples, &c., just one rung up from the great apes & so obdurate to Progress that, like mastadons & mammoths, I am afraid a speedy "knocking off the ladder" – after their cousins, the Guanches, Canary Islanders & Tasmanians – is the kindest prospect.'

'You mean,' Cpt. Molyneux finished his soup, 'extinction?'

'I do, Captain, I do. Nature's Law & Progress move as one. Our own century shall witness humanity's tribes fulfil those prophecies writ in their racial traits. The superior shall relegate the overpopulous savages to their natural numbers. Unpleasant scenes may ensue, but men of intellectual courage must not flinch. A glorious order shall follow, when all races shall know &, aye, embrace, their place in God's ladder of civilization. Bethlehem Bay offers a glimpse of the coming dawn.'

'Amen to that, Preacher,' replied Cpt. Molyneux. One Mr Gosling (fiancé of Preacher Horrox's eldest daughter) wrung his hands in oleaginous admiration. 'If I dare be so bold, sir, it strikes me as almost . . . yes, a *deprivation* to let your theorem go unpublished, sir. "The Horrox Ladder of Civilization" would set the Royal Society alight!'

Preacher Horrox said, 'No, Mr Gosling, my work is here. The Pacific must find itself another Descartes, another Cuvier.'

'Wise of you, Preacher,' Henry clapped a flying insect & examined its remains, 'to keep such thoughts to yourself.'

Our host could not conceal his irritation. 'How so?'

'Why, under scrutiny it is obvious a "theorem" is redundant when a simple law suffices.'

'What law would that be, sir?'

'The first of "Goose's Two Laws of Survival". It runs thus, "The Weak are Meat the Strong do Eat."'

'But your "simple law" is blind to the fundamental mystery, "Why do white races hold dominion over the world?"'

Henry chuckled & loaded an imaginary musket, aimed down its barrel, narrowed his eye, then startled the company with a 'Bang! Bang! Bang! See? Got him before he blew his blow-pipe!'

Mrs Derbyshire uttered a dismayed 'Oh!'

Henry shrugged. 'Where is the fundamental mystery?'

Preacher Horrox had lost his good humour. 'Your implication is that white races rule the globe not by divine grace but by the musket? But such an assertion is merely the *same* mystery dressed up in borrowed clothes! How is it that the musket came to the white man & not, say, the Esquimeau or the Pygmy, if not by august will of the Almighty?'

Henry obliged. 'Our weaponry was not dropped on to our laps one morning. It is not *manna* from Sinai's skies. Since Agincourt, the white man has refined & evolved the gunpowder sciences until our modern armies may field muskets by the tens of thousands! "Aha!" you will ask, yes, "But why us Aryans? Why not the Unipeds of Ur or the Mandrakes of Mauritius?" Because, Preacher, of all the world's races, our love – or rather our *rapacity* – for treasure, gold, spices & dominion, oh, most of all, sweet dominion, is the keenest, the hungriest, the most unscrupulous! This rapacity, yes, powers our Progress; for ends infernal or divine I know not. Nor do you know, sir. Nor do I overly care. I feel only gratitude that my Maker cast me on the winning side.'

Henry's forthrightness was misconstrued as incivility & Preacher Horrox, the Napoleon of his equatorial Elba, was pink-ening with indignation. I complimented our hostess's soup (though in truth my craving for vermicide makes it difficult to ingest any but the plainest fare) & asked if the turtles were caught on nearby beaches, or imported from afar.

Later, lying abed in the muggy darkness, eavesdropped by geckos, Henry confided that the day's surgery had been 'a parade of hysterical sun-baked women who need no medicine but hosiers, milliners, bonnet-makers, perfumeries & sundry trappings of their sex'! His 'consultations', he elaborated, were one part medicine, nine parts tittle-tattle. 'They swear their husbands are tupping the native women & live in mortal fear they'll catch "something". Handkerchiefs aired in rotation.'

His confidences made me uneasy & I ventured that Henry might practise a little reserve when disagreeing with our host. 'Dearest Adam, I *was* practising reserve, & more than a little! I longed to shout *this* at the old fool: – "Why tinker with the plain truth that we hurry the darker races to their graves in order to take their land & its riches? Wolves don't sit in their caves, concocting crapulous theories of race to justify devouring a flock of sheep! 'Intellectual courage'? True 'intellectual courage' is to dispense with these fig-leaves & admit all peoples are predatory, but white predators, with our deadly duet of disease-dust & fire-arms, are examplars of predacity *par excellence*, & what of it?"'

It upsets me that a dedicated healer & gentle Christian can succumb to such cynicism. I asked to hear Goose's Second Law of Survival. Henry grinned in the dark & cleared his throat, 'The second law of survival states that there *is* no second law. Eat or be eaten. That's it.' He began snoring soon after, but my

Worm kept me awake until the stars began weakening. Geckos fed & padded softly over my sheet.

Dawn was sweating & scarlet as passionfruit. Male & female Natives alike drudged up 'Main Street' to the church plantations atop the hill, where they worked until the afternoon heat was intolerable. Before the skiff came to take Henry & me back to *Prophetess*, I went to watch the workers plucking weeds from the copra. Peradventure it fell to young Mr Wagstaff to be their overseer this morning & he had a native boy bring us cocoa-nut milk. I withheld from asking after his family & he did not mention them. He carries a whip, 'but I rarely employ it myself, that's what the Guard of Christ the King are for. I just watch the watchers.'

Three of these dignitaries watched their fellows, leading hymns ('land-shanties') & reprimanding slackers. Mr Wagstaff was less inclined to conversation than yesterday & let my pleasantries lapse into silence broken only by sounds of the jungle & labourers. 'You're thinking, aren't you, that we've made slaves out of free peoples?'

I avoided the question by saying Mr Horrox had explained their labours paid for the benefits of Progress brought by the Mission. Mr Wagstaff did not hear me. 'There exists a tribe of ants, called the slave-maker. These insects raid the colonies of common ants, steal eggs back to their own nests, & after they hatch, why, the stolen slaves become workers of the greater empire, & never even dream they were once stolen. Now if you ask me, Lord Jehovah crafted these ants as a model, Mr Ewing.' Mr Wagstaff's gaze was gravid with the ancient future. 'For them with the eyes to see it.'

People of shifting character unnerve me & Mr Wagstaff was one such. I made my excuses & proceeded to my next port of call, viz., the schoolroom. Here, infant Nazarenes of both hues study Scripture, arithmetic and their A–B–Cs. Mrs Derbyshire teaches the boys & Mrs Horrox the girls. In the afternoon the white children have an additional three hours' tutelage in a curriculum appropriate to their station (though Daniel Wagstaff for one appears immune to his educators' wiles) while their darker playmates join their parents in the fields before the daily vespers.

A short revue was staged in my honour. Ten girls, five Whites, five black, recited a Holy Commandment apiece. Then I was treated to 'O! Home Where Thou Art Loved the Best', accompanied by Mrs Horrox on an upright piano whose past was more glorious than its present. The girls were then invited to ask the visitor questions, but only white misses raised their hands. 'Sir, do you know George Washington?' (Alas, no.) 'How many horses pull your carriage?' (My father-in-law keeps four, but I prefer to ride a single mount.) The littlest asked of me, 'Do ants get head-aches?' (Had her classmates' titters not reduced my interrogator to tears, I should be standing there pondering this question still.) I told the students to live by the Bible & obey their elders, then took my leave. Mrs Horrox told me departees were once presented with a garland of plumeria, but the Mission elders deemed garlands immoral. 'If we allow garlands today, it will be dancing tomorrow. If there is dancing tomorrow . . .' She shuddered.

'Tis a pity.

By noon the men had loaded the cargo & *Prophetess* was kedging out of the bay against unfavourable winds. Henry & I have retired to the mess-room to avoid the spray & oaths. My friend is composing an epic in Byronic stanzas entitled 'True History of Autua, Last Moriori' & interrupts my journal-writing to ask what rhymes with what: – 'Streams of blood'?; 'Themes of mud'?; 'Robin Hood'?

I recall the crimes Mr Melville imputes to Pacific missionaries in his recent account of the Typee. As with cooks, doctors, notaries, clergymen, captains & kings, might evangelists also not be some good, some bad? Maybe the Indians of the Societies & the Chathams would be happiest 'undiscovered' but to say so is to cry for the moon. Should we not applaud Mr Horrox

& his brethren's efforts to assist the Indian's climb up 'Civilization's Ladder'? Is not ascent their sole salvation?

I know not the answer, nor whence flew the surety of my younger years.

During my night at the Horroxes' parsonage, a burglar broke into my coffin & when the reprobate could not locate my jackwood trunk's key (I wear it around my neck) he attempted to force the lock. Had he succeeded, Mr Busby's deeds & documents would now be fodder for sea-horses. How I wish our captain was cut from trustworthy Cpt. Beale's cloth! I dare not give Cpt. Molyneux custody of my valuables & Henry warned me against 'stirring the hornets' nest' by raising the attempted crime with Mr Boerhaave, lest an investigation spur every thief aboard to try his luck whenever my back is turned. I suppose he is right.

Monday, 16th December —

Today at noon the sun was vertical & that customary humbuggery known as 'Crossing the Line' was let loose, by which 'Virgins' (those crewmen crossing the equator for the first time) endure various hazings & duckings, as thought fit by those Tars conducting ceremonies. The sensible Cpt. Beale did not waste time on this during my Australia-bound voyage, but the seamen of *Prophetess* were not to be denied their fun. (I considered all notions of 'fun' to be an anathema to Mr Boerhaave, until I saw what cruelties these 'amusements' entailed.) Finbar warned us the two 'Virgins' were Rafael & Bentnail. The latter has been at sea for two years, but sailed only the Sydney–Cape Town run.

During the dog-watch the men slung an awning over the fore-deck & assembled around the capstan, where 'King Neptune' (Pocock, dressed in absurd robe with a squilgee-wig) was holding court. The Virgins were tied to the cat-heads like a pair of St Sebastians. 'Sawbone & Mr Quillcock!' cried Pocock upon seeing Henry & me. 'Art thou come to rescue our virgin sisters from my scabdragon?' Pocock danced with a marling-spike in a vulgar fashion & the seamen clapped with lickerish laughter. Henry, laughing, retorted that he preferred *his* virgins without beards. Pocock's riposte on maidens' beards is too obscene to record.

His Barnacled Majesty turned back to his victims. 'Bentnail of Cape Town, Riff-the-Raff of Convict-town, be you ready to enter the Order of the Sons of Neptune?' Rafael, his boyish spirits restored in part by the anticks, responded with a brisk, 'Aye, your lordship!' Bentnail gave a surly nod. Neptune roared, 'Naaaaaay! Not till we shave those d—d scales off you sogerers! Bring me the shaving cream!' Torgny hurried up with a pail of tar, which he applied to the prisoners' faces with a brush. Next, Guernsey appeared, dressed as Queen Amphitrite, & removed the tar with a razor. The Cape man howled curses, which caused much merriment & not a few 'slips' of the razor. Rafael had the sound sense to bear his ordeal in silence. 'Better, better,' growled Neptune, before yelling, 'Blind-fold 'em both & shew Young Riff into my court-room!'

This 'court-room' was a barrel of salt-water into which Rafael was plunged head-first while the men chanted to twenty, after which Neptune commanded his 'courtiers' to 'fish out my newest citizen'! His blind-fold was removed & the boy leant against the bulwarks to recover from his hazing.

Bentnail acquiesced less willingly, yelling, 'Unhand me you sons of w—s!' King Neptune rolled his eyes in horror. 'That stinking mouth needs *forty* o' the best in the brine, boys, or me eyes ain't mates!' On the count of forty, the Afrikaner was raised, baying, 'I'll kill every last one of you sons of sows, I swear I will I—' To general hilarity, he was submerged for another forty. When Neptune declared his sentence served he could do nothing but choke & retch feebly. Mr Boerhaave now ended the skylarking & the newest Sons of Neptune cleaned their faces with oakum & a bar of toilet soap.

Finbar was still chuckling at dinner. Cruelty has never made me smile.

Wednesday, 18th December —

Scaly seas, barely a breath of wind, therm. remains about 90°. The crew have washed their hammocks & triced them up to dry. My head-aches commence earlier daily & Henry has once more increased my dosage of vermicide. I pray his supply will not be depleted ere we drop anchor in O-hawaii for the pain unameliorated would shatter my skull. Elsewhere my doctor is kept busy by much erysipelas & bilious cholera on *Prophetess*.

This afternoon's fitful siesta was cut short by clamour, so I went on deck & there found a young shark being baited & hoisted aboard. It writhed in its own brilliant ruby juices for a considerable time before Guernsey declared it well & truly dead. Its mouth & eyes called to mind Tilda's mother. Finbar butchered its carcass on deck & could not altogether ruin its succulence in his galley (a woody scrod-fish). The more superstitious sailors spurned this treat, reasoning sharks are known to eat men, thus to eat shark-flesh is cannibalism by proxy. Mr Sykes spent a profitable afternoon making sand-paper from the hide of the great fish.

Friday, 20th December —

Can it be that the cock-roaches grow fat on me as I sleep? This morning one woke me by crawling over my face & attempting to feed from my nostril. Truly, it was six inches long! I was possessed of a violent urge to kill the giant bug, but in my cramped, gloomy cabin it had the advantage. I complained to Finbar, who urged me to pay a dollar for a specially-trained 'roach-rat'. Later, doubtless, he will want to sell me a 'rat-cat' to subdue the roach-rat, then I will need a cat-hound & who knows where it will all end?

Sunday, 22nd December —

Hot, so hot, I melt & itch & blister. This morn I awoke to the laments of fallen angels. I listened in my coffin, as moments unfolded into minutes, wondering what new devilry my Worm was working, until I made out a booming cry from above: — 'There she blows!' I uncovered my porthole but the hour was too dim to see clearly, so despite my weakness I forced myself up the companionway. 'There, sir, there!' Rafael steadied me by my waist with one hand as he pointed with the other. I gripped the hand-rail tight, for my legs are unsteady now. The boy kept pointing. 'There! Ain't they a marvel, sir?' By the crepuscular light I beheld a spume, only thirty feet from the starboard prow. 'Pod o' six!' shouted Autua, from aloft. I heard the Cetaceans' breathing, then felt the droplets of spume shower upon us! I agreed with the boy, they make a sublime sight indeed. One heaved itself up, down & beneath the waves. The flukes of the fish stood in silhouette against the rose-licked east. 'More's the pity we ain't a spouter, I says,' commented Newfie. 'Must be a hundred barrels o' spermaceti in the big 'un alone!' Pocock snapped, 'Not I! I shipped on a spouter once, the cap'n was the blackest brute you've ever seen, them three years make *Prophetess* seem a Sunday pleasure punt!'

I am back in my coffin, resting. We are passing through a great nursery of hunchbacks. The cry 'There she blows!' is heard so often that none now bother to watch. My lips are baked & peeled.

The colour of monotony is blue.

Christmas Eve —

A gale & heavy seas & ship rolling much. My finger is so swollen, Henry had to cut off my wedding band lest it prevent circulation & cause the onset of dropsy. Losing this symbol of my union with Tilda depressed my spirits beyond all measure. Henry berates me for being a 'silly puffin' & insists my wife would set my health above a fortnight without a metal loop. The band is in my doctor's safe-keeping, for he knows a Spanish goldsmith in Honolulu who will repair it for a reasonable price.

Christmas Day —

Long swells left by yesterday's gale. At dawn the waves looked like mountain ranges tipped with gold as sunbeams slanted low under burgundy clouds. I rallied all my strength to reach the mess-room where Mr Sykes & Mr Green had accepted Henry's & my invitation to our private Christmas Meal. Finbar served a less noxious dinner than is his wont, of 'lobscouse' (salt beef, cabbage, yam & onion) so I was able to stomach most of it, until later. The plum duff had never seen a plum. Cpt. Molyneux sent word to Mr Green that the men's grog ration was doubled so by the afternoon watch the seamen were flown. A regular saturnalia. A quantity of small-beer was poured down a luckless Diana monkey who capped its crapulous mummery by jumping overboard. I retired to Henry's cabin & together we read the second chapter of Matthew.

The dinner wrought havoc on my digestion & necessitated frequent visits to the head. On my last visit, Rafael was waiting outside. I apologized for delaying him, but the boy said, no, he had contrived this meeting. He confessed he was troubled, & posed me this question: 'God lets you in, doesn't he, if you're sorry . . . no matter what you do, he don't send you to . . . y'know . . .' here the 'prentice mumbled '. . . hell?'

I own, my mind was more on digestion than theology & I blurted out that Rafael could hardly have notched up a mortal portfolio of sin in his few years. The storm-lantern swung & I saw misery distort my young brave's face. Regretting my levity, I affirmed the Almighty's mercy is indeed infinite, that *joy shall be in heaven over one sinner that repenteth, more than over ninety & nine just persons, which need no repentance.* Did Rafael wish to confide in me, I asked, be it as a friend, or a fellow orphan, or a relative stranger? I told him I had noticed how downcast he seemed of late & lamented how altered was that blithe boy who had stepped aboard in Sydney, so eager to see the wide world. Ere he framed his reply, however, an attack of laxity obliged me to return to the head. When I emerged, Rafael was gone. I shall not press the matter. The boy knows where he can find me.

Later –

Seven bells of the first watch were just smote. My Worm pains my head as if the clapper strikes my skull. (*Do* ants get headaches? I gladly should be turned into an ant to be freed from these agonies.) How Henry & others sleep through this din of debauchery & blasphemous carolling I know not but keenly I envy them.

I snuffed some vermicide, but it no longer brings elation. It merely helps me feel half-way ordinary. Then I took a turn about the decks, but the Star of David was obscured by thick clouds. A few sober shouts aloft (Autua's amongst them) & Mr Green at the wheel assured me that not all the crew were 'sixteen sheets to the wind'. Empty bottles rolled from port to starboard & back with the swell. I stumbled upon an insensible Rafael curled around the windlass, his corrupted hand gripping his empty pewter. His bare young chest was bespattered by ochreous smearages. That the boy had found his solace in drink instead of his friend-in-Christ made my own spirits glummer.

'Guilty thoughts disturbing your rest, Mr Ewing?' spoke a dybbuk at my shoulder & I dropped my pipe. It was Boerhaave. I assured the Hollander that while my conscience was quite untroubled I doubted *he* could claim as much. Boerhaave spat overboard, smiling. Had fangs & horns sprouted I should have felt no surprise. He slung Rafael over his shoulder, slapped the sleeping 'prentice's buttocks & carried his somnambulent burden to the after-hatch, to keep him out of harm's way, I trust.

Boxing Day —

Yesterday's entry sentences me to a prison of remorse for the rest of my days. How perversely it reads, how flippant I was! Oh, I am sick to write these words. Rafael has hanged himself. Hanged, by means of a noose slung over the mainmast lower yard-arm. He ascended his gallows between the end of his watch & first bell. Fate decreed I should be amongst his discoverers. I was leaning over the bulwark, for the Worm causes bouts of nausea as it is expelled. In the blue half-light I heard a cry & saw Mr Roderick gazing heavenward. Confusion twisted his face; succeeded by disbelief; folding in grief. His lips formed a word, yet no word issued. He pointed to that he could not name.

There swung a body, a grey form brushing the canvas. Noise erupted from all quarters, but who was shouting what to whom I cannot recall. Rafael, hanged, steady as a plumb-lead as *Prophetess* pitched & rolled. That amiable boy, lifeless as a sheep on a butcher's hook! Autua had scrambled aloft, but all he could do was lower the boy down gently. I heard Guernsey mutter, 'Should never o' sailed on Friday, Friday's the Jonah.'

My mind burns with the question, *Why?* None will discuss it, but Henry, who is as horrified as myself, told me that, secretly, Bentnail had intimated to him that the unnatural crimes of Sodom were visited upon the boy by Boerhaave & his 'garter-snakes'. Not just on Christmas night, but every night for many weeks.

My duty is to follow this dark river to its source & impose justice on the miscreants but, Lord, I can scarce sit up to feed myself! Henry says I cannot flagellate myself whene'er innocence falls prey to savagery but how can I let this be? Rafael was Jackson's age. I feel such impotence, I cannot bear it.

Friday, 27th December —

Whilst Henry was called away to attend an injury, I hauled myself to Cpt. Molyneux's cabin to speak my mind. He was displeazed at being visited, but I would not quit his quarters until my charge was stated, to wit, Boerhaave's pack had tormented Rafael with nightly bestiality until the boy, seeing no possibility of reprieve or relief, took his life. Finally, the captain asked, 'You do, of course, have evidence for this crime? A suicide letter? Signed testimonials?' Every man aboard knew I spoke the truth! The captain could not be insensible of Boerhaave's brutality! I demanded an enquiry into the first mate's part in Rafael's self-slaughter.

'Demand all you wish, Mr Quillcock!' Cpt. Molyneux shouted. '*I* decide who sails *Prophetess*, who maintains discipline, who trains the 'prentices, not a d—d pen-pusher, not his d—d ravings & by God's Blood not any d—d "enquiry"! Get out, sir, & blast you!'

I did so & immediately collided with Boerhaave. I asked him if he was going to lock *me* up in his cabin with his garter-snakes, then hope *I'd* hang myself before dawn? He showed his fangs, and in a voice laden with venom and hatred, issued this warning: 'The stink of decay is on you, Quillcock, no man of mine would touch you lest he contract it. You'll die soon of your "low-fever".'

Notaries of the United States, I had the wit to warn him, do not vanish as conveniently as colonial cabin-boys. I believe he entertained the notion of strangling me. But I am too sickly to be afraid of a Dutch sodomite.

Later —

Doubt besieges my conscience & complicity is its charge. Did *I* give Rafael the permission he sought to commit self-slaughter? Had I divined his misery when last he spoke to me, interpreted his intention & replied, 'No, Rafael, the Lord cannot forgive a *planned* suicide, for repentance cannot be true if it occurs *before* the crime,' the boy may yet be drawing breath. Henry insists I could not have known, but for once his words ring hollow to my ears. Oh, did *I* send that poor Innocent to Hell?

Saturday, 28th December —

A magic-lantern show in my mind shows the boy taking the rope, ascending the mast, knotting his noose, steadying himself, addressing his maker, launching himself into vacancy. As he rushed through the black, did he feel serenity or dread? The snap of his neck.

Had I but known! I could have helped the child jump ship, deflect his destiny as the Channings did mine, or help him understand that no state of tyranny reigns for ever.

Prophetess has every inch of canvas aloft & is 'sailing like a witch' (not for any benefit of mine, but because the cargo is rotting) & makes over 3° of latitude daily. I am terribly sick now & confined to my coffin. I suppose Boerhaave believes I am hiding from him. He is deceived, for the righteous vengeance I wish to visit upon his head is one of the few flames unextinguished by this dreadful torpor. Henry beseeches me write my journal to occupy my brain, but my pen grows unwieldy & heavy. We make Honolulu in three days. My loyal doctor promises to accompany me ashore, spare no expense to obtain powerful paregorics & remain at my bedside until my recovery is compleat, even if *Prophetess* must leave for California without us. God bless this best of men. I can write no more today.

Sunday, 29th December –

I fare most ill.

Monday, 30th December –

The Worm recrudesces. Its poison sacs have burst. I am racked with pain & bedsores & a dreadful thirst. Oahu is still two or three days to the north. Death is hours away. I cannot drink & do not recall when I ate last. I made Henry promise to deliver this journal to Bedford's in Honolulu. From there it will reach my bereaved family. He swears I shall deliver it on my own two feet, but my hopes are blasted. Henry has done his valiant best but my parasite is too virulent & I must entrust my soul to its maker.

Jackson, when you are a grown man do not permit your profession to sunder you from loved ones. During my months away from home, I thought of you & your mother with constant fondness & should it come to pass [. . .]*

Sunday, 12th January –

The temptation to begin at the perfidious end is strong, but this diarist shall remain true to chronology. On New Year's Day, my head-pains were rolling so thunderously I was taking Goose's medicine every hour. I could not stand against the ship's roll, so I stayed abed in my coffin vomiting into a sack though my guts were vacant & shivering with an icy, scalding fever. My Ailment could no longer be concealed from the crew & my coffin was placed under quarantine. Goose had told Cpt. Moly-neux that my Parasite was contagious, thereby appearing the

* Here my father's handwriting slips into spasmodic illegibility. – J. E.

very paragon of selfless courage. (The complicity of Cpt. Moly-neux & Boerhaave in the subsequent malfeasance cannot be proven or disproven. Boerhaave wished evil on me, but I am forced to admit it unlikely he was party to the crime described below.)

I recall surfacing from feverish shallows. Goose was an inch away. His voice sank to a loving whisper, 'Dearest Ewing, your Worm is in its death-throes & expelling every last drop of its poison! You must drink this purgative to expel its calcified remains. It will send you to sleep, but when you awake, the Worm that has so tormented you shall be out! The end of your suffering is at hand. Open your mouth, one last time, hand-somely does it, dearest of fellows ... here, 'tis bitter & foul a flavour, it's the myrrh, but down with it, for Tilda & Jackson ...'

A glass touched my lips & Goose's hand cradled my head. I tried to thank him. The potion tasted of bilgewater & almond. Goose raised my head, & stroked my Adam's apple until I swallowed the liquid. Time passed, I know not how long. The creaking of my bones & the ship's timbers were one.

Somebody knocked. Light softened my coffin's darkness & I heard Goose's voice from the corridor. 'Yes, much, much better, Mr Green! Yes, the worst is over. I was very worried, I confess, but Mr Ewing's colour is returning & his pulse strong. Only one hour? Excellent news. No, no, he's asleep now. Tell the captain we'll be going ashore tonight – if he could send word to arrange lodgings, I know Mr Ewing's father-in-law will remember the kindness.'

Goose's face floated into my vision again. 'Adam?'

Another fist knocked at the door. Goose uttered an oath & swam away. I could no longer move my head, but heard Autua demanding, 'I see Missa Ewing!' Goose bid him begone, but the tenacious Indian was not to be faced down so easily. 'No! Missa Green say he better! Missa Ewing save my life! He *my* duty!' Goose then told Autua this: – that I saw in Autua a carrier of disease & a rogue planning to exploit my present infirmity to rob me even of the buttons from my waistcoat. I had begged Goose, so he claimed, to 'Keep that d—d nigger away from me!' adding that I regretted ever saving his worthless neck. With that, Goose slammed & bolted my coffin door.

Why had Goose lied so? Why was he so determined no-one else should see me? The answer raised the latch on a door of deception & an horrific truth kicked the door in. To wit, the doctor was a poisoner & I his prey. Since the commencement of my 'Treatment', the doctor had been killing me by degrees with his 'cure'.

My Worm? A fiction, implanted by the doctor's power of suggestion! Goose, a doctor? No, an itinerant, murdering con-fidence-trickster!

I fought to rise, but the evil liquid my succubus had lately fed me had enfeebled my limbs so wholly I could not so much as twitch my extremities. I tried to shout for aid, but my lungs did not inflate. I heard Autua's foot-steps retreat up the companion-way & prayed for God to guide him back, but His intentions were otherwise. Goose clambered up the hawser to my bunk. He saw my eyes. Seeing my fear, the dæmon removed his mask.

'What's that you're saying, Ewing? How shall I comprehend if you drool & dribble so?' I emitted a frail whine. 'Let me guess what you're trying to tell me – "Oh, Henry, we were friends, Henry, how could you *do* this to me?" [He mimicked my hoarse, dying whisper.] Am I on the nose?' Goose cut the key from my neck & spoke as he worked at uncovering my trunk. 'Surgeons are a singular brotherhood, Adam. To us, people aren't sacred beings crafted in the Almighty's image, no, people are joints of meat; diseased, leathery meat, yes, but meat ready for the skewer & the spit.' He mimicked my voice, very well. ' "But why *me*, Henry, are we not friends?" Well, Adam, even friends are made of meat. 'Tis absurdly simple. I need money & in your trunk, I am told, is an entire estate, so I have killed you for it. Where is the mystery? "But, Henry, this is wicked!" But, Adam, the world *is* wicked. Maoris prey on Morioris, Whites prey on darker-hued cousins, fleas prey on mice, cats prey on rats,

Christians on infidels, first mates on cabin-boys, Death on the Living. "The weak are meat, the strong do eat."'

Goose checked my eyes for sentience & kissed my lips. 'Your turn to be eaten, dear Adam. You were no more gullible than any other of my patrons.' My trunk lid swung open. Goose counted through my pocket book, sneered, found the emerald from von Weiss & examined it through an eye-piece. He was unimpressed. The fiend untied the bundles of documents relating to the Busby estate & tore open the sealed envelopes in search of bank-notes. I heard him count my modest supply. He tapped my trunk for secret compartments, but he found none, for there are none. Lastly, he snipped the buttons from my waistcoat.

Goose addressed me through my delirium, as one might address an unsatisfactory tool. 'Frankly, I am disappointed. I have known Irish navvies with more pounds to their name. Your cache scarcely covers my arsenick & opiate. If Mrs Horrox had not donated her hoard of black pearls to my worthy cause, well, poor Goose's goose would be basted & cooked! Well, it is time for us to part. You will be dead within the hour & for me, 'tis hey, ho! for the open road.'

My next cogent remembrance is of drowing in salt-water so bright it hurt. Had Boerhaave found my body & thrown me overboard to ensure my silence & avoid tiresome procedures with the American consul? My mind was still active & as such might yet exercise some say in my destiny. Consent to drown, or attempt to swim? Drowning was by far the least troublesome option, so I cast about for a dying thought & settled on Tilda, waving off the *Belle-Hoxie* from Silvaplana Wharf so many months before with Jackson shouting, 'Papa! Bring me back a kangaroo's paw!'

The thought of never more seeing them was so distressing, I elected to swim & found myself not in the sea but curled on deck, vomiting profusely & trembling violently with fever, aches, cramps, pinches. Autua was holding me (he had forced a bucket-ful of brine down me to 'flush out' the poison). I retched &

retched. Boerhaave shoved his way through the crowd of onlooking stevedores & seamen, snarling, 'I told you once, nigger, that Yankee's no concern of yours! & if a direct order won't convince you—' Though the sun half blinded me, I saw the first mate land one brutal kick in Autua's ribs & launch another. Autua gripped the atrabilious Hollander's shin in one firm hand whilst he gently lowered my head to the deck and rose up to his full height, taking his assailant's leg with him, robbing Boerhaave of his balance. The Dutchman fell on his head with a leonine roar. Autua now seized the other foot & slung our first mate over the bulwarks like a sack of cabbages.

Whether the crew-men were too fearful, astonished or delighted to offer any resistance, I shall never know, but Autua carried me down a gangplank on the dockside unmolested. My reason informed me that Boerhaave could not be in Heaven nor Autua in Hell so we must be in Honolulu. From the harbour we passed down a thoroughfare bustling with innumerable tongues, hues, creeds & odours. My eyes met a Chinaman's as he rested beneath a carved dragon. A pair of women whose paint & tournure advertised their ancient calling peered at me & crossed themselves. I tried to tell them I was not yet dead, but they were gone. Autua's heart beat against my side, encouraging my own. Thrice he asked of strangers, 'Where doctor, friend?' Thrice he was ignored (one answered, 'No medicine for stinking Blacks!') before an old fish-seller grunted directions to a sick-house. I was parted from my senses for a time, before hearing the word 'Infirmary'. Merely entering its fœtid air, laden with ordure & decomposition, caused me to retch anew, notwithstanding my stomach was empty as a discarded glove. The buzzing of bluebottles hovered & a madman howled about Jesus adrift on the Sargasso Sea. Autua muttered to himself in his own tongue. 'Patience more, Mr Ewing – this place smell death – I take you to Sisters.'

How Autua's sisters might have strayed so far from Chatham Isle was a puzzle I could not begin to solve, but I entrusted myself to his care. He quitted that charnel-house & soon the taverns, dwellings and warehouses thinned before giving way to sugar plantations. I knew I should ask, or warn, Autua about Goose, but speech was yet beyond my powers. Nauseous slumber tightened then loosened its grip on me. A distinct hill rose up & its name stirred in memory's sediment: – Diamond Head. The road hither was rocks, dust & holes, walled on both sides with unyielding vegetation. Autua's stride broke only once, to cup cool stream-water to my lips, until we arrived at a Catholic mission, beyond the final fields. A nun tried to 'shoo' us away with a broom, but Autua enjoined her, in Spanish as broken as his English, to grant his white charge sanctuary. Finally, one sister who evidently knew Autua arrived & persuaded the others that the savage was on a mission not of malice but mercy.

By the third day I could sit up, feed myself, thank my guardian angels & Autua, the last free Moriori in this world, for my deliverance. Autua insists that had I not prevented him from being tossed overboard as a stowaway he could not have saved me & so, in a sense, it is not Autua who has preserved my life but myself. Be that as it may, no nursemaid ever ministered as tenderly as rope-roughened Autua has to my sundry needs these last ten days. Sister Véronique (of the broom) jests that my friend should be ordained & appointed hospital director.

Mentioning neither Henry Goose (or the poisoner who assumed that name) nor the salt-water bath which Autua gave Boerhaave, Cpt. Molyneux forwarded my effects via Bedford's agent, doubtless with one eye on the mischief my father-in-law may inflict on his future as a trader operating from San Francisco. Molyneux's other eye is on disassociating his reputation from that now-notorious murderer known as 'The Arsenick Goose'. The devil has not yet been apprehended by the Port Constabulary nor, I suspect, shall that day ever come. In Honolulu's lawless hive, where vessels of all flags & nations arrive & depart daily, a man may change his name & history between *entrée* & dessert.

I am exhausted & must rest. Today is my thirty-fourth birthday.

I remain thankful to God for all his mercies.

Monday, 13th January —

Sitting under the candlenut tree in the courtyard is pleasant in the afternoon. Laced shadows, frangi-pani & coral hibiscus ward away the memory of recent evil. The sisters go about their duties, Sister Martinique tends her vegetables, the cats enact their feline comedies & tragedies. I am making acquaintances amongst the local avifauna. The *palila* has a head & tail of burnished gold, the *ākohekohe* is a handsome crested honeycreeper.

Over the wall is a poor-house for foundlings, also administered by the sisters. I hear the children chanting their classes (just as my schoolmates and I used to before Mr & Mrs Channing's philanthropy elevated my prospects). After their studies are done, the children conduct their play in a beguiling babel. Sometimes, the more daring of their number brave the nuns' displeasure by scaling the wall & conduct a grand-tour above the hospice garden by means of the candlenut's obliging branches. If the 'coast is clear', the pioneers beckon their more timid playmates on to this human aviary & white faces, brown faces, kanáka faces, Chinese faces, mulatto faces appear in the arboreal overworld. Some are Rafael's age & when I remember him a bile of remorse rises in my throat, but the orphans grin down at me, imitate monkeys, poke out their tongues, or try to drop *kukui* nuts into the mouths of snoring convalescents & do not let me stay mournful for very long. They beg me for a cent or two. I toss up a coin for dextrous fingers to pluck, unerringly, from the air.

My recent adventures have made me quite the philosopher, especially at night, when I hear naught but the stream grinding boulders into pebbles through an unhurried eternity. My thoughts flow thus. Scholars discern motions in history & formulate these motions into rules that govern the rises & falls of civilizations. My belief runs contrary, however. To wit: history admits no rules; only outcomes.

What precipitates outcomes? Vicious acts & virtuous acts.

What precipitates acts? Belief.

Belief is both prize & battlefield, within the mind & in the mind's mirror, the world. If we *believe* humanity is a ladder of tribes, a colosseum of confrontation, exploitation & bestiality, such a humanity is surely brought into being, & history's Horroxes, Boerhaaves & Gooses shall prevail. You & I, the moneyed, the privileged, the fortunate, shall not fare so badly in this world, provided our luck holds. What of it if our consciences itch? Why undermine the dominance of our race, our gunships, our heritage & our legacy? Why fight the 'natural' (oh, weaselly word!) order of things?

Why? Because of this: – one fine day, a purely predatory world *shall* consume itself. Yes, the devil shall take the hindmost until the foremost *is* the hindmost. In an individual, selfishness uglifies the soul; for the human species, selfishness is extinction.

Is this the entropy written within our nature?

If we *believe* that humanity may transcend tooth & claw, if we *believe* divers races & creeds can share this world as peaceably as the orphans share their candlenut tree, if we *believe* leaders must be just, violence muzzled, power accountable & the riches of the Earth & its Oceans shared equitably, such a world will come to pass. I am not deceived. It is the hardest of worlds to make real. Tortuous advances won over generations can be lost by a single stroke of a myopic president's pen or a vainglorious general's sword.

A life spent shaping a world I *want* Jackson to inherit, not one I *fear* Jackson shall inherit, this strikes me as a life worth the living. Upon my return to San Francisco, I shall pledge myself to the Abolitionist cause, because I owe my life to a self-freed slave & because I must begin somewhere.

I hear my father-in-law's response. 'Oho, fine, *Whiggish* sentiments, Adam. But don't tell *me* about justice! Ride to Tennessee on an ass & convince the red-necks that they are merely whitewashed negroes & their negroes are black-washed Whites! Sail to the Old World, tell 'em their imperial slaves' rights are as inalienable as the Queen of Belgium's! Oh, you'll grow hoarse, poor & grey in caucuses! You'll be spat on, shot at, lynched, pacified with medals, spurned by backwoodsmen! Crucified! Naïve, dreaming Adam. He who would do battle with the many-headed hydra of human nature must pay a world of pain & his family must pay it along with him! & only as you gasp your dying breath shall you understand, your life amounted to no more than one drop in a limitless ocean!'

Yet what is any ocean but a multitude of drops?

Acknowledgements

Manuel Berri, Jocasta Brownlee, Amber Burlinson, Angeles Marín Cabello, Henry Jeffreys, Late Junction, Rodney King, David Koerner, Sabine Lacaze, Jenny Mitchell, Jan Montefiore, Scott Moyers, David De Neef, Hazel Orme, John Pearce, Jonathan Pegg, Steve Powell, Elizabeth Poynter, Mike Shaw, Douglas Stewart, Marnix Verplancke, Carole Welch.

The Ewing and Zachry chapters were researched with the aid of a travel scholarship from the Society of Authors. Michael King's definitive work on the Moriori, *A Land Apart*, provides a factual account of Chatham Islands history. Certain scenes in Robert Frobisher's letters owe debts of inspiration to *Delius: As I Knew Him* by Eric Fenby (Icon Books, 1966; originally G. Bell & Sons Ltd, 1936). The character Vyvyan Ayrs quotes Nietzsche more freely than he admits, and the poem read by Hester Van Zandt to Margo Roker is Emerson's *Brahma*.